SLEEPERS

BOOKS I, II, AND III

JACQUELINE DRUGA

A PERMUTED PRESS BOOK
ISBN: 978-1-61868-641-1

Sleepers:
Book 1, Book 2, and Book 3
© 2017 by Jacqueline Druga
All Rights Reserved

Cover art by Dean Samed

PERMUTED
PRESS

Permuted Press, LLC
permutedpress.com

Published in the United States of America

SLEEPERS

1
INSIGHT

I embrace the night because the darkness brings a sense of comfort. When night falls there are no lights of any kind, not even the flicker of a candle. Nothing. A single lantern or even a small campfire can be seen for miles, so no one dares to ignite them. The only sources of illumination are the stars and the moon if the sky is clear enough. They cast an eerie blue upon the deadened streets. If you are smart, quiet, and stay hidden, then you'll be safe and perhaps you can sleep. But never for long and never deeply. You know what is right outside your door. Then, of course, the daylight comes and the sun on even the bleakest of days allows you to see what has become of our world. When the sky is its bluest and the sun the brightest, everything is still gray.

I hate it.

During the day you are able to see every crack in the streets, burnt building, bloodstained sidewalk and the remnants of people who fought for their lives.

Give me the night. It's quiet and it reminds me of the days when I was first married to Daniel. We were kids then, and our biggest worry was how to get enough money to have our power restored, eating cold beans out of a can and laughing about it.

We eat from cans now, but we don't laugh about it. We don't make a sound. Some people, well, the few of us left, fear the night, cry themselves to sleep, drink to oblivion, anything to get through it. Not me. I just listen, rest once in a while and listen.

I know that the nights are the most dangerous.

I don't care. I've gotten quite good at surviving the nights. I think it's because I know it won't be forever. It can't be.

What happened to our world isn't easily described.

It started with a bang and went downhill from there. Many attributed it to God. I didn't, because I refused to believe that God would be so cruel. No matter how horrible a race we had become, God would not inflict that on anyone, especially the innocents who were taken first. It was an event labeled by so many as the Rapture.

It wasn't God's Rapture; it wasn't what I had learned about in the Bible. While there were many events that did mirror those predicted in the Holy Word, the Rapture wasn't one of them. It couldn't have been. It was too horrible.

If God used the Rapture for his chosen and the special, then the rest of us truly are doomed to a life of hell.

They outnumber us thousands to one. I remember the day when they didn't, when we still had some semblance of control. When we all believed it would eventually turn in our favor. But that lasted a day.

Now we wait.

Wait, and hope that eventually things will be better.

I know they will, at least for me. I'm almost home.

2
THE TEXTS

Daniel needed a haircut. His curly light brown hair took on that 'bushy' Greg Brady look, requiring a baseball cap to keep it in control; that of course hung on the bed post. He placed it there when he went to sleep and grabbed it before he was even out of bed, a routine of his until he transformed from his winter look of Grizzly Adams to the clean shaven summer guy. I claimed it was laziness; he claimed that he needed all the help he could get to stay warm since he worked outside.

I didn't want to get out of bed. Who does on a Saturday morning? But our son Jeremy had a baseball game, and for the first time in two weeks the sun was shining. The game would be a go. Then again, it was the first weekend all year that our oldest son, Danny, wasn't making it home from school, so there was still a sense of gloom for me.

Daniel slept in and I didn't want to wake him. With all the storms we had been experiencing, Daniel was putting in a lot of overtime with the power company. The night before was the first night in a long time we relaxed at home, staying up to all hours watching bad movies on cable. He passed out during a *Bigfoot* movie. Wanting a second drink for the evening, mid-reach for the bottle of Jack Daniels on the nightstand, he turned his head and was out. He wasn't an alcoholic by any means. In fact, he was a lightweight, always being responsible and letting me be the one who consumed a few too many when we were out. Although I believe there were ulterior motives to that one. When drinking, I became a huge flirt.

I reached across his thick body and shut off the alarm before it blared. I lightly kissed him once on that small space of skin between his eye and beard, and I slipped out of bed, trying not to wake him.

"What time do we have to leave, Chirp?"

He called me 'Chirp' always, the nickname he gave me decades before. I don't even think he remembered my name is Mera.

"Not till ten, go back to sleep," I said.

He breathed heavily and spoke with morning gruffness to his voice. "Wake me in enough time to have coffee. Okay?"

"Absolutely."

I wanted to tell him to stay in bed, he needed his rest, but Daniel tried with everything he had not to miss a moment in their lives.

He loved our children more than life itself and proudly displayed their names in the form of a tattoo that read, Jessie, Danny and Jeremy on his right bicep.

The day I met Daniel I was pregnant with Jessie, but I didn't know it. It was a stupid kid move, giving into my high school sweetheart right before he shipped out with the Army to be stationed in Germany. I knew I'd never see him again and never in the world dreamt I was with child.

Walking down the street, I paused to fix my shoe when 'slam,' a hardhat fell not a foot from my leg, landing on the sidewalk.

"Shit!" I heard his voice. "I am so sorry." Within a few moments, Daniel was down that telephone pole, so apologetic. "Please, this is my third day on my own. Don't tell anyone."

"I'm okay, you know, in case you're wondering. It didn't hit me."

"Oh, yeah, sorry. Are you okay?"

I shook my head with a smile, told him I was fine and tried to walk away.

He stopped me, we talked, he went back to work, and the next day I saw him again.

Daniel had longer hair back then. Short on the sides, they later named it a mullet. It looked cool on him. After all, he was the bad boy, an older man of 23 who rode a motorcycle and I was this naïve girl of eighteen.

We spent a lot of time together. He actually was pretty sad when we met. He had lost his parents in a car accident and was still dealing with that tragedy.

We grew close, always together, then I realized about four weeks later I was pregnant. I had to tell him. It wasn't his because he and I hadn't even reached that point.

While I saw him as a man, Daniel was only a kid. He wanted to stick by me, but I never gave him the chance to tell me that. I broke it off.

A couple weeks later when I told my parents, they were furious. What I didn't know was that my father went to the electric company, found Daniel, and threatened to shoot him if he didn't do right by me. That night Daniel was there with a ring.

I apologized to Daniel and told him I would tell my parents the baby wasn't his. He wouldn't hear it. As crazy as it sounded, Daniel said he loved me and three months later he and I were married.

We have never been apart. We never broke up, separated, and rarely fought. Daniel claims me and the kids were God's gift to him. I say it was the other way around.

I put on my flip flops and made my way down to the kitchen. I stopped first to check on Jeremy and give him that warning wake up.

"Is it raining?" my twelve-year-old son asked.

"No."

"Sweet. Did Danny change his mind? Is he coming in?"

"No," I said. "You know it's his friend's birthday."

"Fine." Jeremy pouted.

I laughed and prepared to bask in the quiet of the morning. My phone was charging on the counter. I made coffee and knew that soon enough two of the men in my life would be racing around the kitchen.

I poured my coffee, grabbed my phone, and looked at the single text message from my daughter. 'I love you Mommy.' I replied and noticed she had sent it at four in the morning her time, seven my time. My daughter was all the way on the other side of the country at school in Washington. The mother in me was thinking about what she was doing up at that hour. But I knew she was responsible and there wasn't trouble. There couldn't be; she didn't try to call.

Nothing from Danny. Not that I expected a text or call. That wasn't my son. He transformed from a troublesome youth into a semi-obedient young man in his near two years at Carson Military Academy.

I remember when the judge—yes, the judge—suggested it. Danny had gotten into yet another fight and was facing being sent to the juvenile center. I thought my son would scoff at the idea, but he didn't. We tried hard to get him into Valley Forge, a mere twenty miles from our home, but his 'record' kept him from getting accepted.

I was grateful for grants and funding because there was no way we were able to afford the tuition. But every penny we spent on travel, supplies, and uniforms was worth it. Our son went from a fourteen-year-old troubled youth who faced a potential life behind bars to a respectful sixteen-year-old who used 'ma'am' and 'sir' in nearly every sentence.

Although he still got in little bits of trouble here and there, it was nothing like he used to.

So, children placed to the back of my mind, wanting to mentally find solitude, I settled into a game on my phone.

My peace lasted about a half an hour. Jeremy made his way into the kitchen, darted me a kiss, then grabbed juice from the fridge.

"I'll make you something to eat in a minute," I told him.

"That's cool. I'm going up to get dressed, go online."

He was moving fast, brushing into Daniel as he flew from the kitchen.

Daniel got out a 'morning' then made his way directly to the coffee pot. "I'm thinking of getting the hair cut off today."

"Really?" I asked. "It's only May."

"I know, but it's so friggin' hot. I was gonna wait a couple weeks so it was done before we went to pick up Jess, but..." He shrugged. "It's itching."

"Shave, too."

Daniel laughed and joined me at the kitchen table.

Within moments, Jeremy called our names frantically as he raced to the kitchen. "Put on the TV and we have to call Jessie." He flew to the kitchen television set. "Earthquake hit Seattle. Bad one."

My heart dropped to my stomach. Seattle. The exact city in which my daughter resided. The images of destruction greeted us immediately as the television powered on. It had hit there an hour before, largest in history.

Jeremy didn't hesitate trying to call her from my phone. "Mom? It's going straight to voice mail." My son was scared; I could hear it in his voice. "I'll keep trying."

Daniel returned to the kitchen with his phone and he groaned painfully, collapsing to the chair.

"Dan?"

"She sent me a text an hour ago."

The text. The 'I love you text.' How could it have slipped from my mind?

"She sent me one, too." I said. "Did it say, 'I love you?'"

Daniel shook his head, running his hand over his face and showing me his phone and his message from our daughter. His was different. His read, 'Help me Daddy. I'm trapped.'

3
THE ONSET

Daniel had transformed instantaneously, along with the feel of our home. He was level-headed and strong, yet I could see how concerned he was. Immediately he was barking out orders of what I had to do while making calls to local authorities, the Red Cross, emergency workers, the phone company to trace her phone.

We couldn't get a flight out, so I had to pack the car. He was telling me and Jeremy what we had to get ready.

Danny had called in the middle of all that. I felt like I was a bit short to him, only repeating what Daniel told me to convey, "Stay put, we'll get you in a couple hours."

I was a basket case. My heart ached so badly that I could physically feel the pain in my chest. My poor daughter. How frightened she must have been. Was she okay? For as fearful as I was, I felt she was. As a mother I felt it. Surely if my own flesh and blood had left the earth, then I would know.

But despite our best efforts we could not get through to any authorities. Jeremy took to posting on a social network for anyone with family in Seattle to try to help. All of this occurred in the hour or so we were getting ready to leave. The plan was simple, get in the truck, grab Danny in Harrisburg, and go to Seattle.

With each passing minute attempts grew futile. News of yet another quake hit the airwaves, this one in San Francisco. While not as bad as the Seattle earthquake, it left us all bewildered as to what was going on.

A small bag packed, we were minutes from walking out the door when my phone rang.

The call came from Jessie's phone. One would think I'd rush to answer, but I didn't. I froze. Instead of thinking my daughter was calling, I feared it was a police officer, doctor, neighbor, someone other than my daughter calling to tell me the worst news.

"What the hell, Chirp?" Daniel snapped and grabbed the phone from my hand. "Jess!" He spoke in a rush as he answered it.

The second I saw Daniel's eyes close, I knew it was nothing other than a look of relief.

"Baby," he said. "I can barely hear you. Yes. Yes." He mouthed the words to me, 'she's fine.'

I broke. I broke in gratefulness, collapsing into emotions.

"Jessie, we love you. Stay put. Jess…stay put, baby. We're coming out. We'll be there…Jess." Daniel scrunched his face, bringing the phone down away from him in a hard swoop against the air. "It died. She's fine. Reception is bad. She's on campus. They dug her out. That's all I got."

"I'm sorry. I'm sorry I didn't answer."

"It's okay."

"No!" I cried. "It's not. I was scared. I was…"

"It's okay. She's fine." He pulled me close. "Let's take a breath." He stepped back, placing his hands on my shoulders. "Feel a little more at ease and head on out."

At that moment, we both heard it. A double 'thump' above our heads.

Daniel stepped back, head tilted, and aimed his voice toward the stairs. "Jer, you all right?"

No answer.

"Honey!" I hollered. "Did you drop something?"

Still no answer.

"He probably has his headphones in," I said.

Daniel didn't wait to find out, he walked up the steps. "Jeremy. Answer me."

Thinking, *he's not hearing you, how can he answer?* feeling better about Jessie, but still concerned, I turned to pick up a bag to take to the car. I didn't dwell on what was transpiring upstairs. In my mind, Jeremy had dropped something, was listening to music, and never heard us call. Never did I imagine I'd hear Daniel cry out, "Call 911!"

Every ounce of air escaped me and grabbing the phone, I flew up the stairs and into Jeremy's room.

"Call them now!" Daniel ordered. "He's having some sort of seizure." He was on the floor holding Jeremy in an upright position. My son shook, his body convulsed, head going from side to side. A thick white liquid oozed from his nose and mouth, eyes rolled back to his head. His skin was an eerie gray.

"Oh my god!" With hands shaking out of control, I dialed those three easy numbers.

Like midnight on New Year's Eve, the recorded voice said that due to high volume, the call could not be completed. I didn't waste any time. I dialed again.

Same thing.

"What's wrong?" Daniel asked.

"Circuits are jammed."

"Try the landline."

I ran to the master bedroom, quickly racing through my mind what I would say. He wasn't epileptic that we knew of. What was going on, I didn't know. Arriving in the bedroom, I lifted the receiver and was greeted with a buzzing busy signal.

"Fuck!" I slammed down the phone, waited a second and lifted again.

The same thing.

Running back to Jeremy's room, I tried my cell again. No luck.

Daniel looked up to me, so lost. "What's going on?"

"I can't get through on either line."

"Fuck it, we'll drive him." He swooped his arms under Jeremy, lifted our son effortlessly, stood, and charged from the bedroom.

He wasn't waiting on me. I had never seen my husband move as fast as when he bolted down the hall and to the staircase. I almost fell down the steps trying to keep up.

"Hold him in the back, I'll drive," Daniel ordered, grabbing the front door.

I couldn't speak; I was losing it. Right after we stepped outside, I made a dash around Daniel to the car, figuring I'd open both doors, slide in the back, be ready for him to place Jeremy in my arms, and then Daniel would get in and drive.

I did that, focused only on that task.

I slid in the back seat, turned my body, arms extended, fully expecting Daniel to be right there. But he wasn't.

Daniel stood in the middle of the walkway, holding tight to our trembling son.

He stood there staring out as if in shock.

Did he panic? What?

"Daniel?"

His head moved slowly from left to right looking around.

"Daniel, come on!"

His lips moved, but I didn't hear any words. For a brief second he made eye contact with me, then clutching Jeremy, Daniel looked around again.

I stepped from the car and hurried to him. "Daniel, come on. We have to go!"

"What's happening, Chirp?" Daniel asked softly as his eyes met mine. They glazed over like I had never seen them. "What's happening?"

Before I could question, I slowly turned around to see what it was that drew his attention.

We had moved to Hawthorn Street because it was a picture-perfect middle class neighborhood perfect for raising a family. We chose that street because so many young couples were living there, all having children.

And as I looked around, I saw those neighbors. The ones we spent many Little League seasons cheering alongside, swimming with, and attending picnics. I saw the entire block of families all doing exactly what we were doing.

All of them held their children, some held two. All of the children the same as Jeremy. All of us rushing to our vehicles to try to get these children help.

We were not alone.

As I stood there taking in the devastating awe of it all, my mind repeated the question Daniel had just asked.

What was happening?

4
ONE POINT EIGHT

What had I become? A shell of a woman, a weak human being who couldn't talk, think, or move. I could only stare at my son, weeping from the depths of my soul while praying to a God whose existence I had begun to doubt.

But of course that was a contradiction, because God seemed the only logical explanation for what was happening.

Logical? Nothing was logical. Someone needed to tell me something. Someone needed to give me some answers.

My son, who not long before was vibrant, energetic and ready to play baseball, now lay on his bed, his hands retracted, mouth agape, eyes wide and bulging, his body in no less than a vegetative state. His skin was so white he looked almost bluish, and the color wasn't the only thing. His hair began to fall out. He appeared as if every ounce of his life force, his soul, was slowly being sucked from him and there was nothing we could do. Nothing.

And all that deterioration occurred within four hours of his first seizure.

We tried to get him help. We made it within two miles of the hospital but traffic was so jammed we couldn't go any further. Every parent around was seeking help for their child.

Jeremy trembled and moaned in pain and we had no choice but to turn around and take him back to the comfort of his home.

George Lawson was a doctor who lived three streets over. I didn't know him before he knocked on our door and told us that the Masons had sent him over to see Jeremy.

He did for our son what he did for the others: offered us little advice and gave him a sedative that helped the seizures and allowed him to calm down.

We received more from George Lawson than those poor individuals who chose to remain with their suffering children in the gridlocked traffic, waiting for help that they probably wouldn't see.

And it wasn't just our house, our street, our city. It was everywhere.

Every town, every country, every single child under the age of fourteen fell ill at the same instant.

1.8 billion children, all dying at the same time.

For as much as I wanted to doubt the existence of a God, what was happening was no less than an act of a supreme being.

In my heart, in my mind there was no explanation.

None.

Yes, the airwaves flooded with explanations. Everyone was trying to give their theory. But how do you explain an event that affected more people than there were in all of China?

Some said, since viruses emerged daily, this was a new one that afflicted only the young. While plausible, how was it possible that it afflicted them all at the exact same time?

Scientists were working around the clock, but there was no way they could work fast enough.

Religious leaders claimed it to be Judgment Day, with the taking of the young being the first sign, the Rapture.

What?

The Rapture? I was raised Christian. I knew the Rapture to be a selective event, where the young, the innocent, the pure and those believers in Christ would be lifted from Earth, saved, so they were spared the destruction and horrors about to be bestowed upon the Earth.

But if that was the case, what happened to the disappearances, the waking up to find only clothes left behind? What happened to the 'rising' in glory of those chosen for the Rapture?

This was *not* glorification. It was nothing less than a damnation, and the youngest and innocent of them all were the targets.

We watched a child full of life suddenly looking shriveled like a dying 90-year-old man gasping for life. We heard of babies being born without life, babies who, weeks earlier, were developing normally on a sonogram.

Stillborns across the planet.

The Holy Bible Rapture?

If He wanted to make His Rapture so horrifying then do it to me, my husband, to anyone who knew of sin, not innocent children who hadn't even begun to know life.

No, if this was God's work, then He was not a God of love and understanding, He was, indeed, like the Old Testament portrayed, a God of wrath.

And to do this to the children of the world? It wasn't peaceful; it was painful. I heard it in my son's cries.

My child was suffering; he was not spared.

His soul was still there, and with each sedated call of my name, my heart broke and I swore if it indeed was God's work He was not a God worthy of my praise.

Damn my soul, I didn't care. Not at that moment.

Not as I watched my son die.

5
DUST

It was so hard to look at my son lying in that bed. With each passing second, another ounce of life was leaving him. It was not the same child who two days earlier didn't understand why some of his friends weren't allowed to stay over because their parents believed that Daniel smoked pot.

He looked at me with his big brown eyes, questioning with innocence and following up with, "Does he?"

"Does he what?"

"Smoke pot," Jeremy said.

"Do you know what pot is?" I replied, trying my best to be evasive.

"Uh, yeah, Mom, I'm twelve."

The perfect out of a parent in any situation where you don't want to answer a question or want desperately to change the subject is to actually hold the conversation while you cook.

"Just asking," I said. "Could you find me the long wooden spoon, thanks?"

"I hope he doesn't. He has a dangerous job." Jeremy sought the spoon. "He could electrocute himself while under the influence, or worse, cut the power to thousands of homes."

I stuttered some in shock over what he thought was worse than the death of his father.

"Does Dad?" he asked.

At that second, Daniel walked into the kitchen. "Does Dad what?"

Saved.

Jeremy finally handed me that spoon. "Josh can't sleep over because his dad says you smoke pot. Do you?"

"Yes," Daniel said. "And I buy it from his dad."

I'm sure my husband didn't see my mouth drop open in shock. He laughed, darted a kiss to my cheek and started to leave the kitchen. He did pause in exit. "I'm kidding, Jeremy, I don't smoke pot."

Then Daniel left.

Jeremy pulled up a kitchen stool, sat at the counter across from me and propped his face on his hand.

"What?" I asked him.

Jeremy sighed and looked up at me with this huge puppy dog brown eyes. "He does."

Now those brown eyes were lifeless and gray. They stared back at me, but not like they did a day earlier. There was nothing behind them. Nothing. I felt it. As we inched around the twelve hour mark, the only inkling of life remaining was the occasional squeeze of his hand or whimper of my name.

He remained like that for a while.

Daniel appeared to be holding up better than me, but I knew my husband. It was killing him. We took turns trying to call our daughter and other son, but it was useless. Getting a line out seemed impossible. A neighbor suggested to Daniel that communications were shut down to avoid even further chaos. Perhaps that was why the news was sporadic.

There were no answers. None at all.

There was a quiet to the night, a feel to it all like I had never experienced. Complete quiet. I had cried so much, I could barely see and my head pounded out of control. I sipped on some bourbon but that didn't help. Sitting next to Jeremy was all I could do.

Daniel paced, tried to call Jessie, tried to call Danny then sat next to the bed.

Me, I didn't move.

My other two children were not far from my mind, but forgive me, not forefront. Not as I watched Jeremy. They would want my attention on him.

Jessie listened, I felt that. She was safe at school, staying put and waiting, just like Daniel told her. As for Danny, I guessed school officials wouldn't let him leave; he was underage. But not so underage that he fell into the age of children who took sick.

About two in the morning, a massive storm blew in. It blew in quickly and without any warning. It went from a clear, crisp night to something ridiculously violent. The sky lit up with lightning. You couldn't see the bolts, only the clouds as they brightened orange and green as if the sky were on fire. The wind battered the house and I swore we were going to lose the roof. Daniel opened the windows some for fear they'd shatter.

It lasted over an hour, and then the quiet returned. Quiet and dark. The power had gone out. Something told me we had seen the last of the power for a while.

Just before the sun came up my son began this odd breathing. A raspy, wheezing escaped him as he took short huffing breaths.

I remember when it started. My hand shot to my mouth, my eyes closed, and I fought the remaining tears.

Daniel sat down across from me on the other side of the bed, grabbed Jeremy's hand, looked at me and said, "He's leaving us."

I knew it. I felt it. I heaved out a single sob and wanted to die. I wanted to die right there with my son.

Looking at Daniel was useless. I always looked to him for strength, but he had none at that moment. He squeezed Jeremy's hand, bringing our son's frail fingers to his mouth, and my husband cried.

Imagine what it was like. A quiet dark surrounding you, no speaking, and the wind that seeped through the open window carried the distant sounds of parental cries that matched our own. Heartbreaking cries.

I had reached my end as I knew my son was reaching his. I crawled on the bed next to him, scooting up close behind him and wrapping my arms around his curled up body.

I just wanted to hold him. Hold him one last time. I was there holding him when he took his first breaths of life, I wanted to cradle him while he took his last.

It wasn't supposed to be like that. I wasn't supposed to watch my child die.

Feeling as if I wanted to absorb him into my soul, I clutched tighter to Jeremy. The moment I did, Daniel whispered out, 'Oh, God, Chirp," and I felt it.

I felt my son leave me.

In every sense of the word, he left me. The tighter I held, the faster he left. His body crumbled in my arms like a thousand-year-old book.

Crumbled into a fine, gray dust until all that remained were his clothes and hair.

Despite the fact that I was faced with the undeniable realization that what transpired was beyond human control, I lost it.

Slipping into an agony where death would be the only relief from the pain, I was uncontrollable in my reaction until I eventually passed out.

6
STILLBORN WORLD

The world went on pause.

There was no radio, no news, no power. Not a sound of a car or plane. Absolute quiet. Everything and everyone had stopped. How could it not? Nearly one-third of the population, all of whom were so very young, died and vanished.

How do you even begin to comprehend that? I know I didn't, and it made sense that no one else did either. I supposed once the initial shock wore off, things would happen. But people handled grief differently. That frightened me, because there would be a lot of people who just didn't care anymore.

Not a single person on the planet wasn't affected one way or another by the Event.

Although it was daylight, it was dismal and gray, as if another storm was about to roll in.

We stayed in Jeremy's room for a while, both of us crying, and then Daniel carefully wrapped what remained in the sheet, folded his bedspread over that and spoke the first words to me in hours.

"I'm going to go find a place to bury him."

He began to leave the room and paused at the door. "Chirp, I know how this feels. My heart is broke. No, it is completely crushed right now. I know this is horrible, but you, me, we gotta pull it together. We have to. Okay?"

With a hard sniff, my hand clenching the bedspread, I peered up to him. "How?"

"I don't know. Find it," he said firmly. "Find it. We have to. Because we have to find our kids."

With that he turned and left.

It took a moment, staring at the sealed bedspread, for me to realize how right he was.

I had to pull it together. I didn't understand how all my strength was failing me. *I* was the person people ran to when things went wrong; *I* was the person people turned to for wisdom and strength. And here I was so emotionally drained I could barely muster the strength to stand.

But I had to.

Pressing my lips to my fingers then running them over the bedspread, I whispered my love to my son and stood.

My first step in pulling it together would be to help Daniel.

As small as it was, it was still a step.

Daniel had been outside earlier in the morning. Shortly after Jeremy had passed away, he left to get some air. Bill and Jenny from across the street were making coffee on the huge grill they used to brag about. Even with no children of their own, they knew what was happening on the street to us all. They made coffee and some food in case anyone needed or wanted it.

They had to be at a loss at what to do, how to help. The idealistic young professional couple who dreamed of one day starting a family was probably grateful they had chosen careers first.

They moved the grill to the street so anyone could walk up.

I had some of the coffee when Daniel brought it to me. But Daniel brought me nothing else. No news of what I'd see outside.

Our street looked like a war zone. It looked like one of those streets you'd see on the news somewhere in Midwest America struck by a tornado, not a suburb outside of Philadelphia, Pennsylvania.

Cars were battered with tree limbs and dirt, the street was mud-laced, and many homes were missing shingles, siding, even pieces of roofs.

Part of our roof was gone and a piece of our chimney lay in our front yard.

I was so wrapped up in my world with Jeremy that, though I noticed the storm, I didn't think twice about how bad it really was.

I stepped outside rubbing the chill from my arms. Bill was right across the street sitting in a lawn chair. He stood almost cautiously, a tall lanky man who seemed frightened as he walked to me.

"I'm very sorry," he said.

I only nodded.

"If you need anything, let me know. Okay?"

"Thank you." I reached out, placing my hand on his arm, taking in the sincerity of his tired eyes and turned my head.

As I expected, Daniel was digging in the flower bed outside the house. Our beautiful flower bed that we worked on as a family would be where he'd place Jeremy.

As I turned to leave Bill, I noticed the smoke rising in the distance from the city. My face crinkled with curiosity as to what could be causing that much smoke. Bill must have seen my expression.

"Tornados, three of them, ripped through Philly last night," he explained.

"How did you know?"

"I have radios. Army radios from my dad. I heard chatter. Actually, you could see them last night," he said.

My mind immediately went to Danny. "Were they anywhere else, did you hear?"

"No. Just Philly. Well, I'll uh, I'll let you go. If you need anything…"

"Thank you for being here for everyone on the street."

He didn't say anything else. Mouth tightly closed, nearly biting his lips, he extended his arms as if to say 'it's the least I can do' and he stepped back.

I moved to Daniel, who had begun to dig. I looked to see if anyone else was out and about. I saw Tom Mason walking into his home, more like a dragging walk. He set a shovel on the porch and went inside.

The feel of the street was indescribable.

How do you even begin to console or feel for others when you can barely console or feel for yourself?

"Do you need my help?" I asked Daniel.

He shook his head. "I'm fine. I don't really need to dig that far down. Just enough—"

The scream made him stop. It was a woman's scream, loud and shrill. It wasn't like the screams from the night before, those filled with agony and heartbreak. This one was different. It was a scream that seemed to be produced by physical pain, echoing through the hollow, empty streets, long and continuous, intermittently shouting 'No!'

Daniel immediately dropped the shovel and tried to pinpoint the location it was coming from. He took a step forward and then started running across the street.

It wasn't unlike him. I wouldn't have expected anything different from my husband.

I followed and so did Bill, across the street and two doors down. The Masons.

Daniel didn't knock, he raced right in. Me, I knew exactly what was causing her screams the second I crossed the threshold.

We hurried upstairs, all arriving within a split second of each other.

Greg Mason stepped from the bed where his wife Beth thrashed back and forth. A pool of blood soaked the bed between her legs.

Beth was pregnant and I knew she was due. No, wait, she was in labor.

Bill was still clutching the doorframe when he called in, "I'll try to get Lawson on the radio."

Greg nodded and Bill flew from the room. Then with exasperation Greg faced my husband. "Daniel, please help. The baby is coming and she refuses to give birth."

"She doesn't have a choice, does she?" Daniel nearly scoffed.

Greg's eyes shifted to me. "Mera, can you? You're a woman."

A woman? Just because I was a woman didn't mean I knew anything about giving birth. I didn't pay much attention when I birthed my own. How could I make a difference? I wasn't a nurse or a doctor. However, I knew at the moment I wanted to help. I *needed* to help.

I stepped to the bed and before I said anything, Beth grabbed hold of my arm, yanking me to her.

Her voice was throaty, strained, and emotional, and she peered at me with so much hurt, her blonde hair dangling in strands against her face.

"Please!" she begged. "I can't do this. I can't have this child. I can't see another die. Please. Kill me. Do something," she sobbed. "You know." She pulled me closer, dropping her voice. "You know. I can't do this. I can't. I watched my two children die. I can't watch another."

I did know. More than anyone in that room, as a mother I did know.

"Beth," I clutched her hand, "you can't stop this baby from coming, no matter how hard you try."

"Beth," Daniel called out brightly. When I looked, his hands were on her stomach. "Beth, the baby is moving. He's kicking in there. He's alive. Beth, he's alive."

She shook her head back and forth, then, despite her best efforts, nature took over and Beth flung forward and bore down.

From her gut, graveling all the way out of her mouth, she cried out, "No!"

Holding one of her legs, Daniel demanded "Chirp! Please!"

Both he and Greg looked at me as if because I had given birth I was suddenly some sort of guru. But you know what? Something happens. It's odd. As apprehensive as I was, I moved to the bed and I felt as if I knew exactly what do to. It was instinctive and I didn't have to be an obstetrician to know all that blood was not a good sign.

Trying to peer between her legs to see if the baby had crowned was useless. "I can't see anything," I said. "Her legs..."

Beth, with everything she had, kept pulling her legs together, stopping the child from emerging...or at least trying.

It was after about three or four minutes of arguing with Beth, pleading with her in between her worsening contractions, that George Lawson arrived.

George looked as if he had been through the wringer, tired and drawn, dark circles traced under his eyes. A short, stout man, he wasn't big in height but was extremely large in presence. He entered the room, set his bag on the floor, and flicked his forefinger against the already prepared syringe.

"This will calm her," he told Greg and without hesitation jabbed the needle into Beth's arm, plunging the fluid into her.

Beth screamed.

"Beth," George said firmly, "Beth!"

"I don't want to have this baby. I don't. I *don't!*"

"Beth!" George snapped, taking a seat on the bed. "Listen to me."

Like a two year old having a tantrum, Beth thrashed. "It's going to die."

"It will die anyhow!" George stated flatly. "This blood? The placenta has detached. If you don't stop this, the child will die. At least give it a chance."

George's words didn't faze Beth. His hand rested on her belly and I could see her skin and stomach distend, moving, jolting.

Calmly, George turned to Daniel and quietly ordered, "Hold her legs." Then to me, "You too."

I wasn't a big woman, not at all, and while neither was Beth, clearly she was out of control and I feared it would be a struggle to hold one leg down.

Using both hands, I gripped her leg, pushing down. Beth heaved forward with a painful groan then suddenly she went limp, her head lolling to the side.

I thought she'd died.

"She's fine," George said, peering up from his examination. "The sedative kicked in. Greg, I need you to brace behind her back and lift her toward me."

Holding her leg outward was easier, and I focused on Greg taking his position behind his wife.

One hand between her legs, George leaned forward, placing his other hand on the top of her stomach near her ribs. "Now," he said to Greg.

I watched him push on her stomach, manipulating her belly downward.

"Okay, stop," George said, then lowered to re-examine her. "Once more...now." They repeated the ritual.

"Stop." George's expression showed no emotion. "Head is out." He then moved completely between Beth's legs and nodded to Greg. "Again."

Greg did as instructed.

"That's good. Greg, can you get me a towel or blanket please?"

Greg gently placed Beth down and stood straight. "Why is the baby not crying?"

I didn't think anything of it. None of my children cried when they were born. But after Greg questioned, I realized there wasn't a sound.

My heart raced, my breathing became heavier. I felt like I was suffocating and I couldn't get enough air.

A hard stomach twitch hit me when Daniel whispered out, "Oh, God."

Then finally I looked. What was it? I certainly didn't see what Daniel saw. From my point of view, I saw the baby's shoulders emerging as the child rotated clockwise as all infants do upon birth. It looked normal, alive, its shoulders moved and I saw the fingers clench.

He was fine. He was fine...

And then he just flopped into George's hands. His little arms and legs dangled lifelessly over George's fingers and his head titled my way.

The ache shot from my heart causing a sound to emanate from my throat. I saw what Daniel saw. His face. His tiny little face had no features. No nose, mouth or eyes. As if he were an incomplete sculpture with no details ever added.

I had seen enough and I left before George had finished. My heart broke again. For the child that never had the chance to experience life outside the womb, for Beth who would wake to hear the news, for Greg who broke down and sobbed.

"I thought he would live," he cried out. "I thought he could be saved."

Greg repeated those words, releasing his emotional grief against his sedated wife.

How devastating. How truly devastating it was for them to lose both of their other children, then to lose the baby.

To me it was also a vile form of cruelty. The infant kicking with life inside of her stomach was nothing more than a misleading glimmer of hope.

It was surreal and hard to believe any of it was really happening. But it was.

My son, their children, all of the children. The only inkling of light I had remaining was that Jessie and Danny were alive out there.

We just had to find them.

If that were even possible.

7
FOOTSTEPS

It was hard to determine where the gunshots were coming from. Occasional shots and even rapid fire filled the night air. Those alone told us to wait until daylight to leave for Harrisburg and then Seattle.

Smoke from fires blocked out any stars. That mixed with that early summer humidity made the air stifling hot. For some reason I expected quiet. I guess in a sense, even with the gun shots, the world would be quiet in its own way. How could it not? There were no more children to fill our ears with laughter or cries. No more children. How was that possible? It was so inconceivable that a part of me didn't want to believe it was more than our city. Despite the fact that I had heard the news broadcast before the airwaves went dead.

While we are all born with blind faith, the older and more educated we become, we question. Everyone, I truly believe, at one point in their lives questions the existence of God or a supreme being. Somewhere in the back of the mind, there's that spot that has been waiting for undeniable proof. I got it, there it was. And I didn't want to accept it.

Because accepting that God had begun finishing off the world meant no hope for a better tomorrow. I was certain that I was not one of those people chosen for salvation and welcomed with open arms at the pearly gates. Because at that moment, having witnessed my son's death, God was the last Being I wanted to see.

The weather, the lack of a breeze, made staying indoors unbearable. There was no power, no air conditioning. Daniel and I, like many on the street, were on our porch. We sat on that swing that I adored, he on one end, I on the other, both sitting there speaking no words.

What was there to say?

We were packed and ready to leave and were only waiting for the first light of day, and then we'd go in search of Danny and Jessie. Truly, we felt Danny was going to be easy. He was less than a hundred miles away, and Bill via his radio contacts learned through this person and so forth that Harrisburg was good and Carson Military Academy was secure. We didn't hear that directly, but I felt a truth to that. Jessie, as long as she continued to listen to Daniel, we'd find. Hopefully we could get across the country. I didn't know what it was like outside our little Philadelphian world. It could be normal; it could be worse.

Venturing out was the only way to know. And while we had the car packed, Daniel said we needed more supplies, supplies to survive in case we were stranded. I found that hard to believe when he first told me. It was America; how stranded could we be in our own country?

Unlike me, Daniel's faith took a different turn. He immersed himself in prayer, read the Bible. That angered me. I didn't tell him, but I know he sensed my bitterness.

Around nine pm, two single gunshots a minute apart rang out on our street. They were undeniably close.

No one ran to the house, because those of us who had taken to sleeping outside knew. The shots came from Greg and Beth's.

Two of many, I imagined, that would take their life in the aftermath of the Event. I wondered if I, too, would have been moved to take my life if I didn't have hope in finding my other two children.

Probably not. At that moment, I turned into a coward, afraid of everything. Contrary to what people think, it takes a lot of guts to take your own life. More than I had, that was certain.

My head rested on my hand and only lifted once and that was on the first shot. I looked at Daniel, who closed his eyes, made the sign of the cross and brought rosary beads to his mouth, moving his lips again in prayer.

When the second shot rang out, I was a little envious because Greg and Beth were not feeling the pain any longer. They didn't have to worry about waking up the next day and realizing it was another day without their children.

I wanted…no, I *needed* to talk to my husband so badly. But he was trying to reconcile his pain, find comfort, and I didn't want to intrude on that.

My mind wandered to happier places and times. I thought about how I got the nickname Chirp. Daniel gave it to me because I talked too much and ate too little. It was a joke that stuck, although he was the only one who called me that.

Soon though, the silence was too much for me, and I turned to talk to Daniel. He had closed his eyes and rested back. I got up, went into the house and sought another glass of bourbon, hoping a drink would numb me or perhaps even make me sleep.

Drink in hand, I walked across the lawn. The coolness of the grass on my bare feet felt good, and I sat by the flower bed where we had buried Jeremy.

It seemed like I was the only one awake. I wasn't. I couldn't be. Small campfires danced across the lawns. I saw the reflection of Bill's fire in my drink as I sipped it and watched the flower bed.

His wife was asleep in a sleeping bag, while he sat next to her fiddling with a radio. Occasionally a rush of static carried out, followed by some voices.

Who was Bill? He lived on our street for a few years but I didn't even know his last name; I never bothered to ask. Did anyone? Yet there he was. A man barely thirty was trying to find a way to comfort neighbors who never took the opportunity to even get to know his last name.

Perhaps that moment was the one to seize. I sipped again and stood. Just as I did, I heard a flapping sound in the distance. That same sound caused Bill to stand up and look, like me, to the direction from which it came.

Flapping, then the closer it drew I realized it was footsteps, hard footsteps, running, basketball shoes smacking against the pavement.

I moved to the street and within a moment, I lost every bit of my breath and my glass dropped from my hand, shattering on the street.

From the depths of my soul I cried out in relief and my body couldn't move fast enough when I saw it was my son, Danny, running toward me.

I held him for the longest time in the middle of the street. Frozen with my emotions, I didn't want to let him go. I was afraid if I did, Danny would somehow disappear as well.

Something happened in that moment of holding my son, gripping him; I felt a glimmer of hope. A bit more strength returned to me.

"You were supposed to stay put," I told him.

"I couldn't, Mom. So many kids…they…" Danny shook his head. "Everything started falling apart at school and I caught a ride with the first car going east."

"I'm glad you're safe." After realizing how selfish I was being in our reunion, I stepped back, wiped my eyes and grabbed his hand. "Daddy needs to know you're back." I pulled him to follow.

There was reluctance, I felt it.

"What's wrong?" I asked.

"So Dad's okay?"

I wanted to blurt out that it was a silly question. Of course his father was alright. But there had to be a reason that spawned that inquiry. "Danny, why would you ask?"

"Just, you know, with it happening to so many. I knew you were fine; you ran to me. I figured when Dad didn't, he had the sickness."

"Baby," I gripped his hand. "Dad's fine. Jeremy though…" I lowered my head. "Your little brother didn't make it."

My son, so much taller than me, looked down, still such a child, innocence in his eyes. His lips did that pucker thing before he spoke. "I kinda figured."

"I'm sorry."

"Me, too," Danny said. "I wish I was able to see him, though. I wish I wouldn't have stayed back at school. I would have been here."

"You're here now. And Daddy isn't sick, so no worries."

I watched Danny take a step, his eyes shifted to the porch and he stared at Daniel.

"Danny?" I called his name.

"He's got it," Danny whispered.

"Danny, no."

A shift of his body, and Danny looked in another direction. "Mrs. Logan does, too."

"Mrs. Logan?" I questioned. "Who is Mrs. Logan?" Then I saw where he focused. He stared at Bill's lawn and to Bill's wife, Jen. "Oh, Jennie. No, she's fine."

Danny didn't respond. He just watched her. Then he murmured. "No, she has the sickness."

My God, what my son must have seen. How frightened he must have been. To me, that was the only explanation for his paranoia that everyone was ill.

Bill made his way over and I was grateful for that.

"Danny," Bill shook Danny's hand and gave him a half embrace. "Glad you're okay."

"You, too," Danny said.

"Bill," I interjected, "could you tell Danny that your wife isn't ill?"

Bill smiled. "No, she's fine. Out like a light."

"Just like Dad," I added.

Danny's eyes went from Bill to me. "They have the sickness." He said those words so calmly, so matter of fact, it was almost frightening.

I laid my hand on his cheek. "Danny, that sickness, it only hit children."

"Mom?" Danny grabbed my hand. "That was the Rapture."

I scoffed some and stepped back. "It was the Rapture. Oh, please."

"Then what was it?" he asked.

"I don't know."

"The Rapture, Mom. It *wasn't* just the kids. It was entire villages. People are gone. Missing. Wiped out. The weather, the rash of disasters yesterday. Now, this. This is what some are saying is the cleansing phase, starting with the sickness."

Bill asked. "How do you know this, Danny?"

"How do you not?" Danny retorted then looked around. "Oh, okay, I see, no power. Well, we had power at school. We had news. Internet. We had information over the last twenty-four hours and it's insane."

What had I missed? What in the world was going on? Suddenly I felt all the blood rushing to my head. I was so consumed with my troubles, isolated in our storm area that I had no idea what was happening in the world.

Danny looked at me. "Have you slept at all since Jeremy left?"

"Yeah, for a little—"

He turned to Bill. "You? Have you slept?"

Bill nodded.

"Then you're fine. Have they?" He pointed first to Daniel then to Jen.

"I don't know if Daddy slept," I answered.

Bill looked over his shoulder at his wife. "I think that's the first time."

"Then I suggest," Danny said, "if you don't believe me, check them. Go on. Check. Feel them. Then try to wake them. They won't get up."

Bill turned and moved toward his house and to his wife. I watched as he crouched down, reached to her and quickly retracted his hand. He stared our way.

I didn't hesitate after seeing that. I ran as fast as I could to the porch. "Daniel?" I called his name. "Danny's home. Danny's back."

No response.

I refused to believe he was anything but in a deep sleep.

"Daniel." I reached down to him, the moment my hand touched his shoulder, I pulled back as fast as Bill pulled from Jen.

Even through his clothes his skin was burning hot. Hotter than I'd ever felt.

I moved away, stunned and without words. I stepped from the porch to not only face my son but face one more thing that made me question what was going on.

8
CATCHING UP

Bill made a comment that he felt stupid and that the 1990s called wanting their radios back. He felt so proud of them at first, getting information and so forth, but looked at them halfheartedly when he realized they failed him more than helping him. Which wasn't really true, but I am certain in his mind it was.

The radios kept him in the dark and he was relying on them. I reminded Bill that had it not been for his radio, George Lawson wouldn't have been able to make his last round of house calls.

That then spawned a conversation about George. Where was he? How was he? That caused Bill to ask us to watch Jen and he sauntered away. I use the word 'sauntered' because I can't think of another word to describe Bill's walk. He was a tall man that moved slowly. He struck me as a kid in a big man's body.

When he first left and walked down the street, I had no clue where he went.

That was, of course, after Danny had told us all he could tell us. He sat on a blanket on the lawn not far from our SUV, his things in a duffel bag next to him. He wouldn't go near the porch. I had tried unsuccessfully to wake Daniel. His fever raged. The wet rag I used on him immediately dried. I even attempted to get him to lie down on the swing. This only caused him to roll, almost lifelessly, off the swing and onto the porch.

Never once did he respond to the fall.

About an hour after that, I noticed blisters forming on his mouth. His lips were dry and swollen and the fever blisters only made them look worse. I wiped, or at least tried, to wipe him down every twenty minutes.

What was happening with my husband?

For as much as I loved Danny, I tried not to put too much stock in what he said. All except when he said, "Jessie's fine."

"How do you know?" I asked.

"Mom, I told you I had internet. I spoke with her online. She gave me the address of her friend's house. She promised to stay there until we get her."

"When's the last time you spoke to her?"

"About two hours before I left to come here. We lost connection. Things, or rather, the sickness hadn't started there yet."

"Danny? Where did you hear about this?"

"On the news. The internet gave more details though. But you can't believe it all."

He went on to tell us how across the world, shortly after the children came down with the illness, that people started disappearing. Entire villages in China were gone. Israel reported blocks and scores of people missing. This was news I hadn't heard.

The night we had the three tornados in Philadelphia, similar storms and tornados ripped across the plains of the Midwest. Earthquakes shook the coastal cities. Wave warnings were issued and the temperature began to rise. That little tidbit I didn't need the news to tell me.

In the twenty-four hours that I was without power or communication, the world pretty much threw science and virology out the window and prayer took on new meaning. Prayer was the new penicillin.

It wasn't happening. I was in a suspension of disbelief.

Then again I hadn't left my little suburb. I would, and soon enough I would be hit with some sort of reality. Until then I worried for my husband.

What was this sickness? Danny only knew what he had heard and some of what he had seen.

"It kicks in once you fall asleep," he told me and Bill. "Not everyone, but most. A lot of people won't go to sleep now. In China and other places, they're saying that the fever rages a person so bad that when they are finally conscious they are nothing. Some say they get violent, I don't know. At Carson, all the instructors got it. That's when we decided to book."

"What happened with them?" I asked him. "What made you run? Were you afraid of getting it?"

"No, it was freaky," Danny said. "They just stared. They had these sores on their faces, they moved, but they watched you and stared. No reaction. No talking. Like they were thinking about what to do with you."

Bill shivered. "Uhh…" he said, wiping his hands against his own arms. "That's scary."

"Tell me about it," Danny said.

"Every instructor?" Bill asked.

"Every one."

"All the staff?"

"Every one."

"But the kids. Not the kids, right?"

"The ones older than fourteen, yes. The ones that hadn't gone to sleep yet. And only a couple. One kid had it in the car on the way here."

I shook my head. "That can't be right. Every single person on your campus with the exception of a few kids who didn't sleep?"

"Mom, why don't you believe me?"

"It sounds farfetched, that's all."

"Oh, yeah?" Danny raised an eyebrow. "When's the last time you saw anyone but Mr. Logan here on the street moving around?"

That question from Danny was the one that caused Bill to stand up and walk off.

Me, I didn't have an answer, but I was pretty sure I had seen *someone* else, a few others moving about. I don't know what was wrong with me. Perhaps it was my grief, the overwhelming abundance of sadness I was swimming in, I don't know. But I had such a hard time believing the words of my son. It seemed so ridiculous. First, all the children then others disappear, disasters, and now some weird sickness?

It was far beyond the realm of what I could believe. A sickness that kicks in once you sleep. It was out of a science fiction movie. Unreal. And to top it off they were saying it was God? *God?* All my life I believed in God, but at that moment, when unexplained things occurred, I doubted His existence at all.

I had fetched more water to wipe down Daniel when Bill finally returned a few hours later. He looked tired and drawn and had broken a sweat. His locks of hair had turned into wet curls framing his face.

I was with Daniel, saw his approach, but kept doing what I was doing.

"Mera," he called my name, breathless.

"I'm almost done," I replied. "You need to wipe Jen down soon."

"Mera, I walked for eight blocks. At least."

"Look at his lips, Bill. Look at what the fever is doing."

"Mera, listen to me." He laid his hand on mine. "Eight blocks."

"Do you think he's not responding because of this fever?" I stayed focused on Daniel, even though I did hear what Bill had to say. Change of subject, avoidance of subject, to me that made it less real.

"Eight blocks," he said. "No one. Not a single person didn't...Mera, every person I saw was curled up, lying there with a fever. I went into homes, looked at those sleeping on their lawns."

I didn't reply. I just kept wiping down Daniel. It broke my heart that with each swipe against his forehead, the wet cloth became dry.

"Mera, did you hear me?"

After a pause, I replied. "Yes." I dipped the cloth in the water and wrung out the excess. I looked at Bill. "Everyone?"

"Everyone."

I wanted to lay that cloth on Daniel. I wanted to. But I clenched it, water dripping out onto my hand. My forehead went to my clutched fist and I began to sob.

9
AWAKENING

Though it wasn't hot, we still had running water. It didn't matter, I hadn't showered in days and the cold water felt refreshing, especially with the heat. It was hard to believe that it had been two days since I woke up thinking all was right with the world.

There was no steam to clear from the mirror and I was immediately assaulted by my own reflection. It wasn't even fully light out, yet I could see enough. My God, I looked bad. My eyes were puffy from crying, my face drawn and looking thinner than it usually did. I had been crying nonstop. I couldn't even stop crying long enough to take the shower.

I felt refreshed, somewhat. The good shower sobbing episode helped. I knew I needed sleep. But that wasn't an option. Not yet. Plus I was still a little scared to fall asleep. Danny and I were in debate. He wanted to get on the road right away to head to Seattle. I told him there was no way we were leaving his father, to which he replied staying wasn't going to be an option and I'd see soon enough.

I grew angry at that military school, wondering what they had done to my son. When did they remove the compassionate gene in him? Yes, he was a troubled teen, but he had emotions. He cared; that's why he fought. But suddenly my son went into some sort of strange survivalist mode. He removed things from our vehicle saying they weren't needed and replaced them with other items. He collected gas cans that the neighbors had for their lawnmowers, combining the fuel and getting as much as he could.

Roy Littlemen had an NRA member sticker on his car. Danny remembered that about him and went to Roy's house. He returned with two 9mm handguns and a shotgun, along with ammunition.

Danny seemed to not think twice about his looting.

"What you are doing? That's against the law." I followed him as he stayed focused loading our vehicle.

"Mom, please."

That's when I spotted the guns. "What the hell are you doing, Danny? Those are Roy's."

"Yes, they are."

"You can't just take them."

"Roy doesn't know. He's on his couch with the sickness." Danny tossed the items in the car. "We need them."

"For what?"

"Protection."

"We'll get arrested. We don't have a license for those."

"Mom..."

"Oh my God." My hand went to my head. It literally spun. I felt dizzy, scared. I kept thinking, we were going to get in the car, start to drive and Martial Law was probably already in effect. We'd be pulled over.

To me, all of it was temporary. Rationalizing the long term hadn't even begun for me. I wasn't there yet. Danny was. Not me.

"Mom, really? Arrested? You can't possibly be that naïve."

"Don't talk to me like that," I scolded.

"Well, don't be like this. Come on."

"Like what?" I asked. "Honest? Law-abiding?"

"Scared." Danny leaned into me. "You're scared."

"I *am*," I argued with passion. "And adding guns to this makes it worse. We don't need them."

"We do. Ask Mr. Logan." Danny swung around with a point across the street.

Bill was in his yard. He had taken to holding Jen in his arms, rocking back and forth.

"I don't think Bill cares about anything right now except his sick wife," I told him, "like I am with my husband, your father. Your *father*, Danny, remember?"

Danny huffed. "You don't think I care?"

"I'm beginning to wonder."

Danny turned his head with a look that said, 'unbelievable.'

"No," I argued. "When did you get like this? When?"

"Like what?"

"Cold."

"Not cold, Mom. Focused. Right now I'm focused."

"Then focus on your family!" I turned hard and headed back to the porch and to Daniel.

"I am!"

Danny's words made me stop.

He ran up to me. "Mom, I am." He stepped in front of me. "I love my father with all my heart. My baby brother too. I love them." He brought his fist to his chest. "But there is nothing we can do about them. *Nothing.* Jessie, she's another story. We *can* help her. She needs us and we have to go as soon as we can to get her. This is a dying world. Who knows how much time we have to find her?"

I saw it in my son's face and heard it in his words he delivered with marked maturity. But he was wrong and to me stuck in some mode that the school had instilled in him. There was no logical explanation for what was going on, but surely he was exaggerating.

Unfortunately, I was in complete denial, a denial that lessened some when I took another step to the porch and noticed the grass beneath my feet. The night before that same grass was cool and damp; now it was dry and dying.

I raised my eyes and looked around for the first time that morning. The leaves on the trees were turning brown, the flowers in our flower bed were wilted and dead. Everything on our street that once exuded life was quickly losing it.

At that moment I realized there was more truth to my son's label of a 'dying world' than I cared or wanted to admit.

But all that had to be put behind me. I had to worry about Daniel. Just as I lifted my foot to the front porch my attention was drawn to Bill's voice.

The street was quiet, everything echoed and even though he didn't shout, his voice was loud and clear as he stuttered out, "O-oh, shit. Oh my God."

I turned completely around. Bill was on the ground, scooting back from Jen using his hands and feet. He moved back quickly. Had she died?

Danny called out to him and as Bill looked Danny's way, Jen, head still turned toward Bill, sat straight up. As if she had some sort of ejection lever, her head moved smoothly, almost mechanically to look our way, then back to Bill.

Bill looked at his wife, let out a short shriek, then glanced our way and shrieked again as he scurried to his feet.

It the midst of my watching, I felt it against my back, the slightest bump as if someone had moved directly against me.

Slowly, I turned around and the shock of it stumbled me back a few steps. Daniel was standing on the porch, his eyes glossy and encircled by dark rings, his face pale. With his head tilted slightly to the right he just stared at me; without blinking, he stared.

"Daniel." I heaved out a breath of relief. "How are you?"

No response.

"You were so sick last night..."

Daniel took the first of the two steps down from the porch.

"Daniel? Danny's home. He came back last night. I tried to wake you."

Another step and he was on the lawn with me. I didn't know how to react. He wasn't saying anything, just staring and moving slowly to me.

I was intimidated, scared, anyone would be. But this was my husband. What was I to fear about him?

"Mom." Danny's call of my name and grasp to my arm jolted me back from Daniel. "Let's go. Get in the car."

"Danny, he's sick, that's all."

"Mera," Bill approached out of breath. "I have a bad feeling."

Danny added. "Me, too."

My mouth dropped open in shock. I was ready to blast them, ready to ask what was wrong with them, scold them, because our family needed help. When I turned around, words about to emerge from my mouth, I saw.

Not just Jen, but other neighbors were walking from the grass, all moving slowly, staring out, heads tilted and walking in the same direction, toward us. There had to be thirty and more coming from down the street, as if the three of us were some sort of calling beacon.

"Oh, my God," I whispered.

"Yeah," Danny said with sarcasm. "Let's go." He tugged my arm.

"I can't leave your father."

"Start the car, Danny," Bill ordered. "I'll grab her."

"What?" I screeched. "You're going to leave Jen? I can't—"

"Mera." Bill called my name sharply, as if to snap me to reality. He took hold of my shoulders. "Look around. This isn't right. We have to go. We have to go *now*."

I shifted my eyes and looked. It was surreal, like a nightmare. They edged their way toward us. No noise. No sounds. Just closing in. I felt the rush, the urgency, as if we were on the brink of something.

"Mera!"

"Okay." I pulled away from him. "Okay, I'll go. Just let me say goodbye." Instinctively, I knew it wouldn't do any good. Daniel mentally wasn't there, he wasn't *right*. Wiping my hand over my face, I faced my husband and looked up. "Daniel, I am sorry. I have to go get Jessie. I love you." I tiptoed and leaned forward to kiss him.

Before I could even comprehend, Daniel's hand snapped out and clutched my throat. His grip was hard, strong and strangling. Immediately, I felt the pain to my neck, my larynx felt as if it were crushing.

"Mom!" Danny shouted.

I heard Danny, couldn't call out for help. I couldn't even get air. I dug my nails into my husband's hand and tried to plead, but couldn't. Fighting and struggling made it worse, and trying to make eye contact with Daniel was useless; his eyes looked right through me like I was a stranger. My God, he was killing me. Then Daniel exuded strength I never knew he had when he lifted me in the chokehold single-handedly from the ground.

I distantly heard Danny's voice, Bill's voice, their shouts fading and drowned out by the sound of blood, my blood, rushing to my ears. I kicked, struggled to get any breath. I could see through my increasingly blurred vision how Danny and Bill diligently tried to pull Daniel from me.

It was all in vain.

I was fading. I knew it.

The heartbeat in my ears replaced the rushing blood. Thump-thump . . . thump . . . thump.

The beats slowed down. There was no air. My blurred vision grew darker and I no longer had control of my eyes, they rolled behind my head and my arms and legs grew numb and weak. My body shook, but that was all I felt. A peaceful feeling took over. My life literally flashed before my eyes.

I heard Jeremy's voice, his laughter, Jessie's voice, saw her smile. I had a flash of a vision of Danny in his school uniform.

And then I saw Daniel the day we were married. So young, so handsome, he looked down to me. "I love you, Chirp."

At that split second in time, I knew I was dying.

Then the sound of a single gunshot brought me a gasping rush of air and it all went black.

10
COFFEE AND REALITY

Nothing in particular made me wake up. I wasn't dreaming, didn't hear anything, feel anything. I just woke up. It took only a few seconds to realize I was in the back seat of our SUV and we were driving.

As soon as I moved, my neck hurt. It felt as if not only did I have a stiff neck but also a sore throat. If I had an Adam's apple, I would have sworn it was crushed.

I sat up from my reclined position and my groan must have caught the attention of Bill and Danny. Bill was driving and he peered only quickly over his shoulder then used the rearview mirror to communicate.

"How are you feeling?"

"Sore." I smoothed my hand over my neck. "Thirsty. And I have to use the restroom."

"We'll stop ahead, I saw a sign. A few more miles. Can you hold on?" Bill asked. I nodded.

"Are you sure you're okay, Mom?" Danny asked.

"Yeah," I answered breathily, then noticed the clock above the radio. The digits indicated eleven in the morning. "How long have I been out?"

"Hours," Danny replied. "We knew you were fine, so we let you rest."

I peered again at the clock and noticed the radio was on, but nothing was playing. The digital display read 'scanning.' I suppose they were hoping to catch something.

It was as I turned to look out the window that not only did I notice we were cruising along on the Pennsylvania Turnpike, but the reality of what had occurred struck me.

I grabbed my neck. Visions of my husband's expression flashed through my mind, his eyes cold and showing no emotion. His fingers were strong, yet he was still fevered; I could feel the heat on my skin. He strangled me and did so staring out as if I were a pane of glass he looked through.

Then I remembered the gunshot.

It had caused him to release me, and with that memory my insides churned and my heart thumped so hard I swore I felt it hit my stomach.

"Who fired the gun?" I asked.

Danny looked back. "Excuse me?"

"Your father was killing me. Who fired the gun? Who shot him?"

I was in the backseat. Did they think I wouldn't see the long exchange of a glance? Both of them looked at each other then returned to staring forward.

"No one," Danny answered. "No one shot Dad. We...I... fired a shot in the air and it startled him. He let you go."

Bill nervously picked up the story. "And then we put you in here and took off. They were uh, all coming toward us. You know..."

Liars. I wanted to say that out loud, but I didn't. They were trying to protect me from the truth. Perhaps they didn't think I could handle yet one more heartbreak. That little bit of sleep I received did me a lot of good. While the reality of what happened to Jeremy was still with me, the reality of the big picture was a bit clearer. I felt myself being more level-headed, rational. Yes, I was grieving and I would mourn my son and husband when I could, but I also had to keep moving.

The world was different now.

I could see that as we rolled down the highway. There wasn't a car on the road, at least none that I had seen. The spring trees looked more like autumn ones, and the sky was gray and overcast. The whole feel of life felt off-balance.

I saw the 'Rest Area 2 miles' sign just before we passed a tractor trailer that was pulled off to the side of the road. The driver stood outside, staring out with the same expression as Daniel and Jen had had. He watched us as we drove by him.

"Do you think it will be safe?" Danny asked Bill.

"Yeah. Sure," Bill replied, "I mean, we only saw a truck or two on the side of the road, right? And I don't think many people went inside the Roy Rogers and took a nap. That's when it hit."

"True."

"What if they pulled over there and slept in their car?" I asked them both.

"Then...then we'll have problems," Bill said. "We'll deal with it when we get there."

I leaned more toward the front seat. "You're very brave."

I must have suddenly become a comedian because Bill and Danny both burst into laughter.

"What?" I asked. "What's so funny?"

"Brave." Bill snorted a laugh. "I am so not brave."

I looked at Danny. "Why are you laughing? That's rude."

"Sorry," Danny swiped the smile from his face. "It's just that, when you were sleeping he was saying how scared he was."

"I still think he's brave." I sat back. "He saved my life. It took a lot of guts for him to shoot your father."

Danny looked back at me. "He didn't—"

"I saw." My eyes shifted to the window, then quickly back to Bill and Danny to see their reactions. I was lying, of course. I didn't see anything. But I needed to know the truth and it was delivered not by their admittance, but rather Bill's quick change of subject when he nervously announced, "Rest stop."

We pulled over.

The illuminated gas sign told us that the rest stop had power. It had been decided that we'd do what we needed to do inside the restrooms then fill up the tank and canisters with gas before hitting the road again.

We hadn't a clue what was ahead or how far we'd get for the day.

There wasn't a car in the parking lot, yet the lights were on, the doors unlocked. The workers inside up and left quickly, which was evident by the smell of burnt coffee when we stepped inside.

Danny checked out the ladies' room for me as I went into the gift shop and grabbed a travel toothbrush and toothpaste. My mouth felt gross and dry. He gave me an all clear and I went and took care of my business.

Danny was on watch when I came out and I sought something for us to eat.

Someone else had been there before us, maybe even several people.

The snack rack outside the first food stand was wiped clean, along with all the prepared sandwiches. Food that was starting to get moldy and petrified still remained on the tables in the restaurant. I supposed it had been sitting there for two days.

Upon first glance, anything edible in plain sight was gone. But having been familiar with working in restaurants, I went into the kitchen and sought out the dry storage. I emptied the box of ketchup and loaded that box with as much as I could. I grabbed cereal, granola, some stuff in jars. No cans. I couldn't remember if Daniel or I had grabbed a can opener when we were packing food and camping things for the trip to Seattle.

Then again, Danny had removed some things from the car; he could have thrown some of that out. I didn't know for sure. I was out of it then and I wasn't really registering anything that was going on.

I did know that what I grabbed was short term, more so for the ride. Eventually we'd have to figure a way to get real food or none of us would have any strength, and then what good would we be?

For a moment, a brief moment, I dismissed my dismal thoughts of survival and replaced them with hopeful ones. Maybe once we got further west things would get better.

But I thought like that for only a moment. How could I even conceive a better world out west when I stood in the middle of an empty, lifeless rest stop? Nothing on the television, no sounds, no people.

"Mera, you all right?" Bill called.

It startled me some and I jumped. "Yeah. Sorry." Box in arms, I stepped from the back kitchen area. "I was getting some supplies."

"Good thinking," he said. "I know there are boxes with food in the back of your truck, but you can never have enough. Here…" He handed me a Starbucks cup.

I gave a curious look.

"They had one of those Starbucks Kiosks, and I figured I'd make us all one. Danny said you loved your mochas with extra shots."

At that second, I believe it was the first time I smiled in days. "You made me a mocha? Thank you."

"It may be the last we have for a while once power goes down everywhere." He grabbed the box from me. "Enjoy."

I took a sip. "This is very good."

"Geez, I hope so. I worked my way through college at Starbucks." He gave a twitch of his head as a point. "Let's go. Danny's waiting, and who knows how long it'll be safe here?"

I followed, cradling the large cup between both of my hands. There was something about holding it that made me feel a little better. It wasn't the taste, but more so that I got to hold on to a little bit of normalcy, a normal life that was slipping further away with each passing hour.

11
FIRST CONTACT

The 'fasten seatbelt' bell chimed when Bill started the car. But no sooner had he closed the door than it was joined by another sound, the odd, off-key beeping of the Emergency Broadcast System.

A recorded electronic voice told us to 'please standby for further instructions.'

Then Bill acted as if he hit the lottery. Well, maybe not that enthused. He clenched his fist and hit it against the steering wheel.

"Yes. *Yes.* See?" He pointed at Danny. "Didn't I tell you? I was right. See? Yes."

Danny calmly stated, "Yes, you were, but maybe we should go." He pointed out the window.

Across the large lot of the gas station was a parking area for trucks, and a long line of slow moving truckers were headed our way.

"Might be a good idea," Bill agreed. He put the vehicle in gear and pulled away from the pump, and then the gas station. He didn't do so with urgency.

I watched the truck drivers. It was actually kind of funny; they were a good hundred feet away, yet as we drove out, they reached out their hands all at the same time like we were within their grasp.

A mile or so down the road, Bill still had a gloating tone. He played with the volume on the radio, perhaps thinking that would make the announcement come sooner.

"You're the man," Danny murmured sarcastically.

"What did I miss?" I asked. "I must have slept through a conversation."

Bill nodded. "Yeah, I told Danny that I saw this program on the History Channel and they said about thirty radio stations were chosen by FEMA to be operational in an all-out catastrophe, given generators and everything. Danny didn't believe me."

"I didn't say I didn't believe you," Danny replied. "I just didn't think with it being the Rapture that there'd be any need for an Emergency Broadcast System."

"Why not?" Bill asked. "It's an emergency. We had disasters, deaths."

"Seriously?" Danny asked with a chuckle. "Bill, for real, think about this, dude. The whole purpose of the EBS is to help people survive, to know what to do. If

God's ending this world, there's nothing you can do but hang with those you love and wait it out until your number is called."

"Wow, that's really your attitude?"

"Yeah."

"That sucks. I mean I expected more out of you, mister..." Bill changed his voice to be more mocking, almost as if he were imitating Danny, "grab the guns, be prepared, star military school pupil. People are basing this theory of 'God's End' on what? The Bible? Well, you know what? I read the Bible and nowhere in there did I see a length of time for ending this world. I don't know about you, but I'm not gonna hang around for years waiting for my number. I'll survive, thank you very much."

I looked over to my son, watching his facial expression. His jaw went from left to right and he nodded slowly. "That's a good point. Mom? What do you think?" I guess it was my son's way of getting me to join the conversation while awaiting the EBS announcement.

"Please don't ask me," I answered. "I'm still waiting on a logical explanation for all that happened."

The reflection of Bill's eyes made contact with mine in that rearview mirror. "I know what you mean, Mera," Bill said. "I'm waiting for one, too."

"Logical explanation?" Danny directed at Bill. "Isn't God's end a logical explanation?"

"Not at all," Bill answered without missing a beat. "It's not God's end."

"How can you be so sure?" Danny asked.

"Simple," Bill said. "I don't believe in God."

Danny let out this offended 'uh!' and cocked back. "*What?*"

Bill laughed.

"Dude, did you, like, ever hear the old saying, 'there are no atheists in foxholes?'"

"There's that military school coming out," Bill commented.

"No. It's an old saying. Check this out." Danny's hands flew about as he spoke. "Two billion kids die at the same time. People disappear, disasters occur, people get this sickness that turns them into drones...there is no logical explanation except for God. This is the proverbial foxhole."

"Then I am the only atheist in it." Bill shrugged.

"But I heard you say, 'oh my God, '" Danny said.

"Yeah, well, I talked about Santa last Christmas too, did that make him real?"

Did my son think his rambling in offense would cause Bill to throw his hands in the air and suddenly proclaim, 'I see the light, praise the Lord?'

Then again, maybe in Danny's mind he thought it would.

My mind went elsewhere. Bill didn't believe in God? The revelation that Bill was actually a total stranger to me hit me right there when he revealed he was an atheist.

Never would that have dawned on me. Then again, I was traveling across the country with a man I knew nothing about.

"What did you do for a living, Bill?" I asked.

"Mom?" Danny called my name with a hint of shock. "Where in the world is that coming from?"

Bill blew slightly from his mouth and said, "Yeah, that's like a total change of subject."

"Mom, you okay?" Danny asked worriedly.

What was it about the way Danny asked me that question? Sarcastic concern? I didn't know, but I understood what he could be implying.

"I'm not having a mental breakdown, if that's what you mean," I clarified.

Danny bobbed his head. "Well, it was out of the blue. We were talking about the end of the world, God."

"I know. It was," I said. "Maybe subconsciously it was me trying to change the subject. It just hit me I didn't really know Bill."

Bill crinkled his brow. "I lived across the street from you for three years. I went fishing almost every Sunday with your husband."

"You went fishing with Daniel?"

"How did you not know this?"

Danny shook his head. "Bill, if you don't shoot out espresso, have the name Jack across your head, or spit out quarters, she didn't notice you."

"Huh?" Bill asked, apparently lost.

"My mom drank coffee, bourbon, and gambled. Period."

"Oh, please," I defended. "I did more than that."

Bill gazed over his shoulder. "Okay, so what did *you* do for a living?"

I didn't get to answer. The tone of the EBS occurred once more, only this time it was accompanied by a female voice, effectively putting our conversation on pause.

"Virginia Harrison" introduced herself before delivering her speech over the airwaves. To me, she needed no introduction. She was the Secretary of State and the most powerful woman I knew in politics. Her broadcast was laced with intermittent static and blips but was audible nonetheless. It was apparent she was broadcasting from somewhere remote.

"Our hearts and prayers go out to everyone who has been touched by this global crisis," she said. *"And it is a global crisis unparalleled to any we have experienced in history."*

She told of how we had her assurance that the president was safe and alive, but at the time was mourning the loss of his daughter through the Event and coping with the illness of his wife, inflicted by the sleeping sickness.

They were pushing to maintain a strong hub of government, which was vital to keep order.

"*Our top minds and scientists are struggling to figure out the cause of the events that have unfolded,*" she explained. "*While many attribute these events to a higher power, our government, your government, cannot operate on that theory and must proceed accordingly to ensure continuity and survival and that we rise above the ashes. It is pure tragedy, what has happened. We must forge forward but we must do so facing reality.*"

Then she spewed forth the reality.

Natural disasters had ripped across the globe in major areas exactly twelve hours after the Event that took the children. The Sleeping Sickness, as it was labeled, began twelve hours after that. Basically, everything happened within a twenty-four-hour period. Thus far, nothing new had occurred, but those inflicted with the Sleeping Sickness were not predictable. Many showed signs of violence and seemed to be on some sort of automatic operating mode.

According to Ms. Harrison, major metropolises were swarming with the afflicted, and for that reason those who were well were advised to avoid the major cities and highly populated areas.

All that could be done was being done to gather them and aid them; however, the numbers, combined with the reactions and violent tendencies of the infected was making for an impossible task.

Cities were also in disarray. Not just from the afflicted, but from the natural disasters. Ms. Harrison stressed that if they had occurred singularly, they would not have been considered such an ordeal, but since they all occurred simultaneously it put the world on a break. Once the pause button was released, chaos ensued with the confusion.

She assured us that the government was working hard and things would return to semi-normal, eventually. It was a daunting task that was bigger than they ever imagined.

Military personnel were trickling back in, but their numbers were a mere fraction of what they should be. The government was seeking volunteers to help.

Martial law was in effect from 6 pm until 6 am. Those caught traveling on the roads after six would be detained, while those caught looting would be shot on sight. It was temporary but had to be done.

She ended her transmission by telling us, "*I'll update when I have more information.*"

Then the silence returned to the airwaves. Her speech held such heavy overtones I could not help but feel burdened by this overwhelmingly dismal and grieving feeling.

My world as I knew it in every aspect was over.

Bill and Danny returned to some sort of conversation. Not me. I removed myself emotionally and mentally. I curled up against the door, rested my head against the window and pulled out my phone. I knew my battery was dying and I would have to conserve. But for the time being I needed to see my other children. I powered up my phone, ready to open the photo album and stare at Jeremy's smiling face, maybe read Jessie's barrage of text messages she had sent me over the last week. It was then I saw something else I hadn't seen in days. Sitting up, I leaned between the two front seats with my phone.

"Guys," I held out my phone. "I got a signal."

12
THE SIGNAL

It came just three hours earlier. "Mommy, Mommy, I'm fine." Jessie was crying. "Please, if you get this, get back to me. They're moving us from the city to a camp in Maple Valley. I'll wait there for you guys. I'm fine, Mommy, I love you guys. Please be all right."

I listened to her message fully, then I tried to call my daughter. Though I truly felt she was fine, getting that message renewed me, filled me with a focus. What would happen beyond reaching my daughter I didn't know, but I had to get to her.

It took six attempts and another bar of my phone battery, but eventually Jessie answered.

Our conversation was brief; neither one of us wanted to risk the battery power. We agreed we'd shut the phones off to conserve. She had already figured out that Jeremy had passed; what she didn't know was about her father.

I told her Danny was with me and that her dad had the Sleeping Sickness, at which she sobbed. I cried too, and told her how much I loved her. Jessie had arrived at the elementary school with about four dozen people. She had set up her stuff in the far left corner of the gym by the fire extinguisher and promised that if she had to go, she'd leave a note, right there.

For the conservation of power our tear-filled conversation had to end. It did, with my promise to get there, to get her, no matter how long it took. I was on my way.

I took over driving about twenty miles before Pittsburgh. Bill seemed relieved. He relaxed in the front seat while Danny took time to sleep in the back. I should have let Danny drive the Pennsylvania Turnpike. It avoids all major cities, unlike Interstate 80, which wasn't that far away.

Nowhere in the journey did we see another traveling car. That struck me as odd because in my mind, if the Secretary of State was delivering speeches there had to be people out and about. We saw neither travelers nor any people. Well, not in the conventional sense. Some cars or trucks were off to the side of the road and when we passed an interchange called Breezewood, I saw people moving about the street, walking aimlessly. Bill said they probably had been infected; it was something about the way they moved.

The air conditioning was having a hard time keeping up. The heat was stifling and the sun was overpowering but I knew all that would change when the sun went down. It was pushing four o'clock when I saw the sign indicating an end to the toll road. Bill and Danny were both sleeping at that point.

"Bill," I reached over and nudged him. "Bill? Where's the ticket?"

Bill woke with a puzzled look. "Huh?"

I hated to wake him but I had looked in the visor, the console, it wasn't there. "The ticket," I reiterated. "Turnpike ticket."

"Mera, I didn't take the ticket when I went through."

"Why not?"

He stumbled at first for an answer. "I don't know. Maybe because I didn't think anyone would make us pay."

For some reason this sent me into an anxiety frenzy, especially with the toll booth fast approaching. "I cannot believe you didn't take the ticket." My words were emotional, hard and snappy toward him.

"You really think someone is going to be there standing there, waiting on your money?" his voice edged up some.

"Guys," Danny blurted out groggily from the back.

"No, I don't think that!" I barked. "I'm not dumb. I don't think a toll worker is there!"

"Then why do you care if we have a ticket?"

"Come on, guys, stop," Danny said.

Ignoring Danny, I yelled my loudest, the barren toll booth now within a few seconds of driving. "Because how else are we supposed to get through the fucking closed gate without a ticket!"

"Go around!" The man I had believed to be mild mannered, suddenly blasted back at me as loudly as I yelled at him. "Go around the booths!"

Instinctively my foot hit the brake, which caused a 'thump' and a groan from Danny as he rolled from the backseat to the floor.

"Did you just yell at me?" I asked Bill.

"Why did you stop?" he asked.

"I don't know. You yelled."

"No, *you* yelled. I reacted."

I was going to say more, but I didn't. I gripped the steering wheel with both hands and apologized to Danny. "Sorry, honey."

He grumbled, "It's fine," and returned to the back seat.

I lifted my foot from the brake and turned to Bill. "What do you mean, go around?"

He pointed to the small office building to the side of the tool booths. "There, through that lot. Go that way."

"Sorry, I wasn't thinking about that."

Perhaps Bill thought he was mumbling under his breath, but I certainly heard his, "Obviously."

Again, my foot hit the brake.

Thump. "Mom!"

I shot a glare at Bill then continued to drive.

Maybe it was the little bit of rest I had, the coffee, or the phone call from Jess, I don't know, but I felt energized. I wanted to get to my daughter. No, I *needed* to get to my daughter.

A few miles up the road after the turbulence of our quick verbal spar, I slowed down and with good reason.

The transition section between Interstate 76 and Interstate 80 brought something none of us expected to see.

A single military truck blocked the road. Not completely; I could go around and I planned on it. I didn't need the instructions from Bill or Danny to 'gun it.' I was making my own judgment call.

It was a good thing I didn't, because two soldiers emerged. As we drew closer it was apparent they were as shocked to see us as we were to see them.

In the few moments from first spotting the truck to approaching it, many things went through my mind. At first glance, it looked abandoned. Then when I saw the soldiers, I had a sense of the cavalry arriving. Heroes, yes, they were going to save the day. But these young and innocent boys, not much older than my own son, were as much lost souls as we were.

They waved for me to stop and of course, I did.

Only one of the two soldiers approached. "Afternoon, Ma'am," the one soldier smiled. "Really good to see you guys." He peeked in the car, perhaps to check us out. "Can I ask where you're headed?"

"West. Trying to get to Seattle," I replied.

"You taking I-80?" he asked.

"Hoping to. Why?"

He shook his head. "Best if you stay on 76 until just past Akron. Eighty goes through Cleveland and they shut that way down. You do realize there is a curfew, right?"

"Do you think that we'll get stopped if we ignore it?" I asked.

He lifted his shoulders in a shrug. "I wouldn't chance it. You got about two hours before curfew. There's a refugee station outside of Cuyahoga Falls, signs are posted. I'd stop there. Besides, you'll probably need to refuel and they're helping folks do that."

"After that where's the next camp?"

"Another hundred miles or so. Not many camps."

I nodded. "Thank you. We'll try there."

"You be safe."

Before I drove off, I had to ask. "How many cars came through here before us?"

He paused before answering, looking at the other soldier before leaning toward the window again. "I've been here since morning. You're the third car."

I tried not to show my shock at his answer, but I exhaled and gave a single nod. "You be safe, as well," I told him, wound up the window and eased on the gas.

Danny poked his head between the front seats. "Did he say three cars?"

"Three," I confirmed.

Bill whistled. "That's not a lot at all."

I shook my head. "Not at all."

Then Bill's demeanor switched to a more positive one. "I say we keep going. Forget the curfew. I mean, three cars? They aren't stopping anyone."

"I don't know," I said. "It is Martial Law. You heard the soldiers. Danny, what do you think?"

Danny shrugged. "I agree with Bill. Really, Mom. Three cars? We have fuel containers and enough gas to get us across the state. I say go."

Again, I was still in debate. "I'm thinking we'd better head for this refugee station. Play it safe."

Bill waved out his hand as if I were being ridiculous. "Mera, please. Have you seen a car? We went all the way across Pennsylvania without seeing a single military vehicle. No one is out and about. No one is going to enforce the curfew. Trust me," Bill said with much certainty. "We're fine. Keep driving. We're not getting stopped. We're not getting arrested."

It took all of about forty-five seconds before my arms started to hurt from having them raised in the air.

"Yeah, Bill, yeah," I said to him as we pulled up to the military blockade. We had made it about 30 miles beyond the first refugee camp. Truly, even I thought it was going to be smooth sailing.

"They're bored," Bill replied, "That's why they're stopping us. We're not getting arrested."

I looked in the rearview mirror at Danny. He was biting his nails. "Danny?"

He shifted his eyes to Bill then to me. "We're getting arrested."

I slammed my hand on the wheel. "I knew it."

"We're not getting arrested!" Bill nearly yelled. "Slow down, play it cool and most of all, play dumb."

"Play dumb?"

"Yes. Act like you didn't know. Trust me."

"I trusted you to keep goi—"

"Trust me."

"Okay." I slowed down and pulled to the blockade. There were three trucks there and more soldiers, maybe ten. Two stood before the hood of our SUV, while one approached the window.

My insides churned with a nervousness I hadn't felt in forever. Bill whispered, "We're not getting arrested," as I wound down the window.

The soldier was wearing a gas mask, which frightened me. My nervousness caused my face to immediately get hot and a slight buzzing started in my ears.

"Folks, road's off limits to civilians."

I shivered a breath, gripped that wheel and let out a fake chuckle. "Really?"

"Martial Law is in effect," he said. "You didn't know this?"

My heart pounded as my hands released the wheel. "No," I squeaked out. I never was any good at lying. Then quickly I turned to him. "Okay, we knew."

The soldier moved back. "Step from the vehicle. All of you."

"Why?" I asked. "Really, can't we just keep going? We'll stop at the next refugee station."

I don't know why I did it, but when he reached for the door, I locked it and immediately wound up the window.

"Ma'am!" He pounded on the window.

"Why did you do that?" Bill asked.

"Open up the door before I break the window!" The soldier kept pounding.

"We're getting arrested," Danny stated.

"No," Bill retorted calmly. "We're not getting arrested."

"What do I do?" I asked, noticing at that point four more soldiers were at our car.

"Gun it," Bill said, then he must have thought I believed him, because he quickly countered with, "No, Mera, open the door before he breaks the window, please."

Again, Danny repeated. "We're getting arrested."

"No, we're not." Bill said. "Mera, open the door."

I unlocked the lock and wound down the window again. "Sorry," I said to the soldier. "I panicked."

"Step out of the vehicle now. Hands in the air," he ordered, opening my door. " Now."

I looked at Bill and whispered, "I'm killing you."

"Me?" he snapped.

I raised my hands slightly, not too much. It was a difficult task to get out of the driver's seat with my hands in the air. As I emerged, I watched one soldier grab for Danny. A defense mechanism perhaps, a mother's way of watching out for her child, I yelled, "Hey! Leave him alone. That's my son." I reached out, thinking I could intervene, but I was pulled away.

They moved the three of us off to the side while they proceeded to search our SUV. It was utterly ridiculous, the entire Martial Law thing. I didn't get it. Was there something they weren't telling us? I couldn't fathom the world being up in arms or chaos on the street. Nothing I had seen since I left my home indicated anything other than the world was dying.

Yet there we stood, being treated like common criminals. I held on to my son, watching as all of our things were tossed out to the ground. We weren't thugs, thieves or armed terrorists. Okay, we *were* armed, and it didn't take long for the soldiers to find that out.

"They have weapons, Sarge."

We stayed quiet and the one soldier, I guess the one in charge, walked over.

"Do you folks have a license for these weapons? Are they registered to you?"

Without hesitation, Bill replied. "Yes, I just didn't think to bring documentation, we left so fast."

Then that soldier looked at me. "So the weapons belong to him?" He pointed at Bill.

"Yes." I saw the soldier was staring at me. "No. We sort of borrowed them."

I inwardly and outwardly cringed when I realized the true error of my honesty, or should I say stupidity. My simple answer caused a commotion amongst the guards and they rushed over to us as if suddenly we were going to make a mad dash.

It was when they took a firm hold of me that Bill found a moment to whisper my way, "*Now*, we're getting arrested. Thank you."

13
ARRESTED

They actually called it 'detained' and they brought us to the refugee camp set up in a volunteer fireman's hall located in a suburb of Toledo.

The building had probably seen its share of weddings and other festive events, but now housed about a hundred people, each with their own cot and blanket, each with their own heartbreaking story.

We were placed not far from the check-in table, which was close to a small sectioned-off area where occasionally we'd see a soldier go in and out. Like everyone else, after they took our names, they gave us a blanket and cot along with a gross pasty spaghetti meal in a pouch. The coffee, however, wasn't bad.

Danny had his phone and was playing with it. I didn't notice until I heard him say, "Something is going on."

"Danny, save your phone power."

Danny lifted the phone to show me a cord. He was plugged into the socket. The building had power.

Immediately, I wanted to charge my phone, but remembered we didn't have any of our belongings. After that, it dawned on me what Danny had said. "What's going on?"

Danny shook his head. "Hard to tell. Only three of my friends have updated a status in the last three hours. And there's no mention on the news about the Secretary of State's speech. Weird."

To me it wasn't all that weird. This wasn't happening in just one city, one town—this was worldwide. People had other things to worry about rather than posting or reporting news.

"See," Danny explained, "I would think at least the government would have their Martial Law rules on here. But there's nothing."

"Have you updated your status?" I asked him.

Danny stared at me for a second. "No."

I shrugged. "Maybe people are like you. Busy. Traveling. Trying to find people."

"That makes sense."

I reached over and ran my hand over his head. "I can be right once in a while."

At that moment Bill returned with another cup of coffee. "Anyone hear that gunshot?" he asked as he sat on the floor by me.

"No," Danny answered.

I replied, "What gunshot?"

"Guess not," Bill said. "Answers my question."

"Couldn't have been a gunshot," I told him. "I would think we'd hear it in here, it's awfully quiet."

Bill nodded.

"Then again, who would be shooting? I'm thinking you may have heard something that sounded like a gunshot."

"Mera?" Bill scratched his head. "Were you an attorney?"

"Huh?"

Danny laughed.

"You never said what you did for a living," Bill stated. "I was wondering, with all the arguing, if you were an attorney."

Danny interjected. "She wasn't an attorney, she was everything but, sort of."

"What's that supposed to mean?" Bill asked.

"She worked a lot of jobs. She was always changing them. She got bored easily. One day she'd be working at the drug store and she'd come home. We'd ask how her day was and she told us she quit. My dad was pretty good about it. He'd always tell her she'd find something else. And she did. The bet was when she worked in the hardware store. Lasted three days."

"I couldn't determine what I wanted to do, that's all. Waitressing worked out the best. I could get you guys off to school, work the lunch rush, and be home for the bus. You kids were so young, I didn't want to be away from home too much. And Jeremy, he…" I stopped. At the thought of my son, my heart sunk.

Grief has a way of making you physically feel your pain, as if it were a true physical pain. It hurt as much, and thinking of Jeremy was stabbing.

"Mera?" Bill laid a hand on my knee. "You all right?"

"Yeah, I just… I just was thinking of Jeremy."

"I'm sorry."

"It's okay." I took a deep breath. "He's in a better place than we are right now."

"If you believe in that," Bill said.

"Dude, really?" Danny snapped. "Not cool. You're supposed to be compassionate at this moment."

"I'm sorry, that was wrong."

"It's fine," I said softly. It wasn't really. My heart was still broken in a million pieces and would never heal. I was that person that believed in God but refused to believe what was going on was His doing. Believing in God and believing He'd see us through and that my son was in a better place was all I had to hold on to.

I felt myself sinking again, something that happened easily and often. I needed a change of topic.

"What did you do for a living, Bill?"

"Oh, I created video games," Bill answered.

"Whoa…." Danny chimed as if impressed. "Wait. Why aren't you rich? Weren't your games popular?"

"A few were, one especially. But I had school loans, a wife who didn't work but went to school, getting out of debt…"

I turned my head and looked at him. "Don't have to worry about that now, or at least for a little bit."

Bill cracked a half smile. "No, I don't."

"Which game?" Danny asked. "Which was your best game?"

"Ironically…" Bill paused to chuckle, "Rapture."

"Dude! No!" Danny shrieked with enthusiasm. "That was like the best game. Hard as hell to beat."

"I know."

"The entire concept rocked," Danny went on. "Finding survival supplies after you've been left behind. Beating demons. The best is when you beat the game and the bonus feature where you get to play the whole game again as Jesus. Kicking minion butts and defeating the devil. Only doesn't matter how much you died, you came back."

"That last tidbit was all my idea. The Easter Egg."

"That was sweet."

"Thanks."

"Wait." I finally caught up to the conversation. "You, the atheist, invented a video game call Rapture?"

"Yeah."

I looked at Danny. "And you played this game?"

"You bought it for me."

"I had no idea it was a blasphemous game. I would never have purchased it for you had I known."

Danny laughed.

He *laughed*. It was genuine. And that made me smile at him. It worked, changing the subject. The mood had shifted, but only briefly.

Two duffle bags and a small suitcase dropped right behind Bill. They were our clothes and were delivered by a soldier. I didn't get to see much of him; my eyes stayed focused on our bags.

"You're detained until zero six hundred hours. Then you can go. Those are your personal belongings. The rest we have kept."

Bill had barely muttered his thanks before the soldier had turned, walked away and moved straight into that partitioned-off section.

All of my life I had been a contradiction, unpredictable, but always strong. I'd fight one moment then cave in the next. But I had strength nonetheless.

I heard Danny and Bill talking about being grateful for not being arrested, but I didn't absorb all their words because focusing on their bags did something to me. I felt my blood get hot and swore I could feel it pumping through my veins.

"How?" The word slipped from my mouth. I wasn't expecting an answer.

"Mom? How what?"

I stood up. "I'll be back."

Bill reached up for me. "Mera, where are you going?"

"To find whoever is in charge."

"We're not under arrest," Bill said. "That's a good thing. We're free to go in the morning."

"Yeah, but how are we supposed to go? They took our stuff."

"We'll get other stuff," Bill replied.

"Yeah, Mom, we're resourceful."

"I'm sure," I said. "But I want *our* stuff. Excuse me." Focused on the partition curtain, I walked that way, ignoring Bill's statement to Danny that for sure we'd end up arrested.

The partition curtain was closed as best as it could be. Muffled voices carried out to me and had there been a way to knock, I would have. But there wasn't, so I simply slipped through.

The area was small and I faced the backs of four soldiers. They were talking to someone, a meeting of sorts.

I'd wait. Eventually they would move away.

"Can I help you?" the deep male voice asked, silencing the other soldiers who were talking. The voice was softer, yet a bit hoarse, probably from the lack of sleep lately.

Before I knew it, the four soldiers before me sidestepped and parted like the Red Sea to expose the light-skinned black man seated behind the desk. He wasn't wearing the full military camo jacket, just a tee shirt and oddly, a shoulder harness with a revolver. I couldn't determine his age. He wasn't young but he wasn't old. The expedient lighting that dangled in the makeshift partition office reflected some specks of gray in his buzzed close to the scalp cut.

His body hovered over papers and he didn't stand, only raised his eyes and repeated. "Can I help you?"

"Yes." My voice cracked, I cleared my throat. "Yes, I need to speak to the person in charge."

One of the soldiers stated, "She's a detainee, sir."

"Which one?"

"The class four offense."

The man behind the desk said, "Give us a moment, gentlemen. Thank you."

They walked by me and out. Once they cleared the area, his eyes returned to his paperwork and said, "I'm in charge. What can I do for you?"

"I would like our stuff back."

"If I'm not mistaken, your things were returned a few moments ago."

"Some of our things were returned," I stated. "I would like *all* of our things back."

"What could be returned was." He continued to work.

"Not..." I paused. Was he even paying attention? I took a breath with my irritation. "Will you please look at me when we're speaking, mister..."

"Major."

"Mr. Major, can you—"

"No," he interrupted. "You called me mister, call me Major, please."

"Okay, does being a major excuse you from being polite?"

He set down his pen, rubbed his eyes and looked up to me. "I'm sorry. You're correct. I was being rude. Now, I'm being honest. What can be returned was returned to you. I have to get back to work. Now, if you'll excuse me I—"

"No," I said. "No, I will not excuse you to get back to work."

He rubbed his eyes; he was tired. I could tell.

"I need our stuff. It was our stuff. My SUV, I made the payments on it, I didn't steal it. We are not thieves and I don't appreciate being treated like a class four offender, whatever that means."

"It means you are looters and are considered dangerous."

That made me laugh. "Do I look dangerous to you? Really? Just be human. Give us back our stuff."

"You were lucky we gave you back what we did. You had stolen guns—"

"Please," I scoffed. "They weren't stolen. Roy would have given them to us if he wasn't in some sort of viral zone. He passed them out like candy. Big Chuck Heston supporter."

I noticed he wasn't amused by me. He just stared.

"Okay, fine." I told him. "Keep the guns. Give me my vehicle and food and other supplies. Okay? The food was mine."

"It was?" He bobbed his head in a nod with a tightly closed mouth. "So I should assume that you always have in your home super large cans of fruit cocktail and cling peaches with the name Marie's Restaurant on them?"

"Yes." I nodded. "No. I borrowed them."

"Like the gas. The packs of candy and cupcakes. You broke the law."

I laughed; it wasn't a long laugh. Just enough to make him more irritated.

"And that's funny to you?"

"Yeah, actually it is. Have you been out there? Law and order? It's a joke. No one is there! No one. Law and order for what?"

He rose to a stand in his argument with me. I wish he would have remained seated. Somehow there was a lot of intimidation when he stood. He was tall, but it wasn't his height; it was simply the fact that he was big. "Have you even seen or run into a Sleeper?"

"A what?"

"A Sleeper. The ones that had what they call the sleeping sickness. They're dangerous."

"Not all. I saw them. I know some can be dangerous. I was choked by my husband."

His head lowered some. "I'm sorry to hear that."

"But the rest just wander."

"Mrs. Stevens," with closed eyes he shook his head slowly, "answer me this question. When was the last time you saw a Sleeper?"

I had to think, it was early and I told him, "Six hours ago, I dunno. Not up close."

"That's what I thought. Things have changed. That is why we have law and order. And Martial Law is more for your protection. Now," more adamant, he walked around his desk and stated, "if you'll excuse me."

"So you're going to get my stuff?"

"What?" he choked off a laugh of ridicule. "No."

"What are we supposed to do, stay here in the middle of Ohio? Oh, wait, no we'll find another car. Or should we just plan, for the sake of not getting arrested, to walk to the state of Washington?"

"Those rumors haven't been confirmed. No one knows for sure if it's better out west than here. Communication—"

"I know nothing about rumors, Major. I care about my daughter, who I know at this moment in time is fine in Seattle. But for how long, I don't know. It's my flesh and blood. My child." I spoke passionately, my fist close to my chest. "I lost one child already to this madness and I won't lose another. And every second, hour, day, that you and your law and order cost me is another second, day or hour that my child is at risk. If it was your child out there, wouldn't you do everything you could to get to her? If it was your child out there, how well would you deal with being arrested over a few cans of fruit from a roadside diner? Of course, if it *were* your child, you wouldn't be standing here preaching law and order, I can guarantee it. You'd be like me, forgetting law and order just to get to your kid."

His eyes shifted some and I looked over my shoulder. Two soldiers had entered the curtained area. I guess my voice carried. I shook my head slowly, turned from the Major and spoke to the soldiers. "I know I'm a dangerous criminal. But he's fine. No need for back-up." Another shake of my head in disgust, not to mention feeling terribly defeated, I left that area.

What had I expected, really? That I would just march into that little area, ask to speak to whoever was in charge and they'd grant my request? It was stupid all that was happening. The world was fast becoming vacant and I didn't give too much thought to the Major's news about the Sleepers either. My thoughts were on Jessie.

I returned to our little section of the fire hall. I was fired up, disappointed, and every other negative feeling I could think of.

Bill, still seated on the floor, peered up to me.

"What?" I snapped.

He shook his head. "Nothing. I'm not saying anything."

I plopped down to the floor and immediately grabbed the bag I knew was mine. Angrily I unzipped it and reached inside. It wasn't there and would have been easy enough to find. I felt around again as if I were missing it with my fingers.

"Son of a bitch." I tossed my bag to the side. "They took my bourbon. All I wanted was a drink."

Danny cringed. "Mom, shhh."

"No! It was my bottle. I didn't steal it. Assholes." Like an angry child, I pulled my knees into my chest and pouted.

Bill whistled. "Okay, wow. It's all right. We'll get more. I know you're upset."

I don't believe my eyes ever felt so heavy. It felt like they were filled with sand and all I could do for relief was close them. The moment I did I started to cry. I couldn't help it, and I buried my face to hide the tears.

"Mom," Danny said softly, "you tried. You really did. I think you handled it well. We could hear. We'll deal with this as soon as they release us in the morning."

"Yeah," Bill said. "We'll get another car. We'll get what we need. This is only a delay, it's not stopping us."

"Mom, it's okay."

I felt Danny's hand reach to mine and I gripped it, then my head fell to my knees. It wasn't okay; it would never be okay again. Jeremy was gone, who knew about Daniel, and my poor Jessie was alone. Even at nineteen she was still a child, my child.

My entire being wanted to crumble. I wanted to wake up from the madness and find my life the way it was. But for the time being, I just wanted to be left alone. To let my head rest against my knees and be left alone.

I wasn't sitting there like that long before I felt the tap to my head, accompanied by, "Hey."

Slowly I lifted my head and the corner of my eye caught a bottle of bourbon. I followed the bottle to the hand and then up the long legs to the deliverer. I swiped my hand over my face to remove the tears.

It was the Major.

"Here," he said. "Take it. I don't know what they did with your bottle, but you can have this."

With slight apprehension, I took it. "Thank you."

He crouched down to be at my level. "And you're right. If it were my child, I would do anything to find her." He handed over my keys.

I'm sure my shocked expression said it all. I was speechless.

"I'll have your other items released. Not sure about the weapons, but the food and the gas will be returned. They'll be by your vehicle in the morning. It's in the back lot by the garages."

My mouth moved and soon all I could get out was. "Why?"

"I lost my son and daughter in the Event." His voice dropped to a whisper. "More than a soldier, more than an enforcer, I am a father. Go find your daughter."

"Thank you," I said.

He stood up and walked off without another word.

I clutched the keys in one hand and the bottle in the other. I took a drink, only one, and passed the bottle to Bill.

Suddenly I felt better and as if I could rest. I would need to sleep. I wanted to sleep because I wanted to be my all first thing in the morning when we left for Jessie.

14
RANDY BRIGGS

Even though Danny and Bill took advantage of the cots that were given to us, I couldn't. I used the blanket to somewhat soften the floor, lay on my side and rested my head on my bag. Despite their ongoing conversation regarding a plan of action, Danny and Bill's voices faded and I was out like a light before long.

For as hard and as deep as I slept, I thought for sure when I opened my eyes, I would be greeted by a morning buzz of people. But it was silent. Danny and Bill slept. I had no idea what time it was but knew I couldn't go back to sleep again if I tried. It was so hot in the Fire Hall I could barely breathe. The air was humid and thick and my nose was congested. Every inhale was sluggish and loud, leaving my mouth as my only option for breathing.

I knew I needed fresh air and was certain that would help. First I went to the ladies' room to try to clear my nose. I worried that yet another form of a virus had been delivered and I was the next victim. I reasoned that fear away. Not feeling sick, just stuffy, I attributed it to the lack of a good night's sleep, heat and crying.

The bathroom trip helped my nose some, but not enough. Again, really feeling like fresh air would do the trick I walked across the eerily quiet refugee center to the main door. It was held open slightly by an old ashtray and a soldier stood there.

"Excuse me," I said. "Can I go out and get some air? It's really hot in here."

"That's fine. But stay close to the building under the lights," he instructed.

"I'm not gonna run away," I told him. "Really."

"It has nothing to do with you running away." He paused. "Really. Stay close."

His young face, no older than twenty-five, held a look of sincerity. When he held the door for me, I knew for sure that it was a safety rule, one I would follow.

For some reason, I felt scared when I heard that door hit against that metal ashtray. Things were different out there. There was a sense of emptiness. I heard shouting in the distance but couldn't make out what the voices were saying. I peered out across the dark parking lot. At the edge was a long line of military vehicles forming almost a blockade and beyond them, the dancing beams of flashlights.

What was going on?

The shouting didn't send off warning signals to me. Perhaps they were looking for someone, or something.

Thinking I was alone, the single sniff caused me to jolt and turn to my left.

He sat there on one of those folding camping chairs, but he seemed too large for it. He looked in his fifties, I couldn't tell, nor could I tell his height, but he was stocky. He wore old blue jeans and a white tee shirt. He turned about the same time I spotted him, ran his fingers through his bushy hair that reminded me of Daniel's.

"I'm sorry," he said and stood. "Did you want to sit?"

"No, no, thank you." I waved my hand. "I'm good. I came out for air. It was really hot in here."

"Tell me about it." He returned to his seat. "It's better out here. Have that breeze. But it carries that stench with it."

"I can't..." I sniffed a sluggish inhale. "Smell a thing. I'm stuffy."

"I was too, until I came out here." His voice was soft, laced with a hint of country. "You sure you don't want to sit down?"

"Stay seated. I'll sit on the ground. I'm good."

"Don't you even think about it." At that point he stood and inched away from his little folding seat. "I'll sit on the ground. Please." He held out his hand.

"Thank you." I accepted his offer. The moment I sat, I started sniffing more. I brought the back of my hand to my nose.

"Here." He reached into his back pocket and pulled out one of those little packs of tissues. He took a couple out for me and extended them as he sat on the ground.

I looked at the tissues for a moment. They were just tissues, but to me, such a simple gesture seemed to mean so much. "Thanks, I've been crying a lot."

"Yep." He winked with a heavy sigh. "Me, too."

"I'm sorry."

"Aren't we all?"

Taking a moment with the tissues, I stared out again to the activity. "I wonder what's going on out there."

"I don't know. I've been trying to decipher it. No luck."

There were fragments of silence within our skeletal conversation. Both of us overwhelmed, too tired or too emotional to talk. We'd stare out then one of us would say something, almost as if it were obligatory because we were sitting together out there.

"Are you from around here?" I asked.

"No. Outside of Chicago. I uh, stopped here for rest. Figure I'd move on and hit my destination before curfew tomorrow."

"And that is?"

"The ocean." He shrugged. "A beach out east would work."

"Are you looking for family?"

He shook his head. "Nope. I lost everyone."

Saying 'I'm sorry' was appropriate, but it didn't cut it. I knew that myself. "Can I ask you a question?" I waited for his nod. "Do you think it's the end of the world?"

To my surprise he shook his head with certainty. "Nah, I think it's the start of a new one. But I can tell you I don't like it much. I don't like it at all."

Again it was silent. In fact we waded in silence a lot in the hour that he and I sat outside. But I did learn about him. His name was Randy Briggs, an insurance adjuster from Cedar, Illinois. He told me he waited his entire life to find that one woman and it took him until he was in his forties. He had two daughters with her, both under ten years old, both of them taken in the Event. His wife wasn't a Sleeper; she just couldn't take the pain of losing her children and she took her own life.

As he told the story I could envision it all. He had held that gun to his temple as well, but couldn't pull the trigger. I knew his pain. My God, did I know his pain. Now all he wanted was to go east, sit on the sand, watch the ocean and hope for death. He said maybe while sitting there'd he drum up the courage to walk into the ocean and let the waves take him. An easy death, considering he didn't swim.

He called himself a coward for not taking his own life. I suggested that perhaps there was a reason and there was something else planned for him. Those were the only words I could offer.

Randy wasn't looking for pity; he didn't strike me as that type of man. He was talking to me, that's all. Making conversation.

It neared four a.m. and I started to get tired again. I hoped I could grab one more hour of sleep before we were free to go. Randy returned to his little chair and as I headed inside, I stopped to thank him.

"Randy, I know you have a plan in motion, the beach and all, but, if you want to put that on hold or feel you really aren't ready for that yet, you are more than welcome to join us."

"That's pretty nice of you. Thank you."

I gave him one of those closed mouth smiles and turned.

"Mera?" he called.

"Yes?"

"You're going west because you're pretty certain your daughter's alive, right?"

"We are. Why do you ask?"

Randy shook his head. 'No particular reason. Just checking. That's uh, that's a pretty positive goal. I'm a little envious. Good luck to you."

"You too, Randy. You too." And with that, I returned to the stifling Fire Hall.

15
RUN

I never did catch the smell Randy spoke about. At least not while we were outside. Sometime during my rest, my ability to breathe through my nose returned. The scent of something putrid and sour caused me to wake. In fact, it caused Danny and Bill to stir at the same time.

"God." Danny winced. "What is that smell?"

I turned my head as another wave of odor entered along with a breeze. I peered around Danny to see the front doors were wide open.

"What's going on?" Bill asked, drawing my attention. Then I saw. People were grabbing things, moving about. One thing was different. There wasn't a soldier in sight.

Bill glanced at his watch. "It's not even six yet."

Hurriedly, Danny jumped up and grabbed his bag, whipping his phone charger from the wall in the same motion. "Let's go. Something is wrong."

It was a moment of 'stuff and go', shoving what we could into open bags, grabbing them into our arms to make a hastened escape.

"The back door," I instructed when I saw Danny and Bill moving toward the front.

The once-full refugee center, with a hundred people plus soldiers, was thinning down and we moved against the grain of refugees to get to the back.

With our items in tow, we hustled into the kitchen area and out that door. At that point I still had not seen a soldier.

The second we stepped outside, I spotted my SUV. It was all the way in the back of the lot near the garages where they kept the fire trucks. There were three or four other vehicles there. I could see our boxes, as promised, next to the SUV. But I didn't see any people. The moment we started moving quickly toward the car, I heard a gunshot, then two.

It made us run the rest of the way.

"Open the hatch," Bill ordered. I saw him trip a little and catch his balance in his charge to the back of the SUV with Danny. "Pop it."

I opened the driver's door and reached for the lever.

"Mera!" I heard from a distance.

As I popped the hatch and stepped from the car door I saw Randy running our way.

"Randy? I thought you left?"

"I tried. My car is useless. Does the offer still stand?" he asked, speaking rushed and out of breath. "Can I come with you? Please. I can't stay here."

"Absolutely. Put your bag in the back."

It was happening so fast. I didn't notice at the time the fear in Randy's voice. I just wanted to move. The gunfire increased. The feeling that we had to flee took over and I hurried to the back to help put the boxes and bags inside.

"They're not here!" Danny exclaimed.

"What?" I asked.

"The guns, they kept the guns!"

Randy lifted his bag onto the back floor of the SUV. "I have weapons." He unzipped his bag. "Two." He lifted a handgun and handed it to Bill. "It's loaded. Safety is on."

I grabbed another box, tossed it in. "This is Randy. He'll be joining us," I said by way of introduction. "He'll be..." I trailed off when I spotted the man him walking from the back of the garage, moving slowly.

Bill placed one of the final boxes in and looked over his shoulder. "A Sleeper."

Something immediately changed on Randy's face. He pointed to Bill and shouted, "Get in the car! I got this!" He shot a stern look to me. "Mera, get ready to go. *Now.*"

I didn't understand what the big concern was. Yes, the man was clearly inflicted with the sleeping sickness, but he looked harmless. He just stared and moved slowly.

There was one canister of gas left to load; it was closer to the Sleeper. Danny stepped to it.

"No," Randy tugged at him. "Leave it. Get in the car. Now. Mera, drive."

In typical Danny fashion, he defied an adult, and with a sarcastic, "He's harmless," reached for the gas can.

The Sleeper lunged fast at Danny, growling, and bit down hard on Danny's reaching arm.

Danny screamed. I screamed, took a step to my son, and before I knew it, Randy had extended his weapon, shot the Sleeper and grabbed Danny.

"Mera! Go!" Randy yelled as he lifted my son.

I took a step back, barely able to breathe, frightened beyond what I could even comprehend, and as I spun—*slam!* I ran right into the Major.

"Get in. Drive now. *Fast,*" he said and reached hurriedly for the back door.

"My son...he..."

"Drive!"

After a quick glance to see Danny, I jumped in the driver's seat, closed the door and fumbled for the keys as Bill got in the passenger side.

Between peering to the mirror to make sure everyone was in, no matter how hard I tried, my hands shook so badly, I couldn't get the keys into the ignition.

Bill reached over, grabbed my hand and aided me. "Drive," he said calmly.

I started the car and then placed it in gear. Such a simple task seemed impossible to complete. My foot depressed the gas, but I couldn't focus on driving, only on my son.

Bill looked toward the back. "How is he?"

"Bleeding badly," Randy said.

"I'm fine," Danny argued. "Really."

My son had been bitten. All I could think about was that an infected person had bitten him. "Is he gonna get sick?" I asked.

The Major was the one to answer me. "I don't know. Hopefully not. Sir, help lift him up here with me."

Eyes again to the rearview mirror, I watched Danny roll onto the back seat, and heard the unzipping of a bag.

The Major said, "I have you. Hold still. Get me that water, sir."

I wanted badly to see what was going on. I couldn't. I could only listen to the voices of the Major and Randy as they performed first aid on my son.

"This might sting," the major told Danny.

Danny grunted. "I'm good. I'm good."

"Here, use this shirt," Randy said.

"Thanks. Why are you driving so slow?" The Major asked. "Pick it up, please."

I nodded. I'm sure he didn't see it. My eyes lifted to the ripping sound.

Bill asked. "What's that?"

"Field dressing. Temporary, that's why she has to drive faster," the Major said. "Ma'am, please."

I looked at the speedometer. I was barely going ten miles an hour. What was wrong with me? I turned the bend to the final stage of the parking lot and instead of hitting the gas, I instinctively hit the brake.

At the edge of the lot pandemonium ensued. A wall of people formed a blockade that was nothing short of an all-out violent confrontation. Fists flew, people screamed, there were four or five people attacking one woman. It appeared as if a riot broke out with no means of control. Smoke rose from two or three cars. I saw soldiers on the ground, dead. Two men engaged in a tug of war over another man resulted in them giving up and throwing him to the ground, pouncing on him as he helplessly hit the pavement.

"Oh my God," I said breathlessly.

"What?" Bill asked then turned his head from the back of our vehicle to look out the windshield. "Holy shit."

"Drive!" The Major ordered. "We have to get your kid somewhere I can clean up this wound and stitch him. Drive."

How was I supposed to get around these people who had the parking lot blocked?

Then it seemed as if someone yelled, 'stop' because suddenly every single being in that lot halted what they were doing and turned as one to look at us.

"Oh my God," I repeated.

"Drive!" the Major shouted.

"Shit, Mera!" Bill yelled. "Drive! *Drive!*"

"I can't get through them! They're blocking our way!"

Every single person—and there were hundreds—flew toward us.

"Hit them," Bill instructed.

"I can't, they're people and—"

The Major's face inserted between the front seats. "Hit the fucking gas now and plow through them if you have to but get us out of here. *Now!*"

The blasting of his final word caused me to slam my foot to the gas and the SUV jolted then sped forward.

I saw the edge of the parking lot and made that my goal. The people grew closer, running at us in attack mode.

"Don't stop," Bill said his hand on the dashboard. "Please. Just go. It's okay."

It wasn't okay. I was moving at top speed, there was no way I could stop and the second the front end of my vehicle made contact with a person, a sickening knot formed in my gut with the '*thump*' sound of the body hitting the car.

They weren't animals or things, they were *people*, and at that second that was all I could view them as. My entire being shuddered and I cried out as I physically felt it every single time I careened into a body. Every '*thump*' and '*thud*' against the car and hood of my SUV was sickening. It wasn't one or two; it was too many too count. As fast as I drove, they dove in our way as if they could care less if I hit them.

Thump-thump-thump. Thump.

Steady, nonstop. As if I drove down the middle of the road in a construction site hitting every cone and barrel set up. Picking off the people and sending them flying.

My body tensed; it wasn't me. I couldn't have been doing that. I aimed for the edge of the parking lot. It seemed like an eternity when it was only a few seconds. I peeled from that parking lot with a hard right turn and squeal of my tires. It felt like freedom. No more hoards of people. Trying to catch my breath, I quickly looked back to see if we were being pursued and as I turned back around to drive...

Slam!

I hit someone else. This body didn't veer off to the side, he flew up and crashed down on my hood, and his face pressed against my windshield. His eyes connected with mine.

He was there for maybe a split second, but long enough to burn the image of this man's face in my mind forever.

The scream rumbled from my gut and resonated in my throat as I slammed on the brakes sending him flying from my hood.

I had to stop. I just had to. My hands clutched the steering wheel, I lowered my head and broke down and cried.

"Mera," Bill spoke softly.

"Oh, God, Bill, I looked in his eyes. I looked in his eyes."

"It's okay. It is."

"No." I shook my head. "It's not."

"You did what you had to do to get us out of there. You have to drive."

Again, I shook my head as I lifted it. "I can't. I can't now."

Bill turned and looked in the back. The Major stated, "It's clear. Switch up."

I watched Bill get out and I climbed over to his seat. All I wanted to do at that moment was vomit. I felt sick. As Bill drove off, he, Randy, and even my son tried to help me by telling me that I only cleared the way of Sleepers.

Sleepers?

That may have been how they viewed them, but I didn't. I viewed them as human beings whose lives I had mercilessly taken.

16
UNEXPECTED GUESTS

The Major instructed us to keep driving until we were far enough away from major population areas. We stayed on the Ohio turnpike, which was the same as it was the day before. Vacant. The Major informed us he didn't want to wait too long, though; he had to put sutures in Danny's arm, do a better cleaning and assess. He kept his eyes peeled for the place to do that.

I hadn't a clue what 'place' he was speaking of.

I do know I couldn't close my eyes. Every single time I did I felt that knot form in my stomach and remembered the sound and feeling of hitting those bodies. A magnified version of that feeling one gets when they hit an animal or run over one already dead on the road. Very few are immune to that feeling.

Bill did pull over so I could throw up. It didn't make me feel better because I really hadn't eaten yet. It was a ten minute battle of cramping and heaving that left me feeling physically worse. Emotionally, my fears for my son eased as he didn't show any signs of infection. Plus, Danny stated he felt fine. Then again, he had only been bitten less than an hour before.

About thirty miles before the Indiana border, the Major told us to turn off on some pissant exit, one of those exits no one would turn off unless they lived there.

"It's here," the Major said. "I saw the sign yesterday."

Then we all saw the sign: AS Survival Haven.

The Major—whose name I had yet to learn—explained that he hadn't seen the Survival Haven but was willing to wager it was a safe place to stop.

There were no cars on the road, and the haven wasn't as easy to find as the miniature billboard led us to believe. A mile up the road and a homemade painted arrow pointed to another road. That one was only a step above dirt.

I don't know why, but in my mind, I envisioned this Survival Haven to be Wal-Mart size, not some log cabin home renovated to be a store. The dirt parking lot was only big enough to hold four cars, tops. A wide front porch had empty racks, there was an old camper to the left of the building and a conversion van sat outside the garage which was about fifty feet from the main building.

It was the only thing for miles.

"I'll go inside and check for Sleepers," the Major said, and left the SUV.

My eyes were transfixed as he went to the door; obviously it was locked, and the Major disappeared behind the building.

"They have space blankets three for ten bucks," Bill stated.

"I'm sorry, what?" I asked.

"Just pointing out about the space blankets. Ammo is on sale, too."

"Why do I care?"

Bill shrugged. "Just making conversation."

I wanted to say, 'well, don't,' but I didn't. Bill really didn't irritate me; I wasn't feeling well and the worry about Danny was getting to me.

The Major appeared at the front door of the store, stepped to the porch and waved us all in.

I shut off the SUV and looked behind me. "Danny, do you need help getting in?"

"It's my arm, Mom. I can walk."

"I'll help you anyhow," Randy told him. "Just in case. You lost a lot of blood."

Personally, I hadn't seen the wound. The Major had bandaged it with some sort of giant military band-aid he ripped from a package. But Randy had to have been correct in his assessment of the blood loss that Danny suffered. Not only were his jeans covered with blood, there was a lot on the back seat. Which led me to wonder if the 'I'm okay' bit that Danny kept projecting was nothing but a mere front for my benefit.

AS Survival Haven served a dual purpose to its owner; it was both his business and his home. The storefront carried rifles, wilderness survival supplies and other related items, while the back of the building was a larger apartment. Bill was enthralled by the store, checking out every single thing. I was too focused on what was happening in the back apartment.

Through recommendation of the Major, we shut the store front door and the apartment door as well. Just in case.

Someone had lived there and rather recently. Everything was impeccably clean and sterile looking. The cabinets had food and the fridge was stocked. The electricity was still up and running.

The Major had taken Danny into the back bedroom. I actually went back to watch, but the second he started to remove the bandage, I grew queasy and excused myself.

Randy had put on a pot of coffee and said he'd search up something for us to eat before we moved on. I felt funny about that; it was someone's home. Perhaps after I knew Danny was okay I'd be more apt to have an appetite.

"Crackers are fresh." Randy set the box on the table. "Have one. Get something in your stomach."

I reached for one and brought it to my mouth to nibble.

"You guys have to see these," Bill said enthusiastically, walking into the kitchen and dropping an armful of stuff on the table. "This place is the coolest. It has stuff I never even heard of. These meals in this foil pouch, for instance."

Randy reached down to the table and lifted the white bag. "It's an MRE, same thing they give the military out in the field."

"What's an MRE?" Bill asked.

"You're kidding, right?" Randy chuckled. "You have to be. Meals Ready to Eat. MRE?"

"Ah, yes." Bill sat down at the table. "Before we head out, we should see what we can get from this place."

The Major's voice entered the conversation. "Starting with that conversion van. We should see if there are keys around here." He walked to the sink and began to wash his hands. "It will be a lot better for the drive to Washington."

Bill asked. "Are you coming with us? Don't you have a post to hold?"

The Major snorted and shook his head. He reached for a paper towel, then a cup and pointed to the coffee pot. "May I?"

"Help yourself," Randy told him as he set a coffee before me. "I don't believe we've actually exchanged names." Randy held out his hand to the Major. "Randy Briggs."

"Gavin Beck. But please, just call me Beck." With his coffee he sat down at the table.

"Are you sure we're not supposed to call you Major? Isn't that what you told me?" I asked.

Beck's mouth opened to respond. He stammered some then said, "I apologize for that. It was a stressful moment at the refugee center."

"No, I apologize. I'm not myself these days. How's Danny?"

Beck took a deep breath. "He's resting. He needs to. He lost a lot of blood. I don't think he's lost so much that he's in danger of needing blood. It took about thirty stitches to close the bite. I gave him a dose of penicillin and put him on a saline IV. But, as far as anything further, I can't tell you. He may need more. I don't know."

"How did you know to do that?"

"Combat," he answered. "I was just glad to have a field pack on me. When the Sleeper situation took a turn for the worst, we were all issued one." At that moment, he turned to me, laid his hand over mine and looked me in the eyes. "I know you want to get to your daughter out west. I think, though, its best we hang back here for the day. Let Danny recoup. According to my intel there's a small town with a hospital not far from here. Probably wasn't hit too bad in the Event. We can head there if we need something stronger for Danny. Hell, who knows? Maybe there's even a doctor hanging around. Okay?"

I nodded. He slipped his hand from mine.

With a heavy breath, Randy ran his hand over his face and joined us at the table. "What the hell happened? I heard the Secretary of State's message. I thought everything was getting under control."

"It was going to take a while to get things under control," Beck said. "We all knew that. I don't think any of us had a grip on how many people were stricken with the Sleeping Sickness. But it was enough to shut down cities. They had no phone service along the East Coast so it was pretty tough to gauge what was happening there. Last I heard was the order to prepare my men for combat and to ship them out to Toledo at first light. That came around seven p.m. Nothing since."

"I saw the soldiers leaving," Randy said.

"And I stayed behind to close things down. Well, me and about four others," Beck explained.

I wanted to ask questions, too. I had a lot that I needed to know, but my mind spun. Bill had begun spouting out questions about the survival supplies. It was then I heard it. It was hard to hear over Bill, but it was in the distance.

"Do you hear that?" I asked.

Beck held up his hand for silence.

The sound of a motorcycle grew closer and stronger.

"Sleeper?" Bill asked.

"Doubtful," Beck said.

The motorcycle engine stuttered, and it was apparent it stopped at the survival haven. Beck held a silencing finger to us as he stood, grabbed his revolver, and walked to the door.

We all stood slowly.

My heart pounded with each footstep that neared the door.

Beck was ready, he listened, he waited and then, weapon raised, flung open the door only to be greeted with the barrel of a shotgun.

The shotgun handler wasn't a short man, but he seemed it facing off with Beck. Probably in his late thirties, he looked rough and rugged. His dark hair was pulled back in a tight ponytail, his beard was trimmed, and his heavily tattooed arms were steady as he aimed that shotgun without a flinch. He pumped the chamber before he spoke with a arrogant half smile.

"All right, son, care to tell me why you and these people are in my shop when the sign out front clearly says closed?" He nodded to indicate Beck's weapon. "And you might wanna put that gun down. You're in my home."

Beck turned the revolver to be flush in his palm and he raised both hands. "I'm sorry. Look, we're not here to steal anything. We just…" He stopped speaking when he saw it.

We all saw it.

Shotgun man's eyes shifted to the kitchen table and the mound of items lying there.

Bill nervously stepped forward with a raised hand. "That's me. Guilty. I wasn't… I wasn't stealing. We didn't think anyone was coming back."

The man tilted his head quizzically. "What in the world would make you think no one was coming back? The sign just said closed. Not closed for good."

Beck placed his revolver away. "Listen. Again, we aren't here to steal. We stopped by because it looked safe and we need get the boy some help."

"The boy?"

I stopped forward. "My son. He was hurt and was bleeding badly. The Major here needed to stitch him."

Beck corrected. "He was bitten."

The man lowered the shotgun and looked at our faces, perhaps reading us, trying to find a sense of honesty or a reason to trust us. "Where is he?" he asked.

Beck pointed. "In the bedroom."

He walked right by us and I followed behind Beck.

"Please," I pleaded, "he needs to rest."

The bedroom was in plain view once we entered the living room and Danny was on the bed.

The owner of the home rested his shotgun against the wall outside the bedroom door. "What kind of animal bit the boy?"

"Wasn't an animal," Beck replied stepping into the bedroom with him. "It was a Sleeper."

"A Sleeper?" He shook his head with a quirky look as he sat on the edge of the bed. His fingers trailed the tubing of the IV that was attached to the wall with duct tape. "What the hell is a Sleeper?"

I looked at Beck then to the man. "Maybe you don't know them by that name."

He seemed focused on Danny at that second. "Boy's pale. How old is he?"

"Sixteen," I answered.

"You give him something to make him sleep like this?" he asked as he stood.

Beck shook his head. "No, but he lost a lot of blood."

Danny groggily said, "Sleep like what? You guys are so loud." He closed his eyes again.

He shook his head with a chuckle at my son, running his hand over Danny's head. "He needs to be seen by a doctor." He walked over to the closet and opened it, reaching for the top shelf.

"I wish," I said. "But that's not possible."

After retrieving what looked like a black satchel, the man walked to the bed. He opened the larger pouch and pulled out a blood pressure cuff and stethoscope. He placed his hand on Danny's wrist. 'Pulse is good." Then he applied the cuff and took his blood pressure. "Pressure's good. The paleness concerns me." He reached for the bandage. "May I?" he asked Beck.

Beck nodded.

He carefully undid the bandage on Danny's forearm. "Now what did you say bit him again?"

I answered. "A Sleeper."

He finally exposed the wound. "Jesus Christ. This was deep. Nice repair."

"Thanks," Beck said.

"Looks like a human bite," he said, reapplying the bandage.

"It is," Beck said. "Are you... are you a doctor or nurse?"

"No." He gathered his items to return to the bag. "I was a Corpsman in the Navy. Got out, was a paramedic in Toledo for eight years before I decided to chuck it all for my passion. Survival stuff. You know, in case the world ends. But that's beside the point." He set the bag down. "Running from the law or not, this boy's got a human bite. He has to be seen."

Beck shifted his eyes to me. He had to have been thinking the same thing as me. Why was this man talking as if we could just hop in the car and go to the nearest clinic? Running from the law?

"Sir," Beck took a step toward him, "are you aware of what's going on?"

He was about to answer when a high pitched, whiney, female voice called out. "Alex!"

He turned his head.

She called again, getting closer, this time sounding even more southern. "Alex? Why are there men in your kitchen? Alex..." Her voice grew nearer. "Honey, you told me you was taking me home. I ain't seen my babies in four days, can..." She stopped speaking when she arrived at the bedroom door. "Alex?"

Her hair was bleached blonde, to the nape of her neck and poker straight. It was tucked behind her ears and she looked as if she hadn't washed it in days. She presented herself as the quintessential ditzy girlfriend of the bad boy. Short shorts with boots, a tank-top tee-shirt, she was very pretty and petite. But despite her lack of bathing or fashion sense, she still sported lipstick.

But I heard what she said. Four days.

I spun to Beck. "Four days," I whispered.

Alex held lifted his hand to her. "In a minute, Missy, gotta deal with this. Okay?"

"Another group running from the law?" she asked.

"Don't know," Alex answered. "Give me a minute."

"Fine." She folded her arms. "Then I'm using your bathroom. I've been holding it for four days." She flew into the bathroom, but before she closed the door, she looked out at us. "You all may want to ignore what you hear. I refused to go in the woods."

She closed the door.

Beck turned to him. "Have you been in the woods for four days?"

"Yeah, we were camping. Why?" Alex asked.

"Did you have your phone? Radio? Anything?" Beck asked.

"When I go, I shut myself off from civilization. Why?" he asked again.

"You didn't notice the roads or towns when you came back?"

Alex breathed out in frustration. "Son, I had my bike. I took the back way here. Again, why are you asking me?"

"Because you don't know."

Folding his arms, Alex tilted his head and peered at Beck. "Know what?"

17
DISCOVERING REALITY

Alex Sans handled it.

It was actually kind of hard to tell how well he handled it or if he even handled it well at all. He was a composed man whose fingers tapped in an arpeggio manner and jaw twitched once or twice in the aftermath of the news.

A twitch of his head, a swipe of his fingers down the corner of his mouth and Alex stood, went to the fridge and retrieved a beer.

Beck had brought him into the kitchen to tell him. Maybe it was to be outside of earshot of Missy, who was still in the restroom. Or maybe even to see all of our faces together. Whatever the reason, Alex sat at the kitchen table, said, "Okay, I'm seated. Shoot."

Beck did.

He delivered it to Alex like a military debriefing. 'Eleven hundred hours this... fourteen hundred hours that...' Beck gave statistics. Nineteen cities devastated by tornado; three volcanic eruptions; twenty three earthquakes. All in the United States alone. The Sleeping Sickness... the Event.

The Event.

That was the thing that caused Alex after his brief absorption of the news to get up and get that beer. Refrigerator door still ajar, arm resting on top, Alex chugged half that beer and wiped his mouth with the back of his hand.

Another drink of beer, eyes still transfixed on Beck, Alex handed him a bottle.

"There was a chance," Beck stated, opening the bottle. "An inkling of keeping it together. Even after all that. But then the Sleepers turned. I believe that was the final straw."

"Before it went... did they say what caused it all?" Alex asked. "Curious."

Beck shook his head. "Speculation."

Bill spoke up. "A lot of Christians are saying that it's God's end."

Alex gave him a weird look. A combination between a scoff and a maybe. He took another drink.

I asked him. "Did you have children, Alex?"

He shook his head. "No. No, I didn't. And I'm sorry to all of you who..." He took a look around the room at us all. "Who lost. I'm sorry." He finished the beer, set the bottle on the counter, reached in, grabbed another, shut the fridge and leaned against it. "I had a hunch something was wrong." Alex stared down to his beer bottle. That one he didn't drink quite as quickly. "I couldn't catch a fish. We had to rely on the food I had up there. Thought I lost my touch for a weekend." He sniffed and shook his head. "How many kids?"

Beck answered. "One point eight billion."

Alex asked then looked at me as if I were the one with the better answer. "How?"

"I can only say what happened with my son. He started to convulse and then over the course of the day, it was if every single speck of life was sucked out of him until he was gone."

Alex nearly whispered, "It's a lot to take in."

Randy, who had been quiet, finally spoke up. "It still is. Imagine waking up to the fact that not only your child, but in the course of one day, Saturday, every single child under fourteen years old died."

Crash.

We all turned to look. Missy's purse and all its items had spilled to the floor and her perfume had shattered. She chuckled nervously. "Sorry. You guys were talking. I got scared, you know, then I realized..." she nervously picked up items. "You were probably talking about a movie."

The silence in the room was so thick you could swim in it.

"I need a paper towel. Look at this mess." She tried to lift the broken bottle.

"Missy," Alex took a step to her, "while we were away, things happened. That's why you couldn't get a line out. That's why things seemed weird."

She stopped and slowly stood. "What happened, Alex? Did war break out?"

He lowered his head.

She stared at all of us, taking a second to look at each of our faces as if waiting for one of us to have the guts to tell her.

Alex reached for her. "Missy, sit down."

She whipped her arm from him. "I'm not sitting down, Alex. What happened?" Again she looked at us then focused on Randy. "You said something about all the kids. What did you say?"

Randy lowered his head. "Ma'am..."

"What did you *say!*" Missy screamed the last word.

"They're calling it the Event," Randy said softly. "The children are...the children are gone."

No more needed to be said.

"Oh my God, my babies!" Missy said, and flew out of the kitchen. Before Alex could get out her name and began his charge after her, she was out of the house.

Within a moment, the motorcycle started and sped off.

"Son of a bitch." Alex raced into the kitchen, opening drawers. "She took my bike. Where the hell are the van keys?"

Bill approached Alex with the keys extended. "Take our truck. It's right out front."

Alex grasped them, nodded thanks and turned to me. "Can you come with me? She may need someone there who's been through it."

More than anything I wanted to tell him no. I didn't want to face that situation again. But I couldn't.

"Sure," I murmured reluctantly. Before I had a chance to say anything else or even change my mind, he grabbed hold of my hand and pulled me along.

If we didn't need a new vehicle before, we probably would after Alex was done driving it. He drove fast, taking back roads, sending us into the air over bumps and divots. I lifted and banged back down to my seat more times than I could count.

"Sorry, I'm trying to get there before her," he said.

"It's okay. I understand."

"It's just that she has two little ones. Really young."

"How old?"

He looked at me then returned to looking at the road. "Two and three."

My heart sunk. They were babies. That poor girl. I didn't have to imagine what she would go through, I went through it. I felt every emotion she was about to experience, and soon enough relive it, in a sense.

"What is she gonna see when she gets there?" Alex asked.

"Clothes. Hair. Dust."

"What?" Alex squeaked, shocked.

"The children just disintegrated."

"Then it was the Rapture."

At that, I grew angry and defiant. "No. No it was not the Rapture."

"But with what you said—"

"No." I cut off his words. "No, I'm positive. Because this was not kind. It wasn't a moment of glory. It was horrendous. The suffering... That's not God's work."

We pulled on to the street. It was a small one, maybe eight frame houses and a couple of trailer homes. Cars were scattered about the road, not necessarily parked, and I didn't see a soul on the entire street. It was quiet.

Alex explained that Missy's ex-husband Greg and Greg's mother had her boys for the weekend.

We pulled up in front of the house and Missy rode up on the motorcycle out of control and fast. She hopped off before it had even stopped. After tripping, she raced to the house.

"Missy!" Alex called strongly as he stepped from the SUV.

Missy tried the front door. "It's locked." She raced off the porch to the side of the house.

"Missy!" Again, Alex called and this time he and I ran after her.

He caught her, latching on to her arm. "Missy, wait."

"Get," she tugged her arm away, "off of me, Alex." Using all of her body, Missy pulled back hard, freeing herself from Alex's hold. "I have to get in there. What if my babies were spared? Huh? And they're alone. I gotta find out." She turned and ran, calling out, "Greg! Connie!" her voice trailed off as she disappeared behind the house.

We both followed but didn't make it far before we heard a bellowing scream.

Charged with fear, I bolted behind Alex into the back door of the home. It led into the kitchen and as soon as we stepped inside, a sour, rotten odor pelted us. It made me immediately gag and turn my head. If it wasn't the smell that made me instinctively want to vomit, it was the sight of the older woman. She hung from a belt that had been fastened to the archway between the kitchen and hall, a toppled chair at her feet. It looked like a dried puddle of blood was on the floor beneath her. Why that was, I didn't know. Her body swung, I figured from Missy pushing past the body in her race for her children.

Her voice carried out as she searched. Calling, "Kyle, Liam! Mommy's home. Babies? Mommy's here!"

Alex, back against the wall, winced as he slid by the woman's body. Hating to do it, hand covering my nose and mouth, I followed. I tried to slip through, but I brushed against her body and it turned. When it did, I saw the reason for the blood. Her entire midsection was wide open. She looked as if she had been gutted.

That was all it took. I couldn't control it. The knot in my stomach erupted and vomit shot from my mouth and through my fingertips. I turned away, from the body, from Alex, trying to stop. My insides twisted and my forehead rested against the wall. I listened to Missy race around that first floor. The house wasn't that big, maybe it just seemed like she ran about for a while. Then clearly, she hit the steps.

"Kyle! Liam! Mommy's here."

Her voice trailed above us.

"Mommy's..."

Silence.

I closed my eyes tightly. I knew what was coming.

And it did. The gut-wrenching scream of instant heartbreak. It made me stop gagging and unable to breathe.

At that point Alex was already gone, probably up there and I knew, as much as it pained me, as much as I didn't want to see the look on Missy's face, I had to go up as well.

When I arrived upstairs at the last bedroom, Alex was leaning head down against the doorframe. Missy was on the floor between the two twin beds, her back against the wall, knees brought to her chest and she clutched a tiny blue tee shirt.

"It's all that's left." She lifted her head. "That's all that's left of my babies." She sniffled. "I didn't get to say goodbye."

The sadness in her eyes ricocheted into me and I felt it. The look she had on her face pulled at my soul and I broke. I moved slowly to her, dropping on the floor before her. "I'm so sorry, Missy. I am."

Lips quivering, she shifted a glance to the bed and then back to me. "I didn't even say goodbye." Her fingers clutched tighter to that blue shirt and with a hard single sob she dropped her head to her knees and wept.

We stayed in that room for a little bit, not for long, just enough for Missy to pull herself together enough to walk to the truck. She grabbed Kyle's favorite action figure and a car that belonged to Liam. She also took with her the clothing the boys were wearing when the Event took them. I was a little envious of that. I wish I would have kept Jeremy's shirt instead of burying it in the flower bed.

I had my arm around Missy's waist, holding her close to me as we inched down the stairs. The smell was strong once we hit halfway.

Missy looked at me, she spoke in a daze. "Should we take Connie down?"

I looked at her curiously; it took me a second to figure out what she was talking about.

She stopped walking and looked behind her to Alex. "Alex, I think we should take Connie down. She doesn't deserve to be hanging like that. She was a good woman."

"Missy, I don't think she knows," he said.

I had to hide my gasp of offense. I couldn't believe he just blurted that out. No sensitivity at all. Then again, maybe Alex wasn't thinking. A lot had happened.

Missy wouldn't move. She gave a stern look to Alex. "Take her down, please."

Alex grunted. "Fine. Go on out. I'll be right there." He brushed by us on the stairs.

He turned right and as we neared the bottom of the stairs. I tried my hardest to ignore the smell and concentrated on the salvation of the front door.

When we reached it, Missy paused again and looked up to me with her sad eyes. "I want to die."

I pulled her closer and whispered, "I know." Edging her to move, I reached for the front door and opened it.

Missy's head lifted. "Greg?"

He stood there, face gray, head titled, mouth agape and he stared at us through the tops of his eyes. Missy called him Greg, but it was obvious to me who, or rather *what*, he was now.

I slammed the front door. "Alex!" I shouted. "Sleeper!"

Alex rushed our way. "You still have yet to tell me what a Sleeper is."

Just as he finished his sentence there was a bang at the front door. It rattled on its hinges and soon the bangs were steady.

"That," I said, pointing to the door.

"Why is Greg acting like that?" Missy asked.

Alex peered through the window on the side of the door. "He's banging against it with his body."

"Are there any more out there?" I asked.

"Any more?" Alex asked with surprise then looked out the window again. "Nope. He's the only one. Okay," he held up his hand, "step back with her." He inched us from the door and further into the living room. "When I say run, you run with her and get in the truck. Keys are still in there."

"What are you going to do?" I held tightly to Missy.

"Handle this."

"He's a Sleeper," I stressed. "He's—"

"Greg," Alex stated. "I played deck hockey with him. I'll handle it." He bit his lip, twitched his head in irritation and reached for the doorknob. "Goddamn it, quit banging!" He waited and flung open the door. When he did, Greg must have been rearing to shoulder the door; he charged, not realizing the door was open and stumbled in.

"Run!" Alex told us.

Missy wouldn't budge, she kept watching Greg. There was dried blood on his shirt; his clothes were dirty.

Greg was fast, quickly scurrying to his feet. With a tightly closed fist, Alex delivered a punch that I swore would have knocked anyone out. I heard it. But Greg barely flinched.

"What the fuck?" Alex revved back and hit Greg again. Nothing. Greg merely shook his head like a cat that ran into a wall. Alex looked quickly at us. "I said to run. Go."

Just as I saw him sail his fist, using all my strength, I grabbed on to Missy nearly dragging her out the door.

"Alex!" She kept looking back as she ran.

"Come on." I pushed and shoved her along to the truck. When we reached the back door, I too glanced back at the house. No sign of Alex. All I kept seeing in my mind was my son being bitten. How when I plowed through the Sleepers, they didn't care, they kept coming.

When I opened the back door, I saw Randy's gun. He had left it on the seat. Quickly, I snatched it and pushed Missy inside.

"What are you doing?" she asked.

"Wait here." As I went to shut the door, I saw two more Sleepers coming from down the street. "Stay here. Do *not* get out. Okay?"

She nodded and I closed the door.

I hadn't yet looked at the revolver. It was a classic revolver. I was familiar with those. Releasing the cylinder, I checked to make sure it was loaded. It was.

Alex hadn't emerged from the house and the Sleepers were moving slowly down the street. With fear that something had happened to Alex, I raced to the house.

Barely had I made it to the front porch when both men flew out. Entangled in each other's grip, they spun around and dropped off the porch landing on the walk. It looked to me, while Alex was holding his own, he was more on the defensive. I watched as he slugged Greg once more then Greg rolled, flipping Alex to his back. Alex pushed and hit, but Greg had him right where he wanted.

Mouth open, saliva poured from Greg's mouth as he viciously snarled in Alex's face.

I had to do something. I thought of throwing Alex the gun, but there wasn't time. There also wasn't time to deal with how I was going to feel after my actions.

I fought in my mind to remember what Daniel had taught me. What was it? What did he say? All those times he took me to the range and I was drawing a blank. What was wrong with me? Alex was fighting for his life; Greg was on his way to victory.

Then it all came back. Playing fast forward in my head, I heard Daniel's voice. *"Brace it, lock your elbows. Plant your feet, hold it steady, take a breath…"*

Bang.

Greg dropped onto Alex, and quickly Alex rolled him from him. When he did I saw where I hit. The entire side of his head was gone.

Out of breath, Alex jumped to his feet. "Thank you." He took hold of my arm and hurried me to the truck.

"There's more," I said.

"Where?"

I pointed. They were still a good fifty feet from the car.

"We're good," he said. "Get in."

The moment we both got in the truck, I put on the safety and set the revolver between the two front seats. It was at that moment that my hands started to shake.

Alex drove. "Are you all right?"

"Yeah. Yeah, I will be." I brought my hands to my face.

"That was a great shot," he said calmly. "You have amazing aim."

My fingers trailed down my face, holding down my skin and I turned to him.

"I mean, he was inches from my face and you..." He paused when he saw my expression. "What?"

"I could have killed you."

"No. No, you did good. Right on it. Your aim was great."

"No." I shook my head. "It wasn't." I paused. "I was aiming for his legs, somewhere in case I hit you, I wouldn't kill you."

"You...you were aiming for his leg and you hit him in the head?"

"Yes."

He whistled as he exhaled, rubbed his eyes, and continued to drive. "Forget what I said about aim."

We returned to the haven where everyone was waiting for us with obvious worry. They all rushed to Missy and me the second we walked in.

Missy was a mess and it was evident on Randy's face that he felt every moment of her pain. He closed his eyes briefly with a wince then extended his big arms to her. "Come here, darlin'. Come here." You could tell he was a welcoming sight to her. His huge frame was not intimidating like Beck's, but rather comforting. He wore his heart on his sleeve and it was as big as his body.

She whimpered as she pressed against him. "My babies."

"I know. I know." He took a deep breath, wrapped his arms around her almost burying her in his comforting embrace. Like that, he escorted her to the other room.

Beck gave an upward motion of his head to me. "How was it?"

"Bad," I answered.

Beck prepared to ask more, then Alex walked in. His eyes blinked and he did a double take. Alex was bruised and a little bloody.

"I need to know," Alex said, holding the revolver. "Whose is this?" He set it on the table.

Bill looked down at it. "That's Randy's."

Alex pushed the gun Bill's way. "Keep it away from her, will ya? At least until someone teaches her how to shoot."

I defensively folded my arms. "I'll have you know, my husband taught me how to shoot."

"He didn't teach you to aim."

Beck asked. "What happened?"

"I'll explain once I calm down from my near death experience." He walked to the sink and turned on the water, splashing some on his face.

"Sleeper almost kill you?" Beck asked.

"No." Alex grabbed a towel and dried off. "She did." He pointed at me.

"Hey!" I snapped.

Beck held up a hand to silence me, which irritated me more. He focused on Alex. "Are you okay, though, man?"

Alex nodded. "Yeah. Yeah, I'm fine."

And he was. A little bit bumped and bruised, but not emotionally scarred at all. Something told me Alex would always be fine. But that was him and not everyone else was doing so well. Missy was worse than I ever was and Beck informed us it appeared that Danny was showing signs of an infection.

18
THE ARRIVAL

The Survival Haven still held on to electricity, which made Danny and Bill happy because they fired up Alex's video game system. Danny seemed fine to me; I wanted to tell Beck he was nuts, but I saw my son's arm.

I knew it was safe to interrupt when I heard the unison, 'ohs' from Bill and Danny and that telltale toss of the game controller.

Game over.

"Why are you on the floor?" I asked Danny.

"I'm fine," Danny replied. "We're gonna play one more game."

"No, you're going to eat." I pointed to his untouched plate that sat on the floor. "Bill, make him eat."

Bill peered over his shoulder to me. He had this dopey, open-mouth look on his face and when I took a step closer I saw that Bill had touched nothing on his plate either. At that point, I shut off the television.

"Hey!" they both protested.

"Guys, come on." I sat on the foot of the bed. "Eat. Okay? Please. Would you rather go in the living room and—"

Bill answered quickly. "No. No."

Danny slowly stood with his plate. He walked to the desk in the bedroom and sat there. "Yeah, it's weird in there."

"Yeah," Bill added as he sat next to me on the foot of the bed. "Quiet."

I thought about what they meant. Randy sat on the couch with Missy. She sipped a glass of wine, holding on to her children's clothes.

"They're grieving, both of them. Everybody grieves differently. You two talk and take your mind off of things. I'm trying but it's hard." I lowered my head. "I just want to keep going."

Danny asked. "So when do we go? It's not going to take that long to get to Washington. But if we keep stopping…"

I raised my hand to him to halt him. "We have to make sure you're okay."

"I'm fine." He ran his fork through his food.

"Ha!" Bill laughed. "Did you see that arm? It's gross."

- 89 -

Danny shook his head. "This food is gross."

Bill turned to me. "Tell me again why we're eating SPAM?"

I glanced down to the plate. It was the best I could do. The meat product, some rice and corn. "Because our host, the survival guru, has two cupboards full of nothing but Spam." I stood. "Eat, Danny, you need your strength." As I left the room, I paused in the doorway. "And do not turn the game back on until you are done."

Danny nodded his reluctant agreement. I stood there watching. Bill ate and Danny nibbled. He did look pale; his coloring wasn't right. A simple turn and step brought me into the living room. It was dark in there but for one lone candle. It was a plain, simple room, a couch and two chairs, a few little tables. This surprised me, the simplicity and sterile feel of the home. I guess I expected rustic.

Randy and Missy sat close on the couch. He was showing her pictures on his phone. I saw their plates on the coffee table and I bent down to retrieve them.

"Mera, I'll get them," Randy said.

"No, it's fine. I'm trying to stay busy." I glanced at Missy. "How are you?"

She shrugged. "I'm doing. How are you, Mera?"

"I'm doing as well," I told her. "That's all we can do."

"We're sharing pictures of the children," she said. "If you wanna join us."

"Maybe later."

Randy asked. "How's Danny?"

"Feisty, but I can tell something is wrong."

Missy reached up and laid her hand on my wrist. "He'll get better. He will. I feel it."

"I do, too. Thank you. I'll let you guys go, I'm gonna go see what our macho duo is up to."

It felt good to know even at my wry attempt at humor that I elicited a smile from Missy. I carried the plates to the kitchen. I could hear Beck and Alex talking outside. I rinsed off the plates and set them in the sink.

My bottle of bourbon was sitting on the counter and I poured a healthy glass, taking it with me to porch.

Even though it was seven o'clock, it was still bright, although the temperature did drop outside, making it tolerable. Both Alex and Beck sat on chairs on the porch, but they were separated by a distance. It was odd because they were such a contrast of men. Both tried to be the tough guy, one rebellious, the other disciplined.

I didn't feel the need to ask if I could join. I pulled up a chair and sat between them.

"How's Danny?" Beck asked.

"Okay, I guess. What do you think?"

Beck looked over at Alex.

Was I missing something?

Alex said, "We were discussing being proactive." He nodded at my drink. "I have ice if you want to put it in your tea."

"Oh, it's not tea." I sipped. "It's bourbon."

Alex chuckled. "That's a big glass."

I brought it to my lips. "I'm an alcoholic."

"Really?" Beck seemed surprised by my comment.

"Textbook."

Alex raised his beer. "Aren't we all?"

"So, what is proactive? Do you guys think he's going to turn into a Sleeper? Please be honest."

Beck shook his head. "No, I don't believe for one instant that is going to occur. I believe you, me, Danny, the others, all have a natural immunity to whatever virus caused the Sleeping Sickness. The infection that we're worried about isn't the Sleeping Sickness, it's bacterial. Human bites have the highest rate of infection."

Alex added. "That's where the proactive part comes in. I think a healthy IV dose of antibiotics will do the trick. So we're gonna head down to Freeman and hit the small hospital."

"When?"

Alex held up his beer bottle. "When this is gone."

Beck set his empty bottle down. "We wanna go before it gets too dark. Plus, I haven't slept. I want to do that when we get back then switch off with Sans here."

"Switch off?"

"Take a watch, make sure no Sleepers wander in," Beck said. "In fact..." he stood, "we should go."

"I agree." Alex stood as well.

"I'm coming." I took a huge gulp of my drink. Both men looked at me the same way at the same time, as if I were nuts. "What? I can't go?"

Beck moistened his lips. "It may be best if you stayed behind. You know, in case we run into Sleepers."

"Beck, in case you haven't noticed," I folded my arms and looked up to him, "on this little road trip, inadvertently I have taken out more Sleepers than anyone else."

Beck cleared his throat. "Exactly. And um, that's why you should stay back. A sense of protection."

"Sure." Alex set his beer bottle on the porch railing and walked to the door. "We'll give you a gun. Just make sure you aim for the legs." He walked inside.

"What's that supposed to mean?" Beck asked.

"He's an asshole."

"I heard that," Alex's voice carried from the kitchen.

"Beck, please," I pleaded. "I really need to feel like I'm doing something for my son. Let me go help find what needs to be found."

Beck just stared at me.

"I can't sit around. I can't. When I do, all I think about is Jeremy and my daughter. Please. Sleepers or not, it keeps my mind from going there and my heart from breaking every time it does."

Beck peered outward then with a heavy sigh he looked back down at me, laying a hand on my shoulder. "I'll go tell the others we'll be back." He slid it from me as he walked into the house.

I was still holding my drink. Sipping it, I walked to the edge of the porch and stared out. It was quiet at the haven, it really was. A large yard, trees lined up in the distance. Not a sound or smell that was wrong. Peaceful. It made it hard to believe that anything horrible had happened to the world. But I knew I soon would be checked back to reality when I ventured with Beck and Alex to that hospital.

The sky took on the pre-dusk look; still light, yet with that orange hue about it. Alex played with the radio in the SUV, but nothing came up. He told us that back at the haven he had several transceivers and antennas and was going to try to see if he could pick up anything on one of those. When he told us what type they were, Beck was impressed, but I didn't have a clue about radio types and so forth.

The town of Freeman was small. The single national chain drug store was the big icon in the middle of the two stoplight town. No fast food places, and I didn't spot a grocery store. It wasn't an easy off-the-exit stop. Everything was pretty quiet.

After the two main blocks of businesses were houses. We didn't see any Sleepers at all. But then I started to realize that we never did find the Sleepers; they found us.

Like on my street, at the refugee center, at Greg's house. None at first, then they came. I wondered if it would be the same in Freeman or even at the survival haven.

Alex instructed me to take a right on the two-lane tree-lined road, which went for about a mile until it merged onto a four-lane road. That seemed more like a populated area and I got a twitch in my stomach over what we might face. Still, as we drove there were neither cars nor people. We made a turn into the driveway of the county hospital but that was as far as we could get.

Though not nearly as bad, it was reminiscent of when Daniel and I sought help for Jeremy. Cars jammed the entire length of the driveway, even making their own lanes in the grass. The lined cars extended all the way to the hospital and parking lots.

There was no way to drive around them, and to get to the hospital we had to walk.

That scared me, but I was with Beck and Alex. After turning my SUV around in case we had to make a quick escape, we all stepped out. Beck held tight to his M-4; Alex had his shotgun and despite comments from Alex, Beck gave me a revolver.

"Just don't shoot either of us in the leg," Alex commented.

Beck didn't get it. Neither Alex nor I explained. We trudged our way toward the hospital. Both men had a keen ability to stare ahead, focus only on the hospital. I couldn't, I looked inside every car we passed. Every single car was empty. I supposed some parents, gridlocked and desperate, had carried their child home. Others had obviously opted to hold their child until the bitter end.

Alex made the suggestion that noise brought the Sleepers, using Missy's crying out and screaming on a quiet street as an example. So under that theory, we were silent, talking only in whispers when we did speak.

The doors were open at the emergency entrance, and we entered the building that way. It was completely dark, but for emergency lighting on the walls. No one was around. There were tons of hospital beds in the waiting room and halls, but they were all crammed together and pushed to the side. Upon them, IV lines rested on clothing and dust. There was also something else there.

The smell of death. That same sour smell that lingered at Missy's. The remains of the children didn't cause that smell. I knew that.

The plan was to go to the back, search out the IV materials, and get the rest of the stuff from the Freeman Walgreens.

We had barely stepped into the back section when the smell grew stronger. Beck paused and whispered, "There were people here after the Event."

"I agree," Alex said.

"How can you tell?" I asked.

"The beds pushed to the side to make room to walk through," Beck said. He stepped to the nurses' station and ran his hand over the counter. "All the remains of the kids out there, where's the dust? It would have floated about, dispersed and landed everywhere. And ..." He twitched his head toward the desk. His height gave him the advantage to see over the high ledge of that nurses' station. I had to step closer and look.

I brought my hand to my mouth and nose to lessen the smell and to control any urge to regurgitate, something that was fast becoming a regular habit of mine.

Her head rested on the desk surface. She was a nurse or doctor; it was hard to tell but she was wearing scrubs. The entire desk surface was covered with dried blood. It came from a huge gaping wound in her neck.

Alex whispered to me. "Try not to throw up again."

I agreed. Throwing up again was the last thing I wanted to do. I was okay when Beck reached down for her hair. I was even all right when he commented, "She's only been dead about a day." I was proud that I stayed in control when he lifted her head despite the fact that the entire desk calendar lifted with her because the blood adhered it to her body like glue. But the second Beck pulled the calendar from her with a Velcro-ripping sound, I lost it.

I was able to scoot a few feet away to the garbage pail, lifted it and vomited.

"Thar' she blows," Alex said. I ignored him.

My watering eyes searched for something to wipe my nose and mouth, and then I saw the hand extend with a rag. "Thanks." I took it and did a fast cleanup.

"You okay?" Beck asked. Of course it was he that gave me the rag. It wouldn't have been Alex.

I nodded and turned around to see Alex shaking his head. "What?"

"Can you try not to throw up every time we see something gross?" Alex asked.

"I'll try," I said sarcastically.

Alex peered over the counter at the nurse. "Well, she was gross, but all right. At least we know we aren't dealing with the Z word." He looked back and me and Beck. "So when we see a Sleeper we don't have to always aim for the legs."

Beck's lip curled. "Why in the world would we shoot them in the legs?"

Alex only pointed to me.

"Ignore him." I said. "Okay, can we get this done with?"

"There don't seem to be that many rooms," Beck said. "I'm pretty confident if there were any Sleepers here, they'd have heard us and been on us. Each of us will stay in this area, hit a room, and look for the IV bags. If you see a Sleeper, call out."

"Agreed," Alex said, "but if you don't understand what is in the bag, grab it anyway. I will figure it out. I am going to find the refrigerators."

I was nervous. I really didn't want to be doing it alone, but I took stock in what Beck had said.

Beck went to the right; both Alex and I went left.

He went in one room, I went beyond him to the next. I didn't think about how stupid a move that was. It was at least fifteen feet from where Alex went. But the swinging double doors stated 'Emergency OR', and I figured I would hit the antibiotic IV jackpot there.

I didn't see her when I first stepped inside. I was too focused on the long line of cabinets over the sink. But I heard a noise, a slight growl, and I spun to my right.

I didn't scream or cry out with concern; I just said in a slightly louder voice, "Sleeper."

She wasn't a threat, but it was pathetic and sad all at the same time. Her darkened eyes and reactions told me for certain she was a Sleeper.

The younger woman couldn't have been any older than twenty-five. Her hair was long, dirty and stringy. She was on the operating table and she stared at me, mouth snapping as if she were trying to bite. Her legs kicked about, and she thrashed back and forth at an attempt to reach me. But she couldn't. She was held to the table by the restraints on her wrists.

Alex came in with a rush and slowed down when he saw her. "Aw, man."

My eyes never left her. "She's pregnant, Alex, very pregnant."

"I can see that." He slung his shotgun over his shoulder and reached to his waist for his revolver. He pointed it at her.

"What are you doing?" I asked.

"She's a Sleeper."

"But she's pregnant."

He lowered the gun and placed his hands on her stomach. "Nothing, Mera. Nothing moving in there. Nothing. Like every other child. Gone. Just like you told me about all the babies that were born. Dead."

It made me shudder when he said that. Using 'baby' and 'dead' in the same phrase.

"Do you understand?" he asked.

"Yes."

He walked to the head of the table and aimed his revolver at her.

"Alex, you're just gonna shoot her?"

"Would you want to live like this?" he asked me.

"No."

"Neither would she."

Without any further hesitation and a simple pull of the trigger, he fired a single shot into the woman's head and she stopped moving.

I didn't scream, but it caused me to jolt.

He returned the revolver to the waist of his pants. "You can skip this room for supplies. Come on." He touched my arm.

"I will." I pulled back. "Just let me cover her."

"Fine," he said, and rolled his eyes at me, telling me not to dally and left the room.

The single stream of blood poured from the hole in her forehead like an open faucet. Her head was tilted my way and her eyes were still open. The blood hit the floor steadily.

There were a lot of things I felt at that moment, but not one of them was fear. Staring down to her I truly felt bad, certain this was not how she had envisioned her life ending. She was so young. Did she have a family that missed her? Worried about her like I was about Jessie? And the baby she carried…all those dreams she had for the child's life, so close to holding that infant in her arms. Now she lay there, a bullet hole in her head, a victim of some virus that made her into a creature, strapped to a hospital table. Whoever put her there didn't even cover her, barely had her dressed. She was another face, another infected, a person without a name, like she was nobody. But she wasn't nobody. She was somebody's child and almost somebody's mother.

What if she was my daughter? Would I want some stranger to just walk away or would I want that stranger to at least give her a little bit of respect? Respect she deserved in her young life.

My eyes scanned the room. I saw the shelf on the wall behind me that contained sheets and blankets. My foot caught some of the blood and I slid a little in my reach. The blankets and sheets all tumbled to the floor, but I managed to grasp one. Flapping it out, I started with her legs, pulling the sheet up her body. I undid her wrist restraints and laid her arms on her body then before I covered her completely, I took a moment to close her eyes.

"I'm sorry sweetie," I whispered, then pulled the sheet over her.

A week before I would have prayed, but at that moment, I didn't know how I felt about God. If God was responsible for what the young woman endured then he didn't want my prayers for her.

As I turned to go, I caught movement through the corner of my eye. There was a movement of the sheet. It wasn't her hands; the movement was too low. At first I thought it was my imagination then I saw the sheet move again.

Immediately my hands went to her stomach. I felt the full, hard belly and just as I was about to chalk it up to an optical illusion, I felt it.

Thump.

A tiny kick against my hand. I gasped and before I could retract my hands again, I felt another kick, then another.

I couldn't speak, I could barely breathe.

"Alex," I called, and charged for the door, but the floor was wet with blood and my feet caught it. The slickness shot me forward like a speed skater. I had no control and when my shoes hit the clean portion of the floor, my feet stopped, but my body kept going. I flew forward into the wall next to the door.

It knocked the wind out of me and, trying to catch my balance, I reached out, but only caught air and I tumbled to the floor.

"Mera?" I heard Alex call my name.

Still unable to breathe correctly, I couldn't call out. I staggered to a stand and just as I did, Alex blasted into the room. He hit the door with such a force it flew back into me and nailed me in the side of the head and my body hit into the wall.

Blood rushed to my ears and a loud ringing began in them. The tremendous pain to my head was like nothing I had ever felt. I slid down, back against the wall until my rear hit the floor.

"She's not here," Alex said.

"Where is she?" asked Beck.

"I don't know."

Check down here.

Their voices meshed together, drowned out by the ringing in my ears. They were looking for me. Calling me. I was right here. Right here.

Their voices faded.

Faded.

Black.

I wasn't out long; I couldn't have been. I could still see daylight peeking through the window at the far corner of the operating room.

There were three things that snapped me to. One was the pain, the other was the feeling of blood running down my head, and the last was the noise.

A wet, steady noise.

My head spun and my eyes took a moment to focus. Bringing myself to a stand, a sharp pain stabbed through my head and I felt woozy. I probably would have fallen again, passed right out had I not seen it.

Blood saturated the lower portion of the sheet that covered the young girl.

I thought I was dreaming. I had to have been dreaming, because the sheet was moving beneath the bloody mess.

It felt surreal.

My balance was off and I released heavy breaths as I staggered to the table. I was shaken and afraid to look. The closer I stepped, the more seconds that went by, I realized it wasn't a dream. The sheet was moving and I reached out my hand and grabbed it. My dizziness caused me to lose some balance and as I swayed, I pulled the sheet. The entire sheet, still in my grip, slid from her body. Exposed between her legs, the bloody placenta with umbilical cord and attached to that, was the moving newborn.

A breathy scream escaped me without control and I lunged for that table.

The child was moving. It was covered with gunk and blood, struggling to open its mouth and eyes. *Eyes.* It had *eyes.* No, *he* had eyes. It was a boy.

"Oh, God!" I gasped out. "Beck!" I shouted. "Alex!"

I lifted the child the best I could, trying not to detach it from the cord. I leaned close to the table and frantically tried to clear his eyes and mouth. Using my index finger, I opened his mouth so he could breathe. "Beck! Alex!"

Within seconds, Beck flew in. "Mera, what happened? Are you..." Then he saw what I was doing. Beck froze.

"Where the hell have you been?" Alex rushed into the room. "Don't you know..." He stopped at the foot of the bed.

"He's alive," I said. "He's alive and normal."

Alex paused, but only for a second. He swung a point to Beck. "Get a cloth or gauze. Wet it down with the saline on the wall. Then find me a blanket." He spun to me as he rushed to the cabinets. "Mera, keep trying to clear his mouth and nose. He can't breathe properly; his passages are blocked."

I focused on the child. His eyes opened.

I could hear Alex rummaging around. "Try to get him to cry. Did he cry yet?"

"Not yet."

"Get him to cry. Keep his head up. Careful with the cord."

I knew all that. I was the paranoid pregnant woman who read up on what to do if I didn't make it to the hospital.

"Here." Beck handed me the wet gauze.

I lifted my eyes to Beck for a moment. "Thank you." I began to wipe the baby's face. "Come on, baby, cry. Come on."

"Is he breathing?" Beck asked.

"Yes. But it's shallow."

"This is unreal," Beck whispered in shock. "I saw babies born after the Event. They weren't like him."

"Found them!" Alex shouted, and before I knew it he was at the table with me. "Hold him up."

As slippery as he was, I held him.

Alex had a suction bulb; he moved fast and placed it to the child's nostrils. The baby squirmed.

"It's clearing." He lifted his eyes to Beck. "We're gonna need more wet cloths to wash him off. Can you get that?"

"Got it," Beck replied.

Then Alex looked to me. "When did this happen?"

"I don't know. It was sometime after you knocked me out."

"I did what?" Alex asked as he suctioned the child's mouth. "Still not crying." Then without skipping a beat, Alex grabbed his foot and flicked it twice.

The child cried. He sounded like a cat, but he cried nonetheless.

For the first time, I saw Alex grin. "Good boy." He placed a clamp on the cord and cut it then reached for the blanket that Beck had placed by the child, placed it between my arms and the infant and lifted the baby from my hold.

He had to have seen it in my face. I felt heartbroken when he took the child.

"You can have him back when I'm done," Alex said. "But first, Beck, take care of her head, please."

My head? I totally forgot I was injured. A few moments later Beck eased me into a chair and stood over me with some medical supplies. He placed a wet cloth to my head; it stung at first. Wiping my face like a dirty child, Beck said something about it not needing stitches.

I didn't care.

"You have a bad bump. How are you feeling?"

"I'm fine," I answered in a daze. But sitting in the chair, I didn't care if I bled, needed stitches, or my head had a huge bump. Or even that there were Sleepers on the road. It didn't matter. All I worried about at that moment was that baby.

That was my only focus.

19
BUNDLE OF REASON

It had been a few hours and even though I hadn't grown very fond of Alex Sans, I was extremely grateful for his medical knowledge.

He gave me an injection of pain medication before we left the hospital. Not a full dose, but 'enough to take off the edge,' he told me. I didn't have an edge at that point; my adrenaline was pumping over finding the baby.

But after we successfully made our way around the dozen or so Sleepers on the lawn of the hospital, I felt pressure, like a migraine. No pain, just pressure. I realized then what taking off the edge meant.

Alex said he had more if I needed it. I was sure I would.

When we stopped at the Walgreens for baby supplies, I stayed with the baby in the truck, holding him close to my chest and checking every ten seconds to make sure he was still breathing.

He was tiny, maybe five pounds. His eyes stayed open and he stared at me, nibbling on the edge of my finger and whimpering occasionally. He was hungry, but there was nothing we could do about it until we got back to the haven and sterilized some bottles.

Everyone seemed to have a different reaction to the baby.

Alex seemed to not even want to acknowledge the child beyond what he had to do. He seemed more concerned with my head injury and my son, racing straight into the house with that IV bag before I was even out of the truck.

Beck was shocked, but he didn't look at the baby, almost as if it were too painful. I understood why. His own son was only three months old when he was taken in the Event.

When we stepped inside everyone seemed more focused on the fact that Alex rushed into the bedroom with the life-saving antibiotics rather than noticing I had a blanket in my arms. Beck immediately started preparing bottles.

I walked right by Missy and Randy; they didn't even see the baby.

Danny, though, noticed right away. He immediately bounced forward with enthusiasm, only to be told by Alex to hang back.

"Mom? Can I see?" Danny asked.

Bill tossed down the remote to the game and rushed to my side. "You found a baby."

I brought the baby with me and sat on the edge of the bed. "Look how precious." Danny's finger reached out. "He's so small."

"I know."

Bill sat down next to me. "I thought all babies... I mean, all children..."

"Apparently not this one," I whispered.

Bill has a wide, innocent smile on his face, almost as if in awe. "Can I hold him?"

"No," I said. "I don't want to let him go yet."

Alex shook his head. "She's been like that. Hasn't put him down or taken her eyes off of him."

Danny asked me. "Did you find him?"

I shrugged. "More or less. His mother was a Sleeper, pregnant, Alex shot her in the head. The baby came out."

Danny lifted his eyes to Alex who was finishing the IV. "Dude, you shot a pregnant woman in the head?"

Alex nodded. "I also knocked out your mother by accident too. Been a hell of a day." Alex stepped back. "All done. I'm pretty confident that will do the trick. The infection isn't too bad yet. I think it's probably a combo of the human bite and raw surgery. Let's kick it in the ass." He walked to the door. "I'll check on you in a bit."

"Thanks," Danny said. "Oh, hey, Alex? What do you think about finding the baby?"

Alex looked very seriously at Danny. "I don't." He tapped his hand once on the door frame and left.

"Wow." Bill blinked. "That was harsh. Anyhow, are you sure I can't hold him, just a second?"

I shook my head. "No. Not yet. After I feed him. Okay?"

"I'll wait," Bill said agreeably. "This is cool, Mera. A baby. This is hope."

I grinned. "I know."

"What are you gonna name him?" Danny questioned. "Or did you?"

"Not yet," I replied. "I will."

"Call him George," Danny suggested.

"Or Spencer," added Bill.

I laughed. "No. Whatever I decide to name him will be important and mean something."

Bill shrugged. "I'm sure Spencer or George means something."

"I'm sure." I stood. "Okay, I'm gonna go feed him. I'll be back." I waited until I received a nod from them and I turned and walked from the room.

When I re-entered the living room it was evident that Randy and Missy had figured out what I had in my arms.

Missy slowly moved to me. It was clear she was still in shock over her children and the sight of the baby was too much. She reached out, her hand trembling, and she looked at him. The second her fingers trailed over his head she burst into tears, spun and ran to the couch.

Randy was smiling, a peaceful smile, and he lifted the blanket to take a peek. "Probably need some clothes for the little guy. We should make it a point to stop somewhere on the way to Seattle."

"We should." I looked up to Randy and gave a quirky smile. "That's really perceptive of you to pick up that he was a boy. Or did Beck tell you?"

Randy shook his head. "He looks like a little boy." Randy chuckled. "His eyes are open." His huge fingers trailed over the baby's head. "He keeps staring at you like he knows ya."

"He probably knows I have to feed him. And name him. I have to give him a name. But I really want to give it some thought. You know?"

Randy nodded.

"Bill and Danny suggested I name him George or Spencer. You have any suggestions you want to throw out?"

"Nope." Randy replied then closed his mouth tightly with a shake of his head. "That's your duty. You pick out the name. He is a strong little boy. He has to be. Look at the world he has to face."

I cradled the baby closer and closed my eyes, brushing my cheek against the softness of his skin. I didn't reply. There was no need, because I couldn't agree more with what Randy had said.

Beck had impressively made the bottles. He filled enough that he believed would get us through the night and into the morning. He was tired and went to get some sleep. He told me he'd be more than happy to take over baby detail when he woke up to keep watch for Sleepers. He went to bed about nine o'clock.

I fed the little guy, then, because he was so tiny, I fed him again in two hours. He was only taking an ounce, and that was normal from what I remembered.

I was scared. I held him, watching the clock, waiting for another feeding time. About two in the morning, right before Alex went to switch and wake Beck, he went and checked on Danny. Checking on Danny was the only time Alex left his post, which was on the roof of the porch.

I sat on the porch, feeding the baby yet again

"He has absolutely no signs of fever now," Alex told me. "And the arm definitely does not look as red. He'll be good to get on the road by morning."

I thanked him and inside I felt relieved, but a part of me already knew Danny was getting better. Again, that mother instinct overruled the mother worry.

Alex continued. "To be on the safe side he should do a course of antibiotics for ten days. I'm no doctor, but my guess is that would be best."

"I'll make sure of it."

"So will I."

"We're leaving tomorrow for Seattle."

Alex flashed a quick sarcastic smile. "So am I."

That took me by surprise. "I didn't think you would. I mean, you have it all here and—"

"Except people. And Beck is gonna need some help getting your crew across this country. Finding your daughter is a goal. I like goals. Plus, I'm kind of curious as to what all has gone on out there."

"It'll be good to have you with us."

Alex stepped to the edge of the porch. "Beck will be out soon. You may want to get some sleep, too. How's the head?"

"My head is fine. I have a slight headache, but that's all. Why won't you look at the baby?"

Briefly Alex looked over his shoulder at me then continued to stare out. "I did. When he was born."

"Don't you like children?"

"Oh, I like children. I love them. Wanted a crew of my own one day." He sighed.

"So it's not personal?"

Finally, Alex turned to look at me. He had this look upon his face, staring at me as if I were nuts. "What are you talking about? Personal?"

"Like you knew the mother or lost a child."

"No." He answered quickly and turned back around.

"I didn't name him yet. I'm still thinking."

"I wouldn't name him at all."

Slowly I stood. "Why would you say something like that, Alex? Why don't you like this baby?"

He chuckled, and arms folded tight to his body he turned around. "It has nothing to do with like, Mera. It's not personal. I don't want to look at him. I don't want to name him. I don't want to know him, like him or get attached. Okay?"

I hesitated to ask why. In fact, I did hesitate, but the word slipped out of me softly and it cracked when I asked. "Why?"

He pursed his lips, swallowed and stepped closer. "Look at him. He's little. Hell, if he's five pounds we're lucky. He's early, too. You know that. He's a preemie, and his mother was one of those infected. Lord knows what went through his veins or how long he was deprived of oxygen. He doesn't stand a chance. It's hard but it's the truth."

Alex's words cut and took away my breath. I stared at the baby. "Stop it." I told him. "Don't say any more."

"Why? Because you can't face the truth? I don't look at him, Mera, because I don't want to like him or get attached. You look at him like a hero that rose from the ashes. Well, how you gonna feel when you wake up in a day, maybe two and that little guy ain't looking back at you. Did you ask yourself that question?"

"No." I said strongly then lowered my voice. "No. You know why? Because he's not gonna die. He survived, Alex. When all the other children in the world died, he lived. The question I ask myself isn't what am I gonna do when he dies, it's, when other newborns were stillborn, why he was born alive. Why this child? Huh? Why? I'll tell you. Because there's something special about him. We just don't know what it is yet."

Not wanting to give Alex a chance to say anything else or to bring me down, I took the baby and I went inside. And I went inside certain that Alex Sans was wrong.

20
FORWARD MARCH

The thumping headache caused me to wake up but panic caused me to spring from the loveseat where I had fallen asleep with the baby just before dawn.

I moved cautiously so as not to wake or stir the baby, but he wasn't there. He was gone. At first I thought I rolled over on him, but I was still in the semi-upright position. I checked the creases of the loveseat the cushions. My heart sunk. Had he, like the other children, simply turned to dust? I searched for answers to that question.

"You okay?" Randy asked, startling me as he walked up behind me.

I spun around, out of breath, still half asleep. "The baby... I can't find the baby."

Sipping his coffee as if it were no big deal, Randy pointed backwards with his thumb. "Beck has him in the kitchen. There's coffee in—"

Before he finished, I flew by him into the kitchen. Sliding to a stop, I caught my breath when I saw Beck at the table burping the baby.

"Is he okay?" I asked.

"Mera, he's fine. Are *you* okay?"

"No." I shook my head and stepped to him. "I was scared. I thought something happened to him." I held out my hands for the baby.

Beck peered at me with his big brown eyes. "You were sleeping. He was stirring. You needed to rest. You had a head injury. Why are you holding out your hands to me?"

"To take the baby."

"I have him."

"But I can take him now." I wiggled my fingers.

Almost taking offense, Beck said. "I have him. He's fine. I'm a good father, I can handle a newborn. Get a cup of coffee, get your bearings then take a shower."

"Oh my God, do I stink?"

"Huh?" Beck laughed. "No. We'll be leaving soon. You may want to get one. Who knows when you'll see a shower again?"

I nodded. "You're right. Are you sure you don't want me to—"

"I got him."

I walked to the coffee pot and poured a cup of coffee. When I turned around I saw that Randy had slipped into the kitchen and was just having a seat at the table.

Beck's hand smoothed in circles over the baby's back. The child look even tinier resting against Beck's broad shoulders. Then a burp rang out.

The corner of Beck's mouth raised and he spoke in a smooth, higher tone. "Whoa, that's a big burp coming from such a little guy. Yeah. You're a little guy." He brought the baby around to peer at him then brushed his lips against the child's nose, closing his eyes for a moment. A moment I assumed was remembrance and sadness for his own infant boy.

It probably was instinct, but as I sat down I extended my hands once again,

Beck slipped from his moment, opening his eyes and seeing my hands. "Do that one more time, ask to take him one more time, and I won't give him to you at all. I got him. Drink your coffee."

"Sorry." I retracted my hands. "I named him last night."

"Good." Beck smiled. "What did you decide on so I know what to call him?"

"Phoenix." I replied. "His name is now Phoenix."

Randy must have heard the name when he stepped into the kitchen. "You named him Phoenix?"

"Yes," I said. "Actually, though I hate to say it, Alex said something last night that made me think of the name."

"You picked the right name," Randy said. "Immortality. Survivor. Out of the ashes."

I snapped my finger and pointed. "That's what Alex said. Out of the ashes."

Beck kept looking at the baby. "I like the name. It's fitting. Good choice."

"Thanks." I smiled. "Where is everyone?"

Randy answered. "Missy is cleaning up. Bill is messing with that radio unit Alex gave him and your boy is helping Alex get things ready."

Beck added, "Alex wanted to make sure we had everything ready to go."

I huffed. "I wish he wasn't going. I hate him."

"Mera!" Beck laughed and shook his head.

Randy gasped. "Mera, hate is a strong word."

I shrugged. "I'm sorry. I do. He's not nice. He's callous. He knocked me out and has yet, *yet*, mind you, to even apologize, and the worst was he told me last night that Phoenix is gonna die in a day or two."

Beck raised his eyes slowly. "He said that? That's really cold."

"I know."

Randy reached out and rubbed Phoenix's head. "He's not dying. Not at all. He defied the odds already."

"I know he's not dying," I said confidently. "That's why it pissed me off about Alex. I hate him. Actually, I don't think anyone will like him."

At that moment my enthusiastic son burst into the kitchen proclaiming, "Dudes, Alex is, like, the coolest."

I gave up and at that moment, before losing my cool, opted for a shower.

The Survival Haven truly was a haven, even if I hated to admit it. The trek across country for my daughter appeared to be a lifelong dream mission of Alex Sans, one he had been planning for his entire life, but just didn't know it. Making his way across the barren world, although that didn't surprise me from a man who started a business called Survival Haven.

Between him and Beck we were covered. Alex had everything. He pulled out maps and charted where we could run into problems. He checked the vehicles for road worthiness and got them ready. He packed two extra car batteries, had a small gas-run generator which would be used to power up a pump specifically created by Alex to retrieve gasoline from gas stations with no electricity.

As long as there was a gas station, power or not, we'd not run out of gas. He packed up food, protein bars, water, medicine and those thin space age blankets that Bill was in awe over.

There was a lot put into that van. I hadn't a clue what all was there.

I'm sure Alex did.

We would leave my SUV behind and take the trip with two vehicles. A small car and the conversion van, which would be used more for carrying supplies.

While both Beck and Alex stated that we could probably find what we needed en route, it was better to bring it just in case.

But out of all the nifty gadgets and things that Alex packed for us, I was the most grateful for that old-fashioned radio system.

Bill was deemed radio man because Alex called him the Tech-Ru, short for technological guru. The radio wasn't working quite right when Bill sat down with it, but damned if he didn't get it working and we not only received a signal, we spoke to a man in Northern California.

It was a short conversation, but the man assured us that out west, as rumored, things hadn't yet fallen apart.

That was good to hear.

But that was California. I needed to know about Seattle.

The weak signal we had on the phone two days earlier had diminished.

No more speaking to Jessie.

I was in the dark about my daughter and could only hope that like California, Seattle, Washington was holding its own in the dark days we faced.

We were getting ready to move on, and it was pushing noon. We were pretty much waiting on Bill, who was the last to take a shower.

Missy sat on the porch still cradling her children's clothing. She was reluctant to go with us, but Randy talked her into it. Beck was by the van; Alex kept making trips in and out of the house for items. Randy sat on the step of the porch fiddling with what looked like a small pad computer. And me, I was at my wits' end with my son.

Holding Phoenix, I listened to Danny rattle on. Alex this; Alex that; Alex had this and Alex knows that.

"Enough already, Danny, please," I snapped. "Okay? Enough about Alex. If you're going to find a male figure to praise, how about Bill? He developed that game you like. Or Randy?" I indicated to where Randy sat on the steps. "He's nice. Or Beck? He served his country."

"Alex served this country. Why don't you like him?"

"Because he is mean to Phoenix and he knocked me out."

"He said you were standing behind the door, he didn't see you and it was your fault."

I gasped. "He said that? He's an asshole."

Alex came out of the house with a box, stopped and said, "Who's an asshole?"

"You," I replied.

"Man, you're tough." He leaned forward to peek at Phoenix.

"Don't." I pulled him away. "You didn't want to look at him yesterday. Don't look at him today. He's alive, you know, in case you're wondering."

"Good Lord, woman, the mood. It's not conducive to traveling. Here." He reached to the box. "Fresh bottle of whiskey." He lifted a fifth and handed it to me. "If you wanna crack one open for an afternoon hit, you know."

My response to that was a stare. One evil-looking glance his way.

He, of course, laughed, and that annoyed me. He walked to the steps, paused and said to Randy, "What's that you got there, stud? Ain't never seen a computer like that."

"And you won't," Randy replied. "Or wouldn't. My wife worked for the manufacturer. They were going to revolutionize the industry. Solar powered. But the juice is low because I didn't power it up yesterday to charge."

Alex whistled. "Nice. You trying the net?"

Randy shook his head. "Just playing. Passing time. Keeping my journal."

"Hmm. What version of Windows is that? It doesn't look familiar."

"Windows?"

"Ain't that the truth? I'm a Mac man myself." Alex stepped off the porch and headed to the van.

Why was Alex in such a good mood? I didn't get it. Again, I could only attribute it to the fact that he had been waiting on the apocalypse for so long, it was a dream come true for him.

When Bill finally came out of the house, Randy stood. He stowed his computer and reached out his hand to Missy. "You ready?"

"Am I riding with you?" she asked.

"If you want. I'm driving the car."

"Then yes." She grabbed his hand. "Yes, I am."

Missy baffled me, the whole situation. It definitely played a part into my factoring of reasons why I didn't like Alex. This was a woman who went camping with him. His girlfriend. So why hadn't they spoken two words since we returned from finding her children? Why did she need to find comfort and solace with Randy, a stranger, instead of a man she probably knew intimately?

Those were things I'd find out. Not that they were important, but it would help keep my mind off of Jessie and the worry about her as we made our way out west.

It was indeed time to go.

Alex locked up the shop, hung the 'closed' sign and we were off.

21
ANOTHER NIGHT CLOSER

There are certain things that are taken for granted. I know at least I took them for granted. One of them was normalcy. I expected a normal drive and for the most part it was. Interstate 80 was always, to the best of my memory, an easy highway. It was flat and never brought us near any major cities. Although South Bend, Indiana, wasn't a major metropolis, for safety's sake, we took a small detour and picked back up on 80 after South Bend.

It didn't surprise me that Alex liked country music. It wasn't the newer catchy stuff; it was the old twangy country. Thank God Beck kept turning it off and claimed he needed to be able to hear the CB radio, should Randy contact him.

He was in constant contact with Randy who seemed to lag behind. That was a source of irritation to Alex. But I kept thinking that the drive through Indiana had to be painful for Randy. He was returning to the home state that he'd left; the one he had run from after his family had died.

An hour into the drive, I finally broke down and let Bill and Danny hold Phoenix. Bill held him like a china doll, where Danny made me nervous, bringing back memories for me of when Jeremy was born. Danny was all of four and he so much wanted to hold his little brother. But by the time Jeremy was six months old, the tiny infant was nothing than a mere live action figure for Danny.

I had to watch him constantly with Jeremy. He'd pose him, lift him, and hide him. *Jeremy.*

Every single time I thought of my son, I wanted to break down. My chest grew heavy and my heart sunk. I wished with all my might that I would be overcome with good memories instead of thoughts of his death, remembering him with fondness instead of crawling into a pit of despair and envisioning his final, horrible moments of life on this earth. What went through his mind, what was he thinking? Did he see us with him? Did he so want to reach out and ask, "Mommy, what's going on? Help me."

Or did he simply leave before his body was finished? That was what I hoped for.

It would be a while, if ever, that I'd find happiness in memories of Jeremy. It didn't help me that nearly everyone who remained was in the same boat: Beck, Randy, and Missy. Like them, I had lost and I wanted my son back. I wanted everything to change, for it all to be a nightmare.

It wasn't.

But unlike Beck, Randy and Missy, I had Danny and Jessie, too. I was fortunate.

And now I had Phoenix to care for, as well, if I could ever get him back.

It was odd riding in the van with a baby not in a car seat. We didn't have one and we all weighed the consequences, agreeing that a car seat was less mobile should the baby have to be moved from the van in a hurry.

Phoenix wasn't cradled in Danny's arms. Danny had his legs up on the seat and the baby rested against his thighs facing him.

"Danny, please hold the baby. What if we hit a bump and he rolls off of you?"

"I got him, Mom. Honestly." Danny lifted this little hand. "Look how tiny he is. He's not going anywhere." He peered down at Phoenix. "You're tiny, huh?" Then Danny chuckled, playing with Phoenix's fingers. "Man, they don't seem real, do they? So small."

Bill reached across touching the baby's fingers. "And look at these nails. When they grow, how do you cut them? Really. I'd be scared I'd clip his fingers."

From the front seat Beck replied. "Bite them."

"Bite them?" Bill asked.

"Yeah," Beck answered. "Like you do your own. It's safer."

Bill fluttered his lips. "Sounds kind of gross, if you ask me."

"It's not gross when it's your kid," Beck said.

"But it's not anyone's kid," Bill said. "Who will bite his nails? I won't."

Even from where I sat, I could see Beck roll his eyes. "I will," Beck said. "Okay. Why are you worried about his nails right now?"

Bill shrugged. "Just bringing it up. A thought."

I watched as Danny looked super close at the fingernails. "They aren't real nails. Sort of like thick skin. It's weird."

I gasped and shrieked when I saw Danny bring Phoenix's hand to his mouth. "What the hell are you doing?" I pulled the baby's hand away.

"I was seeing if they were bitable."

"There you have it," Beck said to Bill. "Danny will bite his nails. Obviously he's not grossed out by it."

Then Alex interjected. "His nails are soft because he's early. Give it a couple weeks."

"So you're saying he'll be alive in a couple weeks now?" I asked, sarcastically.

Alex lifted his sights to the rearview mirror and his brown eyes caught mine. "Why the attitude?" he asked. "You haven't been nice at all to me this whole trip, actually since last night."

"That's because you're an asshole."

"Yeah, well, you said that already, so how about this time telling me why."

"Two main reasons. One, you knocked me out—"

"And I apologized."

"No you did not," I stated firmly. "Not at all."

"Then I'm sorry. Better?"

"No." I shook my head. "You didn't mean it."

"I give up."

"Good." Exhaling, I reached over and took Phoenix from Danny.

"What's the other reason?" Alex asked. "You said there were two."

"You said you gave up."

"What, the other reason?"

"The baby." I said. "You were cold and callous and said he was going to die."

"That's it?" Alex laughed. "That's why I'm an asshole, because I was being honest with you?"

"You wouldn't even look at him."

"You know what?" Alex lifted one hand from the wheel. "I'm sorry. I am. Can we get past this please? Please."

"And…?"

"And?" Alex's voice cracked as he asked. "I thought you said there were two reasons."

"Three. Why doesn't Missy want anything to do with you?"

Alex laughed. "That's not a reason."

"It is," I said. "She's your girlfriend and wants nothing to do with you."

"She's not my girlfriend," Alex argued. "Why would you say that?"

"You went camping together."

"Doesn't make her my girlfriend; she's my friend."

Beck, trying to change the energy of the van and obviously the subject, spoke up. "You know what? Speaking of Missy, let me radio back there to see how they're doing."

"Yes, do that," Alex directed. "And ask him why in God's name why he has to stay twenty car lengths behind us."

Beck picked up the CB. "Randy, come in."

I just so happened to glance to my right and Danny was smiling. "Is this funny to you?"

Danny bobbed his head. "In a way."

"Well I'm glad that—"

"Shit," Alex said, which made me look up. He was looking ahead. "Brace the baby."

His stern, serious order instinctively caused me to grip my arms and bring the baby to my chest. Before I could ask what the problem was, Beck said, "Braking." And in a split second, my body flung forward as Alex slammed on the brakes.

It wasn't our speed as much as the sudden need to stop that caused the van to skid then turn sideways before it came to an abrupt halt.

I would have been on the floor had Danny not grabbed hold of me.

Halfway off the seat, I checked on Phoenix. He was fine and started to cry. It was a good thing that Randy did travel far behind us, because I believe he would have slammed right into us. Straightening myself back onto the seat, I didn't need to ask why we stopped. As soon as I raised my head and peered out my window I saw why. How could I not? The sight of it made me clasp even tighter to Phoenix.

The road was gone.

It wasn't just gone; a huge cavern had formed in the road. I looked left to right out of the window and it extended as far as I could see. But maybe it was my limited view, I thought. So, like the others, I stepped from the van.

It took my breath away, both in its devastation and in its beauty.

The van perched all but two feet from the edge of where it appeared the earth had dropped.

Like standing on the edge of the ocean, I didn't see an end.

Beck ran his hand down his face. "What could have caused this?"

"Dude," Danny ran close to the edge. "It has to go down hundreds of feet. Straight down."

I reached out but not too close. I never looked to see what was down there or what it looked like. "Danny, get away from the edge."

"Mom, please. You think I'm gonna fall?"

"Yes. Please. Step back."

"Mom."

"Beck?" I shifted my eyes to him.

With one step to the side and swoop of his arm around my thin son's waist, Beck pulled him back for me.

Bill stated. "Sinkhole. Has to be. They're usually round."

"It's like the other half of the country is gone," I whispered.

I hadn't paid attention at first, but Alex went to the van and returned with binoculars. He stared out across the hole then handed them to Beck.

I finally noticed Randy as he stood in shock with Missy. "Randy, you lived in this state. Did you know about this?"

He shook his head. "Not at all. Of course, this is further west than I was." He stared out with almost a sad look on his face. "I can't believe it caused this."

"What?" I asked. "You can't believe what caused this?"

"The uh…the Rapture, or whatever it is."

"It's not the Rapture," I snapped. "Geez. At least it was a good thing you had time to stop."

"I watched him brake a few seconds before Beck said anything."

Beck and Alex kept exchanging the binoculars. I was waiting on what they had to say.

Alex had one hand on his hip. "Fuck!" He paused when it echoed back to him, and smiled as if he were impressed by that.

With a wave of his hand he gathered us all closer. "All right," Alex said. "Good news and bad news. Good news is it looks like the hole is only about three miles across."

Beck took over from there. "Bad news is, north to south we can't determine how far it goes.

I asked, "What do we do?"

"Well," Beck answered. "Staying put is not an option. So we head north and hope to catch where it ends, or go south. I say south to go around it only because the lakes are north. It obviously doesn't extend to the lakes or this would be a river."

We were standing there discussing it when oddly Missy, out of the blue, walked up to me and asked, "Can I take the baby, Mera? Please?"

I really did think it was odd timing, but then again, Missy was so deeply mourning that whether we went north or south didn't matter to her. Truly feeling she needed to hold Phoenix, I handed him over.

Immediately she stepped from me, pressing her lips to the child. She cried. I could see it. Everyone else was too engrossed in which was the best route to go.

I couldn't believe everyone found passion in discussing the matter. To me it was trivial. Pick a damn route.

Go north because that was certain it ended somewhere before the lakes.

Go south where it was less populated.

It went back and forth until Randy had had enough. "South. Okay. I don't want to get near Chicago. Let's go south. I flipped a coin. It said south."

Alex clapped his hands together once. "South it is. Can you try to keep up?"

Randy chuckled. "Keep up? Good thing I didn't. I would be dead when you stopped suddenly. Besides, you were going 90 miles an hour."

"What!" I screeched. "No wonder we spun when you tried to stop."

Then Bill squealed, "Ninety miles an hour! You were going ninety miles an hour?"

"Yeah," Alex answered. "What's the problem?"

Bill shook his head. "No problem. I'm impressed. I had no clue we were going that fast."

"I redid the suspension myself," Alex said proudly.

"Guys," Beck whispered.

I heard his call but all I was thinking about was that we were barreling down the highway at 90 miles an hour. What conversion van even goes that fast?

"Pretty good job," Bill said. "I didn't feel a thing."

"Guys," Beck called again.

"She rides smooth," Alex said then turned to Randy. "I'll slow down a bit. But try to keep up."

"Yes, well keep in mind," Randy retorted, "you may be in a souped-up conversion van, but I am driving a Smart Car."

Alex laughed. Bill laughed.

"Guys!"

When I looked over, Beck had moved closer to Missy. His call was a warning. She stood on the edge of the great divide holding Phoenix. My mouth dropped open.

Alex lifted a hand to me with an assured nod. He spoke as if he saw nothing wrong. "So, uh, let's get moving. Now's the time to change vehicles if you want."

Nervously, I inched closer to Missy.

"Missy?" I called to her. "Would you like to ride in the van and I'll ride with Randy? Or maybe, you and I can drive the Smart Car."

Missy finally turned around. She stood too close to the edge for my comfort. I shifted my eyes to Beck, who was nearing her slowly. She didn't pay attention to his approach. But still she had made it a distance from the rest of us.

"Look at this little guy," she said. "So perfect. Why was he so lucky? How did he live?" Her words were smooth, almost sedated.

No one said anything.

"Look at this world he was born into. It's damned. He don't stand a chance. Alex said he's gonna die, ain't that right, Alex?"

"Actually," Alex stepped forward toward her, but did so cautiously, "he's doing well. I think he is gonna make it."

"Why?" Missy wheezed. "Why? Why him? Why is he so lucky? I lost my babies. My babies are gone."

"No one has those answers, Missy," I said. "If I had them I'd tell you. I lost my baby, too. My son was taken as well. But we need to move on."

Missy closed her eyes. "You don't know. You still have Danny and your daughter that you gotta find. No, you didn't lose it all."

Then Randy moved forward. "But I did. I lost my babies. My wife. I lost it all. I know. Trust me, I know. Now give me your hand." He held out his hand. "And let's get back on the road."

Missy shook her head. "No. My journey ends here. This is a sign. No further. I can't go no further."

"Yes," Randy said with certainty. "Yes, you can. You must move on. Give me your hand. Come with me and we'll talk in the car."

I wanted to scream. I was so angry and wanted to yell at her to give me the baby and I didn't give a damn what she did after that. I watched her footing. She was so close, too close to the edge of that hole, Phoenix in her arms. My entire being shuddered.

Again, she shook her head and at that instant started to sob. "God took my babies. I can't live without them. I can't. I can't."

I understood every single emotion she was feeling. I did. I was sure Beck and Randy did, too.

"There's a better world," Missy said. "But it ain't across this hole and it ain't on this earth." And at the end of her words, she took a single step.

That single step took her over the edge and into that hole.

I charged forth screaming, "Noooo!"

In fact everyone charged forth.

Except Beck. He was right there, waiting. Anticipating, I suppose. Because Beck was ready.

The second Missy stepped forward, he dove for her, reaching out, snatching hold of her shirt. The weight of her falling body caused Beck to slam down hard, chest to ground.

That was all I saw at first. Beck on the ground, his arm extended downward.

She jumped. She really jumped. And all I thought in my run over to the edge of that cliff was that if she had released Phoenix, I swore at that moment, if she did, I was stomping on Beck's arm until he released *her*.

Those thoughts raced through my mind, so many in such a short span of time. I screamed my entire run. *No. No. No.*

In the few seconds it took me to reach them, which seemed like an eternity, I watched Beck extend his body, peer over the edge, and then he extended his free arm down into that hole.

He was struggling, that was evident. But when he raised his left arm victoriously, he did so with Phoenix gripped within his behemoth hand.

"Take him!" Beck called with a grunt. He had snatched the baby from her grip.

I wasn't even taking a chance; no one was getting near that child. With eternal gratefulness, I dove forward and grabbed Phoenix. How she hadn't released him in the jump, I'll never know. She should have. By all accounts and reasoning, that baby should have been at the bottom of that hole.

And I finally saw the magnitude of that hole as I took Phoenix. I was closer than I was before. It seemed never ending. A bottomless pit.

Everyone raced over. They tried to help Beck. But he had her. He had her good. I just stood there.

"Missy," Beck said with struggling words. "You gotta help me out here. Use your feet."

I watched him try to pull her. She didn't aid him in the least.

His huge frame was flush to the ground, his right arm extended all the way down and the top portion of his chest bent unnaturally.

Me, I just stood there. The only emotion was gratitude that Phoenix wasn't at the bottom of that pit.

"Get rope!" Randy yelled.

"I'll get it!" Danny replied.

Still, I just stood there. Watching.

Alex dove for the ground. He wasn't anywhere near as big as Beck so his grip didn't extend as far. "Someone hurry with that rope!" he yelled.

I could see it all: Beck holding her, Missy peering up, Beck struggling to hold onto her shirt, a garment that could rip at any second. It stretched and pulled and Missy moved further down. Calm, cool, she looked up at him with tears in her eyes.

"Missy, you have to help me out," Beck told her. "This shirt is gonna let loose."

Alex was losing his cool, I could see it. "Where's the rope!"

When Bill yelled back that they couldn't find it, Alex pounded his fist to the ground, stood up and ran.

To the van I suppose, I don't know. I stayed transfixed on what was going on between Missy and Beck.

Maybe Beck wanted my help. Maybe he wanted me to convince her to try to save herself. But I couldn't. Honestly, at that second, I teetered between not caring less and knowing exactly how she felt.

Beck tried. His boots pushed the dirt as he struggled for a foothold. "Missy!" he beckoned her.

"Let me go, Beck," she pleaded. There was calm in her tear-laced plea. "I don't wanna live without my babies. I don't wanna live in his world. Please. Let me go. I wanna be with my babies. Just... let me go."

I was the only one on that ledge.

Beck stared at her for a moment.

"Let me go," she said again.

Then with a lowering of his head, Beck did.

She didn't scream. There was no sound. The hole was so deep there wasn't even a sound of her landing.

Just as Beck dropped completely and exhaustedly to the ground, I lowered my lips to Phoenix and clutched him.

Alex, Danny, Bill and Randy all raced over.

Nothing was said.

I half expected Alex to cry out, scream, something. He looked over the edge, his eyes closed tight and face riddled with pain. He took a moment, then tossed the rope with frustration, leaned toward Beck and said, "You tried. You tried." After that, he exhaled, lifted the rope again and walked off.

Each of them—Randy, Danny, Bill—they all walked up to Beck and said the same thing. 'You did good' or 'you tried.'

They thought he dropped her or that she fell.

They didn't know. They would never know.

Beck didn't move. His chest was still flush to the ground, left hand resting on the back of his head that was half over that ledge, his right arm extended as if he were still holding Missy.

He was still.

"Let's move," Alex called.

Baby in my arms, I walked to Beck. I crouched by his midsection, held out my hand, and softly called, "Hey."

A second or two later it registered to him and he lifted his head a little, turned his body and faced me.

"It's okay," I told him.

"Is it?" he asked.

"Yeah. Yeah it is." Slowly I stood up. "Let's go." I showed him my hand.

His eyes locked onto my fingers and he lifted himself from the ground and stood before me. I felt his unspoken request with the simple shift of his eyes to Phoenix, and I handed him the baby.

Beck cradled the baby in his arms as if Phoenix were his life support. Still holding the child he turned, and with his hand on my back, both he and I walked to the van.

It was time to move on.

We switched up vehicles. I drove the Smart Car, which actually belonged to Missy. A crucifix dangled from the rearview mirror, a baby bottle was still on the floor. Beck and Phoenix rode with me. I thought it was best that Beck and I ride together in case he needed to talk. I was the only one who saw what happened at the Great Divide.

He held Phoenix, the passenger seat pushed back as far as it would go. He wasn't comfortable. He couldn't be. The car was small. How Randy endured it for two hours was beyond me.

Beck didn't say much, a few words here and there, but nothing about Missy. I wondered what was going through his mind. I would have bet anything he was feeling guilty, and he didn't need to. I wished with all my heart he would have opened up to me in the car. It wasn't a conversation I could start first.

And Alex? How was he? I asked him before we took off.

"How do you think I should feel?" he responded, and I let it go at that. I did ask him again when we stopped briefly. He was better about his answer and simply said he was hurt, felt bad, but knew it was a different world. One that he was glad Missy had left.

That made sense. Those of us left behind were definitely not the lucky ones.

As for the drive, I kept up well. I attribute that to the fact that I put duct tape over the speedometer to stop me from seeing how fast we were going. Alex felt the need to radio us every so often to compliment my ability to keep up the speed.

That was about all the conversation in the first hour. At least until we found the end of the Great Divide. It wasn't as far as we feared. We had backtracked a mile or so to an exit, then took a back road south for about twenty-five miles. We got on another major highway, had no luck, then tried it again. That time only ten miles south. There we picked up Interstate 70 at Crawfordsville and found the edge of the Divide.

It ended there. The highway was partially destroyed but we were able to go slowly off road to catch it on the other side. From there it was a series of highways north until eventually we were back on track going west on the best route to get to Washington.

It was started to get late, and as much as I wanted to keep going, I knew we had to stop. In the dark we wouldn't be able to see what was ahead.

I was especially convinced after driving through those numerous small towns and farm towns.

Sleepers paced the road, moving about aimlessly, as if trying to remember how to go about their day. Meandering up and down the street, bumping into the cars as if they knew they had to get in them, but couldn't recall how. When they saw us, though, moving vehicles or not, they raced as fast as they could. Angry, attacking, smacking into our cars. We just kept driving.

I wondered, as I guessed everyone did, how long they would last. How would they survive? I remember Beck saying he believed that they operated on pure basic animal instincts. Kill to live and survive. And as long as they had things to kill, they would survive.

There was one moment that was actually pretty funny, and it gave comic relief needed on a road trip tainted with Missy's passing.

Driving through a small town, one set up for highway travelers with gas stations, food places and such, Sleepers were scattered about everywhere.

Alex, with a serious tone, said over the CB, "Guess going through the drive-thru is out for now. Sorry people."

Sure enough, right after he said that I looked to my left. They mobbed around the McDonald's, raiding it. Some walked around eating paper products, some with actual food items. It was almost like they operated on cognitive behavior but weren't consciously aware.

It was strange but it told me a lot. They were still human and alive, but in a different sense.

Just before sundown, a pretty good distance into the state of Iowa, we found a little town about three miles off the interstate. The highway sign advertised a motel, Bucky's Motor Lodge or some ridiculous name like that. Obviously, the Holiday Inn was out of the question, as were any of the lodging options right off the highway.

Sleepers were swarming. As soon as they spotted us, they chased us even when we turned off the main road. They ran at top speed as if they could catch us, until they disappeared in the rearview mirror and were mere specks of maddened beings.

"Do you think they'll still run down the road for us?" I asked Beck.

"Actually, I do." He picked up the CB. "Hey, Sans, I'm thinking staying the night on this road isn't gonna be a good idea. The Sleepers are relentless."

"Yeah, my thoughts too. We'll keep going," Alex said.

Luckily Bucky's place wasn't on that road. A small hand-painted sign pointed for us to make a left. Alex stopped and knocked over that sign, throwing it off to the side, stating it was on the off chance the Sleepers could still read.

My gut told me, though, that we weren't gonna be safe at Bucky's or anywhere. Then again, my gut was wrong about a lot of things lately.

At the top of the tree-lined hill was the small, flat parking lot to the motor lodge. Beck's words echoed my thoughts when he said, "Something is weird here."

Alex stopped the van and I pulled behind him. Bucky's Motor Lodge was one of those long single-floor motels, not kept up the best or modernized but not too run down. There wasn't a car in the lot, yet the light was on in the office and a maid slowly wheeled a cart at the end of the motel.

"Do you think this is so far removed that nothing happened here?" I asked Beck.

"No." Beck shook his head. "It can't be."

Both he and I stepped from the car at the same time everyone got out of the van. Beck, still holding Phoenix, reached for his rifle with his free hand.

Randy held out his arms. "Here, let me hold the little guy for a while."

Beck looked at me for permission and I nodded. My eyes kept going to the maid wheeling her cart.

"Let's head in, Beck," Alex said. "Bill, you keep an eye on her." He tilted his head at the maid as he handed Bill a weapon. "No need to aim for the legs, any shot will do."

Bill started to agree but stopped. "Aim for the legs?"

"He's an asshole," I said and started to follow Beck and Alex.

"Whoa. Whoa." Alex spun around to me. "What are you doing?"

"I'm coming in case everything is cool and you need to pay," I said.

"You brought money with you at the end of the world?"

"You never know."

With a slight grumble then a chuckle, Alex shrugged. "Just don't throw up."

"I won't. I'm good." I followed them, looking one more time to the maid.

We stepped inside the well-lit office and weren't greeted with any raw or foul smells.

"Looks like everything is normal," I stated.

Alex leaned his elbow on the counter and pointed to the rack of keys. "I think we're still back in the fifties. Wonder if Norman Bates is here?" He laughed at his own humor and called out, "Hello?"

Then there was a scuffling sound, but no response. Alex lifted his head, looked at Beck and me then hit his hand once on the bell. "Hello?"

A split second after the ding, a burly, bearded man appeared at the back office door and without warning he barreled at us with a screaming snarl.

As fast as he came for us, that was how fast Alex pulled out his gun, lifted the weapon and fired. A single gunshot to the head and the man was knocked back and down.

"So much for normal," Alex said. He reached behind the counter for a handful of keys and turned back around toward me about the same time I huffed sharply.

"What?" he asked.

"This is a fantasy for you. This is your perfect life, isn't it?"

He shook his head and walked out of the office and I followed.

"Really. Perfect Alex-world. No questions, just shoot to kill."

Outside, in front of the others, Alex stopped walking and spun around to me. "The man was a Sleeper. How many questions do you think he was gonna answer? How about this? Next time, I'll make damn sure they wanna rip my head off before I shoot. How's that?"

I folded my arms, stared and said nothing.

He laughed once. "I cannot believe you're giving me shit about this."

I raised my hand. "I'm not giving you shit. Really, I'm not. I was being sarcastic, that's all. This just seems all too natural for you."

Alex sighed. "Maybe. Maybe you're right. Who knows? Maybe right now is the whole reason I was born." He moistened his lips, prepared to say something else, but his attention was caught like mine by the squeaky-wheel noise that drew closer.

Beck motioned his head to the maid, who was wheeling her way toward us. "You wanna ask her if she's a Sleeper first?"

How stupid we must have all looked, not that it mattered all that much to the older maid. She didn't come for us full speed, but she wheeled our way nonetheless. And we stood there in a long line, all just watching her.

She pushed the cart at an incredibly slow speed, her lifeless eyes fixed on us.

Beck exhaled. "Someone want to tell me why we're all standing here watching her?"

Alex asked. "Anyone want to handle this?"

"You're the expert," Beck replied.

Almost nonchalantly, Alex took long strides toward the maid, peering back at us intermittently, his gun behind his back as he made it about two feet from her.

"Ma'am," he said as he leaned to her. "Ma'am."

At first she slowly turned her head toward Alex and she stared at him. Just stared at him. Then without warning she widened her mouth, snarled and lunged.

Alex stepped back and shot her.

There were no other Sleepers around, at least none that we could see. But even this little place, not even big enough to be a dot on the map, wasn't spared from what happened.

That told me that nowhere was safe from what was happening to the world.

Nowhere.

My poor Jessie.

We didn't see a Sleeper the rest of the evening, which really surprised me. I expected we would. A gunshot carried for miles. Perhaps they didn't have the perception needed to follow. We had supper by a small fire, which we quickly extinguished after the meal.

I had to use powdered formula mixed with bottled water to feed Phoenix, but I didn't need to warm it. The nights were almost as hot as the days.

Beck and Alex chose Room 12, each taking a bed in the deluxe family room. They went to sleep early, just after the sun set. I stayed up for a while taking watch with Randy, not that I could do all that much. I still didn't want to put Phoenix down, but I knew eventually I would have to or else the child wouldn't know how to sleep anywhere other than in a pair of arms.

Randy was good to hang out with. He was optimistic and realistic at the same time. I asked him how he was doing about Missy and he said, like the rest of us, he was sad but not surprised. He knew she wouldn't be on the journey long. He just knew.

He didn't blame her and he reminded me that death had been his plan as well until he met us.

We'd leave at first light and stay on the highway. That was the plan. The only plan. Getting to Seattle to find Jessie was it. No one talked about what would occur beyond that. Would we all go our separate ways, stay together? Maybe even civilization wasn't that bad the further west we went.

No one knew because we had no way to communicate. There wasn't a radio signal at Bucky's motel. We'd stop on the road and try again, but we hadn't had any luck since speaking to the man in California before we left the Survival Haven.

Admittedly, the lack of a long-term plan started weighing heavily on my mind. But honestly, how could I think of a long term plan for my life when I didn't know what had happened to a huge part of my life... Jessie?

She was the entire reason we'd packed up and were heading west. She was my focus to move forward and on. Yes, I had Danny, but I needed and wanted my daughter, too.

But with each passing day, each passing hour that I didn't speak to her, I grew fearful of what I would find when I arrived in Seattle.

I only hoped it was the not knowing that was causing my fear and not my maternal instincts.

22
ALMOST THERE

Was it really over? Had the world ended and civilization was well on its way to extinction? I truly had to ask that. For all the hopefulness I'd carried at the beginning of the journey that was how much despair I took with me as we neared the state of Washington.

A simple trip, pre-Event, across country would have taken three days and that was driving and stopping for two nights. Insane people drove straight through.

But in the post-Event world it wasn't simple. Without the use of GPS, we relied on the old-fashioned map method. Beck charted routes that would keep us furthest from civilization. While there were no more physical obstacles like the Great Divide, we had little obstacles that added up.

Fueling, for example, wasn't as simple as pulling up to the pump. It took a while; we had to open the reserves, lower the pump, fire up the generator, pump out gas and transfer it to the vehicles.

Twice we ran into Sleeper problems, both times at night. But nothing major and nothing that Beck and Alex couldn't handle.

The further west we went, the more civilization grew invisible. We found remnants of refugee centers and leftover military trucks. No one held post, although it appeared they held their posts longer than out east.

We managed to make contact with some guy named Carl in Nevada. He said it was barren there and they were working hard to pull people together. They were dealing with Sleepers, but for the moment, they were under control. He gave us coordinates and invited us to join them after our search. The only hope for continuing civilization was if everyone pulled together. He and about twenty others were preparing an underground place at on old military installation. I couldn't help but think of Area 51.

One week.

It had been one week since it all started. Since Jeremy passed away, since Daniel transformed. Since everything went to hell.

One week.

We were on, at least we *believed* we were on, the last stop before finding Jessie.

It wasn't as easy as one would think to find a place for the night. Sleepers were increasingly more predominant at night, and it seemed they sensed us.

I couldn't agree more with Beck and Alex when they stated again that, after we found Jessie, we had to plan on hunkering down somewhere. Staying put, cleaning house, something long term. While nothing was even remotely close to being a firm plan, it was finally some talk about the future.

If that was what it was called.

Unspoken rules for traveling and spending the nights started to surface, things that grew evident with each passing night before we pulled over.

It had to be remote and away from civilization, although Beck argued a top floor apartment would do the same. It had to have at least two exits, and windows that weren't easily accessible. The structure had to be strong and the vehicles had to be somewhat hidden.

The motel was an easy hideaway. The next night we stayed at a house in a small town, at the far end of a one-way street. No Sleepers were in sight when we pulled up, but by two in the morning we were bombarded and we had to pack up and go, spending the rest of the night in a nearby tunnel.

Beck figured it was a smoke signal that had led them to us. We were grilling that night. Easy enough to conclude.

The next night, we were wise enough from the evening before that we didn't even cook. The meal was cold, we stayed inside, and brought only the minimum in with us. That night we stayed in a hardware store.

Again, by two or three in the morning, the Sleepers arrived.

What was the reason there? The lights, we figured. We had a lot of battery-operated lanterns going.

In a dark world, we were no less than beacons to follow. But we couldn't keep going; we had to stop and rest.

A few hours before finding our next stop, we located a discount department store. Alex went inside for dark fabric. He ran out with two spools and five or six Sleepers following him.

He said he would have shot them but wanted to conserve ammo. However, in the future he'd devise a plan to get rid of them, large groups at a time.

Until we found Jessie, however, it was one at a time.

Just across the Washington state border, we followed the signs to Hilltop Christian Church. Bill saw the sign on the highway and said it sounded like it would be the right place to go.

Coming from Bill I knew it wasn't some praise and prayer reference. I suppose we followed Bill's hunch and as we pulled up the winding road, I too felt it in my gut.

It was the right place.

A quaint stone building with a sign that read 'built in 1892', with six concrete steps in need of repair leading to the red double wooden doors. There weren't many windows and the few that were there were stained glass. The stone was darkened gray, but otherwise the building was well maintained. There was a small bell tower on top. I immediately thought of how that would be our watch tower.

Bill was somewhat argumentative about having to go inside with Alex and Randy to check for Sleepers. Danny volunteered to go, but I quickly slapped that down.

But the truth was, Beck and Alex were the strong guns of the group. Both of them couldn't be inside at the same time anymore.

So Bill went.

It didn't take them long. They gave it a clean sweep. The building was one main room and a back area that had an office and a lounge. The basement was one room as well, with a cafeteria style kitchen. Probably used for church dinners or rented for the occasional baby shower.

We pulled the vehicles to the back, parking closely to the back door of the building and again, bringing only minimum supplies with us.

There was something different about the church when we entered... the smell. There *was* none. No smell of death, dust, or simple emptiness. Before the Event I would never have believed emptiness carried a smell, but it did. The church, however, did not.

Beck's first comment inside the doors, once again, reiterated my own.

"Someone has been here and not long ago."

I thought that too.

Some remnants of dust carried in the last of the light beaming through the stained glass windows. There were two rows of beautiful wooden pews before a simple altar. The walls were white and the high ceiling had wooden beams.

I thought it beautiful. Simple, but beautiful.

Randy stopped midway up the aisle. "It's God's house," he said. "I'm willing to bet many people stopped by here." He exhaled and slid into a pew. "Peaceful."

Bill said, "Doesn't make sense, though."

Danny asked. "What doesn't?"

"An empty church," Bill said. "During the apocalypse. And one, mind you, people think that God did. If I believed in God, I may flock to a church. I'd expect it to be full."

Danny nodded. "That makes sense. But it *is* far out here. Maybe people didn't want to take the trip. Or maybe it's just an old church that's more of a tourist attraction."

"It's maintained well, like a church would be for services." Bill reached into a pew. "Look, the hymnals are modern."

"Shhh!" Randy said sharply. "If you don't mind, I'm trying to get a prayer in here. It's respectful to keep your voices down."

Bill laughed. "Like a library? Didn't know there were rules."

I shook my head with a roll of my eyes. "Let him go. Let him pray. Randy doesn't bother anyone."

"I didn't mean anything..." Bill quickly lowered his voice when I gave a scolding look. He then whispered, "I didn't mean anything. He actually is reiterating my point. He immediately prays. Why aren't others here praying?"

Danny said, "Maybe they're all dead."

"Or Sleepers," Beck added.

Alex's voice echoed through the hollows of the church as he came from behind the altar. "Well, someone has been here."

At the same time we all hushed him with a unison 'shhh.'

"What?" he asked. "Is this a library? I didn't know there were fucking rules about how loud—"

Beck raised a hand and I could see the cringe on his face. "Whoa. Hey. It's a church."

"Whoops." Alex hunched, spun to the cross and looked up. "Sorry." He then faced us speaking softly as he walked. "Someone has been here. Recently, too. Found cooked food remnants in the garbage." He held up the particle no bigger than two inches. "Spam. Fried." He sniffed it. "Fresh. Maybe two hours."

I snorted a laugh at how ridiculous he sounded giving examination results of Spam as if he were a coroner at a death scene. "I'm sorry." I covered my mouth and tried to swipe away my laugh. "You know how fresh or old cooked Spam is?"

"Uh, yeah. I love Spam."

"We knew that, Mera," Bill said. "Remember his cabinets?"

"Not to mention," Danny added, "what he brought with us."

Beck laughed. Probably the first one I heard in a while.

"What?" Alex asked. "Wait. Nothing is wrong with Spam. Great food for the apocalypse." He looked once more at the little piece of meat in his hand then placed it down on the railing just before the altar.

As if he had committed some carnal sin everyone reacted in offended shock.

"Whoa. Geez." He grabbed the meat and stuck it in his pocket. "I'll throw it out later. Man, people get weird in churches."

He stepped closer and filled us in on his find. Alex told of the blanket on the back office couch and the food downstairs. How things had been cooked, he felt, as recently as today.

Yet, there was no one around. Even he commented on the lack of people in a church. He then added he was embarrassed to admit he was fearful that we'd open the doors and be pelted with people who came to pray, turned to Sleepers and were just waiting for release.

The day was drawing to an end, and if we wanted to have light in the church then the windows had to be covered. I was in charge of cutting the fabric and the men would hang them over the windows.

When I finished the cutting I checked on Phoenix. He was fast asleep and comfortable in the wicker basket. I slid him closer to Beck, trusting him with the care of the baby and to keep an ear out while I sought out something for a meal.

Our supplies were near the entrance of the church. With my luck, Alex had probably grabbed spam out of the van. I was about to open the food box when an unfamiliar male voice spoke.

"No need to hang those. They won't come here."

Everyone stopped making noise and I spun around. He came from the altar, stepping toward us. He was probably in his late thirties, though it was hard to tell with the shoulder length brown hair and beard.

Alex said, "I locked that back door."

"I have a key." He smiled and held it up. When he did that, I noticed what he was wearing. Black pants, black shirt. The white collar portion hung open at his neck, but it was there, clearly enough to let us all know he was some sort of man of the cloth.

"Michael Lawford," He said, extending his hand to Alex, the first person he approached.

Randy walked immediately to him with a firm handshake and introduction "Father, I'm Randy. We're sorry for intruding."

"No," Michael shook his head. "I'm a reverend. Not a priest. And no intrusion. This is God's house, right?"

Randy nodded. "It is. I expected people to be here praying."

"They came at first," Michael replied. "Then after a day or so, nothing. No one." We all gathered close to him. He walked to each of us, greeting us with a handshake. I was last. When he arrived at me, he laid a hand on my shoulder as he gripped my hand. "Welcome."

He was tired, his face drawn.

With a sigh, he turned around and said, "Please, just relax. I'll make some food. I have plenty. But you needn't hang those to cover the windows; they won't come."

Bill asked. "Who won't come? The Sleepers?"

Michael tilted his head, "I'm not familiar with that term."

Beck explained. "The ones that were infected with the virus. They wander, attack..."

"Ah, yes." Michael nodded. "Them. That's who I am talking about. I never gave them a name. But the... Sleepers won't come."

"Begging your pardon, padre," said Alex. "But they show up everywhere."

"Yeah, they do," Michael replied. "They tend to seek life. They flock, attack. At first I thought they could sense life. But then I figured out a few days ago, it was just *signs* of life they sought. Lights, smells, that sort of thing. But one tends to follow another. That's why I give them a path."

He must have noticed our confused looks, because after a brief pause he explained. "If one heads to the light, the others follow. The more that are at one place, the more that show up. I set up a house about three miles from here. Lit lanterns all through it, put on music. Once full dark hits, they'll head for that house and never come here. Trust me. Worked the last three nights."

Alex asked. "You set up a decoy?"

Michael nodded.

Danny proclaimed, "Dude, that was really smart."

Michael chuckled. "Thank you...dude. Now if you'll excuse me," he turned. "I'll prepare a meal. I'm sure you folks are hungry."

"You know what?" I said, and he stopped to listen. "As much as I appreciate your hospitality and generosity, I don't want to put you out."

"It's not putting me out," Michael said.

"We have food." I noticed the moment I spewed forth those words that all eyes were upon me. Replaying the deliverance of those words in my mind, I realized I had dealt them to the good reverend in a short manner. "I mean, we have food, so please save yours."

Still it didn't sound good, and really I didn't care. Maybe it was just me, probably was, but I was paranoid. What if the reason no one was at the church was because the reverend had fed them and poisoned them all?

"And," I added, "I would feel much better if we still hung the black cloths over the window. We haven't rested in days."

"I told you—"

"I know what you told us."

Was I that bad? Beck stepped forward toward me speaking softly, "Mera, he's trying to be nice."

"It's okay," Michael said, moving in my direction. "She doesn't trust me."

I stared at him, examining his face. My lips pursed as I sought the right words to say. "It's just that ..." *Think*, I told myself, *think before you speak*. "Why did you stay?"

"Where else was I to go?" Michael asked.

"To family?"

"I have none," he said with a shrug. "Besides, this is God's house; I do God's work. After all, this is all part of God's end."

I laughed.

"You don't believe that?" he asked.

"Not in the least."

"But the Rapture—"

"That wasn't the Rapture," I argued. "Did you see them? Did you see the children that were supposedly Raptured?"

Michael lowered his head. "Yes," he said softly.

"So you saw the suffering? You saw the hell?" I stated. "Why in the world would God want them to endure something like that? Why would he put an innocent child through that?"

"I believe they didn't feel anything," Michael said. "They were taken to be spared from all this. The Sleepers, the destruction. God wants—"

With a wave of my hand and a scoff, I cut off his words. "God can suck my left toe for all I care."

Everyone groaned except Alex. His reaction was priceless. "Oh, hey, now, come on. That offended even me, Mera."

"Alex," I curled a lip, "please. You dropped the f-bomb in God's house."

"Mom," Danny took hold of my arm, "maybe you're tired. You're giving this guy a really hard time for nothing."

Michael lifted his head. "No, let her go. People get confused about what they don't understand."

"And you do understand?" I asked him.

"I think so."

"Then explain the Sleepers. Are they some sort of Rapture gone wrong?"

Michael shook his head. "I believe they are serving a purgatory on earth."

"What about us?" I know I came across as badgering him, but he came across to me as confident in knowing all the answers. If he had them, I wanted to know.

Michael answered without missing a beat. "We could be part of the 144,000 that are chosen or left behind to endure this. Or, we could have been blessed and spared purgatory on earth."

"Please," I chuckled. "I wasn't a bad person, but that good? And what about him?" I swung a pointing finger at Alex. "Do you really think he looks like he earned being spared purgatory?"

"Hey. Quit picking on me," Alex protested.

"She's angry," Michael said. "And hurting."

"I am," I said. "I am so angry. I watched my son die a horrendous death. I have a daughter out there somewhere. My husband, who was a better man than I am a woman, turned into one of those *things*. If God was all that powerful, why didn't he blow us up? End it? No, God didn't do this. He didn't Rapture the children to save them from Hell on earth. If He did, then he made a mistake."

"God has a plan. He doesn't make mistakes."

"Really?" I said, inching to the pew and lifted the basket. "If God saved all the children and doesn't make mistakes, then explain him." I showed the basket with Phoenix to Michael. "Because He forgot one."

Reverend Michael or Pastor Mike as everyone else started calling him, was thrown. His entire theory on everything that had occurred to the world was disproven with the presence of Phoenix.

He was rethinking, I could tell. He didn't say anything, but he was quiet over dinner and then buried his head into the Bible.

He led a prayer after dinner in which I declined participation. I just wasn't feeling it. I was glad that Bill was an atheist because he went with me on my exploration of the small church.

We had passed Michael's small office located off the lounge behind the sanctuary, but were more focused on the cafeteria downstairs. Both he and I wanted to have a look. It was nothing spectacular. Our exploration took only a few minutes.

On the way back to join the others, Bill went into Michael's office. I told him not to, that it was Michael's personal space. And I planned on scolding him further until I heard him whisper out in awe, "Oh wow."

Admittedly, my curiosity got the best of me and I joined him.

He was seated behind Michael's desk looking at a large scrapbook. "Guess this was the last family member he had. Or rather, was from the last family member."

I looked over Bill's shoulder. He had opened the cover. Inside was a note in a woman's handwriting. It simply said, 'Michael, I am so proud of you. I love you. Mom.' Clipped to that was a prayer card, the type you get from a funeral home.

Bill lifted it. "His mother. She died last year. She must have made this for him. Look at this all, Mera."

I only caught a glimpse. The opening was a newspaper article and a picture of Michael and an older woman. I closed the scrapbook. "Bill, it's his. It's not cool to look without permission."

"You're right," Bill admitted. "But some of these headlines…" He took a second to read, then stopped, closed the cover. "You're right. Let's join the others."

The night wound down. Alex took his watch around midnight after catching a few hours' sleep. He perched by the window, peering out.

Hating to admit it, I realized there was something so peaceful about the church. There really was. Yet, no one was sleeping. Beck was reading; Danny and Bill played a board game; Randy was on his computer contraption, writing diligently. I wanted to sleep. I could have but Phoenix inhibited that. He was cranky and crying. I think he had a bellyache because he kept pulling his legs up into himself.

Like I used to have to do with Jeremy, I began walking him around. He whimpered.

The scrapbook was never far from my mind and the more I thought of it, the more I wanted to take a look. At the very least it would distract my thoughts from what would happen the next day when we arrived at Jessie's location.

I was nervous about that, scared and even anxious. I needed to see my daughter, I needed resolution. But for some odd reason, every time I thought of her, my heart ached. A thumping feeling formed in my stomach. It shouldn't have. The last we spoke she was fine. I only hoped it was my neuroticism or the fact that I hadn't seen or spoken to her in so long.

Michael was in the back of the church stringing an acoustic guitar. He looked up when I approached him.

"Would you like me to take the baby?" he asked.

"No, I have him."

"Moot question, padre," Alex whispered from his window seat. "She doesn't let anyone touch that baby."

"Not true," I said. "I just don't let *you* touch him because *you* said he was going to die."

Michael looked at Alex. "You said that? That is very wrong."

Alex rolled his eyes. "I retracted it the next day, but I can't get a break from her." I waved him off and he returned to peeking out the black cloth curtain.

"Did you need something?" Michael asked.

"I have a confession," I said.

"I'm not a priest." Michael smiled.

"Just a little one. When Bill and I were touring the church, he saw a scrapbook on your desk."

Michael nodded slowly and peacefully, "Yes, my mother made that for me. It's very special."

"I figured that. I was wondering if I can look through it. There was a lot of work put into it and I'm kind of bored."

"Please," he said. "Be my guest."

I thanked him, left him alone to string his guitar and headed to his office. There wasn't a door or window back there, so I felt safe from a Sleeper attack. Plus, Alex was on watch.

Phoenix in my arms, I made my away back there, thinking about how quiet and comfortable the lounge portion was. After I was ready to sleep, even if it were only a few hours, I was going to sleep on one of the couches.

The scrapbook was amazing. His mother documented every moment of his evangelistic career from his seminary graduation to mission work. There was a CD cover from his first Christian music album and various newspaper articles, some quite impressive. Most of the articles had been written in the prior couple of years about the little mountain church, how Michael was responsible for raising the money for renovations and rocking the young back through the doors of the church.

I was swept away from my worries of Jessie and lost myself in the last ten years of the life of a minister I had just met. All ten years were carefully pasted and constructed on the pages of a scrapbook made with so much love.

Michael was a good man, from what I read. I believed I misjudged him.

I sat there for the longest time, Phoenix still not completely sleeping, but not too fussy that I couldn't enjoy what I read.

Then the soft guitar music started flowing to me. It came from the church. Simple guitar picking that was soon followed by soft singing.

Within minutes, Phoenix soothed with the music. That surprised me. It was time to close the scrapbook, grab a blanket and try to sleep. But first I thought I'd listen to Michael play.

He was good. There was something about his singing.

While I carried an enormous amount of anger over what had happened to our earth and put a lot of blame on God, I was still moved by how much he felt the words he was singing. That was evident in his voice.

Perhaps like Phoenix, his music could give me an inch of peace.

I left the back office. Alex perched on a bar stool by the window, still staring out. I stopped before I passed him.

"Anything?" I asked.

Alex shook his head and whispered. "Nope. Quiet out there. The moon is really bright." He nodded at the baby. "He's finally asleep?"

"Yeah."

Alex started to reach out his hand but stopped. "Sorry."

"No, I'm sorry. Go on."

"Wow," Alex cocked a sarcastic smile. "I'm honored." Then that smile turned peaceful. First his fingers touched Phoenix's head, and then his entire hand cupped it. "He's a tough little guy, you know that, right?"

"Yeah, I do."

"Four days old and he's like," Alex whistled softly, "alert. Preemie and so alert. He's gonna make it and I'm very, very sorry for saying otherwise."

"It's okay." My eyes lifted from watching his hand to his eyes. "I know you're sorry and I'm sorry for being so hard on you."

He closed his mouth tightly and shook his head. I noticed his eyes were glossy.

"You okay?" I asked.

Halfheartedly, he answered, "Yeah. Just thinking about Missy's youngest. He was my godson, you know."

"No, I didn't. I'm sorry."

"He was early, too." Alex took a deep breath and shivered as he exhaled. "You can put him down right by me. I'll watch him. He won't stop breathing."

His words caught my attention. "Why did you say that?"

"Because I know that's what you're thinking. He's early, little, if you keep holding him at night and he stops breathing you'll know."

He was right. I was scared that if something happened to Phoenix while he wasn't in my arms, I wouldn't know.

"Besides," Alex continued, "you should get some sleep without something attached to your chest. Then again, your son is attached to your hip."

"Dude," Danny called out across the quiet church, "I so am not."

I laughed. Alex laughed. Then I decided to take him up on his offer and I sought out the basket for Phoenix, placing him in the pew nearest to Alex.

I thanked him for the nice conversation. And it was nice to talk to him without arguing or hearing an 'aim for the leg' comment.

There was one other man I needed to speak to before retiring for a few hours.

Making my way to Michael, I noticed Beck was dozing off while reading. Randy was out. Really out. And as I passed Bill, I noticed he had Randy's pad computer thing in his hands.

"Randy let you use that?" I asked with shock. "He's so protective over it."

Bill moistened his lips as he innocently gazed to me.

"Give it back," I told him so motherly.

"I'm not gonna read his personal private stuff," Bill shook his head. "I just want to see this thing. It's cool. I am a computer guy. However..." he lifted it and turned it all about, "I can't figure out how to turn it on. Odd."

"He waves his hand on it."

"Really?" Bill waved his hand around it.

"Up top," I instructed.

Bill tried it again. Nothing. "Wait." He stood and walked to Randy. Carefully he lifted Randy's hand, moved it over the computer and it turned on. "Cool. Thanks for the tip."

I wondered if Randy would get angry about Bill checking out his toy. I doubted it. Randy was a nice guy. It was an interesting and unique computer. But I really didn't get into that sort of stuff.

Michael was still playing his guitar in the back of the church; he stopped when I approached. "You look more peaceful," he said.

"I feel better, thank you. And I wanted to say that you have had an amazing journey as a minister."

"It's my calling," he shrugged.

"And I am sorry for not trusting you and throwing the monkey wrench into your theory on what was happening to the world."

He produced a puzzled look. "What do you mean?"

"Phoenix."

"Ahh," he nodded. "I didn't change my mind, if that's what you mean. I still believe it's God's end, probably even more so now that I met Phoenix."

"How?"

"Mera, did you ever think that maybe the Rapture didn't turn out as intended? Or maybe Phoenix wasn't left behind by error, but rather on purpose? For you to find? Maybe?"

"Why me? Why us?"

"I don't know. Maybe we have to get him somewhere. But I'm thinking Revelation 12:5, where the pregnant woman gives birth."

I smiled gently. "I may be Catholic, but I know the Bible."

"That's funny," he said. Then he paraphrased the section of the Bible. *"And she gave birth to a male child who was destined to rule the nations."*

"But, Michael, that child was immediately taken up to God, like in the Rapture."

"Yes," Michael said, "to another battle, if you remember correctly. The child battles demons. Heaven versus hell. What if this child's battle is here? Right here on earth?"

"But that section, that woman is symbolic of another Mary and the child is a second Jesus. Are you saying you think Phoenix..." I paused, I didn't finish. I didn't know whether to laugh in ridicule or express shock over what he had said.

"Possibly," Michael said. "The Sleepers, the death, the destruction...that child defied the odds, like the baby in the Bible, born into a crazy world. There is something special about him, I can feel it. Babies were stillborn, children taken from this earth. But he remained. He alone. Think about it, Mera. It is possible that he wasn't left behind. It wasn't a mistake, but rather like the Bible states, the Second Coming."

23
JESSIE

Michael's words stayed with me until I fell asleep. They were farfetched, but deep. Then again, I was having a hard time believing it was God's end. I still believed in God, but Him ending the world? No. Not that I believed Phoenix was the Savior, but did God leave him there for us for a reason? Yes.

I woke and washed before heading out to join the others. I really enjoyed the privacy of that back office. The sun had just risen, and as soon as I entered the church Michael handed me coffee and a biscuit. I thanked him and spotted Randy zipping his bag. Everyone else was getting ready to go.

He was the one I wanted to talk to in regards to what Michael had said to me.

Randy, in my opinion, was the best one. Bill was an atheist, he'd scoff; Danny was too young; Beck would shake his head in disbelief; and Alex would ridicule. Randy's opinion would be honest. He, like me, believed in God and he, like me, wasn't convinced that the Book of Revelation was suddenly upon us.

"Got a second?" I asked him.

Randy smiled, one of those half smiles. "What else do I have but time? What's up?"

"I was talking to Pastor Michael last night while you were sleeping. And he said something interesting. He brought up Revelation 12:5."

Randy looked to the ceiling for a moment as if he remember what exactly that passage was. "Refresh me."

My voice, like his, was a whisper in the church. "The woman who gave birth. The male child."

"Born to lead nations," Randy said.

"That's the one."

"What about it?"

"He brought up that, what if Phoenix is that child?"

Randy exhaled heavily, causing his lips to nearly flutter. "That's a hell of a burden to place on an innocent baby. Not agreeing or disagreeing, but there *is* something about this baby, you know."

"I agree. He also said that what if Phoenix was left for me to find? That there's a reason I found him."

Randy stared at me for a moment. "Are you asking my opinion?"

"Absolutely," I said. "Do you think that Phoenix is an anomaly and we coincidentally happened across him or do you think there is a reason for Phoenix and we just don't know what it is?"

"I think he was left for us to find," Randy stated. "I don't think he's the child in Revelation, the Second Coming. Mainly because I don't believe this is God's end. I do believe that there is something we need to do with him, somewhere we need to take him. He has a purpose."

"Where?"

Randy shook his head. "That I don't know."

About that point in the conversation, I noticed Bill creeping up with a 'hand in the cookie jar' look about him.

I knew that look. I just never expected to see it on the face of a thirty-some-year-old man. My kids would give that look when they thought I was tattling on them to Daniel.

Bill's worries had to have been with the computer antics he'd pulled the night before. I excused myself from Randy and scooted to Bill.

"You want something?" I said.

He nodded nervously, shifting his eyes.

"What's up? And if you're worried that I told Randy—"

"No." Bill stopped me, took me by my arm and pulled me further aside. "I need to talk to you."

"About what?"

Bill moistened his lips, looked around and whispered. "Something I learned about Randy."

At first I was wondering what he meant, then it dawned on me, Bill had been reading Randy's computer. More than likely he was nosy and went into the journal.

"Do I want to hear this?"

"You need to hear this," Bill said. "Actually, everyone does. But they may think I'm nuts, and I don't know how to go about it."

Immediately I dismissed that Randy was gay. That was the first thing that popped into my mind. Not that he acted gay, it just popped into my mind. What Bill discovered wasn't good, or at least Bill didn't think it was. It made him nervous.

Was Randy a murderer? Child molester? Something awful?

"Bill, if he's a criminal..."

"What?" Bill shook his head again. "No. Not a criminal. That computer, it's not what you think." He took a deep breath. "Mera, Randy is—"

A short, high pitched whistle silenced Bill.

It was Beck. "Let's go. We're moving." Then Beck made his way to us. "Mera?"

I held up a finger to Beck and turned to Bill. "Do you wanna finish?"

Bill shifted his eyes to Beck, then to me, and shook his head. "No. No, it can wait."

"Are you sure?"

"Yeah, it's not bad. It can wait." Bill turned and walked toward the doors.

"Is he all right?" Beck asked.

"Yeah, he said he had something to tell me, that's all."

"Must not be too important if it can wait. Ready?" Beck asked, then smiled "Let's go get your daughter."

On the way out of the door, I passed Michael. I joked with him about lagging behind, to which he informed me he wasn't coming with us. He didn't want to leave the church, not yet. If we showed up then someone else could, and he didn't want to take a chance on missing anyone.

We were welcome back to stay or rest, whatever we chose, after we got Jessie.

He said he'd pray for us.

Although a huge part of me was still so angry, meeting Michael did open my eyes some. Not that I believed I carried the new Savior in my arms, but rather, Phoenix was an answer to a prayer I didn't ask.

God had left him there for me to find for a reason. Maybe to show me all was not lost. I don't know. I was still confused, but I do know, for the first time since Jeremy's death, I said a short prayer.

I just wanted to find my daughter.

I suspected at first that Bill would sit next to me in the van, his imperative news regarding Randy swirling around his brain, waiting to get out. I know every time I thought about it, it drove me nuts not knowing. But I figured it had to be something embarrassing or Bill would have brought it up in the van. After all, Randy and Alex were riding in the Smart Car. It was a perfect opportunity for Bill to spill his guts.

He probably found porn on that contraption and was fearful that Randy was some sex addict. Something private. My paranoid mind started searching for things that it could be; it at least took my mind off of worrying about Jessie.

But every few seconds my oldest child was forefront again in my mind. My baby girl, no matter how old she was, would always be my baby girl. So special to me. We didn't have those teen moments where we fought as mother and daughter. We always got along. Daniel called her my mini-me, stating she aspired to be just like me.

I loved Jessie with every ounce of my heart and soul. She defined me as a person and as a woman, and was the turning point in my life. She was never in trouble… ever. No matter what, she was always there for me.

I felt so lost not knowing about her.

My heart broke thinking of any trouble she could be in. Was she scared? I was.

It would take three hours to get to Maple Valley. The school was a private school and I hoped not too hard to find. If it were a military refugee center, there would be signs. I hoped.

Already having his days and nights mixed up, Phoenix slept. I dozed off a few times, but not much.

Danny was quiet on the trip. At first I thought he was tired. But then I realized it was more. He kept his gaze out the window, occasionally looking at Phoenix, running his fingers over the baby's head.

One of those times, I noticed a slight tremble. I grabbed his hand and held it. "You all right?" I asked him.

"Yeah." Then he looked away.

I knew my son. Short answer. Quick answer, no eye contact. "Talk to me."

He shook his head, still focused out the window. "Nothing to say. Just being quiet."

"Danny." The whispering, pleading call of his name caused him to turn and face me. Then I looked at him, really looked at him. As a mother you stare at your infant, they grow into toddlers and you watch them, but somewhere you just stop staring at your child. You look at her or him, you see them, but you don't study them.

Then again, sit there and study a teenager's face while they sleep or read and you're bound to be told 'you're weird.'

But I looked at Danny. Studied his face. My God, he was still so young.

"Danny?"

He sighed heavily. "If I tell you, do you promise not to get mad?"

"Why would I get mad?"

"Promise."

"I promise." And I was able to make that promise because I couldn't figure out for the life of me what he would have done to make me angry.

"I don't have a good feeling, Mom."

Danny didn't need to say about what or whom, I knew. He was speaking about Jessie. Instantaneously, upon the deliverance of his words my gut was struck with that heart thumping feeling. The heavy twitch. I started to ask him why, and I tried to speak but a heavy phlegm mixed with air caused me to choke. I cleared my throat and tried again.

"Why do you say that?"

"You're mad."

"No." I shook my head. "I'm not mad. I just want to know why you think that."

He tightened his lips, shaking his head slowly from left to right. "I don't know. It's a gut thing. Maybe because we haven't heard from her. Maybe because things are getting bad. I don't know." He shrugged. "What do you think?"

I took in a deep, shivering breath. My eyes shifted about; I sensed Beck and Bill were listening, how could they not? Perhaps they wanted to say something, add to it, but they didn't.

"I want to believe she's fine." I said. "That she's with a group of people and is just out of touch. I want to believe that. But like you..." I rested my hand on Danny's. "I just don't know."

Danny's gut instinct was right on and my fears seemed to come alive the moment we pulled into the lot of Maple Valley Christian Academy.

There were four abandoned military vehicles, papers strewn across the lot, and it looked as if it could have been the refugee camp we left behind in Ohio.

Bodies of soldiers and civilians lay about, not many, but enough to show a struggle had ensued.

The doors to the gymnasium were open and I gasped the moment I took it all in.

No movement, no people, no Sleepers. It was quiet.

I whimpered. "Oh my God." I clasped Phoenix tighter to me.

Beck stopped the van and looked over his shoulder. "We'll go inside and check it out. Stay here."

"No." I shook my head. "I have to go."

"Mera," he said softly, "that may not be a good idea."

"I have to go," I repeated calmly. "This is my daughter."

A simple nod told me Beck understood.

Randy stayed behind with Phoenix and Bill kept a watch outside. I accompanied Beck and Alex into the gymnasium. And for obvious reasons Danny came as well.

There was no set plan as to what we would do once inside; we really didn't know what to expect. Beck and Alex had their weapons ready.

Stepping inside was like opening a refrigerator with spoiled food. A thick, foul, rotting stench permeated the entire place. It made me sick to my stomach in more ways than one.

The beam of Beck's flashlight cut through the large, dark room. Streaks of light illuminated the chaos that had occurred in that aid station.

At first I saw cots, some overturned, some standing. Belongings of the refugees were scattered about, clothes, papers, food.

Then I saw the blood. Some of it glistened as Beck's flashlight hit it.

Fresh. Or at least within a few hours.

There was no movement at all in the gym, none. As we stepped hesitantly forward I saw the first body, then I saw a leg, an arm, then my stomach churned.

The second Alex looked at me, I knew what he was trying to convey with his glance. *Keep it in control, don't get sick.*

It was a tough struggle, and my mouth filled with saliva with each gag I fought to keep under control. I turned my head away from the scene to try to keep it together. Once I felt my stomach settle and my glands relax, I lifted my head.

My eyes adjusted to the dark, and then I saw the fire extinguisher in the far left corner of the room. Jessie was set up there, right below it. She told me that if she had to leave she would leave a note.

She promised.

Jessie had never broken a promise to me. With renewed strength and determination, I raced across the gym, never seeing another thing except that extinguisher. My feet hit into things, I almost lost my footing, but I didn't look to see what I touched or nearly tripped over. The extinguisher was a good fifty feet away; as I was closing in, I heard my son call out.

"Mom, stop!"

I did. Cold and fast.

Something in the way he yelled stirred a cramp in my stomach and caused my feet to immediately cease moving. My body swayed forward from the momentum.

What did he see that I didn't, was what crossed my mind. Slowly I started to look back to him when Danny approached me.

"Why did I stop?" I asked.

"She's not there. No one is there."

"But, Danny, she said she would leave a note if she left. Obviously she left."

Danny's head lowered. "Mom..."

Beck laid a hand on my shoulder. "How about I go over and look in that corner for a note."

"Beck?"

Then Alex said, "Danny, take your mom outside. We'll look in here."

Danny reached for me.

I swung out, swatting him away. What did they see that I didn't? Then I realized it was dark. Only Beck's flashlight really brightened anything to a visible state. Perhaps when I had turned my head to stop myself from vomiting, they saw what I didn't.

Quickly, I grabbed the flashlight from Beck's hand and aimed it in the direction of the corner.

It felt as if someone grabbed my insides and twisted them to the point all the air squeezed from me.

The entire wall around the extinguisher was splattered with so much blood it looked like abstract art. An overturned cot was next to one covered with blood. Another cot by that wall contained a leg. But far more disturbing than seeing the lone limb was something I recognized.

On top of the cot, directly beneath the extinguisher was a teddy bear. I knew that bear because I gave it to Jessie when she was six. She treasured it. Even when she grew too old to cuddle with that bear at night, it perched on her dresser always. But there it was, on its side, half torn apart and obviously splattered with something I could only assume was blood.

My mind heard her voice that day she left for college:

"*I'm not leaving him behind, Mom.*"

"*Jessie, you don't need to take him.*"

"*I do, Mom. When I miss you guys, I have him. He's home. He's... you.*"

I exhaled heavily and blinked. My focus grew blurry from the welling tears.

"Mr. Biggles," I whispered, sad and shocked. "Mr. Biggles." I ached out a sob, dropped the flashlight and ran out.

The fresh air was like the opening of an emotional valve for me. The second I stepped out, I broke down and cried. I couldn't stop. I didn't want Randy or Bill to touch me, talk to me, or look at me. I leaned forward against the front of the van, waving my hand to keep them away. I was there for only a few moments, and lifted my head when I heard Randy call out.

"Beck?"

There was too much question in his voice.

I looked.

Beck emerged with Danny and Alex and then I saw Beck had the bear. I went from sadness to rage in a split second.

"What the hell, Beck?" I raced to him, blasting, "Why would you bring that, huh? Why? Do you think I need to see that?"

Beck tried to answer, "Mera, I—"

"Why didn't you leave that in there?"

"Because!" he yelled, then lowered his voice. "Because she may want it." He handed me a small sheet of paper. "She's not in there, Mera. She left."

The note was crumpled and there were smudges of dried blood on the corners. The note didn't say much, but it said enough to tell us where she went.

'Mom. Saint John the Baptist Church. Love you.'

After reading it, I peered up to Beck.

Beck nodded. "Let's go find her."

As soon as we pulled close to Saint John the Baptist Church, I knew something had occurred there, that had Jessie been there, she was long gone. Everyone was.

It was nowhere near as violent a scene as the school gym, and no bodies out front. Beck commented that it looked like people left in a hurry, because items were strewn across the front walk and lawn of the church. Almost as if they were dropped as they ran to get away.

Actually, the only indication of violence was the message sign out front. The front glass was shattered on the board that boasted the message:

We that
praise on
are saved!

It looked as if it were smashed with a baseball bat. The black letters against the white backdrop were crooked and some even had fallen from their spacing.

The only way to know for sure was to go inside and check it out. Like the gymnasium, maybe there was word of where they went.

We all stepped from the van. I was instructed to wait outside, which irked me, but I understood.

The church was a simple Catholic church. Not like what I was used to seeing out east. Red brick, not monstrous. The entrance was a mere set of double wooden doors, each with a small pane of stained glass above the handles.

They were open.

Bill stated he wanted to stick by me, if that was alright with Danny. It was, so Beck, Alex and Danny went inside while Randy, Bill and myself waited at the base of the stairs just before the entrance.

Phoenix cooed and moved. I cuddled him as I kept my eyes focused on the doors of the church.

Bill cleared his throat. "So, uh, Randy, mind if I ask you something?"

I wasn't really thinking much about it then it dawned on me. I wondered if Bill was bringing up what he discovered on Randy's computer.

"Sure," Randy answered. "What's up?"

"Well, the other night..."

Bill was about to ask when Beck's voice carried out of the church. "Come on in, it's clear."

I turned around. Randy was waiting, apparently for Bill to finish.

"I'll ask later," Bill said and walked to the church doors.

I followed until I noticed Randy lagged behind. "Are you coming?" I asked.

"No," Randy replied. "Someone has to keep watch out here. You go on."

I knew it was useless to go inside. Why did Beck even call for us?

I stepped into a small foyer that led into the church. It didn't have the charm that Michael's church had; it seemed plain, too plain.

"Stay by the door," Beck said. "Just in case." He was up by the altar.

"Where is Danny?" I asked.

"In the back with Alex; they're looking for clues, for anything to say where everyone went."

"So they were here?"

"Without a doubt." Beck walked up the altar. "Clothes are here, food, sleeping bags. They went somewhere; there isn't any blood. No sign of attack; that's good news, right?"

"Yeah," I spoke softly. "That is."

"We'll find where they went," Beck pointed. "I'll be back. Bill, keep an eye out."

Bill nodded. He moved about the pews, lifting items. "Maybe somewhere in here is a clue to where they went." He lifted a blanket. "Just odd." He moved slowly around the front pew to the piano to the right of the altar. "I always wanted to play." He tinkled a few keys. "But I'm better on a computer keyboard that a Rhodes."

His comment made me chuckle. "Bill, what were you going to ask Randy?"

Head still looking at the keys, he spoke as he slowly depressed a few notes. "I was calling him out. I know, that's not fair, right?"

"I can't say what's fair and what's not, I have no idea what you're calling him out on."

Another note, then Bill's hand slammed down to the keys hitting a sour chord. "On that computer, future e-book reader, or whatever you wanna call it, there's stuff about Phoenix."

"Oh my God!" I gasped. "He's a child molester?"

"What?" Bill squeaked out a surprised laugh. "No. He..." Bill looked at me, and suddenly his whole demeanor changed. His facial expression went from smiling to serious and his tone was deep with concern and warning. "Mera, run!"

Instinct didn't have me moving; it made me look behind me. Nothing was there. I produced a quirky smile and turned back around. "Bill? Not cool to joke like—"

"Move!" he bolted my way.

I was confused, but I took a step forward. No sooner had I done that than the first of the Sleepers dropped to the floor from the choir loft above me.

I clutched Phoenix as tightly as I could. The Sleeper was in front of me, arms extended in attack mode. I spun to bolt out of there when another dropped, blocking my way. Then another. They dropped from above me fast and furiously. How many were there? They reached and grabbed. I screamed.

I lost my bearings and didn't know which way to run, where to go or what to do. I was completely surrounded and all I could think about was protecting Phoenix.

With everything inside of me I believed I was done for. Their hands reached out. One pulled my arm away from Phoenix. I tried to yank it from his grip, but he was too strong. I watched as his mouth widened and he came in for the bite. Just as I felt his saliva and the slight graze of his teeth, I was yanked backwards, hard and fast. I landed on my backside and must have slid five feet from the force.

Thank God I still had Phoenix in my arms.

I went from being in the midst of trouble to trading places with Bill. He snatched me, threw me, and in doing so, put himself in harm's way.

"Beck! Alex! Help!" I screamed and scurried back, struggling to get to my feet. Despite my cries for help, the Sleepers didn't worry about me.

There had to be thirty of them.

Bill was completely enveloped. His large frame fought diligently but he was overpowered. I had never felt so helpless in all of my life.

His face was red as he struggled to get free, calling out for me to run. He had saved my life and I couldn't do anything to help him. I wasn't armed.

I could only scream. "Someone help! Please. Someone!"

I know it wasn't that long but it seemed like an eternity for the first shot to ring out and it didn't come from the church.

There was one shot, then another and as I moved to the side, backing up, I felt my body grabbed.

Fearful it was a Sleeper, I swung out with one arm.

"Mom!" *Danny*.

"Get her out of here. Now!" Beck rushed by, pointing backwards. "Now!"

Danny pulled at me but I couldn't stop watching Bill. His eyes were connected with mine. To break that would be to abandon him. I kept that eye connection even as Danny moved me away.

A few more shots and I saw a few Sleepers behind Bill fall down. Beck flew into the mix, grabbing Sleepers, then Alex joined in.

The confrontation grew further from my sight as Danny dragged me to the side door. As we readied to leave, finally, Bill broke free. He moved only a step forward. I saw the look of relief on his face.

Then a Sleeper lunged at him, wide mouthed, and bit down hard upon his neck. From my heart I cried out a long and loud, *"Nooooo!"*

I was still crying out as Danny pulled me outside. He slammed the side door closed and spun around to face me. "To the van. Now!"

"Bill…"

"Now!" Danny took hold of my arm and pulled me along. The gunshots inside increased.

We ran round the side of the church.

Danny stopped before we made it to the front, held a hand out to me and peeked around the corner to make sure all was clear. I knew it was when he came back for me and grabbed my arm.

Just as we made it to the front lawn, Randy bolted out of the door. "Danny, help me secure this door!"

"Go to the van, Mom," Danny ordered and raced to Randy.

"Get ready," Randy said, holding one side.

Danny took the other.

Before I knew it Beck and Alex raced out of the church dragging Bill with them.

"Now!" Randy shouted, slamming the door shut and Danny did the same with his side.

Too much. Too much was going on.

I was only a few feet from the steps.

Beck and Alex laid Bill right by my feet and Beck, after releasing Bill, raced to the van. My eyes went to Bill, then to Randy and Danny who struggled to secure the doors of the church.

Randy used the weight of his huge body, but we knew he couldn't hold the determined Sleepers at bay for long.

My eyes went back to Bill. His shirt was saturated with blood.

I lifted my eyes when I heard Randy call out. "Hurry, I can't hold it."

Danny was securing the door.

"Mera, I need a free hand," Alex said. "Please."

Again I looked at Danny and Randy, then finally I was able to focus and I crouched down to Bill. Alex took off his shirt and placed it over Bill's neck wound. "Hold this as tight as you can. Okay?" He instructed. "Pressure."

One arm clutching Phoenix, I pressed my other hand tightly to the wound. Bill's body shook from pain and the loss of blood. My heart squeezed and I wanted to crumble.

Bill opened his eyes. "Mera."

"You saved my life. Bill, I'm sorry. I'm sorry, this happened."

He shook his head. "Listen... listen..."

"Watch out!" Alex returned. He slid to the grass on the other side of Bill, joined by Beck, who was preparing a syringe.

"Mera," Alex made eye contact. "I have to do this fast. When I'm ready, you lift. Okay?"

I nodded.

My attention drew from Alex only a moment when I heard Randy call out. "Got it!" he shouted.

I peered up to see him and Danny backing from the now secured door.

I returned my attention to Alex. He was preparing a suture. He glanced to Beck and said. "I think it hit a jugular. He's bleeding way too bad. Get ready, Mera."

"Can you get it?" Beck asked.

"Let's hope. I'm gonna clamp it then suture. Ready with the syringe?"

"Ready," Beck said.

A single nod, then Alex said "Now!"

I lifted my hand.

Bill tilted his head my way. "Mera..."

"Don't talk," I told him.

"Have... have to." Bill struggled for a breath with each word.

"Motherfucker's deep," Alex said.

"Can you get it?" Beck asked.

"I'm trying. Hold it closed with your hand."

Bill kept his focus on me. "Ask...ask...Ran...Ran..."

"Randy?" I asked. "Bill, this isn't important."

"Is. It is," Bill struggled.

"I can get this," Alex said. "Come on, guy, hold on one more minute. Mera, he has to stop talking."

"Bill, please." I laid my hand on his face. "This can wait. Let them fix you."

He shook his head. Then Bill's hand lifted and dropped. "2633." He breathed out, short huffing breaths. "Get...Phoenix. Get... get to New...Jerusalem." He sighed, raising his bloodied hand.

"Almost there!" Alex grunted. "Almost."

"Get..." Bill placed his hand on Phoenix's head, "baby there. He... saves."

Bill's last word trailed out as his fingers slid down from Phoenix's head leaving a bloody trail. Then Bill, head tilted to the side, went still.

"Alex," I whispered.

"Done," Alex said. "Closed."

I lost all ability to breathe. My throat swelled with emotions and I wanted to scream. Not him. Not Bill.

"Alex," I whimpered.

Still reeling from the adrenaline rush of his emergency medical procedure, Alex, breathing heavily looked at me.

"What?"

I couldn't say it; I could only nod toward Bill.

At first, Alex murmured "No," and then, more emotional than I had even seen him, he screamed, pounding his fist to the ground. I thought for a second that Alex was going to break. His face reddened, the veins in his neck protruded. He dropped to his rear, hand to his head and looked away.

My face tightened up and I couldn't hold back the tears.

"No," Alex said strongly. "No, this will not happen." He spun around, hands on his knees and faced Bill. "Beck, prep a syringe."

"Epinephrine?"

"Yeah."

"Got it."

I slowly stood up, backing away to give Alex room. He was determined and vigilant. Nothing going on around him mattered. Not me standing there with Danny and Randy, not the Sleepers as they broke the glass on the doors and reached through the windows.

Nothing.

"This is not your day to die, Bill. Not your day." Alex grabbed the syringe, raised it high above Bill's chest and slammed it into his flesh.

It was so hard to watch, yet I couldn't look away. Bill's eyes were still open and Alex worked on him.

I wanted it to work so badly my heart was breaking. It *had* to work.

Alex focused like I had never seen another human being focus and worked to revive Bill with his heart and soul.

His determination was a saving grace that I firmly believed, with each compression, each breath of CPR, Alex was giving Bill his lifeline.

24
CAGED IN

It didn't work.

Despite his best efforts, Alex was unable to bring Bill back to us. He stopped the bleeding and fixed the wound, but it was too late. Bill had passed on.

We were all in a state of shock and left emotionally a mess. No one expected it to happen, not at all.

My mind reeled in Bill's final moments and the words he diligently delivered to me. I heard his words and kept thinking of that old saying Danny said not a week back.

There are no atheists in a foxhole.

What did Bill read on Randy's computer to cause a staunch nonbeliever to rattle off Biblical information in his final moments?

I needed to speak to Randy about it. I needed to find out what Bill had read.

But that had to be later. We dug a shallow grave on the front lawn of the church. The Sleepers stopped trying to escape and a wave of quiet swept over us.

We'd left Pastor Michael's church not even five hours earlier, yet it seemed as if we'd experienced another week of heartache.

Bill had lived across the street from me for years, yet I didn't get to know him until the last week.

I felt bad about that, because he was such a good soul. During my tragedy with Jeremy, during everyone's tragedy, Bill tried to help out. He died trying to help.

I was crouched there, holding Phoenix and staring at the grave not far from the van, when Beck laid a hand on my shoulder. "We have to get going."

Slowly I stood. Beck, Alex and Danny stood behind me. Randy's attention was elsewhere. I finally looked at Danny, I mean really looked at him. He didn't look well. Bill's death wasn't something he was handling. They seemed as if there were waiting on me.

"Where?" I asked. "Go where?"

Beck shrugged. "I don't know. To find Jessie. Maple Valley is not that big. We'll start here and look around."

Alex stepped forward. "They obviously left this church in a hurry. They're around somewhere. We just have to find them."

"Yeah," Beck added. "We didn't come all the way across the country to quit now, did we?"

"No." My head lowered. "At least at the gym Jessie left a message, we knew she was alright. But this time they left in such a hurry, we haven't a clue where they went. No one left a message."

Randy finally spoke up. "That's not true." He turned around. "They did. Look." He sidestepped, exposing the sign in front of the church.

Alex whispered in shock, "Oh, wow."

"Oh my God," Beck followed.

And Danny said, "How did we miss that?"

Miss what? I was still missing it. I raised my free hand and let it drop.

"What do you see that I don't?"

Danny hurriedly looked over his shoulder at me. "You were never good with puzzles. Read the sign."

I sighed and, head tilted, read with some sarcasm, "We that praise on are saved." I paused. "What?"

Danny huffed. "Read it again. Look at the letters."

My huff of breath matched his. "We that praise..." Then I saw it. How had I missed it? How had any of us not noticed?

I thought it was part of the destruction we took for granted. But a message was clearly left for someone.

The 'T' and the 'H' of the word 'That' had fallen some, as had the 'A' and the 'E' in the word 'Praise', and when I read the sign without the dangling letters, it clearly read:

We at
Prison
are saved.

I shifted my glance to Beck. It made sense, a perfect place to hide and wait. Safe. Secure. Locked.

They had gone to a prison.

But which one?

Though I wished fervently, I doubted very much that it was going to be as easy as driving to the Maple Valley Police Station and finding everyone there. It was empty and the only people we found on our travels were Sleepers.

Randy used his computer and was able to find out there were two facilities large enough to be considered prisons. One was Monroe State Penitentiary and the other, Kings County Jail. Monroe was about 40 miles north and Kings County, well, was right smack in the middle of Seattle.

We discussed the matter. None of us wanted to go into the heart of the city. Not with all the Sleepers. The state prison had to be the place. That was the wishful deduction.

Unfortunately, when we arrived nothing remotely indicated any survivors were there. We couldn't even get in.

We'd wasted two hours of our day, and we headed back to Seattle.

I feared what was in the city. I feared the Sleepers because they were growing increasingly dangerous. We had all packed into one vehicle, leaving the Smart Car and the contents behind. I felt relatively safe in the van; it was strong and sturdy, and I had accepted the group decision that should we hit more Sleepers than we could handle, then we would simply turn around.

If the city were overrun with Sleepers, then in our minds there was no way survivors were locked down with them.

As we drove into the metropolis entering from the freeway we saw the first sign. A handwritten cardboard sign read, 'John the Baptist', with an arrow.

The next sign stated 'Freda's Grocery' and another arrow. All along the freeway ramp were names of businesses and places that we could only deduct were once safe havens for survivors.

But why the signs?

"The Sleepers read," Beck said. "That's the only thing I can think of. Or these people *think* the Sleepers can read and just to be sure, they make sure the Sleepers don't understand the signs."

It was a scary notion that the Sleepers could read or reason. I doubted that, not seeing the way they attacked Bill.

I guess whoever placed the signs was being cautious.

There wasn't a vehicle on the freeway entering the city and oddly there were none leaving. An exodus was a common sight as we passed major cities, but not in Seattle.

No cars. No Sleepers.

It looked empty until we pulled off the ramp to enter the city. Around the bend was a huge barricade made of cars and trucks.

Beck slowed down the van. "What is this?"

The cars extended all the way across the ramp with two school buses parked diagonally in front.

Alex lowered the binoculars. "Stop the vehicle."

"Sleepers?" Beck asked.

"I don't know." Alex said then raised them again. "I don't know. The guy is waving."

At that second I thought that perhaps the Seattle Sleepers were different, maybe even smarter. I looked around the front seat to glance out the windshield and did so about the same time Alex announced the man was coming our way.

I saw him. He held a rifle over his head and waved his other hand high.

"Pull up a bit," Alex instructed. "Let's see what's going on."

I asked. "Is it safe?"

"He's waving his weapon in the air," Randy remarked. "He's trying to tell us he's safe."

With a nod, Alex said, "Pull ahead."

Beck moved the van slowly forward.

The man trotted our way and Beck rolled down the window.

"Nice to see you guys." He smiled. "Really, it is. Always glad to see survivors."

"Thanks," Beck said. "We're looking for someone. Her daughter, Jessie. She's nineteen." Beck pointed back to me.

The man peered in the window. "We have a lot of people that came from different camps. You can head on in and check for her. This road is barricaded; it's a safe passage. Head down another block, make a right. You can see the county jail."

Beck thanked him again and began to drive. Cars were piling up and a huge crane perched to our left. It was obvious where all the cars had gone. Whoever these people were, they were piling them up as a blockade.

The fortress of cars grew stronger the closer we drove to the prison.

Beck parked. "What do you think?" He looked directly at Alex when he asked that question.

Alex inhaled loudly and sat up a bit to look through the windshield. "I don't think these people mean harm. Isn't gonna hurt to ask, right?"

Beck nodded.

Alex turned around to me. "I don't think we should take the baby in. Not yet. Not until we case this place out."

"I can stay out here with him," Randy offered. "I don't mind. I agree with Alex. I don't think we should let anyone see him. Not anyone we can't trust."

Anyone we can't trust.

I thought about Randy's little computer secret that Bill had discovered and hadn't had a chance to tell me. My instincts told me Randy meant no harm and wanted to protect Phoenix.

"Or you can stay here and we'll take Danny inside," Beck suggested. "Your call."

I handed the baby to Randy. "Thank you. Watch him."

"With my life," Randy smiled.

I took a deep breath. "Let's do this."

There was a guy standing front smoking a cigarette who waved to us as we stepped out of the van. The glass front doors to the jail were open, and as we made our approach I could see another man inside; he had a clipboard.

Alex and Beck were armed with their rifles and Danny had a handgun.

My hands and arms felt empty, I needed to hold something to absorb my nervousness. Then I saw that clipped to Beck's belt was none other than Mr. Biggles.

I had no idea he had it on him until that moment. "May I?" I asked, my fingers pointing to the bear.

"Absolutely." Beck unclipped the bear and handed it to me.

Mr. Biggles smelled sour and his fur had rough spots from the dried blood, but I held him anyhow. The ten-inch bear fit nicely in my grip as we stepped inside the doors.

The man with the clipboard was wearing a blue tee shirt and a pair of gray uniform pants. Probably around fifty years old, he had a receding hairline, but the rest of his hair was buzzed. Not tall, not short, average.

He turned to us, his hand extended to Beck first and said pleasantly, "Nice to meet you folks. My guys said you were heading in."

"Beck," he gave his name with a firm shake. "You?"

"Miles. John Miles. But everyone calls me Miles." He made his round of handshakes. "You folks coming from a camp? Shelter?"

I answered. "Neither. We're looking for my daughter. She was in college here in Seattle. I spoke to her three days after the Event."

"We've had a lot of camps, refugee centers, churches and so forth join us," Miles said. "I sent out men and a radio call."

Alex said. "We saw the signs."

Miles nodded. "Yeah, we keep adding them every time another place joins us. You know, in case someone is looking for a loved one. Like you."

Back commented, "This is quite a set-up."

"Well..." Miles chuckled a little, "I wouldn't say that. Not yet. It will be. We've only been at it a week, really only throwing ourselves into long-term survival over the last few days when people started joining us."

He told us how he had worked at the prison and had no family. He actually was working the day of the Event and no relief came, so he stayed and was also there when the Sleeping sickness took hold. Miles said it was horrible because there were some cells that held a Sleeper, and the cell partner wasn't infected. About sixty percent of the prison population fell to the Sleeping Sickness.

When they first turned, they were robotic and not that violent. It was shortly after that they received word from the government to release all prisoners. There was no reason to keep them and the healthy could be useful.

Miles released them and set them free.

Knowing what was happening to the world, Miles also knew that the jail had a good food supply and could be secured. He conveyed this to the prisoners. Half of them stayed; the other half left.

The ones that remained helped move all the Sleepers to the third floor high security area. After all, when they did that, the Sleepers hadn't turned violent and to Miles, they were just sick. Who knew if a cure was forthcoming?

After about three or four days, when no more was heard from the government and the Sleepers turned violent, Miles and the men realized they had a potential sanctuary for people. He sent out men to build a protective blockade against the Sleepers, to scout weapons, forage for more food and water, and find survivors.

Danny, who had been quiet, asked. "How many people do you have here?"

Miles paused to think. "Has to be over 500 now. Maybe more."

"My daughter was moved from Maple Valley Christian Academy." I pulled out my phone and turned it on. "Then she went to John the Baptist Church."

"That group came here," Miles said. "I know Father Craig personally."

"Her name is Jessica or Jessie Stevens." I pulled up her picture on the phone.

"The name doesn't sound familiar."

"Do you recognize her?" I handed him the phone.

He did look, long and hard. "I'm sorry. I haven't seen her here. We have only about two dozen women and most of them aren't young. Only a few."

Alex questioned. "Only two dozen women out of five hundred people? That seems skewed; is it because of the prison population?"

Miles shook his head. "No."

Beck said, "Maybe you're mistaken. There are a lot of people here..."

Again, Miles shook his head. "I know our women. There aren't a lot. We keep them safe. You're welcome to check, but I'm really sorry, I know for a fact she isn't one of them."

I believed him, he had honest eyes. My head hung low.

"I am sorry. You..." Miles hesitated. "It might be difficult, it might be painful, but it may bring you resolution if... let's just say you're welcome to check the yard."

Immediately my head lifted. I saw Beck, Alex and Danny all held the same confused expression as I did. What did he mean? The yard? What was so painful about that?

A hint of daylight peeked through the small window on the bronze colored security door. Concrete encased it and Miles raised his hand to the keypad. Before he inserted a code, he turned around to us.

"Just be prepared, okay? When we walk through there is a fenced-in walkway. Try to stay away from the fence." He punched in a code. "The walkway goes around the entire yard, so you should be able to get a good view."

The second that door opened, the answer to the mystery was clear before I even stepped through.

I could hear them. Smell them.

Sleepers.

Hands tried diligently to squeeze through the small fence and only fingers made it. Reaching for us, gnawing at the fence. Hordes of Sleepers pressed against the fence.

Every ounce of air escaped me. There were hundreds of them. There were more Sleepers than there were survivors in the complex.

I backed away from the fence, but I made sure I looked at every face, or at least tried to.

Some were pale, very pale, eyes dark. Some were pasty white with injuries that were beginning to heal badly.

"Please don't let her be here," Danny whispered.

I closed my eyes for a second and said a quick prayer. I didn't want my daughter to be penned up with the Sleepers either.

Beck was very tall and he was able to see beyond any of our scopes.

"Anything?" I asked.

He shook his head.

Miles explained as we paced slowly. "We've not had much time to learn them, but we will. There are three types of Sleepers. The ones that turned in the Event, they get violent, most of them. Most often it's when provoked or even just approached. They attack in waves and without rhyme or reason. They also calm down in waves. The second type are those who were bitten or scratched by the Sleepers and became one. They're violent most of the time, if not all the time."

"Wait," Danny said. "I was bitten. I didn't become one."

"Then you must be immune," Miles replied. "I was bitten too. However, that fella there," he pointed to a black man in the yard; his neck was stained with blood, "he wasn't so lucky. He'll pass on soon. They're almost on auto pilot. Alive, moving, but eventually the serious injury takes its toll. We've seen it happen. They are the third kind. Bitten by a bite-wound Sleeper, their wounds are usually near fatal but the virus revives them enough to live. They aren't zombies or undead. Close to it. Most Sleepers sleep during the day when they aren't in here. That's why you don't see many on the streets during the day. Most of these were captured at night or turned when they got here. We found if you provide them food, they're less violent."

Danny asked. "How do you feed them?"

"We bring in food once a day and leave it for them. Whatever we can. Some eat. Some don't. Some get weak and some are getting stronger. We have those suits men wear for attack dogs; that's how we bring it in without injury."

"Why?" Alex asked.

Miles looked startled. "Excuse me?"

"Why are you feeding them, allowing them to live like this?"

"Why not?" Miles retorted.

"Aside from the fact that they're dangerous, do you really think they want to live like this?" Alex questioned further.

"I don't know." Miles shrugged. "Ask them."

Alex snorted.

"I'm serious, young man. I wouldn't want to, I have stated my wishes—put a bullet in my head. However, they haven't stated their wishes."

Alex laughed in ridicule. "I'm pretty sure they don't want to live like this."

"I am too, but it's not my call," Miles said. "I'm also pretty sure that right now, we're left behind in God's Rapture, end of the world, whatever you call it. He made this virus. He made the Sleepers. He'll take them when He's ready. They do die on their own. God has a plan, and I don't think me killing them is part of His plan. I'm not taking that chance. I'll keep them away from people, give them basic needs and let God do the rest."

Alex didn't agree. His face clearly showed it.

"A lot of folks disagree with me," Miles admitted. "That's fine. They can do what they want to the Sleepers out there, but in here, they live."

Beck sighed. "This isn't living, sir."

We were so engrossed in talking, and not looking, that I must have wandered too near the fence. A Sleeper reached out. The hand slipped through the fence and grabbed hold of my belt. Then the fingers went to Mr. Biggles.

I jumped back a little but the fingers held on.

Danny whimpered out, "Mom."

I was engrossed in the struggle with the bear until Danny's call snapped me out of it. The tone of his voice could only mean one thing. My eyes shifted from the fingers to the hand, then followed the arm until I saw the Sleeper's identity.

Jessie.

25
LIFE DECISIONS

It was plain to see that she was injured, badly, too. Her beautiful face had scratches, a bite mark removed a section of her cheek nearly to her chin, and her forearm bore a gaping hole that was well into a later stage infection.

My daughter seemed to emerge from the masses, making her way to the fence. My heart beat in my ears and my eyes connected with hers.

She was still in there. Behind those lifeless eyes surrounded by a pasty white face, my Jessie was still in there.

She knew the bear. She wanted that bear. But did she know me?

I moved my index finger to swipe across her hand and the second I did so, Jessie let go of the bear and grabbed hold of my fingers. She grabbed my hand.

My lips quivered, eyes still making contact with her, and she opened her mouth wide. I prepared for a growl, snarl, something vicious. I wasn't prepared for what I got. It was as if she tried to speak. A streaming whimper filled with pain and agony emerged from her open mouth like a baby seal crying out for help. Only through those sounds, my heart heard, "Help me, Mommy. Help me." That is what I felt in my soul and I crumpled right then and there.

Releasing a hard, built-up sob, I fell to my knees and to the concrete. Her frail fingers still gripped my own, and I brought my lips to her hand.

She continued the groaning with each touch of my lips, each trail of my hand up her arm. I didn't want to let her go.

"Oh, baby, I'm so sorry." My tears fell to her hand and I swiped them. "Mommy is so sorry."

My heart was broken; another of my children, my flesh and blood was lost to the madness of the world. Lost to the senseless plague of whatever that swept across the globe.

No. No.

Looking at my child, again, I was convinced there was no God that had caused this. No way.

I felt my son, his hand gripping my shoulder as he hunched behind me, sharing his sister's hand with me. His head pressed to my back and I could feel the shaking of his body as he cried.

"I just... I wish I could hold you one more time. I wish I could hold you." I sniffed hard. My daughter. My oldest. The child that held such a special place in my heart. My best friend, a hole was placed in my heart right then. I grasped a final moment as a family, bringing Danny's hand into mine with Jessie's. I pressed my lips hard to her hand and held them there. My eyes squeezed tightly closed at the sounds she made and I stood.

Trying to pull myself together, knowing I could break down at any second, I avoided really looking at Beck. Because the moment I did, I saw the gloss of welled up tears in his eye. He felt emotion for my family. He knew my pain. Looking at him was hitting at my core and I was fearful I'd fold. There was something I had to say.

"Miles, thank you for this resolution," I said. "They can't tell you what they want. But I'm her mother. I know she doesn't want to be like this. I know this." I turned to Alex. His forefinger and thumb were pressed tightly to the corner of his eyes and he looked away. "Alex?"

Alex cleared his throat. His voice cracked as he said, "Yeah?"

"You're the only one that can do this. Please, for me, you know what needs to be done."

"Mera..."

"Please." I placed the teddy bear firmly in Jessie's hand and gripped her hand while looking at her. Did she know me? Would she understand my words? I believed she did. "I'm sorry, baby. I love you. I love you so very much." I brought her hand to my mouth and kissed her one last time. "I love you."

Releasing that hand was the hardest thing in the world I had ever done, I took a step, turned around to see Danny.

"Goodbye, Jess," Danny whispered then an ache seeped from him, and he spun to me.

I took my son's hand and, without looking back, without thinking about what I had asked of Alex, I left that hall, the yard and eventually the prison.

Randy had pulled out his little folding chair and was seated right outside the prison in the shade of the van. Phoenix in his arms, he stood when he saw us.

"I was worried," he said and walked only a step.

I moved quickly to him and my head fell to his broad chest.

"Oh my God, Mera. What happened?"

I could smell Phoenix. My head balanced between Randy and the baby. I felt his hand on my back.

"What..." Randy moved back when we heard a bang of metal. I raised my head then turned to where he looked.

Danny. Poor Danny.

He kicked the van, hit it, pounded his fist and gurgled out a scream as he grabbed on to his head. He unleashed.

Not once since he returned home from school had my son shown emotions like that. I was worried that he had become cold but I saw at that moment he was trying to stay strong, and his strength had left him.

"Danny," I called out.

"It's not fair!" he kicked the tire again. "It's not fair!" With a heavy, heart-wrenching sob, he spun around, back against the van and slid down to the ground, sobbing.

"Danny." I started to cry as I walked to him. Randy stood behind me.

"No, Mom. Why?" Danny peered up to me.

"I don't know."

"All of this. Why? Jeremy. Dad. Bill and Jessie? Jessie, Mom? She never hurt a soul. She of all people didn't deserve to be a Sleeper. Not her."

"Dear God," Randy said. "Mera, I'm sorry, I'm so sorry."

"What happened to this world? I hate this!" Danny cried, dropping his head to his knees. "I want my life back. I want it back. And that will never happen."

He really was just a child. Despite how badly he wanted to portray his maturity, that he was strong, he was a teenage boy and not only had the world placed the burden on him, I had as well.

There was little I could say or do except comfort him.

He was right. I hated what had become of our world. I hated it too. I wanted my life back.

But things would never be the way they were.

If it had been God's work, why didn't He just end it? End it, damn it, put us all out of our misery.

We stayed together, huddled close to the van for a while. I wanted to leave and wondered what was taking Beck and Alex so long. Randy offered to go in and check, but I wanted and needed him outside with us.

Randy agreed but stated he was only giving them a few more minutes before he had to go in and make sure things were all right. After all, there could have been problems. They were in there close to a half an hour.

Right about the point Randy was going to go in, he urged us to get into the van. He even opened the door, but stopped when Beck and Alex emerged.

It wasn't them walking out that knocked me physically over, it was the fact that over Beck's shoulder was Jessie. Her limp body bounced with every step he took.

Alex stopped a few feet from the entrance and looked back at Miles. "We'll be in touch and let you know. Thank you," Alex told him and trotted to catch Beck. "To the back." He instructed with a motion of his hand.

"Oh, my God," I gasped and approached them as they moved to the van.

Jessie was wrapped in some sort of cloth restraining outfit. Arms secure, legs secure. Her eyes were closed.

Beck passed me and went to the back of the van.

Both Danny and I rushed over as the back doors opened.

"Lay her down," Alex instructed. He tossed in a tan bag.

"What's going on?" I asked.

Alex looked at Beck then to me. His eyes cased Danny and Randy as well before he spoke.

"She's sedated. Should be out for a little bit. But we need to hurry before she wakes." He tossed the keys to Beck. "Beck, you drive. Everyone in the van. Mera, you can stay in the back with me."

"I don't understand. I thought..."

Alex adjusted Jessie to lie inside, then he helped me in. "You asked me to take care of it, of her," Alex said. "You told me I was the only one who could do it and I knew what needed to be done. Well, you know what? I do know what needs to be done. I spoke to Miles, to Beck, after I saw her grab your hand. Look at you. Cry for you. I saw that, Mera. I saw her do that. I know what needs to be done. At least let me try."

He climbed inside and nodded to Beck.

Beck closed the doors.

Soon everyone was in that van.

I reached out and grabbed Jessie's hand; her head tilted to the right as Beck sped off.

Alex pulled things out of the bag, medical supplies, an IV and so forth.

"What are you doing?" I asked.

"Like I said," Alex raised his eyes to me. "What needs to be done." He lost slight balance when Beck turned the van hard and fast. "Take those turns a little easier, please."

"Sorry," Beck replied from the front. "Just trying to move fast."

"Where are we going in such a hurry?"

"I need to get there before she wakes up. The only place safe enough to work on her," Alex said. "Back to Pastor Mike."

26
TRYING

The return trip to Pastor Mike's didn't take three hours. Beck flew. We probably would have made it there sooner had we not stopped to refuel.

Once I saw that Jessie had become a Sleeper, and obviously one of the ones bitten by a stage two, I resolved to myself that my daughter was gone. When I asked Alex to take care of it, I never expected him to emerge with my sedated daughter over his shoulder.

Not the man who put a bullet in the head of a pregnant girl.

Alex explained that initially it was Beck who said something. Beck told Alex he couldn't watch him do it. Not with what he had seen.

Then Miles added that he had never seen a Sleeper show any signs of memory. None.

They didn't need to do much convincing. Alex, after witnessing Jessie with the teddy bear and crying out almost for help to me, made him leery about pulling the trigger.

She still had life, Alex told me. He felt it and saw it. And before he or even I made that decision to put her out of her misery like a sick animal, Alex knew he had to try.

When I told him only he could do what needed to be done, something else besides killing Jessie had come to his mind.

Miles had been bitten. He was immune so he didn't turn. Others had been bit and they did turn. We never turned or got sick… immune. Danny was immune.

And with Miles' comment on how he never saw a Sleeper behave like Jessie, it dawned on Alex, what if Jessie had *some* immunities? Not a lot, but some. Those immunities were fighting but weren't strong enough.

Alex planned to see if he could strengthen them.

He had hooked up Jessie with an IV in the back of the van and I held it. But there was still much he had to do once we returned to Pastor Mike's. Much he had to get if Mike didn't have it.

The mountain church was safe and secure and afforded Alex an opportunity to work safely. He wanted to implement a therapy based on a theory he had developed.

One he talked about with Miles and Beck, before Beck put on the dog trainer suit and went into the yard amongst the Sleepers and grabbed my daughter.

I couldn't believe what they did for my family.

I was an emotional wreck.

Danny was, too. If my head was spinning, I could only imagine what his was doing.

Alex's plan was complicated yet basic. He had to hydrate Jessie and give her nourishment all via IV lines. What she had flowing through her veins in the van was a basic saline solution.

Her body sucked down that bag immediately and Alex switched it for antibiotics.

Jessie's wounds were infected; some were fresh, indicating she'd probably turned in the last day or two. She was also fevered.

Nourish, hydrate, fight infection, fix and clean the wounds and then give her an Immune Globulin IV to build her weakened immune system. Not to mention he had to find an anti-viral medication as well.

But he didn't have anything except that one bag of antibiotics and another dose of sedatives.

Once we arrived at the church, I was to get my daughter cleaned up. Beck would tend to the wounds while Alex and Randy sought what was needed.

Michael wasn't at the church when we arrived. Doing his rounds, I hoped. He said he liked to look for survivors.

The church was open and we didn't expect any problems.

Alex and Randy immediately left. Danny took watch while holding Phoenix, and I commenced tending to Jessie.

There wasn't any running hot water, so I drew a bath and Beck boiled water to heat it.

Jessie began to rouse and Beck wasted no time sedating her again. We couldn't take a chance with the violent behavior.

Michael arrived as the bath was finally prepared. Having received the Cliff Notes version from Danny, he had knowledge of what was going on. He helped me with Jessie while Beck readied to clean and dress the wounds he could.

After removing the restraints, Michael and I literally had to peel her clothes from her. Her shorts, tee shirt, socks and undergarments stuck to her like glue, adhered by blood and body fluids.

My daughter smelled horrendous, a mixture of every horrible odor you could think of. Before we lifted her and submerged her in the bath, Michael sought out a bar of homemade lilac soap his grandmother had made. It was strong in scent and would do the trick.

It took us both to submerge her. Her limp body was especially heavy. My heart ached with every swipe of the soapy cloth, cleaning my poor child and imagining the suffering she had endured.

Beck did the honors of lifting her from the tub. We wrapped her in warm blankets then dressed her with one of Beck's tee shirts.

Beck had finished ministering to her wounds and dressing them. He reattached the IV. Michael had made us a simple supper, and it was right before sundown when Alex and Randy returned.

They had to travel quite far and ran into an abundance of Sleepers, but had retrieved the necessary items.

The therapy was underway.

It was just a matter of waiting.

I had long since finished my bowl of canned beef stew when Danny came into the room. I sipped bourbon, watching Jessie. Just watching.

Michael had given up his bed for her. He said he didn't need to sleep; he planned on spending his evening praying.

It was barely evening and it felt like the middle of the night.

"Mom?" Danny whispered, laying his hand on my shoulder.

"Hey, baby." I reached up and grabbed his hand.

"How is she? She looks a lot better."

And she did. Her coloring was better. Her wounds were closed, she was clean and peaceful. "Yeah, she does," I said. "Her fever's down."

"That's good. Any response?"

"She woke when we cleaned her, but that was it. Alex wants to keep her sedated for a little bit."

"How long are we staying here?"

"A few days. Why?"

"I don't know." He shrugged. "Our entire goal was to get her. But now what?" Another shrug. "Bill kept badgering me about us needing to have a long-term plan after we found her."

"And we have nothing. We will though." I paused. "Bill…" I sighed out his name as I stared at Jessie. "It breaks my heart, you know."

"Mine too." Danny inhaled. "So," he reached down to the floor, grabbed my bottle and glass, "orders from Beck. Take a break."

"So the major is giving me orders now?"

"Yeah, you need it. Go talk to the others. I have this."

"Where's Phoenix?"

"Get this…*Alex* is holding him. And just fed him."

"No way."

"Way."

"That's so odd." I stood.

"Maybe because they know we're stalling a few days." Danny said, taking my vacated seat. "And they're all relaxing."

"Odd, isn't it?"

"What?" Danny asked.

"It feels very safe here."

"Yeah, it does." Danny reached out, laying his hand on Jessie's. "Do you think that has to do with God?"

I paused for only a moment and then I answered him with the honesty of what I felt. "No."

Danny laughed.

"I'll be back."

I left the door open. I could hear the men's voices as I walked from the back area across the altar.

Alex laughed when he saw me. "Aren't you just the budding alcoholic holding that bottle as you walk across the altar?"

"Check me out." I held up the bottle and walked to him. Leaning forward, I believe I took him by surprise when I kissed him on the cheek.

"What was that for?" he asked.

"Thank you," I said and walked to Beck, kissing him on the cheek as well. "Thank you both for what you are doing for my daughter and what you have done."

"You're very welcome," Beck responded softly.

"You know…" Alex seemed to 'burp' out those words, with a hint of carelessness and as if he was going to say something sarcastic.

"Here we go," I said.

Alex smiled. "It was a pretty down day with Bill. Sucks, you know? He was a really good guy. We were all down from that. We needed hope. Besides…when this eclectic group of people came to my survival haven, I had no idea what I was in for. I had everything I needed at the haven. Everything to survive, but I didn't have a reason.

You need a reason to survive and stay put or you aren't living." He shifted his eyes to Michael. Maybe he was trying to convey to the good pastor it was time to leave his own haven. "Amen to that, padre?"

"Amen to that," Michael said.

"Anyhow," Alex continued, "you folks gave me the reason. Your daughter. Search her out. We did. Now, we just have to try. I can't make promises that what I am doing will work. I can't. If it doesn't, then we'll have to make those decisions. You, Mera, will have to make those decisions. But I didn't think it was quite fair to not try."

Suddenly Randy stood up. It was abrupt, as if agitated. He exhaled a huge breath bigger than his body. Hand on the back of his neck while his other hand held the computer thing, he turned from us.

"Randy?" I called him.

"It works. Sort of." Randy turned back around. "It does. The Sleepers aren't meant to be cured. They can be, to a degree. The virus, combined with infection and fever ravages the brain. It pinpoints the reasoning portion first and starts to burrow itself. The longer the virus and fever are a team and hit the body, the more damage they do, hence why the Sleepers weren't violent at first; it took a few days. The virus embedded itself, taking away all reasoning and memory, until they are nothing more than mere living zombies. They walk, move, eat and survive all on instincts. Like a two-year-old will bite to get what they want, fight, hit, eat anything...so will a Sleeper."

Beck exhaled as well, blowing air through his lips. "Wow, you've been taking notes."

"It's more than that," Randy said. "By the time people started figuring things out, the Sleeper virus had taken hold. Initial victims took three days to get violent, five to lose all memory. Their victims or subsequent Sleepers took a day or two to get violent, three to lose all memory. Jessie was bitten two days ago. She's almost at total frontal lobe deterioration. This is why she knew the bear. In another day, had you not given her this treatment, Alex, she would have been too far gone. Her digressive progress will be stopped, but the brain cannot repair itself in this instance. What's done is done, no reversal, no turning back. Her speech is gone, reasonable thinking all but gone. Her memories are instinctive, meaning she knows she knows you, knows she loves you, but can't process that. Make sense?"

"No." Alex stood up. "Awful lot of big words and knowledge coming from an insurance man."

Beck shifted his eyes. "I was going to say that myself."

I knew it all had something to do with that computer and what Bill had read.

"Will she stay violent?" I asked.

"It doesn't really say," Randy said. "But I'd still watch her closely."

"Wait. Wait. Wait." Alex held up his hand. "Mera, why are you asking this man questions as if he holds the gospel truth?"

"I do," Randy said.

Michael interceded with offense in his tone. "You do *not*. Only God knows. This is God's work and in His hands."

Randy turned and looked at Michael, speaking respectfully but firmly. "With all due respect, I do know. I am a spiritual man, and I believe God knows. But this is not God's work. This is not in God's hand. Of that I am certain." Slowly he lifted that computer thing. "Bill," Randy paused and closed his eyes. "Bill read it, I know he did. He left his prints all over… never mind, see for yourself." He handed me the computer. "You look first since Bill probably mentioned it to you. You go on. I have it ready for you. Ask me anything after you read, okay? You probably won't get through it all. But use my notes and references back to the Doctrines. It's all there."

I took the computer into my hands.

"The truth shall set you free, isn't that right Pastor Mike?" Randy asked him.

"That's what we are told," Michael answered.

"Well, I'm setting myself free." Randy turned slowly. "I had planned to tell you after a decision was made about Jessie so as not to influence it, but I think now is a good time to let it out."

Beck asked. "What is it? What is she reading?"

"Everything that happened. Everything that will happen." Randy paused, passing emotional glances to everyone. "The truth."

27
LEAST EXPECTED

I knew I wasn't going to understand what I was about to read the second I swiped my hand over the screen and was greeted with big scientific words. Words I thought I had heard of but really didn't know what they meant.

Reading no more than the first paragraph, I stood and walked over to the men.

"What's wrong?" Randy asked.

"I don't understand," I told him. "I really don't understand what I am reading. It says you're from the future? Twenty-six thirty three? Am I reading that right?"

Alex laughed.

As if he were slugged with the physical punch of an insult, Randy summoned up a confused look. "Why is this so hard for you to believe?"

No one said anything.

"Here." Randy set down the tablet, swiped his hand over the pad as it set on a pew. He spoke in a directive voice, "Geno-Corp entry 3312-1…"

And what occurred next truly did silence us all.

Out from the tablet shot a life-size, three dimensional, holographic image. At some point it was damaged, because the figure was distorted, flickering in and out.

The image was of a shorter man, thin with a bald head. His voice was almost electronic. "T-minus three hours until Project Savior. My name is Doctor Hanninwall and I am chief designer of the project. I will be one of twenty-six travelers to embark on this mission. Godspeed to us all." The image went on pause.

"He sounds like that because the computer is interpreting what he is saying," Randy explained. "Language is a bit different in six hundred years." He paused. "Go to the next entry after release."

The same man switched on and looked worn, his face dirty and drawn. "We erred. Man has evolved so much that we didn't take into account that our very own germs would hold such devastating effects. I must get in contact with the other travelers. We must contact the leaders of this time and convince them—"

The image cut off.

Randy faced us and gave us an explanation that we found hard to believe, but what choice did we have but to believe it?

Time travel became possible in the 26th century, but it was outlawed because time travel caused 'burps,' or disasters, whenever the traveler landed. He told us that in the third millennium, many years after him, man felt the need to make the human race more superior. There was never really an explanation. Believing they could do so with DNA manipulation, they went back in time to release a virus they thought would manipulate the DNA of the young and create superior future generations. But the plan backfired. Instead of helping, it killed. The night of the earthquakes, tornados, storms, was the night the travelers arrived to release the virus, a virus that killed the young and infected millions more... the Sleepers.

The virus was never cured; it carried on for centuries, killing the young before they reached a certain age. Randy, who had lost two of his own children, decided he was going to come back in time and correct a wrong.

On his computer were the Doctrines. They documented the virus and the survival of man. They followed a mythical child that was supposedly immune to the virus. Randy came back to find that child and get him to ARC, a government facility developed to protect and preserve mankind. If he could get the child there, he could stop future generations from dying of the virus. The child was believed to have the cure in his blood. The child... was Phoenix.

I could see Danny was listening to Randy's every word. Michael was trying to understand it. Beck was in shock, Alex still didn't believe and me, I moaned.

My poor son, my Jeremy. Somehow it was easier to believe that God had caused it than a man from the future. Easier because at least if God caused it, I knew for certain my son was in a better place.

"Why haven't they cured it?" Beck asked. "You say you're from over six hundred years from now. Things are advanced, man is so smart. Why haven't they cured it?"

"They try," Randy answered. "They fail. It has become a genetic disease. In order to beat it in the future, the cure has to be found at this time. Supposedly it lies with him." He pointed to Phoenix. "His DNA changed, mutated somehow. He has the answers and the cure within his bloodstream that can stop future generations from dying. I'm here to follow the Doctrines, which have been almost one hundred percent true. Things have changed some."

"Doctrines? You mean Bible?" Michael questioned.

"Another leg of it. It has become a legacy of man's rebirth."

"And they state Phoenix is immune?" Michael asked. "How did they know?"

"Since he was the only surviving child, they tested him when he arrived at New Jerusalem, the ARC."

Once again, Alex did his Doubting Thomas act. "Stop. Hear me out. If the Doctrines state that Phoenix is immune and he holds the cure, if they knew it, why didn't they use that to cure it?"

Randy paused before answering and he did so gently. "Because by the time Phoenix arrived, the injuries he had sustained were too much and he died before they could use him to help."

I gasped. "He dies? Oh my God, we can't let that happen. We can't."

"We won't. We know how it happens," Randy said to me. "If any of you want to read the Doctrines you can."

"Who wrote it?" Beck asked.

"The original Doctrines were called *Logan's Log*," Randy said. "It was written by Bill."

This caused me to cock back. "*Bill?*" It didn't make sense. How would Bill write Phoenix's death unless we missed something? "Did we stop something from happening to Phoenix? How did Bill write them?" I asked. "He's dead."

Randy walked over and lifted the tablet. He read, "*And the mother, holding the Phoenix Child, stood watch in the house of worship with her son while the three men went in search for clues of the whereabouts of the young female paler.*" He paused. "The Doctrines refer to the Sleepers as Palers." He continued. "*A large attack commenced. Palers descended upon the mother for the Phoenix Child, hungry for the child, instinctively knowing the child was special. It was there the son fought diligently and gave his life for his mother.*"

"*I died?*" Danny gasped.

I felt my heart hit my stomach. Immediately I remember Bill adamantly insisting he stay back with me. Perhaps he thought he could handle them. "Bill knew." I whispered. "He knew and switched places with Danny."

Randy nodded solemnly.

At that moment, I didn't know how to feel. There was no way I could repay Bill for the gift he had given me. I didn't know how to react. My lips puckered, my face grew tense and eyes watered as I struggled with emotions.

"So we're all in there?" Alex asked.

"Yes. Except me," Randy said. "I'm not."

Michael waved his hand dismissively. "I don't want to read it then. I don't want words on a computer screen to dictate what I did or don't do."

"I'm with you," Beck said. "I don't want to read it. I just want you," he pointed to Randy, "to buffer the pain. Got that? If something is coming and it can be stopped, you stop it or damn well do all you can."

"I've tried," Randy replied. "But I've failed."

"Fate," Michael said. "This is where God's will comes in. If it's God will to happen, there's nothing we can do."

"Bullshit," Beck snapped. "I'm sorry, Pastor, but bull. Those words are from the future, they haven't happened yet, therefore they can be changed." Beck growled in frustration. "This is screwed up. It is. Who knows what do to?"

"We keep going," Randy said. "East, like the Doctrines says. You can read it, Beck, if you want."

Beck shook his head. "No. No. You just let us know. Buffer. Okay? I don't want to read it and I don't want to know too much."

"Well, I do," Alex stated. "I want to know. Hell, I'm in it, right?"

Randy nodded.

"Do I die?" Alex asked. After a moment of silence, he raised his eyebrows, and bit his lip. "I'll take that as a yes. When?"

Michael shot out a hand to Randy. "Don't answer him. No man should know."

"When?"

"Don't," Michael said stronger. "Don't answer that."

"When?" Alex asked again.

Randy looked directly at Alex, and ignoring Michael, he stated, "Tomorrow."

28
HOLDING OUT

I returned to watching over Jessie and holding Phoenix as close to me as I could. The more I thought about it, the more I felt like Beck. I didn't want to know or read too much about what was going to happen either.

Although, knowing me, I could see me turning the page and saying just one more section.

It was obvious that the Doctrines were rewritten several times and simplified. The only name that stood out was Phoenix. Everyone else had a title. I was the Mother, Danny the Son. Bill was the Man of Technology, Alex was the Warrior, and Beck was the Strong Man.

Pastor Mike was the Preacher. According to Randy he travels with us. The Doctrines were huge, over a thousand pages long. A part of me longed to read it, but then I knew how much of it was changed.

I did have Randy find me the section about the church and how Danny died. How did we learn about going to the prison?

It was stated in the Doctrine as a sign from God. It kind of made me chuckle, because I could see Bill writing '*it was written on the church sign*' and it being translated as '*a sign of God.*' I guess in essence it was.

In the late hours, I sat with the computer on my lap, debating on whether to read it.

"How is she?" Alex said, walking into the room.

"Um… about the same. Not fevered, but not responding."

"She's sedated."

"What do you make of Randy saying she gets well? You don't suppose, though, she's the reason Phoenix gets injured, do you?"

Alex shook his head then pointed to the computer. "No. I know why you would think that, but I don't. It's here if you want to know."

"I don't want to know that. That's a choice I have to make, you know."

"I do."

I sighed. "Randy has been my Cliff Notes until I read it. I'm hoping that we change it so much that it does become fiction. According to Randy we're not far off from getting to New Jerusalem."

"But it's out east, right?" Alex asked.

"Randy is trying to decipher that with Danny since he's not familiar with landmarks and everything is different since the Great Quake of the Twos."

"Great Quake of the Twos?" Alex smiled. "What the hell?"

"No kidding. Randy said on February 2nd, 2222 a huge quake hit and totally changed the face of the eastern seaboard."

"Whoa." Alex sat back. "So the east may not be so east."

"Who knows?"

"Did you ask for the Cliff Notes about me?"

I bit me lip. "I read that part."

"And?"

"I can't figure it out."

"What do you mean?" he asked. "Doesn't it say how I died?"

"It says how you die, but the circumstances don't make any sense."

"Maybe if I read it," Alex suggested.

"Maybe."

"So in what manner do I die?"

"You...you get shot in the head."

"What?" Alex laughed. "How the hell does that happen? Were you aiming for my legs?"

"Not funny, Alex."

"Yeah, it is." He crinkled his brow.

"No, it's not. As much as we fight," I laid my hand on his, "we need you. I need you. I don't want you to die."

Alex smiled gently. "You may not say that in a year. But it's not gonna happen, Mera. Trust me." He squeezed my hand. "Come tomorrow, those Doctrines change again. I'm not going anywhere."

29
FLIPPING A PAGE

"I'm sorry, Mera," Beck told me. *"There was trouble and we lost Alex."*

Those words were spoken to me in the dream and they seemed so real, they caused me to jolt awake.

I don't know how long I had been sleeping, not long, but long enough for Jessie to have stirred as well.

I sat up in the chair to see Jessie sitting on the bed, legs on the floor, staring at me. Just staring.

Her long hair dangled in her eyes as she locked a bone chilling stare on me.

"Jessie, sweetie?" I whispered, standing slowly.

Her head raised and her eyes took on a better look. My heart was at ease. A few more steps toward her, then Beck entered the room.

"Hey, look who's up," he said walking to Jessie, "Lie back down, sweetie, you're still hooked up." He gently guided her and Jessie resumed lying down. Beck checked her IV. "As soon as this is done, we'll start one more and see where it goes." He touched her arm. "Feel her skin; it feels good."

Jessie sat up a bit, slowly, not the robotic and rigid movements usually made by Sleepers. She lowered her head to his arm.

"Beck," I peeped out in a warning voice.

"I'm good."

I was fearful my daughter, even subdued, would snap and take a chunk out of his arm. But she didn't. She merely brought her nose to his arm, inhaled, then rubbed her chin against his skin.

A soft whimper rolled from my chest in gratefulness.

"Look what I got you," Beck said and held up a plate. "Are you hungry?"

I noticed what was on the plate. "Beck, she hates Spam."

"I'm thinking, she may not know." He winked.

Hungrily Jessie grabbed the slice of Spam, lifted it from the plate and brought it to her mouth. She shoved the entire thing in her mouth, chewed twice and gagged. It rolled out of her mouth in a slow vomiting manner.

"See," I said.

"We'll try something else."

"Where are her restraints?" I asked.

"Alex took them off," Beck replied. "She's not showing any signs of violence. She's almost like a two-year-old." He stared at Jessie. "You know, intense therapy could give her some things back, like a stroke victim. We can try. I'd like to," Beck turned and looked at me. "I would."

"I would really love that, thank you." I stretched. "So is Alex sleeping?"

"No." Beck shook his head. "He went with Michael a little bit ago."

As if I touched an electric socket, a shock went through me and I gasped. "What! No!"

"Mera?" Beck asked as he stood. "What's wrong?"

In a whimper, Jessie held out her hand.

"It's okay," Beck told her. "She's fine." He looked back at me. "What is wrong?"

"I can't believe you let him go. I can't believe *Randy* let him go."

"Why?"

"It's how it happens. He's with Michael when he dies." I flew from the back calling out for Randy as I emerged from behind the altar.

He and Danny were huddled with the computer.

"What's wrong?" Randy asked.

I was enraged; so many emotions twirled inside of me I didn't know which one to grab onto first.

"How could you!" I blasted at him. "You promised to buffer. You *promised!* And you just let him go!"

"I don't know what you're talking about," Randy said.

"Mom?" Danny asked. "What's wrong?"

"*Alex.* Alex went," I explained. "With Michael. I read the Doctrines. That is how he dies."

My voice was loud, grating. I was about to open my mouth and continue on with my rant when I heard gibberish screaming coming from the back. It was Jessie.

Spinning on my heels, fearful for Beck, I flew back to that room. Jessie was seated on the bed and Beck in the chair next to her. "What's going on? Are you guys okay? I heard Jessie screaming."

"Actually," Beck ran his finger down the bridge of his nose as if he were using his hand to cover his smile. "She heard you and like a toddler was mimicking."

I heaved out a smile that came from a breath of relief. Jessie was responding and not violently. She was trying to be human. "I'm okay, baby," I said to Jessie. "Mommy's just mad." I walked to my daughter, laid my hands on her cheeks and kissed her forehead. "I'm fine."

Her hands reached up and touched mine.

My forehead to her forehead, eyes locked with hers, I giggled an emotional laugh. "Beck, she used to scream like that when Daniel and I fought."

"My daughter did the same thing."

"It's amazing, isn't it?" I shifted my eyes to Beck.

"Yeah, it is. It's a gift, Mera."

I was caught up in that moment, my daughter's face in my hands. A child I had condemned to die was alive and coming back.

"Mom." Danny's strong voice came into the room. "You can't…"

I stepped back from Jessie.

"Is she okay?" he asked.

"Yeah, yeah, she is," I smiled.

Jessie held out her hand to Danny.

"Oh, wow," Danny said in awe, reaching out to Jessie's hand. "She's not growling or trying to bite us. Alex was right."

"Speaking of Alex," my words sharpened and then I saw Randy. "Why did you let him go?"

Randy replied. "Is there any stopping Alex?"

"I read the Doctrines," I explained. "After sunup Preacher and Technical Man go out for supplies and to set diversions—"

Randy cut me off. "And after they were gone too long, the Warrior Man sought them out."

"Yes," I said. "There was trouble at a farmhouse and he walked into it, getting shot."

Randy held up a finger. "Stopping Alex was one thing, stopping Michael from doing his work was another. Worse. Alex and I went through the scenarios. We couldn't stop Michael from going. If Alex stayed behind and Michael went out and didn't return, what would Alex do?"

"Go out for him."

"Just like the Doctrines. So Alex's theory was, be Bill."

"But that doesn't mean—"

"You're right," Randy said. "But all we can do now is wait for Alex and see. That's all."

The wait was killing me. They had been gone for several hours, and as much as Beck wanted to seek them out, I put up a fight and wouldn't let him.

In fact, at one point I threw such a temper tantrum that I actually saw Beck get angry.

Danny was submerged in the Doctrines. But he focused more on the immediate and what had happened. He, like Beck, Michael, and me, fell into the fear of not wanting to know. Not for his own safety, but Danny feared learning about me and Jessie.

Randy told Danny that if he skipped to the sixth chapter, then he wouldn't know any people. Bill was moved into a technological position and wrote the remaining Doctrines to his death, and most are based on what people had told him.

I didn't understand the Doctrines and why they were so important. They weren't the supposed word of God like the Bible.

Randy explained, "It's more than just the story of the Phoenix Child. It really is. It goes beyond the walls of the New Jerusalem and how people survived, the lessons learned. There's a lot to be said about the forefathers and their struggle to rebuild beyond an iron wall."

"What does it say about us finding it?" I asked. "I mean how do we find it? Does the Doctrine say?"

"It says Prison Man—Miles—was the first to hear from them and it was during Bill's contact with Miles that they learned, or rather you learned."

Again with his name, I sighed. "Bill. He always played with that radio."

"Yeah, and now that we have someone to communicate with, Bill's gone."

Danny's softly read aloud: "*And shortly after, those behind the prison sanctuary were brought to the safety of the New Jerusalem and the Palers were unleashed upon the city for their reckoning.*"

I raised an eyebrow. "Reckoning?"

"It never was clear what that meant," Randy answered. "Some say it meant that they roamed until they passed on. Most believe it was God."

"It says here," Danny stood up, "that we stay at this church for two moons. Does that mean nights or moon cycles?" He walked to us, reading. "*It was then word was received from the Prison Man, and the Technological Man urged the group to move east in search of the New Jerusalem because the reckoning was at hand.*"

Speaking my understanding of this passage, I said. "So Miles and his people get rescued and Bill urges us to go to find the New Jerusalem."

"Hold on," Danny said. "I'm looking up the word Reckoning."

"No need," Randy explained. "It's gonna tell you that once they had retrieved all survivors that they could and taken them to the New Jerusalem, then the Palers roamed free and the Reckoning commenced. Like I said before, some say it was God, and all the Palers left the earth, but it still took a year for the survivors to be able to leave Jerusalem."

It didn't make sense to me, and I knew that soon enough my son would lose his fear of reading the predictions and make it through those Doctrines.

I also knew my son, and he would be a far better buffer than Randy for trouble.

About four hours into my worrying about Michael and Alex, Beck spotted the truck pulling up the driveway.

Michael made his way into the church first, carrying a box. I was frightened when I saw this, wondering where Alex was. Then in a few moments, Alex returned as well. He told Beck there were other things in the truck.

I never thought I'd do it, but I hugged Alex tightly, scolding him for going.

"Bill didn't die," Alex stated, "so I took his place. The Doctrines talked about trouble at a farmhouse; we avoided it."

"To my dismay," Michael added. "I believe that is a stronghold for attraction and to divert the Sleepers."

"And just when he had me convinced that I was making a mistake," Alex said, "we headed to the farmhouse and saw the trouble, therefore avoiding any unnecessary shots to my head."

Beck stepped forward. "What took you so long, guys? We were worried."

Alex set the box down. "There're a lot out there, and it took creative diversion to get them off our tail. Plus there are things we needed to get, and we needed to put in motion our diversions for the next few days." He looked around. "How's my patient?"

"Resting," Beck answered. "She ate breakfast and lunch. The calm things seem to be working."

"They do," Randy said. "I told you this."

Beck said, "Alex, tell me about the Sleeper situation. Should we stay here or should we leave?"

Michael answered. "I think for the time being, and until we see what becomes of Jessie, you should stay here. I have well water. The walls are strong."

"And here we find out about where the New Jerusalem is," Danny added, "through radio contact that Bill made."

Alex corrected, "I'll make that radio contact now. But to answer your question, Beck, it's bad. It'll get worse. We can strengthen this place. But for the time being, this is our best survival option."

"What about going back to the prison?" I asked.

Alex shook his head. "It's getting bad out there, almost as if the Sleepers sense areas where there is life. We won't make it back, not through that town again. We can try east. In fact, I plan on setting up an escape route with Michael here, should we need it. But where are we going to go? For now we fend them off as best as we can. We obviously, according to the future Doctrine thingy, make it to the radio transmission. So I'll go by that. And," Alex held up his hand with a serious expression, "spoiler alert for those of you who don't want to know. This little fortress here, according to the Doctrines, sustains a hell of an attack."

Danny groaned, and I did as well.

"Alex!" I scolded. "Why did you tell us?"

"I *said* spoiler alert."

I grunted.

"And," Alex continued, "spoiler alert again, I was dead in that scenario. Beck can't keep constant watch if I am not here. He and I can do a great job together, so I don't foresee the attack, if it happens, coming as any big surprise. Plus, I got explosives while we were out, just in case."

Alex finished talking about his and Michael's little plan for staying put. Again reiterating how he based it on not only the amenities along with the safety the church offered and the fact that we had nowhere else to go, but also he was putting faith into Randy's Doctrines.

He and Michael, aside from setting up the evening diversion for the Sleepers, got a lot of things from many surrounding areas. Hence they were able to give a knowledgeable account on the Sleepers and it was why they were gone for so long.

Aside from ammo, food, and explosives, Alex got radio supplies, more medical supplies, and things for Jessie.

He got her clothes and items that would aid me in taking care of her because Jessie, like a two-year-old, needed to be taught control of her bodily functions. If that could happen and teaching her that much was even possible, because Jessie, according to the Doctrines and as Alex always added, 'spoiler alert,' was like a toddler again.

Alex even got me a body baby carrier so I would be able to have Phoenix in my arms at all times.

The items that Alex and Michael retrieved ranged from basic and critical survival gear to entertainment items.

By what they unloaded, it was clear to me that we were at the church for the long run, or at least until the call arrived about the location of New Jerusalem.

DOCTRINES 7:12-18

And the walls of valor set around the roadways leading the fortress house of worship could hold no more. They came like a wave of invaders, from all directions, ascending upon the place of worship.

There were more than the weapons could handle, and the group of seekers sought their escape. Like lava, the Palers poured in through the broken glass of the church. The doors were not strong enough to hold them.

In order to escape, another diversion was needed and the Preacher called upon his favor with God.

The young Paler woman was the sacrifice, and the Preacher offered her to the attacking Palers. Was this what they wanted? Would that satisfy them?

It did for the moment, and as the Preacher, the Mother, the Phoenix Child and the Technological Man sought the safety of the vehicle, the Strong Man saw the diversion did not hold.

After seeing them safely to the vehicle, the Strong Man raced outward, away from the seekers, causing the Palers to follow him.

The Mother, Phoenix Child, Technological Man and Preacher were able to flee safely.

The horde of Palers engulfed the Strong Man, drowning him like a tidal wave. Strong Man was taken by them and killed. Through his own self-sacrifice, he saved the Phoenix Child and others.

They prayed for him as they moved east.

30
TIME

DOCTRINE 7: 12-18

7 weeks later ...

I had found my niche in our eclectic little group. I was actually a better cook than Michael and was in charge of preparing all meals, not that there was all that much to do.

What else was there to do? I did help to carry water.

It got boring over the weeks, but it was nice not to run or move. Once in a while Alex would take us out on journeys, his safe routes that he knew were protected from the Sleepers.

But still there was only so much we could do. Thank God, the grounds of the church were safe. I never realized how hard Alex, Beck and Michael worked to keep us safe. There was a daily set of occurrences, a chain of events that had to be completed.

Every day.

But each day when they returned we were told it wasn't going to be much longer and we'd have to move forward.

The van was already packed and ready to go. Survival supplies were in there.

They had to resort to blockading the driveway and wooded areas around the church. After a week, one or two Sleepers made it onto the grounds. Within a couple of weeks there were five to ten. By six weeks we were fighting off dozens a day.

It kept things interesting.

Phoenix was doing so well. A baby born a mere five pounds had easily doubled his weight. He was alert and cooing. Alex took to feeding him solid foods too early to plump him up, stating that—spoiler alert—Phoenix was super advanced and spoke by the time he was three months old.

Randy quickly dispelled that tale.

Jessie was making amazing progress. In so many ways she was just like a small child, a toddler, learning things over again. She fed herself and babbled. She giggled at the silliest things.

Beck had taken such a liking to her. I really credited him with her progress, although I was realistic as to the fact that many abilities would never return to my child.

But she was alive and she no longer was one of those *things*.

Miles was grateful for the news and implemented Alex's therapy on two individuals who had turned but were caught early enough.

The rest had been Sleepers far too long for help, although Miles admitted to trying it on those who had been Sleepers for a while. It didn't work.

One thing Miles conveyed was that he had to find a way out of Seattle.

It was getting bad and his concerns echoed those of Alex's, stating he was certain the Sleepers were sensing those who were not infected.

Seattle got ahead of them and they were overrun.

They had about another month's worth of food and then they had to figure out something.

We were in daily contact with Miles, hoping that one of those times he would tell us he was contacted by New Jerusalem.

Randy kept trying. He told us that at the time of the Event, there were close to 1,000 functioning satellites in orbit around the earth and that his computer device and those of the other two travelers could link to a satellite and eventually to each other. But 1,000 satellites was a lot to try and the odds of trying the same one at the same time as one of his friends was slim.

He didn't give up.

Just when I started to believe that somehow the Doctrines weren't prophetic, we received word from Miles that his camp had been contacted.

Miles relayed to us that several key members of the government, including the President and Secretary of State were hunkered down in a secure living area.

They were actively seeking survivors to begin civilization. Their numbers were growing but there weren't enough.

They asked Miles how many there were in their camp, alive and well, and informed him that transportation would be forthcoming.

Not including his Sleepers, Miles had nearly five hundred people. He didn't see how they were getting out of their sanctuary.

Miles and his people were imprisoned in their own jail by the massive amounts of Sleepers that had descended upon the city.

There were two days of radio silence, and we didn't hear from Miles.

Alex didn't call out at all over the radio, fearful that it was a trap and that perhaps Miles' camp was simply wiped out.

It was two days before the eight week mark, or the second moon cycle, that Beck got Jessie to make the 'B' sound that progressed rapidly into 'Ba.' Beck rejoiced in his victory. Jessie said his name first.

"Oh, please," Alex ridiculed. "She did not. Ba is not Beck. Besides," he paused and looked at Michael, "spoiler alert."

Michael groaned, covered his ears and started humming.

Alex laughed and continued. "She says my name first. Crystal clear. Says so in the Doctrines, she calls for me."

Randy chuckled with a shake of his head. "Then she must call for your ghost; remember, at this moment in the Doctrines, you're dead."

"Yeah, that's right." Alex scratched his head.

"Besides," Randy looked at Michael, "spoiler alert."

Michael covered his ears again and stood.

"She never spoke in the Doctrines, so, Beck, you have done well."

"So like, dude," Danny said to Randy, "did you ever stop to think what the people in your time will be like since everything is gonna change?"

"We'll be a happier race of people and not a dying one," Randy answered. "We worry because we'd be extinct in a few hundred years just from dwindling population."

"Can I lower my hands now?" Michael asked.

"Yes," we chorused.

"Thank you." He walked back over to the group. "You," he pointed at Alex, "need to stop with the spoiler alerts. I really think you do that to me on purpose. How much can you spoil over two months? I think you make things up."

I looked at Michael and nodded. "He does."

"I knew it."

Then the radio stunned us by breaking the silence. *"Alex, come in. Alex, come in."* It was Miles.

We all flew over to the radio as if our presence would make a difference.

"Miles," Alex said in relief. "What's going on? We were worried."

"Sorry about the lack of contact. We've been evacuating. It took the good part of two days."

"We?"

"We made it, Alex," Miles said. "We're in the compound. It's set up for long-term protected survival. We're still processing but it is very organized. They airlifted us by chopper. This is serious."

Alex lowered his head then looked at all of us. It was a look of gratefulness he produced. "Life does go on."

"Alex," Miles said, "I told them about you folks. They said they'd see what they could do, but…their exact words were they didn't know if there was time."

"Time?"

"Don't know, Alex, but there seems to be a sense of urgency around here."

Urgency. There was that word and all of us knew that word was significant in the Doctrines.

Alex took a deep breath, "Tell them...tell them about the baby."

"But we don't know if that's a good idea, Alex. You and I discussed that."

"I know. I know. But tell them. We have to get the baby there, Miles. We have to get the baby to safety."

"Will do."

"Miles, where is the compound?"

"You aren't gonna believe this. It's—"

Static.

"Miles," Alex called. "Miles!"

Beck slammed his fist. "They cut him off." He turned to Randy. "Do you even have a clue what this urgency is?"

"No. No, I don't," Randy said.

"Okay. Okay," Alex stood straight. "Danny, any thoughts on the location of New Jerusalem?"

Danny first glanced at Michael. "Spoiler alert." Then his attention turned back to Alex. "It's east, we know that, but it can't be too far. A day's trip, maybe two by the Doctrines; they arrive not long after Miles."

"So they airlifted them by chopper; they can't go too far. And it's not that far from here," Alex said. "Where would they hide a bunker?"

"Nevada?" Beck suggested.

"Possibly," Alex said. The moment he said that, there was a distant sound of breaking glass and Alex spun to the door. "What the hell? It's not even nighttime." Leaving the radio, he moved to the lookout point at the front of the church.

I guessed he, like the rest of us, thought that one or two were making their way onto the property.

The Doctrines didn't even cross our minds at that second.

Alex peered through the small opening in the front window. "Fuck." He spun. "Grab the baby. Get Jessie. Out the back. *Now.*"

Beck manned his weapon. "What's going on?"

"We're overrun. There are hundreds." No sooner had he said that than the window in the front of the church smashed and arms reached in. Alex backed up.

"Everyone out!" He looked once over his shoulder. "Danny. Do it. Don't let go of her."

Danny grabbed hold of Jessie and dragged her with him to the back. "Mom, come on!"

"Beck?" I called out for him, following Danny.

"In a second." Beck reached into a bag. "Alex, catch," he said, tossing him a grenade. "I'll plow them out; use that when we're clear."

Alex caught it and had backed up near the altar.

We hadn't even crossed the sanctuary when windows in the church burst one right after another. Arms reached in, fighting, and soon they used each other as leverage and poured through the windows.

A group of them battered down the double doors of the church.

I was standing with my children, Phoenix tight in my arms. Randy and Michael were urging us through when Beck called out to Alex, "Don't be a martyr! Do it now."

Beck charged to us, bodily forcing us through that back door and when he did, Alex was a second behind. He slammed and locked the door the second the grenade detonated.

"To the back!" Beck yelled, and he and Alex pushed us to the back door.

Michael was there first. He looked out then turned to us. "Van's surrounded."

Even I could see the Sleepers in the backyard. They hadn't hit the back porch yet; they were all around the van as if they actually reasoned we'd be running to that. They blocked it and guarded it at least ten deep all the way around.

"No. No. No!" Beck edged through and looked. "Okay, think, think."

"Diversion?" Alex suggested.

"We have to," Beck said. He jolted and looked to the locked door behind us. They were banging on it, trying to get in from the church. "They'll be in here in a minute. All right, I'll run out. Alex you get them in the van and—"

"No," Michael said firmly. "No." He grabbed the doorknob. "I met Bill. I have a hard time believing he portrayed me as such a coward. Just know I would never ever use a child. That is not me." He shouldered his weapon. "God be with you." He turned the knob. "And Alex, I read those Doctrines. It's been an honor to know you all."

On that, he opened the door and squeezed out.

Instinctively, I cried out, 'No!' squeezing Phoenix even tighter.

Jessie buried her head on Danny's chest; Randy held on to both of my children.

Beck looked out when we heard three shots. "He's running. They're… they're… following."

Alex added. "A little more. A little more."

"You have the keys?" Beck asked.

"Right here." Alex jingled.

"One more second."

I didn't want to look, I couldn't. I let them be my guides. They'd let me know when to go.

"He's clear!" Beck yelled. "Now!"

Randy flung open the door and the rest was such a blur.

I felt as if I weren't even in control of my movements. Did Beck have me? Did Alex? Both? I didn't know. I was moved with urgency out the door, across the porch, down the steps and to the van.

It was seconds. Mere seconds from the church to the van, but I was able to catch a glimpse just as Beck pushed me inside.

I saw Michael. I saw the mob, and then after a few more shots, Michael disappeared within it. The massive amount of Sleepers swallowed him.

Just before Beck closed the door, I heard him whisper, "Thank you, Michael." Then he, too, jumped into the van.

Alex sped off before Beck's door was even closed.

"Hold the baby," Alex warned as he made a sharp turn.

Had Danny and Jessie not been next to me, I probably would have slid out of the seat.

I couldn't see what was going on. I could hear the thumps and bangs against the van. It rocked some even as we moved.

Finally it seemed as if we broke free.

"Randy?" Alex called to him. "What's behind us?"

Randy was in the back and he peered out the rear window. "They're running but not catching us."

That was good to know, good to hear, but I still didn't feel any sense of relief in the van. We were all still tense and reeling from what had just occurred.

After twenty minutes we were on the highway. Alex finally stopped the van in the middle of the highway in the middle of nowhere on top of a high bridge.

Far enough from anywhere, he reasoned, that the Sleepers wouldn't come. It was there we took an hour to absorb all that had happened.

I stepped out of the van to take it all in. The sun was about to set, and the entire valley below was peaceful and quiet.

Not a sound or soul was heard.

It seemed as if there was nothing left, but that was far from the truth.

We made it to a truck repair station a few miles down the road and away from civilization. We moved the van inside the garage and all took turns keeping watch in case we had to make an escape.

We were so used to being in that church, settled and calm, we forgot how to run.

Like a bad habit, though, it came right back.

We waited through the night in the dark, staying silent but keeping the radio on. Waiting to hear something from New Jerusalem.

But no one called.

31
CONTACT

"Calling Alex Sans, 22, this is CSCM, do you read us, over?" A brief pause. "Alex Sans, are you there? Over."

The radio cut through the silence of the garage in the early morning as Alex flew from his spot at the window to the radio.

It could only be The New Jerusalem.

"This is Sans, I read you."

"Sans, this is an official from the government rebuilding site, we hear you have a group of survivors."

"Roger that," Alex replied. "Seven of us."

"What is your approximate location?"

"About fifty miles inside Idaho, off of Highway 26."

"Are you mobile?" the man asked.

"We are."

"Are you able to refuel if needed?"

"Yes, sir," Alex said.

"We're gonna see if you can make it to us If not, we need to get you in chopper range We are on fuel conservation Need you to head straight on highway 26 until it meets up with 84 At that junction go east on 80, and avoid Salt Lake City; it is infested I repeat Infested."

"Roger," Alex said. "Then what?"

"Remain in contact. Let us know when you get close to the Colorado border. We'll arrange a pickup if need be. Once you hit Colorado, we'll be able to tell you a safe route."

"Where in Colorado are we going?"

"Colorado Springs." There was a delay and the man came back on. "Is it true you have a small child with you?"

Another hesitation, yet Alex did reply. "Yes. He was born after the Event."

"What is the state of his health?"

"He's fine and very healthy."

"That's good to hear," the man said. "Be safe in your journey; this channel will be clear for you. Let us know if you run into problems. Our doors are set to automatically close in three days so we need to get you in here. Out."

And that was it.

That was the radio transmission. Probably similar to the one that Miles received. Of course, Miles was probably the reason they used all their fuel.

I didn't understand why, when we had the child, they weren't coming for us as they had Miles' group. Maybe they felt because we were such a small group that we could trek across the godforsaken land easier than five hundred people.

Beck deduced that if we were headed to Colorado Springs that could only mean one place—NORAD.

They were hunkered down, alright, in the safest place in the world. But the doors were closing and sealing. Why?

We didn't have time to question. With the hope of our journey ending soon and finding a home in New Jerusalem, we packed up and made our way east.

31
CLOSER

It was apparent to me that Beck was a great father and that he had truly suffered a loss when his children were taken in the Event. He took an immediate liking and protective mode to Jessie, and Phoenix, well, that went without saying. Although it seemed everyone was Phoenix's parent.

We stopped for the night without any incidents. It was a pretty clear drive and we made as much distance as we could. I finished reading the Doctrines up until the entrance of the New Jerusalem.

I felt the need to speak to someone about what I read. Beck didn't want to know, but Alex stated he was ready.

Ready for what? Everything had changed from what occurred in the Doctrines. Suffice to say, further outcomes would change as well. They had to. With Beck and Alex still alive, there was no way we would be overrun by Sleepers and placed in a compromising position.

Pastor Mike was also gone. According to the Doctrines, he sacrificed himself when we were encompassed and waiting for the New Jerusalem to arrive.

The self sacrifice was already made.

Also, according to the Doctrines, Phoenix, Bill and I were the only ones to arrive in New Jerusalem. But that was only after some huge battle and the Doctrines stated, '*While the Technological Man fought with diligence, a paler snatched the Phoenix Child from the confines of the Mother's chest, plunging its teeth into the infant's flesh. The Mother challenged and won in a fight with the Paler, regaining the child. However, the Phoenix Child was not without deep injuries.*'

All of that couldn't be deciphered and thwarted because all of that had changed already. Right after we stopped for the second night, Alex made radio contact with New Jerusalem, informing them that we had crossed the Colorado border.

We felt confident that we would make it before the doors sealed. And New Jerusalem felt confident that we would arrive. They were waiting.

The highway route kept us out of any major cities and there was only one unavoidable city we had to encounter.

Denver.

Just before that, while still safely on the highway, Alex and Beck stopped the van to do a weapons check. Everyone, including me, was armed and ready. We were to be ready to disembark the van if need be. Phoenix was positioned in the carrier to my chest.

We hadn't a clue what we'd run into.

New Jerusalem told us that Denver was bad, overrun, drawing attention from other areas. Sleepers were congregating there. I only hoped they left the highway alone.

We had followed directions precisely. We were almost there, just outside of the suburb of Thornton, Colorado when the van died.

Thornton was about eight miles north of Denver.

The white steam from the front end confirmed Alex's fears.

"Engine block is cracked. She was running hot, but I thought we'd make it," he said. "This is the end of the road. She isn't going any further."

"What now?" Beck asked.

"We radio and see. We should be in chopper range," Alex answered.

It seemed safe, from the highway point of view, until Danny indicated to the area to the west.

There were Sleepers, lots of them.

Beck paced back and forth. "Everyone think. Look. Spot somewhere to go. This isn't good."

I peered around, as did Randy and Danny.

"What about there?" Danny pointed across the highway.

A building five or six stories high. It would be a jaunt, we'd have to go back to the exit and possibly run all the way there. But it appeared as if very few Sleepers were in that area.

Beck nodded. "It's a hospital. Yeah. It's daylight. Not a lot of Sleepers. Let's do this."

Alex raced to the radio. He sent a message out stating where we were, what had happened and where we were headed. He also stated he would try to take the radio but if he had to, he would lose it.

We would be inside, and we would head for the roof so the choppers could pick us up.

No one replied.

We couldn't let that stop us. We were sitting ducks on the open highway, nowhere to go. It wouldn't be long before the massive number of Sleepers spotted us. How could they not? We were life and what they sought.

We stayed close and moved at a quick pace. Beck took the front, Alex the rear. We cleared the highway without incident and encountered only a few as we headed down the ramp.

They reached for us, moved our way, but it wasn't threatening.

The medical center was in plain sight and not that far away. The area it was located in wasn't the best, but I didn't see a soul. A Sleeper here and there. I felt confident, I really did.

Until we turned the bend off of a side street and more toward the medical center. As soon as we hit the lot, we stopped.

There were hundreds, if not thousands of Sleepers. The main entrance of the hospital, not more than three hundred feet from us, could as well have been a mile.

"Back it up," Beck ordered.

"Not an option," Alex replied. "We have them behind us."

I thought, *This is the attack, this is the big one Bill talked about.* I cradled Phoenix tightly.

"Fuck!" Beck said vehemently. "Okay, listen. We have to run for it. As fast as we can. Alex and I will lay fire to try to clear a path. No matter what, don't look back, keep moving, and run fast."

"What if they're inside?" I asked.

"I'll try to get there before you," Beck replied. "On my call."

We were ready to bolt, ready to run, and all I could think about was one of the Sleepers grabbing Phoenix from my grasp. With that in mind, I lifted him quickly from the carrier and extended him to Randy. "Take him. Hold him. Tight. Please."

Randy knew. I could tell by his eyes, he knew why I had handed Phoenix to him. He nodded.

Beck hollered "Now!" and with that he opened fire.

I latched on to Jessie, telling her to run. I searched for Danny as well. He kept up, but like Alex and Beck he kept shooting.

I felt crushed between all the men, but I forged ahead. There were so many, I don't know how we moved across and through them.

They reached out for us, clawing, gnawing with their jaws. Just as we got to the end of the parking lot, I was grabbed by two of them.

Danny fired, then Beck.

The short distance seemed like it took forever. The salvation of the main doors wasn't that far.

But the Sleepers pursued and did so with vengeance and diligence.

We broke free of the pack just at the end of the parking lot, keeping up a faster pace than they could. The front doors of the medical center were closed and signs were posted indicating they were closed to new patients.

Beck tried the door. It was locked and he did the only thing he could. Telling us to step back, he broke the glass then cleared the way.

It wasn't the smartest thing to do, but it was our only option to get into the building quickly.

It did tell us one thing, though. If the doors were locked, there weren't many Sleepers inside.

We hurriedly made our way in. The hospital was dark and reeked of death.

As we rushed through the lobby, Beck and Alex looked for the stairs. For a moment, just a moment, there was peace.

After they spotted the stairwell, the Sleepers broke through and poured into the lobby.

There wasn't time to think; we had to move. Beck led the way. I followed, pausing only when I heard Alex call, "Go, I'll catch up."

I didn't know what he was doing, or what he was up to.

We had made it to the third floor when I heard the bang of the staircase door and Alex raced through below us. He held an ax but he wasn't alone.

Multitudes of Sleepers lunged after him and he ran at top speed to catch us. He fought them off wielding the ax and laying fire.

The Sleepers gained on us and the distance between us grew smaller.

Reaching the top, Beck pushed the rooftop door.

It wouldn't budge.

"Open it," Alex stated in a rush. "Hurry!"

"I'm trying!" Beck said, pushing against it. "Something is against the door."

Alex joined him in pushing on the bar.

The Sleepers grew closer, from a few flights of stairs below us to only two. Contrary to what I wanted, Randy handed me the baby and lent his strength to pushing the door.

They struggled. I pleaded for them to hurry and just as the first of the Sleepers reached us, Jessie flung forward snarling at them.

They stopped.

Her head tilted as she growled and snarled out a long whining cry as if to say, "Stop!"

And they *listened*. I reached for her, fearful they were going to get her. But they were stunned, halting their pursuit.

She held them at bay long enough for the door to finally be opened.

Beck took hold of the back of my shirt, pulling me away from Jessie and to the door. "Go."

Just before I crossed the threshold to the roof, I handed Phoenix over to Beck as I stepped through, sun in my eyes, only to be faced with a Sleeper.

He reached out viciously, clawing down and ripping the carrier from my chest.

A single shot from someone tore through the Sleeper's skull and he flew back.

I looked at the tattered and torn baby carrier then turned back around.

Randy was putting his gun away. "You okay?" he asked.

I nodded, looking for my children.

Danny was on the roof; he now had Phoenix. Jessie was safe, too, and Alex and Beck bodily held the door to stop the Sleepers.

How much longer they could hold them back, I didn't know. The items that had barricaded the door earlier were scattered about. I ran to them, pushing what I could find to help Beck and Alex.

Then Randy grabbed the downed Sleeper and dragged him to the door. He tossed him on top of the items.

Everything and anything was used as a barricade. The heating unit, ax, roofing repair supplies, a Sleeper body.

Everything.

It took several minutes, but it was holding. The door moved; the Sleepers on the other side kept trying, but not with any luck.

We finally had a moment to breathe.

But we were stuck now. Trapped.

Alex walked to the roof's edge and peered over. "Going down this way is useless."

"Can we radio?" Beck asked.

"I had to drop it."

Beck lowered his head.

The noises of the Sleepers from beyond the roof door and the ones on the ground were loud, too loud, and almost unbearable.

We were at a standstill.

Until Randy called out, "I did it. Connection!"

We all turned. He had his computer unit out.

"New Jerusalem?" I asked.

"I don't know," he shrugged and within seconds, a three-dimensional figure appeared.

"Randy? You're safe," the man said. He was older and looked worn.

"Barely," Randy stated. "Tell me. Are you at New Jerusalem?"

"Yes, we both are," he answered.

Randy lowered his head. "Thank God. Demetrius, we're trapped. A whole group of us are on the roof of a medical center outside of Denver."

"So you are with them?" Demetrius' voice lowered. "Did you find the Phoenix Child?"

"Yes," Randy answered. "We did. But we're trapped. And as of right now, he is not injured."

"That is good news. Randy, they are on their way. They tried to radio back but didn't receive a response."

"See if you can get in touch with them," Randy said. "There is a heliport here."

"I will do that. I will see you soon, my friend. I am so proud you found him. And Randy, it's good you are found now. The Reckoning takes place in four hours. You need to be in here for safety's sake."

"I don't understand. How can we assume to know when God does the Reckoning?"

"Because it is not God. It's man. All major cities first, then over the course of the next week, the smaller ones. Wiped out. It is the only way to get rid of all the Sleepers."

"Nuclear weapons?" Randy asked. "That would mean people would have to stay underground or sheltered for a while."

'No," Demetrius answered. "Because the Sleepers are alive, they'll be using oxygen bombs. So whatever you do, make sure the Phoenix Child gets on the helicopter."

End of transmission.

Oxygen bombs? I turned to Beck. "What is he talking about? Oxygen bombs?"

Beck ran his hand over his face. "The bombs explode in the air above each city. Creates this huge fireball and sucks all the oxygen out of the air. Anyone in or around them will die. The buildings are left intact."

Alex added. "Sleepers will die along with any survivors left out here, unless they are far from the city or in a remote area."

"We're sitting ducks if they don't come," I said.

Alex nodded.

"Maybe the Sleepers will retreat," Beck said. "Back off in enough time for us to get out of here. We don't know."

Danny asked, "What if we're in the building or go to the basement?"

Alex shook his head. "Doubtful."

"No need to worry," Randy said in a near whisper. "Look." He walked slowly to the roof's edge and pointed at the sky.

It was a speck of light at first, then the bigger the light grew the more evident it was from the noise that it was a helicopter.

We cheered and jumped, all embracing each other as the helicopter circled twice then lowered to the heliport.

I had never been that close to a chopper. I couldn't believe the amount of wind that came from the blades. My hair whipped out, dust blew in my eyes, and I grabbed for my son and Jessie and brought them close.

The engines from the chopper slowed down and finally stopped. In a few seconds a man in a dark military-style uniform emerged from the chopper. Leaving the chopper door open he ducked and made his way across the port and down to us.

"Who is Alex Sans?" he asked.

"I am," Alex approached him with a firm handshake. "Glad to see you."

"I bet." He smiled. "I saw it down there. Unfortunately the situation is worsening. More survivors became infected, everything is overrun. It's a miracle you folks survived."

The man turned and looked at Danny holding the baby. He reached out his hand and softly touched Phoenix's head. "This little one is probably the end to this all. You realize this."

Danny nodded. "Yeah, we do."

The man reached out his hands for Phoenix.

Danny stepped back. "Sorry, dude, no can do until we get to the place."

"I understand." He rolled his hand into a fist, smiled politely and stepped back. "All right, if you all…" Suddenly he stopped. His eyes shifted and he looked at me then to Jessie. "She's infected."

"No," I stated strongly. "No, she's not."

"She is." He stepped closer to her. "It's evident."

How? I wondered. How was it evident? To me she looked normal. All but her… her eyes. Her blue eyes were now a dead brown, despite all that Alex had done. She had that non-pupil look to her.

Alex intervened. "We cured her."

"There is no cure," he said.

"We gave her antiviral meds, antibiotics. We were able to turn it back," Alex stated.

"But unfortunately, she still carries the virus. We know this for a fact. We have tried the same remedy. A simple kiss, touch, a scratch, and the Sleeper virus starts all over again."

Beck tossed his hands in the air. "What do you want us to do?"

"I don't care," he said. "I care about the baby. What you do is up to you. *She* can't come."

I looked at Jessie. Her head lowered and her eyes glossed over. She knew. She really knew what was going on. My heart broke.

Danny, in his rebellious way, adamantly stated. "Then if my sister doesn't go, the baby doesn't go, and I won't go."

Alex repeated the sentiment. "None of us will. All of us or none."

"How chivalrous," the man stated. "None of you go. The child dies; you all die when the bombs go off to eliminate the Sleepers. She doesn't know." He said passionately. "Save yourselves and leave her."

At that second, Jessie whimpered. Her head dropped to my shoulder. I put my arm around her waist and brought her close.

"It's okay," I whispered to her. "It is."

The man looked at all of us. "I beg you to at least give me the baby."

"No," I said. "We'll go. Our group will go. Phoenix needs to survive."

He sighed in relief. "Good."

Beck called my name, as did Alex, and Danny said, "Mom?"

I gave my hand to them, kissed Jessie on the forehead and stepped away from her. I looked to Alex. "Get on the chopper. I need you to watch my son." I then turned to Beck. "I need you," I chuckled nervously, "to watch them all."

"Mera?" Beck questioned.

I shook my head and faced Randy. "Get on the chopper. Thank you for all you have done."

"Are you sure?" he whispered. "You're meant to—"

"*Phoenix* is what is important. You're a father, Randy. What would you do?"

He leaned toward me and placed his lips to my forehead. "The same."

I gave another nod as he stepped back.

My lips felt big, swelled as I fought with my emotions and turned to my son. "Danny..."

"We aren't leaving Jessie, Mom. She knows."

"I know she knows."

"So what are you doing?" he asked. "Why are you telling him we're going?"

"Because *you* are." I stepped to him. I placed my hands over his and had him hold Phoenix tighter. "You'll get on that chopper with Phoenix, and you'll live." I planted my lips to Phoenix's cheek then spoke softly to the baby. "Thank you, little guy. You are a part of me."

"No." Danny shook his head. "No. You want the baby to live, fine. I'll give him to Randy, but I am not leaving you and Jessie."

"Danny," I laid my hand on his face, "my heart is breaking right now. It is. I lost your father and Jeremy and I will not lose you too. You have to get on that chopper and go." I sniffled, filled with emotion. "Alex?"

"Yeah..." He moved to me.

"Get on the chopper, please." I kept my eyes on my son.

"Mera..." Alex's voice cracked.

"Please. I need you to watch him."

Alex nodded and moved closer to me. "Maybe the Sleepers will disperse. If you go to the basement you have a chance."

"I'll keep that in mind," I replied. "But if I don't, please take care of my son and Phoenix."

"With my life." He wrapped his arms around me and I sank into his embrace.

"Thank you, Alex Sans, for everything."

"No, Mera," he pressed his lips hard to my cheek then to my forehead, "thank *you*." He hugged me again. "Are you sure?" he whispered in my ear. "If you want me to stay or if you want us all to stay…"

"Go. Please." I pulled from his embrace.

Alex had an emotional look on his face, one I had rarely seen. His eyes glossed over as he ran his hand down my face. He stepped to Jessie and hugged her. "I'm proud of you, Jessie. Take care of your mom."

He inched back.

"Danny," I said.

"No." He shook his head. "No, Mom."

"Danny, please."

"Mom. No!" His words were ragged with emotion. "I love you. I can't leave you and Jessie. You're my family!"

"And you're my son," I laid both hands on his face. "My son. Please, please, live. Please. I can't leave your sister. I can't. I can't leave her alone on this roof knowing she is going to die. But I can watch you get on that chopper knowing you are going to live."

Danny whimpered, trying not to cry. "I can't leave you alone, Mom."

"She won't be alone," Beck said softly. "I'm…I'm not going."

Both Danny and I looked at him.

"Beck, no," I told him.

"Mera," he said calmly, "no argument. Okay? I'm not going. I don't want to go. So I'll be here, Danny, with your mom and sister. If I can get us out of this, I will."

"Beck," I whispered his name. "I need you to…"

He shook his head. "Do you know why I am still alive? Because I met you and Danny and wanted to help you find Jessie. We did that." He smiled. "Mission accomplished. Can't top that one, so I stay put." He looked at Danny. "Get on the chopper, son. It's okay."

After a huge intake of breath, I embraced my son. Without any more spoken words it was no longer an argument. He was going.

Despite that I knew what could happen to me, I was grateful that my son would live on, and so would Phoenix.

I held him for the longest time until I knew I had to let him go.

"I love you, Danny," I said. "I am so proud of you. Know that. Okay?" He folded like a child in my arms. "I love you." I lifted his chin and glanced in his eyes.

"I love you too, Mom." He embraced me once more and stepped back. "I love you, too."

That was it. I allowed my fingers to touch my son until he had stepped beyond my reach.

Alex stayed with him, helping him into the chopper. Danny still held on to Phoenix and looked once more over his shoulder before getting in.

Alex did the same. He waved to me then saluted Beck.

They were inside.

The chopper doors closed.

I clutched Jessie and Beck. Standing on the other side of Jessie, he held her as well as the chopper lifted from the port.

A total emptiness engulfed me, causing a lump to form in the pit of my stomach. I watched my son for as long as I could, absorbing the final moment of seeing him until the chopper was out of sight. And even then, I stood there watching.

32
FINAL LIGHT

There were three reasons I broke down and cried on the roof of that building minutes after the helicopter left.

I filled with a pain that radiated through my body and I sobbed.

I cried for my son's loss, for Beck and me staying behind, and for my daughter. My poor daughter. She was innocent before it all occurred and now, she was just like an infant. So helpless, yet there she was, condemned to death, and there was nothing I could do about it but hold her.

I pulled myself together for Jessie's sake. I wanted to be brave for her. We had to be brave.

It finally grew quiet as the evening hours drew near. The Sleepers stopped pounding at the door but they were still there, crammed in the stairwell. I honestly think they didn't know what to do next or how to get back down. They were a stairwell thick and Beck kept checking.

Below us, they swarmed. Even more showed up as if the helicopter noise was a calling card for every Sleeper in earshot. And in a dead silent world, sound traveled far.

They were still wandering to the hospital, gathering like ants.

We thought after a couple of hours they'd thin out, but they didn't. Beck said we probably only needed to make it a mile to be safe; we could run that at top speed in less than ten minutes.

But we had to get out.

And at T-minus 45 minutes until the bombs, we were still trapped.

We had finally resigned ourselves to the fact that we weren't going anywhere. We took a seat on the roof. Jessie sat between Beck and me. One moment she'd cuddle closer to me, the next closer to Beck.

Beck held her with as much love and emotion as if she were his own child. She sensed it. I know she did.

Her face held an admiration for Beck. How could one not admire him? He was so noble and such a great guy.

I wished I had known him before the Event. I think we would have been great friends.

The night crept up quickly and we both knew what that meant. The city was dark but the sky was lit by a bright full moon.

It was a perfect night, the weather, the stars.

Perfect.

"Beck?"

"Yeah?"

"Do you regret staying behind?" I looked over to him.

Jessie's head rested on his shoulder. "Not one bit."

"Thank you for being here. I mean it."

"I wouldn't have it any other way, Mera. You know that."

After a pause, I asked, "Did you think you could get us out of this?"

"I hoped. I didn't think so, though."

"It isn't fair." I sniffled and wiped my nose, really trying not to cry. "We made it so far. Never once did I think they wouldn't take Jessie."

"I did."

That caught my attention. "You did?"

"Yeah, actually it crossed my mind. No matter what we did for her, she is a carrier."

"But Phoenix is the cure."

"They don't know that; they can't take that chance." Beck said. "I thought about it and made up my mind that if they didn't take her, I was staying with her."

"Did you think I wouldn't stay behind?"

"To be honest, I wish you went with Danny. He's going through hell right now, but as a parent," he let out an airy chuckle filled with emotion, "I know why you did it. Everything you did on this whole trip you did for the love of your family. Why would you stop now?"

"I couldn't leave her, Beck. She was alone when this all happened. She was alone when she got ill. I couldn't leave her now."

"Even though it means your life?"

"I'd give my life for any of my children. At any time." I inched closer to Jessie, sandwiching her tighter between me and Beck. When I did that, Beck wrapped his huge arm around us both. I felt safe.

I felt right in my decision.

I heard him exhale.

"How much longer?" I asked.

"Minutes." He leaned over and kissed Jessie, running his hand down her face.

"Ba." She smiled.

"Ba, that's right," he said. Then with his huge hand encompassing the back of my head, he leaned to me and planted his lips to my forehead. He left them there. "It has been an honor and a privilege to have known you, Mera Stevens."

My eyes locked onto his. "The pleasure is all mine, Major. All mine."

Basking in the security of his arms, I moved into him even more. Jessie wrapped her arms around my waist and placed her head against my chest. I leaned down into her, and Beck leaned into me. Though differently than we thought, we'd be reunited with our families. We'd be home. We were fine with that. We really were.

We hoped until those final moments that another chopper would come, that they changed their minds or the Sleepers would just leave.

None of that happened, and time was counting down.

Beck's fingers gripped my side, holding me tighter and then he and I, as we held my daughter close, peered to the sky.

We waited.

Any minute.

Any second.

It would be over.

We were ready.

SLEEPERS 2

SLEEPERS 2

INTRODUCTION
RANDY BRIGGS

My existence is yet to be determined. While I live and I breathe in this world, now I have to wonder if my presence has marred my own future. I, like many others, watched my children die, watched them succumb to a horrible death on the eve of their maturity from a centuries' old virus, one with no cure, no prejudices. A virus embedded in their DNA and activated with the simple release of a hormone meant to bring about the next stage of life, not death.

I am a traveler and I wish I could say like none before me, but that would not be true. My travels are to stop the travesty of death in the future; theirs was simply to deliver it.

I believe with every iota of my heart and being that I have accomplished the mission on which I embarked, to find and deliver the cure. In doing so, I discovered something else.

Humanity.

On a spring morning, a virus was deliberately released, intended to enhance the human race. However, it spiraled out of control. In the course of a single day, every child under the age of fourteen died. The virus raged through their young bodies at an unbelievably fast rate. The death was painful, horrendous and took not only their lives, but their beings, leaving nothing but dust as an indication of their existence.

The virus didn't stop there. It found other hosts. The virus ravaged the bodies of their adult victims differently. It took their lives by taking their minds, their humanity. It made them into ravenous, raging murderous beings that survived by their vicious animal instincts.

They infected others and the virus spread.

Before we knew it, the planet found itself infested with Sleepers.

However, amongst the darkness there is a cure. It lies within the blood of a single newborn baby boy who defied all odds.

It was in the search for this child that I joined with others, people who would forever change my view of the human race.

You see, I come from a time and place where people just...exist. They live without *living*. I always believed I was different, and it took meeting the others to realize how different I was.

I love life. I want to *live* life. I want my children to live. I want all children to live.

While I was fighting to stop man's extinction, I came to realize the battle had started centuries before.

Despite the ruins, the death, the human race has a desire for life and a will to survive that I had not believed existed. If I succeed in anything, I hope that I not only succeed in bringing the cure to the future, but the passion for life and survival that encompass the people who I have met.

They have taught me. Man will not become extinct, not without a fight.

I witnessed with my own eyes their perseverance, that man just would not lie down and die, no matter how tough the odds or horrendous the heartbreak. He won't.

He just doesn't have it in him.

1
ALEX SANS

I was ashamed of myself, so much so that my stomach wrenched and twisted in disgust. Every second I spent in that helicopter gnawed at me. I stared out the window watching them longer than I believed they could see me. I knew from the second the helicopter door closed I would regret the decision to go.

How could I leave them? They were helpless on the roof of a hospital a mile or so outside of Denver, watching us leave, knowing that their fate, their deaths, were less than a few hours away.

From any perspective, the roof or the air, there was no escape. Sleepers filled the stairwell trying to burst through the blocked roof door, and they swarmed on the ground below. Every Sleeper for miles seemed to gather at that hospital, their arms raised high as though somehow they could reach those on the roof.

Even though the Sleepers had no thought processes, they somehow knew what they wanted. It was as if, even though they were unable to comprehend it, the Sleepers had a mission: To eliminate everyone who had retained his or her humanity.

At least, it seemed that way.

I know, I know. I had to go. I *had* to get on the chopper. I didn't want to. I did not want to leave Mera; neither did Beck. I supposed it was because he had reached the end of his line. Finding Mera's daughter in a world turned upside down was his goal after losing his own kids. Mera's daughter, Jessie, was a Sleeper. Granted, we were able to reverse some of the damage, the dangerous side of her. The truth remained that she was infected.

When the rescue helicopters arrived to take us to the protected bunker, Jessie wasn't allowed to go.

Mera wouldn't leave her daughter. I didn't blame her. At the age of nineteen, Jessie's mental age had regressed to that of an infant. The remnant of the Sleeper virus made her that way. How does one leave a child behind to die alone, especially one with a helpless innocence?

Mera didn't.

Her eyes focused on a noble goal, Mera had trekked across the country in search of her daughter. I felt honored to be a part of her journey, to get to know Mera, Beck and the others.

I watched them through the window of the chopper as long as I could see them. I wanted badly to say to the pilot, "You know what, guy? Stop. Let me off. Just let me go…" Yet, I didn't. I couldn't. I told Mera I would take care of her teenage son, Danny. I would guard him with my life.

Danny was beside himself. He was trying to be brave; I could see it. He buried his head against the baby, Phoenix, protectively cradling the infant in his arms. Maybe for comfort, but whether for him or the baby, I don't know.

He lost his father, his brother, and now he was going to lose his mother and sister. I promised Mera I would take care of him, and that promise was the reason I didn't get off of that helicopter.

It's funny, you know. Mera found Phoenix dangling between the legs of his dead mother. I killed her. A young pregnant woman, a Sleeper. I didn't know much about Sleepers, just that they were deadly.

Phoenix was born alive when all other infants born after the Event were stillborn. I figured it was an anomaly, chalked him up as dead, giving him no more than a day or two before he died.

How wrong I was. It was ironic; the child I mentally condemned to death held within his blood hope for all of mankind's continued existence.

He held more life than I could even imagine.

Finally, we pulled out of sight of the city and I sank a little in my seat.

"How you doing?" I asked Danny.

The young man, I think he was sixteen or so, only nodded. Randy, another member of our group, was silent. He stared out the window, not saying much of anything.

They were taking us somewhere, whereabouts unknown, at least to us. They called it the "ARC." I guess after Noah or something. I believed it was an acronym, for something stupid like Apocalypse Renewal Center.

Who knew?

Who cared?

"It's not fair," Danny whispered.

"I know." I laid my hand on his head.

"Alex, I feel so guilty. I shouldn't have left. I shouldn't have left my mom." Danny finally looked at me, his eyes glossed over.

"I feel guilty too. Trust me," I said. "But your mom, she wanted you to live. And she couldn't leave your sister."

"What do I have to live for?" Danny asked. "Huh? I have no family left."

"What about him?" I nodded to the baby. "Your mom loves him."

"They're gonna take him," Danny said. "Don't kid yourself. They'll take him. Isn't that right, Randy?"

Randy, a big guy, breathed out heavily. "Probably. Once they see him, see that he actually exists, they'll take control of him, so they can find a cure. My guess is most people in the ARC maybe aren't immune."

"See?" Danny said, looking back at me. "Unfair. They get to live, and my mom and sister die. Not a fair trade." He closed his eyes again, laying his cheek against Phoenix's head. The sadness he projected was contagious.

When he said that, something clicked in my head.

Trade.

It wasn't a fair trade, was it?

I cocked my head in thought and looked at Phoenix. That little baby was crucial. They wanted him. They needed him.

An idea hit me; trust me, it wasn't well thought out. It was a spur of the moment thing, one I thought I'd wing and hope for the best.

I didn't know if it would work, but it was worth a shot.

I looked at the clipboard-wielding man who'd hurried us aboard the helicopter. The callous, arrogant shit with no feelings, telling us that he couldn't take Jessie.

He didn't actually show care or concern that Mera and Beck were staying behind, offering no other alternative other than stay and die, or go and live.

Asshole.

The more I looked at him, spinning my idea in my brain, the more my gut raged with anger, disgust and sadness.

"Lower the chopper."

Clipboard Guy chuckled. "I'm sorry, that's not possible."

I pulled my revolver from the back waist of my pants and extended it point blank at his head.

"Alex," Randy scolded gently. "What are you doing?"

Danny looked at me with a look of relief, one that conveyed to me that he believed in me, and I wasn't letting him down. It was that look that drove me to push on. I shoved the gun hard against Clipboard Guy's temple. "The bird will go down one way or another. So, save yourself, save him, order your pilot to lower the chopper. We're getting off."

When I saw the arrogant, confident look drop from Clipboard Guy's face, I realized that my radical plan stood a chance.

2
ALEX SANS

Truth be known, I sucked at gambling. I tried it; I loved it; I never won. On that helicopter I finally spun the right combination.

They didn't land; they didn't let us off. They picked up speed, taking us to the ARC. I asked Danny to give me Phoenix. I needed him in my arms until the plan followed through, and Danny obliged. I wasn't going to take the baby, but Randy whispered, "It won't work. They'll shoot you immediately," and I decided I needed Phoenix to protect my life as well.

That was all it took. It would work.

I wasn't asking for that much.

It made perfect sense, and I recognized the mountain range as we made our approach.

Colorado Springs. NORAD. A perfect place to lock down and preserve what was left of humanity.

The flight took all of fifteen minutes, which helped. The Reckoning, as it was called, would begin in a few hours.

As we flew overhead preparing to land in a fenced-in area, even though it was dark, it looked like a sea of people was waiting for us.

They were Sleepers, tens of thousands of them outside the fence. There was no way that fence would hold them back for long.

Even with the engine of the chopper blasting, the moans of the Sleepers carried like a low electronic hum in the air. It reminded me on a smaller scale of what we'd left at the hospital.

"How can there be this many here?" I asked, getting off the chopper.

"At least two thousand of them," Clipboard Guy answered, "were once inside."

I glanced at Randy; he was right. Those in the ARC weren't fully immune. Phoenix's price tag had now gone up.

Do not think for one second that infant child's life meant nothing to me. It did. My friends' lives were hanging in the balance, and Phoenix was all I had to save them.

After leaving the chopper, we walked a short distance to the guarded entrance. We were told that typically there was a processing protocol, one that took hours. It was one long process that the four of us were allowed to bypass. Danny, Phoenix, Randy, and I were immediately escorted to a back room.

"Wait here," Clipboard Guy told us.

The room was stark; it contained a sofa, a table and two chairs, and a soda machine. I wondered if the Coca-Cola was cold.

I walked to the soda machine. Listened. It was running. "I don't suppose anyone has change?" I asked. I pressed a button for the heck of it and out rolled a can. "Sweet."

Randy paced. "I'm in debate here, Alex."

"What do you mean?" I asked, snapping open the tab.

"I mean if they are going to do it, why bring us here? We're stuck now."

"He has a point," Danny noted.

I gulped a healthy drink of the soda. Months, it had been months since I had one. It tasted really refreshing.

"They have us," Randy continued. "Not saying that your plan won't work. It might. But what's to say they won't lock this door and trap us in here? That's all I'm…is that good?"

I noticed him staring at the can of soda. "This? Yeah." I extended it to him. "Have some."

"I've never had one. Ever." Randy took it. He apprehensively took a sip. "Wow."

"See?" I nodded.

"You're confident," Danny said. "You have a good feeling in your gut, don't you, Alex?"

"I do."

The moment I said that, the door to the room opened. Two men stepped in, then an armed guard, and behind the guard…the President.

I found out through quick introductions that the other two men were scientists.

"My finder," the President stated, and I believe he was referencing Clipboard Guy, "told me that you are in a bartering mood." He smiled.

I realized now why I didn't vote for him. There was something untrustworthy about his smile. "Yep."

"It seems you're here, and you want to leave and take the immune child." He shrugged. "You saw it out there, Mr. Sans. Where are you going to go? How are you going to get there safely?"

"Well, sir," I stepped to him. "Had your boy with the clipboard lowered the chopper when I asked, we wouldn't be faced with this, would we?"

"It seems as though you're out of bartering power," the President replied.

"How many folks here aren't immune?" I asked.

"Many."

"This child here, he's your cure. Ask them." I nodded to the scientists. "His blood holds the key to the cure. You immune?"

The President didn't answer.

"I didn't think so." I said. "You need him."

"We have him. You are here, Mr. Sans. The baby is now within our reach," the President said. "I'm sorry, your attempt to blackmail us has failed."

The president turned, visually giving an order to those with him to follow.

"If you open that door before giving the order to stop the bombs, I'll break his neck."

He halted as he reached the door, turned around. "You wouldn't do that. I've read the doctrines; that isn't you."

I braced Phoenix's head with a grip that would have looked threatening to them; I gave a cold stare, but, damn it, I folded. My head lowered. "You're right. But you know what? We brought this child. We found this child. If it weren't for us, you, sir, could very well be one of those people out there. We brought him to you. We are giving you years of life. Years." I stared at him, instilling my plea with heartfelt passion. "All I'm asking for is one day. One day. That's it." I paused. "Sort of."

3
ALEX SANS

There was a glimmer in the President's eye; one that said, 'I'm listening.' Those damn scientists weren't quite as congenial.

I wondered, though, if they knew they had us, if they knew I was out of bartering power, then why bring us to that little back room? Why bypass the check-in stuff? Like the president said, they had us; they had Phoenix in their grip.

Something inside told me there was still a sense of gratefulness to us for bringing Phoenix. Or maybe it was Randy's scientist friend on the inside.

In any event, I made it a point to show my human side, not the one that threatened to snap the neck of a small baby. I apologized to the President for the loss of his children and his wife, who had turned into a Sleeper. His head lowered, he thanked me. After a brief, quiet moment he asked, "What do you know about the Sleeper virus?"

"Not much," I admitted. "I know that you can reverse some of the effects if you catch it right away."

"They remain carriers and able to infect others," the President said. "This baby is vital. You know that. Not only, as I am told, to the future, but for now. He holds the key to the cure, or at least an inoculation. He has to. There are so many that are infected, that are carriers..."

"You mean like the ones we reversed?"

"No. They fell victim to the original strain, fell asleep, raged with fever, but they recovered. This is how it spread so fast. It's airborne and highly contagious. These folks are contagious. If you aren't immune, you'll get sick. We had to force many people out of this shelter because of it, because there are many here that are not immune. If you did not sleep that first night, and you weren't immune, the virus didn't get a chance to take hold. You weren't out of the woods unless you were isolated, like us."

Immediately my mind went to Danny. I didn't look at him, but I thought about that bite, the one he received from the Sleeper. How Danny got sick and recovered. How the President was toast if Danny was indeed a carrier.

"For those reasons, and because you found this child and brought him to us, I will listen to you. Out of gratefulness."

"Okay, then let me play it straight," I said. "This boy here, Danny, his mom Mera is the one that fought for this child. Her daughter Jessie was a Sleeper that I reversed. Your people wouldn't take her because she is a carrier. Mera stayed with her daughter, trapped on a roof, surrounded by Sleepers. Mera, Jessie, and a man named Beck will die when your bombs go off. They don't deserve that. I'm not asking for you to bring them here. I'm asking you to hold the bombs for one day. Spare the fuel, fly there, lift them to a safe location, and give them a fighting chance."

The President stared at me for a moment, and then glanced at his scientist buddies.

One scientist shook his head. "You don't need to do that. A day can be costly. We need to eliminate the Sleepers that are outside. You know that. We have to seal this place completely."

Danny stepped toward the President and spoke with a pleading tone. "It's my mom. *Please*. I've already lost my father, my brother...please don't let me lose my mom."

"Please," I said. "Give them a fighting chance." Then I asked the question I believe was the deciding factor. "Didn't they give *you* a fighting chance?"

4
ALEX SANS

I would be lying if I said I didn't hold my breath when they took Danny's blood. Turns out he was immune. Suffice to say I was relieved, but not as much as I was over the fact that they delayed the bombing of Denver and its suburbs. They didn't have enough bombs to take out every major city, but they were planning to eliminate anything close to or on the same side of the country as the ARC.

Then the doors to the ARC would be sealed for six months. No one would go in or out.

I promised Mera I would watch Danny. This weighed heavily on my mind. Here was the problem: they had agreed to delay the bombings, and they would send out a flight to airlift Mera, Jessie, and Beck to a safe location; in return, they had to have access to Phoenix.

I wanted to go to the safe location with them, as did Danny. Surprisingly, Randy did, as well. However, the deal was they had to keep Phoenix to use as a cure. Mera would have my head if we left Phoenix in their care without one of us there.

Personally, I didn't want to leave Phoenix behind. In fact, I wanted Danny safe within that ARC, as well. So, after hashing out some things as if it were a freaking peace treaty, we made a decision.

The next day when the chopper flew out to get them, I would go and take Phoenix with me. That would be my assurance that they weren't pulling anything funny. Danny wanted to go, too. And this time, his goodbye to his mother wouldn't be final.

We'd airlift them, bring them to safety. Then Danny, Phoenix, and I would return to the ARC. They could have Phoenix for those six months, but I would be there, along with Danny and Randy as the baby's caretakers.

Six months. That was all Beck, Mera and Jessie had to survive without us. It wasn't long, really. After all, we were in that church with Pastor Mike for two months. And I was confident in Beck.

When the doors to the ARC opened, we would be able to go, along with everyone else. It wasn't a prison; we would be free.

Those officials in the ARC believed that six months would be ample time for the Sleepers to die off.

We'd meet up with Beck, Mera and Jessie.

That was the plan.

They gave us a meal. It wasn't much, but they made a big deal out of it, like it was some gourmet supper or something. However, I liked my Spam, and Pastor Mike was one of the oddballs like me who had plenty of it, so I was used to eating Spam regularly. After all that salt, everything tasted bland.

Our small group was kept away from everyone else for some reason, and no, I didn't allow them to take Phoenix from us until we returned to the ARC.

Danny fell asleep, but Randy was just as nervous as me. I kept thinking about Mera and Beck on that roof, how they looked when we left them, how they had to be feeling.

They were faced with their own demise, waiting on their deaths. I kept looking at my watch, counting down the minutes, seconds to when the bomb was supposed to go off. I imagined them staring at the sky, watching and waiting.

I prayed they felt a sense of relief and knew something was up when the sky didn't explode.

Would I? If I had stayed with Mera, not Beck, would I assume they'd cancelled the bombs?

I didn't know. Of course, knowing me, I would think it was a mental tease or something, that, at any second, it would happen.

I'd find out soon enough when we flew out to get them off the roof. For the night, though, I was out of my head. I couldn't sleep, couldn't relax. I wished the baby had colic or something to use as my excuse to walk the floor with him. Even Phoenix seemed to be annoyed because I couldn't settle down.

So I decided to hit the Doctrines, those Bible-wannabe passages written by a man in our group, Bill, who had died before he could fulfill his destiny of writing the Doctrines in the future. I wondered who would take over that role. Man, I hoped it wasn't me.

Randy was more than happy to give me the Doctrines, I figured to shut me up. Like Mera and everyone else, I had only read until our arrival at the ARC. To be honest, I really didn't give a shit what happened after that. We'd already changed so much. The baby was the only one from the original Doctrines that lived. Personally, I thought they got a little boring when I bit the dust.

The Doctrines stated that I was shot in the head. I doubted that. I think Bill went fictional for a while. Then again, according to Randy they had gone though several translations, just like the Holy Bible.

I settled into my bunk above Danny and let the baby cuddle with Randy. I asked Randy to make sure he didn't roll over on the baby and suffocate him. He didn't think I was funny. I didn't mean to be. Randy was a stocky guy, kind of hefty.

It wasn't my intention to keep him from sleeping, at least not consciously. But between my laughing comments while reading the Doctrines and intermittently asking Randy if Phoenix was still breathing, the typically mild-mannered man huffed at me.

I think it was my last burst of laughter that threw him over the edge.

"You know, Alex," Randy stated with irritation, "reading isn't one of those activities that usually warrants commentary."

"Really? You met Bill—you seriously think he didn't exaggerate? He was creative."

"I don't think it was Bill," Randy said. "I believe it was the translators and those who made interpretations of it. We highly regard and respect the word of the Doctrines, Alex. It's necessary to our culture. There are valuable lessons in there. Very valuable. Man begins again."

"I honestly don't mean to laugh," I said. "Okay, I do. This has me..." I read the latest passage aloud, *"And the Technological Man and the Mother found love while in the New Jerusalem. There they raised their new child together..."*

I realized Danny wasn't asleep when he barked out "What?" He sat up so fast his head hit the bottom of my bunk.

"Why do you two find it so hard to believe that Mera and Bill found love?" Randy asked.

"Because," I replied, "for one, it's *Bill*. Really." I rolled my eyes. "And two, Mera can't have any more kids."

"Yeah," Danny added. "Mom can't have any more kids. Wait. How did you know that, Alex?"

"Um, we were in that church for two months, guy," I told him. "One night your mom asked me why I didn't ever have kids. I told her I never had the chance. And when I asked her why she didn't have any more, she told me she had her tubes tied after Jeremy was born. Hence, why this is fiction and Bill got creative."

"Her sterilization process means nothing," Randy stated. "Keep reading."

"And you read this whole thing?" I asked.

"Yes, hundreds of times. I'm waiting for you to get to the 'Oh shit' moment."

It took Danny aback as much as me because he commented on it before I could even open my mouth. "Randy, did you just swear?" Danny asked.

"I did." Randy held Phoenix close to him. "And I believe he's close."

"To an 'Oh shit' moment?" I asked.

"Yes."

I glanced down to the small computer thingy then noticed that Randy was staring at me. "Are you gonna sit there and watch me read?"

"Yes, while making sure I don't suffocate Phoenix. You're close. Read."

"Fine." I settled back again, feeling self-conscious. I promised myself that I wouldn't laugh while I was reading and, even if it surprised me, not to show it. I had every intention that I wouldn't give Randy the satisfaction of hearing me have an actual 'Oh shit' moment. Besides, there wasn't anything that could cause me to do that.

Was there?

I read...three, four scrolls of the screen later...

Bam. The ceiling wasn't high enough, and I repeated Danny's action only I sat up and whacked my head on the suspended ceiling tiles.

Randy grinned. "There it is."

Danny jumped from the bunk and stood. "Oh shit?"

I swung my legs over the edge, rubbing my head with the computer in my hand. I looked at a smiling Randy and at Danny.

"Oh shit."

We reveled in the 'Oh, shit' moment for quite some time. It actually wasn't clear at first, merely a guess on my part and a good one, at that. I wanted to read more, but obviously, more time had passed than I thought, because just as Randy began to explain things, they came for us.

The chopper was getting ready to go.

I swaddled Phoenix in a blanket, and I kept him zippered in my oversize coat, close to my chest. They provided me with earplugs for him, and were also generous enough to pack a small survival duffle bag for Beck, Mera and Jessie. Some water, some MREs, antibiotics, things like that. Another thing I was grateful for.

Danny and I were both nervous but excited. Randy stayed behind, not because he wanted to but because they made him. He was their assurance that I wouldn't take a jump off the chopper and keep running.

I liked Randy, but did they think I'd return for him? Okay, that was wrong. I would find a way to go back for him. If they kept Danny, that would be another story. But Danny had to go; he needed to see his mother once more. Six months would be a long time for him.

I would return to the ARC, not because of Randy, but because I made a deal. I gave them my word. I would go back. In a new world, just beginning over, I don't want to go down as the person who broke their word and caused the loss of a lot of lives, lives Phoenix could easily save.

The trip to the city was short. It seemed to take longer, but I think that was because we were anxious. It was the same pilot as the night before, and he made the comment before I even noticed.

"Sleepers moved."

Both Danny and I peered out the window. They swarmed as they did the night before, but seemed to be further away from the highway and the medical center.

"There's where we got you guys," the pilot said, pointing. "Give me a second to swing around and…" he paused. "Something's not right."

My heart sunk to my stomach. Surely, he saw they were dead. I looked at Danny; his face was pale.

The pilot hovered, and then I saw what he'd seen. I knew Danny did, as well.

The roof was empty.

The stairwell door was open, and no one was on the roof. Not even a Sleeper.

Had the Sleepers broken through?

"Can you pull back to look at the street?" I asked.

The pilot did, tilting the bird. "Nothing down below. No movement. Just a few Sleepers."

I was afraid to look at the sidewalk myself, fearful of seeing a splattered body or two. The pilot circled the roof again; there were no signs of blood. Nothing. Just an open door and an empty roof.

"Beck's black bag and gun," Danny said. "They aren't there."

I breathed out so heavily it formed condensation on the window. My hand cradled Phoenix. "Can you circle around?"

"Sir, the fuel—"

"Please?" I asked with sincerity. "You had enough gas to drop them somewhere, right?"

The pilot didn't refuse. I felt the bird lift up and maneuver away.

He circled the city then branched out. We hovered over the streets looking for movement, checking all rooftops. Our van still sat on the highway ramp as we left it.

We even went out toward the roads, the woods.

We flew around and searched for over half an hour until the pilot called it quits and we headed back to the ARC.

We headed back with our mission unaccomplished. The bombs would be going off. We would be locked away for six months without any answers regarding their circumstances.

All we knew as we flew away was that Beck, Mera, and Jessie were gone without a trace.

5
MERA STEVENS

My legs burned, my stomach twisted and my fingers ached. I felt physically beaten, worse than I had felt in a long time. My head was throbbing so badly I thought it was going to explode.

However, no matter how poorly I felt, I was alive.

We were alive.

I tried to rest some on the ride, but my head kept bouncing against the window or the seat; it didn't matter where I laid it. Jessie slept with her head on my lap, her arms cradling my legs. She was peaceful, completely unaware.

I was probably in a state of shock. No…I know I was. How could I not be?

The world had become a place that I had resigned myself to leaving. I had said my goodbyes to almost everything before I ever faced my death. As I stood there on that roof, I never would have imagined that I would go through the five stages of grief in four short hours.

I had stayed behind with my daughter. The little girl I adored had grown into a beautiful young woman. I called her my best friend, my lifeline. When she was born she became the air that I breathed, and I could not abandon her. I *would* not abandon her.

And Beck, well, he didn't want to abandon us. He was a quiet, complex man who was extremely levelheaded and smart. He was a career soldier who'd left his post for a new mission: the search for Jessie. He completed that mission with me, and I guess he thought that if it was going to end, he was going to end it with us.

He stood there waiting for his death as well, and he did so with such bravery. It broke my heart to know he was going to die, that he had a full life ahead of him, and he chose to end it with us. It was a sacrifice that he didn't have to make, and I would be forever in his debt.

I don't know what I would have done without him there.

When that helicopter lifted my entire being sunk.

Stages of grief commenced.

Denial.

No, it wasn't happening. We didn't just search and find Jessie, cure Jessie, find a way to the ARC to have them refuse to take in my daughter. I fully expected they would see it as some sort of mistake; that some soldier on the radio would tell them to turn around. I expected that helicopter to come back.

It didn't.

It was quiet, except for the eerie moans of the pursuing Sleepers.

Anger.

I got angry, for stupid reasons, mostly. Why didn't Beck go with them? Why wasn't Alex doing something? He was on that chopper; why didn't he fight for us? Why didn't he argue with them to turn around? Then my mind strayed to the silliest of all reasons: Alex would be raising my son. I liked Alex. He was a good man, but he wasn't Beck.

Beck was a father; he was reasonable. Alex would have my son inked up, let him grow his hair long. He'd have Danny dropping the 'F' bomb as if it were a normal adjective.

That anger issue was short-lived. It was based more on jealousy that I wouldn't get to see my son grow up. I wouldn't be there when he met his first love, had his first child.

I wouldn't be there.

I heard my son's voice in my head. He'd said to Bill early on, '*There are no atheists in foxholes.*'

That would be me.

The loss of life, watching my son Jeremy crumble in a horrendous death, left me bitter against a God who would allow such a travesty to happen.

While I ranted and raved how God had abandoned us, I realized that *I* abandoned God, and there on the roof, I decided to seek Him out. I prayed for the first time in a long time, a real prayer. I begged Him to help Beck, my daughter, and me, find us a way off the roof. Get us out.

The moans of the Sleepers only grew louder and they banged even harder against the stairwell door.

I gave up on the prayer.

I was a little too late in asking for help.

Grief.

I cried. It was a loud, full body sob, until I realized my daughter didn't need to see that. She was already confused as to what was happening. I knew she knew something was up; she sensed our sadness, but she didn't comprehend it.

I cried inwardly for the losses I had suffered and the losses my son would experience. I cried for a world that had turned into no less than a nightmare; for my daughter who would never know being a woman. I cried for Beck and all that he'd done for us.

After a while I realized no amount of crying, anger, pleading, or praying was going to stop the inevitable.

We were going to die. It would be fast, painless and we probably would only see a flash.

Acceptance.

I sat down on that roof and embraced the end.

Jessie sat between Beck and me, his large arms wrapped around us both. We said the things that needed to be said and looked to the sky.

We waited. We were ready.

It was time.

"Any second," Beck whispered, drawing us closer.

Nothing happened.

Now, when nothing happened, my body didn't feel an immediate sense of relief. Anxiety unleashed and my heart raced, blood rushed to my ears and every tremble my body made ricocheted against my eardrums.

Come on, get it over with!, I beckoned. I couldn't take it. We were there. I was ready.

Neither Beck nor I said anything; we just waited and stared. Finally, he looked at his watch.

"It's been over an hour," he said.

When he stood, I wanted to scream, in fact, I did scream. "No!" I grabbed his hand. "What are you doing? Don't walk away."

Suddenly I had this vision of Beck at the roof's edge and the flash occurring. He would turn and, instead of feeling him hold us close, drawing from his strength, I would only catch a glimpse of his face.

That was not how it was supposed to happen.

Beck held out his hand to signal 'hold on' and walked to the roof's edge. He looked for a moment and turned around.

"What's going on?" I asked.

"They aren't coming. The bombs, they aren't coming."

"What? How do you know?" I stood, helping Jessie to her feet.

"Because I have been in the military long enough to know that if there's a scheduled drop, it's coming, unless there's a delay or an abort." He drew up a look of perplexity, scratching his head. "How..." Then his eyes grew wide and he cocked his head. "Alex."

"What about him?"

Beck smiled. "Alex did this. He got them to hold off. Somehow, he did it."

"How do you know it was Alex? How do you know there wasn't a malfunction? Or Randy, or Danny—"

"My gut says it wasn't a malfunction. There is a backup plan. This drop was delayed or aborted. It had to be Alex. Danny is too emotional right now to think clearly. Randy is only focused on Phoenix and the future, but Alex...nah, come on, Mera. We know Alex. Do you actually think he'd calmly sit by and let them blow us up without a fight?"

My face flushed and I was immediately emotional again. "No," I whimpered. "No, he wouldn't."

"No." Beck shook his head and walked closer to me. "He did something. Caused a stink. Hell, I wouldn't even put it past him to threaten to take Phoenix or kill him if they didn't stop."

I gasped.

"I would threaten to do that if they wanted him that badly." Beck tilted his head. "Phoenix is their only bartering tool. But that doesn't matter right now." He placed his hands on my shoulders. "We were given, by some chance, more time. Now we have to think. Think." He gave a slight jolt to my body. "How can we get out of here?"

"Ink! Ma!" Jessie inched to us; she smiled, wanting badly to join the enthusiasm.

I laughed; it was nearly a sob. "Think," I repeated. Then I looked at Beck's eyes. They had a spark to them, a look of life.

For as much as we portrayed that we were ready to leave this earth, right then and there, it was evident that we weren't ready. We didn't want to die.

We stared at each other as though we were trying to do some sort of intense mental planning. How could we get out? Sleepers were like a river below us and relentlessly pushing at the stairwell door. Our bright moment of salvation seemed quick and short lived.

We were still trapped.

Then we heard...*music.*

At the same time and the same pace, both Beck and I turned our heads to the distant sound. It was several blocks away, but it was loud. Of course, anything would be loud. And it wasn't just normal music; it was 1980s pop rock.

Bon Jovi's *Living on a Prayer* will forever hold new meaning to me.

The music blasted and a huge bonfire erupted on another rooftop. It was as bright as the North Star.

As the music played and the fire burned, the Sleepers suddenly turned their attention to it.

It was a diversion. A huge diversion.

My body went from trembling and heart racing to feeling as if all the air had been sucked out of my lungs. I wheezed out a breath, raced to the edge of the roof and gasped. "They're leaving!"

Like a wave pulling back into the ocean, the Sleepers moved away from the hospital. The pounding and banging on the stairwell door slowed down and then finally stopped. The song played over and over.

Halfway through the fourth repetition, Beck ran to the other side of the roof. He enthusiastically spun around to me. "The parking lot over there is clear; we can get to the road! Maybe run for it, find a car."

I nodded, and then paused. "What about the stairwell? There are Sleepers in there, I'm sure."

"We'll face it. I'm positive there aren't as many. If there are, we'll shut the door and wait it out some more." He ran and picked up the black bag, tossing it over his shoulder as he grabbed his rifle. He also checked his revolver.

Leading Jessie and me to the stairwell door, he placed us flush against the wall behind the door. "I may need to use Jessie," he said. "They won't attack her. I'm gonna open the door, let them run through, then we bolt. Got it?" He slipped his belt from his pants.

"What are you doing?"

"Once we get through the door, I'm securing it to the railing. It won't hold for long, but it'll buy us time."

I understood what Beck wanted to do. He was hoping to hide us behind that door, open it, and those Sleepers that stayed behind would run onto the roof and we'd slip by.

It sounded frightening, but it was plausible. The longer the music played, the farther away the Sleepers moved.

Quietly, Beck removed the blockade from the stairwell door. My heart raced and I awaited his signal.

The second he opened that door, eight or ten Sleepers plowed through and raced onto the roof.

Beck sidestepped in front of the door, raised his weapon, slammed one in the face, then called out, "Come on!"

He yanked me as I held on to Jessie, and he flung us into the stairwell. It was nothing like it was when we first climbed up there.

Beck moved fast, tying his belt against the doorknob and then to the railing. I wasn't going anywhere without him. Perhaps I shouldn't have been so focused on what he was doing, because I was grabbed by a Sleeper. It grabbed my arms, and I felt its nails dig into my flesh. I barely had time to scream.

I pulled hard to get away but the Sleeper was too fast and too strong. It was a tug of war and I lost. He jerked and the momentum of the fierce pull sailed me forward onto him and we flew backwards down the staircase. I felt my body roll with his, tumbling body over body, hitting hard on every metal step until we halted on the first landing and my head cracked against the concrete wall.

Jessie cried out "Ma!" while I tried to get my bearings.

The Sleeper had my legs pinned and his mouth was agape, ready to attack. For sure, I believed I was losing my thigh.

Jessie jumped on his back, screaming and grabbing for him. He threw her from him. I kicked and tried not to not to draw any more attention.

Beck was fast. Jessie hit the stairs just as the Sleeper's teeth touched my skin, and Beck jumped down on the landing, grabbed hold of the Sleeper, braced his head, and in one hard jolt, snapped the Sleeper's neck. In what looked like a seamless move, Sleeper still within his grip, Beck extended his right arm, aimed his revolver and fired a single shot into the forehead of an approaching Sleeper.

For the moment, the stairwell was cleared. I knew it wouldn't stay clear for long—the sound of the gunshot would call those remaining in the hospital.

"You all right?" Beck asked, helping me to my feet.

"I guess. Yeah. Yeah. I am. Let's go."

Sandwiching me between him and Jessie, we rushed down the staircase, his left arm reaching all the way back to hold on to Jessie as he aimed forward with his weapon, leading us at a high speed down the four remaining flights of stairs.

It was like a video game. Doors would fly open bringing Sleepers toward us. Beck would try not to shoot; he'd fight them off and keep running with us.

He did, however, have to fire four more times, four more warning bells for the Sleepers.

The music was muffled in the stairwell, and I was beginning to think it had stopped, but once we reached the lobby, I could hear it again. It was louder and was probably the reason for very few Sleepers remaining there.

In the months that I had known Beck, I had never seen him fight for his life—for *our* lives—as he did in that hospital lobby.

He punched them, hit them, threw them, driven by an unstoppable force, a desire to live.

I could only imagine that he felt as I did. We were given a second chance and we weren't going to waste a second of it.

The best I could do was follow him and hold my daughter close as he determinedly cleared a path.

Once outside, the parking lot looked empty and that Bon Jovi song had never sounded so sweet. It filled the air instead of Sleeper groans and snarls.

Filled with adrenaline, I ran with Beck and Jessie across the parking lot, down the street and to the ramp where we had left the van.

One Sleeper followed us at top speed, but he seemed to give up at the bottom of the ramp, turning his attention to the music and running in that direction as if the music were much more easily attainable.

We caught our breath. To be honest I was wheezing and my heart beat so fast, I swore I was going to have a heart attack.

Bent over holding my knees, I could not only feel the pain from my fall start to creep upon me, but also a wave of nausea hit. I was going to vomit.

Beck leaned against the van. Jessie seemed fine. She was young and fit, and was only slightly winded.

I was still unable to stand straight I was so out of breath, and Jessie patted my back believing I was choking. I looked at Beck. "What now?"

His raised his hand, breathing heavily, then coughed. "Take a second and head out. As far as we can on the..."

He stopped talking, slowly stood up straight and looked. Was it a Sleeper?

Fearfully I turned my head.

About a hundred yards away was a truck. There were no lights on the highway and the moon was the only illumination, but I clearly see that the truck door was open. A male figure stood there waving and then headlights flashed off and on twice.

A moment's reprise and they did it again.

Off. On.

He was signaling us. He had to be the one who caused the diversion. He had to be. He'd saved our lives.

I looked excitedly to Beck. "You think it's Alex?"

"I'm betting." He reached out and grabbed my hand. "Let's go."

I giggled for an instant like a schoolgirl. I never thought I could be so happy. We were safe. We were going to make it out of the city before the bombs arrived.

Beck, Jessie, and I, we weren't going to die. At least not on *this* night.

The three of us, Beck holding my hand as I held Jessie's, moved at a quick pace toward the truck, picking up speed as we drew nearer. Our gratefulness and eagerness pushed us to the vehicle.

We were running then, and when we got to about ten feet before the truck, the figure stepped from behind the driver's door and into view.

"Thank God it worked," he said. "Thank God."

I had all of about ten seconds to comprehend. I looked over to Beck who stopped cold in his tracks with a look of shock. Jessie shrieked and raced to him.

Me, well, I don't know what happened after Jessie let go of my hand. Everything turned black and I passed out.

JACQUELINE DRUGA

It was the shock of seeing him.
It couldn't be.
But it was.
Pastor Michael.

6
MERA STEVENS

I thought he was dead. I *swore* he was dead.

I *saw* him die.

"No, you didn't," Michael said, handing me a bottle of water.

I guess they loaded me in the truck and drove off. When I came to, water was being rubbed on my face. We were off the road, and from what I was told, only a few hundred yards from where Michael picked us up. I was out only briefly.

"We can't stay here long," Michael told me. "We have to keep moving, at least until daybreak."

"I...I saw you die. I saw you killed."

"No, you didn't. You saw me get covered by Sleepers. You saw them swarm around me," Michael explained. "Imagine the scariest, freakiest movie you've ever seen. It pales in comparison to that moment in my life." He exhaled and stood up. "It still makes me shiver." Michael shuddered. "They reached for me, grabbed for me, their mouths were open and then...they just stopped. They stopped. They didn't move, didn't attack, they just stared at me." Michael lifted his head; his focus was elsewhere, his mind almost entranced. "Stared. Their eyes were blank, and they were looking at me as if they were trying to figure out what I was. I was on the ground and...I got up and pushed my way out. By the time I got out of the crowd, you guys were gone."

My hand shot to my mouth. "Why do you think that was?" I looked at Beck. "Beck? Do you know?"

Beck glanced at Michael for a few seconds, then to me. "No. I haven't a clue. How did you find us?" he asked Michael.

"Wasn't that hard." Michael stood. He finished his water and tossed the bottle. "When you left I had to find transportation, but I was safe in the church. The basement. The Sleepers never bothered me again." He shrugged. "I kept calling out on the other radio. Eventually Miles got a hold of me, told me where you guys were headed. I was already a day behind, but I figured if I didn't stop for the night, like you would, I might catch you. Plus, I figured, you know, maybe I was blessed and the

Sleepers wouldn't get me." He shrugged again. "I was smart enough to realize they were lifting you out. The Reckoning mentioned in the Doctrines would probably take place and the rush had to do with sealing the ARC. To me that meant they were burning out the Sleepers. Nukes, maybe."

"Why didn't you stay put then?" Beck asked. "Why put yourself in danger?"

"Alex said something to me once," Michael said pensively. "He said that he had everything he needs at his haven to survive, but he didn't have a reason. A person needs a reason to survive or they aren't really living."

Beck smiled peacefully. And then he added, "Amen to that, Padre."

"Indeed." Michael smiled. "In those two months, you guys became my reason. I'd rather die trying to live than to live without ever trying."

There was so much truth in his words that an agreeable solemn silence surrounded us. We had sat long enough and Michael reiterated that we had to go. He finished his story in the truck.

He told us how he had arrived too late. He saw the chopper leaving and sat on the highway for a while debating what he would do. He knew in his heart something was up because the Sleepers were like ants at a picnic surrounding one crumb. They still reached and cried for the hospital. Something or someone had to be where they were. So he went across town to another building, and using binoculars, he spotted Beck, and that's how he figured out we were trapped.

Then Michael did what he was the master of…he created a diversion.

We all debated on whether to head to Colorado Springs, the location that we were last told to go. But Beck and Michael felt it best to drive northeast, away from civilization, away from populated areas, away from the infected. To drive into isolation and wait, until at least The Reckoning was over. If, indeed, it still was going to take place.

I tried to rest on the drive, but my body started to feel the effects of the tumble down the stairs, scratches from the Sleepers, and the running.

I was exhausted but I was grateful and for some reason, I felt extremely at peace.

7
ALEX SANS

The feeling of failure radiated through my bones and swirled in the pit of my stomach forming a sickening knot. Sitting in the huge hollow Chinook chopper didn't help. It was designed to lift many people. We were just a few. We sat close to the front, and the chopper looked and felt empty.

Phoenix felt my anxiety. The little guy, who usually cuddled, squirmed and whined as I held him. I ended up handing him to Danny.

I told Danny I was sorry, but I honestly felt I couldn't apologize enough. There I was, this big shot with the big foolproof plan, and I had failed.

"They got away, Alex, trust me, I know they did. *You* know they did," Danny said. "Beck's stuff was gone."

"How?"

Maybe I needed someone else to say it again. This time it was the pilot, Tim.

"Sleepers moved," Tim said. "They moved far enough away from the clinic for them to get away. We're talking nine hours maybe? They got clear."

Danny nodded at me. "See?"

But I didn't and I didn't feel any better. Even if they escaped that roof, where could they go?

I couldn't believe I was worrying as badly as I was. Beck was resourceful, I knew, but I feared for Jessie and Mera in that world.

Part of me felt we were stronger as a group, safer. You know, the old saying, safety in numbers. But now we were separated. And we weren't just apart for a short period of time. We would be apart for six months.

I prayed they'd thought of us and left clues. They had to. Mera loved Danny and Phoenix. Surely, they would know we would go looking for them once the ARC opened again.

Or maybe they planned to be there when the ARC doors opened.

I didn't know.

I couldn't think. I was sick over the whole thing. I wanted to close my eyes and pretend it was all a bad dream.

It wasn't.

The nightmare was six months from being over.

I had to wonder if a dinner bell was going off around the ARC. I hadn't noticed how many were there when we left but it seemed as if every Sleeper for miles, hundreds of miles maybe, had congregated in the area surrounding the ARC.

How were we going to deal with them without jeopardizing those inside?

Nowhere was safe. The fence surrounding the landing area wobbled from the weight of them.

Through the chopper noise, I couldn't make out what Tim was saying on the radio, but he had a look of urgency. Readying to lower the chopper, Tim looked back at us.

"This is going to be rushed," he said. "Sleepers already made it through a lot of the fenced-in area. Once we're inside, they are initiating The Reckoning."

I don't know why but my heart dropped with a sickening feeling. I thought of Mera and Beck and Jessie and I hoped with everything I was that they were safe.

"I'm gonna set down. As soon as I open the cargo door, bolt for the lift. Got that?" Tim instructed.

I turned to Danny. "Let me have Phoenix." Danny handed the baby to me. "You run, you got that?" I told Danny. "Don't look back. Don't stop, just run. I'm good with the baby."

"I got it."

The chopper began to lower. When we were fifty feet from setting down the fence gave in and, like a tidal wave, the Sleepers flowed through. They fought each other, climbed over one another. It was disturbing.

Twenty feet.

The Sleepers ran for us.

I spun in my seat looking for the doorway to the elevator that would take us below. It was a good fifty feet from the heliport. There was no way, in my mind, that Tim could lower that cargo back door and safely allow us to run out. No way.

Ten feet.

The Sleepers raged our way in masses.

"We need some help out here!" Tim yelled into the radio and then I felt the helicopter jerk.

Sleepers had reached us.

"Sorry," Tim looked over his shoulder. "We have to get out of here."

Seriously? Leave the ARC? Don't go in at all? That was fine with me until I fel the jolt of the chopper when Sleepers leapt for us.

"This is Nomad84," Tim called into the radio, struggling with the bird. "We are lifting out. We cannot land. Repeat, we cannot land. Attempt to lift. What is your directive?"

It was apparent that Tim was trying his hardest to gain control. But the weight of the Sleepers hanging on the hovering chopper made it impossible, and this was a huge chopper. The blasting chopper blades with wind forces equal to an F2 hurricane blew back dozens of Sleepers. It was actually sort of comical, like a wind bomb, but there were Sleepers that still held onto the bird.

"Take Phoenix, Danny."

"What are you doing?"

Immediately following the transfer of the child into Danny's arms, I pulled my weapon and crossed over him to the cabin door just as a Sleeper slammed his face against the window.

I grabbed for the door.

"Alex!" Danny yelled. "What are you doing?"

"Hold him tight!" I looked at Tim as I grabbed the handle. "Get ready."

Tim nodded. I could hear him speaking into the radio, but I couldn't distinguish his words. He was trying his hardest to work between communicating, pressing things on the digital control panel, flying, and dealing with what I was about to do.

I readied my revolver and whipped open the cabin door.

The one at the window flew sideways and another jumped to the floor of the chopper. I kicked him then shot another. There were two more hanging on and I was able to pick them off with ease. Another reached up, grabbing my foot, and I don't recall if I unloaded on him or kicked. I may have done both. Everything happened so fast, it was a blur.

Once the chopper was free from the imbalance caused by the Sleeper attack, it lifted. As it tilted to fly out, I nearly fell to my death. I slid out of the small door and my feet caught air, but I managed to get a grasp and climb back in.

I swore my heart beat out of my chest and my breathing was erratic. In no way was I calm. I peered out to see every square inch of ground covered in swarming Sleepers. It was if they knew their death sentence was being delivered from that location and they were trying their damndest to stop it.

We were airborne.

"What now?" I asked Tim.

"We have to fly out into a safe zone. They already initiated The Reckoning. We have about twenty minutes. We should be able to make it into Nebraska, at least to the forest. That should be a safe distance. They'll come for us in a few days."

I looked to the black bag containing survival supplies we had for Beck and Mera. Little did I know when I packed it that it would be for me, Danny, Phoenix, and Tim.

I felt safe as we flew on, leaving Colorado Springs, leaving behind the multitudes of Sleepers, closing in on Denver and where I had hoped to find Beck, Mera and Jessie.

It was starting out to be one hell of a day. Nothing had gone as planned and I worried what else could go wrong.

8
RANDY BRIGGS

"Hawk Center, Hawk Center, this is Nomad84
Falling Angel
I repeat, Falling Angel
Grid to follow."

While I wasn't certain what that meant, internally I knew.

I was never far from the President or his men. I was the man from the future. I was there when the pilot reported a failed mission, that the 'forgotten,' as they referred to Beck, Mera, and Jessie, were not there.

The roof was empty.

I was also present when the pilot placed the very quick distress call and the President instructed that as soon as Alex, the baby, and Danny were inside, The Reckoning would commence.

I felt like a prisoner, a hostage, a bartering tool. Something inside of me told me all that would change the second the final radio transmission came in.

The landing area outside was overrun with Sleepers, making it impossible for the helicopter pilot to land. The pilot was given directives to fly north at least 150 miles and wait in a mountainous area.

About 50 miles into the trip, they lost an engine.

Falling Angel meant one thing: the helicopter containing Alex, Phoenix, and Danny was crashing.

At that moment, I began to question what this meant to me, all my work, all those years, reading and studying the Doctrines. Going back, searching for and finding the Phoenix child, making sure the baby got to the ARC unharmed and healthy enough to be a cure for the future.

All that was out the window now. The chopper went down.

Was it ever meant to be?

Were we as a people meant to become extinct? I lived in a time where, for the first time ever, the birth to death ratio wasn't scaled in favor of living.

There was no fear of overpopulation, because children died. They died every day. As routinely as people taking out the trash, they buried their children. I was born with a gene that made me care, a gene that crushed me when my children died.

No one understood that.

Well, my cohorts in this endeavor did. They were like me.

I recalled a conversation during the planning stages. We were Time Keepers, entrusted with the protection of the Time Vehicle and we were about to break that trust for our own good, for the good of humanity. Should the past be changed? *Could* the past be changed?

It was argued that if a man invented time travel to go back and save his wife, then he would never be able to save his wife because that was the reason for the invention of time travel.

A paradox.

My argument was, once you went back, you were no longer in the past but the present and everything was fair game, even if it meant the lack of our existence in the future.

My thoughts weighed heavily on me as I waited in the silence after the crash in that control room.

I kept going back to 'what was meant to be, was meant to be.'

Perhaps Phoenix, while depicted as some sort of savior of humanity in the Doctrines, was not intended to make it into the ARC to save humanity.

There were several emotions that swarmed around that control room: anger, sadness, regret.

The President listened to the military man state that they had a lock in on the location where the chopper went down and that the pilot probably did a roll on landing, which gave a probability of survival.

The President seemed relieved to hear that. However, there was no further communication with the chopper.

To get to them, they'd have to fly out again.

There was no way out of the ARC, not unless they initiated The Reckoning. After they had done so, and the area was semi-safe, in a few days they'd send a rescue squad for them.

Hopefully, they'd survive the few days.

I was confident in Alex Sans and that he'd see them through. He was the Survival Haven guy.

I wanted to hear more, needed to hear more, but oddly, I was escorted out of the control room and told simply that they would come for me when and if they needed me.

It wasn't until I was off the elevator and had walked down a long dark corridor that I realized something was up.

The hallways weren't like the ones I had seen already. They weren't new, clean, brightly lit. These halls were dingy, dirty, and rusty. My escorts opened a manually locked door that was heavy and solid, like a prison door.

For some reason I wasn't brought into general population. I was taken far from everyone. Hidden like a criminal or leper in no less than animal-like conditions.

There was a reason for it and I was certain I would find out.

9
MERA STEVENS

I hated the fact that Beck had disappeared, playing an apocalyptic hero of some sort when I really felt we needed him more.

Was that selfish of me?

I faced two things the next day not long after I woke.

One was The Reckoning. The sound of the explosions echoed across a dead land and it was hard to pinpoint where they had come from.

Before that, Beck swore he saw and heard a helicopter go down. Michael said he did too. I was sleeping. I had only been asleep for a couple of hours.

Beck, so convinced that he and Michael saw a chopper in distress, took off.

With no real direction, no radio contact, no way of knowing, he left. Before The Reckoning commenced.

It pissed me off.

Then again, that was Beck. That was who he was. He never really had any regard for himself. If someone else was in trouble, he went to help them.

He assured me before he left that I was safe.

It was a madhouse. The world had gone mad and Beck had gone off.

We convinced him to take the truck. I was with Michael, the Sleeper repellent, as we joked, safe on that ranch.

We had arrived just before the sun came up. The moon was still eerily bright in the sky, yet the horizon was starting to lighten.

We lucked out. Michael brought out a map and the main road took us to a secondary, then to a dirt road, which wound around into the mountains, ending at a farm.

I truly felt this would be home.

We found several Sleepers when we arrived. They roamed the property dining on the horses. The untouched horses ran amok, I suspect trying to stay alive. Six of them had been eaten already, and when we pulled up the Sleepers were devouring the horses' innards like a buffet.

Beck put them down. The Sleepers, that is.

To be honest I didn't know how I felt about that. Jessie was, in a sense, a Sleeper. If she knew me, if she experienced feelings, then how did we know other Sleepers weren't just trapped within their own out-of-control minds?

According to Beck, they were dangerous. Chomping on a heart of an animal, looking like something from a George Romero movie, they needed to be put down.

He calmly killed them all without flinching.

He took the night watch to make sure no more came. We were so far removed from the city or even a town that I doubted any would.

Until it was light, we camped outside. Michael lit a small fire for warmth and pitched a tent. The ranch-style home wasn't too far away and we'd see what it had to offer in the morning.

I had barely spoken to Beck at all since our escape from the city. He cleaned and dressed my wounds and checked me for signs of infection. I was doing well.

Jessie was exhausted and passed out in the bed of the truck before we even had a bite to eat.

Everything seemed surreal. I was still reeling with how to handle Michael, or rather, how to feel about him. In my mind and in my heart I had watched him die. Even the Doctrines stated he had died. Why was he alive? Why didn't the Sleepers get him? Maybe, just maybe, it wasn't the church at all that was protected but Michael himself?

Beck shrugged when I presented that thought to him. I was certain he had his own idea of why Michel was spared.

Michael was special, though. He cooked Spam over his little campfire. I thought of Alex immediately. I recalled that, at one time, Alex called it Michael's most endearing quality; not that the man ran a church, was a good Christian, helped so many people, but because he liked Spam.

Then again, that was Alex.

Deep in my heart, I knew he was responsible for the delay in The Reckoning.

The night before, just after we arrived, Beck was quiet, more so than usual, a man of few words.

I offered him a plate of food. He took a single bite then said he was fine.

It was quiet. Michael was dozing off inside the cab of the truck as well. I didn't know why he pitched a tent.

"Thank you," I told Beck.

"For what?"

"For everything. For being there, for staying behind, for getting us out of there."

He turned and looked at me giving me a peaceful smile. "You're welcome."

"Are you...have you given any thought to what is next?"

"No, but I do know we have to find a way to leave a clue where we are, or stay in one place. We need Alex to find us. He has your son."

"I know. What about…in a week or so, you head to the ARC?"

Beck cleared his throat trying to stop a laugh. "And where is it?"

"NORAD. We know this."

"We *think* we know this. We can try." He laid his hand on mine. "For now, let's take a breather and be grateful we're alive to watch the sun come up."

A groggy and half awake Pastor Mike murmured, "Amen to that."

Beck winked. "A blessing from the padre."

It seemed right that night. The moon was bright enough for me to get a good look around. The horses settled some; the ranch home looked empty and dark. It seemed like the type of place that would be perfect to wait things out.

In the morning, things were different. Despite the fact the ranch was untouched when The Reckoning took place, and despite his promise to return, Beck was gone and had been for several hours.

The feeling of ease from the night before was gone.

10
ALEX SANS

I was dead, a soul trapped in a lifeless body. There was no heaven, no hell, no otherworldly existence, simply the cessation of my body's life force.

I was unable to move; the air around me was thick and I could see nothing.

Was it really death? I started to fear that the Sleeper virus had somehow mutated and I was an animated corpse, that despite being in control of my mental faculties, my decaying body would eventually stand and ravish the living.

I was feeling hungry.

Damn it. How did it happen?

The pilot announced we'd lost an engine and we'd have to crash land. He promised he would do his best to land in a safe area, but silly me, I believed somehow, on a large hillside filled with trees, there'd be a safe place.

Unfortunately, not for a chopper the size of a Chinook.

Tim aimed for the small road below.

We had ample warning to strap in, but my concern was with Phoenix. I put him inside of Danny's coat, strapped my belt around the baby, told Danny to hold him with his life, then secured them both in the crew chief's seat.

It wasn't a general knowledge of aircraft that I knew to do that. Tim had shouted that the crew chief's seat was crashworthy and faced the rear of the craft. Upon impact, there was less chance of Phoenix ejecting away from Danny's grasp.

I strapped myself in the second pilot's seat and watched our descent.

It looked good at first, then we tilted as we neared the ground. We smashed belly-down with a fierce force, then flipped to the side and rolled for what seemed forever. I felt every bump in the road. My body was flung so far forward I could almost taste the windshield.

Then we careened into something. A hillside? A vehicle? I don't know. I only felt the crushing impact on my body.

That must have been when I died, because everything went black, dark and thick.

My ears were clogged for some reason and everything sounded like a fading echo.

"Alex! Alex!" Danny screeched. "Oh my God."

Phoenix cried. It sounded like a healthy cry.

They were fine, and that was all that mattered.

I waited to drift off. The buzz of silence became deafening, and I suspected at anytime a bright light would appear.

When I came to, if that's what I could call it, I started feeling guilty.

Was I one of the living dead?

My leg twitched and so did my hand. I moved slightly, and thought there it was, I was rising.

Then I realized I was trapped beneath something. A body. It was Tim the pilot. Something warm seeped against my leg, saturating my pants. It came from Tim, probably his final bodily functions.

I couldn't believe I was feeling that. It was a revelation for me that the living dead felt and thought.

My stomach growled again.

Damn it.

A bit more maneuvering and I was able to move Tim from me. He rolled with ease once I got the strength.

Tim wasn't a small man and suddenly, the air felt thinner, and it was easier to breathe.

I wasn't really breathing, right? I was dead.

It was a memory of living, yeah, that's what it was.

I had been pinned by the pilot's seat, no wonder it was dark. Thankfully, I'm not that tall or bulky and I could stand.

My head hurt, my legs were sore. Then again, I was pushing forty so they hurt anyhow.

When I was fully erect in the tipped chopper, I saw Danny through the window.

He stood about fifteen feet from the chopper, Phoenix in his arms, staring out into the distance.

The rear ramp was down and open, and even though the cabin door was above my head, it made my awkward exit through the back easier, especially in my state.

The whole bird was tilted and I walked on the troop bench until I slid out and dropped to the ground.

I was stiff. My legs didn't seem to want to move as I staggered around the chopper.

Rigor mortis had to be setting in.

Once I could survey the scene, I saw that our pilot had made an impressive crash landing.

The road was on a large hillside. How we didn't careen into the ravine below I didn't know, but we were hundreds of feet above the valley.

Danny stood looking out. I must have made a noise, because he turned.

The look on his face would forever be embedded in my mind.

He screamed.

God. How bad did I look? I kept thinking, '*Run, Danny, run!. Don't let me near you. I don't know what I'm capable of.*'

"Dude!" Danny said in shock. "I thought you were dead."

Was he stupid? Of course, I was dead. I was an animated corpse. Then I tried to speak, knowing full well that all that would emerge was a moan.

I opened my mouth. "Run, I'm...I'm..." I stopped.

"You're what?" Danny asked.

"I'm..." I looked down at my arms; they seemed fine, then I felt my skin. "I'm alive?" I laughed.

"Yeah. Did you think you were dead?"

"Um..."

Danny laughed. "You thought you were dead?"

"Didn't you?" I asked.

"Well, yeah."

I stepped closer to Danny. "Are you guys okay?"

"Not a scratch on us. You look pretty good, too. Just a cut on your head."

I stammered for the words shaking my head in disbelief. "W-why did you think I was dead?"

"Tim was."

"Did you check for a pulse?"

"On Tim. Not you. You were under Tim and you weren't moving."

"You still should have checked for a pulse, Danny, what the hell?"

"I was scared. I thought you were dead, I wasn't touching you and then...then I saw..."

"Saw what?"

"I saw it happen, couldn't miss it. I'm glad we're far enough away."

He pointed and I turned. They were still there, burned like a photograph in the sky. Glowing mushroom clouds, two of them. It struck me breathless.

"Oh, my God. They said they weren't using nukes."

"They lied," Danny said solemnly.

I took a moment, assessed my physical condition, and then took in the surroundings. "All right, we aren't gonna have a lot of time, just in case there's a wind shift and the radiation comes this way. Our best bet is to get deep in the woods, a safe distance from here."

"The bug-out bag they packed for my mom and Beck is still on the chopper."

"Good. Good." I nodded. "You wanna carry that or the baby?"

"The baby."

"I figured. Let me go check to see what else we can scavenge from there. Okay?"

"Yeah."

I backed up.

"Alex?"

"Yeah?" I spun around.

"Glad you aren't dead."

"Me too." With renewed vigor, I walked faster and more freely back to the chopper. I didn't have it in my mind anymore that I was a walking corpse. I climbed in the rear ramp; the bug-out bag hadn't been secured and lay right at the door. I needed weapons and I wanted to grab the first aid kit, maybe some flares and anything else I could find.

I wasn't on that chopper more than a couple of minutes when Danny called for me. Only this time his voice was loud, almost excited.

"Alex! Alex, hurry!"

I peered over my shoulder; Danny was standing with Phoenix at the back of the chopper.

I secured a weapon in my grip in case there was a problem. Leaving the other things behind, I hurried to the ramp and jumped out instead of sliding this time.

I hit the dirt road at the same time a truck slid to a grinding halt, blowing so much dirt in the air it created a cloud.

The truck was only ten feet away and I could hear the opening of the creaking driver's door.

The towering figure emerged and he was unmistakable. His face was happy and relieved the moment he locked eyes on us.

It had only been a day since I had seen him, but it felt longer.

I was so grateful. We…were so grateful.

It was Beck.

11
ALEX SANS

Out of respect for a brother-in-arms, we took the time to bury Tim, a good man whose expertise in flying had saved our lives. We were at a safe distance from the blast, it was time well spent, and it really didn't take long. It was good to see Beck. At first I thought, *'what are the odds?'*, then I realized they were pretty good, considering we were all in the same vicinity.

He patted me on the back like an old comrade and embraced Danny as if he were his own child. And Phoenix...man, when Beck saw Phoenix, the big guy's eyes watered and he brought that child into his arms. I swore Beck stopped breathing for a moment he held his breath for so long.

He said it would take us an hour or so to get back to Mera. I drove the truck with him giving directions. He wanted to hold Phoenix.

"How did you find us?" I asked.

"I saw and heard the Chinook go down," Beck said. "I could tell that he was going into a roll on landing, so chances were someone was alive. I figured the chopper was from the ARC. My gut instinct was they had a change of heart about us or were bringing us supplies. What the hell are Phoenix and Danny doing out here?"

"It was part of my deal," I told him. "They could have Phoenix for the six months but he never leaves our sight. In order to have him and us, they had to save you guys, meaning halt the bombs and lift you safely somewhere else. We went looking for you and you were gone."

"What gave you so much control?" Beck asked.

"The baby."

"Yeah, but you were in the ARC. They had you already."

I kind of turned from Beck for a moment and kept driving. "Do I stay on this road?"

Danny poked his head in between the seats. "Alex threatened to kill the baby," he announced.

Beck shot a look at me.

"What?" I asked. "I didn't mean it."

"Dude, seriously," Danny said. "You should have seen it. Alex had his hand over the little guy's head, looked like he was gonna snap his neck. Had this mean glare on his face. He did it right in front of the President."

"I really don't see where you had a choice," Beck said. "I probably would have threatened the same thing."

"Thank you."

"How long did you keep up the ruse? Did they know when you left that you were gonna kill him?" Beck questioned.

I opened my mouth to speak but Danny did first. "Man, it was funny. The President called his bluff and Alex folded in like ten seconds."

Beck laughed with a shake of his head.

"Will you knock it off, mister '*They taught me nothing in military school?*'" I snapped at Danny. "I folded and then I reasoned. The President listened. Bet he's pissed now."

"Yeah," Beck said with a nod of agreement. "Did you hear if the pilot sent a grid?"

"Yeah, so as soon as it's safe they'll come looking for us." I exhaled. "I don't want to go back, but Phoenix here is the cure, so we're gonna have to. Maybe we can talk Mera into going and we can hang with Jessie."

"My mom's not gonna leave Jessie," Danny said. "And for sure won't leave Beck after what he did for her and my sister." Danny reached up and grabbed Beck's shoulder. "Thanks, man."

"Speaking of which…" I said. "Beck, are you okay? I mean, that was scary for me, I can't imagine how it was for you guys."

Beck replied, "I tried to keep my cool for Mera and Jessie, but it was sobering and sad. Then, you know, it turned like a switch and we went with it."

"How?" I asked. "I know I got the bombs to be delayed, but the hospital was overrun. How did you get out?"

"We had help."

I peered to the rearview mirror to Danny, who perked with interest.

Then Beck did something I rarely have seen him do. He smiled an arrogant smile, one of those pretty-boy half smiles.

"What?" I asked him.

"Well, I know you read the Doctrines and all. I don't know how far you got or even if it is there, but…" The smile grew wider. "I've been waiting to tell you this."

"What? *What?*"

Beck grinned. I thought for a second he really shouldn't do that because he stops looking threatening and more like a teddy bear when he smiles.

"Who helped us. Spoiler alert," Beck said. "Pastor Mike is alive."

"Oh yeah?" I said with little surprise and peeked again in the mirror to Danny. "Well, big guy, I knew. Ha! We both did. I read more of the Doctrines while at the ARC. And, as they say, spoiler alert." I reached over and patted him on the knee. "The Doctrines state the Padre is the Son of God."

12
MERA STEVENS

"You saw the flash," Michael said. "You know what that means."

"But what if it was the other types of bombs and they were close?"

Michael's hands closed firmly on my upper arms. "No. That was blinding white light. But I couldn't tell you how far."

I whispered, "Beck."

"He probably took cover and that's what is taking so long. And Mera, we need to shelter up. For a few days, in case of radiation."

I crinkled my brow at that. He had to be insane. Radiation? If I didn't feel any rumbling of the ground, nor hear an explosion, that meant the bombs went off far enough away. How could we get hit with radiation?

There was a look on Michael's face that conveyed he was concerned and if he was, I would be too.

The ranch wasn't far, but it was still a trot, and leaving our things, Michael, Jessie, and I made our way to the house.

It was a beautiful home that exuded a sense of eeriness. It appeared dark even in the daylight. It had a long front porch, the kind I had always wanted.

The curtains were drawn.

I looked at Michael. "You think someone's here?"

"No. Not with Sleepers eating the horses. No. But, just to be sure..." he raised his voice and called, "Hello! Anyone home?"

Pause. Nothing.

"Hello!"

We waited. Nothing.

"Let's leave Jessie out here and go check; she's fine," Michael suggested.

I wouldn't say she was fine. Yes, she was safe from Sleepers, but not from her own state of mind. Jessie was like a child; I had to have some assurance. I thought about it a moment, checked out what was around. I spotted the garden hose on the ground next to the swing. Taking Jessie's hand I led her to the bench.

"Mommy's gonna play a game, okay?"

"'Kay." She smiled.

"I need you to sit, Jessie."

Her face brightened when she realized the bench swung.

"Yes, you can swing," I told her. "Stay here." I lifted the garden hose. I knew I didn't have to tie it, just secure it lightly around her, enough to hold her down. "You have to stay put."

"'Kay." She smiled, touching my hair as I secured her with the garden hose. I was brought back to when she was three and how infatuated she was with touching my hair. It made me smile. Just as I brought the hose around her, I caught movement.

The window was right behind the swing. While the curtains were closed, there was a slight parting, maybe an inch or so, enough to get a glimpse. I finished my task and inched behind the swing.

"What do you see?" Michael asked.

It was hard to make out. Whoever lived in the home had placed plastic over the windows, perhaps thinking it had been a biological attack. I could see inside through the small curtain gap, but the plastic gave a foggy effect. Despite that, I clearly saw two figures. It looked as though one person was seated directly in front of the window, the other on a sofa. With an airy exhale of disbelief, I turned and looked at Michael.

"There are people in there. They're ignoring us."

"Maybe they're dead."

I looked again. This time I saw movement and though it was dark, I could make out what they were doing. I huffed out a laugh. "They're alive. Eating off of TV trays."

"Why wouldn't they answer us?"

"Afraid."

Michael opened up the screen door and reached for the doorknob. "It's locked. Keep looking, see what they do."

I nodded.

"Hello!" Michael knocked. "I know you're in there. We mean no harm!" He looked over at me. "Anything?"

"Ignoring you."

"Unbelievable." He pounded harder. "Hey, we need help! We need shelter. Just for a few days. I don't know if you know this but bombs have gone off. Nuclear warheads. We have a young girl with us!"

They kept eating. "They aren't budging. Maybe they're deaf."

Michael tried another approach. "I'm a minister. I swear to you, we only need help." He hit his fist one more time.

I saw the person in the chair; their head jolted toward the door then returned to eating.

"They heard you." I said. "They're hoping we go away. They obviously are harmless or else would have shot at us."

"Look! We took care of those things out here. It's safe." He lowered his head then exhaled. "Hell with it."

"What are you doing?"

"Going in." He brought around his weapon, flipped it butt-side down and at the same time, he slammed the weapon against the doorknob while blasting against the door.

It opened, and Michael nearly rolled in.

"Stay here," I instructed Jessie and followed Michael.

I don't know how he stood there without vomiting everywhere.

The stench was unbearable. It blasted me the second I stepped into the long hallway. Immediately I brought my shirt over my nose. I couldn't pinpoint the smell as one single thing. It was urine, feces, vomit, and a sulfuric rotten-egg smell, laced with a sour presence.

Unbearable was an understatement.

"Breathe through your mouth," Michael instructed. He cleared his throat, and then coughed. A cough I was certain was an attempt to hold back a gag.

Breathe through my mouth? The stench was so strong, I'd probably taste it. No, I kept my mouth shut. The living room was immediately to our left. I have to say I was proud of myself for not throwing up, but I knew I would at some point. That was just me.

With his shotgun extended, Michael stepped cautiously into the living room. "Oh my God."

The stunned sound of his voice made me step forward with him.

There were two people. The woman was in the chair, the man on the couch; both had a television tray in front of them, watching a powerless TV.

They didn't acknowledge us. They kept eating. Their faces were smeared with blood both dry and fresh. Both of them had that 'dead' Sleeper look to them, pale and pasty. I don't know what that was on their full plates, but whatever it was, it reeked and was rotten. Maggots swarmed about, covering their fingers as they brought the food to their mouths.

"God forgive me…" Michael pumped the chamber on the shotgun.

For some reason that caught their attention and they stopped. At the same time and in the same movement they stood. As the man rose, I saw strands of fecal matter pull from his saturated pants, stretching like taffy from the fabric of the sofa.

They moved towards us. Heads tilted, mouths open, eyes wide. Watching us, studying us. Of all the Sleepers I had seen, these were the vilest looking. They looked different, somehow.

Processing the scene, fighting the urge to vomit, I stared at the face of the woman. Remnants of whatever she had eaten flowed from her mouth. The blast of Michael's shotgun jolted me out of my daze.

He had put the man down. I didn't see it, I heard it. When I turned to see the man's body sprawled ten feet away from the women, Michael shot the woman.

He lowered his weapon and his head. "We need to check the rest of the house. Maybe look for a basement. We can't stay in here."

No kidding, I thought. Using Jessie as my excuse, I poked my head out of the door, heaved in a breath of fresh air and told her I would be right back, reminding her to stay put.

I was good. I gained control. I lifted my shirt over my nose and entered the house again.

To our right looked like a dining room. "I'll go check the kitchen," Michael said. "You okay to go down the hall?"

"Yes," I told him, patting my revolver.

"Just shoot any Sleepers you find," he instructed.

Another nod. I didn't want to breathe. He moved into the dining room and I walked down the hall. The first door was a bathroom; the door was open, and no one was in there. There were three other doors, and perhaps one of them was a basement door.

I grabbed the first doorknob. The door was slightly ajar.

"Mera!" Michael called just as I stepped into the room.

I paused, readying to run back.

"I found a radio. A good one."

"Good!" I shouted back.

"It works."

I walked into the bedroom. And then I lost it.

Any battle I waged to keep my stomach contents from erupting was lost right then and there.

There was a woman on the bed, her age hard to tell because her face was so badly decomposed. Her head was tilted to the right, one arm crossed over her forehead. She wore a dress and her legs were spread wide open. Between them, on the bed, was a huge pool of dried blood. The placenta and umbilical cord, which looked like some badly discolored beef jerky, was still attached and it partially protruded from her vagina. In the center of that blood stain, between her thighs, was the child she'd delivered. A child stillborn into the world, it was evident by the missing facial features. Even decomposed, it was still smooth like an ivory statue.

The sight of the woman and child alone wasn't what caused the final straw in my attempt to hold back my regurgitation. It was the fact that her body, everything but her face, had been picked apart and eaten. Flesh removed right down to the bone in some spots. She was there like a buffet for the Sleepers, available for them to take their pick at her when the urge to feed hit them.

And that tiny newborn, the one who never got a chance to take his first breath? His precious little body wasn't immune to the hunger of the Sleepers either.

That was it for me.

Michael shouted that he had something. What it was, I didn't get because my ears rang, my throat swelled and with a mouth full of vomit I raced from the room.

I heaved out my stomach contents in the hall and after a brief reprieve, I raced for the front door.

Air. I needed air.

I blasted out the screen door full speed, hoping that the open air would somehow save me. Just as I leapt to the front porch, I saw the front end of the truck.

I gasped so hard in relief that I nearly choked on the remaining vomit in my mouth.

Beck had made it back.

I spat, wiped my hand over my mouth, and readied to call Beck's name but stood in shock at the next voice I heard.

"Why is this poor child all tied up with a garden hose? Now, that's bad parenting. At least use a rope."

Speechless, breathless, I slowly turned my head to the right to see Alex untying Jessie. Was I dreaming? Was it real? Did I pass out in the house and was somehow having delusions?

"Mera?" he called, tilting his head with a smile. "Did you just throw up again? I know that look."

I wasn't dreaming.

Releasing the biggest gut wrenching scream of happiness, I flew to Alex at such a force that when I connected with him, I nearly knocked him over.

"Whoa. Whoa." Alex put his arms around me. "Good to see you, too."

"You were part of saving us. I knew it. I *knew* it." I spoke rushed and out of breath. I placed my hands to his cheeks and kissed him quick then I did those mother-type kisses, quick, jabbing, over and over. "Thank you. Thank you."

"Wow, this is pretty cool." Alex laughed. "But, uh, I think your boy over there is getting jealous."

As fast as I hit Alex, that was how fast I spun around.

Danny.

Oh my God, Danny. I thought I'd never see my son again. And there he was standing next to Beck. I raced to him, throwing my arms around him. He mumbled my name, but I guess I was smothering him. I clenched him tight, and turned my head to look at Beck. Then I saw Phoenix.

Buried within the hold of Beck's huge arms, Phoenix squirmed. I smiled so widely that my face hurt. It was unbelievable. I didn't know who to hug first.

I had to catch my breath. Get my bearings. I brought my hand to Beck's arm and gripped it tight. "You amaze me. You know that?"

"You say that now..." Beck smiled peacefully.

"Randy." I peered round Beck. "Where's Randy?"

Beck bit his lip, Danny looked away, and then I turned to Alex. Alex had his hand on the back of his head with an apprehensive look.

"Oh, God," I gasped. "He's dead?"

"No. *No!*" Alex held out his hand and walked to me. "No. He's fine. He's safe. He's at the ARC. He wasn't with us. We came out to make sure you guys were safe. I'll see him when we take Phoenix back."

A squeak of the screen door brought Michael to the porch. I saw Alex and Danny ready to greet him, but Michael spoke before they could.

"You can't do that. You can't take Phoenix there," Michael said.

I turned around and looked at Michael. He was pale, he looked as if he had seen a ghost. My first thought was that he'd seen the woman on the bed.

Beck chuckled. "What do you mean?"

"If you want to figure out a plan to get Randy, you do so," Michael said. "But you can't take Phoenix there."

"Padre," Alex moved to him in a pacifying manner. "It's good to see you alive. Listen, Phoenix is the cure. As much as I would rather not have him there, for the future of mankind, he has to get the ARC."

"No, the Doctrines state that mankind's only chance is to get him to the New Jerusalem," Michael said.

"Same difference. That's what we're saying," Alex argued. "He has to get back to the ARC."

"No, he has to get to the New Jerusalem," Michael said passionately. "*Not* the ARC."

Beck moved to Michael. "Mike, isn't that the same place?"

"No," Michael said, "we were wrong. All wrong. Randy was wrong. The ARC isn't the New Jerusalem."

Alex asked. "How do you know?"

Michael pointed back to the house with his thumb. "Because I just spoke to them."

"The ARC?" questioned Beck.

"No," Michael answered with a shake of his head. "The New Jerusalem."

13
MERA STEVENS

The open kitchen windows provided enough of a breeze to ventilate the house and relieve some of the smell, but not enough. Alex sprayed air freshener every chance he got. We had to go into the kitchen because the radio was in there. That's where it was when we picked up the signal and we didn't want to take a chance that we'd lose that signal if we moved it.

"I heard them. I thought they'd keep talking," Michael said.

"What did they say?" Beck asked.

"Dude," Danny said, "I gotta get out of here." With Phoenix in his arms, he took Jessie's hand and led her outside.

Alex watched them leave then turned to Michael. "What exactly did they say?"

"Their words were, 'We are a second facility. We seek others and trust with the appropriate elements we can make a secure future.'"

I interjected, "The appropriate element, meaning Phoenix."

"I didn't say anything about Phoenix. It was a chance call. I asked where they were after the announcement ended and got nothing. No response."

"It could have been a recording," Beck suggested.

"What the hell is this?" Alex threw out his hands. "It's the ARC playing games."

Michael shook his head. "I don't know. I do know this, they began their announcement with 'This is the New Jerusalem. We are with people from Project Savior.' That, my friend, is what makes me think they are the real thing."

Alex heaved out a breath. "Fine. Pack up the radio and remember the frequency. We need to make a plan." He took another breath. "I can't take this smell." Alex walked out, taking the can of air freshener with him.

Beck and I followed, leaving Michael to pack up the radio.

Project Savior. That title stuck in my mind because Randy had used that name when he explained the virus to us. The virus wasn't supposed to be deadly; it was supposed to enhance those who were exposed to it, and those people from the future were part of Project Savior. The deliverers of the virus.

It made sense to me that if those with Project Savior made the virus, then with Project Savior's knowledge and Phoenix's blood they could create a vaccine and cleanse the virus. For some reason, I had a feeling that Beck and Alex would strongly disagree.

I walked around the house to the front yard. Alex had a map spread out on the hood of the truck. He was discussing strategy with Beck. Danny listened in, but Jessie seemed focused on something on the side of the house. I glanced around, didn't see anyone and called for her.

She dragged her feet in the dirt and reluctantly made her way to me, still looking back at the house.

I grabbed her hand and pulled her. She pointed.

Ah…the storm hatch on the cellar door of the home intrigued her. She knew that we'd looked for a basement.

By the time I returned, Beck and Alex had hatched a quick plan, and I was out of the loop. Of course, so was Michael.

"So that's it," Alex folded the map.

"Excuse me?" I moved closer. "What is it?"

Beck replied, "We both agree that the bombs probably came from Denver, maybe Colorado Springs. So if we move north through Nebraska into South Dakota, we should be good."

"So we're not hunkering down here?" I asked.

"This isn't a good place," Beck said. "You know that, and I'm sure we will be safe from fallout if we take that route. I'm not worried about the Sleepers as much as what occurred here."

"You didn't see those Sleepers, Beck." I said. "Something was wrong."

Alex laughed. "Mera, they're Sleepers. They're never right unless they're Jessie."

"No, they were different. I can't put my finger on it." I shook my head. "So the plan is to move north, and then stay or go or what?"

Alex looked at Beck and then to me. "I'll travel with you guys until we hear from the ARC. At that time, I'll go to them with Phoenix."

My mouth dropped open. "What about the New Jerusalem?"

"Mera," Alex said, "we don't even know if it exists. We know the ARC does, and we know it's a fully functional facility. They have to have access to Phoenix, not for the future, but for now. You saw those people in there." Alex pointed to the house. "That kind of thing can't be allowed to continue."

I laughed in disbelief. "And you think that they'll cure it that fast, so fast that they can keep anyone else from getting sick?"

Alex shrugged.

"Mera," Beck said softly. "Me, you, Jessie, and Danny, we'll head north, then maybe east for a while, organize and try to come up with a plan for the winter. Right now, we aren't thinking about the winter because it's so damn hot. It'll come around."

"That's why we should head east, to the New Jerusalem."

"What's out east?" Alex asked. "The what?"

"The New Jerusalem. They radioed."

"You heard Michael; they made no mention of east." Alex laughed at me; that irritated me.

"The Doctrines said east."

"Yeah, well, the Doctrines also said the padre was the Son of God. You wanna believe that, too?" He looked up. "Sorry, Padre."

I looked over my shoulder and saw Michael standing there with the radio.

"That's totally blasphemous," Michael stated.

"Well, that's what the Doctrines said," Alex replied. "I got as far as your rising from the grave, the St. Francis of Assisi thing with the Sleepers, or Palers as the Doctrines call them, and that's it. I didn't get a chance to talk to Randy because we left to find Mera and Beck."

"Well, that's ridiculous," Michael whispered.

"I'm beginning to think the Doctrines aren't all that prescient, and maybe they're a bit fictional. Just sayin'." Alex tilted his head. "Aside from saying you're the Son of God, supposedly Mera here and Bill hook up, fall in love and live happily ever after." He looked me.

"What?"

"I was expecting a response. I don't know, like a laugh."

"Um, did you *see* Bill?" I asked. "Bill was very handsome."

"Yeah, in a geeky way," Alex snorted.

"Enough," Beck held up his hand. "Bill's gone, so that is not even an argument. However, and no offense, Michael, I don't think you are the Second Coming."

"No offense taken." Michael replied.

"So with that in mind, we can't bank on the New Jerusalem being anything but the ARC," Beck said. "We don't know what's east. They bombed the west. We're clear here of Sleepers, but how far east did they drop bombs?" Beck shook his head. "I say we all go north and wait to hear more from this place. In the meantime, we'll plan on Alex taking Phoenix back to the ARC. Danny doesn't have to go with them."

"And I go back because I gave my word," Alex looked at me.

"I don't want you to," I told him.

"I don't want to go, either. But afterward I'll meet up with you guys with Randy and the baby. Beck's promised to leave a message when you move on. I'll find you.

Going north is best. Maybe you, Beck, Padre, and the kids will settle somewhere, and I won't have to look far."

It was when he used the word 'kids' and 'settle' that I turned my head to look for a glimpse of Jessie. She had wandered off again. She was standing next to the cellar hatch.

"Jessie," I scolded. "Sweetie."

"Ma!" She pointed to the hatch.

"Come on." I pulled her arm.

She pulled away. "Ma. No. Ma!" She pointed at the cellar door.

It took a second, but then her stubbornness registered. If I hadn't been so distracted by all that was going on, I might have noticed that she was adamant. Too adamant.

"Beck," I called then waved my hand to summon him.

It didn't take him long to come over. The others followed.

"What's up?" Beck asked.

"I don't know. But she's really focused on this hatch."

Beck stepped closely to her. "Jess, hon, what is it?"

Jessie only pointed.

"Is there something there?" Beck asked.

Then Alex arrogantly stepped forward. "Okay, now, really? Why are we asking her? Just open the damn hatch and show her it's clear." Alex reached down.

I wanted to tell him to stop, even though I believed myself that the hatch was clear, and my daughter was showing juvenile curiosity.

Michael muttered, "Might not be a good idea," but Beck stepped back, raising his weapon.

Alex confidently opened the hatch.

Did I expect anything to be in the cellar? A Sleeper maybe, after my run in with Ma and Pa Cannibal Kettle, but I didn't expect—nor did I think Alex expected—to be face to face with a shotgun.

I heard it rack a shell into the chamber.

Alex raised his hands. Beck charged forward aiming his gun. I grabbed for Danny and clutched Phoenix tightly.

I'd never heard Beck use such a harsh, soldierly voice. "Sir, lower your weapon."

"No, you lower your weapon," he said. "You're on my land."

I couldn't see the man in the storm cellar, but I could see Beck. He aimed and stared into that hole. It was a standoff.

"All right, all right," Alex intervened. "This isn't the OK Corral. No one is shooting anyone. Only reason we opened your little hideaway was to see what the girl was pointing at." Alex shifted his eyes to Beck then look down into the cellar.

"We aren't here to hurt you or steal anything; we just stopped by. We're leaving. We'll let you keep hiding." Alex showed him his palms and slowly reached for the hatch. "I'll close this, and we'll be on our way."

"Wait," the man called as Alex began to close the hatch.

I watched Beck lower his weapon, indicating to me that the man I couldn't see had obviously lowered his.

"Wait." The man's voice softened, and I watched a bare arm reach to hold open the hatch.

A moment later, surprising even me, the man emerged.

14
MERA STEVENS

He was sweating, and it was obvious that the sunlight bothered his eyes. He asked for a moment and walked to a hand water pump that was hidden by a garbage can.

He pumped a bucket, poured it over his head, then pumped some more.

"You all are welcome to help yourselves; there's plenty."

Water had never truly been a problem with us, especially at the church, but it had been a couple of days since I had actually washed or felt clean. We'd all appreciate a bucket of cool water to wash off the sweat and grime.

"I'll fill one up," Alex said without hesitation.

The man handed Alex the bucket with one hand and extended his other. "Sonny Richards."

Alex took the bucket. "Thank you for the water, Sonny." He promptly dumped it over his head.

Sonny flashed a quick, nervous smile. He was about Alex's age. He probably was blond; it was hard to tell with his wet hair. He had a familiar look to him; something about his demeanor was familiar to me, but I couldn't put my finger on it. I knew I would remember eventually.

His body looked strong and healthy, although not muscular. He wore a pair of tan work pants cut off around the knee, a wife beater, and boots without socks.

He walked toward the house and reached behind a bush, lifting two more empty buckets. He turned. "Anyone else?"

Beck and Danny each took a bucket.

Alex asked me if I wanted to dump a bucket over my head. "Um, no, I'll only use the water to wash."

"Wash Phoenix; he probably can use it." Alex sniffed. "I know he needs to be changed." Alex cringed. "Man, he reeks."

I ran my finger down the baby's precious face. "Is mean Uncle Alex making fun of you?" Then Phoenix smiled for the first time. My heart leaped. "Did you see that?" I asked Alex.

"Yeah. Do we even have diapers?"

"No," I answered.

"Eh, let him go commando," Alex joked.

Then Sonny said reverently, "Oh my God." He walked over to me. "I didn't even see him in your arms. Oh my God."

There was something about the way he said that. His eyes glossed over as he inched even closer to look at Phoenix.

"Is this your son?"

"Not biologically, but in every other way, yes. I was there when he was born."

"Alive," Sonny whispered. "He was born alive."

"Was this your home, Sonny?" I asked.

"Yes," his words cracked. "I was supposed to be a father by now. My son...he..." Sonny took a moment, cleared his throat and shook his head. His hand hovered over Phoenix's tiny head, and it trembled. "May I?"

Alex scoffed, "Sonny, she doesn't let anyone..."

Before he could finish, I had handed Phoenix over to this stranger. I don't know why; there was something about his blue eyes. I trusted him.

Obviously, this didn't sit well with Alex or Beck, who, dripping wet, walked over as if I had committed a crime. He stared at me for a bit then watched Sonny as if he were timing him. I had never before seen that protective, even jealous side of Beck.

Alex looked annoyed.

However, that tense moment, at least for me, was broken when I heard laughter. *Laughter*. It astounded me. Danny and Jessie were laughing, playing a game of water tag with Michael. Michael actually didn't look too thrilled about it, but he smiled when they laughed.

True laughter. Just like when they were kids.

For a moment, I was swept away. It wasn't the end of the world, it wasn't the apocalypse; I was in my backyard. At any moment, I would tell them not to forget about their brother Jeremy; he'd want to play. Then Daniel would come out and yell that they were gonna turn the yard into a mud bath, and they were wasting too much water.

I didn't hear anything else, didn't see anything else for that moment. Then I snapped out of it.

"Guys, come on," I called to them. "Don't waste water."

"It's okay," Sonny said soothingly, still focused on Phoenix. "I have plenty. In fact, in the house, if one of you wants to go in there, there's a nursery. We were ready." Sonny's voice cracked. "Fully stocked. The diapers may be a little small, but they're better than nothing."

"I'm sorry," I told him. "I am really sorry for your loss. I know. I lost my son, too."

He nodded and handed the baby back.

Beck heaved out a breath as if he were holding it the whole time Sonny held Phoenix. "I'll get the diapers."

Sonny instructed, "Second door on the left."

"Beck," I said as he stepped away. "Inside it's not…"

Beck held up his hand. "I understand."

I watched Beck go into the house. I thought of what he'd see, the woman on the bed, the baby. They were Sonny's wife and son. I felt sick. Did he know what had become of them? I was snapped from my thoughts by a single word from Sonny.

"Bathroom." Sonny said as if he had a revelation. "I have a toilet in my man cave. Actually a bathroom. It works if you take a bucket with you and fill the tank."

Now, *that* made me gasp with pleasure. "You have a toilet I can use?"

Alex asked, "You call the basement your man cave? Is that new, or did you always?"

"Oh, it was always my spot," he replied. "Just head down, you can't miss the bathroom; it's to your right."

I was thrilled. I handed Phoenix to Alex. "I'll be back." I almost skipped to the water pump. "Danny, can you carry two buckets of water down into the basement for me?"

"For what?"

I boasted proudly, "I'm going to use the toilet."

"Two buckets?" Alex joked. "You have to go that bad?"

"Ha. Ha. Ha. No, I need to clean up. Hurry, Danny! This is so great."

Danny murmured, "Oh my God." I only looked back once more before darting down the steps into the cold cellar.

Or, as Sonny called it, the man cave.

To be honest, I didn't even look at the basement when I got to the bottom of the stairs. I turned to my right, saw the gleaming toilet, and flew into the bathroom.

"Where do you want them?" Danny asked as he stepped in.

I looked around. The bathroom was enormous. There was some laundry hanging, probably left there to dry. A bar of soap was on the sink. I lifted and smelled it; I recognized the scent. Fells Naphtha. Potent. Perfect. At least for one day I'd smell fresh. "Leave one bucket on the floor and…" I lifted the ceramic lid to the back of the commode. "Pour one in here, please. Thank you."

I know I was rattled. I spoke quickly and enthusiastically. Danny didn't look all that thrilled; he didn't seem to understand. He poured the bucket in as I danced in anticipation.

"Thank you, Danny. This is so great."

"Mom, it's a toilet."

"Exactly. But I am still a woman, and in the apocalypse, this…" I pointed. "Right now this is a luxury."

He smiled, laughed a little even. "I'll leave you to enjoy your toilet." He walked out, pulling the door closed behind him. When he did, my whole attitude changed. Hanging on the back of the door was a mirror, and for the first time in months, I saw my reflection.

Michael's belief that Sleepers attract Sleepers had him placing mirrors everywhere facing away from the church, so the Sleeper would see its reflection and follow it. There were no mirrors inside the church. There were old religious relics and a few other things that we used, but our reflections were distorted.

Before me was my true reflection, the Mera of the Sleeper world.

I wanted to cry.

Every bit of heartache, every moment of pain that I endured had etched itself onto my face.

My eyes were dark; I had grown lines around my mouth. My face not only looked dirty, it was drawn and pale. What did I expect? Really? I wasn't high maintenance or a beauty queen, however, I always took pride in my appearance. I always kept my hair styled in an easy cut. Daniel loved my hair longer. I never went out without wearing some sort of makeup, even if it was just powder and lipstick. I was that, 'yeah, I think I'll get in shape' woman, starting a new diet when I gained weight. When I dropped a few pounds, I rewarded myself with ice cream or cake. I started exercise routines but never truly kept up with them. Still, despite the halfhearted attempts to keep fit, I was proud of my appearance and always tried to look good.

I did it for Daniel, because Daniel always told me that I was beautiful. Always. For all the years we were together, I never wanted to let him down. I loved the way he looked at me when I attempted to look special.

Sleeper-world Mera was not beautiful.

She was haggard, had lost weight, her clothing inappropriate for a screwed-up world. Nevertheless, Daniel would still tell me that I was beautiful.

How I wished he were with me.

Despite my best efforts, I broke down and cried. It had been a long time since I'd cried for my lost family. I buried it, tucked the pain inside of me. However, it exploded from me with this evidence of all that I had seen and felt. The world's pain, every mother's grief, I looked at it right there in that mirror.

And I sobbed.

My time in the man cave bathroom was not long. I knew we had to get on the road. I was in there long enough to use the bathroom and wash myself thoroughly, including my hair. Admittedly, I smelled like my grandmother's laundry. That wasn't a bad thing; it was one of those smells that brought back memories. I took a shirt that hung on the shower rod.

I heard voices in the other room, and I knew it was time to face them. I did feel a little better.

"She emerges," Alex said when I walked out. He was smiling as he looked at me. His eyes shifted to mine, and he took on a serious gaze. "You okay, Mera?"

"Yeah, I am. Thank you." I inhaled and noticed Sonny was packing. "Are you coming with us?"

"Yes, Alex and Beck invited me."

"That's great. I'm glad." I tried to add some enthusiasm to my voice, but everything had just hit me, and I was wearing down. "I hope you don't mind that I borrowed this." I pulled at the shirt. "I have no clothes. I kind of lost everything at the last place we stayed."

"No, I don't mind at all. In fact…" Sonny snapped his fingers and turned around. He grabbed a rubber storage container. When he did that, I realized why he seemed familiar.

It was his boots.

I stared at them. In fact, I stared so long that Alex nudged me and whispered. "Are you staring at his backside?"

"No," I chuckled sadly. "His boots."

"His boots?"

"Yes. Sonny? Were you a line worker for the power company or in some sort of electrical job?"

Sonny gave me a strange look. "I worked for the power company restoring lines. How did you know?"

Alex answered. "Your boots."

"I recognized your appearance," I said. "The boots clued me in. They're ASNI approved. God, I saw Daniel go through many of them." I looked at Alex. "My husband worked for the power company. It's weird…every career has a distinct appearance. You can tell a soldier, a fireman, a railroad worker…a power line guy… sorry. I'm rambling."

"It's fine," Alex said. "In all the conversations we had, you never mentioned that Daniel worked for the power company."

"I kind of tried not to think of Daniel. It hurt." I choked on my words, trying not to cry.

Sonny handed a pile of clothing to me. "Some of my wife's clothes. She was pregnant and stored these here. They may fit."

"You sure?" I asked.

"Positive."

"Thank you, I'll go change." I stepped back and watched Sonny for a moment. He continued packing. Alex helped by handing things to Sonny. Another person had joined our little group. We were almost complete with the exception of Randy.

I worried about him. Was he okay? Concerned for us? Were they treating him all right? I was sure they were. After all, Randy was special.

Very special.

I knew that no matter where we went, one thing was clear; I was not going to be satisfied until Randy was back with our little group.

I was convinced that everyone felt that way.

15
RANDY BRIGGS

The slow but steady trickle of water was the only disturbance in my room. The odor was rusty with a hint of mold. The single cot, however, was new, still wrapped in plastic. At least I had new bedding. My single bag of belongings perched on top.

They decided my fate long before they told me.

While it was extremely hot outside, it was cold in what I could only call my cell. They had locked the door. Despite the fact that no one said anything to me, I knew they wanted to keep me away from everyone.

I had done nothing. I realized there was anger regarding the helicopter going down, perhaps because they hadn't left Phoenix behind.

Hours passed. I was in that room without food, water, or contact for hours.

Finally, the door opened.

Slipping through the small space was my friend, Demetrious. He and I had travelled together with one other man to find the Phoenix child.

The door shut and locked behind him.

I wanted to run to him, grab him with enthusiasm, but I was taken aback by his appearance. He was thin, frail, and dirty. He looked exhausted, like he had aged ten years since I'd last seen him.

"My God, what happened?" I grabbed his shoulders.

He closed his eyes and lowered his head. "I'm sorry."

"For what?"

Demetrious exhaled and embraced me weakly. "May I sit? I don't have much strength."

I nodded as he made his way over to the cot. Immediately, I thought that something we had done had caused this deterioration in him, some ripple in time. If so, why hadn't it happened to me?

"Forgive me, I haven't eaten in days," he said. "I had to beg them to let me speak to you. My time is short. Every day I think it's my last."

I moved to him, crouching before him. This man of forty looked in his sixties. "What is going on? Are you unable to eat?"

Demetrious laughed weakly. "No. You'll eat. You'll get food, minimally, until they don't want you anymore. They need you for radio contact, I am certain, although they don't tell me anything anymore."

"Demetrious, what is going on?"

"I...I had to see you." He coughed. "I'm glad they let me. I want to say I am sorry. I am truly sorry. With everything I am, I am sorry."

I was confused. Why was he apologizing?

"Miles, the man from the prison," he went on, "he knew. He overheard. He and I talked. We tried to break contact. We tried to keep you away, but they forced our hands. They used Miles' people against us."

I was as impatient as I was confused. "Where is Anthony?" I asked of our third traveler. "You said he was here."

"I lied." Demetrious' head hung low. "He was killed in a Paler attack on the way to the New Jerusalem."

"On your way here, you mean?"

"This..." he raised his eyes, "this is far from the New Jerusalem. We picked up a radio transmission and tried to follow it using the wisdom of the Doctrines. They have the answers, the facts we didn't know. One of them was here. I spoke to him."

"One of those from Project Savior?"

Demetrious nodded.

"My God."

"He made the mistake of telling them everything. We tried to go to the New Jerusalem. This place got a hold of me before I could reach them. This place... here...we're prisoners on death row awaiting our execution."

"Prisoners?" I stood, catching my bearings. A part of me wanted to scoff at that. I had always known that Demetrious could be overly dramatic, but this was different. "You have to be mistaken. Exaggerating."

"Do I look as if I am exaggerating?"

"No. But what crime did we commit?"

He looked seriously at me with eyes that lacked luster. With a cracking voice, he told me, "We saved the Phoenix child."

16
ALEX SANS

There was still a lot to put together about Sonny. A lot we didn't know, like who he was, what was his story, how long he was in his man cave. However, we had time. Mera kept trying to pick information from him, and I had to remind her we needed things to talk about when we settled for the night, and to let it alone for now.

I didn't worry that he was a bad person. I had a good feeling about him, and I always trusted my gut. Of course, we had Mera as a backup who was adamant that power company workers were extremely reliable.

Sonny had a much better vehicle than the truck Pastor Mike had brought, a work van. We definitely needed a bigger vehicle, so we switched up. Sonny packed a little bit, not much. Some personal items. He filled some large water jugs and had a little gasoline left in a tank on the side of the house. We punctured the tank on the truck and drained that, as well.

Finding gas was not a significant concern for me.

When we originally headed to the ARC, our van broke down, and we abandoned it to run for the roof of the hospital. We left many things behind.

It wasn't until we transferred things from Mike's truck to Sonny's van that I realized our recently identified Son of God had grabbed some things from our abandoned van, a few bags, including my medical bag and the case of survival things I had brought along.

I was grateful because in there was one of those wristwatch Geiger counters.

Yeah, I carried them at my Survival Haven. It was a popular seller at certain times of the year.

I think Mike just grabbed random stuff, because he didn't take a thing of Mera's. Radiation levels were acceptable, and we were hundreds of miles away from the blast, so we made a stop to pick up some personal items.

There were one or two Sleepers meandering around the parking lot of the discount department store we chose. I pulled up front, and Beck went inside to check. It was clear, so he and Mera went in. I felt it best if the rest of us stayed put.

We waited in the van. Danny held Phoenix, who was getting a bit fussy. We were cramped in there, even though it was a bigger van. Our supplies and belongings weighed down the roof and filled all extra space inside. It was hot, though getting out wasn't an option.

The only one who seemed to accept everything was Jessie. She kicked her feet back and forth like a child, just sitting there staring out.

My eyes constantly darted as I watched the wandering Sleepers, the front doors of the store.

What was taking them so long?

Phoenix wailed; I knew he had to be hungry. I looked up to the rearview mirror. "Hurry up, Danny, and give him some of that Spam to suck on before your mother comes out."

"Okay," Danny said. "You sure it's cool?"

"Yeah. He doesn't have any teeth, so he won't bite any off."

Mike gasped. "What?? You can't possibly be serious. Give a newborn Spam?"

"You got another option?" I asked.

No reply.

"Didn't think so." At that point, I heard the loud sucking coming from Phoenix.

"Dude, he likes this a lot," Danny announced.

"See? I know what works." I returned to my watch, but during our Spam exchange, Bargain Store Sleeper woman was making her way closer to the van.

It was the first Sleeper I saw wearing a blue smock.

She walked toward us, her head tilted, clutching a candy bar wrapper in her hand. I watched her.

Within seconds, she was at my window. Her hands clawed, and her lips pressed against the window as if she were trying to eat it. I wanted to put her out of her misery, but I also didn't want to attract more Sleepers.

Her eyes, void of true color, stared at me, she watched me. She stopped clawing and biting and watched me.

"This is kinda creeping me out," I said. "Where are Mera and Beck?"

Mike replied, "They've only been in there half an hour."

"Christ...oh, sorry, Padre. Half an hour," I grumbled. It was like a train wreck, watching the Sleeper woman in the bargain store blue smock. She was quiet as she watched me. Did she think she knew me? There was a moment there that I felt sorry for her. She actually looked like she was going to speak, and then she shocked the hell out of me by opening my driver's door.

"What the hell!" I almost wasn't fast enough. I didn't expect it. I had never seen a Sleeper open a door. She struggled with me over that door, shrieking a noise that sounded like a dying cat.

"Two more are coming!" Sonny said. "Should we shoot them?"

"We can't," I said. "We'll attract more attention. Lock the doors."

"This is ridiculous," Mike sneered. "I'll handle it."

"Stay in the truck."

"They won't bite me," Mike argued.

"I'm not chancing it. Stay in the truck!"

I fought to close my door, wondering where she got her strength, while I argued with the padre to stay put. Just as I was about to lose the battle with the padre and the door, the Sleeper woman sailed to the left when the butt of a rifle smashed her in the side of the head.

Beck hit her again, waved an arm to Mera in the doorway then walked around the vehicle.

Beck had no problem with the older male Sleeper. He tossed him out of the way as if he weighed nothing. However, the younger one...man, Beck gave it all he had. He slugged the guy in the face and the man kept coming.

The size difference between Beck and this Sleeper was enormous, with Beck having the advantage, but the Sleeper wouldn't go down. Finally, after struggling with him, Beck gave up and shot him.

Mera got in, and then Beck tossed two large bags in the back, squeezing them in tightly. He walked around and got up front with me.

"Everyone all right?" he asked.

"What the hell took so long?"

"Don't ask."

I started the van to pull out of the lot. "What the hell did she get?"

Beck only glanced at me. "Don't ask."

I couldn't help it. I looked in the mirror. "Mera, what the hell did you get?"

Beck said, "I told you not to ask."

"Things," Mera replied. "I have nothing. Okay, I needed almost everything. Jeez. And I'm sorry, I love that store."

"And you picked *now* to go shopping?" I asked sarcastically.

She pouted. "I needed stuff, and I can't help it. Every time I go in that store I get more than I need."

I looked at Beck.

"I told you not to ask," he said.

I tapped my hands on the steering wheel and looked at everyone in the vehicle. Sonny stared out the window, Danny smirked, and Michael looked as if he enjoyed the fact that Mera annoyed me.

"Mera, dear..." I said as passively as possible, "I fully understand your need for *things*. However, two nuclear weapons detonated not far away, we're facing being exposed to radiation, and did you happen to notice when you came out of the store that we were being attacked?"

"I'm sorry," Mera said. "You said we were safe, and I didn't think there would be a problem."

I gave up. I dropped my head to the steering wheel then took a deep breath and concentrated on driving. The highway was clear. Sonny told us about a campsite that wasn't much further. He was sure it would be safe enough to hang tight and wait out a few days.

Shucking my annoyance over the shopping spree, I enjoyed hearing Mera gripe about Phoenix smelling like Spam, and then I focused on getting us to the camp.

I hoped that Sonny was right. We all needed to stop, settle in, and come up with a plan.

17
MERA STEVENS

My instincts were not solid evidence, yet with each passing moment, I felt there was something different about the Sleepers. They were…changing. Since the beginning, they had gone through phases, so was it inconceivable that they'd begin another stage?

I didn't share my thoughts, not yet. I would talk with Beck later when he and I had some time.

It was hot in the van, suffocating. Understandably, Alex wouldn't turn on the air conditioning, but even with the windows open it was unbearable. Not a single window opened all the way. They cracked open. It was not enough.

I tried to think of other things apart from the heat.

My mind went to the Doctrines, or Logan's Logs as they were originally called when Bill wrote them. As with the Bible, how much had historians and translators changed them? I wished that I'd read them during our two months in the church.

Michael was the only one who tried, and he never finished, though he said he'd gotten pretty far into them. I asked him about the part where he was called the new Savior, but he told me to let it go.

I couldn't see for one moment Bill Logan, the atheist, writing that Michael was the Son of God. It had to have been interpreted incorrectly. When I asked Alex about it, he said he only got as far as Michael's appearance at the New Jerusalem. When he asked Randy about it, Randy informed him that the Doctrines called him the Second Coming.

If the campground panned out as Sonny expected it would, we'd have plenty of time to talk.

Jessie's hair was soaked with sweat, and I was glad when Alex announced he was pulling over.

My poor, smiling daughter didn't complain. I wish I had her level of tolerance.

There was a gas station off the exchange before we veered east on the highway. Several stores were on the strip of road, but it was deserted. The windows in the station were broken, and it clearly looked picked through.

Where were the Sleepers? We had not yet hit a town that didn't have Sleepers. Then again, this wasn't a town. It was a small shopping strip in the middle of Nebraska.

The van doors opened, and the air rushed in. It felt like air conditioning although I was certain the temperature outside wasn't any lower than eighty degrees.

"The Settle Ridge campsite isn't much further," Sonny said as he stepped out. "Ten miles, maybe. Most of it is traveling through the woods, so it'll be cooler."

"Everyone stay close to the van," Alex ordered. "Beck and I just wanna fill up our cans. Sonny, you got this?"

Sonny raised his rifle in answer.

I watched Beck and Alex take the gas canisters, the hose and the little pump to remove fuel from the reservoir. It was something they did well by this point.

Shouldering his weapon, Sonny reached into the van, lifted a jug of water, poured some in the container and handed it to Danny. "Cool the baby down."

"That's a good idea, thanks," Danny said.

We stood by the van's open door, Michael keeping a vigilant watch.

Sonny turned to Jessie. "Hey," he said. "Put your head back like this." He tilted his head all the way back.

Jessie imitated him, and when she did, he slowly poured water over her head. She giggled, trying to catch it, dancing around from the chill.

"Feels good, huh?" he asked her.

"That is nice, thank you," I told him. After a few minutes, I saw Alex and Beck return, then I noticed an untouched soda machine by the side of the dilapidated gas station. "Oh look." I pointed.

Danny laughed.

"What's so funny?" I asked.

"They had one at the ARC, and Alex was excited about it too. You gonna ask if anyone has change?"

"No, should be easy to break in. It may be warm, but man, won't that taste good?" I smiled. Danny had Phoenix, Jessie was occupied with Sonny, what would it hurt if I went the fifty feet to the machine?

Beck spotted me and called out, "Mera, where you going?"

"Gonna get a Pepsi. I'll be right over there."

"Too far," Beck said. "Give me a second to finish and I'll walk with you."

"Beck," I whined and laughed at the same time. "It's right there. Jeez."

"I'll go with her," Michael cut in. "She'll be safe from any Sleepers with me."

"Padre, you're taking this 'Son of God' thing a little serious, aren't you," Alex said. "You keep saying that."

"I take offense when you make fun like that," Michael countered. "I am certain the Sleepers avoid me like poison."

Another laugh from Alex. "I'll believe it when I see it."

I waited for Michael to join me, and I told him to ignore Alex. He'd obviously forgotten that Michael had been overtaken by the Sleepers and had survived his encounter.

The soda machine was a bit farther than I thought, but the van was still in our sights. It looked like Alex and Beck were packing everyone back in.

Michael and I pressed all the buttons, hoping for some magical release of the beverages, but had no such luck.

Michael reached into his back pocket and pulled out a screw driver. "I'll pry, you pull."

"Sounds good." It dawned on me that, in all of our journeys, pulling that soda machine was probably one of the only physically useful things I had done.

"Almost there," Michael said.

Jessie called out, "Ma."

"One second, sweetie," I said, remaining focused on the soda machine.

As soon as Michael made some leeway with that soda machine door, there was a series of calls for us.

"Mom!"

"Mera! Michael!"

Before Michael or I could register why they were calling our names, we found heard the sound. It started as a rumble nearby, sounding as what I could only describe as a stampede, like horses on a racetrack.

Michael turned his head to look, and the screwdriver dropped from his hand. There had to be at least fifty Sleepers running full speed our way.

They were close. Too close.

"Get in the van!" I shouted to the others.

I couldn't determine whether they did or not. The wall of Sleepers blocked my view as they came straight for Michael and me.

He grabbed my arm, I think to try to make it to the store, but there was no time. Before we even made a move, they were on us.

Michael slammed me back first into the soda machine, tucked my arms to my chest then pressed his body firmly against mine, shielding me the best he could.

They attacked us.

I felt fingers reaching for me as Michael held me tightly. There was so much pressure, I swore I could feel each Sleeper as it slammed into him trying to get to me.

I could hardly breathe because my face was plastered to his chest. His heartbeat was loud and fast.

Michael was as scared as I was. Nevertheless, he held on, protecting me.

"Don't move. Don't speak," he whispered. "Still. Stay still."

He spoke rapidly, then his voice dropped even more, and I couldn't understand what he was saying.

The moans and cries of the Sleepers were loud. They pushed and pushed.

Oh, God. Make it stop! I screamed inside.

Eventually, Michael's strength would give out. He was only human.

Or was he?

I don't know how long we were under attack. It seemed like forever when I knew it wasn't long at all.

In the distance, muffled within the noise of the attack, I heard Beck's voice shouting, "Over here!"

Beep. Beep. Beep. The van's horn.

"Hey! Come on! Get me!" Beck shouted again. He was close to us, closer than the horn. He fired a gun. "Come on! You don't want them. They're Happy Meals. I'm an all-you-can-eat buffet. Come on!"

The pressure started to lift, bit by bit.

I felt the battering lessen until finally it felt like hundreds of pounds were lifted from my chest.

I still couldn't see anything, but I could hear that the stampede was moving away from us.

The van door slammed, I heard the van pull off with a screech of its wheels, and the sounds of running feet faded into the distance.

Michael moved away and looked at me. "You all right?"

I peered to my right to see the van turning with the Sleepers senselessly running in pursuit.

After a deep exhale, I grabbed onto Michael and embraced him. My fingers clutched him, and I didn't want to let go. "You saved my life. Thank you."

He pulled back. "We should try to go inside until they come back for us. The Sleepers will be back at full speed."

I nodded my agreement. As soon as we moved a foot from the soda machine, the door popped open, and cans rolled to the ground.

Not able to keep it in after the emotional turmoil, I coughed out a laugh. I crouched down, my fingers reaching for a can when I heard the van's motor. The van sped toward us from the opposite direction. Alex must have led the Sleepers away and lost them. I didn't see them.

Before the van screeched to a complete stop, the passenger's side door flew open, and Beck jumped out.

He didn't say a word, just took a single long stride toward me. He grabbed hold of me, almost crushing me in what felt like a grateful embrace. This surprised me—Beck never showed emotion.

"Oh my God, I thought I lost you. I thought I lost you. You scared the hell out of me," he said. "You okay? You hurt?" he stepped back.

"I'm fine."

He laid his hand on my cheek in one of the most natural touches I had ever felt.

"Good."

"Thanks to Michael," I told him.

"Yeah," Beck smiled. "Thanks to Michael." Then pushing me away, he did another thing that was totally out of character for him. Like an excited parent, out of breath, Beck placed both hands on Michael's cheeks, yanked him closer, and smacked him hard with a kiss to the forehead. "Yes, excellent job."

Alex cleared his throat. "I'm sure I didn't leave those Sleepers that far behind. Can we wrap up the post-traumatic reunion and head out?"

Beck opened the back for Michael and me. "Get in."

Michael stepped in first. I started to get in, then I paused.

"Mera, let's go!" Alex shouted.

I couldn't help myself. For all the trouble they'd caused, I just had to. I spun, bent down, grabbed a couple of cans of soda, and then I got into the van.

18
MERA STEVENS

I felt like an idiot.

Somehow, when Sonny had said campsite, I envisioned tents, not an operating mini community for trailers and campers.

He was right, though, it *was* secluded, two miles up a winding road to the top of a hill. It wasn't as popular as some because the lake wasn't as easily accessible.

There were four Sleepers there when we arrived. Sonny recognized them as people who hadn't left the camp on that fateful weekend when everything went to hell.

Alex took it upon himself to take care of them. After that, he decided the site was secured. Sonny's trailer was perched on a good lot, not far from the edge of the hill with a breathtaking view of everything down below. It would be perfect for night watch.

On the way from the gas station after the attack, my children held tight to me. Danny pressed against my side, Jessie had her head on my lap, and I held Phoenix in my arms.

I was told it was a difficult, emotional moment in that van when the kids saw the Sleepers crowd and surround us.

Beck said that Danny was freaking out, screaming, "Do something! Someone do something!"

And Jessie had cried, "Ma-ma! Ma-ma!"

When the van pulled off, Beck said they grew frantic, which made him even more emotional. No matter what he said or did, he could not calm them until they saw us standing by the soda machine. Then both of my children had screamed for joy. Beck said everyone in the van did.

Beck.

Yet another aspect of this situation that made me feel like a complete idiot.

What a selfish, self-centered person I had been.

Here was a man who'd broken the rules for us in the first half hour after he met us at the refugee center, who was our guardian and protector, who joined a journey with a group of strangers to find a teenage girl all the way across the country.

The same man who was prepared to give his life so that my daughter and I did not die alone on that roof.

Beck was a complex, quiet man who barely spoke and rarely smiled. For over two months, I had been with this man. He lost everything—his wife, his two children, one of which was a newborn. For all that he did for us, for all that he did for me…I never asked the names of his children.

I never bothered to find out who Beck really was. He didn't volunteer information like Alex, Bill, Randy and Michael did.

Why had I never taken a moment to ask him a question that would show I cared? I did care.

All of that hit me when Jessie and I were in the bathroom of Sonny's trailer.

The trailer was a pleasant one, and I knew I'd get a decent night's sleep.

She and I shared the shower, giggling like girls, just as we used to do when she was a child. I washed her hair, she washed mine. It was extremely easy with her intellect and demeanor to forget she was nineteen years old. When I looked at her, I saw a child. She was learning again.

We were combing our hair after we dressed when she said Beck's name. Not 'Ba', as she usually did. This time she added the hard 'K' to it. I smiled and thought about how Beck had worked with her all the time.

At the church, he was always trying to get her to speak. I paused and took in all that he had done for us when a knock at the door startled me.

"You guys all right?" Beck asked.

I opened the door. "Yeah, we're fine."

"Wow, you guys look good and smell fresh. Good job." He reached his hand into the small bathroom, stroking Jessie's hair from her eyes. "Look at you. Pretty. Pret-tee."

Jessie smiled. "Tee."

Beck laughed. "Close enough. Oh!" He snapped his fingers. "Alex scavenged about the camp. For you." He extended a brand-new unopened bottle of bourbon.

"Oh my God! Thank you." I smiled. "You'll have some, right?"

"Absolutely. But there's more. People in this camp liked to drink. I'll let you guys finish, but hurry, okay? We're all waiting to eat." He turned.

"Beck?" He stopped. "I know you showed me pictures, but what were your kids' names?"

He turned around and faced me. He seemed bowled over by the question.

I stepped to him. "I'm sorry I never asked you. I am really…really sorry, it was wrong, it was selfish, and I should have—"

"Dakota and Levi," Beck answered, and then cleared his throat. "Levi was the baby. Just born. And it's okay that you didn't ask. It's been really painful."

"And your wife?"

A pause. "Robyn."

"Can we talk about them one day?" I asked. "I'd like to."

"Yeah, we can. We'll find time, sit down, and talk about our families."

"I'd like that. And I am sorry. I really am...for all that you have done—"

"Mera," he cut me off, "I didn't do anything."

"Yes, you did," I argued. "You sacrificed, you put yourself in harm's way, you were there. We owe you."

"Everything I did, I did because I wanted to do. You, Danny, Phoenix..." He paused to give a small smile to my daughter. "Jessie. You guys are the only reason I keep going. You won me over with your lame excuses at the refugee center. Danny, when he was bitten, all I saw was a boy I wanted to help. And your passion for finding Jessie became mine. I didn't care if I lived or died until I jumped in the truck with you guys. So, no, I owe you. And...I've said too much."

"You said more than you have in two months."

"Nah. I talk, just not much. Finish up, we're hungry."

I nodded my agreement, realized he said all that he could say, and let him walk away. He was comfortable talking for a moment, but I could feel his uneasiness after he was done.

I exhaled, placed the bottle of booze on the sink, and grabbed the brush to finish Jessie's hair. "I'll be done in a minute," I told her.

She reached up, and her fingers touched the bottle.

"Yeah, that would be called Mommy medicine. Good stuff, too. Stuff Daddy wouldn't let Mommy buy." I lay down the brush. "You know what? It's been a couple of days." Lifting the bottle, I unscrewed the cap, sniffed it, and took a small sip. "Yeah, that's good stuff." Recapping the bottle, I set it back on the sink and finished Jessie's hair. I also reminded myself to thank Alex for thinking of me.

I should have known to expect Spam since Alex and Michael were in charge of making dinner. We all sat around a small campfire. It was relaxing.

I discovered Sonny's name was a nickname. His last name was Wilson. He told us that his father, like Alex, had a habit of calling everyone 'Son', young or old, so the nickname stuck.

Sonny told us his story.

The campsite was a place he and his family went every single weekend during the season. He was at the campsite opening and stocking the camp when the Event took place.

He and many others rushed home, Sonny especially worried since he heard that women were spontaneously giving birth. Maria, his wife, was seven months pregnant.

When he got home, the town was in hysterics over the death of the children. Hospitals were packed, traffic was jammed, and for a town of ten thousand, the chaos matched that of a big city.

His wife did not give birth to a stillborn, not then, anyhow. The baby stirred and kicked in her belly, and they believed they were spared.

In fact, the entire town, nestled in the mountains, believed they were spared by the massive Event that shook the world.

It was not until about two weeks after the Event, Sonny said, that the town started falling ill. One by one, they were sent into the elementary school gymnasium because they were showing aggressive tendencies.

While we were tucked away in the church, Sonny's town was in the thick of things. This didn't make sense to me. The whole world spiraled into a deadly Event, and one town was spared.

If Sonny's town had been spared that long, then others had to be spared, as well. At least, that's what Sonny thought.

"When most of the town started to turn, I loaded supplies and hunkered in the house," Sonny said. "I thought we were okay. My mom, father, sister and her family, my wife, we were doing fine. Then one morning, I woke up, and my whole family was pale. Even my wife, and she was still pregnant. She never had that baby."

I looked up at Michael. I didn't have the courage to tell Sonny about his wife and son.

"They stared at me with this eerie look," Sonny continued. "I knew. I knew they had turned. I couldn't do anything about it. I wasn't going to kill them, so I went below. I was there about a month when you guys showed up. Funny thing was I never saw a Paler on our property before that day."

I saw everyone's look of shock.

Alex asked, "Why did you call them Palers?"

"That's what the mayor in town called them. It just stuck. Why?"

Alex looked at all of us. "That's just what Randy called them."

"The Future guy?" Sonny said with a hint of disbelief.

Alex nodded.

"Well, I can tell you, I don't know why the future guy would say that, I can tell you why *we* called them that. Maybe the future liked the name Paler better than Sleepers."

"Maybe," Alex said, "at least the translators did."

Sonny tilted his head and looked at Alex. "I'm confused."

"Randy brought with him these things called the Doctrines," Alex explained. "They're like the Bible to the people of the future. Originally, they were called Logan's Logs. Later, in the translated Doctrines, these people called them Palers."

I added, "Logan's Logs probably wouldn't have called them that."

Sonny shook his head, his lips parted. "What were these Doctrines called?"

I answered. "Logan's Logs."

"Wow."

"What?" I asked.

"Nothing. Go on," Sonny said. "Tell me about Logan's Logs."

"Apparently they were written by a man who was with us," I said. "They describe the Event, our journey to find Jessie and our arrival at the ARC, and even beyond that. They've been translated, because there was no way he would have written that Michael was the Son of God. And he called them Sleepers as well."

"And where is the author of the logs now?" Sonny asked. "At the ARC?'

"No, he died a while ago."

"He died?" Sonny asked. "So, let me get this straight. Some guy from the future tells you he came back to save the baby because he is the only cure?"

Alex held up his hand. "Cliff Notes version. One thousand years from now man wants to make us better. They come back in time, release a virus, it backfires and creates the Sleepers, kills the kids. The virus continues to kill half the kids in the future. Randy, a product of the viral future a few hundred years from now, time travels here because the Doctrines talk about the immune child. He figured, save the child, save the future."

Sonny coughed on his sip of water then looked at me, ironically as I was filling my glass with a hefty helping of bourbon. "No wonder you drink so much."

His comment caused everyone to laugh.

"I'm sorry," he said. "That was rude."

"No, it's no problem. It's not the reason I drink this much," I replied. "I always did. I'm a functional alcoholic. At least that's what my friend Kelli used to call me." I lifted my glass.

Sonny stood. "So, Randy follows the Logs like they are a guide, but the guy who wrote them died? How accurate are they?"

Alex fluttered his lips. "Not very. All of us here are supposed to be dead according to the Doctrines, except Mera. And, of course, Padre, but I haven't seen him perform miracles or shoot fire from his fingers like the Doctrines say."

"You know," Michael spoke up finally,. "if I weren't such a God-fearing man, I'd call you an asshole, Alex Sans. The Doctrines make no mention of me shooting fire from my fingers. I read almost every word. I'll prove it. I'll go get my notebook."

"Your handy-dandy notebook like in *Blue's Clues*?" Alex taunted.

Michael growled his frustration and wagged a finger. "You…you…I'll pray for you."

Alex found pleasure in that. He laughed.

"Dude," Danny said. "Quit picking on Mike. What are you gonna do when you find out he is, like, a chosen one? You saw him save my mom. That shit was not normal."

My son's words caused Alex to become silent. He grabbed for my bottle.

"Please forgive me," Sonny said, "but it's really hard to believe. I know you folks have your reasons, but if the guy who wrote the Doctrines is dead, why are they still incorrect? If this time travel stuff is real, why didn't the Doctrines change?"

Alex sprayed out the booze that he had just taken into his mouth. "Exactly. I saw *Back to the Future*, I thought the same thing. The moment Bill died, theoretically, the Doctrines should have changed or disappeared all together."

"Yeah," Sonny nodded. "I mean, right now to us, time travel is fiction, but we all saw enough movies to know that those Doctrines would have changed. The moment that man died, the words would have changed. But the last you read them, were you dead?" Sonny asked Alex.

"Yeah. I was a goner."

"See? So it's hard to believe."

"That's because they're fiction," Beck said softly. "Historical fiction." He reached across to me, grabbed the bottle, and refreshed his drink. "When Bill wrote them, he wrote his own version of what he wanted people to think happened, not the whole truth. So then the words were translated and rewritten, and the translators changed it so much, it didn't matter what he wrote. It turned into fiction." He downed his drink.

Beck's opinion made some sense, but the whole thing was mindboggling. My head spun from the conversation, and I could only imagine how poor Sonny was trying to process it. We had been living with this information for months. He was learning it, and we didn't have anything to support our stories. We had to have sounded ridiculous to him.

We set the conversation aside for the night and moved on to something else, plans on what we'd do, where'd we go, stuff like that.

Despite the fact that I had been living with the knowledge of the virus, the Doctrines, and Project Savior for a while, I couldn't help but think there was a piece of the puzzle still missing.

A big piece.

❖   ❖   ❖

I dozed off, not for long, and I couldn't fall back asleep. It was close to three in the morning. Sonny was courteous enough to give my children and me the back bedroom. Phoenix slept between Jessie and me, with Danny on the floor.

I could hear movements on the roof and knew it was Alex keeping watch.

Quietly, I made my way through the darkened trailer and outside, calling out in a whisper to Alex, so he didn't shoot me.

With ease that impressed me, I climbed the ladder to join him on the roof of the trailer. The view was breathtaking.

"Nice, huh?" Alex asked.

"So beautiful." I walked to him. "May I?"

"Please, sit."

I did, dangling my legs over the side of the trailer as he did. "You can see for miles up here."

"Yep, very few clouds."

"How's the radiation?"

"Nil."

"That's good." I rubbed my hands together; it had chilled some. "So what do you think?"

"About?"

"Do you think we're safe here?"

"For the time being, yeah," Alex said. "You do know, we really are gonna have to find you guys a safe place to settle in and maybe wait it out until Phoenix and I get out of the ARC."

"You're really going back there?"

Alex nodded. "I gave my word, and you know what Randy said. Phoenix is the cure for the children of the future. Plus Randy is there. We have to get Randy. It's only for six months. I was out at sea longer than that."

"And you don't think the New Jerusalem is where we should take Phoenix?"

"I think if Randy's friend said the ARC is the place, then this New Jerusalem is a copy cat or something. My main concern is to get you safe and far away from the Sleepers."

"But the bombs—"

"I believe," Alex said, "that they didn't reach every place. They couldn't. I also know they concentrated more on this side of the country."

"So why can't we stay here at this place?"

Alex stared out then turned to me. "Not so sure this place will be safe for that long. The moment it gets cold, and we use any heat, there'll be steady smoke signals rising to the sky. I don't what place will be safe, really, any place that's not a fortress. The Sleepers...they bother me more now."

I sighed. "You, too?"

"Yep. When I first joined up with you guys, they wandered more than anything. You know. The biting, like with Danny, was rare. When we ran into them at the clinic, they were just...I don't know...testy."

I snickered. "Good word."

"Then they got more insistent, mobbing, chasing. Then they got violent. Even the violent ones I could deal with. These Sleepers, Mera..." He looked at me, dazed. "The Sleeper today opened my car door. They never open doors. She had a candy bar in her hand. And I saw what was in Sonny's house. They may not attack each other, but they sure as shit eat their dead. Plates, Mera, they had *plates* on TV stands..."

"I know." I closed my eyes. "It was freaky."

"No, it was downright scary." He took a sip of his water. "The transformation is too scary. If they're starting to think or act on instinct, they're gonna be a hell of a lot harder to control, because they outnumber us big time."

Think?

For as much as I felt the Sleepers were changing, that hadn't crossed my mind. I leaned more toward them just reacting to old memories.

"What do you think is going on with the Sleepers?"

"Don't know for sure. If I didn't know any better, I'd say," Alex heaved in a deep breath then exhaled loudly, "our Sleepers have awakened."

19
ALEX SANS

My father loved to fish. In fact, he loved it so much it led him to divorce my mother. I remember being in basic training and getting to make that two minute, once a week phone call. My mother had said, "Alex, your father went fishing."

"He always goes fishing," I'd replied.

She then added, "For good."

I thought it was a joke, and then I feared she meant he died, until she gave me the short version of how he just packed up and left.

Never once did she let on to me that it bothered her. She portrayed normalcy in her letters, and while I detected a hint of sadness, I never quite knew how much it broke her heart.

It devastated her. Twenty years of marriage, and he left without warning and moved on before I even got out of boot camp.

She was the only one that came to graduation. It was on the eve of her fiftieth birthday, and she and I celebrated both events. I was proud of her; she seemed as if she was doing fine.

I came home for a brief leave before training, went out with my friends, kissed my mother, told her I wouldn't be late, and while I was out…she took her own life.

Put a gun to her head and pulled the trigger.

She left a simple note saying, *"I'm sorry, Alex, I can't take the pain any longer."*

I never saw my mother as a weak woman, but to me, suicide was weakness. That tainted my view of women as being strong. To me, every woman who said or presented she was strong was putting on a front.

I also never forgave my father and never saw him again.

If he hadn't died in the twenty-plus years since he left, then I prayed he was a Sleeper.

I didn't think of my father often over the years until the day Danny and I walked the mile to the lake to fish.

Danny boasted he was an extreme angler, whatever that meant, and had learned from his father.

Daniel was a good man from what I'd learned. If he truly was a lot like Sonny, then I would have liked him.

My father never taught me. He gave me a rod, said to fish, and he went off in his own direction.

I learned, though. I'd put him to shame.

When we got to the lake, I saw what I believed to be one of the most bone-chilling sights, which confirmed many of my fears about the Sleepers.

In the middle of the lake was a boat; sitting in it was a man with a fishing rod. He wasn't casting, he just let it sit there.

Both Danny and I were excited at the prospect of another survivor, until I raised my rifle and peered at him through the scope.

"Fuck."

"What?" Danny asked.

I handed him the rifle.

"Oh my God. A Sleeper?"

I nodded. See, I had this theory, especially since visiting the prison in Washington and seeing the Sleepers in the yard. Those Sleepers barely ate, and had even looked as if they were dying. So my theory was that in a short amount of time the Sleepers would die off from starvation. However, Sonny's parents with their plates of flesh, the bargain store clerk with her candy bar, and the fisherman showed me that, even if they didn't have a real clue as to what they were doing, they lived instinctively.

The only thing that put a hole in my theory was when Fisherman Guy spotted us and flailed his arms frantically trying to reach us. He did that eerie growl and cry, which echoed in the hollow of the valley.

We both kept an eye out for more Sleepers.

The Sleeper fisherman had probably headed to the hills and, while out, transformed.

A few times he rocked his boat trying to get to us, but he didn't attempt to paddle. I wondered how long he had been out there.

We kept watching him, but we also cast our lines. The lake was full of fish.

Within an hour, we caught several bass, strung them up, and prepared to head back to camp. I lifted my rifle again, scoped out Sleeper Fisherman. He looked at us, and I fired. The shot was dead on but the sound rang out so loudly birds flew from the trees, squawking and disrupting any peaceful feeling.

I radioed that we were fine and on our way back.

Sonny built a cooking hole that seriously impressed me. Little smoke escaped it, and it buried a lot of the aromas.

We ate our meal of fresh fish and canned vegetables and talked about the situation. I probably would say it was the best meal I had since before the Event.

Beck was obviously tired of debating the Sleepers. "We established it wasn't a God-driven event. Therefore, not every place would feel it at once. That's my opinion."

"How do we know it's not God's event?" Danny asked. "Really, dude, seriously. Explain Pastor Mike."

Beck inhaled deeply though his nostrils, ate a bite of his food and said, "He's a Sleeper."

That did not go over well. Everyone thought he was joking, though I saw validity in his reasoning.

"Plus, adding to what Beck just said," I said, "they said at the ARC that not everyone walking around today is immune. The President is not; they sealed him in an airtight environment fast enough. Me, Danny and Randy are. We were tested."

"And going by Beck's theory," Danny said "it's probably in the air, and those out in rural areas like Sonny's family are taking longer to get it."

Mera gasped. "I may not be immune. I could become one, then."

"I doubt that. You're immune." I reached out, grabbed her leg, and indicated the deep scratches. "So is the big guy. He didn't break a fever with that bite."

"Bite? What bite?" Mera asked. "When were you bit, Beck?"

I answered. "When he was trying to save Bill. Never knew he was bitten, never flinched. It was a little one."

For some odd reason, Mera seemed to fade after being informed that Beck had been bitten, and she hadn't known. I saw all over her face that it bothered her. I wanted to say right then and there that she'd been wrapped up in Jessie, and all of us were crushed by Bill's death.

I almost said it, and then we heard the sound. It was a loud pop followed by a bang.

There wasn't even one of us who didn't jump up trying to find out where it was coming from.

"What was that?"

"I don't know."

"Where did it come from?"

"Over there."

Voices meshed. Me? I ran to the edge of the hill to look out.

I stood there, Beck right next to me, and spotted the source of the sound.

A school bus with a blown out rear tire was on the side of the road.

"Holy shit," I gasped.

"What are the odds it would stop right here where we are?" Beck asked.

Danny's mocking voice entered into the equation. "Pretty good if you guys didn't continuously rule out the God thing."

Both Beck and I looked at him. "Son," I said, "you need to stop listening to the padre so much. Grab a rifle. You're heading down with us."

I'd be lying if I said it didn't cross my mind that a Sleeper was driving the bus. I *had* just seen one fishing. It would not have surprised me.

Beck, Danny, and I took the hillside straight down to the bus and arrived about the same time that Mera and the others did in the van.

That pissed me off. They should have stayed put. We didn't know who or what was driving that bus.

No one emerged, and that raised my suspicions higher.

I signaled to Mera and the others to be quiet and motioned for them to stay back while Beck and I moved closer to the front of the bus.

It struck me as odd that all the school bus windows were covered by blankets or something, all but the front two windows.

I lifted my weapon and called out, "Hello! Anyone there? Are you hurt?"

No answer.

I fully expected that, at any given moment, a busload of Sleepers would pour out and charge us. I turned and motioned to Sonny to get in the van and get ready.

I called again, "We're harmless. We're a safe group with women and young people. Are you hurt?"

A voice emerged, a woman's voice. "Need you to look into the side view mirror real good, so I can see your eyes."

"I'm not a Sleeper."

"I know that!" she shouted back. "Haven't run into one that talks, yet. I judge a man by his eyes. Look in the mirror."

"What?" I chuckled . "Hell, Beck, you look in that mirror; you look more reliable than me."

Beck stepped forward. "Ma'am, I'm Major Beck of the United States Army, not that there's a military left. I can assure you that you're safe. We mean you no harm."

"Are there any of those Sleepers around?"

"None that we see or hear. We're armed, so you're safe."

"Hold on," she said. After a moment, we heard the bus door open.

We didn't see her at first. Then she emerged around the front of the bus, a woman in her fifties with short red hair. She held a rifle, but it wasn't aimed. The moment I saw her, I could imagine that she worked on a cattle ranch. Her appearance, her blue jeans, and her earthy appearance gave me that feeling.

She shifted her eyes around, looked back at our people, then nodded. "None of those things is around?"

"No," I answered.

"You a good shot? Fast?"

"Yes, ma'am. Big guy is, too."

"Good. Good. Need to remove some weight from this bus, so we can change this tire."

I couldn't figure out what she had. She walked around the other side and hollered. "Come on. Come and get some fresh air. Cool down."

Others? I thought. *More people?* I had turned to Beck, so he saw them first.

One frightened little girl peeked around the front end of the bus. She stepped into the road. She was maybe ten, but she wasn't the only one.

There was a boy, then another and another.

Before we could take it all in, more than a dozen children stood on the road by that bus.

A dozen.

It doesn't sound like a lot, but in a world where every child died and turned to dust, a dozen children weren't just a bunch.

It was a miracle.

Of everyone in our group, I was the only one who didn't experience, in one way or another, what happened to the children in the Event.

After seeing the kids, admittedly I was dumbfounded, shocked, and speechless.

Beck dropped his weapon.

Danny spun to Mera with a questioning look. Michael dropped to his knees. And Mera rushed forward.

She raced to the line of children, all of them looking as if they had seen better days. Her hand extended to the face of a little boy about eight, and then Mera dropped to her knees, Phoenix still in her arms, and sobbed.

She sobbed uncontrollably, her head resting on the pavement, her body curled in.

The maverick woman who drove the bus walked up to Mera, rested her hand on her head then kneeled to the ground next to her. A stranger comforting a stranger.

It was an emotional moment.

To believe that we lived in a world void of children, void of all young life with the exception of Phoenix, then to see that indeed, somehow, some way, we were wrong.

So many questions raced through my mind. Where had this woman found these children?

I wanted to ask, however, we were all in shock. Finally, Beck snapped out of it, picked up his weapon and asked, "Do you have a spare tire, ma'am, or should we try to find one?"

"I have one, thank you," she said. "And, please, call me Bonnie. It's under the bus, strapped on. Everything you need to change the tire is on the bus. I thought ahead."

"Bonnie," I said, "we have a camp at a big campsite, about a mile from here. Sonny…" I pointed to him, "and Pastor Mike can take you guys up there while we fix this tire. I promise you, you and the children will be safe."

"Oh, I feel that." She smiled. "He has trusting eyes," she said, indicating Beck.

I felt the need to apologize for the silence and for all of us acting strangely. "Please understand that we aren't usually this slow or strange. It's just the kids…"

Her head lowered. "Don't think for one second I didn't have the same reaction when I found them. Or rather," she laid her hand on a little girl's head, "they found me. I'd like to say we'll pass on the camp, let you fix that tire and be on our way, but the truth is, I need help. *We* need help. This is far too much for us to handle."

At that moment, Mera finally lifted from the ground. "We'll help. We'll help in any way we can."

Bonnie smiled and placed her hand on Mera's face. She reminded me a lot of my mother, feisty, beautiful, tough.

"I don't suppose any of you has any medical knowledge?" she asked.

"Alex does," Mera replied before I could speak up. She grabbed my hand and pulled me forward. "He's incredible. He saved my daughter and my son; he's our chief life saver."

I think I blushed. It wasn't all that, I just did what needed to be done. I liked helping people, which was why I had been an EMT.

Bonnie asked, "You have any medical supplies?"

"Some. Not much. Find me a clinic around here and I'll get what I need," I replied. "Is someone hurt? Ill?"

"I don't know how you'd describe it. Really, I don't." Bonnie took a deep breath. "Follow me please."

Convincing Mera to stay behind wasn't hard at all. She immediately walked to the kids, touching them, giving them hugs. I could only imagine what was going through her mind.

Beck and I walked around the front of the bus, following Bonnie. As soon as we walked through the doors, I heard a little whimpering sound. I turned around and looked at Beck.

"A baby?" I said to him.

"It is." Bonnie pointed.

Another woman was seated toward the back of the bus, her arm securing a basket next to her. A little boy sat in the seat in front of her. He couldn't have been older than six.

"Look, Mommy, two men."

"I know, Calvin, sit, please."

Bonnie introduced her; her name was Jillian.

"Jillian and her son were hiding out when I found them. They were nowhere near the other kids, but were in the same town where I was looking for supplies. I spotted a Sleeper. She was dead, bleeding from between her legs. I noticed the partial placenta."

Jillian picked up the story. "I heard the Sleeper cry out, but I was scared and stayed with Calvin. Then I heard the bus and ran for her."

"I made Jill stay with the kids while I followed the blood. I had a weird feeling, you know," Bonnie said.

Immediately, my mind flashed back to the Sleeper that had given birth to Phoenix. Was it possible, *another* Phoenix baby?

Bonnie continued. "And that's when I found the baby lying on the ground. I clamped the cord as best as I could. Lord knows how many of these Sleepers gave birth. I was under the impression that every birth was stillbirth."

"Me, too," I said.

Beck asked. "How long ago was this, Ma'am?"

"Two days ago. I can't believe he's still alive."

"So is he sick? Injured?" Beck questioned.

She answered just as my hand reached for the child who was in the basket. "No," she said. "He's an abomination."

I lowered the blanket exposing the tiny infant. Beck heaved out a breath; I felt it against my neck. I looked back at him then to the boy. I had heard Mera, Beck and Michael talk about it, but I hadn't witnessed it with my own eyes. Something they all called the Ivory Statue stillbirths.

Only this child wasn't stillborn. He was alive, but how, I didn't know.

From what I saw, his body was normal. He had a small mouth that moved and a tiny hole that could have been part of a nostril, and something that could have been an ear canal. Oh my God, it was so hard to tell. I didn't know. But the rest of his face was smooth, formless, as they described…an ivory statute.

No eyes, no ears, merely smooth.

I didn't even know where to start.

20
MERA STEVENS

Alex went with Sonny to the nearest medical center, which was thirty-two miles away. Bonnie told us that she had passed the place, and it wasn't Sleeper-infested, which made me feel better. Alex wasn't convinced that the child could breathe while he ate, and he needed items to create a feeding tube for the baby. It saddened me that they hadn't even named him yet. Bonnie's reasoning was that naming him made him more real and it would be all the more painful when he died.

I didn't quite agree with that.

Beck sectioned off the camp to let the kids play, and they did.

Jessie joined them. Not a single child out there was over twelve years old. How had they escaped the Event? How were they this fortunate?

I was overjoyed, yet a part of me was extremely sad. Why couldn't my son Jeremy be one of those few exceptional children not touched?

If there were those twelve, there had to be more.

Many things went through my mind while waiting for Alex to come back, in addition to my concern. I thought a lot about Randy, how he carried the Doctrines, and nothing was mentioned about other children, at least that was what Michael said.

Could those in our group who believed much of the Doctrines had been embellished have been right? That could be the reason they didn't change.

I wondered if Randy was all right. Was he was hungry, scared, lonely? Did he miss us? It had only been a few days, and I missed him with all my heart. We, as a group, had become such a close-knit new family.

The new woman, Jillian, was sleeping in the lounge chair and her son, the cutest little red-haired boy I'd ever seen, ran about, playing mostly with my daughter.

The new baby was sleeping in a Moses basket, and I felt awful for him. I hadn't touched him. Actually, no one wanted to. Then again, Phoenix was in my arms. I looked down at Phoenix. His hair was fair and starting to come in, although I suspected he'd lose it again.

His eyes were bright blue and staring at me, and he cooed and smiled all the time. He had progressed so much since we found him. I wished Alex would stop giving him Spam to suck on, though. He tried to put off that he didn't, but I knew.

Alex and Beck had grabbed a car seat from Sonny's house, brand-new in the box, and it had become quite handy when putting Phoenix down for a nap or feeding, not that I would ever strap him in the seat when we travelled. To me, the ability to free him easily in case Sleepers overran us outweighed the dangers of holding him in my arms.

I couldn't imagine trying to get him out of a car seat or the car seat out of the van in the midst of a Sleeper attack.

I moved the car seat nearer to Michael, who was peeling potatoes, cutting off the bad spots while listing to static on the radio.

"Can you keep an eye on Phoenix?" I asked him.

Michael looked surprised. "Wow, yeah, sure. Absolutely. Everything okay? Are you sick?"

That made me smile. "No, why?"

"You never ask anyone to handle him when you can."

"I want to spend some time with that baby. I feel bad for him. No one holds him. Alex said when he was fixing his umbilical cord, he seemed to enjoy being touched."

"The mother in you emerges." Michael smiled. "I think that's a great idea. Maybe with some warm, loving arms to hold him, he may actually figure out how to eat and breathe at the same time."

"I'm sure Jillian and Bonnie have tried."

Michael didn't respond, just looked at me.

"What?"

His eyes shifted to Jillian, who was sleeping, and then to Bonnie, who sat in a chair watching the children. He dropped his voice to a whisper, even though I was positive they couldn't hear him.

"Beck said they referred to him as an abomination."

When I heard that, my heart sank, yet, I found it hard to believe. "Maybe...maybe they are unaware of the true meaning of the word."

"Doubtful."

"Any luck with the radio?" I asked. "Anything from the other New Jerusalem?"

"Nothing yet, but I've not given up hope even though it's been three days."

"Keep trying." My words of encouragement lacked originality, but he knew I meant it. I left Phoenix in Michael's safe hands and walked over to the basket.

"Bonnie, can I hold him?"

She looked over her shoulder at me as if I had said the most disgusting thing. She hesitated and then said, "If you want."

I lifted the baby, keeping the blanket in place. The moment I looked down at him, my heart broke. He didn't look right from the nose up. I parted the blanket, peeking at his body. His skin looked dry, and the diaper that Alex had placed on him hadn't been soiled even a little.

Reaching down, I placed my hand on his little chest, and he curled into my touch. When he did that, a lump formed in my throat, and I brought him close to my chest. I wanted to cry. I felt my whole being tremble, and my throat thickened.

Sonny's trailer was cooler, so I took the baby there. All of the new things I'd gotten for Phoenix were in there as well. When I stepped in, Danny was sleeping on the couch.

Immediately, I started rummaging through the items I got for Phoenix and the newborn things we took from Sonny's house, placing things I needed on the countertop between the kitchen and living areas.

I found the bottle with the tiniest and newest nipple, filled it with some formula powder and room temperature water, and placed the bottle aside to dampen a washcloth. Sonny had generator power and warmed a tank of water in the morning for us, so the water was warm.

"Everything all right?" Danny asked, sitting up on the couch. "Something wrong with Phoenix?"

"This isn't Phoenix," I said. I placed the baby on the counter and opened the blanket.

Danny came over to watch. "Oh, man," he said. "Poor little guy." He reached for the baby's hand and the tiny fingers wrapped around Danny's.

I guess Danny brought it out of me. I don't know, but I just started to cry. *Poor little guy* was right. What a horrible start to such a hard life. To me, Phoenix was the golden boy, the child who had it all. This little guy...words could not describe.

Sniffling, I grabbed the cloth and gently began to wash the baby.

"He likes it," Danny said. "Look."

I washed the baby with my most loving touch, my tears rolling from my cheeks, dropping onto his little body. I wiped them away, then gently caressed him with baby lotion, and when I finished, I paused, lowering my head to him for a moment. After I swaddled him, I lifted him close to my chest and picked up the bottle.

"Bonnie said he can't eat," Danny said.

"I know." I wiggled the nipple near his mouth. "I don't understand why though."

"Because he doesn't have a nose. He can't eat and breathe."

"He has a nostril; he has to be able to breathe," I insisted.

"Alex said he wasn't sure."

"Alex is allowed to be wrong. I won't be satisfied until I see for myself."

Admittedly, I watched my son more than I watched the baby. I just cradled him so close to my chest, afraid to look in case he wouldn't eat. The moment I saw Danny's eyes brighten, I looked down.

He was taking the bottle and swallowing it. It didn't trickle from his mouth, nor did he choke or turn blue.

"Oh my God, Mom." Danny grinned and ran his hand over the little guy's head. "He's eating."

Many ordinary things had started to make me happy in this new life. Seeing the child eat was on that list. More tears flowed from my eyes. "You're eating," I said to him. "Yes, you are."

"I have a feeling he's gonna be okay, Mom," Danny said. "He has you now."

I smiled at Danny and then placed my lips on the baby's head. Holding him close as I fed him, I started to hum a song, trying my hardest to resonate it against my ribs so even if he didn't hear me, he felt my vibrations.

Danny said he was going to be okay.

I didn't know how much of that was true. The small, unloved, unnamed, newborn baby boy might defy odds and live, but to be okay?

The whole world was far from okay. And this newest addition to our group had far too many obstacles ahead of him.

"You've been crying," Beck said to me as soon as I approached him.

"I don't know how I should take that," I said. "Do I look that much of a mess?"

"Nah, you're actually pretty cute when you cry. Are you all right, though?" He leaned against the hood of an abandoned car, our lookout then reached down to the baby. "He looks different. Is he the reason you're crying?"

"I feel so sorry for him. I bathed him and rubbed lotion on him, fed him."

"How did that go?"

"He ate."

With surprise, Beck turned to me. "He ate?"

"Three ounces. Two more than a child his age should eat, and he burped. A good one, too."

"Wait. Bonnie said he wouldn't eat."

I motioned with my lips, looked back at the kids and at Bonnie and inched toward Beck. "Please keep this between us."

"You don't think she fed him?"

"I think she wanted him to die. I don't know. That's terrible of me to say. Please forget I said it."

"I can't, Mer, I think it too. But in her defense—"

"Her defense?" I echoed, appalled.

"Yes, Mera, in her defense. He has no eyes, no nose, and no ears. He has little chance of survival in this world without someone constantly caring for him. We don't even know her story, but we do know she's caring for a dozen kids already. That is a lot. Now there's a baby that needs attention. It's a cold, cruel world, babe."

"I know. But she has Jillian."

"Come on, Mera." Beck motioned his head. "She's hopped up on something. Probably hit every available drugstore to ease the pain of the world's end. Bonnie's doing this alone. Not saying she's right, but if she deliberately allowed the child to slip away, then she did it for the baby's sake, too."

"Why save him in the first place? Why cut the cord? Why do that?"

"It was the humane thing to do," Beck replied. "Then reality hit her. Again, her choice."

"She didn't name him."

"Her choice."

"Wow," I said.

"What?"

"You've been hanging around Alex too much. This right here…" I swirled my finger at him as I stepped even closer, "is all too reminiscent of that major I met at the refugee center."

Beck lowered his head. "I'm sorry."

"It's okay. It was a brief slip."

"So name him."

"I did. You're the first one I am telling. Don't make fun."

Beck threw his head back. "Oh my God, don't tell me that you named him Falcon or Hawk or Eagle."

"What? No. Why would you say that?"

"Because you named Phoenix after a bird."

"Oh. I guess I did, huh? Not this one. I named him Keller."

Beck opened his mouth to speak but paused, then blinked. "Like Helen Keller."

"Yep. She was blind and deaf and made an impact on the world." I lifted the baby. "And so will you, right, Keller?" I spoke to him then I raised my eyes to Beck. "What do you think?"

"What do I think?" He looked up then back down to me. "I think you're pretty special, and that baby is lucky to have you."

"I don't deserve that compliment."

Just then a rushed and panicked call from Michael made my heart thump to my stomach. He was running to us.

"Mera!"

"Oh my God, Phoenix, is he all right?" I asked.

"Huh? Yeah, why would you ask?"

"Because you're screaming my name. Where's the baby?"

"Danny has him. Mera...." he lifted a journal. "I was reading.... I was...did you name the baby?"

I gave a curious glance to Beck then nodded at Michael.

"Did you by some off chance name him Keller?"

It shocked me that he asked me, and it showed on my face. "How did you know?"

"So you did?"

"Yes. Why?"

"Later. We'll talk later." Michael rushed off.

Beck's eyebrow rose. "We'll talk later? You didn't tell anyone the name but me?"

"No, I didn't."

"That's weird."

"You think?" I turned and looked at Michael. How did he know? He looked frazzled, almost thrown for a loop. However, I did know one thing for sure. Michael had survived a seemingly inevitable death sentence, he'd found us again and saved me, and now he knew Keller's name. There was definitely something different about Michael, I just didn't know what it was.

I was convinced we'd find out.

21
MERA STEVENS

When Alex returned with Sonny, I was unable to tell if he was happy or annoyed that Keller was eating on his own. He was probably irritated that he hadn't tried to feed the child himself. However, he still insisted on starting an IV on the baby to rehydrate him.

We didn't have a clue how long it had been since he had eaten sufficiently, if ever.

I wanted to question Bonnie about it, but under Beck's and Alex's advisement, I let it go, especially after hearing the story of how she came across the children.

I guess I thought that she picked them up one by one, but we discovered that wasn't the case. About a month or so after the Event, around the same time that Sonny's town went south, Bonnie emerged from her hideaway to see what had become of the world.

She had been hiding at her brother's farm in Iowa when he turned suddenly after a trip into town and a run in with, as Bonnie referred to them as well, Palers.

Unlike Sonny, though, she'd had some contact with the New Jerusalem and then the ARC.

She told us that she was about to give up three days into her solo journey to find one of the two salvation centers, and that's when she met Ray.

She was running for her life in a town overrun with Sleepers when she saw the school bus and realized it would be a safe hiding place.

Little did she know when she boarded the bus that Ray and the children were already there.

She never did get much of the story from Ray. He, four other adults, and the kids had been on a camping trip with their church. He was in charge.

The Event occurred, and he stayed with the children because none of them had turned. They stayed at the campsite for a long time, but when they left and pulled into a town an attack occurred.

The children were still safe on the bus. Ray was the only adult who survived.

Bonnie told us the details after dinner, after the kids were sound asleep and couldn't hear anything. The night had cooled a little, and we sat in a circle around the small fire listening as she finished her story.

"I never questioned the children," Bonnie said. "Jillian wanted to ask about the adults, but they've been through enough. The past couple of weeks it's been difficult to keep them fed and hydrated."

I understood the problems she'd faced. Alex and Sonny had stopped for supplies, and I knew from speaking to them that we'd have to go somewhere with fresh water wells soon. We had gone from seven to twenty mouths to feed.

We were in for a long winter if we didn't find a safe place to live. I was hopeful we'd find the New Jerusalem. For some reason, I was worried when Bonnie went over the maps with Alex and Beck to try to locate it.

Beck asked. "What happened to Ray?"

"He was killed a few days later," Bonnie answered. "His daughter, Amber, was devastated. She still isn't talking. She's smiling more lately, though, than she did at first."

"You said you had radio contact with the ARC and the New Jerusalem. Did Ray talk to them by any chance?"

Bonnie nodded at Beck. "The ARC, yes, but he told me that they weren't aware of the children, and we should aim for somewhere else. He had a bad feeling. He was smart, really smart." She exhaled loudly. "When we found the..." she paused and looked at me, "found Keller, I wish Ray was around. He said he was a doctor. I wasn't sure what kind, but he would have been better than me."

"That's why we're grateful for Alex," I said. Grabbing my bottle, I poured a drink, offered it around, and Bonnie obliged. Jillian did as well, and that scared me, especially if Beck was right, and she was taking pills.

It was actually a pleasant evening. We were relaxed, but it also felt like the calm before a storm. It was probably my imagination, however, I kept my guard up. I learned all too well after the church incident that things could turn on a dime.

Michael played background music. He occasionally sang, which I loved because he had such a fantastic voice. I realized only after a while that it was all Christian music.

Sonny retrieved a beer for himself and Alex and out of courtesy offered one to Michael. It shocked me that he accepted.

I think it shocked Alex more than the rest of us because he choked on his beer. He laughed, but his eyes glanced across the fire. He seemed to be studying Bonnie and Jillian.

"So," Alex said, "this Ray guy checked out in a Sleeper attack?"

"Ah, come on, guy," Danny said. "Be gentle, man. Use some tact."

"That *was* tactful," Alex argued. "Just was curious. I mean, I was wondering what happened to their men."

I coughed out a laugh. "Their men?"

"Yes," Alex said. "Their men."

My voice squeaked in disbelief. "Their men? What? This isn't the OK Corral, the 1950s or even an episode of *The Walking Dead*. Their men? Please. They're doing okay without their men."

"Like you?" Alex pointed his beer bottle. "Padre here is a man. Without him, you'd be Sleeper fodder right now."

"I'll give you that," I retorted. "However, at that soda machine, I stood a better chance than you."

"How do you figure?"

"Michael wouldn't have covered you with his body."

Alex looked at Michael, who stopped playing.

"It's true," Michael said.

"Man, that's rough."

Beck spoke up. "Can we…can we change the subject? No Sleeper talk tonight?"

Sonny lifted his beer bottle. "Here, here, Major. We are in a safe location for the time being. Let's enjoy it."

"And on the subject of changing," Alex turned to Michael, "I know you're playing and singing for your Dad. How about changing up?"

At first, Michael appeared to be insulted. With a shake of his head, he looked up. "I'm not sure I remember much that I didn't play in church." He tapped his finger on the bottom of his guitar. "All right, I got one, I'll take you back." He looked at Danny. "You may not even know this one."

He struck a chord and sang the first line of the song, 'It's Only Make Believe.' "*People see us everywhere…*"

It was as though a valve released. Everyone, including Danny, because I was sure he knew the old song, sighed. We had been listening to Michael play Christian songs, and that was the only music we had heard in months.

This was a song from everyday life. It was a breath of fresh air. It wasn't the end of the world for a moment; we were just people sitting around a fire.

We weren't scared that Sleepers would follow the noise and come rushing out of the woods, because we hadn't seen one in days.

Bonnie laid a hand upon her own chest with a reminiscent smile. "My husband and I always played this on the jukebox when we were out. No matter how old it is, it's a great tune."

I smiled. "Daniel and I did the same thing. How funny. And we danced every time, no matter who was around."

"Nathan and I did, too. There was…" Bonnie's eyes lifted, and I looked up.

Alex was standing before me with his hand extended.

"What?"

"Don't make me feel like I'm back in the eighth grade asking Mary Jane Wymer to dance and she shot me down after I made it all the way across the gym."

"You only made it across the fire."

He wiggled his fingers.

"Alex, I don't think…"

He walked behind me, grabbed my hand, and tugged me to my feet, then pulled me a few feet away from the group. He gripped my hand as he danced with me.

I whispered, "Do you really think it's a good idea to dance with all that's going on?"

"I think it's a great idea to dance. It's been about three months, Mera. Are we supposed to mope forever? It's the end of the world as we know it, but you're alive. Your son, your daughter. You have Phoenix. And you guys didn't die on that roof. Sometimes, we have to celebrate life instead of canonizing death. Appreciate the positives, Mera, instead of feeling guilt over the negative."

"You trying to tell me something, Alex Sans?"

"Could be…" He stepped back, extended his arm, turned me once and snapped me directly to his chest. He whispered, "Or I might be looking for an excuse to touch you."

I giggled. I couldn't help it. That certainly wasn't something I had done much of lately. Alex made me laugh, and his breath tickled my ear. I stepped back away, ready to end the dance and thank him for that moment of normal life that I'd just experienced. Before the words left my mouth, I noticed Beck.

He looked sad. He stared, looking at his drink, lifting his eyes to me. I was caught up in his look, wondering where his mind was. He probably was missing his family, his wife. My expression reflected his as we stared at each other.

Alex, though, broke that with a hard kiss to my cheek.

"Thank you, that was nice," he said.

Alex returned to his seat, and Michel kept playing non-Christian music.

I moved to sit down again, and Beck finished off his drink and stood. "I think I'm gonna call it a night so I can relieve Alex of watch in a few hours."

Sonny spoke up, "You know, you guys have me as well. I can take a watch."

"I think Alex and Danny first watch," Beck said. "Me and you, second. Thanks. Good night, all." He bid his goodbye and headed to the trailer.

"Will you excuse me?" I said, and I followed. If Beck needed to talk, needed someone, then I was going to be there for him. I was selfish early on, but no more.

When I walked into the trailer, it was still. Jessie was sleeping on the couch. I didn't need to call out for Beck; he was standing over the cradle.

"Everything okay?" I whispered.

"This is amazing." He waved me over to him. "Come look."

Arms folded, I walked to the cradle where for the time being we were able to fit both Phoenix and Keller.

"I wanted to check on them," Beck said. "And look."

I peered around Beck to the cradle. Both babies were on their sides, Phoenix so much bigger than Keller, but I saw what Beck did, and it made me gasp. The precious sleeping babies were holding hands.

"They're meant to be brothers," Beck said. "There is something remarkable. They feel it, I feel it."

I grazed my finger lightly across their joined hands. "How am I going to give him up for six months? He won't know me when Alex brings him back."

Beck backed from the cradle. "Why don't you go with Alex to the ARC?"

"What? No. And leave Jessie?"

"You couldn't leave her before because we were waiting on a death sentence. You can now. She'll be fine. I'll take care of her. This baby needs you."

"And what about Keller?"

"I can take care of Keller. We have a lot more people now, Mera. We'll find a place, and we'll wait it out. Wait for you guys," Beck said. "I'd feel better if you went with Phoenix."

I shook my head slowly as I exhaled. "I can't go. I can't leave my daughter. Plus I don't really want to stay away from you for six months. You've become my rock."

He smiled gently. "I appreciate that. Okay, how about my plan B? What if when they call for Alex we tell them Danny is MIA after the crash. That way he doesn't go back."

"Why don't we say they are all MIA, Alex and the baby as well?"

He tilted his head. "You know as well as I do, Phoenix has to go back to the ARC. He has the cure in his blood. He has to go. As painful as it is for us, that call for him is going to come." Beck turned again to the cradle and reached his hand to Phoenix.

22
ALEX SANS

I heard the engine of the yellow bus long before I saw Sonny drive into the camp. He and Beck had finished the tire the day before. Since we had to get on the road, it was time to bring the bus to the camp. How else were we going to manage the trip with all the children?

I asked Bonnie where she was headed, and she didn't have a clue. She was just moving forward. I felt sorry for Sonny, Mera, Beck, Danny, and even Jessie. None of us had signed on for taking care of a bunch of kids. I sure didn't.

From what I witnessed, Bonnie did a good job, but the children weren't important to her. She offered to leave with the kids but stated she'd appreciate being part of our group.

Not to mention the news that Sonny brought.

"Eight. I counted eight," Sonny said. "Moving slow, but straight up the highway."

"Did they follow you?" I asked.

Sonny shook his head. "I climbed to the roof of the bus to take a look. I don't think they even saw the bus. But they probably heard it."

"Damn." I picked up my radio. Danny had ended up on the night watch and was still out there on the cliff. "Dan, you there?"

"Yeah."

"Any Sleepers?"

"None that I see."

"Keep me posted," I told him. "Sonny spotted several on the road."

"Got it."

I munched on a cracker while I looked at the map. How I missed the days of just being able to go on the Internet and find things. The original concept of the Internet was to survive a nuclear war, to keep the county running, but damn if it hadn't lasted longer than a week.

"Here's a thought," Sonny said. "I'm pretty well stocked at the ranch. Big Bear Grocery warehouse is fifty miles from here. If it hasn't been hit, we can stock up even more. My land is good. What about sending a cleanup crew to clear it? There's plenty of room there."

"Yeah, but we need to be secure. You saw how many Sleepers were at the Bargain Mart. I saw firsthand at the ARC that a fence doesn't cut it."

"What about a prison or a work farm? There's one in Kentucky that actually has a wall. It's a boys' detention work center."

"That might not be a bad idea. How'd you know about it?"

Sonny gave an embarrassed smile. "I grew up in Ohio, got locked up there."

"No shit? An Ohio boy? I'm from Ohio, too," I said. "Dude, what did you get locked..." I paused. "You know what? I don't want to know. New world. New start."

"Appreciate it."

I looked at the map. "Anywhere you guys go should buy you enough time to think of winter prep."

"You really are going to the ARC?" Sonny asked.

"Man of my word." I said with little enthusiasm. "Okay, boys' work center, good idea, we'll pitch it to the others. Any other ideas?"

"We can go high," Sonny said. "Like a skyscraper. But then water will be an issue. Underground is out."

"True. Unless it's one of those decked out government...oh, shit."

"What?" Sony asked.

"That's probably where the New Jerusalem is." I peered over my shoulder to Mike who was starting breakfast. "Padre?"

The padre immediately stopped what he was doing and turned to me, looking frustrated. "What's up, Alex, are you going to insult me?"

"What?" I laughed. "No. Hear anything from that place that claims they're the New Jerusalem?"

"No, nothing in days," he snapped.

"What's wrong with you?" I asked when I heard his sharp tone.

"Lots. Number one being the fact that I can't figure out how we are going to feed all these people all the time. Dinner, yeah, you and Danny plowed the fish."

I rubbed my chin and looked at Sonny. "Wherever we go, a lake is our number one priority. Maybe Mike here can turn a few fish into a miracle, and we won't have to worry about feeding everyone."

Michael bobbed his head. "Yeah, yeah, make the jokes. I'm really tired of it."

"You said you read the Doctrines," Sonny remarked. "Did you get to the place where you returned, and everyone thought you were the Savior?"

"I did. Long before we even left the church, I read it. I was pretty sure," he shifted his eyes to me, "not that I was the Son of God, but that I wasn't going to die. Then again, according to the Doctrines, I didn't die until we were almost at the ARC."

"How did they think you were the Son of God?" Sonny asked. "I'm curious."

"Yeah, me, too," I added. "Randy never really got to that part."

"Mera," Michael stated. "The Mother, as the Doctrines called her, convinced them. Apparently they were going to kill me. She said I rose from the dead, and they tossed me out with the Palers. When they didn't eat me, and they backed off, they were convinced I was there as the Savior. The Second Coming."

"Then what?" I asked. "What became of you?"

Michael lowered his head. "I was crucified."

"Oh my God." I stumbled back. "That's horrible. Really?"

"No, I'm lying, Alex," Michael said. "Consider it my payback for all the times you mess with me. Actually, I became a teacher and was highly regarded, I think. I don't know; it was weird. It read like fiction."

Sonny laughed. "Isn't that what you said, Alex?"

"Yep." I nodded. "Reads like fiction. I'm convinced someone made it all up and the interpreters made it sound Biblical."

"Along those lines," Michael said, "fiction, I mean. Something extremely odd has happened." He looked at me then Sonny. "You know how I took notes on the Doctrines? I have three notebooks. Well, I looked through them, and they—"

"Alex!" Danny's panicked voice rang through my radio, interrupting Michael.

I lifted the radio mic. "What's up, Danny?"

"Pack it up dude, seriously, get everyone moving. Like now. I'm on my way back to camp. We got Sleepers on the highway."

I laughed. Really, that showed his youth. "Dan, come on. We can handle eight Sleepers."

"Eight? *Eight?*" Danny asked. "Leading the pack, yeah. Try hundreds. Too many to count."

"Shit!" I told Danny to haul ass to camp and turned to Michael and Sonny. "Pack it up. Grab the radio, rustle up everyone. Grab all we can. Let's load the bus."

"If Danny just spotted them," Sonny said, "and they're moving at a steady pace, we have a little time until they get to the entrance."

"Let's not chance it," I replied and turned, fully intending to shout out a wakeup call to everyone.

Then we heard static.

"Alex Sans, calling Alex Sans."

The call came from Michael's radio.

"This is the ARC. We just lifted your voice. Come in."

I walked over to Michael's radio and whispered to him, "Go wake everyone. Hurry."

"Alex Sans, do you read me? Come in."

I don't know why, but I just stared at the radio. That was it. It was my call to leave. To take Phoenix and go. My heart sank.

"Alex Sans, repeat, come in."

I was reaching for the radio when the creak of the trailer door caught my attention. Beck stepped out, pulling a shirt over his head.

"ARC?" he asked.

I nodded and reached for the microphone.

Beck grabbed my hand, stopping me. "Mera and I were talking last night. Whatever you do—"

"Alex!" Danny came barreling through the woods. "The whole pack is moving pretty quickly. We have to pack it up or prepare for battle."

Beck looked at Danny. "Sleepers?"

"A ton," Danny replied.

I cringed. I had to buy more time. I couldn't just go to the ARC and leave everyone. I had to know where my group was going.

"Alex Sans," they called again.

I faced Beck. "I have to answer. How do I buy time?"

"I don't know. I'll get things packed, but whatever you do, please, tell them Danny is MIA with the pilot."

"I had planned on that." Finally, I lifted the radio. "This is Alex Sans. Look, I've got to move out right now; I have a major Sleeper attack headed my way."

"Sans, we located the chopper wreckage. We have men in the air. Give us your location and we can give you air support. Do you have the Phoenix child and the teenager?"

"Danny is missing. He was thrown from the wreckage when the chopper crashed." I said.

Bonnie laid her hand firmly on mine, shaking her head.

I released the button so she couldn't be heard. "What?"

"Ray was so adamant about the ARC," she said. "As if he knew. Don't you have one of your people there? Speak to him first, before you say anything further. Okay?"

I nodded. "Is my friend, Randy Briggs with you?" I asked on the radio.

"Yes," the ARC person replied.

"I'd like to speak to him before I say anything else, just to make sure he's all right."

"Hold please."

I took a deep breath, snapped my fingers to get everyone moving. At that moment, everyone scurried. The children moved about quickly as if it were a familiar routine for them to escape from Sleepers.

I looked at the faces that surrounded me. Mera had emerged holding Phoenix, Jessie holding Keller, Beck.

Michael and Sonny rushed about gathered our things.

"Alex," Randy's voice spoke over the radio. "Alex, are you there?"

"Randy. Man, are you okay?"

"Yes." He paused. "Alex, is the baby with you?"

I hesitated, moistened my lips, finally answering after a brief pause. If anyone did, Randy knew the importance of getting Phoenix to the ARC. "Yeah, he's fine. He's good. We're together, and with new people."

"Good. Alex, they need your location," Randy said. "A county, city, somewhere they can find you. Can you give that to them?"

I hadn't a clue how to explain where we were, so I turned to Sonny. His finger pointed to the map.

"Yeah, I can."

"Good," Randy said. "Then I want you to...run."

My heart dropped.

His voice picked up speed. "Run, Alex, take the baby and go. Run. Hide. Whatever you do, don't let Phoenix—"

He was cut off.

End of transmission.

I didn't try to call back in case they were tracking the signal.

As best as we could, as fast as we could, we would follow Randy's behest.

We would run.

From the Sleepers and from whatever it was that Randy feared.

23
RANDY BRIGGS

The butt of the M-4 not only silenced me in the midst of my sentence, it broke my front tooth.

My warning was heeded; at least, I believed it was. Alex Sans was a smart man. All he needed to hear from me was the word 'run.'

I expected to die in the moments after that radio call. I was supposed to get the information from Alex, find out where they were, and set him up as Demetrious had done to me.

However, I couldn't.

Alex was my friend. He was a remarkable man with extraordinary instincts and abilities. If anyone could hide and protect the Phoenix child, he could.

They used my life against me. Told me that they would kill me if I didn't get the information, that my life meant nothing, but what did I care? I would perhaps be born again.

That's what I thought.

They couldn't use Demetrious. He died within two hours after he visited me in my prison room. His body stayed there, reeking of death, for nearly three days.

They came for him when they believed the heard Alex's voice on the radio.

Actually, they came for me and only removed his body.

They needed and wanted the Phoenix child.

I found out a lot of things in those last few hours with Demetrious, things I needed to know, things Alex needed to know. I had to chance getting that information to him. I knew when they said they'd probably require me to find out his location that I'd get my chance on the radio to either tell him what I found out or tell him to run.

I opted for running, especially after I asked to see the President and found that he had become a Sleeper. Some demented man named Leonard was now running the project.

Demetrious had told me that those from Project Savior were the ones in the New Jerusalem, and with that knowledge, I prayed Alex could find them.

I was still alive because Leonard believed that since Alex asked for me, Alex would eventually negotiate to get me.

Alex was smarter than that.

My life wasn't important.

Phoenix's was.

The ARC wanted the child. They wanted him for many reasons—none of which were good. They would pursue him relentlessly.

24
ALEX SANS

Run.

I never realized the impact that the three-letter word could have until Randy blurted it out.

Run.

I got the message; he didn't have to say any more.

I prayed that God would protect him as much as Randy was trying to protect Phoenix and me.

Run.

That told me so much. The intentions of the ARC were not what we thought, and either Phoenix or I was in danger, or both of us were. Either way, my friend warned us, and I listened.

Our immediate thoughts were about the ARC finding us, and about the band of Sleepers that were homing on our sound and the smell of the breakfast fire. So much so, they picked up speed.

Two things came at us not ten minutes later.

One was the stampede sound of running Sleepers, and the other was helicopters.

The bus was large enough to haul us all safely off that hill and plow through the Sleepers, but the bus was also a prominent yellow target for the choppers.

The idea of staying in the camp held two scary prospects. One, the Sleepers would invade us and be too much for us to handle, and two, the choppers were going to be looking for activity.

Beck loaded a clip in his M-4 then attached two more clips to his belt. "What do you wanna do, Alex?"

I had to think fast. My eyes caught Mike's and a thought hit me.

I tossed Sonny the keys to the bus. "Take it down the hill. Take out as many as you can, then get them to follow you. Got it?"

"Excellent idea." Sonny gripped the keys. "I'll pull out on the highway as well and try to get the choppers to spot us."

Bonnie rushed to the bus. "I'll go with you. They won't buy for a second only you in this big bus."

"Good idea," I told her then swung around to Danny. "Take your mom, the babies, Jessie, and a few kids into Sonny's trailer, lock it, keep them down, quiet, and stand guard."

Danny nodded.

"Michael, take Jillian and the rest the rest of the kids into the Hoss trailer, same thing. Down. Quiet. Lock it. Watch them."

"Got it." Michael began gathering children. The Hoss trailer, as I called it, was a double wide, permanent trailer directly across the main road from Sonny's trailer.

"Beck, you and I will take high watch. Shoot anything that makes it into the camp. I'll take the check-in station by the gate, you take the rec center. That way you can get anything that I don't."

I got his agreement and watched him move in the direction of the rec center. He paused to look at Mera and Jessie as they went into Sonny's trailer, telling them to please stay down.

I gave my final instructions to Danny and Michael. "Don't be a cowboy, and don't try to be a hero unless you have to be. No shooting. No noise, no matter what happens out here. One sound can jeopardize the whole lot of you."

I could tell by the looks on their faces that I was preaching to the choir, but I had to be sure. I didn't want one of them to race out to save Beck or me.

The bus started to roll away. It covered the sound of the helicopters, lessening my ability to pinpoint their location. I was hopeful that the bus would cause the diversion I needed.

It was an easy climb to the roof of the check-in station. I got a clear view of the road and watched the taillights of the bus disappear around the bend. I gave the camp one last look. The door to Sonny's trailer was closed, and I breathed out in relief that Mera and her family were in there. Beck was already on the roof of the rec center. There was one thing wrong.

Jillian.

She struggled with Mike as he tried to get her inside the trailer. I wanted to yell, but I was too far; my voice wouldn't carry.

I couldn't hear what they were saying, but it was obvious that Beck had words with her. Finally, Beck's hand flew out in a 'screw it' motion to Mike.

Mike backed up into the trailer. Jillian, holding her son's hand, slammed the trailer door and took off with the red-haired boy into the woods.

Maybe she wanted to protect what was hers. Maybe she didn't see the safety in numbers. Whatever her reasons, they were her reasons, and he was her child. My job at that moment was to protect the camp.

I turned back to the road. Sonny wasn't going to be able to run over all the Sleepers or, like the Pied Piper, lead them all away. Nevertheless, I hoped he would lead enough away from our camp to give us a fighting chance.

25
MERA STEVENS

We had done it again. We became complacent and let our guard down. I found myself hiding under a thick comforter with four terrified young children.

It wasn't their first time hiding from a Sleeper attack, and for that, I was grateful. They knew to be quiet.

Danny had hustled four boys and a girl into our trailer. Confident that Sleepers wouldn't touch Jessie, I hid Jessie, a ten year old girl named Marissa, and the two babies in the closet.

Jessie, like Michael, was a source of protection. The little girl was there to help her with the babies, almost like a sitter. Marissa was intelligent.

We stayed in the hallway near the rear bedroom so we had an escape route out the back door. All the blinds were closed, lights were out, and we waited.

It happened so fast. I had just woken up, taken a sip of soda for some caffeine. Beck had changed both babies, handed Phoenix to me, gave Keller to Jessie, and walked out.

I heard the voice and only had time to open the door before I was overwhelmed with instructions.

Run here. Run there. Do this. Do that.

Danny rushed at me. "Mom, come on. We have to stay low."

Danny was barking out instructions to the kids that went into our trailer, and I was still in the dark.

"Danny, what the hell?"

"The ARC radioed. Randy got on, said for Alex to run. It can't be good, and we have hundreds of Sleepers barreling our way, more than likely from the Bargain Mart."

I called out, "Beck?"

"Get inside, stay quiet," he told me. "It'll be all right. Alex and I have this."

He spoke with confidence. Even thought I didn't know what was going on, I brought the children into the trailer.

I was still trying to understand if Alex was told to run because of the impending Sleeper attack or if something else had happened.

Then I heard the helicopters. I told the kids they had to be quiet, not to cry, shout, or make any noise. We muffled any sounds with the comforters and blankets in the hallway.

It was rush, rush, rush. My heart beat out of control; I helped Danny to lock all the doors, close the blinds, and secure everyone.

He was armed with a rifle, and I had a pistol.

We were ready, and I had faith in Alex and Beck.

Just as we settled, I heard Beck's voice. He was arguing, using a deep growling voice to command, "Get in. Now."

I was under the blanket when it started, and I emerged.

"Mom, get under," Danny told me.

"I'm fine. What's going on out there?"

"Beck's arguing with Jillian," Danny said ruefully.

"Why?"

He replied, exasperated, "I don't know!"

The voices stopped, I heard the slam of a door and figured it was over.

It grew quiet again.

I could no longer hear the bus engine, and the helicopters sounded so far away.

It was quiet.

But not for long.

In the distance, it sounded like war had broken out and we were on the front line, or close to it. I heard rapid gunfire. I closed my eyes and feared for Sonny. Within minutes, Beck and Alex were firing, not much, an occasional pop-pop-pop here and there. I envisioned Alex aiming at the Sleepers and Beck picking off the ones he missed. From the sound of things, it was worse in the distance.

I truly believed that we were spared, but in a brief moment of quiet, a spine-tingling sound rang out in the form of a child's voice.

"Mommy!"

My eyes popped open, and my head cocked. I looked at Danny.

He had the same look on his face.

"Mommy! Where are you?" It came from behind the trailer in the distance.

"Calvin!" Jillian returned the call.

I sat up. "Oh my God."

"Mom," Danny warned.

My heart raced.

"Mommy! Mommy, I'm scared. Where are you?" Calvin's words were breathless and echoing; he had to be in the woods.

"Keep calling me, Calvin! Keep calling."

My mind screamed. *No! No! No, don't call. Please be quiet, Calvin.*

"Mommy! Mommy!" His voice sped up with terror. "Mommy there's a group of them!"

"Keep calling my name, so I can find you."

"Mommy!"

My jaw tightened, my face burned, and fear raged through my entire being. "Danny?"

He closed his eyes tightly, his face clenched with pain as he dug the palms of his hands into his head.

In a flash I saw little Calvin in my mind, lean and agile, his red hair tossed about, his face dirty, running, looking behind him, trying to escape, trying to find his mother.

Danny and I locked eyes when we heard the shrill, long, chesty scream preceding the most horrifying cry of, *"Mommy!"*

I jumped up.

"Mom, no."

"You stay here. Watch the children." I checked the clip on my gun; it was full.

"I'll go."

"No, Danny, you have to stay. Lock and barricade the door behind me. I'll be back." I moved as fast as I could to the back door and quietly moved the barricade. Standing off to the side, I peeked out. I didn't see any Sleepers. I nodded to Danny, readied my gun, and waited for him to open the door. I had to be fast.

I didn't even know what direction the sound came from, only that it was behind the trailer and more than likely in the woods.

I heard him cry out again. "Mommy! Help me!"

Oh, God, they had him. The sound of his voice, the crying, the shrill screams tore at my heart.

The door opened, I slipped out, and I heard the door shut.

Two feet out, a Sleeper jumped at me. I fired. I don't know where I hit him, but it moved him away from me. I looked left to right and didn't see any more of them.

"Mommy!"

"Calvin!"

"Mommy! Help me. Ow! Mommy!" Scream.

My feet pounded, weapon ready, and I raced in the direction of the voice.

Nothing. I saw nothing.

Calvin's cries for help were drowned in heart wrenchingly painful sobs and each one burned my ears.

"Mom…Mommy…hurt…me…." Another scream.

The woods became a maze. The sun darted through the leaves and blinded me as I ran. I could hardly breathe.

"Mommy! *Please!*"

He was close.

"I'm sorry, Calvin. Mommy's sorry! Mommy's so sorry!"

"Mommy!"

"There's too many...Mommy's..."

I stumbled upon Jillian as she cried the word, "Sorry." She dropped to her knees and sobbed.

My jaw clenched when I made eye contact with her.

"There are too many." Her shoulders bounced with her sobs.

About fifteen feet beyond her I saw a group of Sleepers, maybe six. They were on the ground, arms flailing.

"*No!*" I aimed my gun and shot indiscriminately.

I hit one, then another. They fell over, and I saw small legs.

Oh God!

I aimed to fire again but before I could press the trigger fast, consecutive, single shots, accurately fired, knocked off the rest.

I looked to my left and saw Beck on the other side.

The Sleepers were down, and I raced over. My heart beat so loud that I heard it, I felt it, and when I caught sight of Calvin, all that swirled in me, every emotion, every bit of sadness, anger, ignited like a split atom and burst from my being in a cry that I was sure echoed through the woods over and over.

All hope that Calvin would be all right was instantly dashed.

His midsection was torn to shreds. His little head was tilted to the right, eyes open, mouth agape as if he looked, searched, prayed for help.

I dropped to my knees, leaned forward, and cradled his head, then lifted him to me. This poor child, one of few left in this childless world, lost his life as he cried for help that did not come, only to die alone in pain, without loving arms reaching out to him.

I sobbed as if he were my own. My heart broke for him and all that he endured. How scared he was. That poor baby. That poor, poor baby.

I couldn't stop crying.

"Mera," Beck walked up to me, speaking softly.

I lifted my eyes. "Where were you?"

His head rocked back, and he stammered for words. "W-What?"

"How could you let this happen?"

"Don't, Mera." He ran his hand over his mouth. "Don't put this on me. Please."

His eyes closed and he dropped down. One knee raised, he looked at us, brought his hand to his face, and turned a little. "Please." His shoulders bounced once, and he released a cry of sadness. "I tried. I looked. I tried. I couldn't find...the trees. It was..." Another sound of sadness. "I'm sorry, I failed him."

"No. I'm sorry, Beck. I shouldn't have said that. I'm sorry." My crying continued. My left arm held Calvin to me as I reached out my other hand for Beck. He moved closer, gripping my hand, still not looking at me.

Sleepers could have been upon us, encircling us. It didn't matter. I didn't even hear Alex coming, just his voice.

"What happ.... Oh my God."

Alex was standing there. He looked away. I couldn't say anything.

Alex said, "I saw Beck take off. I'm sorry."

I sniffled hard, tried to stop crying.

Beck finally lifted his head. "I'll be back. I want to get a blanket to cover him, so the other kids don't see him."

I nodded.

He stood, and I saw how much sorrow he carried. Head lowered, shoulders slumped, he hurried from the woods.

"It's safe now," Alex stated. "No Sleepers that I saw." He took a deep breath. "His poor mother."

When he said that, something inside of me snapped.

"Jillian, I am so, so sorry," Alex said.

He looked beyond me. I turned to see her standing ten feet behind me.

"We saw them," she said weakly. "The Sleepers. We were hiding and—"

"Don't speak," I said, turning from her.

"Mera?" Alex said.

Jillian continued, "I thought if I sent him farther..."

My eyes fluttered. *Sent him farther? Alone?*

"Don't. Speak." I repeated.

"I saw them chase...I couldn't see him."

"Please..." I begged. "Don't speak."

"There were so many, I couldn't—"

"I said don't speak!" I screamed.

"Mera!" Alex blasted.

I gently placed Calvin on the ground. I closed his eyes, looked at him for the last time, and stood.

Beck had returned with the blanket. He paused when he saw Jillian.

My facial muscles were tense, and my gut wrenched. I slowly turned around as Beck covered the child. I inhaled deeply.

I was always obedient. I never raised my hand to my children. I never fought in school. Violence was not in my nature.

Yet, when I saw Jillian, I raced toward her with a tightly closed fist, and I nailed her with everything I had.

She fell backwards and scurried away as I went for her again. Alex intervened, bodily moving me away from her.

"Mera!" he scolded. "What the hell? She just lost her child!"

"She...she" I tried to catch my breath. "He cried. He begged, Alex, *begged* her to help, and she just stood there and watched."

She wiped her nose. "There were too man—"

"There are *never* too many when it comes to your *child*!" I screamed. I went for her again, and again Alex stopped me.

"Knock it off," Alex scolded. "Beck, do something."

"No, I'd rather stay out of it, thank you," Beck replied without malice.

Alex growled. "Mera, let's go." He took hold of my arm led me away.

"I can walk," I snapped at him, snatching my arm from his grip. "I'm fine." I stalked away from Alex, looking over my shoulder.

"Let it go, Mera. Let it go for now," Alex said. "Calm down."

I honestly didn't care what he said at that moment. I continued walking toward camp. I did need to calm down, though. Not just for me, but for the others in our group.

However, what I felt right then was too hard to let go. I wouldn't let it go for a long time.

26
ALEX SANS

We'd gotten a bit of a reprieve, just enough time to pack up and move. I still didn't know what was going on with our pursuers from the ARC.

Mera marched angrily back to camp ahead of me. I had never seen her that far out of control.

She wasn't even rational. I didn't have the story yet, but whatever it was, Mera forgot that Calvin was Jillian's son. Jillian had lost her son. No matter what Jillian had or had not done, her son was dead.

I couldn't understand Mera's position at all. I just couldn't. Beck passively sided with Mera, as usual. At that moment, I didn't know if Beck reacted to Jillian or to Mera's opinion of Jillian's actions.

One thing was for sure, when we arrived back to camp, it wasn't good.

The kids knew what had happened. They, like Mera, had heard Calvin scream. Their response was surprising. Quietly, unemotionally, they watched Beck carry the body past, and then went on with what they were doing. Not Jessie.

She screamed and freaked out when she saw the blood on her mother. How do you explain to a person with the mentality of a toddler that the blood wasn't her mom's?

We tried, but Jesse wouldn't stop screaming until Mera cleaned up. She followed her mother into the trailer to shower. I hoped that, despite the early hour, Mera would hit that bottle of bourbon. If she didn't, I was going to shove it into her mouth.

In the months that I had known Mera, I only once saw her with an attitude, and that was for a short time after she met Pastor Mike. However, that time she got over it quickly. Now, I was even a little bit afraid of her, so I thought about other things.

Like where we would go. We had to go soon.

Beck returned holding Calvin's blanket-covered body. Jillian followed ten paces behind him.

The look on the big guy's face told me that he was broken up over the death of the little boy. We hardly knew the boy, but I figured it wasn't who he was, it was what he was a *kid*.

The children all stood around and stared as Beck took the body and placed it to the side.

"Danny," Beck called out, "I need you over here."

I followed Danny. Mera was still in the trailer. I didn't need to keep an eye on her any longer.

Beck told Danny, "I'm gonna go dig a grave. Can you keep the kids away from him, please?"

"Yes," Danny replied. He looked down at the body. "How bad, Beck?"

"Bad." Beck placed his hand on Danny's shoulder when he walked by him.

Michael told his group of kids to sit on the road where we used to have our campfire and then walked toward me. His hand shot to his mouth. "I heard him cry." Michael's eyes watered. "I could swear on my life, Beck would have saved him."

My heart thumped in my chest. "Me, too, Padre, but, uh, do me a favor, don't say that to the big guy, okay? He's taking this pretty hard. So is Mera."

"As is his mother," Michael said.

My eyes shifted to where Jillian was sitting a few feet away from the children. "Yeah," I said. "I'm sure."

"I'm going to pray for him, right now." Michael walked to the body and knelt by him.

"Why?"

He shot me an angry glance.

I raised my hands. "Just asking."

The school bus returned then, and I was glad to see it. The bus looked as if it had seen better days.

Sonny and Bonnie emerged from the bus like excited champions.

"We plowed through a lot of Sleepers," Sonny said.

"I don't think any more than a couple dozen came through," Bonnie said. "We figured you could..." her eyes lifted.

It was obvious she'd picked up the atmosphere of the camp.

"What happened?" Sonny asked.

I lowered my head. "We lost Calvin."

Bonnie gasped. "Excuse me," she said, and brushed past me straight to Jillian.

Sonny looked confused. "How? Weren't all the kids together?"

"The details are still sketchy," I said, one eye closed. "Now tell me what happened."

"Hundreds of Sleepers. Once we ran over a bunch of them, we waited until the rest followed. We actually moved pretty slowly until we hit the highway. Your buddies really saved the day though."

"What do you mean?"

"The choppers fired on the Sleepers. They hit them with small explosives. The highway is littered with them." He paused. "I think they thought you were on the bus 'cause they landed."

"And?"

"And they asked for you. I said I didn't have a clue who you were."

"You think they believed you?"

Sonny shrugged. "I don't know. They did say if I ran into you, I should tell you that you have three days. After that, they're coming after you, and they aren't gonna make it easy."

My face crinkled. "I'm not a criminal."

Sonny chuckled. "Bonnie asked that. She asked them if you were a criminal, and they said yes."

"What?"

"Yeah," Sonny continued. "They said you stole mankind's future."

A little melodramatic. But okay, I guess I did. Something about the three-day warning didn't sit well with me. I had a lot of thinking to do and plans to make. My first decision was to move our entire group off the hill and away from the campsite to another, safer location.

However, we first had to solve a significant problem. Where in the world was it safe?

Sonny knew the area and that was a blessing. He knew where to find anything we needed.

The Sunnybrook Food Warehouse was located nine miles off of Route 80, a good seventy miles southeast of our campground.

With the ability to draw gasoline from the reserve tanks at stations, I made the suggestion that we get another vehicle. Not that the bus wasn't large enough, it was, but we were crowded. Sonny's van served us well and was a lot more comfortable when it wasn't weighed down.

Mera rode in the van with Beck, Danny, Jessie, and both babies.

I got stuck on the school bus with all the kids. However, they weren't too bad; they were actually sad and unusually quiet.

We rolled down the hillside road. Sonny was spot on with his description of the carnage on the highway. Where had all the Sleepers come from? Like Michael had suggested a while back, they followed each other, gaining members of their pack and picking up momentum when they found a trail.

If there were that many remaining, I was left to wonder how many the government had killed.

The bus bumped up and down as it rolled over bodies. I tried not to believe that they were people, especially since they had started to evolve.

A little girl named Marissa made her way up to the front of the bus and sat right next to me. It surprised me. None of the kids had actually talked to me. They were an odd bunch. I mean, I only knew Missy's kids and a few others, but this busload was strange. They barely spoke, were well-behaved and seemed immune to shock and despair. Unfazed by much, they glossed over Calvin's death.

Suffice to say, Marissa's behavior took me aback.

Her hair was blonde. I suspected it would be a lot lighter-colored if it were clean. It was tangled, messy, and needed to be brushed. In fact, all of the kids needed a good bath. If Bonnie or Jillian didn't take care of that soon, I'd get Mera on it. She apparently liked that motherhood stuff.

"Hi," she said.

"Hey," I nodded.

"I'm eight."

"Oh, yeah?"

"How old are you?"

"Why?"

"We are curious."

"Hmm…" I paused. What would she know? So I lied. "Twenty-five."

"Wow, that's *old*."

"I know," I said, thinking to myself how shocked she'd be if she knew how old I really was.

"Maybe you will live a long time."

"Let's hope." I tried to hide my smile.

"My father, he lived to be forty-one!"

"I'm…I'm sorry?"

She crinkled her face in curiosity at me as if I'd said the oddest thing. Then she exhaled. "I hope to be forty-two."

"Well I hope you live to be eighty-two if not more. Heck, a hundred and two."

She gasped. "Is that possible?"

"Yeah, it is. Sure, why not?"

"True." She bobbed her head. "It's a fresh start. So…are you mean?"

"No. Do I look mean?"

Again, she nodded. "All the kids think you look mean."

"Why is that?"

"Because you drew all over yourself."

I looked down at my arms, my sleeves of ink. "You mean my tattoos?"

She gasped.

"What?"

"Tattoos are the devil's work."

"Yeah, I know. Perhaps you should talk to the padre about that. He can pray for me. He's the Son of God, you know."

"I will." She hurried away.

The devil's work? I wondered if the kids had all lived in a religious commune or something. They *were* on a church trip when the Event occurred. That would explain their oddities. They probably were a cult, and the Ray guy, who was the doctor, was probably the cult leader.

About four more kids came up to me asking the same questions. I hadn't a clue why they were like that with me. I was a likeable guy. Perhaps I needed to put forth a little child-friendly effort.

I did know one thing: next bus ride, Beck was riding with the kids.

We didn't see a Sleeper until we pulled into the Sunnybrook Food Warehouse parking lot. I thought that we'd hit the jackpot. The warehouse was a massive structure. The whole place was surrounded by a tall fence. There would have to be thousands of Sleepers in order for them to break through the fence as they had at the ARC.

Four Sleepers wandered the property; they'd be easy to take out. The warehouse was near a small farm where their food distributor grew their own produce. A few houses were scattered along the road leading to the warehouse, and a small housing community was two miles away.

It was perfect for our needs.

We took out the Sleepers with ease, then Beck, Danny and I went inside to look for more of them.

Sonny and Bonnie took his van to examine the area and would report back to us. We locked the fence behind them. I had a good feeling.

The warehouse bays were open; that told me that survivors had come and taken their pick. I didn't believe that much would be left.

The Sunnybrook distributors handled superstores that carried more than just food, so the warehouse did, as well.

I wanted to dance a jig. The warehouse would not only tide us over for a few days until we figured out the next step, it would also give us supplies for the near future.

I reminded myself to hug Sonny the moment he returned.

It took us over an hour to go through the entire complex. We had located several more Sleepers, but that was it. Just about the time we finished, Sonny returned.

They'd only found a few Sleepers, which they killed.

We secured the fence once again, brought the vehicles into the warehouse, and locked it down.

The vast, empty bay area used for bringing supplies to trucks served well as a gathering area.

We immediately set up bedrooms for the kids in the offices off of the bay. There were brand-new sleeping bags in aisle seven. They were eight shelves up, so Danny had to do some climbing.

The kids had room to run, play, and make noise. That drove me nuts, but then again, the warehouse had room for us to have privacy.

Mike was messing with the radio again, just listening, he said. I asked him about what he wanted to tell me in regards to his Doctrines notes, and he said he'd tell me later.

I accepted that.

Mera stayed away. She set up her sleeping area in a small office and made a makeshift bed for the babies. Phoenix was learning to roll over, so I told her that it wasn't going to work for long.

She glared at me.

And Marissa accused *me* of doing the devil's work. Apparently Marissa hadn't ever seen that look Mera gave me.

She stayed in sight nearby; she just didn't talk to us.

She spoke to Beck...of course.

As the evening wore on, the kids quieted down. We used lanterns to light the area, and no one said much. Jessie and the babies were asleep. I invited Mera to join our group, but she declined, choosing instead to read by the office door.

We talked occasionally about trivial things, and then Jillian, who had been silent, made the fatal mistake of speaking.

That was what Mera was waiting for.

The moment Jillian opened her mouth, I looked across the bay at Mera. Her book went down.

"It doesn't seem right," Jillian said softly, "without kissing him goodnight."

Man, that just shot us all down.

Jillian exhaled. "It was for the best. He's better now. It's the way it had to be."

Stomp. Stomp. Stomp.

I grumbled. I knew what would happen when I saw Mera making her way over.

"What do you mean, it's the way it had to be?"

"It's better that he not suffer any longer," Jillian replied. "This world is no place for a child to live. Don't you agree?"

"No." Mera barked. "I have three children, four if you count Keller, that are living in this world. No matter how hard this world is, I'll do what I have to do to keep them safe."

I stood. "Mera," I said soothingly, "come on."

"Come on what, Alex?"

Jillian stood. "Why are you like this with me? You struck me. You hate me."

"I'm mad at you. No, wait, words can't *describe* how angry I am with you."

"Why?"

"Because you did this on purpose."

At that instant, everyone except Beck jumped at Mera, calling out her name, telling her to stop.

"No!" Mera said harshly. "Sonny, you didn't hear. Neither did you, Bonnie. He cried. He cried and *begged* for help. He screamed. You told him to run ahead on his own."

"He was my son!" Jillian argued.

"He was eight years old!" Mera shouted.

"And? He was *my* son. Not yours or anyone else's. It was my choice. It is my right as a mother to decide what happens with my son."

"Not when he is a living, breathing child. Then it's murder."

"Mera!" Michael yelled.

"You sent him out there alone," Mera continued. "It wasn't for his safety; it was for yours. You used him to distract the Sleepers so you could live."

"Enough." Michael stepped forward. "Mera, enough, that is cold and wrong and—"

"It's the truth," Mera growled. "Look at her. Look at her eyes. She sent him out there alone on purpose."

Michael looked at Jillian.

Quietly and with a spine-chilling tone, Jillian said, "I didn't want him on this earth any longer."

Mera heaved out a sobbing breath. "They tore him *apart*."

Jillian sat back down. "It was my choice."

Thankfully Michael was there to grab Mera when she lunged toward Jillian.

"This isn't your concern, Mera." Michael placed his arm around her waist, holding her back. "This is out of your hands."

"No, it's not. She's cold and calculating and should not be a part of this group," Mera argued. "I don't want her here."

I made my way over to assist, help calm things down. "And what should we do?" I asked. "Send her out there?"

"Yes," Mera answered. "Send her out. Who cares? An eye for an eye." She turned to Michael. "Isn't that what the Bible says, Michael?"

"It does," Michael said calmly. "But Jesus, he turned that phrase around."

"Oh, fuck Him," Mera said sharply. "Take her out. Or I will." Surprising even me, Mera pulled her revolver.

Quickly, I reached out and snatched it from her hand. "Enough. Okay? This isn't *your* group, it's *our* group. And if the group decides she should stay, she stays. Beck?"

Standing quietly in the back, he lifted his head in acknowledgement.

"Can you take Mera for a walk somewhere?"

Mera sneered at me. "Why are you always calling him to control me?"

"Because you people live like one big happy fucking family," I snapped. "So now he can play Papa Bear and calm you down." My voice rose. "Now! The kids don't need this, Danny, Jessie, no one needs this now. Go! Walk."

Beck walked over and said softy. "Come on, let's go for a walk."

After a moment, Mera huffed, "Fine," and stepped back. "Danny, watch the babies," she said as she strode past him, pausing to grab the bottle from Sonny. She stopped, looked at me, and just before she walked away with Beck, she pointed at Jillian. "Know this. Next run in with trouble...you're Sleeper bait."

And then, with Beck, she walked off.

After she had gone, we were quiet. We weren't just reeling in the aftermath of Mera's outburst and anger; we were reeling in the revelation that Jillian let her son die on purpose.

It was a harsh reality for us to accept. I don't think there was a single one of us who knew how to handle it at that moment.

27
MERA STEVENS

We hadn't walked too far away from the group when my breathing normalized, and my heart rate steadied. I tried to recall the last time I felt so out of control with painful emotions. The closest I came was when I thought that Daniel was having an affair.

What was wrong with me? Perhaps I just needed to go on a good drunk. However, I didn't drink to get drunk; I only drank for the calming effect alcohol had on me.

It wasn't that I didn't have a legitimate reason for my anger. I know most of it stemmed from the fact that precious few children were given an opportunity to live. 1.8 billion had died, and only a dozen or so lived. They were exceptional, they were meant for something else, and Jillian decided to let her son die.

No one would ever convince me otherwise. The Sleepers were attacking, she didn't want to die, and she sent out Calvin. Then again, it could have been she felt it was time for him to go. She was finished with protecting him and didn't want him to be scared any longer.

Still, in my mind and my soul, I knew that decision was wrong.

I didn't think Beck would scold me. He took me to the farthest door in the bay area, only stopping to grab a lantern and a couple of paper cups from the supplies. Then we walked.

"Where are we going?" I asked. It seemed as if we were heading pretty far away from the others.

He walked ahead of me as if looking for something. His head moved up and down with the movement of the flashlight beam. "Just want to get you away from the group. Far enough away so you'll feel free to say what you want."

"I'll say what I want anyhow."

He stopped walking and looked over his shoulder. "Yes, I know. How about I rephrase that? I am taking you far enough away, so they don't have to hear you."

"Better. What are you looking for?"

"I saw it somewhere in this aisle." He raised his eyes toward the ceiling.

"Well, we're almost at the end."

He stopped, faced a box above his head, pulled out his knife and cut the box. "Yeah." A bag of chocolate kisses rolled out. He turned and handed them to me. "They say chocolate has something in it to help a bad mood. So here."

I couldn't help but laugh.

"What's so funny?"

"When I was mad, my husband Daniel used to bring me chocolate. Kisses." I gripped the bag and handed him the bottle.

"Smart man."

"So are you." I opened the bag while he poured, and we exchanged goodies.

"Feeling any better?"

"I didn't get it all out of my system."

"You will." He winked.

I took comfort in that wink, and then I absorbed that heavenly chocolate. I didn't care how well or how badly it mixed with the whiskey, I enjoyed it. I took a healthy swallow, finishing off my glass.

"That was fast, even for you." Beck refreshed my glass.

"I know." I sighed. "Let's just go."

"What do you mean?"

"You, me, Jessie, Danny, the babies, let's pack up and go our own way. Let's leave, set up somewhere, and do our own thing."

"Leave the group?"

I nodded.

"That's really not fair to Michael or Alex. We've all been together a long time. They have as much vested in your family as you and I do. Besides..." Beck finished his drink, "you don't want to leave the group. As much as you and Alex butt heads, he gives you a spark that I don't think anyone else can."

"You're right, I don't want to leave the group. But Alex...oh my God. He kills me. He really does. He makes fun of Michael all the time, and he's just so damn arrogant."

"He's a good leader."

"So are you."

"Maybe in other circumstances," Beck said ruefully. "Not in this one. He makes decisions based on the good of us all."

"Don't you?"

"Not really. I make decisions most of the time based on the good of you."

A part of me twitched inside when he said that. After hearing his words, I understood what he meant. From the moment he met me at the refugee center, when he broke the rules and gave me back my belongings, he had been doing things for *me*.

"Everyone out there is a good person."

"Except Jillian," I said.

"I'm sure she is, somewhere under her Mommy Dearest exterior."

I laughed.

"I know what happened hurt," he said. "I know it. I felt it. And I know her actions angered you more than anyone. However, it'll come around. It will. Don't put that bad karma on yourself. Okay?"

In shock over his words, I stepped back. "Wow. That was good."

"Thanks." He took a sip of his drink. "Plus, Bonnie isn't really a mothering type. I don't know if you noticed. All those kids need attention. She can't do it alone; she needs you."

"Somehow I think that if we left those kids in the middle of somewhere, all alone, they'd be just fine. Not that I would do that."

Beck turned his head to the side and looked at me through the corner of his eyes. "Why would you say that?"

"Oh, come on. You haven't noticed that those kids are weird? They hardly reacted to Calvin's death. And that one boy, the one with the brown spiky hair and mischievous smile—"

"Nick."

"Nick, yes. He told me that he knew Calvin from the trip and that he and his mother left the camp early."

"Really?" Beck seemed surprised by that.

"Really, and I think I want to sit." I started to sink to the floor; Beck stopped me, and pulled out a large box, placing it in the aisle then pulled out one for himself.

"Will these hold us?" I asked.

"Oh, yeah, it's a case of Spam."

I burst into laughter as I sat down. "Please don't tell Alex or Michael."

"Trust me, I won't." Beck positioned himself directly in front of me. "And you're right; there is something different about those kids. I can't put my finger on it."

"Kids are resilient, I know that. They seem way too tough. Has Michael said anything about them to you?"

"No," Beck said, "but then again, they just joined us, so maybe they're just shy. You heard Alex's opinion, right?"

"No. I didn't talk to Alex much today." I said. "What is it?"

"He thinks this church group that went into the mountains was like a cult. Isolate the kids and all. He thinks that's why all the girls wear dresses. Bonnie found them in South Dakota. Supposedly they were in Montana when the Event occurred."

"That makes sense, with their demeanor and all."

Beck nodded and drank, refilled my glass.

"Thank you for taking me away."

"Not a problem. I was glad to."

There was a brief pause in the conversation, and then thoughts about things Alex had said swirled through my mind, and I laughed out loud.

Beck smiled. "What?"

It took a second for me to get the giggles under control; the mixture of emotions and alcohol was taking its effect. "Alex..." I laughed again, "called you Papa Bear."

Beck laughed. I enjoyed when he did that, he rarely smiled widely or laughed. "Alex is funny. He has the best one-liners."

"Oh my God, what he doesn't say to Michael. He takes the Savior thing as far as he can."

"And pushes it," Beck added. "I thought for sure Michael was going to kill him when we were discussing the flat tire on the bus, and he asked Michael if he could levitate the bus or something."

"I wasn't there for that," I snickered. "But you know there's something about Michael too. I know you're convinced he's a mutant Sleeper, but I don't know."

"You think he's a Chosen?"

"I don't know anymore." I lowered my head, looking at my drink. "There *is* something special about him."

Beck used his index finger to lift my chin. "Mera, there is something distinctive about every single person here. All of us, good or bad, survived for a reason. There's a dying world out there, yet we live. We lost everything, yet we keep moving forward. We all have a reason for living, and that makes us all unique."

"You're pretty quiet," I whispered. "You ought to speak more often. You have some valuable things to say, Gavin Beck."

His mouth dropped open a little, and the corner of it rose in a smile. "You said my first name."

"It surprises you that I knew it?"

"Uh...yeah."

I laughed. "Did you think I thought your first name was Major?"

"Yes." He smiled, laughed a little, and then turned serious.

In that quiet moment, our eyes locked.

His index finger was still on my chin. It slid to my cheek, and then his whole hand cupped my face. His fingers stroked my skin then slipped to the back of my neck. He pulled me closer.

I felt his thumb brush my face. He was so close to me, only a breath away, waiting for some kind of approval.

Our lips brushed. A mere hair's breadth separated us.

I trembled.

There was no way I had ever envisioned myself that close to Beck in that way. In my pain-filled world, there wasn't time for fantasy or to think about a human connection.

He was waiting. I could tell he was waiting on me.

My heart had been broken by grief, by tragedy, so much so that I didn't even know if I had a real heart to feel with anymore.

Never did I imagine that, for one brief moment in time, the pain would subside, and a rush of peace would take its place. Never did I imagine, for an instant in time, that the world hadn't ended.

However, that was where I was.

Right there. So close.

I closed my eyes and allowed my lips to meet his.

Right decision? Wrong decision? I didn't know. Wrong time? Wrong place? It didn't matter.

He kissed me.

A slow, soft kiss intensified in a heartbeat, bringing a moan, an intensely human sigh that came from my soul. At the same time that our lips locked in that kiss, we both stood, and then we embraced.

It was like nothing I had ever felt.

After all the heartache that I had experienced in the previous months, his arms were the first real arms to hold me. I felt almost happy.

I loved how it felt to be held by him, and I know he felt the same way. His arms moved around me, feeling me, holding me, his body pressing tightly against mine, taking me in, almost as if he wished he could consume me.

And I tried, oh, God did I try to let him to consume me.

Time was suspended. Everything was suspended, the hurt, the pain, the world.

Everything felt right. For as long as I could, as long as he would, I would stay in that moment…with Beck.

28
ALEX SANS

Finding a way to the roof from inside the warehouse was like looking for a needle in a haystack. Not that I minded going outside to climb the outer portion of the building; I just thought it would be safer to go to the roof from inside.

Sonny and I searched for a while after everyone else went to sleep. We found it the last place we looked, naturally. I found the stairway in the closet of the office that I assumed belonged to the big boss.

I was a little irritated by that point. I had Jillian and her actions on my mind. I supposed we'd have to discuss it as a group. What she admitted to did warrant being ousted from our group.

I briefly checked out the roof, climbed back down, and shook my head.

"What?" Sonny asked.

"Just a pain in the ass." I looked at my watch. "I'll take first watch; come and get me in three hours. Beck will be your relief. We'll do round the clocks between us all from here on in."

"Sounds good."

"And uh, find Beck, will ya? Wherever he went."

"What do you mean?"

"I mean, find him. Let him know he'll be on watch in a few. Since, you know, he disappeared with Mera." I headed back to the ladder. "I told him to walk her, not leave for the night."

Sonny laughed. "What the hell are you talking about? Guy, they came back a while ago. They weren't even gone that long."

"How did I miss that?"

"You probably were outside with Mike looking at that ladder," Sonny said.

"Okay. Thanks." I started to climb again.

"Jealous much?"

"What?"

"Just calling it as I see it…. green's not your color."

"Thanks for the tip. But I'm not jealous." I reached the top of the ladder.

Jealous.

I wouldn't call it that. Irritated would be more like it. It wasn't over an interest in Mera; it was over the fact that if they paired off it would upset the balance of our group.

I didn't know. I'd have to soul search for that one, and I wasn't in the mood to do it.

The roof was perfect for our purposes. I had a good view of the surrounding area, and a keen eye and ear would hear a Sleeper coming from a long distance.

The roof was also a good place to think. It wasn't my responsibility to take care of everyone, yet I felt it was. I felt the pressures of where to go, what to do next. Sonny talked to me a lot about it, and that helped. He was a dependable source.

I was also confused.

While I was outside the warehouse, walking the perimeter, Michael joined me. I thought it was a good opportunity to bring up again what he tried to tell me about his notes and the Doctrines. I needed information.

As much as I hated to admit it, the Doctrines, even if they were fictitious, were a good set of guidelines.

"Don't rely on them, Alex, really," Michael said. "Follow your heart and instincts."

"What was it that you wanted to tell me?"

"It's hard to explain. See, when I originally read them, I was taking notes on what I read. They go decades beyond what happens now, you know that, right?"

I nodded.

"Well, it dawned on me that the Doctrines mention Keller."

"By name?"

"By name. But he's older, twenty I think."

"That's impossible. Keller won't survive that long."

"Kind of an odd coincidence though, huh? Keller isn't a common name."

"Who is he in the Doctrines?"

"I don't know. I missed something, it doesn't make sense. We need Randy to explain them."

Randy.

Randy was a virtuous man, a sensible man, and, in addition to his knowledge of the future, he had a considerable gift of giving advice that worked.

We needed him back, but I didn't even know if Randy was alive.

He had warned me to run. The same man who gave up his life to ensure Phoenix made it to the ARC was telling me to run.

If Phoenix or I was in danger, then it was safe to assume that Randy and maybe everyone else was, too.

I believed we were all alive because of Randy. And because of that, I had to make it my priority to do everything in my ability to get him back.

29
ALEX SANS

The radio broke silence for the first time in a while, other than transmissions from the ARC, and it was from those claiming to be the New Jerusalem. Unfortunately, our enthusiasm was short lived over the fact that Michael said it was the same statement that had been broadcast earlier:

This is the New Jerusalem. We are with people from Project Savior. We are a second facility. We seek others and believe with the right elements we can create a strong future…

It was a recording. It had to be.

It was no wonder they didn't respond to any calls he had made. I was left to conclude that the recording was played automatically, and there wasn't a New Jerusalem.

There was something familiar about it, however, I couldn't put my finger on it. I had only caught the tail end. Michael, on hearing it the second time stated, not only was it a recording, it was also vaguely reminiscent of the voice on the holographic message Randy played.

To be honest, all I recalled about that man from Project Savior was that he said they had erred, and their germs were too strong for our time. His voice was like a computerized recording. Randy attributed that to the age of the recording and the fact that it had been processed to make it clear. In other words, edited to save it.

"The same man?" I had asked.

Michael was sure it wasn't. Because he, unlike us, had listened to the message on Randy's tablet more than once. No, it wasn't the same man, but it was done by the same process, electronic and repeated.

Then more we discussed it the less we believed in the existence of a New Jerusalem. In a way, that made our decision easier, at least as far as where to go.

One decision wasn't going to be that easy: What to do with Jillian.

I wasn't her judge, jury, and executioner. While I believed that her actions were morally reprehensible, was it my place in this new world to say she was wrong? It hadn't been her hands that tore the boy apart; it was her motives.

Still, with her actions, there was the possibility that others didn't want her around.

It was time to make that decision and stick with it. There was a lot of tension the next morning. After I grabbed a limited amount of sleep and dived into hot instant coffee, I told the others we would gather to decide.

I sought out that bright little girl with the knotted hair. I figured she was miles above a normal girl in wisdom and would use her to entertain the others. I almost didn't recognize Marissa; her hair was smooth and combed.

"Look at you, all pretty with your hair done."

She smiled. "The mother woman fixed it. She sprayed this stuff on it, and it combed right through."

"Looks good."

"Thank you."

"I have a favor," I said. "Can you gather the kids, take them off to play?"

"We play all the time."

"Yeah, I know, but I need you to keep an eye on everyone, and if you can, take Jessie."

"The pretty, tall girl that doesn't talk?" Marissa asked.

"Yes, her."

"And do what?"

"Hide and seek?"

She tilted her head. "Why would we do that?"

"It's a fun game."

"But isn't 'Hide and Seek' our lives? We live that; why would we play that? Besides playing the Paler game is much more fun. It's like freeze tag."

I laughed. Hide and Seek was real, but the 'Paler' game wasn't? And man, Paler must have been the backwoods term for Sleeper.

"Well, play whatever you like," I said. "I need to have a meeting with the grownups and need the kids to stay away."

"So you can decide Miss Jillian's fate?"

Hearing her say that made me stop for two reasons. One, how did she know? And two, her manner of speaking was off, as if she was too mature for her age. The cult she was in must have thoroughly schooled their young.

I took a moment and replied as best as I could. "Something like that."

She stepped back. "I'll get the others and the tall girl."

"Thank you."

She started to walk away but stopped. "Will the man of God be part of the decision?"

"Yeah he will be."

"Oh, good. He'll be just. He knows God personally, you know."

I scratched my head. "So I heard."

As she darted away, her hair swaying as she ran, all I kept thinking was, *Man, what an odd little girl.*

My short time with her was a pleasant distraction, but it was time to get to the serious matters.

There were seven of us, so no chance of a tie: Me, Beck, Michael, Danny, Sonny, Bonnie and Mera.

Jillian didn't get a vote.

I wished with all my heart that we could just move on, but in the back of my mind, I knew it would stay with us until there was an agreed-upon settlement.

"This isn't a trial," I told Jillian. "Really, it's not. See, we're a group, and we have to stick together. We have to be able to trust everyone." I stared at her for a second looking up at me, unfazed, unemotional, almost as if she expected what we were going to do. "I'm not cut out for this. Anyone else want to take the reins?"

No one stepped forward.

"We're gonna take a vote, whether you stay or go," I sighed, looking at Jillian. "Majority rules."

Jillian nodded. "I understand."

"Some people," I said, "think you...they think Calvin's death wasn't an accident. Or rather, was avoidable. Now, obviously, you didn't kill him. What happened, Jillian?"

She looked at Mera. "It wasn't a diversion. I didn't send him out to save my own life. I didn't..." She stared down to her hands, fingers touching, then looked back up. With each sentence, she glanced at a different person. "It wasn't supposed to be like this. It wasn't. There was no forewarning, you know. Just the wooded area, a camp site, wait it out, emerge after a while. Well, after a little bit, every day, those things... some guy on the radio with Ray called them Palers, they'd make their way into camp. Every day, more and more. I thought it was a death trap up there."

"So you were part of the original group of kids?" I asked.

"Yes, but we didn't go there to die," Jillian said. "We stayed there to wait out the plague. People got sick, society broke down, the virus was in the air, people would die for a long time. Ray said we had to wait six months. No one knew about people turning into those things."

"None of us did," Bonnie said. "You left the camp to protect Calvin. Did you think you could do the same again?"

Jillian shrugged. "It seemed where there were groups of people, those things went to them. I saw the adults of our group torn apart trying to protect the kids. At first I thought, Calvin would grow up. He could live beyond forty. However, every day I saw it wasn't getting better. It was worse."

I crinkled my forehead. "What are you talking about?"

"I'm talking about this isn't a life for him. He'd run today but die tomorrow. He'd eat today, starve tomorrow. That isn't a life. Some mothers would do anything to ensure their child lived." She stared at Mera. "At the cost of running, being scared, having no food, never settling. But is that living? And for how long? Calvin came into this world to live a long life with no one running."

Sonny then asked, "Did you intentionally send him out to the Sleepers?"

"Not at first. We didn't go into the trailer because I don't believe in safety in numbers. Numbers attract. Then…" She paused and quickly looked at Michael. "I gave it to God."

I turned to Michael. "What does that mean?"

"She simply put it in God's hands," Michael answered.

Jillian nodded. "I told Calvin to run. If God intended him to live, he would lead Calvin to hide somewhere. If not…then he would call Calvin home. Calvin didn't go quietly. I think he thought I was going to follow him, so he started calling for me. And then I panicked and tried to find him. But the Palers were on him; before I could reach him, they surrounded him. There were too many. I gave to my son to God, and He gave him to the Palers." Her head lowered.

I had one more question. "If we let you stay, do we have to keep you on suicide watch?"

"Suicide watch?"

Beck clarified. "Do you want to die now?"

"No. My son is better off dead, but why would I want to die as well, when we all went to so much trouble to live?"

I peered around the faces of the circle. "Jillian, is there anything else you want to say."

"No."

"Anyone else have questions?" I waited. After a few seconds of silence, I said, "Then we vote. Bonnie?"

"Stays. It was her son, her choice."

"Agreed. I vote we let her stay as well," I said. "Beck?"

"Goes."

I secretly chuckled, I figured as much. "Danny?"

"Goes."

I knew that, as well. I also had a gut feeling about Michael. "Padre."

"Stays."

I avoided asking Mera because I knew her answer. I wasn't sure what Sonny thought. But I knew at three 'stays' and two 'goes,' Sonny could turn it, leave no tie to break. "Sonny?"

"She should go."

I wanted to scream, *Are you kidding me!* I breathed out slowly, gave an apologetic look to Jillian, and, defeated, called Mera's name.

Mera paused and then she stated, "She stays. For now."

I was blown away. The look on Beck's face confused me further. He swiped his hand across his mouth to hide his grin. *What the hell?* What got me was no one seemed to react to Mera's sudden change of heart. A woman who had a gun to Jillian's head not twenty-four hours earlier, screaming to kick her out, suddenly voted in an opposite direction?

Mera walked off, and I followed.

She was headed to the office that she considered her bedroom. "Mera, wait," I called her. "Wait."

"What's up?" she turned around.

"What is going on? Yesterday you call her Sleeper bait, and today you're okay for her to stay?"

She moistened her lips, looked beyond me, grabbed my arm and tugged me away. "Come here." She stared at me.

I lifted my hands. "Well?"

"Did you hear what she said?"

"Yes, so what she said changed your mind?"

"Absolutely."

"So you don't think she was wrong now?"

"What?" Mera rocked back. "She is so cold. She let her son die on purpose. 'Give it to God, in God's hands,'" she mocked. "Please. Give me a break. Michael gave her that 'Give it to God' line three times yesterday. It's a crock. She let Calvin die *on purpose.*"

"Then what the hell, Mera? You had the opportunity to throw her out."

"Because did you hear what she said?"

"Yes, she let Calvin—"

"No, Alex, not that, about the plague. It was supposed to be a plague for six months. Societal breakdown, people would die. I don't know what plane of existence she lived on but running for the hills didn't save a damn child on my street or Beck's kids. They didn't have a chance to run anywhere."

"So what are you saying?"

"I don't *know,*" she said with some frustration. "The whole lot of them are odd."

"They're cult members. What do you expect?"

"The whole world died, Alex, every child, and those kids lived because they were in the mountains."

"Maybe…" I held up my hand. "Let's just go out on a farfetched limb here."

Mera folded her arms. "Go on."

"Talk of the padre being the Son of God, of the kids coming from a cult, maybe they got a message, maybe this whole thing is really more religious than we've thought all along."

"Do you really believe that?"

I answered without hesitation. "No."

"Neither do I."

"Then what did you think?"

"I don't know."

"Then she's not Sleeper bait anymore?"

"Oh, she's still Sleeper bait, but until I figure out what the hell doesn't make sense with this story…" Mera peered over my shoulder, "she's off the hook."

"No pun intended to the term bait?"

Mera twitched her head. "Maybe some."

At first I thought Mera was a little off her rocker, but the farther I walked away, and the more I thought about Jillian's words, the more I wondered if perhaps Mera was right.

I gave careful thought to what Mera said, and I watched the children and Jillian. I spoke to Bonnie and asked her if she thought the kids were a little odd. Her explanation was similar to mine—children who lived sheltered lives in religious communities were often different.

I asked her about Ray. She didn't know much about him; he died shortly after they met. He was a doctor, that was all she knew, and as far as the children surviving, Bonnie wasn't as close to the death of billions. It wasn't any more real to her than it was to me. Had I run into a bunch of kids instead of Mera and Beck, I wouldn't have thought twice about it either.

I don't know why it bothered me, why I jumped on the Mera train and automatically assumed there was another story to this crew. My first thought was that this group of kids had gotten the untainted form of the virus; hence why worked on them the way it was intended. But how?

From what Randy showed us in the holograph, the future people had sent a virus to improve man. The future man in the video said: "*Ugh. We screwed up. Our germs compromised Project Savior.*"

Okay, maybe he didn't say ugh.

These kids, if part of a cult, hadn't lived normal lives. Would they have? They would have always been secluded, and maybe hadn't even had inoculations. Maybe they were spared because there were certain elements never introduced into their systems.

Admittedly, within twenty-five minutes the whole thing was driving me nuts. The day before I didn't think twice about it.

The old saying 'out of the mouths of babes' crossed my mind.

It was time to learn about this cult.

I grabbed the first kid I saw, a little boy. I wasn't sure of his name, but he was young. "So, you went camping?"

He looked at me.

"The field trip. It was a camping trip. Did you have fun?"

"Fun. Yes."

"So how long were you on the trip?"

"The trip. Not long."

"How long?"

"Seconds."

"How old are you?"

"Eight."

"Yeah, makes sense, I'm getting nowhere with you. Go play." I patted him on the head and sought a bigger child. Where the heck was that Marissa girl when I needed her? Then I spotted the spiked hair boy, Nick. I whistled and waved him to come to me. He looked somewhat apprehensive at first, and he kept his distance.

"Yes, Mr. Alex Sans."

"I want to ask you a few questions, is that okay?"

"Yes, sir."

"Good boy." I gestured for him to sit down next to me. "So, where did you go to school?"

"School?"

"Yes, the place you learn to read and write. Can you read?"

"Doesn't everyone?"

I twitched my head. "Maybe now. Who taught you?"

"The elders."

Elders. That was it. That was the evidence of a cult that I was looking for. I moved on to my theories on why the kids were never really sick.

"Nick. Did these leaders keep you from seeing other people?"

"You mean people in our community?"

"No, I mean outside of the community. Did you kids ever go and meet other kids from other communities?"

"No, Nick said, "there was only us. Anything outside was bad."

"Ever get a shot?"

"With a gun?"

"No, a needle."

"Why would I get shot with a needle? That doesn't seem useful."

"No, it doesn't."

"Unless it went in my eye."

I laughed. "So you didn't see anyone but those in your community. No needles. How about…did you grow your own food, or did the elders go to a store?"

"No stores."

"So you grew your own food?"

"Doesn't everyone?"

"No," I answered and saw the look of shock on his face. "This place here is where people get food. Well, they don't come here, or they didn't. This warehouse we're in shipped it to stores, and consumers such as myself bought it."

"Seems like a lot of steps to take to eat."

Nick made me laugh; his innocence was impressive. I thanked him and told him to go play. At that moment in time I had it all figured out. I figured out why the virus didn't affect those children the way it did billions of others. At least I believed I understood.

No immunizations, no processed foods, no exposure to other people. Purity. And that filled me with confidence that the group of kids were probably not the only ones who were isolated. There had to be other cult-type communities. The Amish for starters, not that the Amish people were a cult.

We very well could have been missing the boat.

Excitedly, I decided to share my views and theories with the others, thinking about mapping out areas that could include kids, especially out east where I was familiar with Amish country, particularly in Ohio.

I checked out the kids playing some crazy game of chase, and as I headed over, I heard Michael call my name.

A moment after, I heard my name again. Only it wasn't someone from our group. "Alex Sans. Alex Sans come in."

I bit back my reply, wanting to blurt out the biggest, loudest 'fuck,' but I didn't want the kids to hear it, and I didn't know what wicked things the padre would do to me.

He was sitting near the radio and he looked pretty sad.

I walked across the bay, toward the radio set up. Everyone else started to gather, and they were looking at me waiting for an answer. Like a bad debt or bill collector, they were a reminder I couldn't run from an obligation.

"Don't answer them," Beck said. "Don't give them a chance to hone in."

I nodded. Then as I did, the voice on the radio said two words: "Sunnybrook Foods."

Every ounce of air escaped me, and my heart dropped to my stomach.

"Alex Sans, we know your whereabouts. The world may have gone to pot, but there are these functioning things called satellites."

"What do I do?" I asked Beck.

Mera stepped forward. "Ignore them. You heard Randy, he said to run. Ignore them."

The radio man spoke again. "Three days, Sans. You agree to a meet, or we come to you. We don't even care if you come with us. You know what we need. Don't make this difficult for those in your group."

My head dropped again, and I walked to the microphone.

Difficult for those in my group.

Was it fair for all these children to be put in danger because of me and my failure to keep my word?

Randy's warning weighing heavily on my mind, I reached for the radio despite everyone yelling *No!* After taking a deep breath, I depressed the button. "This is Sans. If I agree to set up a meeting place, I'll do it on one condition. There's something you need to bring for this group."

"Go on."

I took a moment. "Randy Briggs."

That was my deal. If I agreed to go, agreed to leave with Phoenix, the group had to get Randy in return. They needed him and his knowledge and wisdom more than they needed me.

30
MERA STEVENS

It was a plan in which I was not privileged to know the details. In fact, only Alex, Beck and Sonny knew.

I was not happy about that. Bonnie was indifferent as long as we were all safe.

Sonny scouted out a farm not far away, about 100 miles south. He spent that whole first day going through the place. It was twelve miles from a small town. A quick scope from a distance didn't raise any Sleeper concerns.

In fact, the ranch wasn't too far from Lincoln, Nebraska, which, according to Sonny, was hit with some sort of bomb. Not a nuclear warhead, though, because bodies of decomposing Sleepers lined the street.

He was gone an entire day and returned on the second to load a truck and tow supplies.

Again, alone.

Alex stayed with us at the warehouse in case they were tracking him again.

He needed to be spotted leaving the warehouse as a decoy for those of us who would head south.

That alone told me that he had a plan, and that was to get Randy.

I asked him, "What about Phoenix?"

And he simply replied, "Don't worry about him."

I brought it up to Beck, and he told me, "All we need to do is stay alive, Mera. All of us. That has to be our priority. The moment Alex leaves and goes west, we travel south."

Alex set up a meeting place far from the warehouse, in the opposite direction.

I truly believed those in the ARC were smarter than Alex was giving them credit for.

The message from The New Jerusalem was playing three or four times a day.

Always the same:

This is the New Jerusalem. We are with people from Project Savior. We are a second facility. We seek others and believe with the right elements we can create a strong future.

Despite how much Alex and Michael tried to get a reply, no other response came.

The radio was to be the last thing we packed. Alex insisted that he took his turn on the air so the ARC could hear him.

It was winding down. It was D-Day—Deliverance Day. The school bus had to be left behind; it was too easily spotted. We picked up vehicles from neighboring areas and acquired as much gasoline as we could get.

I was glad I wasn't going to be riding in a bus or van since it was so hot. We placed a case of water in the sun, and it made a nice, warm bath for the babies. They enjoyed it, and it soothed them both. I hated leaving our gold mine of supplies, but Sonny was right; it would be there if we needed to make a run for more.

I had the babies in their Moses baskets, set outside the car. Jessie would ride in the back of the car with them, Beck and I up front. Danny and Bonnie were driving a truck with several children and Michael, with Jillian, was driving the van, and that was packed.

We were nervously prepared.

I expected that we'd all get in our vehicles at the same time. Three of us would go one way, and Alex and Sonny in the red pickup truck would go the other. In several hours, we'd be reunited with Sonny, Alex, and, hopefully, Randy.

I was more concerned making sure the children were safe in the van and knew the rules about staying still for Michael. The plan, even though I didn't know what it was, was set in stone.

We completed our packing, and Michael tossed the radio in the van. I was ready to put Jessie and the babies in the car.

Alex said his goodbyes, in case there was trouble. Sonny got in the truck, and just as Alex was about to get into the driver's seat, Bonnie yelled out, "Stop!"

Alex did. "What's wrong?"

"Aren't you forgetting something?"

Alex startled and looked around. "No."

"Yeah," she snapped rather quickly. "Alex, my God, please don't tell me that you are going to try to pull one over on the ARC people."

"What do you mean?"

"You haven't said anything. I figured you were just making a trade. I had no idea you were pulling a scam."

"Listen, Bonnie—"

"No, *you* listen, Alex," Bonnie scolded. "This isn't just you. This isn't just *your* life. These people threatened us. They know where you are, and if you think they won't find you, you are utterly mistaken. What are you and Sonny going to do, make a false exchange, get this Randy guy, and shoot the pilot and everyone on that chopper?"

"It is our only option."

"The hell it is!" she blasted. "My God, Alex. We have children here. Many children. Including the babies and teenagers there are close to twenty. You want to be accused of stealing the future of mankind, then damn it, put them in jeopardy and you have screwed mankind's future. Look at the faces, Alex. *They* are the future."

"I don't know what I can do. They want the child because he is immune, he holds a cure. Yet, our friend Randy said to run, which tells me there's danger."

"I agree," Bonnie said, "and if you think they won't take it one step further when you pull the wool over their eyes and don't give them a potential cure, an immune child, then you're wrong. The danger is there. They'll come for us. There are far too many of us to run and hide on a moment's notice."

"What do you want me to do, Bonnie?" Alex tossed out his hands. "Huh?"

"Do the right thing."

I thought, I honestly thought, Alex would just get in the truck, and we'd all head south.

"What's the right thing?"

"Give them what they want," Bonnie said.

My eyes widened. "He can't do that."

"He can." She stared at Alex. "He can and has to. It's one life against many. Do the right thing. The child was born and lived when all others died. He is unique." She stared intently at him. "Give them what they want."

"What if they only want to kill him?"

"Why would they do that?" she asked. "Really? He was born alive; he holds the key. But go without a baby and they will hunt us down. Do you want to risk the lives of this entire group over one baby?" She paused and locked another serious stare on him. "Do the right thing."

I couldn't believe it. I couldn't believe my ears or the case she presented. My heart raced and beat loudly. Alex grabbed hold of the door, looked at Bonnie, put his weapon in the truck, and then without hesitation walked to our car.

"She's right."

"What?" I gasped.

"I'm sorry, Mera. I'm sorry."

Before I could say anything else, Alex reached down, grabbed the baby basket and bolted to the truck.

Jessie screamed.

I screamed.

"Alex! Stop!" Beck blasted out, and charged full speed after the truck.

Alex peeled out. After my brief moment of shock, I ran as fast as I could run, chasing that truck. But he was long gone.

Alex didn't just rip a baby from our possession, he tore a part of my soul from me. I felt it physically tear from my gut. The pain blasted through me as if I had been stabbed. Crying out again, I dropped to the pavement in defeat.

Beck stooped down, wrapping his arms around me. "I'm sorry."

"We have to go after them," I wept. "We have to."

"Mera, we can't. We have to move everyone, and you know it."

My throat closed, and I could barely speak. "He took the baby."

"I'm sorry. I am so sorry." His lips pressed to the back of my head as he helped me stand.

"What was he thinking?"

Beck's voice was soft. "I think…he was thinking of the group. The many in the group. I can't say what was going through his mind, or what he'll do. I just know we have to go."

I accepted that explanation. With heartbroken reluctance, I turned to go back into the warehouse.

I would leave as we planned, but I would leave knowing that a part of me would never look at Alex Sans the same way.

With all that I'd lost, he'd taken another thing from me. I wasn't sure if I could ever forgive him. In addition, I was not sure if I even wanted him to return.

31
ALEX SANS

The minor league baseball stadium was the perfect place to meet. While the parking lot had its share of Sleepers, only a few wandered about inside the small ball field. Some in the stands and several on the field had met their final fate via the ARC people.

The chopper, blades idle, sat not far beyond second base. We made our way to the side entrance and had to be quick about it. Sleepers caught our tail and chased us.

Once through the gate, we secured it. About twenty Sleepers hit the fence. We were safe, but it wasn't going to be an easy exit for Sonny.

We talked very little in the truck. I couldn't even convey to another human being how horrible I felt for grabbing the baby. But I knew what I had to do.

I wasn't leaving the baby; I was leaving the group.

I told Sonny that Randy had a lot of answers and was pretty smart. While they wouldn't have my medical knowledge, they would have to make do. And whatever he did, he was to leave word where he went. A note at the ranch. Whatever.

I needed to be able to find them when I left the ARC. That was, *if* I left the ARC.

We weren't late by any means. In fact, I was willing to bet the chopper had arrived early, possibly clearing the stadium if it had been necessary. No one was around when we pulled in.

It wasn't until I stepped from the truck that the side of the small chopper slid open.

It wasn't like the first time. Men in black, carrying clipboards didn't step out. The first person that emerged wore a full biohazard suit and carried a weapon.

He waved his arm behind him and then I saw Randy.

Cleaned up and looking okay, Randy stepped from the chopper carrying his little bag, hopping to the ground. I immediately felt relieved, glad that Randy would be reunited with the group.

Two men in biohazard suits followed him out. Neither man was the pilot; from that, I knew there was a third man on board.

Randy stepped further away from the chopper.

I realized that my intention to take out the two or three men on the chopper would have been ineffective. They were waiting for me to try something, I could feel it.

With that plan scrapped, I went the congenial route and reached into the truck. "Good luck, Sonny."

"Godspeed, Alex." He handed me the Moses basket.

I grabbed my backpack and with the basket I walked to the chopper.

Randy crossed the baseline and headed toward the pitcher's mound. I paused in front of him; the first bio man wasn't taking chances. He was close behind.

"Take care of them all, Randy." I reached out and embraced him.

"Alex," he whispered in my ear, "don't go. Don't. I can't guarantee what will happen with you, but the Phoenix child…he'll be like an alien experiment."

Before breaking from the embrace, I told him, "Mera is alive. So is Beck, Jessie and there are others. Sonny will take you." I gave the man pat to his back. "See you in a few months."

"Alex, don't. I beg you."

I kept walking.

Before we reached the chopper, the bio man reached his gloved hands into the Moses basket. He nodded and pointed at the chopper.

As I neared, the blades began to rotate, and the engine whistled in pre-takeoff. They weren't wasting any time.

Bio Man stood with me at the door and then he climbed inside.

I took another look over my shoulder and waved goodbye to Randy and Sonny. I didn't know if I would ever see them again. I could only hope.

I lifted the baby basket to the floor of the chopper, and as I raised my foot to climb inside, all I saw was the butt of the rifle.

With no time to react or understand what was happening, it slammed hard into my face, my nose to be exact. The pain was unbelievable. I had been shot once, and even that hadn't hurt as much as this did. Perhaps because it was my nose. I didn't know. It was a hard, direct hit. It sent me reeling back. How far down I went or how hard I hit the ground, I didn't know.

I was out.

Engine noise and a wet cloth were deciding factors in my coming to, but not as much as the pain.

It shot through my face and to my temples. I didn't even want to open my eyes because I could tell the sun was bright and knew the how terrible it would feel.

I expected to see a man in a biohazard suit. I didn't expect to open my eyes and see Randy's round face staring down at me.

Was I…resting on his lap?

Oh my God, I was. In the back of a pickup truck, speeding down the road, I was cradled across the big man's lap.

I tried to sit up, not having a clue why that disturbed me.

"Hey, hey, easy," Randy said. "Easy. Stay down."

I didn't oblige. I inched from Randy and sat up on my own. One of those shake and cool bags flopped to my lap. At one point, it must have been on my head. I lifted it. "Where did this come from?"

"We uh, stopped at Walgreens. It wasn't hit too hard. We needed to get some first aid stuff for you. Sonny wiped out a lot of things. We have some good supplies for the winter and for cold and flu season."

My head spun, not to mention hurt like hell. *Cold and Flu season?* I wasn't out that long. It was only the end of July.

"How long was I out?"

"Long enough for me to think you had brain damage."

I tried to look at my watch, but it was blurry, so I peered at the sky. It looked like an afternoon sky. I could see the sun to my left, and we were headed south.

My stomach churned and flopped. "Can we stop for a second?"

"Yeah, feel sick?"

I nodded.

Randy reached out to the cab window, gave a couple of knocks, and pointed. I felt the truck pull over and then stop.

I thought I'd make it. I moved to my knees, began a crawl to the back of the truck, but my stomach had other plans.

I leaned over the side of the pickup, unable to stop myself from throwing up, and my head and face throbbed.

I heard Sonny. "Everything okay?"

"He's sick," Randy stated.

"Man," Sonny said. "You were right. Head injury."

"He hit his head pretty hard when he hit the ground. Then again, it could have been the morphine."

Morphine? my mind screamed. I stomached being sick long enough to sit up straight. "Morphine?"

Randy nodded. "We gave you a shot of morphine. We had to. We didn't want to take the chance that you might wake up when we set your nose."

Lifting my hand to my face, I felt the bandages.

Sonny said, "It was pretty bad, Alex. He hit ya on the side of your nose and sent it almost to the other cheek. Never seen a nose that bad, and I used to box."

No wonder I couldn't breathe. "It was that bad?" I tried to focus.

Randy pointed to his own face to demonstrate, "The rifle hit you square on the side of the nose and face. Caught your eye." He winced. "Not pretty. And your cheek bone. I think that may be busted. Hard to tell." His tone changed to an optimistic one. "But, we set your nose straight."

"How long was I out?" I grumbled. "Obviously long enough for you guys to shop and perform minor surgery."

"We're about fifteen miles from the ranch," Sonny replied. "You've been out a while. We didn't move for the longest time. Randy thought you had brain damage."

"I did," Randy said. "Nose injuries can cause brain injuries. Plus, you lost a lot of blood."

"Oh my God. From one hit?"

Sonny looked at me with an eye closed. "It was a good hit. Hey, we picked up Zofran in case you got nauseous. Want one?"

I shook my head. "I'll be fine."

"Yeah," Sonny said, "you may need it later after we get Beck to stitch ya. Neither of us wanted to attempt that."

"I need stitches too? Just...just get us back. Thanks."

Sonny left me and Randy in the back of the truck.

I don't know why I was in such a hurry. I had totally screwed up everything. Nothing went as planned. I was supposed to be on that chopper. I was supposed to be with the baby, so I could keep watch over him. The pain in my face and head paled in comparison to what I felt in my soul.

How would I face them? How would I face Mera? She was going to hate me. I didn't blame her. I hated myself.

I sank against the side of the truck. "Randy, why do you think they did this to me? Why didn't they take me along?"

"You gave them what they wanted." Randy handed me a bottle of water. "Maybe they didn't want to chance any more trouble with you."

The water was good. My mouth was dry and tasted like blood. "Are they going to kill him?"

"Not intentionally, but they will after they are done," Randy answered with a somber tone. "It's not what we thought. In fact, it's not what they thought either with Phoenix."

I sighed heavily. "What do you know about this Keller in the doctrines?"

"Keller?" Randy cocked back in surprise. "Really? *Keller?* I didn't think you read that far."

"I didn't. Michael did, and he—"

"Michael?" Randy smiled. "He's alive?"

I nodded.

"Like the Doctrines said. He rose from the ashes. He is the Son of God."

I winced. "That's debatable. And, well, talk to him about that. He took notes and didn't understand them. Who is Keller?"

"According to the Doctrines, Keller is equivalent to the Antichrist. Doctrines state he couldn't speak, hear or see, yet, he was so extraordinary he communicated using his mind. But he did so with the Pale...I mean Sleepers," Randy said. "That was the part I thought was metaphorical. Why are you asking about Keller?"

"Because..." I took a sip of water, wetting my dry mouth and lips. "It wasn't Phoenix in the basket. The ARC took Keller."

32
ALEX SANS

"I swear to God, Alex," Beck's deep voice was grim as he hovered over me, preparing to fix my wounds, "if this face wasn't as bad as it is, I'd deck you."

"If I didn't feel so bad already, I'd let you."

"I should just let this gash stay open and get infected, at the very least look bad."

I hadn't even made it to the ranch house yet. Sonny had brought me into the heavy equipment shed and sought out Beck. I didn't see the Randy and Mera reunion, or Danny's reaction, or even Beck's.

Lying on that work bench, I waited in the shed, like a criminal. And it was by my choice, because that's how I felt. Like a criminal.

Beck was less than gentle with his sutures. He was so angry that he grunted in disgust.

"Come on, Beck," Sonny said. "Ease up, okay?"

"Do you know what he did?" Beck asked.

"Yeah, I was there, remember?"

"And you condone it?"

"Let me ask you this," Sonny said. "What choice did he have? I was there when we arrived at the field. The original plan would have failed. Big time. They had four armed men, at least from what I saw. Three of us came back. Had we proceeded as planned, none of us would have."

"It was a baby, Sonny. An innocent baby he turned over to them for experiments."

"He didn't plan on handing him over; he planned on going with him. They did this to him so he couldn't go."

I exhaled loudly. "I'm here, you know. I can defend myself."

"Then why don't you?" Sonny asked.

"Well, Son, I'm a little busy right now," I replied. "Plus, what I did was wrong."

"I knew that baby as long as you guys did," Sonny said. "Yeah, you know what? It was heartbreaking to hear Mera. It was heartbreaking to take him. But how much more heartbreaking would it have been if we'd gone without a baby, got shot up on that field, and Beck and the kids were defenseless when the ARC came looking for the child? How many kids then would have to die?" He looked at Beck. "How would you feel then, Beck, if they came, started shooting and Mera or Jessie got hit? All because we failed to give them what they wanted."

"It wouldn't have come to that."

"Then I think you need to talk to your friend Randy. From what I got from him, the ARC is for continuation of life, at all cost."

"I don't believe that." Beck snipped the sutures and stepped back. "I don't believe they'd shoot or chance that with Phoenix, why would they take a chance on killing their cure?"

As I sat up, Randy's voice entered the shed with the answer to Beck's question.

"Because Phoenix isn't the cure; he's the hub."

Both Beck and I looked at him with surprise. "He's like a queen bee; he exudes something. They say the only reason I was born, that everyone in the future was born, was because the Phoenix child died. He was never able to keep the virus alive. As long as he lives, so does the virus in its active, current form. Any child born, anyone with a latent form of the virus...done. They believe if he lives, man dies. He'd have to die or be locked away airtight for his entire life."

"How do they know this?" I asked. "He was the only one of us that they didn't test."

"Because every single person that came within fifty feet of him in there breathed his air," Randy explained. "If the people in the ARC had the dormant virus, they were Sleepers the next day, the President included. It wasn't me, you or Danny. Everyone was okay until Phoenix showed up."

I blinked several times, my head spinning. The news just delivered was mind-boggling and a little unbelievable.

"What else is screwy?" Randy went on. "Days later, the germ is still lingering. He carries the purest form of the virus, from what they said. Then again, they didn't tell me as much as I wanted to know."

Beck asked. "How come?"

"They told me that they were preserving mankind's future. And I and the others were a threat. I knew too much, I don't know enough, germs I carried, I don't know. They kept me locked away, like a prisoner. Barely fed me. My friend died."

"Well, really," I said, "no disrespect, Randy, but if you think about it, you'll remember you didn't come here to protect our time, but to protect the future, meaning *your* time."

"Agreed."

"Wait," Sonny called out. "Why are you still here, Randy? I'm confused. If Phoenix died in these Doctrines, and they're saying that Phoenix can cause mankind's extinction, why are you here? That has to be wrong. Theoretically, if that's true and

Phoenix is man's ruin, you would have never been born; therefore, you wouldn't be here." He scratched his head. "I think."

Not that I was a science fiction aficionado, but that made sense. "Maybe Phoenix does die. We still have to arrive at the real New Jerusalem."

"Perhaps, like Alex said," Sonny commented, "the doctrines are fiction."

"I take offense to that," Randy said. "The Doctrines are very sacred teachings to my people."

"Yeah, so is the Bible in this time," I said, "but man has doctored it up a lot."

"It's conceivable that Phoenix never died," Sonny remarked. "That maybe the events written by this guy actually took place, but to protect Phoenix from this exact scenario, he wrote that Phoenix died to protect everyone. Write that everyone who has the baby died."

"I'd think that in order for Bill to fictionalize on purpose he would have to know about the time travel stuff," Beck said.

"The Doctrines are written from the perspective that Logan had no prior knowledge of time travel or Project Savior."

"Doesn't make sense," Sonny said.

"Maybe Keller is the Phoenix child," Beck suggested.

"No, Keller is in the Doctrines." I said. "The Antichrist or something. Maybe he battles with Michael."

"That isn't funny, Alex," Randy said sharply.

Tossing a cloth to the side, Beck gathered his things. "I'm going to the ranch. Mera still isn't good. And Antichrist or not, you handed a human being over to the ARC. An innocent helpless baby. It sickens me to think what they'll do to that baby. And worse, what the ARC is going to do when they find out it isn't the Phoenix child." Beck moved to the door. "When you are done hiding your balls you need to join us to come up with a plan. Come on, Randy, I'm sure Mera is waiting to see you."

I looked up surprised to learn that Randy hadn't seen Mera yet. "You haven't seen her?"

"I wouldn't be here, Alex, had you not gotten me out. I thought it was right to wait on you."

"Go on. I'm not quite done hiding my balls."

That was actually putting it mildly. I insisted on being alone for a little while longer. I needed to draw up the courage to face Mera and everyone else I hurt by taking Keller.

Inwardly, I felt what I did was morally wrong, and I never intended it to end up the way it did.

When I grabbed the baby, I thought I'd just stay with him.

Every time I thought about my actions I felt that lump in my gut. I didn't have a clue as to how to make it right.

I kept thinking of that poor baby who craved loving arms and just as he had them, I took them from him and handed him over to a cold lab. He couldn't see, he couldn't hear, he could only feel, and I'd condemned him to a life of feeling pain instead of love.

As I lay back on the bench, every part of me felt too heavy to move.

The head injury, the morphine, whatever the reason, my eyes were heavy, and I shut them.

Think, Alex, think of a solution before you face them. Have something to say. Something to offer to Mera to right your wrong.

After some time, the creak of the shed door caused me to open my eyes. The door was ajar, but I didn't see anyone.

Not at first.

In pain, not thinking clearly, I immediately thought a Sleeper walked in.

I heard the shuffling of feet. I looked to my right. Then the little head popped up. Marissa.

"Hi," she said. She must have been standing on something. She folded her hands and set them by my arms.

"Hey."

"I heard you were back safely. You don't look very good."

"I don't feel very good."

"That has to hurt. Sonny said your nose fell off, and they put it back on."

"It feels like it."

"It looks like it. Your face is very blue," she said. "I didn't think the devil's workers could be injured."

"Probably can't. But..." I winked with my one good eye, "I'm not a devil's worker."

"Then why do you have the devil's work on your arms?"

"They're called tattoos. Each one means something. See this here..." I rolled over and pointed to a woman's face.

"She's pretty."

"That's my mom. I got this when she died. And this..." I pointed to another, "symbolizes the division of the Navy I served. This one, the wars. And this one," I showed her a tattoo of a pocket watch, "is for the old man who made me think that it is quality of life versus quantity."

"How did he do that?"

"He had a heart attack; he was very old. I brought him back."

"Like Jesus?"

"No, like a good paramedic. And he asked me why I saved him, why I didn't just let him die? I don't know...just stuck with me. So you see, I decorated my arms. The tattoos are permanent, like the events and the people that marked my life. A little secret...I'm not a bad person."

"No, Alex Sans, you are not. That's why I came in here. Bonnie said you felt bad because they left you behind and that they took Keller."

"I'm feeling bad mainly because I handed them Keller."

"He was a sacrifice."

"Pretty big word for a little girl."

"Not really." She tilted her head. "Alex Sans, I am not mad at you for what you did. None of us children are mad. You made a choice. Doctor Noah once told us that the needs of the many must outweigh the needs of the few."

"Mr. Spock."

She shook her head. "No, Doctor Noah. Were you not listening?"

That comment made me smile. "I'm sorry."

"That's okay. You're hurt, both inside and out. I just wanted you to know, I'm not angry. I'm glad you're okay and that you're back." Then, surprising me, she leaned forward and placed her lips to my cheek then whispered in my ear. "You're our protector. I feel safe with you around. Thank you for coming back."

That was it for me. I closed my eyes tight, a huge lump forming in my throat. I reached up, cupping her head and holding her near me. I tried, God knows I tried to stay calm and in control. But I couldn't. Not after her innocent words.

A tear had not crossed the creases of my face in decades, yet there it was, rolling down my face.

"Are you crying, Alex Sans?"

"Trying not to."

She whispered, "It's okay. I won't tell anyone. I'll let you rest." She kissed me again and stepped from whatever it was she was standing on.

I was about to break down, right then and there. Sob like I never had. I felt the sorrow rise in me, felt it build. I would have had bawled had she not stopped at the shed door and looked back.

"Alex Sans?"

"Yeah?" I sniffled.

Ever so innocently and pure, she said, "I overheard Beck. Just know, I'm praying you find your lost balls."

She darted out with a skip, and alone in that shed, I laughed. But my laugh was indeed laced with tears.

33
MERA STEVENS

There was an ache in my soul that wouldn't go away. Keller hadn't been in my life very long, but he left his mark. It felt unresolved. What would become of him, what would they do to that poor baby? And there he would be, vulnerable to it all.

There was a basement bedroom that was large, and I chose it as the place for my family. I was there with Jessie. We had just cleaned up, and I was brushing her hair. While I did that, she brushed the wispy hairs on Phoenix's head. His eyes were so bright, and he stared at Jessie with so much love.

She cradled him like a little girl with a baby doll.

I hid from everyone because I didn't want to face them. I was the only one feeling so strongly about Alex handing over Keller. Beck was angrier over what it did to me, I was sure of it. Danny didn't say much. He, like Michael, accepted Alex's reasoning.

After a while, I emerged with Jessie and Phoenix. Supper was waiting. There was a sense of security on that ranch, but I knew it wouldn't last long, especially after speaking to Beck and Randy about the bait and switch.

We expected to hear from the ARC, but we hadn't. I only hoped a missile wouldn't fly our way.

Alex didn't join us, but that didn't matter to me. I still didn't want to face him. I was bitter and angry and unsure if I would forgive him.

Things quieted down about nine p.m. I joined Bonnie in tucking in the children. The living and dining room combo was like one large dorm room with sleeping bags neatly laid out.

They all prayed at the same time, the same way, the same prayer out loud.

"Father of light, protect us from the storm…"

It was creepy and weird, but then again, probably something they learned in their cult.

They all laid down the same way at the same time. I felt as though I were watching *Village of the Damned*. I made sure I said goodnight to each one of them before leaving the room.

Jessie was getting tired. She'd started showing interest in using the bathroom but still hadn't grasped it. I freshened her and placed her in bed with Phoenix in the basket next to her. The battery-operated baby monitor was between them, and I took the receiver with me. I listened to every breath they took. I was going to get a drink, talk to Beck before he took the watch, and I wouldn't stay away from them long.

When I emerged into the kitchen, my heart dropped to my stomach when I saw Alex. I fixed my drink and walked to the door.

He spoke my name, but I held up my hand to him and continued outside.

"Mera," he called again.

"Don't, Alex." I spun to face him. "Please, don't look at me and don't speak to me. Please."

He lowered his head. "I'll make this right."

"You can't. You turned that baby over to the ARC. My God, what that child must be thinking, feeling. You can't make this right. Ever."

"I'm sorry. If I have to, I'll go to the ARC."

I laughed. "They kicked your ass to keep you out. They'll kill you next time. Not that it's a bad thing." I turned and walked over to where Michael, Danny and Randy were sitting at a picnic table.

"That's harsh," Michael said. "You know, Jesus tells us to—"

"Don't throw Jesus at me, okay? Not now. I'm still extremely angry. I may say something unpleasant."

Danny chuckled. "Like you haven't before."

I sat down. "Where's Beck?"

"Checking the fences with Sonny," Randy answered. He raised his eyes. "Mera, I know you're hurting. But for the sake of us all, you are going to have to let this go. Alex did what he did for the sake of everyone. I know it's painful, I know it seems wrong." He lowered his voice. "He can't forgive himself. Can we try?"

"Um, no."

"I'll pray for you, Mera," Michael said.

Randy said, "Please do, you have the gift."

"Really, I don't," Michael countered. "I think Beck is right. I'm a Sleeper, somehow, or have it in me like Jessie. And really, this is pathetic..." He lifted his hand. "Alex, join us."

I huffed. Michael and Randy both said my name with a scold.

Alex slid in at the picnic table, he tried to make light. "Maybe I should make friends with Jillian since she and I are on the outs with Mera."

"It's not funny," I said then looked at him. He honestly did look pathetic. Face all bruised and swollen, nose bandaged. "Alex, I'm trying. I don't want to hate you. I don't want to hate Jillian. I'm just angry, okay?"

"I understand. I'm angry with myself."

"This is a start," Michael said. "Maybe I'll play with the radio and have some luck reaching the New Jerusalem."

At that, oddly, Randy chuckled.

Michael turned to him. "That's funny?"

"I was just thinking. One of the times they released me was to talk to Alex. They were picking up that recording, too. Swore up and down it was Alex. Said the voice analysis was coming up a match. I thought it was funny, because no sooner did one of the communication guys say it was too far away, that satellite picked up your life signal."

That immediately caught my attention. "Too far away, did they mention where?"

"I think south, they didn't say much. I was stuck on the fact they thought it was Alex. Had it not been for that satellite, they'd have chased that signal."

Danny asked, "Can you pick up the satellite with that computer thingy of yours?"

"I'll try, but it needs to charge in the sun for a while," Randy answered.

"Think I'll play with the radio and try to pick up…" Michael said jokingly, "Alex." He walked to the radio a few feet away and turned it on.

"Yeah, can you either try to tune it in better or turn it down," Danny said. "I know you guys are into it, but I don't know how that beeping doesn't drive you nuts."

We all looked at him as if *he* were nuts.

"What?" he shifted his eyes about.

"What beeping?" I asked.

"During the recording," Danny replied. "It's annoying. Like feedback."

Michael scratched his head. "I don't know what you are talking about."

Just then the recording played.

This is the New Jerusalem. We are with people from Project Savior. We are a second facility. We seek others and believe with the right elements we can create a strong future.

"There!" Danny said. "Hear it? Right there."

I looked at Randy, then Michael then even Alex. We were clueless.

"You guys are joking me, right?" Danny smiled and then the smile dropped. "You're not joking? How can you not hear that?"

I honestly didn't know what he was talking about. At first, I thought my son was making a joke, but he was dead serious.

"You can't hear that?" Danny asked. "It's freaking annoying."

"What do you hear, Danny?" Alex asked quizzically.

"The voice, and mixed with it is the feedback. It's going 'Beep. Beep-beep. Beep.' Constantly. Fast."

Alex jumped up. "Don't turn that off," he instructed Michael. "I have to find Beck."

It was another half hour before the message played again, and Beck, along with Sonny, looked as stunned as I did.

Danny, however, was insistent.

"Does it sound like a pattern?" Beck asked Danny, "Possibly a code?"

Danny's eyes widened. "It could be Morse code."

Alex asked. "How are we not hearing it?"

"Could it be on a different frequency?" Sonny suggested. "Maybe the code is coming in on an ultra high frequency that we can't hear."

"Mosquito!" Danny shouted.

I jumped, looked, didn't see anything. "Where?"

"No," Danny said. "Not a bug. Technology. People over a certain age can't hear certain frequencies."

Beck's head flung back. "Kilohertz."

Alex nodded. "Has to be at least 17 kilohertz. Maybe even higher. He can hear it and no one over twenty-five can. We need to be sure it's there."

Beck rubbed his chin then turned to me. "Can you grab one of the kids? One of the older ones. If they hear it, then we know they hid a code in the message."

"Why would they broadcast at such a high frequency?"

Randy answered, "To hide it from the ARC. If most adults can't hear, they can't."

Beck looked at me. "Get Marissa."

I nodded and hurried to the house.

My stirring of Marissa brought out Bonnie and even Jillian. We didn't say anything to Marissa as to why she was awake. She yawned and almost fell asleep at the table.

It was another hour before the message played again.

This is the New Jerusalem. We are with people from Project Savior. We are a second facility. We seek others and believe with the right elements we can create a strong future.

Beck asked her, "Do you hear anything?"

Disinterested, Marissa yawned. "Yes, the message. The man." She sleepily propped her face in her hand.

"Anything else besides the man's voice?" Beck asked.

She squinted. "That's Potter's code."

We all shouted, *"What?"*

Marissa crinkled her brow. "Potter's code. Beeps, short and long that spell words. It's mixed in there." She listened. "Yeah, it's there."

"You mean Morse code," Alex said.

She snickered. "That's an archaic term. But yes." Her head cocked. "Hmm. W-a-i-t-i-n-g. Waiting?" She sat up straighter.

Alex moved to her. "You know Morse code?"

She scoffed. "Doesn't everybody?"

"No!" he blasted. "They don't."

Jillian said with surprise, "I do."

Alex tossed out his hand. "You can't hear that?"

She shook her head. "No, they probably want to reach young people."

"And she's young and can hear it." Alex smiled. "Someone get me a pen and paper. This girl is not going to bed."

"Hey!" Marissa whined.

"You're a godsend." Alex kissed on the head. "God bless that survival cult of yours." Sonny slid a notebook and pen to Marissa. "Ignore my notes. There are blank pages."

"What am I doing?" Marissa asked.

"Listening. And writing down what they are saying in the code," Alex told her.

"You know anyone can do this. You don't need me."

"Yeah, I'm sure. We want you to do it," Alex said. "Just wait. He'll come on again."

Marissa, pen in hand, opened to an empty page and sighed.

I was dumbfounded. Marissa seemed to think we were overreacting. She didn't recognize the talent she possessed. Her community taught her well, gave her practical skills at an early age.

Amazed, we waited. Even though I wanted to go to bed, I had to see what the hidden messages said. So, with the baby monitor nearby, along with everyone else, with bated breath I hung around that picnic table with Marissa and the radio.

Doctrines 42: 3-14

And they came upon his village. He was an enigma to all who had not seen him. He stood tall and dressed in a long black cloak. The hood covered every part of his face but his chin and neck. Keller did not speak. It was well known that he had the gift of unspoken communication. He was able to get into the mind of others to convey what he wanted, to sway them. Mostly, he communicated with the Palers. He gathered them, prepared them for battle. If he did not fall, his rise to power would be strengthened by the Palers. And they would survive ordinary man for generations to come. They already outnumbered him. The Keller had to die.

34
RANDY BRIGGS

I read several passages of the Doctrines to Sonny because he showed interest in Keller. I found Sonny to be bright and strong with a hint of ambivalence to him. He reminded me of Bill.

Marissa was only able to listen to two more messages before she fell back to sleep. I was impressed at the knowledge of this little girl. Admittedly, I didn't know about religious cults. We didn't have them where I came from and what I did know was what I read in history books. None of the cults that made it into history books was viewed as positive.

Another child was placed on the task, and Marissa had the next day to listen. She was able to pick up that they were looking for a Dr. Javier, a name I didn't recognize. The message said they were with people from Project Savior.

Explaining things to Sonny was a bit more difficult, not that he didn't understand, but he already had some doubts.

"So this Keller guy was a telepathic leader who led the Palers into battle against normal man?"

I nodded. "Yes, it was the Paler-Man wars that took place about twenty years after the plague."

"Then it couldn't be the baby we handed over," Sonny said. "That baby, sadly, isn't going to see his first birthday. He is a sickly thing. The name has to be a coincidence."

At that point, Alex joined us as we sat in what was probably the family room of the home.

"How are you feeling?" I asked Alex.

"Better, thank you. Need to sleep." He nursed what I assumed was a warm beer. Sonny said, "Go to bed."

"Not yet. Just waiting. We put another kid on the radio with Jillian. She can't hear, but can translate what he writes."

"Why is that?" Sonny asked. "Why did this group know Morse code?"

Alex shrugged. "Survival stuff. They taught them all young."

"Weird." Sonny sat back. "Just like the Keller guy in the Doctrines."

"He was," I said. "There are chapters of the Doctrines dedicated to him. He was quite evil, feared by our people, portrayed as the Antichrist."

"And you never bought it," Alex stated.

"Wouldn't say I didn't buy it," Randy answered. "I just thought it was over the top, too supernatural to make sense. I always saw it as a metaphor. Maybe it was originally written as a metaphor and the translators took it further."

"And really, think about it," Sonny said. "Two decades after the plague. How did the Palers survive? Wasn't there a Surmising?"

"Reckoning," I corrected. "And there was. The Doctrines made it sound like God cleansed the land, but we know now it was man. The Doctrines stated the Palers hid and survived. We know now the Government didn't make a clean sweep."

Alex said, "I think what Sonny is getting to is how did they survive twenty years to fight."

I looked at Alex and then Sonny. "You're kidding, right? They...evolve. Reproduce."

Alex shrieked like a little girl. "They *reproduce*? Out there right now they are having sex?"

"I don't think yet," I said. "But like animals, they will. And yes, they reproduce. In one hundred years, they are hunted like deer."

Sonny whistled. "Are you shitting me? Do they at least calm down?"

"No, they are violent. Always violent. In my time, we are divided fifty-fifty. It's scary. The virus keeps taking many of our young, so our numbers dwindle. The percentage has grown through the decades. Mankind as we knew it was facing extinction. Without the cure, this running from Sleepers doesn't stop. Man just gets better at it."

Sonny sat back with folded arms. "This is where I don't get it. You came back to find Phoenix, to save him and deliver the cure. So...that your children don't die? So, that maybe there are no more Sleepers or Palers?"

I nodded.

"From your understanding, Project Savior came back to our time to deliver a virus meant to enhance the human race, make us better, to be ready for some sort of takeover."

"Yes."

Sonny shook his head. "Theoretically, it won't work. If you guys were smart enough to have time travel, then you should have been smart enough to know you cannot go back and change the fact that causes you to time travel in the first place."

"What do you mean?" Alex asked.

I knew what he meant; my colleagues and I had discussed it many times.

Sonny explained. "Time will adjust itself. Randy cannot change the circumstances that caused him to come back. How was the future able to release viruses that would change their own existence? You can't. It would create a paradox that could collapse."

"But it didn't," I said. "Nothing collapsed, so theories are wrong."

"That's because it may still have the same outcome yet," Sonny stated. "Or again, the Doctrines were tweaked to mislead. Let's face it, they're fiction. At least in part. No names were ever given. It was the Mother, the Technological Man. In any event, nothing can change. It won't."

Alex fluttered his lips. "I hate time travel shit. Can we stop talking about it? It makes my head spin. You can go in circles repeatedly, and it still doesn't make sense. Accept it and move on."

But I had to know. "How do you know about time travel and things like that?"

Before Sonny answered, Alex did. "Television. *Star Trek*. Movies."

Sonny nodded. "Yep. It's all speculation. I was a big science fiction nut. I loved to write it, too. Time travel stories were my favorite genre to write."

"I thought you worked for the power company?" I said.

"I did," Sonny replied. "But I loved to write."

"Were you published?" Alex asked.

At that point, Sonny did something odd. He grew silent, relaxed a little, and took a sip of his own drink. "No. Not yet. However I...I have a feeling I will be, and it will be a monster hit."

Alex chafed at that. "Dude, really, I don't think you're landing that dream publishing contract. And you have a captive audience. Probably you're the only writer alive."

"No, I'm serious. I hadn't said anything. Take a..." Sonny reached into his back pocket and pulled out his wallet.

Alex, in his usual manner, joked, "You have your wallet?"

"Yeah. Identification. What if I need it?"

"Go on," I encouraged. "What were you saying?"

"I was saying, I didn't mention it before, but I think I may end up being a very famous writer." He tossed his wallet on the table and it opened, exposing his driver's license.

Alex, of course, laughed, and that was short lived because at that second Michael raced into the room.

"We have a location," Michael said, out of breath. "We got the location of the New Jerusalem."

He ran out after that announcement. Alex ran out right behind him.

Sonny swept up his wallet and ran out as well.

I saw it.

Alex didn't. I'm not sure if Sonny knew that I saw. But I did.

Sonny was possibly right when he said he was going to write the biggest book of the future.

The Doctrines were originally called Logan's Logs, named after the man who'd penned them. That part was true. And after I met the group of survivors, I believed and conveyed to them that Logan's Logs must have been written by Bill Logan, one of our group who died.

What I read of the Doctrines to the others, what they had read, probably was written as hearsay. The author of the Doctrines wasn't there. That would explain why they weren't written in first person.

The author wrote the story as he heard it or as he wanted it conveyed. This meant much of the Doctrines had to be fiction. Written by a fiction writer.

I believed they were written by Bill. Until Sonny tossed his wallet on the table.

Sonny was his nickname. His driver's license had his real name.

His last name was Wilson, but Sonny's first name was Logan.

35
ALEX SANS

There was an air of enthusiasm and excitement as if we had struck gold, and we had. Nick didn't just translate a location—the New Jerusalem gave an address.

Or close to it. Three letters.

They were both eerie and ironic to me, although I had to be the one to explain it to everyone, not all picked up on it at first.

The three letters: TPL.

The code stated, 'We are at TPL. Eldorado. Clean sweep. All clear.'

I smacked myself on the head when I heard it. It made perfect sense, and I wanted to kick myself for not thinking of it as a place to go. I was thinking about prisons and such.

TPL. The Promised Land, or the Fundamentalist Church of Latter Day Saints compound in Eldorado. It was built as a self sufficient community, farm land, water treatment, sewage disposal and, most of all, those inside were protected from the outside modern world by concrete walls, twelve feet high. Some said it was equipped with high tech security around the perimeter, but that didn't matter. To me, twelve foot fences were safeguards against Sleepers.

It housed about a thousand people. No one remembered it until I reminded them of the raid in 2008 when child abuse allegations ran rampant, with televised images of child brides, images of women in long dresses and braided hair.

Clean sweep, all clear, I took as meaning they had cleared either bodies or Sleepers. Or heck, maybe, like the bus children, no one turned or got sick. After all, like Marissa and crew, they had lived secluded lives.

Another cult.

I had to laugh when Randy asked, "What is it with your society and cults?"

Mera shuddered at the idea of what all went on there, and Beck said, "It's not what happened; it's what *will* happen there that counts."

Self-sufficient. Protected.

Ironic because of Marissa and the others.

Perfect because its nickname was a Fortress for God. Fortress for God? How about New Jerusalem.

How much more sense could it make?

Much more sense than NORAD, I can tell you.

We missed the mark the first time. We wouldn't make that same mistake again.

We couldn't talk to them, nor did we want to try. We did radio a message that we knew the location and would be en route. I wished we could replicate their frequency, but we couldn't.

Everyone patted Nick on the back, thanked Jillian, then Marissa must have heard the buzz and came out to see what was happening.

She looked so dejected that I kind of felt sorry for her.

Beck returned to roof watch, Mera went inside, Sonny and Randy engaged in a conversation about something, and Marissa stared at the radio.

"What is it?" I asked her.

"I wanted to be the one to solve the mystery."

I smiled. "You did really well."

"Please, Alex Sans. I just heard that they are looking for a Doctor. I don't know that name, do you?"

I shook my head.

"Nick is nowhere near as smart as me. I can't believe he solved it."

"He didn't solve it; he just was the one to hear it."

"Did I miss anything else?"

"Not much."

"I'm still going to listen."

"Good. Good." I laid my hand on her head. "I think it is amazing and very cool that you know how to understand that code."

"Why did no one teach it to you?" she asked. "Was it not standard education when you grew up?"

"No."

"But you were in wars."

"I was supposed to learn it. It didn't stick with me."

"Then you didn't have a good teacher," she said. "I will teach it to you one day."

"I'd like that."

"How is your face?" she asked.

"Hurts."

"It looks much better."

"Really?"

"Oh, yes." She nodded. "It's not as big. And your eyeball isn't all red, just mostly red."

"That's good to know. So, are you gonna go back to bed?"

"No, I'd like to stay up and listen. Maybe they'll give more information. What about you?"

"I think I'll sit with you."

She smiled at me. "I'd like that."

Just as I reached for the radio a call came through.

"Alex Sans."

My entire being sank when I heard that. My name being blasted over the radio meant it was the ARC. I hoped that they were calling to thank me, but a part of me knew they weren't.

I peered up, it didn't take long for Michael, Randy and Sonny to inch their way closer.

"Alex Sans, if you are there can you please respond?" he repeated.

Marissa looked at me with her enormous eyes. "He is saying please; maybe you should answer. He has not said please before."

I wanted and needed permission from someone. Michael nodded.

I lifted the transceiver microphone. "This is Alex Sans. Over."

"Alex, we're not gonna play games, mince words, or make threats. This radio call is about as serious as it can get. Do you copy?"

"I copy."

"The child you gave us is useless. It is not the same child. The infant won't survive despite our abilities. The infant is also immune to the virus. Over."

"Isn't that what you wanted?"

"We have plenty of immune people. We followed what people said of the Phoenix child, that he held the cure, not just immunity. Mr. Sans, I'm not a soldier; I'm a doctor. Phoenix infected a lot of people. Instantaneously. He is like a hive. We believe he breeds the virus. We don't know how or why; we need to find this out. If he is out in the open, out with the general population or those who survived, he will infect anyone with a dormant strain. Any pregnant woman around him will not give birth to a healthy child. Do you understand? Over."

I lifted the radio. "Yes."

"We can't confirm any of this until he is tested. If he carries the pure virus, he may be contagious, but he may also be the key to stopping it. He may also be the key to curing some of the infected. We do not, I repeat, do not want to kill the child. We need the child. We need to acquire him and contain him. Is that clear? Over."

"It's clear. But why was our man so insistent that we run with the baby?"

"Perhaps he didn't have a clear understanding. I don't know. He did know the child is a highly contagious carrier. We need that child. That is not an option. The only option is when you deliver the child. We will return the defective child to you. We need the Phoenix. Each day that goes by, more of our five thousand in the ARC are vulnerable. Each day that goes by, you, your group, all of you may be immune to this particular strain, but one common cold, one flu bug caught by the Phoenix child, and that virus can mutate. All of you are in danger as long as you possess the child."

"And if we don't hand over the child?"

"I'm afraid they will find you. With ease. They know where you are now. They'll follow you and take him at all cost. It is that important. I can assure you, he will not be harmed. Mr. Sans, I give you my word."

I chuckled. "Your word? I don't even know who you are."

"My name is Doctor Albert Javier."

Javier? I looked around at everyone.

Marissa tugged my sleeve. "That's the guy the New Jerusalem is looking for."

I whispered to her, "I know." I glanced to Michael. Michael just shrugged as if he didn't know what to tell me.

"Mr. Sans," Javier continued, "do the right thing. We need him, humanity needs him."

He followed up with they'd be in touch and a single "over."

That was it.

The man New Jerusalem was searching for had radioed us. Both places needed Phoenix, but the New Jerusalem needed Javier. A heck of a Catch-22.

It was too much, too confusing, and it was getting late. My face hurt and my mind swirled with questions that went unanswered. We all sat in a heavy silence following the radio call. It was a call we'd have to tell the others about in the morning.

Until then, we'd try to rest.

36
MERA STEVENS

Jessie ran the soft bristled brush over Phoenix's silky hair while I rubbed lotion on his body. He smiled and cooed over the pampering. I didn't want to leave the Ranch. We had been there two days, and it took that long to get things ready. The kids needed rest.

Sonny and Randy hid a truck with supplies.

The ARC made several more pleas to Alex, and I felt the urgency in each one.

"We're moving out," Beck stepped into the room. "You ready?"

"Yeah," I nodded. "Beck, are we doing the right thing?"

"We have to go to the New Jerusalem, you know this. Phoenix needs to get there."

"But they're looking for Javier. If they're looking for him, then they need him for the cure."

"Mera, I don't know what to tell you to make you feel better. We're going south. It's a safe place."

"They know our every move, Beck."

He lowered his head. "And they're playing mind games."

"So you don't think Phoenix is a danger to any of us?"

"Look at him, Mera. Look at him. Does he look like a danger?"

I glanced down to the baby. He was so innocent, so special. It was hard to believe it was the same baby that was smaller than my forearm not three months earlier. "What about Keller? What will they do?"

"I don't know. We have to go. Jessie, honey..." Beck motioned with his head, "go on to the car, me and Mom will be right out."

"Kay Ba," she smiled and ran out.

Laying his hand on my shoulders, Beck turned me from the baby. "Listen, I know you're worried. I am, too. Sonny and Randy spotted a small town on the map they think may be a decent place to stop for the evening. Midway, you know. We're gonna be fine. We're gonna go to this place in Texas, and we're going to start a new life."

"What if they come for Phoenix?"

"Then I promise you, with everything I am, I will protect him. I will die for him if I have to. I'd die for all of you."

He meant that. I felt it and heard it and with his words I moved into his embrace, baby in my arms, taking comfort from him. Stepping back, I stared at Beck for a moment, searching out that last reassurance before we left. He placed his lips softly to mine.

"Ugh!" Danny blasted. "Dude, are you kissing my *mom*?"

Beck did his rare half smile and stepped back with a shake of his head. "I *am* kissing your mom. I like kissing your mom."

"Oh my God," Danny gasped in a joking manner. "And here I thought everyone was teasing me."

"Well get used to it." Beck winked. "We're all gonna work on being a team, us guys. You, me, your mom, Jess, Phoenix. Okay?"

Danny smiled. "Works for me. And uh, Beck…even though there aren't many guys around, I wouldn't have anyone else watch out for us." He stepped back. "We're heading out."

I looked at Beck, and he truly looked happy. It was the vote of confidence from Danny that I think we both needed. After another embrace, and with deep breaths, we headed toward the caravan. Toward the next and, I believed, the last step in the journey to our new lives.

We were so close.

It wasn't even eight in the morning when we had left the ranch. Our first stop of many was just before noon. We fed the kids, let them move around, but we couldn't dally. The ARC made it quite clear that they knew we had moved.

In what they called their final appeal, they requested that we stop, and they would bring Keller back, no conflict, no harm, if we just turned over Phoenix.

More than anything, we wanted to keep moving, but that was impossible with children and babies.

We hoped the small town a few hours away would give us some security and could hide us. According to Sonny, the town was nestled in hills.

Get in there, hide the cars, and don't respond. In our brief lunch break, we knew we were moving toward some sort of climactic finish with the ARC. A chopper flew overhead, circled, and then flew off.

I was pleased at that time we had already loaded the kids in the cars. For some reason, I didn't want them to know we had more children. Randy argued that if the

ARC knew about the kids, it may keep them from doing anything rash, like firing upon us. My argument to that was what they might do if they thought the kids were like Phoenix.

We had no way of knowing, and we certainly didn't want to stop and find out.

Before we moved on, before we arrived at that small town, I had to speak to Alex. It had been days since he and I had spoken.

We looked at each other, no words. He looked scared and to be honest, I was still angry. But with the increasingly calm threats from the ARC and our arrival at the real New Jerusalem on the horizon, something inside of me told me to make peace with Alex Sans.

He looked somewhat surprised when I approached him. I didn't know what to say or how to introduce an end to our current silence even though I knew I was the key.

"Your face looks much better," I said as I sat down next to him. Maybe that wasn't the best start, but it was a start. "How does it feel?"

"Better, thank you."

Again, silence, no words; we just stared.

"Do you hate me?" he asked.

"No. Not at all. I understand now why you did what you did."

"I'm trying, Mera," Alex stared at his hands. "I am trying to figure out how to get Keller back. They don't want him, and I don't want them to do anything to him."

"Me either," I whimpered. "My heart breaks for him, Alex. It truly does. Then I keep thinking about what Randy said about Keller in the Doctrines."

"Mera, you know my feelings on them."

"But you know they've been right so much of the time."

"I don't think Keller is the Antichrist." He gave a gentle smile and reassuring wink.

"I don't think that either. I don't think that the part that tells that he was abandoned and left to the wild is too far from the truth."

Alex reached over and grabbed my hand. "If I can change that, I will."

I nodded.

"So..." he exhaled. "What brought this on? You haven't looked at me in days or talked to me."

I hesitated before answering. "I'm scared, Alex. We have all these kids. We can't run, we can't hide all that well. Every so often, a chopper flies over. They're waiting, you know. I'm scared if we don't willingly hand over Phoenix, things could get ugly. Especially since they think he's a threat to mankind. And I have to take that seriously."

"Because of Javier?"

"Yes, yes. If the New Jerusalem is looking for him, he has to be important. If he is respected, and he's saying Phoenix needs to be contained and used, then to what lengths will they go to get him?"

"He's just a baby."

"I know. But he's a baby who can bring an end to the tragedy. So, I don't hate you Alex. I appreciate you. I want you to know that in case trouble brews, in case I don't get a chance to tell you that I appreciate all that you have done. Know that and that I love you."

Alex shot a swift glance at me, apparently stunned. He crinkled his nose and looked at me seriously. "I love you, too."

My breath shivered as I leaned into him, kissing him on the cheek. I then whispered in his ear, "I am so scared right now. Tell me something, Alex. Anything. You're good at that. Tell me something to make me not afraid."

I wasn't looking at him, but I felt him shake his head before he answered softly, "I can't. I can't tell you that with all that's going on. Everything seems to be coming to a head and..." He pulled back, looking at me. "I'm scared, too."

37
RANDY BRIGGS

It was better for us to cut back in toward the west. We still faithfully checked radiation levels, which they were minimal as we neared the border of Colorado where it met Kansas.

Cuttersville was the last town nestled in the hills that my tablet showed me before the flatter land. From what I picked up, it seemed safe. We had a storage truck one hundred miles from there. I was able to link to a satellite, but not the ones that the ARC was tapping into.

Our caravan of cars was growing. While the hand held walkie-talkies were intended for the children, they served their purpose for the short distance between vehicles, especially for stops for bathroom or vomiting breaks.

I rode with Pastor Michael. It was nice. We had about five kids in the vehicle. It was good to be around children. Bonnie and Jillian were behind us in the van with more kids, Beck, Mera and Mera's children held up the rear, while Sonny and Alex led the way in that pickup truck. Only one child rode with them, Marissa, who'd taken a liking to Alex.

I did find pleasure in the fact that one of us was always telling Alex to pull over, and he'd always complain.

We took a lesser known road, and it was hard on the gas and the kids. The heat index was unbearable, and we had to keep stopping.

A two-day trip would surely turn into three. Hopefully the town would be a safe place to stop for the night. I needed to rest myself and hopefully find a dentist's office where I could extract my front tooth. It was broken at the nerve from the hit I took, and it was starting to throb and ache.

About fifteen miles away from the road, we could see the town. When we were about five miles away, we pulled over to try to take a look before getting too close.

"It's an old highway town," Alex said. "It was probably kept alive by people taking the scenic route."

"Population could commute, next big city is about thirty miles," Sonny said taking the binoculars. "I'm not seeing anything."

It was bigger than it looked on the screen of my tablet. One main road ran through town, but there were a lot of side streets that branched off.

Beck had his own binoculars. "No movement that I can see. We'll come in from the northeast, head straight through. Looks like the main road has a bank, store, one of those doc in a box places. Oh. Wait. Far end. Jackpot."

Alex looked and then handed me the binoculars. "Take a look all the way to the end of town, off a little. Service station."

I looked. There was a gas tanker there. "Do we want to take gas from that?" I returned the binoculars.

"Hell, no." Alex said. "I want to take the whole thing. We won't have to stop again if that thing's got gas."

"Hold on," Beck announced. "Movement. To the right."

All of us turned around.

"Sleepers?" I asked.

"Hard to tell," Alex said. "Can't see the faces from here. Looks like a man working on his truck. Hood is up. Oh, wow, a woman pushing a stroller." He handed Sonny the binoculars. "I think we have survivors."

After we took another look and decided it was more than likely safe, we turned to gather everyone.

Bonnie was approaching.

Alex asked. "Everything okay?"

"We need to have a talk," she said. "All of us. It's important." She peered over her shoulder and called Mera and Michael to join us.

Mera was by the cars, we were more off the road. She handed Phoenix to Jessie. Danny stayed behind with the kids. They sat in a grouping.

"What's up?" Alex asked.

Bonnie had a tough appearance, but it was obvious that she was worried about what she was going to say. "Another chopper grazed by. They want Phoenix, and I don't think they're going to stop."

Alex nodded with one eye squinted to block out the sun. "They aren't rescue choppers, though, they're infantry birds. Scouting, attack choppers. It's possible they are part of The Reckoning."

That was a valid point, and I had to agree, adding, "No one knows how long The Reckoning will take. We assumed it was a one-day thing. It could take six months. Alex is probably right."

"You know I'd be apt to believe that," she said, "if that doctor hadn't radioed and given a final warning."

"Honestly don't think they're gonna lay fire on us," Alex insisted. "I don't."

"I wish I had the same feeling, Alex, but I don't," Bonnie stated. "They might not bomb us or hit us all, but they have us on the run. Do you think this place we're headed, you think they want that? And what if this doctor is right? What if Phoenix is harmful?"

Alex stood. "Bonnie, he's gonna be a lab experiment. Isolated. What kind of life is that going to be? And we don't even know if they'll hurt him."

"You made a deal." She pointed at Alex. "You made a deal. Wasn't it that they could take him for six months?" She shifted her eyes around. "Randy?"

"That's true, but that promise and deal were made before they realized that Phoenix was a virus hive."

She tossed out her hand at me as if I were foolish. "I don't believe that for one second. They knew; they just didn't know how contagious he was."

"There's no way they knew," I argued. "The Phoenix child was a legend in the Doctrines. The virus is new to them."

"You're actually still thinking the people from the future released that virus?" Bonnie snorted. "Never mind, that is an argument you and I will have at another time. My concern is, there are twenty of us. Over half are under the age of twenty. Is one child worth it?" She stared at Mera. "One child worth every life here? Life you gave birth to? And it is six months. If Alex keeps his word, I think they will, as well. They wouldn't have saved our asses when we were overrun. In six months, Phoenix may not remember you, but he'll love you and learn you again. I promise."

Mera dropped her head. "I don't want to give him up. I don't, but honestly, if it would come down to everyone in danger, then I would have to consider it."

Beck's strong voice rang out. "No. Phoenix will not go with them. I don't give a shit. You wanna worry about everyone else, I can respect that, but if need be, we'll leave. Me, Mera, the kids, we'll go off on our own. No radio contact. Nothing. You go your way, we'll go ours. That's my opinion. No one takes Phoenix."

Alex drew a sharp breath. Hands on hips, he shook his head once projecting that Alex attitude. "While we all appreciate your noble *Father Knows Best* notion, don't you think that might be an option on which Mera may want a say so?"

"If Beck feels that's what we should do," Mera said, "we all agreed that's what we'd do."

"What!" Alex blasted. "That is such bullshit."

A twinge of annoyance hit Beck's face. "No. It isn't. Mera lost her son and her husband, I lost my family. They are my family now, and I'll be damned if she and I will lose our family again."

"Well, fuck me, right?" Alex said. "Did it occur to you that all of you are my family now, too? And I'll be damned if I'm gonna lose a single one of you. No. No. It won't come to that." He turned to Bonnie. "I'll figure out something. I will. We'll work this out, I promise. First things first. Let's pack everyone up. Fuel up in town. If it's safe, we'll stay and think of a plan. Okay?"

Bonnie nodded.

Alex turned to me and Sonny. "Okay?"

Neither of us had a problem with that.

"Padre?"

Michael shrugged. "Fine with me. I'll do what everyone decides."

Then finally to Beck. "Okay?"

Beck seemed to ignore him. Placing his hand on Mera's back, he led her to the car.

"Beck!"

"Yes, Alex, yes," He snapped. "It's okay. Check your ammo, everyone, just in case."

There was a look on Alex's face I couldn't quite place. Sadness, disappointment. It wasn't anger. A lot of unspoken responsibility had been placed on Alex's shoulders. I felt sorry for him. He just wanted to make the right decisions and make everyone happy.

Problem was, not everyone wanted the same thing.

38
ALEX SANS

There was an odor that permeated the town. I knew the second it carried through my open window that something wasn't right.

We rolled into town on the main street all together, Sonny and I leading the way. Two blocks before the town were the chain stores, one of which was auto parts store, and I think that was what sent the first warning sign. If it was me and my truck broke down, I'd pretty much raid the hell out of the auto parts place. Yet the truck was parked, hood open in front of the gas station at the other end of town.

Then again, the driver might have come in from that end of town.

We soon pulled into the shopping area on the main drag. Local shops, businesses, a bank and the doc in a box all were on that street. I pulled close to the small-town police station. At the very least, I was thinking about obtaining ammo. I stopped the truck.

"Hang back, everyone," I instructed over the walkie-talkie. "Sonny and I are gonna pull up. See if it's clear up ahead and get to that tanker."

"Why does it smell so bad?" Sonny asked. "I thought at some point bodies would stop smelling."

"You're right. In this heat, you got a thirty day tops decomposing stage before the body starts petrifying. Something isn't right. Leave the shotgun, take the automatic. Too much reloading."

Sony looked at me. "No one's here."

I grabbed my weapon and opened the door.

I grunted in disgust at the smell. There was a feel to the street, to the town, that just wasn't right.

Randy and Michael were about twenty feet behind us, with Bonnie on their bumper and Beck ten feet behind her.

Marissa was waving. I was glad she wasn't still mad at me for making her ride with Randy again.

"Something's not right," I said, looking to Sonny who had binoculars raised to his eyes.

"He's gone."

"What are you talking about?"

"The truck survivor. The woman with the stroller. Gone."

I looked to my left and to the small grocer. It was the only shop on the entire street with broken windows. Out front was the stroller. Again, I spoke in the radio. "Stay in the cars, please."

"What's going on?" Beck responded.

"I don't know. Just get ready to move. Don't see anyone, but call it a bad feeling." I motioned to Sonny. "Check the buildings on that side."

I walked to the grocery store and to that stroller. My stomach twitched, my heart beat strong, and the smell was beginning to make me sick.

Just at the store windows, an enormous tattered advertisement for bread flapped down and hit me. I jumped a foot from my skin. I cleared it from my head with a slight laugh and moved to the stroller, which was covered with a blanket.

Reaching for the stroller, ready to remove the blanket, I caught a glimpse of the inside of that store.

A thump in my gut involuntarily churned my liquefied lunch up my esophagus and into my mouth. That had never happened like that to me. I spit. Got a hold of my bearings.

Bodies. No, wait. Carcasses. Human, animals, you name it. Sprawled out across the floors, some even neatly piled. Barely an inch of floor could be seen through the bodies. Some eaten, some waiting. It gave new meaning to food store.

I turned in a rush, and as I did, I caught the blanket on the stroller, and it whipped off the carriage.

Two, three—possibly more, it was hard to tell— ivory statue stillborn babies were in that stroller, layered and twisted together. Badly decomposed, but their tiny bodies clearly picked through.

That was it, I was done.

It was at that moment that I realized Beck had been calling my name over and over, asking if I was all right.

No. I wasn't.

I readied to raise the radio to tell them pull out when I saw her, the woman who had been pushing the stroller. She came out of the store.

Clearly, she was a Sleeper.

I lowered my walkie-talkie and raised my gun as she stared at me. Just stared at me.

Blood covered her hands and mouth, and I determined she needed to die.

Then she opened her mouth.

I expected her to try to attack, but instead she screamed.

It was an ear piercing, ungodly long, never-ending scream. One like I had never heard in my life. That scream was a siren. A call.

Pouring out of the store came more Sleepers than I could count. I didn't have time to pull off a shot or raise my radio. I figured they all knew they had to take off.

"Sonny!"

I looked back and saw Sonny was backing up. I could hear the Sleepers running down the road.

I ran to the truck at the same time as Sonny. We'd barely reached it when Sleepers came from the other shops and stores. Fifty or sixty of them immediately went to Michael's SUV, surrounding it, making it impossible for them to move.

Smash. Smash. Smash.

They broke windows, pulled on doors.

We both jumped on top of the truck. I started firing, Sonny started firing. We shot, we kicked.

I felt helpless.

I could hear the kids screaming and then I saw David, one of the little boys, as he was pulled through the SUV window by six or seven Sleepers, kicking and screaming for help.

Michael was trying. He and Randy got out of the vehicle and fought.

Michael couldn't save David and his muffled cries of pain faded beneath the grip of the Sleepers.

Then Michael crawled back in the car, but not before another child was pulled out.

Marissa.

39
MERA STEVENS

I screamed the moment I saw them running down the street, coming from the stores, from everywhere.

"Danny, take the wheel. Back it up and get them out. Now!" Beck ordered.

"Yes, sir."

From the back seat, I cried out Beck's name, but he opened the door and jumped out firing. I couldn't see anything—we were a full twenty feet behind everyone.

They, not us, seemed to be the focus of the attack.

With the van surrounded by Sleepers, Bonnie did something I could only call a brilliant move. She couldn't go forward or backward, so she jerked the wheel and crashed full speed through the window of the Fargo First National Bank. The van barricaded the window.

Beck looked like a football player as he fought his way through the Sleepers. He swung out, hitting Sleepers with his rifle, quickly scaling the van and hoisting himself to the bank sign. I could only guess he was headed for the roof.

Danny peeled in reverse and spun the car around.

"We can't leave them!" I cried. "We have to do something."

"We will. We are."

Danny drove quickly, recklessly. I kept looking behind us, thinking he was trying to get the Sleepers to follow us, but there were too many, they had everyone else to worry about. We were unnoticed.

At the end of the street, he made a turn and then another. We headed back to town, this time down a small back street that was more of an alley. There wasn't a Sleeper in sight.

He pulled the car up to the back of the bank, as close as he could.

"Get in the driver's seat and get ready to go, Mom. Turn the car around quietly. If this back door is open, we are piling everyone in."

I nodded, holding Phoenix close. Jessie was crying, calling Beck's name. "Be careful," I told Danny.

Danny grabbed his rifle and stepped out. With the baby in my arms, I climbed in between the two seats, slid into the driver's seat, and quietly shut the door.

Danny peeked inside the bank. The back door was indeed open.

Please, please, I begged in my mind, *please don't let there be Sleepers in there.*

Gun shots rang out, and all I could do was pray.

I turned the car and reached to open the passenger door. I kept checking for Sleepers. Sooner or later they were bound to show up.

The bank door burst open and out ran Bonnie with two kids, then Danny carrying two and Jillian leading three.

"Oh, thank God!" I gasped as Bonnie tossed in kids.

She grabbed them from Danny, hoisting them inside. "Pack it in, sit on each other, I don't give a shit. But stay down," Bonnie ordered.

I was grateful it wasn't a tiny car. Two more kids got up front, one sat on the floor, and Danny held one on his lap.

The stampede of Sleepers was coming down the alley from behind us. There were so many that they didn't all fit in my side view mirror. "Jillian, get in! Sit on Bonnie's lap!"

She shut the door.

"Jillian!"

She walked to the passenger window and looked in at me. "Drive. Go."

"Get in. We can fit you. Come on!"

"No, Mera. It's my time. They'll not follow if I stay. Sleeper bait, remember? Go." She winked, smiled bravely, and then walked toward the Sleepers.

"Go, Mom!"

"Hit it, Mera!" Bonnie yelled.

"Thank you, Jillian," I whispered and hit the gas. I planted my lips to Phoenix's head and I drove that clear and straight shot out of town.

I looked in the mirror again. My heart sank. I couldn't see Jillian.

I heard Bonnie whimper, but the children were quiet. Not crying. Not moving. Not saying anything.

We were out of there. We were safe. But we weren't running. I knew what I had to do to help the others.

40
ALEX SANS

The last I saw of Randy Briggs was his hand.

Arm raised high, almost in victory, it stayed that way, despite the fact that his entire body was overtaken by Sleepers.

His sacrifice allowed Michael to crawl back into the car and open a window of opportunity for me. I left my post, forgot about shooting, forgot about everything when I saw those three Sleepers with Marissa.

What made it worse for me was that she called my name.

"Alex! Alex Sans, help me!"

Oh God.

I was failing her.

It took only a few seconds to jump from the truck and run to her, but it felt as if I were running in slow motion.

Hold on, Marissa. Hold on.

the Sleepers pulled and tugged at her. She screamed and cried, tearful calls of pain.

I shot one, slammed another, and then shot the third.

I didn't look, I couldn't look, my only focus was getting Marissa out of there.

The poor little thing lay on the ground, her body convulsing as I swept her into my arms and took a quick look around.

The police station.

Marissa in my hold, my weapon at the ready, I ran to the station and bolted inside.

Right into a Sleeper.

I shot him without a second's thought and shifted my eyes to the hallway and the sign that read "Holding Cells."

"Hold on, baby, hold on," I told Marissa. Racing down the hall, I spotted a first aid kit on the wall. I hurriedly opened the box and grabbed everything I could hold. I heard the crash of the front doors and the sounds of Sleepers barreling in after us.

I prayed that I could get us somewhere safe.

Turning the bend, I spotted the three holding cells. They were old fashioned but would serve their purpose.

How we'd get out wasn't a question on my mind, but I knew inside, we'd be safe.

Only one was empty. With a barrage of Sleepers on my heels, first aid items falling from my hands, I dove into that cell and slammed the door shut.

It clicked and locked.

Sleepers slammed against the cell, arms reaching through trying to get us. I backed up until I hit the wall and then I slid down.

I felt it.

The blood.

So much of it.

I didn't want to look, but I had to. I could see Marissa's rib cage. The flesh had been torn from it, and in the tug of war for her body, they had ripped her right arm entirely from her body.

She had lost so much blood.

There weren't enough bandages in my hands to help her, to save her. How much pain she must be feeling, how scared she was, and I had failed to reach her in time.

I tossed the gauze in defeat and dropped the weapon, focusing only on holding her.

Reaching for the blanket on the cot, I held it to her body to try to slow the bleeding.

"I'm sorry. I'm so sorry," I told her, trying to be strong, but it took everything I had not to break down. I rocked her back and forth. There was nothing I could do. Nothing.

I wanted to scream. I felt my throat tense up, and it was strangling me. A swirl of horrendous emotion hit me, and it was sheer agony.

Marissa's eyes opened. "Thank you, Alex, for saving me."

"I'm sorry, baby," I told her, my hand stroking her face. "I'm sorry they did this to you. I'm sorry this happened. I am…"

" It's okay…it doesn't hurt anymore."

I lowered my head.

"Are you crying, Alex Sans?"

"I am." A weak sob emerged from me.

"That's okay. I won't tell anyone."

Her words made me cry harder.

"You saved me."

I shook my head.

"You did. I'm not out there. I'm with you."

I didn't think I even had the ability to talk.

"Alex, could you hold me tight? Real tight. No one has ever held me tight. I'm scared."

Everything I had heaved out in a breath as I brought Marissa to my chest, flush against me, my arms held tight, and my lips planted to her head. "I have you."

"I feel your heart," she said. "I'm not scared anymore. Thank you, Alex Sans."

"Thank *you*."

In that cell, Sleepers loud, reaching, screaming, grabbing, it didn't matter. Marissa was the only thing that mattered.

I felt her fingers hold tightly to my arm. Clawing away as if trying for one more touch.

She said nothing else.

I rocked her with comfort, with love.

Her fingers clenched, released, clenched and then with a single sighing breath, her arm dropped.

Marissa was gone.

She died in my arms.

I lost it.

For the world ending, for everything that had happened, I lost it all right there in that cell, my back against the wall and that little girl in my arms.

I brought her close to me, holding her with my arms, legs, and soul.

My heart broke in a million pieces, shattered in an irreparable nature.

The pain of the heartbreak was more than I could bear.

On that floor, Marissa's lifeless body in my arms, I didn't just cry, I sobbed. From the deepest depths of my soul, I sobbed.

41
MERA STEVENS

We needed only to make it as far as the auto parts store and we were in the clear.

The second we pulled over, Danny checked for Sleepers and the kids unloaded, racing into the store.

I pulled out the radio and placed a call to the ARC for help. I knew they had choppers in the area, and knew they wanted Phoenix. I told them that I had escaped the town and that the baby was still there. The last I saw him, one of our women was trying to save him.

"I know you hear me," I said into the mic. "I know you've been following. Help us."

I described Jillian.

I wasn't even done with the radio call when the first helicopter swooped into town. Within minutes more showed up. They rained fire upon the town. Soldiers in gas masks leapt from the choppers as if engaging in ground battle.

We could see smoke, hear the fighting.

None of us knew the fate of anyone other than Jillian. Beck, Alex, Sonny, Randy, Michael, the other kids...we didn't know.

We stood listening to the gunfire, steady and strong, then it slowed down.

It was like popping corn. Every shot was fired, slowing down until every kernel was popped.

Then a call came over the radio. "Ma'am, how many of your people were in town?"

I had to do a count, telling them that, including Phoenix, there were twelve.

They relayed that the town was safe, requested us to go there, and said they looked for our people.

Looked for our people.

None of that was good.

I thought about leaving Bonnie, Jessie and the kids behind, but then I thought about a Sleeper attack. No, we'd be safer if we walked back to town together.

But I didn't want them to see Phoenix.

I couldn't leave him at the auto parts store, and I couldn't allow the ARC people to see him.

Emptying Beck's camouflage backpack, I placed Phoenix inside, left the zipper open and carried it close to my chest.

I held my daughter's hand, my son walked ahead of us with Bonnie. The children remained by me.

I didn't know what the officials from the ARC would do once they saw the children up close and knew that they were real. I was scared that they would take them.

Just about in town, the smell of bodies and gunfire pummeled us. People in biohazard suits, soldiers in gasmasks moved bodies into a pile.

It was, without a doubt, a war zone.

I didn't realize how many Sleepers there were until I watched them dragging out the bodies. Out of the scope of vision of the ARC, I spotted him.

Beck.

I breathed out heavily when I saw he was alive, but clearly something was wrong. He sat near the side of the building, hidden back against the wall, looking totally exasperated.

"Keep it slow, I have an idea about Phoenix," I told Danny.

"Is Beck okay?"

"I think so. I'll be right back." I hurried to Beck with the backpack in my arms. I didn't say anything. I waited until he looked up.

"We lost," he said. "This was a bad one. I don't know who lived, who died." He closed his eyes, stood and grabbed on to me. "Just so damn glad you're alive." His lips pressed to my head, and I stopped him. "What's wrong?"

"I had to call for help. I radioed the ARC."

"Is that why they came?"

"I told them Phoenix was here in town with Jillian. I described her, they'll find her. They'll think—"

Beck finished my sentence. "Phoenix was killed."

With a smile, I nodded. "Yeah. So here..." I handed him the backpack. "The most precious cargo you will ever carry. Wait until they are occupied, take him, and go to the auto parts store."

"Why won't you take him?"

"They asked for me. I'm a great diversion right now."

"You're a great everything right now." Beck gently took the bag and embraced me. "I have this. No worries."

I reached up to his face. "You are wonderful. I'm so proud to have you with me."

Beck, emotional, nodded. "Ditto. Let's finish this up and head to our new home. Our new life."

"I couldn't agree more." I pressed my hand firmly to his cheek, stood on my tiptoes, kissed him and slid my hand from his face. I left him against the side of the building with Phoenix.

Hurriedly, I joined the others in the group and grabbed Jessie's hand as we neared the bank where we left the van.

The first person I saw in the midst of it all was Sonny. He was speaking to a soldier. He turned and saw me. Despite that fact that I was overwhelmed that he was alive, Sonny wasn't smiling. I then noticed through the maze of numerous ARC people...there was Michael.

He was alive, too. He looked awful, he had taken a beating. With him were three children. More joy...But...

Three.

There'd been five children with them.

That was when it hit me. *The nightmare.* My hand slipped from Jessie's grip, and I turned slowly, looking around. A buzz filled my ears, and things began to spin. On the ground by the SUV was a tarp covered body.

Sleepers weren't covered with tarps; they were piled into mounds.

This body was small. We'd lost another child. My hand shot to my mouth as my chest filled with emotions and then beyond that body I saw another.

"Oh God," I gasped and ran that way.

"Mom!" Danny called, grabbing my arm, but I shook it off and continued my run.

I bent down to the tarp, and as I did, Michael approached.

"Mera, please just...just don't. Okay?" Michael said. "The kids don't need to see."

Sonny stood over us. "The Sleepers got him pretty bad."

Danny hollered, "Who is it?"

I lifted the blanket and saw the curly brown hair. Despite the fact that it was caked with blood, I knew who it was. I looked over my shoulder to Danny. "Randy."

Danny's head went back, and his eyes closed.

I lowered my head to Randy, grabbing onto him through the blanket. "Thank you," I whispered. "Thank you for all you have done for us. I'm sorry." I felt the first of many tears roll down my face.

Beck was right.

We had lost.

I was just about to ask about Alex when I saw him emerge from the police station. I was hoping against hope that he would emerge with the last child, and he did. Unfortunately, that child, covered by a blanket, was in the arms of an ARC soldier who walked beside Alex.

I looked at the faces of the remaining children. I knew which children we lost. David and Marissa. And by the look on Alex's face, his little buddy was the body that came from the station.

I raced to Alex. He was saturated with blood and looked to be in shock. Without words, I embraced him, and his arms wrapped tightly around me.

"I tried, Mera," he wept.

"I know you did."

"She died in my arms."

"I'm sorry."

With a hard sniff and breath, he broke the embrace. "Beck?" His eyes shifted about looking. "Phoenix?"

I moved back into his hold to whisper. "I told the ARC that Phoenix was here in town. Beck has him now."

Alex nodded.

"Ma'am?" a voice, sounding as if it came through a respirator, called out.

I turned. He wore a biohazard suit, and he handed me the Moses basket. "The child is okay for now. None of our experts believes he'll live much longer like this."

I reached inside the basket and grabbed Keller.

He was so tiny, and he squirmed as if he knew I was holding him. I was willing to bet not one soul had touched in him days.

"May I?" Alex asked, extending his hands to hold Keller.

I handed him over. Alex needed to hold that baby.

"Hey, little one," Alex cooed softly, cradling the child. "I promise, from this moment forward, I won't let you down. Ever."

"Ma'am," biohazard guy said again, "my name is Doctor Javier. Our men located the woman you described with the flowered dress." He shook his head. "She didn't make it."

Alex pulled Keller tightly to him. I tried to show some sort of shock.

"The Phoenix child wasn't there," he said. "We'll keep looking. Hopefully, since he carries the infection they won't hurt—"

He stopped speaking when, in the distance, a younger male voice called out, "Sarge, straggling Sleeper."

I looked over my shoulder. They were somewhere behind me, and the Sergeant replied, "Take it out."

It didn't seem like a big deal, and I returned to looking at Javier.

But only briefly.

The young soldier shouted. "He's big one, too."

And my heart sank.

No.

No!

I spun around. I looked out, then up, saw the soldier aiming. And I raced forward, shouting, "No! Don't!"

The shot rang out.

And I watched the shot hit...*Beck.*

I heard Danny scream, then Jessie, and I kept running.

To me, it appeared that Beck fell in slow motion. Blood splattered out of his back as if he'd been hit with a red water balloon. His body arched, one arm went out, and after a few struggling steps, he fell down to his knees and then forward, landing on his side.

"No!"

My scream echoed all the way to him.

He lay on the street at the edge of town. I reached him seconds after he hit the asphalt.

Alex and Danny weren't far behind, and neither was Jessie. In fact, everyone there ran to him.

I couldn't breathe; I couldn't get enough oxygen inside of me to make audible words.

It wasn't happening. It didn't happen.

The backpack was still in his arms, and that was covered in blood.

I heard the cries and screams from Phoenix.

I knelt beside Beck, but before I could roll him over, Alex arrived.

"The baby, the baby," I said, rattled. "I can't look, I can't look." My hand hovered over the backpack.

"He's crying. He's okay. Son of a bitch." Alex examined him quickly. "Beck, stay with me. Can you hear me?"

"Yeah," Beck answered groggily. "The baby. Phoenix."

Alex yelled out, "Bonnie! Michael. Run to that med clinic stat. Start clearing a clean area and find anything that can be used to operate." Alex took off his shirt. "Sonny!"

"Yeah, Alex?"

"Get the people from the ARC. See what they have."

I didn't hear Sonny's reply, or even look to see if he went. Beck reached up, grabbed Alex. "Phoenix."

Alex ignored him and examined the gunshot wound. "The bullet went straight through..." His eyes closed.

"Oh my God." My heart sank.

Alex grabbed the backpack and reached inside, pulling out a bloody Phoenix. Alex's eyes closed tight, and he rocked for a second, looking as if he were holding back a scream. "Someone, give me a shirt! Now!"

I took mine off, whipping it to him. He immediately wrapped Phoenix.

I didn't know what to do, what to say, how to process anything that was going on. Danny had dropped down to Beck and started to cry, and Jessie was hysterical.

"Mera," Alex said out of breath. "I don't have time. Pick one. One has to be worked on stat. Either Beck or Phoenix. I can only help one right now, and I don't know if I can save either."

I looked to Phoenix in his arms, then to Beck.

Beck's lips parted, and he stammered, "The b-baby."

My son's aching cries of sadness rang in my ear. Jessie was hysterically calling Beck's name repeatedly.

I ran my hand over Beck's face, then looked to Alex. "Save him. Do what you can." And with that, I grabbed Phoenix from Alex's arms and ran.

Javier wasn't far; in fact, he was making his way over when I raced to him and handed him Phoenix. "Help him. Please."

Javier looked down. "Oh my God, the injured Phoenix child." I knew, at that second, he'd read the Doctrines.

"Save him, please," I begged.

Cupping Phoenix in his grip, Javier nodded. "We'll do what we can. I promise."

A second, just one second, and I prayed it wouldn't hurt. I stopped Javier, leaned over Phoenix, and laid my lips to his head. "I love you. I love you, little man. See you soon. Please live."

As I kissed him once last time, Javier moved back quickly. He shouted out that he would be in touch, and with Phoenix in his arms, he raced as fast as he could to the closest chopper.

I watched that chopper waste no time in spinning its blades and lifting off. It flew like a bat out of hell from that small town. In less than two minutes, Phoenix was gone.

Out of my arms, out of my sight.

I didn't have time to comprehend what I had done to the child. All I knew was he was hurt. He needed help we couldn't give him. If he was to have a chance to live at all, his only chance was with the ARC.

I felt as if I didn't say goodbye to him, as if it were forever going to be unresolved.

I took a second and tried my damndest to gather my bearings.

Turning, I watched as Alex was aided by Sonny, Danny and two ARC soldiers. They lifted and carried Beck. I rushed over as they approached the clinic doors.

I needed to see him, speak to him, and touch Beck one more time before Alex did what he could do.

The ARC soldiers muttered that they had a medic with them who could help Alex, and they were getting more supplies.

My hand was on Beck's arm. His eyes were struggling to stay open. They focused on me.

"Mera," Alex said. "Mera, we're only going to field stabilize him. Okay? Then they'll airlift him to the ARC."

So focused on Beck, it took a second for Alex's words to register. "What?"

"I can't repair all the damage. I'm not good enough," Alex said. "Me and the medic will stabilize him. He'll have to go to the ARC."

"They have doctors there," one of the soldiers said. "They'll help him."

I only could nod. At that point, we were inside the small clinic. They were moving Beck faster than I could keep up.

Michael emerged from the back. "In here. There's a table. We got it as clean as we could."

Alex stared intently at me. "I'll do all I can. I promise."

"I know." I squeaked out those words, and then looked at Beck. "Fight. Please."

I wanted him to say something, anything. But he was losing strength, and he struggled so hard to breathe and keep his eyes open.

They pulled him from me and into that back room. My hand grazed from his arms to his hand. I felt his fingertips grab for me as he looked at me one last time before he disappeared into that room.

The moment he was out of my sight, out of my reach, I collapsed.

The arms of my son and daughter held me up.

In that hallway, I sobbed.

I felt the gentle touch of a hand on my back, and looked up at Michael.

At that second, I wanted so badly for the Doctrines to be correct, I wanted them to write that he had unusual powers, for Michael to be that Savior we all waited for. He wasn't. I knew it.

"Mera, I'm going to gather the children. I know this doesn't mean much to you, but we're gonna go pray. Okay?"

There was something about his words that shot into my being. A shock radiated through me. And no, Michael wasn't the Savior, but he certainly was remarkable in more ways than one. That, there was no denying. Perhaps God did have a purpose for him.

"Thank you."

He leaned forward, placing his lips to my forehead for a moment. His gentle touch to my head then to my children was reassuring.

He left with Bonnie behind him, and Sonny followed them both.

I was alone with my children. That was what I wanted and needed. We were too emotional to do anything else.

We would wait in the clinic reception room as long as we had to. Until we knew something. Anything.

Our lives were in the balance right along with Beck. Because he was a part of our lives.

42
MERA STEVENS

Despite Alex's best efforts, despite any help the ARC tried to give...Beck died.

They were in that back room for a long time. And I knew.

Telling me was probably the hardest thing Alex had to do, but his words were no surprise to me or my children.

We heard Alex calling Beck's name. He begged and begged Beck to hold on, to stay with him. He cried out to God and to anyone that could hear.

Don't go. Don't die. Please stay.

Damn it Beck, come back.

We heard it all.

His anguish and struggles ripped though my soul.

Beck fought. Alex fought. We all fought.

But in the end we all lost.

Beck was gone. Randy, Marissa, David, Jillian...

Gone.

The ARC had arrived with six helicopters and about thirty men. By the time Beck had passed, only one chopper and three men remained.

Then they left, too.

Nothing was said about the children. We weren't asked if we wanted them to go. They left.

Those of us who remained stood amongst the rubble of a small town, burning Sleeper bodies and the remains of those that we loved.

We gathered what remained of Jillian, Randy, Marissa and David, along with Beck's body, and we drove with our supplies out of that town. We drove a few miles, and just before sunset, after hours of digging, we were able to bury our losses.

Unfortunately, we couldn't bury the pain.

I cried the remainder of the day and into the night. I just couldn't stop crying. My heart broke for Randy. For all that he went through to die such as he did.

The sense of loss I felt over Beck was immense. I clutched tightly to his dog tags, the only thing of his I had. They were splattered with his blood. I would never clean them or be without them. In fact, I would wear them always. He had made such a deep impact on me.

The pain was tremendous, and there was no closure. No goodbyes. No way for him to know how strongly I felt about him. How much he meant to me and my children.

Danny, who barely shed a tear over his own father's death, was inconsolable about Beck. I believe it was because his father was gone—in a way—before he actually died.

Jessie didn't understand. She cuddled close to me and wouldn't leave my side. She knew Beck was gone, but couldn't grasp it fully.

Alex wouldn't let Keller out of his sight or out of his arms. I wanted, needed to hold the baby because when I did, there was something about him that sent a message to me that he knew he was safe. He arched his body into us when we held him as if it were his newborn deliverance of the words thank you.

Keller was home, and he knew it.

The only bright spot to the dark day was the radio call from Javier letting us know that Phoenix was stable. They removed the bullet, and though he wasn't out of the woods, they were optimistic.

They'd keep us posted.

I felt they would keep their word. They didn't have to radio about him at all. But they did.

I wasn't able to make out Javier's face through his biohazard suit, but he sounded honest. In his last transmission to us, he said, "If all goes well, he'll back with you one day. I promise. One day."

I'd hold on to that.

That first night, in the depth of our losses, I held on to my children.

There wasn't a single one of us who spoke.

Next to the graves of those we lost, we lit a small fire and spent the night.

Some dozed, but no one really slept.

The next day was going to be our last day on the road, one way or another.

New Jerusalem or not, we were settling. We would stop.

The end of the road was near, and it was time to move forward. As hard as it would be without Beck, Randy, and the others, we would. We had to.

43
ALEX SANS

I remembered the newspaper pictures, those sprawled across the internet. Pictures of the white building, the cross upon it, and accusations of horrendous things that took place on the grounds of the Zion Ranch.

Stories of torture and so forth. Stories that faded from the minds of the public, and the residents of the ranch moved back in and started their lives again.

All that was surreal and fictional to me the second we saw the white building in the distance.

I wondered if those in the cult-like community were alive, or if they were gone, dead, Sleepers.

The area of Eldorado was clear. Gold stars were painted on the doors of homes and windows of businesses. I guessed the stars meant the building had been cleaned out.

Not a body lined the street, not a Sleeper walked.

There was a long dirt road with a cheesy gate just outside of Eldorado. That road led to the TPL ranch. The twelve foot high wall with its brass gate greeted us.

It was closed.

It was pushing late afternoon when we finally arrived in Eldorado.

New Jerusalem or not, I knew the ranch would be a perfect point for all of us to start over.

During our lunch stop, Javier radioed one last time. He asked us to let him know if there actually was a New Jerusalem. He eventually wanted to get there.

He added Phoenix was doing better.

She didn't say much about it, but I knew, not only was Mera crushed by Beck's death, she was burdened with guilt over Phoenix. Only time could help her to recover.

And maybe getting Phoenix back with her.

Our caravan of vehicles was down to two—the tanker we retrieved from that small town, along with another school bus.

There was no need to hide anymore from the ARC. They stopped following us, and we stopped seeing choppers.

We parked the tank inside Eldorado, and all of us together rode in the bus down the dirt road to the ranch.

None of us knew what to expect.

We had supplies in case no one was there, and a damn high wall to keep us safe.

I stopped short of the locked gate and beeped.

Sonny scolded me as if I were a child. "What if there's Sleepers?" he asked. "You're calling them."

"We'll find out," I replied, opening the bus door. "Okay, I know Sonny, and I don't have a very strong track record, but stay put. We're stepping out."

Sonny and I stepped from the bus. The moment we did, we saw a man, thin, in his thirties, and bald. He waved his hand high in the air, and then ran to the gate to greet us.

The closer he drew, the more I knew he wasn't a Sleeper. He was smiling.

"He's fine!" I hollered. "A survivor!"

I could hear the cheers coming from the bus, and then the man unlocked the gate.

He opened it, his grin wide. He opened his mouth to speak, but no words emerged. Holding up a finger, he reached to his pocket but halted when a child's voice shouted.

"Noah!" Nick, one of the children, cried out with enthusiasm. "Noah!" Nick leapt from the steps of the bus to the gate and into the man's arms.

The man ran his hands over Nick's head and smiled again. Then he did speak. *"Ta-ta get to a chu."*

Nick said, "We picked up the Potter's code. Was that you?"

Noah nodded. He stepped back, spoke again to Nick, then waved out his hand.

Nick faced me. "He can understand but can't speak your language. He's one of our people. He said come in. Bring the bus in."

Nick didn't return to the bus with Sonny and me; he walked with the man.

I immediately thought of Marissa. How she would have totally buried Nick, she was so competitive with him. They were older and the wiser of the bunch. She probably would have tackled him to get from that bus first to let me know she knew Noah.

I got on the bus and informed everyone we were headed in. I didn't know exactly how Nick knew the man. One of his people? That confused me. I'd find out. But one thing was certain I knew as we rolled the bus through the gate.

We had arrived to the New Jerusalem.

It was overwhelming.

At first, we saw only Noah. Then, as we moved further into the complex, there were more survivors, people who looked as if they had been there for a while. They paused to greet us, to wave.

The number one thing that got me was the fact that when the bus stopped and the children stepped off, they knew these people.

And there were a lot of people.

None of us knew what we were going to do, where we would go. What exactly was happening? The welcome wagon consisted of at least one hundred people.

Then another man enthusiastically broke through the throngs. He grinned and looked about.

He grabbed Nick and another boy, embracing them quickly, but he searched our group, looking for someone. Nick pointed to me, and he approached me.

"Levi Minx," he introduced himself. "You are?"

"Alex Sans."

His eyes widened. "You're pretty famous over the radio. Your name is called daily." He looked at Mera. "Is that the child they search for?"

Mera replied. "No, he was injured. We had no choice but to allow the ARC to save him. I…" she lowered her head. "I handed him over."

"I'm sorry," Levi said. "Where are the adults that were with this party of children?"

I shook my head. "They've passed away."

Bonnie clarified. "All of them were killed in Sleeper attacks. We also lost three children."

"The Reckoning, as they call it," he said, "hasn't taken hold. There are many still remaining." He appeared to take a moment to compose himself. "The children are fine here. Please…come with me. I am sure you have a few questions."

He wasn't kidding. A few questions? That was an understatement.

Danny stayed behind with Bonnie, at my request, to watch Keller, Jessie, and the rest of the kids. I know Levi said they were fine, but just in case…I really didn't know these people yet. A part of me was fearful they'd throw a Bible at me and tell me that I had to act and think a certain way to stay there. I prepared for that.

I wasn't prepared for all that Levi told us.

We followed him to a building that had a large gathering room, many couches and chairs in a circle. We sat as close together as we could.

A woman brought us a beverage. It was red, and I didn't drink it. It was a weird cult flashback to the stories of the Jonestown cult and the cyanide-laced drinks they gave their members.

He asked us what we knew, and we told him. We told him about Randy and all that he had informed us about the Doctrines, Phoenix, and so forth. I kind of thought at first I was delivering a newsflash, but he chuckled.

"Things, you know, get lost in translation." Levi smiled. "Your people have the Bible. I am sure if Jesus Christ or any of his apostles or even Moses would come to this time period, they'd say, 'That's not how it happened.'"

His words made me smile as well. "Kind of like we kept saying to Randy."

"Yes," Levi replied. "See, we knew not of these Doctrines." He swiped his hand over his mouth. "You have to forgive me; I'm not as fluent in your language as the children are. They have been taught their whole lives, to make it easy for them. There were two sets of time travelers. We'll call them Group A and Group B. I am from Group A. We came 1300 years from this date. Randy, Demetrious, Anthony, they are Group B. They came from five hundred."

Sonny then stated, "So you're Project Savior."

"Yes. And we had run into Anthony. We have his…" Levi grunted. "What do you call them back in this day? Tandy. Yes. His Tandy."

I couldn't help it, I burst into laughter. "Tandy? Just say tablet or computer. Tandy is *really* ancient."

Levi held up his hand. "I apologize. Anyhow, we worked this. Found a few messages that claim they were from us. They weren't. I don't know this man who was speaking as if he were from Project Savior."

My head itched; it always did when I got anxious. With a slight growl, I scratched my head frantically. "I hate time travel shit. I can't keep track. It makes my head spin."

"Nothing really to keep track of," Levi said. "We're here."

Mera, who really hadn't said much, asked, "Why are you hiding?"

Michael added. "Yeah, really. Why the cryptic, hidden code?"

Levi replied simply, "The children. We needed them to hear. Our group was separated. We knew most were under the age of twenty-five, and they knew the code. We also knew many from the Project wouldn't know the language. So we targeted the children."

I asked. "So why the announcement, the recording?"

"For everyone else," Levi answered. "I think I put too much faith in your technology. I thought you could track the signal to us. Plus, we didn't know the language well enough to make sure we were saying the right thing, so we just played a recording. We retrieved the recording from the…computer we got. It was actually made by the original New Jerusalem. Someone here today or maybe someone who will arrive will make that same announcement."

We all must have been thinking the same thing, because Michael asked, "So Javier came with you? That's why you're looking for him?"

Sonny added. "Yeah, he wants to be informed if this place is real."

Levi clapped his hands together once and sighed in relief. "It would be beneficial to have him here. If he has the child that is the hive like the ARC said, then he can cure this thing for generations. Javier is the creator of the virus. But he…" Levi shifted his eyes around to look at each of us. "He wasn't in our group. He didn't come with us. He's from your time."

My confusion caused me to get more frustrated, and I stood. "I am so freaking lost right now. You used a virus created in this time? I thought you guys created a virus to enhance the DNA? I thought that's what you released. Twenty-seven scientists."

All color left Levi's face. "Mr. Sans, you truly are confused. We didn't come here to release a virus. We came here to live. Not twenty-seven scientists—twenty-seven groups. We are all that remain of the human race in the future. We are overrun by creatures that are genetic descendants of this plague. Your Sleepers. We came back in time to try to save our children, to give them a longer life to live beyond forty years. Elements and nature makes it impossible to live long. History books told a different story. The history we knew told us that seventy-five percent of the world was wiped out by a virus. We came to wait it out, to start over. So our children could play without fear, feel the sun without hiding. That's all."

At that second, my thoughts raced to the Black Plague, how that occurred one thousand years before my time, and I wondered if historians had skewed that story.

Project Savior was only a project to save what was left of the human race. They came back in time to live. They thought they'd blend into an empty world. They were ill-prepared for what they found.

Randy thought Project Savior had released the virus. He followed the Doctrines, that obviously had been tweaked over time. The story in the Doctrines wasn't one hundred percent correct.

Levi continued. "We thought that seventy-five percent died of the virus, not turned into those things out there. We thought the creatures of our time didn't arrive for centuries. Evolution from your plague. Because your plague, or virus, was made by Javier to manipulate the DNA and, sadly, control population. But it killed more than it helped. It transformed anyone who was not immune."

Mera said. "So it was an accidental release?"

Levi shook his head. "No. I'm sorry. It was released a year before it reached its peak. It worked its way through the population for thirteen months, and then it exploded and became deadly. Your people did this to themselves with all good intentions." He paused. "And it backfired."

A silence swept through us all in the aftermath of his words.

Through all the surviving, the running, the hiding, I had an unsettling feeling about everything Randy told me. Not that I didn't believe Randy; it just didn't feel right to me.

At that moment, after hearing Levi, as much as I hated what he said, it sank into me, it felt…right.

We did it to ourselves.

There were no mysterious men from the future trying to kill us in a freak science fiction twist of nature.

We did it.

The future didn't create us; we created a future, one that wasn't very good.

One thing was true; the future was no longer set in stone. We could indeed change it. We had Javier and Phoenix. We had knowledge.

Despite it all, the world as we knew it was over. It truly was time to start anew. We as a human race had screwed things up altogether, and it was up to the few of us who remained to make it right.

I vowed to do what I could.

In the words of Ronald Wilson Reagan, '*Let us be sure that those who come after will say of us in our time, that in our time we did everything that could be done. We finished the race; we kept them free; we kept the faith.*'

I would.

44
MERA STEVENS

Eighteen months later...

A small section of the 1700-acre property was dedicated as the 'In Memory' section, or, as some called it, the Reflection Area. It was outside the safety walls. Only two areas were actually protected by walls, I guess the two areas that were most crucial, the sectors where we all lived and spent most of our time.

Although the bodies of those we loved were not in the ground, we placed white crosses as markers for them. It looked like Arlington Cemetery.

I was visiting my family. I did every day. I spoke to Daniel, Beck, Jeremy, Randy, and Bill. They were whom I chose to mark in memory.

Even though I was outside the protected perimeter, I felt safe. Sleepers could be seen long before they entered. They came alone or with only a few. Twice we had been hit by a wave of them, but we prevailed.

They never made it to the wall, and of course, they'd never make it in.

Saying my daily farewells to those I lost, I spotted two Sleepers on the edge of the wooded area.

They stared with that slanted stand they had. Watching. Waiting.

I'd report them, and they'd be dealt with. I didn't worry.

The population in New Jerusalem had grown. At last count, population was 514.

We had nine births since we arrived. Four of them were stillborn. The virus was still prevalent everywhere.

I attributed the rise in population to Alex; he was diligent about trying to reach someone every day on the radio. For a while that first winter, people came daily, and then they trickled off until spring.

Everyone had a job. My job was the social, functioning coordinator of the kids, or rather, the community mom. I was happy with that. Even though others offered to take the children from Project Savior under their wings, nine of them opted to stay with me. It wasn't a difficult task. I had help.

Bonnie tended to the animals, mainly the horses, and we had a lot. For several months after we arrived, she was always going out and scouting for horses. Sonny loved that because he loved horses.

But that wasn't his job. He was called the Tech Man, because he got technology up and running again, mainly power. Sonny kept the lights on.

I passed the stables on my way through the main gate. Bonnie was out front with Jessie giving her a riding lesson.

Jessie was doing wonderfully. She spoke more and even was self-sufficient with her bathroom needs. I figured she was nineteen years behind the curve and would get there eventually.

"Look, Mama, look. I ride," Jessie boasted proudly, led by Bonnie.

"I see that," I smiled.

Bonnie said, "I'll bring her back when we're done. She was distracted earlier. Coming back from the Reflection Area?"

"Yeah, it's peaceful. Saw two Sleepers out near the woods."

"Better report them."

"Headed there now. Thanks." I moved on with my hands in my jacket pockets. Bonnie was the most indifferent person I had ever met. She never was happy or sad; she was just Bonnie. Occasionally she hung around with a new man in the community, an older guy in his seventies. But that was it. She rarely socialized with any of us.

Well, except for Jessie. She taught Jessie a lot.

The security office wasn't far from the barn, and I made it a point to stop there on my way home. A man named John ran our security force and was inside with Danny doing a weapons check. I knocked once and stepped inside.

"Hey, there," John smiled. He was former military. In fact, he came from the ARC, he and about nine others. They came on their own and were phenomenal at helping us keep the Sleepers at bay.

I was stunned at how many Sleepers there were. I guess over a hundred million people turned, and that was a lot of Sleepers.

"Hey, John," I said. "Just wanted to let you know I saw two Sleepers."

"Thanks, our gate guard spotted them beyond the Reflection Area."

"That's where I saw them."

"We're on it."

I cleared my throat. "Hello, Danny."

"Oh, hey, Mom." Danny nodded at me.

"When did you get back?" I asked.

"This morning."

"Can you let me know when you get back? I'm still your mom."

Danny cringed. "Sorry. But hey, I found three people near Hays, Kansas. One is a nurse."

"Oh, that's awesome. I'm gonna head home. School is out soon, and the kids get hungry."

I started to leave.

"Mom, is it true?" Danny asked.

I stopped in the doorway. "Is what true?"

"I saw Michael. He said Phoenix is coming here soon."

I laughed out an airy chuckle. "Phoenix has been coming here for six months. I'll believe it when he and Javier arrive."

Danny tilted his head. "I think tomorrow. That's what Michael said. Final tests were done."

John looked up at me. "I heard the same from Alex an hour ago."

"What the hell? No one tells me?" I hurried from the office. I had been out and about and back to the house. I don't think I saw Alex once since all of us had breakfast.

Leaving the main compound, I went to the second gate and rushed inside. Our home was there, or rather, our massive living complex. It was designed so multiple families could live under one roof, and in a sense, we were all family. Our original group, with the exception of Bonnie, all lived together. We stuck together.

I was going to stop at the school and ask Michael, but I heard the music and knew he was teaching and busy with the kids. So I went straight to the source.

Getting my hopes up was something I rarely did. Over the last year and a half, Phoenix had gotten better; Javier reported that he had made progress with the cure, but the numerous blood transfusions Phoenix received to save him tainted his blood, making him less and less of a hive.

Javier said he was walking and talking some. Not much.

Miles, who we had all met at a prison with survivors in Washington, the place where we found Jessie, was Phoenix's caretaker.

That made me happy.

I thought of that baby every single day and hoped he would welcome me into his life, when and if he ever arrived.

As soon as I walked into the house, I saw Sonny kicked back on the sofa with a pad and pen.

That surprised me.

"You aren't working?" I asked him.

He lowered the notebook. "I work every day. I got done early. I wanted to write. Try to make some progress before the troops arrive after school."

"Which is soon. I better start lunch. Is Alex still here with Keller?"

"Yep," Sonny said. "Did you hear? Javier is leaving the ARC tomorrow, heading here. Levi is running around telling everyone. I'm happy for you."

"Is it true?" I asked. "Really true this time? You know how many times he said it."

"Sounds it," Sonny shrugged. "You know Danny said last time his crew swung by the ARC it was nearly empty."

"Thanks. I'm gonna talk to Alex."

"Oh, hey," Sonny called out stopping me, "what was the name of Michael's church where you met him?"

"I don't remember. Jeez, ask Michael."

"Eh, I'll make it up. No one will know."

He returned his pen to his paper, and I darted from the room. A short hall led past the kitchen. Next to that was the radio room. Alex was in there. Keller was on the floor, his hands moving about the blocks, feeling them, lifting them, bringing them to his face before setting them back down.

"I'm here," I announced, and then bent down by Keller. Alex had this thing about putting a beanie cap on him to cover where his eyes should be. It unnerved me, but I stopped fighting about it. I touched Keller's hand so as not to startle him, ran my fingers up his arm, and kissed him. I brought my fingers to his palm, traced a circle, and then brought this hand to my chest. "Mommy's here." I ran his hand down my face. "I'll feed you in a minute." I moved his hand from his stomach to his lips.

"How was your...whatever it is you do?" Alex asked from in front of the radio where he sat.

"Is it true?"

"Hello to you, too." He turned around and faced me. "I think it is this time."

I wanted to shriek, scream, but I contained myself. I wasn't going to face another disappointment when Phoenix didn't show. Too many times, I waited at that gate. I exhaled loudly. "Let's hope. How was Keller today?"

"Quiet. Very quiet."

"Oh my God," I whined. "Let that joke go."

"Sorry, can't resist. Are you making lunch? I didn't eat."

"Yes, I am." I bent down, grabbed Keller's hand, and led him to stand. "Give me half an hour."

"Thanks."

Holding Keller's hand, I started to walk with him. He did soon his own; the children had taught him. He felt outward as he moved and was quite skilled at it. I wanted to pick him up and carry him, but he wasn't going to be self-sufficient if I kept doing that.

I told Alex, "I'll leave you to do whatever it is you do."

He laughed. I knew what he did.

- 408 -

Within a few months, Alex had moved straight into a leadership position in the New Jerusalem. He was our official leader. A good one, too. Kept everything in check, everyone fed, and stocked our supply room. He spent hours each day on that radio, calling out. I never met another human being so determined to make the world better than it was.

Alex was on that mission.

I heard him start transmission again as I walked out. It was the same message. He said it so often, he sounded robotic.

"Hey there, world. Calling out for survivors. If anyone is out there, we're in Eldorado. This is the New Jerusalem. We are with people from Project Savior. We are a second facility. We seek others and believe with the right elements we can create a strong future."

His voice carried as I walked into the kitchen with Keller.

I had prepared the soup earlier in the day and had to pull it from the fridge and heat it. I set Keller on a chair, guided his hand to the crackers, and then gave my signal to him to stay put. He was a smart baby, and I was proud of how well he was doing, despite his disabilities. I attributed that to all the kids around him and to Alex being relentless.

Opening the fridge, I pulled out the pot. Soup and buttered bread would work just fine. As I carried the huge pot to the stove, I laughed again at Alex and then I heard a little voice.

"Mama."

My head cocked.

"Mama? Milk?"

The voice was young. Very young. I set down the pot and slowly turned around. I gasped, and my heart thumped hard in my chest. Stunned, I jumped back, hitting the stove.

"Mama." Keller stood before me; he walked to me holding up a baby bottle.

My eyes widened. I heard his little voice. I heard him clear as day and loudly, too.

"Mama? Milk?" he requested again, holding that bottle to me. I watched him speak. I watched and heard him speak his request.

Yet...his lips did not move.

SLEEPERS 3

PROLOGUE
THE TEACHER

25 PE (Post Event)

I am not my brother's keeper, nor he mine. Despite what we have been taught and how we have been raised, we are individuals bound not by blood but by circumstance.

Our parents are not even the ones who created us. We were found.

One of us was tossed aside to die like a deformed animal, the other caught in the seconds following his birth in the grasp of the woman he would know to be his mother.

Both of us are anomalies.

We were both born in a world where all children died, when the unborn lost their lives in the womb.

A virus raged throughout the world, taking the young and transforming most of the others.

Our mother was not touched by the virus, nor was our brother Danny. Our sister, though, was infected, but our mother praises the fact that she was saved.

Was our sister really saved? Or was she condemned to live a tortured life, never knowing what she was or could have been?

None of us, the young, the few who remained in the beginning, know anything of a green world filled with happiness and laughter.

We know hunger and sickness, and we know fear.

Fear is not a fictional tale to us; it is reality every night when we close our eyes to sleep.

We are trying, all of us, to make the world a better place for those who are now being born. For the children who defy the odds of the virus that still lingers in the air.

Not all who are conceived gasp their first breath of life in this world.

They are born without breath, life, or a soul.

Things have to change.

Growing up, we were coddled within a parental shelter. The love of our mother was never questioned. She taught us to be strong; she protected us when we were weak. Fought for us. More than anything, she instilled the basic human values in us both. She made me believe that I could be whatever I wanted and could do whatever I needed to do.

She never treated us any differently, yet I know when she sees us now, she knows.

She knows my brother and I want two different things.

We fight for two different things.

We, as brothers, are as divided as this world, one side against the other.

I will do what I need to do to ensure this world goes on, that this place becomes better for the generations to come.

They have taken this world and destroyed it. *They* grow in numbers and their offspring will be just as deadly to us.

Because of that, I will lead the battle. It will be a war that has only been imagined yet never waged.

For the woman who bore me that I never knew, and for the mother who loved and raised me…it is time.

It has gone on for decades and must stop now.

The so-called Doctrines of the future, a guidebook to us all, predicted the outcome.

I put no stock in the Doctrines because I know who wrote them. I was there as his pen moved across the page and his eyes glanced to the ceiling, thinking of words he could use to create a false story.

Even if they do hold some truth, they are words from a future.

The future can be changed.

I was destined to do it…and I will.

THE DOCTRINES 13: 9-11

The Reckoning failed. The land around The New Jerusalem was poisoned by the fire. Food could not grow there for a long time, and life there was not possible. The New Jerusalem had done to itself what Man had done to the earth. And because of that, those who lived within The New Jerusalem began to leave.

THE DOCTRINES 13: 9-11

PART ONE
THE SECOND YEAR

Still Remembering

1
MERA STEVENS

18 Months PE

I called it the day the laughter stopped, but it really didn't. It was only muffled for a short time. It returned, not as loud, more of whisper really, and I hope that one day it will grow louder.

We live in a place we have now named Grace. Often, Alex Sans jokes about it being Graceland. His infatuation with Elvis, I suppose.

He does well by us as a leader and a fighter. He wasn't supposed to be a leader, but anyone who knew Alex knew he would not idly sit by and let someone else take the reins of his life.

I remember the day that Beck followed Alex's dictate and told me it was because Alex was the leader, not him.

I didn't get it or agree until we moved into Grace.

Grace is a small taste of normal. Well, normal to those who lived in the 1800s.

We grow our own food, mend our own clothes. Although I don't get that because there's a Wal-Mart and a mall not fifteen miles away.

Occasionally I'll whine enough where Alex gets annoyed and has Sonny take me and a few other women out with a security team.

We are still dangerously outnumbered.

In a desolate world, you'd expect quiet. The world is not quiet. Sure, there isn't the sound of traffic, or the annoying young person playing his stereo too loud. No planes. But there is one sound that carries through the dead silence of the night.

The call of the damned.

The Sleepers.

They are there. Always there. They're everywhere.

There are so many nights where I sit in bed longing, not just for the old days of turning on the television or listening to music, but for my old life. Every single day I miss and ache for my son, Jeremy. He was taken in The Event. His life withered before my very eyes. I crave Daniel's type of companionship, my husband who was no less than my best friend. My daughter Jessie, though still alive, had to, in a sense, begin life again. At twenty years old, she is no more than four years old mentally.

She is also a Sleeper.

I yearn for a life of normalcy and opportunity for my son, Danny. That kind of world is a world he will never know. He'll grow up knowing only struggle, running, work, and death.

I miss Gavin Beck, God, do I miss him. A man who was a hero in my eyes after The Event. A man I loved and believed would always be there with me and my surviving children. He died so we could live.

He died so Phoenix could live.

Phoenix was one of two babies born after The Event when all others were stillborn. It was believed that Phoenix held the cure for the virus, that he could save the future of mankind.

The truth was, or at least we were told, that if allowed to live, Phoenix would actually eliminate the future.

His blood was thick with the Sleeper virus. He seeped it. He exhaled it. Now, after months of testing, failures, and some success, Phoenix is coming home, or at least, back to me. That's what I heard.

It's the gossip hotline in Grace. No phones, just word of mouth, '*I heard this*' and '*I heard that*.' So many times people talked about Javier being en route that I stopped believing it.

Javier is the doctor who worked on Phoenix. No, he saved Phoenix after his tiny body was shot.

Last I heard, he had contained the virus within Phoenix, whatever that meant.

Miles was coming, too; he was Phoenix's caretaker.

A part of me was scared. I mean, poor Phoenix spent fifteen months in a lab and under the guidance of a former prison guard. He didn't have a mother's love, and I vowed once I had him with me, he'd be inundated with it.

I was on my way home from the Reflection Area when I started hearing the rumors. I didn't think much about them though everyone had something to say as I passed them. Until I went to security to tell them about the two Sleepers I saw near the field.

My son informed me, and I rushed home to find Alex. If Alex said it, then it was true.

He confirmed it. Still, I didn't allow myself to get too excited. Not yet. I focused on my daily tasks, which mainly were caring for not only my children, but others as well.

Alex and Sonny shared in the child rearing duty. We all lived together like some weird commune. We were friends with the same goals, so it worked.

After getting my confirmation regarding Phoenix, I rescued Keller from Alex. I hated when Alex was in charge of watching Keller, even for an hour. Not that he was reckless or careless; he just was weird. He constantly felt the need to teach him. In my eyes, impaired or not, Keller was still a baby.

Keller was now my own child, having found him when he was a few weeks old. He was born with no eyes, no ears. He was deaf and blind. At first, looking at him brought to mind the many stillborn children who were born without features. We called them Ivory Statue babies.

That was at first. Keller's smoothed-over eye sockets became normal and we no longer saw him as a reminder, but as a blessing.

Of course, I hated that Alex kept putting that stupid beanie over his head to cover his eyes. He looked like a throwback from the seventies cartoon, *Fat Albert*.

It was a normal day, with the exception of waiting for Phoenix. I took the baby into the kitchen with me while I prepared lunch for the masses. We had a huge kitchen table that seated twenty, and we almost filled it.

Lunch and breakfast were easy meals, something fast, simple.

I had prepared the soup earlier in the day and just had to pull it from the fridge and heat it. I set Keller on a chair, guided his hand to the crackers, and then gave my signal to him to stay put. He was a smart baby, and I was proud of how well he was doing, despite his disabilities. I attributed that to all the kids around him and to Alex being relentless about teaching him.

Opening the fridge, I pulled out the pot. Soup and buttered bread would work just fine. Too many mouths to feed.

As I carried the huge pot to the stove, I heard, "Mama."

My head cocked at the young voice.

"Mama? Milk?"

The voice was young. Very young. I set down the pot and slowly turned around. I gasped, and my heart thumped hard in my chest. Stunned, I jumped back, hitting the stove.

"Mama." Keller stood before me, holding up a baby bottle.

My eyes widened. I heard his little voice. I *heard* him clear as day and loudly, too.

"Mama? Milk?" he requested again, holding that bottle to me. I watched him speak. I watched and heard him speak his request.

Yet... his lips did not move.

Stunned, I stumbled back and yelled, "Alex!"

2
ALEX SANS

How in the heck were my feet getting bigger? It took a struggle to get into my boots. I'd had them off while doing my annoying daily calls out.

Each time I made the calls, I got annoyed. I know, as weird as it sounded, it was my own voice that called to us when we were trying to find Grace.

Okay, let me see if I can sum this up in forty words or less. The folks from the future who came to this time just after the onset of the plague were looking for the other parties in their group. They hid a code that only the young could hear, which provided the directions to Grace or, as they called it, New Jerusalem. They used an archived recording that supposedly the original people of Grace made to call out for survivors. Recorded in the 'now' time, they had it in the future and brought it with them. A tweaked, electronic voice, but it was me.

That was more than forty words.

In any event, because I felt I had to, I placed those calls. They helped, brought some people in, but this place, at least for me, is temporary.

I never wanted to be a leader; I just wanted to live my life.

Sonny, our resident electrician and gospel taker, said he wanted to venture out to find a new place for the kids and us. Kids, you know, that weren't born in this time, but came from the future for a better life.

Really? If this, right now, is a better life, then I hate to think of how they lived in their time.

Levi was a man who came with them from the future, along with my friend, Randy, who passed away.

Levi said they had one time trip remaining where we could physically go back in time. That was a scary thought. There was also one ne cerebral time trip. It was a mental thing, like astral projecting. It was conceivable to go to the future just to check how things turned out and use the other for something else. That would be cheating.

Plus, what the hell is a cerebral time trip? Is that like astral projecting or something? Who knows? Who cares? I hate time travel shit and hope it doesn't come up again.

Even with the Doctrines.

The Doctrines, brought from the future, penned in the now. Sonny deemed himself the Doctrine writer because he swore he was the one. So now he sits daily, writing the events that happened, even if they really hadn't.

The scary thing is, Sonny didn't look at the Doctrines brought from the future. I did. And they are eerily similar.

I wonder why he didn't mention my feet getting bigger.

I got my second boot on; it was tight too. I wanted to grab something to eat and head out to the Reflection Area where a few people had spotted two Sleepers.

It wasn't uncommon. More and more showed up, lingering, lurking, and staring. Most of our residents didn't know. I wanted to clear those Sleepers and check for more.

Javier and Miles were on their way to Grace with Phoenix, and the last thing I wanted was for them to be caught in a Sleeper attack.

Only a few of us ever ventured outside of the perimeter of Grace. What we've seen, done and learned is known only among a select few of our group.

I want the people of Grace to feel safe. They *are* safe. But if they only knew...

"Alex!" Mera screamed.

I ignored her, and laced my boots. Mera screaming my name was nothing new, especially the way she just had. Sharp, shocking, maybe even angry.

"Alex!"

I shook my head and stood up. My feet were gonna hurt, I could feel it. What the hell was up with my feet?

"Hey," Sonny said, poking his head into the office. "You don't hear Mera calling you?"

"Yes, Boots, I do. And I'm ignoring her. Lenore made those pickles and I know Mera has been saving one."

"You ate it." Sonny smiled, shaking his head.

"I did. I'm betting that is why she's screaming. If you're concerned, go find out."

Sonny scratched his head, ruffling his always-pretty blonde hair. "You know what? I'm writing."

"I figured." Just as Sonny started to leave, I called for him. "Hey, Boots? You ever heard of someone's feet getting bigger overnight?"

He gave a weird smile and shook his head. "Maybe your feet are swollen?"

"Nah, I must be imagining it. Go write for the future, I am gonna need you, though. Soon."

"What's up?"

"Well," I exhaled. "I'm thinking—"

"Alex, I swear to God. Come here!" Mera yelled.

"Son of a bitch." I stomped my foot for that final fitting. "I'll talk to you, I want to see what the hell she's screaming about."

I stepped from my office and walked directly to the kitchen. When I walked in, Mera's back was plastered against the sink. Keller stood before her holding his bottle.

"Mera," I said as I walked in, "what the hell is the matter?"

"Keller."

"What about him?" I leaned down and sniffed him. "He smells fine. What did he do?"

"He..." Her eyes shifted. "He...spoke."

"I'm sorry," I tugged my ear. "Say again."

"He spoke."

"He spoke?"

Mera nodded.

Now, granted, she did have a scared expression. Her eyes were wide, and she wasn't moving. It was almost the exact same look she had when a rat wandered into the kitchen one morning.

"Keller?" I asked. "This boy here." I placed my hand on his head. "The one with no eyes or ears...spoke."

"Yes."

"A-ha," I said sarcastically, stepped to Mera and smelled her.

"What are you doing?" she asked.

"Seeing if you were drinking."

She smacked me away. "I wasn't drinking. It's the middle of the day."

"Never stopped you before."

"Alex," she growled then looked at Keller. "Honey, talk. Say it again."

"Mera..."

She waved her hand at me for silence and pleaded with Keller. "Please, talk."

Had she not been so desperate, so serious, I would have sworn she was drunk. But she had this look, one that honestly believed what she was saying.

"He spoke, Alex, he spoke."

I nodded. "Okay, let's suppose he did. What did he say?"

"He said he wants milk."

"All right, then." I exhaled. "Get him milk." I bent down, darted a kiss to Keller, took the bottle from his hand, used his own hands to sign that I was leaving, and then I handed the bottle to Mera. "See you in a little bit."

Barely out the door, I heard her curse, "Asshole." I laughed, but almost out of the house, I stopped short.

The vision of the baby and Mera snapped into my head. When I walked into the kitchen, he was holding the bottle, extending it to her as if he knew she was there.

For a brief moment...very brief, I thought about it. What if? Could he?

Then after reminding myself that the child was not only blind but couldn't hear, I dismissed it and left the house in my very tight boots.

3
MERA STEVENS

Alex Sans frustrated me like no other. He had since the first moment I met him. His arrogance and ability to charm anyone annoyed the hell out of me. I don't think I ever stopped getting frustrated with his attitude; I think I just got numb to it.

There were times, though, that I allowed that emotion to slip through with him. His attitude about me being drunk or hearing things when it came to hearing Keller speak was just the latest.

Many times, I was right, and I wasn't drunk, drinking, or imagining it.

Keller spoke. I *heard* him. I know my son hasn't any ears or eyes, and has never made more than a groan or whimper, but I *heard* his voice.

Perhaps it was a psychic thing. I wouldn't dismiss that, not after all that happened. It would occur again, of that I was sure, and Alex would hear it.

I don't know why he chose so many times not to believe a word I was saying.

It started with Phoenix. No, wait, it started before we found Phoenix, when he knocked me out with that door. Alex didn't believe it and refuted it adamantly.

I saw Phoenix come into this world, expelled from his dead mother. When all other children were stillborn, he was alive and normal. Tiny and early, but alive.

Alex wouldn't even look at him. Swore up and down he didn't want to get attached to the baby because he would die.

Well, Phoenix didn't die. In fact, at eighteen months old, he is alive and well and only a few seconds from my embrace.

I put the Keller talking thing in the back of my mind, confident it would happen again and careful not to tell too many about it. I was already considered the nut job of Grace, even though most of what I said was true.

Two weeks after we first arrived, I swore up and down a Sleeper was roaming the property. I was so convinced of it, I was on the brink of being neurotic.

I wouldn't let any of the kids out of my sight or out of the house.

I'd see it everywhere I went. One day I was doing dishes, looked up and the Sleeper was standing on the other side of my kitchen window. I grabbed Keller and ran. Why I ran outside was beyond me. Surely, it wasn't a good move if there was a Sleeper lurking.

"I know you believe you saw what you think you saw," Alex said.

"What the hell kind of talk is that?" I asked.

"I'm trying, Mera. I'm trying to not get upset, but you're seeing a Sleeper in a community with a huge wall and some damned good men watching. No one else sees this Sleeper."

"No one is looking."

Alex held up his hand. "Listen to me. If there was a Sleeper being a peeping Tom while you did dishes, then don't you think someone would have seen him wandering around?"

"When I see him he leaves, and like I said, no one goes looking."

"No one needs to look."

"Well if Beck was alive...he'd look."

"Beck's not alive."

I believe I growled in frustration; I always growled at Alex. To him, I was some nut job. He asked me to speak to Pastor Mike, our resident religious man. Mike had me talk to Levi, a psychologist mind-man from the future. No one believed I saw a Sleeper. They all put it as a product of my imagination.

If I was imagining it, I had a pretty detailed imagination, and sense of smell, too.

It got to the point I doubted my own sanity. Until that night.

It was raining, thunder and lightning, the entire scary works. Keller was in bed with me, just a tiny baby, sleeping soundly, when the thunder boomed, shaking the house. I sat up in bed. Lightning flashed, brightening the room an eerie blue and with it was the vision of the Sleeper standing at the foot of my bed.

I grabbed Keller, holding him tightly, and raced through my mind on what I needed to do. All weapons were locked up with Alex.

Alex.

The children!

If the Sleeper made it to my bedroom on the second floor, how much damage had he already done? Had he hurt someone? Those thoughts hit me in a split second's time, and I reached for the lamp next to the bed. Holding Keller, I whipped the lamp towards me, pulling the cord from the wall, cried out an ear-piercing scream and jumped from the bed.

It didn't move. Didn't attack. It was reminiscent of the early days of the Sleepers when they stared eerily, just stared...

The door to the bedroom burst open and, of course, Alex in all his heroic half-dressed glory barreled into the room.

The Sleeper turned and lunged for Alex. Alex hit him and hit him again, but the Sleeper wouldn't go down. The thing was much bigger than Alex, and apparently much stronger. A fearful turmoil swirled in my gut as I called out for Sonny.

Sonny. Danny. Someone.

Alex went down. His hands held on to the tattered and dirty clothes of the Sleeper, trying to push his biting jaws away.

No one was coming. Baby in one arm, lamp in my hand, I ran over, and with all I had I swung down. But at that instant as the lamp careened full force, Alex flipped and rolled the Sleeper from him and on to his back.

The lamp smashed into Alex's head.

Alex fell sideways and to the floor. The Sleeper sat up, grabbed on to Alex, and opened his mouth. I had nothing. I thought to kick him, but I didn't need to. A small hatchet came down into the head of the Sleeper, and I looked up to see Danny breathing heavily. Sonny hurried in right behind him.

I caught my breath and raced toward the door. "We need to check the kids. Check the kids."

"Sleeper," Danny said.

He and Sonny joined me in checking on the children. They were unharmed and sleeping. I guess one of us checked on Alex, because he was bleeding pretty badly. He ended up needing eighteen stitches.

That night and all before leading up to the Sleeper incident defined my relationship with Alex. He never gave me credit for anything, never believed me, nor trusted me. And sometimes one of us got injured by the mistake of the other.

He apologized for not believing me about the Sleeper.

I said "Fuck you."

Mike said, "Hey, hey, now."

Sonny wanted to get past it all and figured out how this one Sleeper managed to be in Grace for days without someone knowing, or rather, me being the only one to see him. To him that problem needed to be managed and we'd have to tighten down. We never did figure it out. The Sleepers slipped in; they always do some way.

To me, Alex was the problem. He was overly confident. Perhaps if he weren't, we'd find those holes. Back when we first arrived, it was as if those who were there, Levi and the others, those who came from the future to live in our 'better' world, handed all authority over to him.

People sang his praises and placed him in the category of hero because, like Moses, he led the children across a wicked world. Well, if I recall correctly, Alex didn't do it alone. Levi told me that he thinks I resent Alex's stature because Beck is in some way being slighted.

Yeah, maybe, because I feel I am the only one who keeps his memory alive. I have to. I owe my life, my daughter's life, to Beck.

I don't really hate Alex, although times it seems like I do. It's more of a love/hate thing. Some days we get along great; we actually laugh together. Other days I get so angry and frustrated with him that I want *him* to be Sleeper bait.

Nevertheless, I suppose, no matter what my feelings, I have to deal with Alex Sans.

I hate to give him credit, but he does do a good job of leading the community. I just wish he would give me more credit as an intelligent person, rather than treating me like some post-apocalypse Donna Reed whose only purpose is to take care of the young. Then again, that *is* my job. That's all I do around Grace. Perhaps that's why my imagination takes off and I see things along with hearing a deaf, blind, and mute boy talk.

4
ALEX SANS

It was a cemetery, despite what Mera called it. She liked to label it the Reflection Area, because she goes there and reflects. On what, God only knows.

I grabbed hold of Sonny, AKA Boots, and asked him if he'd join me in the hunt for the two Sleepers that a few people had spotted on the edge of the Reflection Area.

A huge wall encircled the main compound, but most of our fields and that cemetery were not enclosed. A wooded area on one side and barren land on the other bordered them.

It's hard to say where they came from, because they could have walked the perimeter of the compound at night.

However, spotting two was worth checking out.

I paused to pass on a moment of respect at Beck's grave. It was neat and tidy, as were the other graves of people we knew. Courtesy of Mera, who went there every single day. Every day for a year. Who does that?

Mera Stevens.

She had a weird obsession about Beck. She didn't know him that long, yet she mourned him and missed him like a partner she'd had for years.

"Leave her alone," Sonny said as I stood after my moment of silence.

"I didn't say anything."

"You were going to," Sonny told me. "You always do. You visit Beck's grave, you do what it is you do. Pray, count, whatever, and then you say something about Mera."

"I do not."

"You do."

"But don't you think it's weird that she is that dedicated to—"

"Stop." Sonny held up his hand. "She is eternally grateful to him. Let it alone, and let's see if we can find these Sleepers. I want to get back. Javier is arriving with Phoenix."

"If Phoenix arrives while were gone, he'll still be there when we get back." I dusted my hands on my pants and peered around.

"Now, see, that's what I don't get. You were there when he was born. Why aren't you more excited?"

"I'll believe he's coming when I see it. Speaking of seeing..." I shaded my eyes. "I'm not seeing the Sleepers."

"That was an hour ago. They left."

"Where'd they go? Reports all said they were just standing over there." I gestured at the wooded area and suggested to Sonny we head there. It was probably the only place they could retreat without being noticed. We readied our crossbows. Never guns; the sound of shots not only attracted Sleepers but also scared the residents of Grace.

"You never did say what Mera was yelling at you for," Sonny said as we headed toward the woods. "Was it about the pickle?"

"No, but I'm sure that's coming," I paused in walking. "Get this. Mera said Keller...spoke."

"She said what?"

"He spoke. Said words. Asked for milk."

Sonny crinkled his brow. "Spoke, you say?"

"Now why would you do that?"

"Do what?"

"Say it like that. 'Spoke, you say?' What the hell kind of talk is that? Mera said he spoke."

"You don't believe her?"

"No." I shook my head. "And you do?"

"Well..."

"Well nothing. The boy has no eyes, no ears."

"He has a mouth, he breathes and has vocal chords, and I've heard him whimper."

"But he'd have to hear words in order to know how to speak them."

Sonny shrugged. "Maybe he *can* hear."

"He doesn't have any ears."

"Or...they're blocked and he can hear some things."

I shook my head and resumed walking. "No. I tested his hearing once. Banged pots. Made all kinds of noise. No response. He's deaf."

"That's odd that you would do that," Sonny said. "I mean, if you're adamant that he's deaf because he has no ears, why test him?"

"Because..."

"Because what?"

"Because sometimes when I watch him, he does weird stuff. Leave it at that."

"Okay, I'll leave it at that." Sonny started to walk. "Just don't dismiss Mera so quick when you just told me he does weird stuff."

"Shut up."

"This is why you two bicker all the time. It's fine for you to think something odd, but when Mera says it, it's not. Almost as if you're afraid she may—"

"Sonny," I halted him. "You are not the resident therapist. Levi is."

"Man, you're tough. I think I'm gonna write a passage in the Doctrines about you."

I shook my head again. "Why do you make things up? That's supposed to be a future document. A Bible."

"Who says I'm making things up? Maybe I'll tell a true story about you." Sonny stopped talking, and I heard why. Just as we reached the edge of the woods, not a Sleeper in sight, we heard an ungodly moan. Almost a cry of the damned laced with pain.

I whispered, "Where did it come from?"

The sound rang out again. It echoed through the woods making it harder to pinpoint. After a few more moments and a few more cries, we followed the direction. Was it an animal? It was hard to tell.

"Stay alert, stay focused, and keep an eye out for Sleepers," I told Sonny as we quietly tromped through the woods in search of the sound.

Then we found it. I held back my arm to Sonny to stop him. Not because I feared what would happen, but rather, I had to think of what to do.

The sound didn't come from an animal or a person, it came from a Sleeper. A lone woman, dirty, pasty white. Her long, dirty hair flung about as she used the leverage of the hillside. She was oblivious to our presence. Naked, on her hands and knees, her legs were spread and with each wave of cries, she pushed back, bringing her rear end out and closer to the ground.

It was apparent by Sonny's face that he was confused what was going on.

I knew exactly what was happening.

That Sleeper, alone in the woods...was giving birth.

5
MERA STEVENS

"And how did that make you feel?"

Seriously? Levi, last name some number, asked the same question every time I went to see him.

"It made me mad. Again. I got frustrated with Alex, again."

Levi stared at me. "Did you convey to Alex this makes you feel this way?"

I laughed. "Levi, are you programmed? You say the same thing every time I come to you and I have been coming to you since Pastor Mike told me to take it elsewhere."

"I am not programmed. I say the same thing because *you* say the same thing."

I gasped. "I do *not*."

"Yes, Mera, you do. It's the same complaint, different situations. What was it today? Keller was staring at you."

That's what I had told him. Believing that he followed the so-called Doctrines and the Doctrines talked about the 'evil' child, I was careful not to convey that Keller possibly was communicating telepathically.

"Maybe it's time you and Alex come in together, and we'll talk."

"You say that, too." I sat back. "How did you help people in your time?"

"Typically, insidious neurotic targeting of an angry nature stems from an unresolved issue. People tend to remember things differently than how they happened. The more time passes, the less accurate the memory. For example, a man is sorely damaged emotionally because his wife left him. He can't get past it. Her words were bitter and angry the day she left, and he was a victim, feeling like a victim."

"Okay..."

"Well, in that instance, he is a prime candidate for cerebral passage. A form of time travel that doesn't put you physically in the same space and time as your counterpart, just in the mind of that moment, and you can relive it. Oftentimes facing that one moment changes an outlook. The man goes back, sees he said some horrible things to the wife as well, feels less of a victim when he returns."

"What if he went back and killed his wife?" I asked.

"It is not possible to physically control your cerebral counterpart. In addition, there is the assurance. Now, he could have influenced the *words*, but then again, if the wife were leaving then, he couldn't have stopped her."

"He could have stopped himself from saying mean things to her."

Levi nodded. "In turn perchance she wouldn't have blasted him. Same resolution."

I sat back. "Hmmmm. So you don't physically leave this realm?"

"No. And you and your people hate the time travel topic, so why are we bringing up?"

"You brought it up. I'm just curious as to what it is."

"Two people," Levi held up his fingers. "One is assurance. The assurance is a person who was there, at the same time, the same moment, nearby. For example, the husband or wife, perhaps a friend in the next room. They *assured* the main traveler doesn't change anything."

"So it's like hypnosis, only you're actually there? That's risky."

"No. Never had a time instance change."

"How would you know?"

"Mera," he snapped, rubbing his brow, "the *assurance*. In addition, the trip isn't long enough to do damage. The experience is one minute in the past. One minute, one moment."

My mind started spinning. "Can you do that to me?"

"What are we resolving?"

"Beck."

"I don't understand."

"He sacrificed for me, Levi. He was going to die for my child. I feel that he died without knowing how I felt. We had one moment that was actually the start to an 'us.' I don't recall it. I need to know that I told him how I feel. I need to see him one more time. Maybe if I did, then maybe I'd stop hating Alex so much for being the one who lived."

"Ouch." Levi stood. "In all our sessions—and there have been many—never has that come up. I thought it, but it never came from your mouth. Do you really resent Alex for living and not dying?"

"Yes," I answered without hesitation. "Especially when something happens and I know Beck would have handled it differently."

"All right. But I need you to go through the application process."

What was he talking about? Like a job interview? Was I up against someone else in use of the cerebral trip?

"As you know, Noah is the only other remaining quantum traveler. He holds the keys as well to the two remaining trips. I need you to write for me why this is important. If Noah agrees and we both feel this will stop your anger toward Alex and embrace what he is to—"

"Please stop." I held up my hand. "Don't praise Alex to me. Please." My gut twisted.

"Will you write it?"

"Yes, I will."

I was just about to ask him what all it needed to include, how long it had to be when Danny burst into the room. "Mom!" He caught his breath then grinned. "Javier is driving up the road. We just spotted them."

"Phoenix?"

"Hard to tell, but it looks like Miles has him."

I jumped up. "Oh my God!" My hand shot to my mouth, and with a huge smile I faced Levi. "I gotta go."

"Possibly seeing Phoenix can be the answer, Mera," Levi stated. "He's been missing from your life just as long. See how you and Alex are when you see him."

"Maybe." I looked at Danny. "Did you get Alex?"

"Um, he went out and I don't know where he is."

"Well then fuck him. I'm not waiting." And I left. To me, I'd rather write the essay. Just Alex being gone knowing full well that Phoenix was en route was enough to get me angry again. I didn't want any anger in me. I wanted only happiness. I raced next door to get Keller from Mike, and then all of us ran to the gates.

Phoenix was returning.

6
ALEX SANS

The seal had been broken, birthing was imminent, and even from twenty feet away, I clearly saw the explosion of fluids gush from the Sleeper woman's posterior.

Then an eruption of fluid gushed from Sonny. He vomited.

"You been hanging around Mera too much," I chided him.

He ran his hand over his mouth. "It's barbaric. It's not right. Something doesn't feel right."

"No shit. This whole thing is wrong. What the hell…?"

The woman screamed long and shrilly, a noise that came from her gut. Immediately I knew that those in Grace stood a chance of hearing it.

I raised my crossbow.

Sonny reached out. "What are you doing?"

"Putting her out of her misery."

"She's giving birth."

"Yeah, well, then I'm putting us out of our misery. " I took aim, but didn't have time to press the trigger. More Sleepers ascended and fast.

Five of them came over the crest racing our way. One stopped and stood guard by the woman and the other four came for Sonny and me.

I fired immediately. The first arrow sailed forth, landing dead center of a Sleeper's throat. He still came at us. Sonny fired at the same Sleeper, taking him out.

That left four, three of them raging our way. I hoped it wasn't going to be an instance of hand to hand, because those maddened bastards were strong. They didn't feel pain or fear and operated only on emotion and anger. They attacked brutally, without caring how it affected them. I could slug one with all I had, hit him a million times, and he wouldn't react to the pain.

Before I could even engage another arrow, a Sleeper jumped for me. I struggled for my knife; it should have been more accessible. What was I thinking? Never in all the times I'd gone out had I been attacked by a group. It was almost as if they baited us into a trap. Like they'd *waited*. Went to the field until they knew they were spotted, retreated to the woods, and waited.

Were they that smart?

I felt the teeth sink into my arm.

My first ever Sleeper bite. A burning pain, deep within my arm. The way his teeth attached to my skin, I swore he was going to rip the flesh from the bone. I was going to either succumb to the Sleeper virus or bleed to death.

Despite my pain, my free hand finally grabbed hold of the knife, and I ejected the sharp object up, into his throat, retracted, and nailed him in the temple.

His jaw stayed clamped.

I had to fall down with the Sleeper or risk losing my arm.

"Sonny!" I called out, but Sonny was busy. He was running. I was ready to blast him for being cowardly when I realized what he was doing. He was trying to outrun the Sleeper, put distance between them and buy enough time to raise his crossbow and take out the Sleeper.

Ten yards away, Sonny did just that, and then hurried back. I watched him run toward me, and another Sleeper leapt on me. His hands immediately went full force into my gut. I felt the pain, and I reconciled my life. I was done. Before he could rip me open, Sonny got him.

The jaws of the dead Sleeper were still locked on my arm. With a tromp of those oh so infamous boots, Sonny smashed down on the Sleeper, crushing into the side of his head and breaking the jaw.

I owed him. I owed him big time.

My arm was bleeding pretty badly. I needed help, but we still had two problems: The woman giving birth and the man guarding her. I whipped off my belt, making a tourniquet, even though I knew better than anyone they weren't good.

All was quiet. The scuffle with the Sleepers caused us to miss the big event, although another was taking place.

The Sleeper woman had given birth. I was unable to determine whether the child was alive or dead. It simply seemed to be discarded off to the side. Was it even a person? It was curled up, covered with blood, streaked with a white substance.

The mother and her henchman were too busy consuming something. What looked like the umbilical cord dangled from her mouth and something was in her hands, something thick, big, and bloody. He shared it with her, taking a bite, pulling away and slurping in the substance.

Were they eating the newborn baby or the placenta? I honestly couldn't tell. Then I saw Sonny on the ground, one knee quickly fussing with the laces from his boot.

I started to question why he would pick now to tie his shoes, and then I saw him with the lace. He stood and rushed to the discarded item.

I wanted to call out to him, forewarning him that what he believed was the child may actually be afterbirth. But he raced to it.

"Son of a bitch." I lifted my crossbow, aimed at the male Sleeper. He seemed to see me the second I caught him in my scope. Mouth red, blood flowing from his raw meal, I fired a good clean, dead center forehead shot.

The woman snarled outward and sloppily stood.

"It's still alive," Sonny announced, kneeling on the ground.

I prepped my crossbow as the woman, carrying the placenta, walked toward me. The cord fell from her mouth, and that's when I realized what Sonny was doing. He was clamping the cord. She chewed, and he didn't want the baby to bleed to death. That's what I guessed.

She didn't move fast or in a stable manner. I didn't think she could; she'd just given birth. Then again, she was replenishing like any wild animal, feeding off the afterbirth of her young.

"I need a blanket. Something," Sonny called out.

"Sonny, what the hell?" I yelled then looked at the woman. She wasn't a threat; she was actually pretty pathetic. Every step she took, blood poured down her legs. Her stomach still appeared pregnant. Unable to take it anymore, and needing to end it, I shot her.

She went down, afterbirth still in her hands. A stabbing pain shot up my arm, and I grabbed it. "Sonny, come on, I gotta get back. Gotta try to get an antiviral or I'll turn Sleeper."

Sonny took off his shirt and I reached for the baby.

"What are you doing?" I asked.

"Taking him."

"You can't do that." I walked toward him and looked down.

"He's trying to cry, but I think he's hurt," Sonny said. "Look at him."

"Stop looking at him."

"Alex, he has his eyes, ears, a nose. He's not stillborn or an ivory statue baby. Look at him."

"And I said stop." I lifted my crossbow. "Turn away."

"What the hell!" Sonny blasted. "What are you doing?"

"Killing it."

"It's a baby," Sonny argued.

"It's a Sleeper."

"We don't know that."

"Well, considering it's been over a year, I'd say two Sleeper parents make a Sleeper baby."

Sonny whisked up the child into his arms. "Then you'll shoot it while I hold it."

"What the hell is the matter with you, Sonny?"

"No, Alex. What's wrong with *you*?" Sonny snapped. "How about I shoot *you* right now, too. Okay? You were bit. How 'bout I just end your suffering right now? Have you become so hard and callous that you'd kill a baby?"

"No, I'd kill a Sleeper."

"I won't let you." Holding the child wrapped in his shirt, Sonny turned to leave.

"This is a mistake!" I shouted. "I'm telling you, taking that child is a mistake."

Sonny stopped. "No, you have Sleeper virus racing through your veins and I'm holding a dying child. Standing here arguing is the mistake and I'm not doing it."

Sonny didn't just walk off; he hauled ass and left me there.

Alone, injured in woods filled with Sleepers wasn't a good situation, so I followed. I don't know, perhaps, I wasn't thinking clearly, I don't know. But my gut screamed that everything that just happened wasn't right and I kept thinking, somehow, we just witnessed the start of a chain of events we'd regret.

7
MERA STEVENS

I was there when Phoenix came into this world. Tiny, frail and premature, he was barely given a chance.. But he lived. At that time, and to the best of our knowledge, he was the only child born alive. Not only was he not stillborn, he was physically perfect.

The Doctrines portrayed him as the savior. Not like a second coming of Jesus Christ, but a child whose blood contained a cure to the Sleeper virus, a virus that carried on and mutated for centuries.

We could stop it the virus with Phoenix.

But that wasn't so. Like most of the Doctrine information, that tidbit was muddled and changed.

No one knew for sure if Phoenix was the cure, because Phoenix was killed before anything was learned. We assumed he was the cure because he was born alive.

Doctrines be damned, the presence of our future travelers changed time and Phoenix wasn't killed. But Phoenix wasn't the cure.

Yes, he was physically perfect, but internally he carried a pure form of the virus and in a sense was a hub. He exuded it in high levels like a walking, breathing biological weapon. As long as he lived, the virus would as well. As long as he was around those not immune, he would infect them.

Javier was the doctor in our time who had invented the virus. Its intentions were good. Levi said for population control; Randy said to create a genetically superior race. That backfired. It created a genetically mutated race alright, but they were emotionless monsters.

Javier lived at the ARC, a place we believed was the New Jerusalem. They'd created it to protect humanity and ensure that life went on.

The ARC wanted Phoenix. I thought they wanted to kill him. I really believed that. Had I known differently, I would never have hidden Phoenix in that backpack and given the pack to Beck.

Beck was mistaken for a Sleeper and shot. So was Phoenix.

Javier took Phoenix and vowed to save him and work on the virus.

Eighteen months later, while he hadn't cured it completely, Javier had contained it in Phoenix.

His work could be continued at Grace, but he was bringing Phoenix home, as promised, back to me.

When Phoenix left me, he was a few months old. Now he was pushing two. Would he remember me? I doubted it.

I arrived at the gate before the truck came onto the main driveway. As they moved closer into my view, my heart raced, I found it hard to breathe, and a lump formed in my throat when I saw the blonde hair in the cab of the truck.

He was no longer a baby, but a toddler. A little boy. I couldn't wait to see him, to hold him and never let him go.

They had radioed when they arrived. They'd flown to one location, then driven to the next. Had I known that ahead of time, I would have been so worried. How they survived the trek across Sleeper land was beyond me.

But they did, and they looked the worse for wear when they stepped out of the truck.

Miles was in good shape, but he was dirty and tired-looking. He carried Phoenix, stepped out, and set him down.

Noah greeted Javier, and I heard him tell him that they ran into problems, but were able to escape.

I stared at Phoenix. I wanted to rush to him, grab him, but I didn't want to scare the child. I also had Keller by my side. At first I thought Keller would be a selling point, but I worried that he would scare Phoenix. I had so many unanswered questions.

"Go on," Miles told Phoenix. "That's her."

Holding Keller's little hand in mine, we approached Phoenix. He wasn't very tall, shorter than Keller, and thinner. His hair was white blonde and curly. It needed a cut.

Phoenix looked up at Miles. Miles nodded with a wink. The child looked at me.

"Hey, there," I said softly then crouched down just as I drew closer.

Phoenix smiled. "Mama. Mama?" Then, like nothing I expected, he ran to me.

The second his tiny body pelted into me, I was barreled over. My jaws clenched and a warmth of crying swept across my face. "Oh, sweetie." I felt how tightly his tiny arms went around my neck and I couldn't do anything but hold him with eyes closed.

When I had a second, I looked up at Miles. "Thank you."

"Been telling him all about you so he was excited to come home."

My heart melted. It literally felt like it melted. I truly felt love from him. Then he whispered, "Brother."

"Yes." I sniffled, pulling back some and searching for Danny. He stood a few feet away behind me, and I waved to him. "Phoenix wants you."

I turned back around and Phoenix was reaching to Keller. "Brother."

Finding it curious, I watched this first interaction. It was odd. When Phoenix touched Keller's arm, he smiled. Then Keller, feeling the touch, smiled as well, and the two boys locked hands.

Phoenix looked at me. "Brother, Mama."

"Yes, brother and…" I grabbed Danny's hand, "brother. He's your brother." I pointed up to Danny. "And you'll meet your sister, too."

"Hey, little dude." Danny crouched down. "You know me, right? I came out to see you."

"Brother." Phoenix had a look of euphoria on his tiny face. His eyes shifted around, one hand holding Keller's, the other Danny's. He grinned widely at me. "Home."

8
ALEX SANS

Sonny didn't say a word to me. I guess he was pissed. I knew he'd get over it. We made it back to Grace before Javier even arrived on the main driveway. My intention was to clean up and head down to see Phoenix. I grew more excited when I heard he actually was en route. However, I needed stitches in my arm and Levi wanted to start an immediate course of antiviral medication. He said we'd fare much better once Javier arrived and could assist.

I wanted to be at the gate. Perhaps I should have thought of that before I went Sleeper hunting. Then again, those five Sleeper men waiting in the woods could have been waiting to attack anyone.

I was dejected and lying in the hospital bed, hoping that someone would give me news on Phoenix, tell Mera I was injured, and inform me that the Sleeper baby died.

None of that happened.

What did occur wasn't really a surprise. I was alone in the room, staring out the window from the bed, IV in my arm, and Jessie walked in. Jessie was a great kid, almost like a daughter to me as well.

Jessie was Mera's oldest child and only daughter. Nineteen when The Event occurred, she was all the way across the country at the onset. Mera was determined to find her. I had nothing else to do so I went along.

Beck took on that focus as well.

The Sleeper era had just started. People were turning, and then they started turning the healthy. Jessie had called Mera a few times before the phone went dead. We went to Washington State where she was in school, and we found a bloody cot.

We didn't stop. Like pieces to a puzzle, she'd left clues everywhere, and that led us to the prison and to Miles. Miles ran things with compassion for everyone, even the Sleepers.

He kept them in the prison yard, fed them, and prayed that a cure would be found. Unlike us, he didn't kill them. That was a good thing because that was where we found Jessie. She was a Sleeper. Well, she had just turned.

With a right soup mixture, we were able to reverse some of the virus. Unfortunately, however, the Mensa Society girl of nineteen was reduced to the mentality of a two-year-old.

But Mera had her daughter. She had her child.

Jessie was so childlike it was hard to see the woman that she had become. She probably would never mentally grow beyond the age of ten, and that was being optimistic. The virus has done a lot of damage to her brain. Not like the others, but enough. However, the bottom line remained. Despite the fact that she was gentle and not dangerous, Jessie was still a Sleeper, my constant reminder that the Sleepers were still human. Jessie was the only Sleeper I liked. The rest I could care less if they were human; I needed to kill them all. Well, except for Pastor Mike; Beck was convinced he was Sleeper.

For our sake and for the sake of our future. Because see, by what I have been told, and that wasn't much, the Sleepers are the future. They mutated and took over. We and those like us are the minority and are almost extinct.

Jessie inched her way into the room.

"Hey, Jess, not joining Mom at the gate?"

"See you." She smiled. "You sick?"

"Nah, just got a boo-boo." I patted the spot on the bed next to me. "Come here." She hurried over like an excited child. She sat down and kissed me.

"Thank you," I told her. "This means a lot."

"Mommy coming."

"Does Mommy know I got hurt?"

Jessie nodded again. "She's showing Phoenix to Michael."

"Oh, so Mike sees him first?"

"She likes Michael."

I groaned. At that instant, the door opened. I expected Mera. It wasn't her; it was Levi. The disappointment on my face must have been evident.

"I'm sorry, it's just me," Levi said and walked inside. "Jessie, honey, can I be alone with Alex?"

"Okay. I'll go find Mommy and bring her to Alex."

I rubbed Jessie's back. "You do that, thank you." She darted a kiss to my cheek and I smiled. After she left, I asked Levi, "What's up?"

"Alex, do you know what you brought back with you?" Levi asked.

"A bloodstream full of Sleeper virus?"

"That, too. But I am speaking of—"

"That too?" I asked, shocked. "That *too*? I'm that infected?"

"Yes, anyhow—"

"No. No stop. Anyhow? Get back to my infection."

"We're battling it," Levi replied. "That's the best I can tell you."

"Are you confident?"

"Uh…sure."

"Uh, sure?" I plopped backwards. "That doesn't sound confident."

"I'll be more assured when Javier looks at your blood. Now I would like to talk about this baby you brought back."

"Is it dead?"

"No." Levi shook his head.

"I didn't bring it back. Sonny did. I wanted to kill it."

Levi exhaled. "I understand that. But it's giving us a chance to examine a Sleeper newborn. First glance of the blood, it doesn't carry the virus. However, I'm willing to wager its DNA shows it."

"Mutation."

Levi nodded. "The first step in the evolution process to what we had in the future."

"We should kill it. They discarded it anyhow. Tossed it to the side."

"And my guess is it would have been retrieved after the parent stopped eating the afterbirth." He paused. "Sonny told me about it. Plus, Alex, really, it's a child. An innocent child. We don't know, at this point in evolution, if the Sleeper is inherently violent or it's a learned experience. We may be able to raise this child normally."

"They're reproducing, Levi." I told him. "We haven't changed the future one bit. It's still going to end up that way unless we kill every single Sleeper."

"They outnumber us in vast amounts."

"But they are reduced to violent animal beings. They don't carry the ability to reason or plot at this point. Now is the time for us to declare war and take them out."

"I don't think that it is possible."

"It is," I said. "At first I held out hope that the Sleepers would die out, but survival instinct took over and they thrive. Now they are multiplying. In order to eliminate the virus, we have to eliminate every single one."

"That includes those who carry the virus that we know of," Levi told me.

I knew of whom he spoke…Jessie. He wasn't aware about Pastor Mike. Both he and Jessie were technically Sleepers. Maybe not in the way the rest were, but they carried the virus, the ability to prolong it, to lead it to the future. What to do with them was a bridge I'd cross when I got there. The fate and future of mankind was hanging on what we did in the present. The clock was ticking; it was now or never on what had to be done. One Sleeper, one town at a time if we had to. We just had to do it.

9
MERA STEVENS

I didn't need to be a doctor or a scientist. I didn't need to look at blood work to know that the newborn baby was a Sleeper. His eyes gave it away: round, dark eyes with pupils that faded into the dark color. His skin, while still newborn pink, showed early signs of discoloration. His cry was not normal, either; it ached out of him, almost a painful whimper. Was there something about him that hurt or was that just the sound he made?

I did not intend to see the baby; in fact, I didn't even know he existed. No one told me.

I grew worried when neither Sonny nor Alex showed up for Phoenix's homecoming. Then I got angry. How dare they miss it? I was bringing Phoenix to the school to see Michael when Jessie told me about Alex's boo-boo.

Immediately, I went to the clinic. I brought Phoenix with me, but Levi wouldn't let me see Alex or Sonny. While Sonny wasn't injured, they were watching him, they told me.

Alex, on the other hand, had been bitten. The viral levels were high, and until they could bring them down he was staying and being observed.

I'd be lying if I said I wasn't worried. Dinner had come and gone. I fed the troops and then summoned Michael to sit with the kids until I returned. I sensed he'd rather not stay back, but agreed.

It was pushing the ten-hour mark since I had seen Alex and I honestly started to fear the worst.

I believed my fears were confirmed when I walked into the clinic and saw Sonny with his head down, hands joined.

"Sonny!" I gasped and hurried to him. "What is it? What happened? Did Alex turn?"

Sonny shook his head. "Alex is fine. I'm fine. They'll let Alex go after one more confirmation test."

"Then what is it?"

Sonny raised his head. "I wanna leave Grace, Mera. I don't want to live here anymore. I think I'm gonna bug out and look for another place to go. Maybe... maybe you and the kids can come. We'll live there. A farm, something. Anything but here."

Apparently, something had occurred and Sonny was either intentionally being vague, or he thought I knew.

"What happened?"

"Priorities. Humanity. Sometimes I wonder if we are here to be protected or prisoners in a dictatorship or what." He shook his head once. "Do you know who runs this place?"

"Everyone," I said. "Alex would be the leader in protecting us and ensuring our survival. But there's Levi and Noah. I can't say who makes decisions because there's never been a decision to make that was brought to the community since we arrived a year ago."

"You know we were attacked today." Sonny slowly stood. "Five of them. Waiting. It was obvious we walked into a trap. This isn't the first time Sleepers wandered into Grace. It isn't the first time we followed and killed them. We've done it a lot."

"Okay, stragglers..."

"It's more than that. I feel it. They're coming from somewhere."

"Have you said this to Alex?"

"Yep. They won't go out and look any further than one sector. Or that town we hit for supplies."

"Why?"

"Afraid of what they'd find. And the fear of the unknown is causing them to lose all humanity. I could be wrong." Sonny began to pace. "I see their point to an extent."

"Sonny, I love you, but you are talking in circles."

On my words, Sonny only pointed to the closet door behind him. "What's in the storage closet?" I asked.

"My reason for being upset."

At first, I thought Sonny had completely lost it. I opened up the storage closet and heard it, the simply painful whimper. Then I saw *him*. The baby. He was placed in a drawer that had been lined with a blanket. I reached sympathetically for the infant, and then I saw his eyes.

"He's a Sleeper."

Then Sonny explained to me what had happened. How he found it, how Alex wanted to kill it. Hating to admit it, I saw Alex's reasoning. So did Sonny, but like me, Sonny also saw a baby.

"Why is he in the closet?"

"Because they are waiting for him to die."

While we were standing in that closet, me in shock over what Sonny had just said, Javier came in.

"What's going on?" I asked. "Sonny says you are waiting for this child to die? Are you killing it?"

"We are thinking about it," Javier said. "Something humane."

"Killing a baby is not humane," I argued.

"He is a Sleeper. Not only that, it's not a virus: it's his genetic makeup."

"He's still a baby."

"Have you held him?" Javier asked. "I know Sonny hasn't since he was brought in, but that was a while ago. Have you held him? Picked him up?"

"No."

"Go on." Javier nodded. "Pick him up."

Was he seriously thinking I wouldn't pick up a child? Me, the master of motherhood, the one everyone turns the children over to? I ended up with most of the orphaned children because it was something I did well. Certainly, I could handle a newborn Sleeper. I reached down, bracing his head, and brought him to me. He wasn't in my hand five seconds before he made this God-awful cry, thrashing his arms and legs, as his head went back and forth, his little hands darting out.

I jolted and placed him back in the drawer.

"See?" Javier said.

No, it isn't right, I thought. I took the blanket, bringing it up and around him in a swaddling manner and lifted the child. His head thrashed. I was convinced that in time he'd calm.

"Mera," Javier said compassionately, "I know your instinct is to hold that child, break that child, and believe everything is going to be alright. He will never survive."

"That was also said about Phoenix."

"He's an abomination."

"They said that about Keller. And look at them both."

Javier nodded. "He is a Sleeper thought, Mera. He will not tame. The mere fact that he has attacking instincts at birth tells me he is born to be that way and that it isn't learned. Chimpanzees are cute at first, then they grow up and become violent."

"Is this why you have him hidden?"

"We don't want anyone to know about him."

"They why haven't you killed him yet?" I questioned.

"We have tests to run."

I laughed in disbelief.

"Mera, stop. I have you upset. Sonny is depressed as if I am committing genocide. This is not your child or his. This, sorry to say, is a product of something I created.

Euthanizing him after we are finished is the humane thing to do." He pointed to the child in her arms. "He is a future we cannot let happen."

"What if…what if he can be normal or behave normally?"

"He cannot be taught. The moment he gets teeth he becomes a danger."

"What if we taught him or tried?"

Javier nodded. "Your arguments are noble. But what if…you can't? What if we did attempt it, but in six or seven months he can't be tamed? What then? How will you feel when you have known him for months?"

I felt Sonny's hand lay upon my shoulder. I knew instantly it was an argument he had been having all day. That was why he was so worn down.

I placed the baby back in the drawer. "Can you tell me before you do it?"

Javier nodded. "We will."

"Can you at least put him in a normal bed? Treating him like a normal baby is a start."

Again, Javier only nodded.

I left with Sonny. I assured him that though our argument was over for the moment, the battle hadn't been lost.

10
ALEX SANS

I read a book. An entire three hundred-page novel penned by an author named DiLouie. Javier had it in his personal collection, and about the four-hour mark he gave it to me to read. It dealt with an apocalypse of the undead. I thought at first, why would I read something about the dead rising when I was close to living it? Then I realized as I read that the story was different. It wasn't a typical, B-movie zombie horror novel; it was different. The 'cause' was different and the characters had to face something unbelievable as the reason for the dead rising, much like we had to face the unbelievable.

Shit happens.

Sometimes we can't control it and sometimes it is out of the realm of our suspension of belief. Not everything is as cut and dried as we want to believe. I learned that through that novel, and it gave me a different approach.

It made me focus more on survival.

Who was important, what was important, and where the hell was Mera for the last twelve hours?

Levi looked like he needed to go to sleep. His eyes were dark, his shoulders slumped, and had I not known better, I would have sworn he was an early-stage Sleeper.

"Twelve-hour mark. All clear. You are free to go." Levi said.

I was already dressed, showered, and Patty, who made most of the clothes, sent me some stew.

"Am I okay?" I asked.

"Javier's antiviral worked great. All good."

"Excellent. Can you make sure Javier gets his book back?" I pointed to it.

"Absolutely."

"Tell me something...I was bitten, on my Sleeper deathbed. Was it my imagination, or did no one give a shit?"

"By no one, are you meaning Mera?"

I nodded.

"Alex, Sonny sat outside this room all night. He just went home a couple hours ago. Mera was by twice, once right away with Phoenix. We just couldn't take a chance."

"Was I that bad?"

"Your levels were that high."

I whistled. "Bet you were scared to come in here and do tests."

"Yes," Levi smiled, "we were. When Mera was here the second time, Sonny told her about the baby. She saw him."

"Christ." I rubbed my head. "Knowing Mera, she got upset. Did you tell her what's going on?"

"She's not happy."

"I'll talk to her. Could be after she spends time she'll see we aren't the bad guys, we're making the right decision. No worries."

I just wanted to get out of that room. I had been there long enough. I thanked Levi and headed to the door. I was almost home free, door open...

"Alex, before you go. Before you try to talk to Mera, we need to talk. We really need to talk."

His words were laced with seriousness, as was the expression on his face.

I closed the door.

11
MERA STEVENS

"I'll pray about the situation," Michael said.

I liked Michael. I really did. Maybe not from the second I met him, but at least in the first half-hour. He was genuine and kind and the least selfish person that I knew. He was also pretty smart.

Michael, though, had a mutated form of the Sleeper virus. We learned this when the Sleepers didn't attack him. We never let this tidbit out. No one but a select few were even aware.

Pastor Michael saved me, and I would never tell anyone about him. No one needed to know. Michael was different, which was an internal argument for me with that baby.

I told him about the child when I arrived home and asked that he not tell anyone. It was a delicate situation. Sometimes when I looked at Michael, I worried that he was lonely, that maybe we didn't spend enough time with him. He was always with the children and those who needed spiritual guidance. He didn't take an oath of celibacy before The Event, but did after, just to ensure he never infected anyone or wasn't a participant pushing the Sleeper gene into the future.

"How were they tonight?" I asked him.

"Good. Sleeping. How was Phoenix on his first evening?"

"Amazing. Odd."

"How so?"

"He took an immediate protective instinct over Keller. Sat with him, ate with him, and watched him. It was odd."

"Then you need to see this," Michael said and waved his hand for me to follow. He led me to my bedroom and slowly opened the door. My heart instantly warmed when I saw the boys on my bed. Phoenix and Keller sound asleep; both on their sides, facing each other, and their hands were locked.

Immediately my mind flashed back. It was déjà vu.

When we first got Keller, I had been outside and Beck was putting the kids to bed, also making sure Jessie fell asleep, too. When I went into the trailer, he was standing over the cradle with an odd look on his face.

"Everything okay?" I whispered to Beck.

"This is amazing." He waved me over to him. "Come look."

Arms folded, I walked to the cradle where, for the time being, we were able to fit both Phoenix and Keller.

"I wanted to check on them," Beck said. "And look."

I peered around Beck to the cradle. Both babies were on their sides, Phoenix so much bigger than Keller, but I saw what Beck did, and it made me gasp. The precious sleeping babies were holding hands.

"They're meant to be brothers," Beck said. "There is something remarkable. They feel it, I feel it."

"Mera?" Michael called.

I snapped out of the memory. It was the same scene, only the boys were older, and Keller was the one who was bigger. "When we first got Keller, he and Phoenix held hands in the cradle. Beck said it was like they were meant to be brothers."

"I believe that."

"You know, Alex didn't expect either Phoenix or Keller to live. He was wrong about them. What if he is wrong about this baby?"

"You saw him. You said he was a Sleeper. You said he seemed to attack like an animal. Mera, he's a newborn. If he is the next breed, imagine how deadly each generation can get."

"But what if we can tame him?"

"Like an animal?" Michael said. "Not all animals can be tamed. I am one for preservation of life, Mera. You know that. But this situation…it's different."

"When I first met you, you believed it was God who did this. Have you have gone back to that thought?"

Michael smiled. "That's out of the blue. And no. No." He lowered his head and shook it. "We as people always want an explanation, and God is a believable explanation for us all. While there are so many religious implications in all that has happened, truth is, God did not do this. God did not cause this, nor did he cause people to turn into murderous creatures. Man did this. Man killed the children and turned the people. Not God. And as cold as it sounds, at any extreme, if man can fix this, I believe God is going to be just fine with it. Even if it starts with just one baby."

Michael was trying to make me see reason. I wanted to. Maybe more than just an innocent-appearing baby, I was still reeling in the reality that a child was born to the Sleepers and getting rid of that baby was going to do nothing. We had already lost control long ago.

12
ALEX SANS

Mera was doing exactly what I expected when I approached our home after being released from the clinic. She was sitting on the porch step, doing her nightly thing of having a drink, the bottle next to her and a glass in her hand. She looked up at me and passed on a slight smile.

That made me feel good.

When I got closer, she stood, stepped to me, and kissed me on the cheek. "I'm glad you're okay," she said. "I was worried."

"Thank you."

"Join me? Or are you too tired?"

"Mera, I've been in a room all day." I sat down on the step next to her. "Is Phoenix sleeping?"

"Yeah. He's great, Alex. Wait until you see him and talk to him. Oh boy, can he talk at his age. I don't remember any of my kids talking that well." She poured another drink then handed me a glass. "I was waiting for you."

"I really appreciate that."

"Do you want to see Phoenix?"

"I'd love to see him. But he's sleeping, so I'll just peek in on him in a bit. I want to talk to you."

"I tried to see you today. To bring Phoenix, but Levi and Javier didn't think that was a good idea."

I exhaled slowly from my mouth as my lips hovered over the glass. "How about how close I was to being a Sleeper?"

"Yeah, I heard." She took a sip. "Speaking of Sleepers..."

"How did I know this was coming?"

"He's a baby, Alex, and I have a hard time looking beyond that."

"I know you do. But you can't mother and save all the children or abandoned babies. Some aren't meant to be saved."

"You said the same about Phoenix and Keller."

I nodded. She was right. "I know I did and if you don't think that weighs on me, you're wrong. It does. But this baby, a day old, is showing violent tendencies. It's like something about us as noninfected makes it react. This is what Randy didn't want to happen. This is why Randy came back. In his future, man still had a chance. In other futures, like where Marissa lived, man was dying. These things continued, populated, and destroyed the planet. We have a chance to stop it."

"With one baby?"

"With all babies. No Sleeper child should be allowed to live. Stop the species before it gets going. I don't want to be the King Herod here, I don't."

"Sonny says he's leaving. He wants to go. He thinks me and the kids and him should be on a farm away from Grace. That here, we're in trouble."

I moistened my lips and took another drink. "I don't know about the trouble. But moving to a farm isn't going to change the future. It just makes you immune from it."

She sighed heavily. "This is a weighted decision."

"It's a very weighted decision. This means eliminating all Sleepers. No more living here peacefully and getting them as they come. This means going out for them."

"What about Jessie and Michael?"

"I'm not talking about them."

"What if the decision is out of your hands?" Mera asked.

"Then we leave." He shrugged. "We can trek somewhere else. No one is hurting Jessie or poor Mike."

"I'll accept and believe that," Mera said, refreshing my drink.

"Thanks. So..." I exhaled, "I hear you hate me because Beck died instead of me."

Perhaps I should have waited until she fully swallowed, because Mera started to choke.

"I'm sorry." I patted her on the back.

"Who told you?"

"Levi."

She gasped. "So much for patient-doctor confidentiality."

"I don't think that applies when you're asking to use the Cerebral trip."

"In my defense," she lifted her glass, "he brought up the trip. And I didn't say I hated you. I said I got angry with you. Resented you. I didn't want to, Alex. I didn't."

"If it makes you feel any better, I wish I was the one who died instead of Beck."

Quickly, Mera looked at me.

"Yeah," I nodded. "He was such a good guy. His decisions were for the good of you and the kids, not the good of the many. He had a quality no one could touch."

"I think I resent you because you would never have made the decision I made. You would have handed Phoenix over."

"Yeah, I would have."

"I blame myself for Beck's death."

"You can't."

"I do. I blame myself for asking him to take Phoenix. To hide him. To break the rules. He did it because I asked."

"He did it because he wanted to." I placed my face closer. "Trust me. It broke my heart to see him go down. It broke my heart to watch him die."

That simple memory for an instant brought back the pain.

"Mine, too. We don't talk about Beck, you and I."

"You have him in some sort of sainthood; I can't mention him. I can't be Beck, and not that I tried, but I wanted you to depend on me like you did with him. Be a team with me. You never did. You just pulled further and further away."

"Because you could never *be* Beck," she said. "And I'm not saying that to disrespect you or hurt you; I'm saying that because that is where my anger comes from. You two handled things and decide things completely opposite. So when you didn't give me a 'Beck' response, I got mad."

"Let me ask you a question," I waited until I had her attention. "Do you think the Cerebral thing is gonna do anything, if indeed it even works? What do you hope to get from it?"

"I need to see him. Hear him. Know things were said that needed to be said. Perhaps, just some resolution will help me move forward."

"Can it hurt? In your opinion, can it hurt?"

"Unless I remember things differently. Alex, this is a man who made the decision to die with my daughter and me. This man walked into a pen of Sleepers to get my child. If I got to hear him, see him one more time, it would be enough for me to just get on and past it. Maybe even stop resenting you."

I raised my glass to her and clinked. "Then let's go."

"Let's go what?" Her eyes lifted as I stood.

I held out my hand to her. "Then let's go see Levi."

"Don't you think it's late?"

"Nah." I shook my head. "He told me all about this thing. It takes a minute. One minute to resolve a lifetime ahead? That's nothing, and we need that resolve to move ahead with any plan. Especially if we want to be a team."

"We?"

"We." I left it at that. If Levi agreed, and I hoped he would, then I had a feeling what point in time Mera was going to choose. If I was right, I knew what I was doing. I knew what I remembered, and I remembered more than she thought. I needed resolution for that moment as well.

Science fiction time travel stuff, I hated it. But if it could help, I'd use it and never bring it up again. At some point in all the madness, we need a break, some relief. It was worth a shot. After all, we weren't physically going anywhere, just taking a detailed and vivid trip down memory lane.

13
MERA STEVENS

The fact that Levi was getting a visit from us at a little after one in the morning didn't seem to surprise him as much as the fact that we wanted to do the trip right then and there. We explained how it could help resolve things and allow me to accept Alex's decisions as leader. He summoned Noah, and they made the decision.

We would go.

There were two tiny vials; they reminded me of perfume samples that they used to give away at the department stores. Of all the things I envisioned regarding the Cerebral trip, never did I think it had to do with a drug.

"You will take the vial in one dose," Levi explained.. "It is potent, so before you down it, set your destination. If anything else enters your mind, you'll end up there. And that can get messy for the assurance. Choose your destination carefully."

I looked sharply at Alex who sat in a chair across from me. He had laughed. "What is so funny?"

"I feel like I am one of the *Ghostbusters*."

I shook my head in annoyance and returned to Levi. "What about him? What about if he thinks another place?"

"Doesn't matter. His vial merely connects the trip to you. You're driving. When you arrive, you'll see through your own eyes, feel what you felt back then. You will be inside of you. It will be very real."

"Will the 'me' of the past know I am there?"

Levi shook his head. "No. Anything you say or do, your past body will think it was its own thought. So be very careful." He looked at Alex. "You'll experience the same. So be prepared."

Noah, who had been silent, added. "And for God's sake, don't try to change anything."

"Once you arrive, you have fifty-four seconds," Levi said. "When that Cerebral Travel drug is done, at the fifty-four second mark, there's no fading, nothing. It leaves and you are back. You may have trouble breathing because your heart rate will instantly speed back up and you'll open your eyes as if awakening from a dream.

"You'll take the drug, close your eyes, and be asleep for one minute. Hopefully you'll find what you need." He handed me the vial. "Prepare your destination." He then gave Alex his. "Good luck."

I was all too aware of the destination I wanted, but before I secure it in my mind, I said a small prayer. I just needed everything to work out. I needed to move on.

14
ALEX SANS

I believed, I really, really believed the entire Cerebral time travel thing was a bunch of bull, especially when they handed me the vial. I was certain they were feeding us some sort of mind-altering drug like LSD and we would tap into a memory.

All that changed after I took the drug was that flashes of light appeared before my eyes. I held on to the fact it wasn't real until I felt the pain. My chest crushed and it felt as if a hand reached into me and twisted my heart and gut.

I knew Mera's destination; I just forgot where I was in that moment.

Her moment and my moment were simultaneous.

When my past came into focus, my body trembled, and I was crying. I wanted to scream. I had this urge to bellow my agony as if doing so would release it. The first thing I saw was that precious little girl Marissa, her limp and bloody body in the arms of a soldier.

She had died in my arms, asking me to hold her. I'd failed her. I failed a little girl who wanted nothing more than to live. Sleepers had gotten her and all I could do was cradle her in the final moments of her life. Locked and protected in the jail cell.

That was nothing.

I was condemned for my mistakes and doomed to relive it.

"I'm sorry," the soldier said. He had just opened the cell. "I am very sorry."

I winced in pain. It was not the moment I thought I wanted or needed for reconciliation, though as I looked at the soldier, I realized that perhaps it was.

15
MERA STEVENS

It was real, it was happening, and I knew it the second everything flashed and I sped through some sort of dark passage. Before I saw anything, I felt grateful. I knew the moment, when everything came into focus, that I was face to face with Beck.

My God. *Beck.* I was there. I was with him.

I didn't need to say anything; inside my past self, I was happy to see him. I just wanted to absorb it. Take it in, pay attention, let the past lead what happened, relive the memory and know exactly what happened at that second.

I handed him the backpack that had Phoenix tucked inside. "The most precious cargo you will ever carry. Wait until they are occupied, take him, and go to the auto parts store."

"Why won't you take him?" he asked.

"They asked for me. I'm a great diversion right now."

"You're a great everything right now." Beck gently took the bag and gave me an embrace. "I have this. No worries."

"I don't." I reached up to his face. "You are wonderful. I'm so proud to have you with me."

Beck, emotional, nodded. "Ditto. Let's finish this up and head to our new home. Our new life."

Stop.

That was it. That was the moment. I would be lying if I said I didn't have it in my mind to change it all. To take back that pack, say it wasn't right and for us to trust Javier.

But I didn't.

I had the moment, the precious seconds, the opportunity to change it all. To bring him back. However, what happened in the past had a reason. I was given a moment with Beck.

For that, I was grateful.

"I couldn't agree more." I told him, pressed my hand firmly to his cheek, stood on my tiptoes, kissed him, and slid my hand from his face.

Our last moment. The last time I touched him, and he knew. I told him how I felt. He knew.

That was what I truly needed.

Then I was gone.

As if in the blink of an eye, all went black for a second and I opened my eyes with a heavy gasp. Levi was right. I had a hard time breathing. Everything was dark. Alex was no longer sitting across from me in Levi's house. Levi and Noah were no longer standing by. I was in my bed.

What the hell happened?

When I opened my eyes, I had gasped and sat up in my dark bedroom. Had the drug caused a blackout like a bad night's drinking? I was drinking beforehand; I should have told Levi that. What if that caused a bad reaction? How did I get into my bed?

"Mera, you all right?" a deep male voice asked from next to me.

Slowly, I turned my head. Beck was staring back at me, lying in bed next to me.

I screamed. That was about the best I could describe it. I screamed. Long and deep, scared half out of my wits, my entire body not only jolted a foot off the bed, but I rolled out and onto the floor, hitting my head against the nightstand.

Knocked out again. If I hit my head one more time, I'd get brain damage. I had a headache, it throbbed at the temples, and for a second, everything was surreal, like Beck being in bed with me was all a dream.

The sound of Alex's voice caused me to stir. It didn't help my headache.

"I told you not to let her drink like that before bed."

"You try telling her not to drink," Beck said.

What the fuck?

Just as I was about to open my eyes, something weird occurred. Flashes of memories I had no recollection of having.

"I have to go, you know that," Beck said. I saw him. In that town where he had died, standing there holding Phoenix. Javier was behind him.

"We'll bring them both back when we're done."

"For us, Mera, I need to watch Phoenix."

I saw him step from that truck, the same truck that had pulled up with Javier. Beck was holding Phoenix. He had a beard. He had a beard? I ran to him.

"Mera?" Beck called.

My mind kept racing. What did I do? What should I say? How did this happen? I opened one eye first and couldn't help it, I screamed again when I saw Beck.

"I shaved the beard," Beck said.

"Sorry. I just...I just..." I stammered for the words. "Seeing you."

Beck nodded. "It's still new. I've been gone a while."

"I'd say." I reached out and touched him. He was real. I looked around, I was in my bed. But the bedroom was different. There weren't any toys or kids' things. Where was Keller's dresser and crib?

"Where are the boys?"

"Which boys, Mera?" Beck asked.

Oh, God, who did I kill with my changing of time?

"We have a lot. Seems while I was gone you took on all the strays," Beck said.

"Keller and Phoenix."

"In their room. Oh..." Beck nodded in understanding. "Okay, you're confused. We moved Keller into a room with Phoenix tonight. He's been sleeping with you while I was at the ARC."

"The ARC." I sighed. "You were at the ARC all this time?"

Here a part of me was scared that he actually knew he had died. Or did he?

"Yeah," Beck said in response to my rambling. "You must have really hit your head."

"May I speak to Mera a second alone?" Alex asked. "It's really important."

"Sure." Beck leaned forward and kissed me on the forehead. "I'll be right outside."

I nodded, but before he could pull away, I grabbed onto him. I grabbed him and held him, allowing my hands to feel his back, neck, head, and then face. It felt so good.

"I'm glad you're back."

"Me, too." Another kiss and Beck stepped back. "Alex, please don't drive her nuts."

Alex waited until Beck had left and we were alone. He then walked over and sat on the bed next to me.

"So check this out, Mera. One second I'm downing this vial and looking at you, the next I'm on the porch downing a shot of whiskey. I nearly fucking choked."

"I'm sorry." I grabbed his hand. "I'm sorry. I really am. I followed the rules; I did nothing. Said nothing. I don't know how this happened? Did it happen?"

"You mean suddenly that Beck isn't dead?"

"Yes."

"Oh, he's alive. To you and me he's been dead. To everyone else he's been at the ARC."

"Alex, I'm sorry to put you in this. I swear to God, I don't know how it happened."

"Of course, you don't."

"I'm serious, Alex, I don't."

"And I'm serious, Mera, of course you don't know how it happened. *You* didn't change it…" Alex said then lowered his voice. "I did."

16
ALEX SANS

From the moment the soldier said, "I'm sorry," I knew who he was.

Back when it happened, he had taken Marissa from me, then handed her to another as he walked me out. Back then, when it happened the first time, I didn't speak. I couldn't speak.

But when I took the Cerebral trip and saw him, I couldn't help it. It blurted out. "I'm sorry," he said.

Thirty seconds. I had maybe thirty seconds to get it out.

"Then please, when we're out there, in a few minutes, someone is going to think they see a lone Sleeper. You will say he's big. He is, but he's not a Sleeper. Do *not* shoot him."

He looked at me confused, nodded and then I was gone. I had no idea if my words would affect the situation.

Unfortunately for me, when I returned I was sipping a whiskey, inhaled from my abrupt return, and choked.

Of course, I wasn't at Levi's house. If I was correct, we didn't need to take the trip because there wasn't a need for resolution, so we ended up right where we'd be had Beck never died.

To figure out what all was different was going to be a challenge, but a part of me felt confident it wasn't going to be that big of a difference in Grace.

How convenient that Beck went to the ARC with Phoenix. Instead of dying in that small town and never coming to Grace, he lived and went to the ARC, arriving here after all that time.

Was I wrong in what I did? Morally, I was. I had no right to cheat fate. But I did it for me and, most of all, for Mera.

In the midst of those thoughts, I felt a slight throb in my arm and looked down at the bandage. I had still been bitten, which meant the confrontation still took place.

Everything had to be very similar or the same. Beck wasn't around in either scenario.

Everything but Mera's and my relationship, that had to be better.

Maybe not.

I returned to sitting on the porch, having a drink, and absorbing the sudden onset of memories that I never lived through. However, in essence, I had. Memories that felt real, but seemed more as though I had just watched them on a movie of my life.

Whether Beck was back or not, one thing remained the same. I was bitten, which meant we found that baby and the declaration of Sleeper slaughter was still in effect.

It would prove interesting now, how it would be handled with Beck in the picture.

One thing was for sure: Mera's relationship with me would forever be different. It had to be. We shared a secret that no one would or could ever know about.

PART TWO
A NEW ORDER

Avenging Jessie

17
MERA STEVENS

A part of me was still having a hard time determining if anything was real. When I woke the next day, I had two sets of memories, one where Beck died, and the other where he didn't.

Which was real? It was like a very vivid dream that stays with you as if the events had really transpired. In my case, they had, and I had to adjust emotionally.

It was especially confusing when I woke up alone in bed. When I fell back to sleep after hitting my head, Beck was lying next to me. Then I smelled food—eggs, and coffee—and I tossed the covers from the bed. Alex was probably cooking again, and I hated the way he made eggs. Sunny side up with crispy edges, doused with a ton of salt and pepper.

But the kids loved his crazy eggs, so after freshening myself, I went to the kitchen.

The children, all of them, including Danny and Jessie, sat at the long table. So many kids, a dozen in all, and Phoenix was positioned next to Keller. It was an odd sight, watching him guide Keller's hand to the food.

Beck turned from the stove with a pan. "Morning."

My stomach twitched; it was so good to see him.

"Mera, how do you do this? How do you feed all these little people?" Beck asked. "I feel like I am nonstop cracking eggs."

"You have to crack them at night and put them in the fridge. Make do with meals that go far." I shrugged. "Alex has his own method. Why didn't you wake me?"

"I wanted to see how it works around here. They have to get to know me again. I made coffee."

"Thank you." I walked over to the pot and jumped a little when he darted a kiss to my cheek.

It was going to take some getting used to. After I poured my coffee, I saw the bags and boxes by the kitchen door.

"What is all that?" I asked.

"Mera, you know what that is," Beck replied. "Sonny is leaving."

Before any words could escape my mouth through my shock, I saw Sonny loading the back of a pickup truck. I hurriedly took a large swig of coffee, set down the mug, and walked outside.

Sonny looked at me and headed toward the porch.

"What are you doing?" I asked him.

"Mera, I'm leaving. Looking for a new place. I told you this yesterday."

"No." I shook my head. "You said you were *thinking about* leaving Grace."

"No, Mera, I told you I was without a doubt leaving."

"You can't go out there alone, Sonny. You can't. It's dangerous."

"Then it's a chance I'll take, because you know I feel this is going to be dangerous. The sooner I go, the sooner I can find a place for all of us."

I exhaled and turned my head. It wasn't how I recalled the conversation going.

"Why are you acting like this again?" Sonny asked.

"Things are different today."

Sonny looked beyond me to the house. "Does Beck seem different?"

"More than you know."

"I know you were hoping, like me, that when he got back here, he'd side with us the second he saw that baby. But come on, we should have known." Sonny tossed his head. "It's gonna backfire on him. That is the main reason I am finding a new place. So you and the kids have somewhere to go."

I didn't have a clue what Sonny was talking about, and I couldn't ask him. Apparently, things were not as I thought.

"You're so angry, Sonny."

"So should you be. A year. A year spent subduing the virus in Phoenix. If Javier can do that, why can't he create something that subdues it in all Sleepers? Instead of Beck's Reckoning plan, why not cure them."

Beck's Reckoning plan?

"I have to get my stuff."

"Wait." I grabbed Sonny's arm as he brushed by me. "If I said I didn't know what you were talking about or what you mean by 'Beck's Reckoning,' what would you say?"

"That you were lying," Sonny said. "So why would you say that?"

"Because I don't know."

Sonny scoffed. "Mera."

"I don't. I really don't," I conveyed with emotions and convictions so he'd absolutely not doubt me. One thing about Sonny, he believed people. I know, unless something changed, Sonny believed me.

"Was it from hitting your head?"

"No." I brought my hand to my face. "Sonny, you know how Levi had that one cerebral time trip left?"

"Has."

"Had." I corrected. "Probably still does, but didn't yesterday. We used it. I went. Alex was supposed to be the assurance, but instead of assuring that I didn't do anything stupid, Alex did it."

"What are you talking about, Mera?"

"Beck died." I whispered. "I went back to resolve that last moment and I did, but Alex stopped his death. I had no idea until I woke and saw Beck in bed with me."

"That's why you screamed?"

I nodded then saw the look on his face. "You don't believe me."

"I want to. I believe you believe it."

"And you know what? That's fine. Just tell me about Beck's Reckoning and how..." I paused when I heard the back porch door open. I turned around to see Alex stepping off the porch and had an idea. "Watch. He'll be clueless about you leaving. Test him. You'll see."

Sonny glanced at me and then to Alex.

"Hey, Sonny," Alex said. "Going somewhere?"

I replied. "Sonny is leaving Grace, Alex, you know this. He told us all yesterday."

"Oh, that's right. Yeah, sorry to see you leave."

"You're an asshole," I told him. "Sonny is leaving and that's all you have to say?"

"We'll hear from him. He's just looking for another place. Isn't that what you said yesterday? He's not gonna go find one and not tell us." He reached out and gave a squeeze to Sonny's arm. "Good luck. I'll catch you before you're gone. I have to go to the clinic; Levi called about the Sleeper baby. No, he didn't die." He started walking away.

"Alex," Sonny called to him. "Um...why did you sleep here last night?" he shifted his eyes to me.

Alex stopped walking. He turned around with a quirky smile. "I'm sorry."

"You slept here," Sonny continued. "Did you have a fight with your wife? I can't see her being okay with you staying here knowing yours and Mera's past. You were fighting?"

Alex blinked. "Uh..."

"It'll work out. I'm sure. You'll be back home tonight."

"My wife. Yes. We will work it out. Thanks." After a hurried look of horror, Alex spun and took off.

I looked up to Sonny. "He doesn't have a wife, does he?"

Sonny shook his head and faced me. "Nope. Who would marry him? Beck's Reckoning." He exhaled. "When Beck was at the ARC, he organized the remaining four thousand military and started moving them out to clean sweep areas. They are using everything and anything on that side and plan to keep moving east."

"But the remaining people at the ARC started leaving. When Danny went there it was pretty much empty."

"Danny?" Sonny asked. "Why would Danny go to the ARC?"

"Well, they'd survey the area for Sleepers and they went to check on Phoenix."

"Beck did that from the ARC. I don't know about the change, but there was no need to send anyone to look after Phoenix."

"Beck was there."

Sonny nodded. "Mera, I know I am writing the Doctrines, but did you ever stop to think that we aren't supposed to change the future? Randy tried; it didn't work. Maybe mankind does have an extinction timeline and this is the beginning."

"If you don't think it can be changed, why are you leaving?"

"This is gonna get bigger than Beck. This cleansing, this Reckoning, this killing every Sleeper. I'm leaving because I have to. The world may end, man may become extinct, but it won't happen in our lifetime. I have to find somewhere for you and the kids to go, when the time comes—and it will—that you have to run." After a solemn look, Sonny touched my shoulder gently as he walked by me to the house to gather the remainder of his things.

18
ALEX SANS

I tried not to show the look of sheer confusion and panic on my face when I hightailed it from the house. I'd catch up with Sonny before he left. I had things to give him and I wanted my goodbye to be private. Despite Mera's stock name-calling of me, I wasn't cold or callous about Sonny leaving. It saddened me.

But at that second, I was in a whirlwind of disbelief.

I had a *wife?*

I panicked.

How the hell did that happen? Beck wasn't even in Grace; how did I end up getting married? The only thing I could rationalize was that in the Beck-is-dead time, I never tried to find anyone because I was too busy worrying about Mera. More than the how I got married, I really needed to find out 'who' I married.

I know women. If I didn't fight with this wife, then I was going to be in trouble staying out all night.

What the hell? Who was it? I started thinking of every woman in the camp. Who was eligible, who was nice, who could I tolerate?

Arriving at the clinic didn't help, I needed to think clearly, I needed to find out, but I also didn't want to alert anyone. Not that they would know, but how does one forget his wife?

Heck, it didn't even come to me with all the new memories that flooded in. It could have and I ignored it. Maybe I hate this woman and am trapped.

Maybe...

I stepped inside the small clinic and didn't see anyone. Levi summoned me to speak about the baby. Maybe he found out more through the DNA, not that I would know. So since I couldn't see Levi, I knew where the baby was last seen.

I walked by the nursery on my way to the closet and was surprised to see the Sleeper baby in there. Not only had they moved him, Pastor Mike was holding him with a smile.

I waved through the window and walked inside.

"Hey, Mike. Man you have the magic touch. He isn't so beastly today." I looked down at him. "His eyes are still weird."

"He's still a beautiful child." He showed me the baby. "Want to hold him?"

"Nah, I'm good. I didn't wash my hands. What...uh, brings you here?"

"I wanted to see for myself the child that everyone fears."

"That would be Phoenix or Keller." I said. "No one knows about this one."

"I'm not talking about the general population; I am talking about the select few who want to put this child to sleep." He gave a nod toward me. "Present company included."

"This baby is proof that they are evolving. We can't have that. We can't have our future belong to them. They already outnumber us."

"Them?"

"Sleepers."

"They *are* us, Alex, just different."

"Uh, Padre? They kill people."

"So do we," Michael replied.

"Without reason and with deadly instinct."

"So do we."

I grunted and tossed out my hand. "I'm not arguing with you."

"Argued enough last night?"

My eyes lifted and I felt a bright relief hit me. Michael mentioned me fighting; Michael knows my wife. "So you heard about the fight?"

"Yes. She told me."

"She has a big mouth."

"Alex, please. Be nice. She has a valid point."

"To her."

"To me as well," Michael said.

"Damn it."

"What?" he asked.

I shook my head. "Where is she now?"

"At home."

This time I thought it, *Damn it.*

"Weren't you just there?" Michael asked.

"It's complicated." As I reached up to the back of my head, I spotted Patty. Patty had stepped into the nursery. She didn't work at the clinic. Besides the sewing goddess, she was like the town nut roll and food queen. She was putting something on a table right inside the nursery door. Apparently, the babies weren't eating anything. She had to be there looking for me. She was single, halfway normal. A leftover from the religious cult that lived there, but still, perhaps it was her. She was looking at me as if she had a bone to pick with me. I excused myself from Michael and approached her.

"Hey, Patty. What are you doing?"

"Leaving cookies for the caretaker."

"Are you mad at me?" There, I thought that was better than asking if she were my wife.

"Why are you asking?"

"Because I stayed out all night."

"I don't worry about how late you stay out, Alex. That's your business. Not mine. You are the man, I am the woman."

I grumbled inwardly. It was that darn subservient upbringing. No way was I married to her. But just on the outside chance, I asked her, "Why didn't I come home, then?"

"I am getting nervous speaking so much to you. Perhaps this is a question you should ask the person you live with. Or maybe if you did not drink so much of the devil water, you would not stumble around calling out names in the middle of the night."

"Yeah, yeah," I shook my head. Before I grunted again, Levi appeared in the door. Saved. I wasn't asking him. By the look on his face, he wasn't there about my marriage; he looked worried.

At his request, I joined him outside and he closed the nursery door.

"Don't you want any of Patty's cookies?" I asked.

Levi just stared at me.

"What did I do?"

"Why is that happening?" He pointed at Michael.

"The baby was crying, maybe?" I guessed.

"No, the baby is content."

"Okay." I was lost.

"Alex, no one could touch that baby. It thrashed. Michael came in here and it didn't react. Why?"

Shit! I inwardly freaked. It didn't take a rocket scientist to know why. Okay, maybe a genetic doctor couldn't figure it out yet, but I knew the reason. A Sleeper baby is not going to attack a Sleeper. Sleepers don't go after Michael.

"You know," Levi said.

"Yeah, so do you."

"No, I'm afraid I don't. I want to test him to see if…"

I gasped loudly and dramatically. "You'll be damned."

"I'm sorry. What is that?"

"I can't believe you don't know. You of all people. I mean, you're from the future. I can understand Noah, because he just started speaking our language, but you... the Doctrines."

"What about them?"

I pointed to Michael. "He's the Holy Man. The Chosen. He rose up unharmed."

Levi's eyes widened. "He is the one they call the Holy Man? Why was I not told?"

"He doesn't want to be treated differently. And that's why he can hold the baby. God loves all creatures, big, small, and evil."

"I see." Levi nodded. "The scripture also states that the Holy Man was attacked by Palers. Good thing I don't buy into scripture. In any event, with how he is right now with that child, it's going to make another person very upset when we put it to sleep."

For some reason, some strange, odd reason, it caused an odd twitch in my gut. Seeing the child act like a child in Mike's arms made the decision to 'put it down' sound and seem so inhumane.

"Do we still need to?" I asked.

"The Second Reckoning has been underway for four months. Keeping this child is against the rules, you know that. Now if you'll excuse me, I have some blood to get."

"That baby is going to run out."

"Not the child, your Savior."

I held in the wince until Levi had walked inside, and then I left the clinic. He'd brought me there to tell me something was up with Michael.

I wasn't quite sure what the Second Reckoning was, another thing new to me. The Reckoning thing, my wife.

When I walked outside, I started getting worried. Bonnie was walking up the street with Jessie.

Bonnie had joined us a year ago. She had saved a bus full of kids, all that came here from the future for a better life. A better life. Weren't they mistaken?

She also was the one who found Keller.

Over the course of time living in Grace, Bonnie didn't really bother with us much. She hung out with Jessie, taught her things, including how to ride a horse.

I worried because what if Bonnie were my wife? I always did have a thing for older women. I could see it. She also had a maddening glare on her face. I had to find out. Bonnie was a Montana cattle chick, rough and tough, probably the only person in Grace older than me.

They headed my way and I stepped into their path. "Morning."

Bonnie stopped cold and stared at me. "Why are you blocking our path? You said your piece yesterday."

Yes, I thought. Bonnie was my wife.

"I'm...I'm sorry?"

"No. Don't worry about it. I am well aware of my responsibilities around here. Make no bones about it, Alex Sans—once Sonny settles and finds a place, I'm going. And if Mera knows what's good for this girl, she'll join him. Come on, honey." She grabbed Jessie's hand.

"Are we married?"

"Are you insane? Why would you ask me that?"

I forced a laugh. "Trying to joke?"

"It's not even remotely funny." She started to walk, but Jessie didn't. "Jessie, honey, come on."

Jessie stared at the clinic. She slowly lifted her arm and pointed at the clinic. "Baby."

"No, no baby there." Bonnie tugged her. "The babies are at home."

Jessie smiled. "No, *new* baby."

"I'm sure, and you can see it later. Let's go." Bonnie pacified her then tugged harder, pulling Jessie along.

Me, I was floored. Could Jessie mean the Sleeper baby? If so, no one really knew about it, so how did Jessie?

19
SONNY

Leaving Grace wasn't easy; after all I had been there a year, but it was what needed to be done. I had been thinking about it for a while. The Sleeper baby was the final straw that broke the camel's back.

I hated to go since Beck just got back. If I stayed any longer, I would be party to the slaughter of the innocents.

Not that the Sleepers were all that innocent, but they weren't aware of what they did. That, of course, was the argument for the Reckoning. Yes, they weren't aware, but eventually their offspring would be.

Their offspring was not my call. The future wasn't really my concern. The here and now and the future of the kids concerned me, which, according to Randy, wasn't as bad as, let's say, the future where Levi lived.

I realize that Beck initiated and regrouped the military personnel remaining at the ARC. According to Javier, he got the Secretary of State back on her horse as well. But all that...genocide of the infected wasn't for me.

I was the man who lived in a basement bunker for months while his Sleeper-infected parents walked about the house above him.

Alex loved the idea of a Sleeper Reckoning, taking daily stats from Beck over the radio as if the death tallies were scores to sporting events.

Alex Sans. The time thing that Mera mentioned would explain his demeanor when I left. He genuinely didn't want me to leave. He checked, then double-checked that I would stay in contact. Then Alex gave me the address to his survivor haven store. Said he had a lot of things in there, and a lot of land.

He knew I was heading to Ohio. I knew Ohio, and there were places I wanted to check out. Alex asked what I planned to do if there were Sleepers at my destination.

A bridge I would cross when I got there.

Bonnie wanted to come along. "Hurry, Sonny. Find a place and hurry before winter. The Reckoning is in Oklahoma."

I knew, however, they'd come to a stop or a delay when they hit the Great Divide.

Mera had told me about it. A huge cavern formed in the United States following all the natural disasters that occurred the fateful day of The Event. It spanned from Lake Michigan down a thousand miles south, hence why I decided to go east then north.

Two things happened as I left. One, Javier stopped me and told me, "I'm not giving up on a cure. Please keep that in mind."

There other was a surprise passenger. I wasn't to be traveling alone. Miles, a man I had never met and had only heard about, joined me. He was waiting by the gate for a ride and said he'd explain when we got on the road.

Everyone knew him before we got to Grace. Everyone but me. All I knew of him was that he was the guy who ran the place they'd found Jessie.

He was silent in the car. A man who, despite being at the ARC, buzzed his hair. He never let his gun out of his sight and chomped on the end of an unlit cigarette, one he'd light in a little bit.

We pulled out of Grace down the dirt road and through that town nearby. A few Sleepers moved about the street, waving their hands as if they could get us when we rode by.

When we hit the highway, Miles finally told me why he decided to come.

"When The Event happened," Miles told me, "I was working at the prison. I boarded us up in there. Then I went straight to the ARC. Locked in there. When I got here and saw that wall, I knew I couldn't stay here long. We can't be locked down in fear. We can't. That ain't no way to live. When I heard you were going, I figured, why not? Plus, safety in numbers. And...I wanted to see what's happened to the world."

"What are your thoughts on the Reckoning?"

"I don't know. Some ways I think it's wrong, others, what choice do we have? They rule the world. Mindless as they are, they have control while we're locked behind walls, scared of them. I just wanna find a place where I'm not hiding and they aren't coming."

"Javier told me he's still looking for a cure. They dropped a biological weapon on Billings. If they can do that, what about a cure? Drop the cure."

"Early stages can be fought," Miles said. "I turned a few. Mera's daughter, for one. But here comes another problem—we cure them, and their mind is gone. They're like babies and are gonna die anyhow. There aren't enough of us to take care of them. So it's a Catch-22 situation. I didn't kill them at the prison. I kept them. I hoped a cure would be found, but I thought, honestly, that if a cure wasn't found, they'd die. They weren't eating; they were withering away. But they found a means to survive. Their instincts kicked in."

I listened to what he said. Maybe my fight for life was in vain and it was a no-win situation. I myself had killed Sleepers in self-defense. However, I never went out looking to kill them.

And that was Miles' philosophy. Don't look for them, just kill them as they come, move on and do the best you can.

That's what I guess I was planning on doing. Moving forward, finding a place where they wouldn't find us, and just live.

Who knows? The eastern half of the country could be different now. No one knew; no one had been there. Miles and I would soon find out.

We moved down the highway without seeing a soul. No people, Sleepers, nothing.

Baby steps to Ohio. Put some miles behind us and then stop for the evening.

One step at a time.

20
MERA STEVENS

There are tiny moments in life that cause massive reflection. Mine came as I fought to squeeze a sponge into a tiny sippy cup. There I was, washing dishes, like I had done eighteen months earlier.

I lost everything that day. My entire being sunk to a depth that I never thought imaginable. Waking up and expecting normal only to face the biggest nightmare of my lifetime. Watching my child, my young son, convulse, then shrivel and die killed me. It killed me.

I was not the same person after that.

Any love inside of me was sectional. My love for Danny and Jessie was the same, but for Daniel, that brief moment in my grief, turning cold, it haunts me. I never imagined that Daniel, my husband and partner for decades, would no longer be with me.

Absorbed in my own loss, disregarding what Daniel felt, I wanted to be left alone. Daniel slept and then Daniel...turned. Like most of the world.

I was grateful for my son Danny's survival and for finding Jessie. But not only my world, but the *entire* world was different.

We, as a race, were at a loss.

For months, we lived off the land, running, sheltering, and hiding, every once in a while finding a safe place, becoming complacent, and then finding ourselves facing one wall of danger after another.

A year ago, I was still grieving. I hated the world and what it had left to offer.

It had nothing.

Sometimes the thought of death was welcoming.

A little over a year ago, I would never have imagined that I would be standing in front of a sink, washing a sippy cup, bathing daily, eating food that I prepared.

In some sort of life consolation prize, I got another shot.

Not a day goes by when I don't think of my lost husband or precious little boy. Not a day. But now, a year later, those days of thinking of them are also filled with smiles. Filled with children that were delivered to me to protect. I savored each and every moment. Life is so precious.

I was a little saddened by Sonny's departure. I knew I'd see him again, and I knew his quest was for the good of me and my family. But the boys, Phoenix and Keller, brought a huge amount of warmth to my heart after breakfast.

The other children were at school, and it was just the three of us.

Beck went to watch Jessie ride and spend time with her. Alex was doing whatever Alex did, and the boys were moving about the house, playing.

Yes, playing.

I had raised three children. Never in my entire life had I heard a toddler speak like Phoenix did.

He put words together to create sentences, and he comprehended more than a child his age should have. Beck attributed that to the fact that they talked and taught him constantly at the ARC, especially Miles.

They were sitting on the floor in the kitchen; Phoenix naturally taking the role of mentor. He was bringing toys to Keller's hands, speaking to him, as if he had been prepared for a blind and deaf sibling.

Admittedly, it sent a chill up my spine.

Phoenix was a natural, as if he had never left Keller's side. Many times as I cleaned the kitchen, I'd pause to smile at the one-sided conversation Phoenix had with Keller, wondering if it actually *was* all that one-sided. After all, I swore I too had heard Keller speak.

Maybe...just maybe...Phoenix heard him as well.

Just as I finished the dishes, I heard Phoenix say, "Let's go."

"Whoa. Wait," I called out. "Where are you going?"

Phoenix had placed a couple toys to Keller's chest and wrapped one of Keller's arms around the truck and figures. He picked up his own toys. "Play."

"Stay where I can see you. I'll be right there."

Phoenix nodded, and with his free hand grabbed Keller's hand and walked into the adjacent room.

As soon as they left the kitchen, there was a single knock on the door, and Michael stepped in.

"Hey," he said, smiling brightly.

"Hey, Michael. What brings you by? Aren't you teaching?"

"Not yet. I wanted to see the boys. Plus I was at the clinic." He held out his hand and showed me a bandage in the bend of his arm.

"Are you sick?"

"No, they took my blood. I held the baby and the baby...he didn't react. He was good."

I closed my eyes. "Michael, if they're testing your blood…"

"I know. I don't worry. I wanted to see Phoenix."

"He and Keller are amazing. Wait until you see them together." I tossed down the dishrag. "They just walked in here." I led the way calling for the boys, but froze when I entered the empty room. Where were they?

Ten, twenty seconds, and they were gone.

"Where did they go?" Michael asked.

I shook my head and called out. "Phoenix." I didn't think much of it; they were two toddlers together, they probably were hiding or in another room.

"Oh my God," Michael whispered and flew by me when he saw the front door at the end of the hall was open.

It was Grace. There were no cars to hit them, the animals were pretty far away, and they weren't getting out of the gate.

Unless…

The back of the living section was indeed protected by the wall, but a small section was left open during the day for ease of access to the farming area.

But there was no way they could make it there.

I had forgotten how fast toddlers moved.

We looked left and right. I didn't see them.

"Michael, go ask neighbors to help, I'm gonna run around back to see if they went to the farm area."

"That's a jaunt."

"Yeah, I should be able to get them before they make it through." I hurried around the house. They weren't in the backyard.

I worried more about the creek that ran the edge of the property, because I didn't see them anywhere. At that point, I started calling Phoenix's name with every step I took. Within moments, everyone around was calling out for the babies.

I ran, headed straight to that open gate. My head was saying no way that they made it that far, but my heart and parental gut instinct said otherwise.

Racing as fast as my legs would carry me, heart beating rapidly and breathing difficult, I had almost made it to the open section when indeed I saw them.

There they were, holding hands and happily racing across the field.

"Phoenix! Stop!" I screamed, pausing to catch my breath. Half bent over I saw that they stopped and turned to face me.

Both of them.

Grateful, I heaved in some air, hands on my knees half bent over, I lowered my head for a second, and when I lifted it not only did I see my two small boys standing with their backs to me, but a wall of Sleepers lined up on the edge of the field where it met the woods.

"Don't move. Don't move," I implored them. I ran toward them and when I made my charge, so did the Sleepers. "Phoenix, run to me!" I screamed.

Neither he nor Keller moved.

I had the shorter distance, but the huge number of Sleepers were closing in. The boys were still a good fifteen feet from me. My arms extended, blood filled my ears. I wanted to cry, to scream, and then through the corner of my eye I saw a blur of a person shoot by me.

Michael passed me, charged to the boys, swept them into his arms, and shouted, "Go! Go!" He turned and ran back toward me.

It took me a second in my momentum to stop and turn, and by that point, Michael had caught me and was quickly beating me to the wall.

"Don't look back!" he shouted. "Keep running!"

You can't warn someone in a dangerous situation to not look down or look back, because instinctually they will. I did.

The Sleepers were catching up to me.

Michael was at the wall with the boys and crossing into the safety of Grace while I was still vulnerable. That was fine with me; he needed to get the boys safe and sound.

I can do this. I can do this.

All I saw was the opening in the wall, and I saw Michael put down the boys, holding the door, waiting on me. Sanctuary...I was close.

Just about there, a breath away from the gate, something jumped on my back. The weight and force brought me down to the ground face first. It knocked the wind from me and I could smell the horrendous sour-meets-fecal smell of the Sleeper.

Everything seemed to be moving in slow motion, my face hitting the ground, my head bouncing back up, the force, the weight, the odor, and hands. One grabbed my hair and the other hand of the Sleeper locked on to my face. His or her fingers pulled at my mouth. The force was so fierce that I swore my skin was ripping. I tried with everything to lift, to move, and the weight of one suddenly became the weight of more. Not only was I feeling the pain of the pull, I was suffocating.

What seemed like a long time of suffering was probably only seconds, because in an instant, the weight lifted. I heard something, a thump, I wasn't sure. I do know that a hand grasped down and lifted me to my feet. Again, it was Michael.

The Sleepers lunged as he put me behind him. There had to be hundreds. Where they came from, I don't know. Michael stood before me and the Sleepers stopped. They just stopped.

He whispered, "Run. Go to the wall."

"Michael..."

"Go."

I was so close to that wall, how they even caught me I don't know. But I looked once more and after moving backwards a few steps, I spun and ran with all I had to that open wall. As soon as I passed into Grace, I turned. Michael was backing up. The Sleepers didn't move, not until he turned and ran.

Then they came. Full force.

It was hard to tell who was around. I watched Michael, and as soon as he stepped through, someone slid the steel gate closed, and the second it connected, I heard the Sleepers slam against it.

The babies grabbed onto me. One each held a leg. I reached for Keller and lifted him and held my hand to Phoenix. Keller on my hip, I felt his tiny hands grab my injured face. He leaned his forehead against me.

"Mama, it will be fine." I heard Keller's voice.

My head lifted. "I hear you, Keller," I said in a barely audible whisper, then pulled him closer into me.

Phoenix tugged my hand. "Hurt?"

I shook my head and watched the gate. It was all starting to register, especially when Alex, Beck, and a whole force of Grace men ran by me and charged to the wall.

Michael backed up, lifted Phoenix, and placed his arm around me. "I'm sorry."

"No, no. Thank you." I stood there in shock. What were Beck, Alex, and the men going to do? And what was Danny doing there?

I could hear the Sleepers banging against the wall, screaming, groaning. They were loud. They were a large, angry mob.

"Everyone, back it up!" Beck ordered. "Back up." He swung his arm out in a point. "Bring those carts. We need to get up on this wall now."

Four men rolled the carts we used for the horses; another brought a ladder. Boxes were stacked in the carts to create steps for the men to climb.

"Once up there, take them out. Watch your shots!" Beck yelled.

My son Danny, weapon slung over his shoulder, was the first and most ambitious to climb up there. He took that wall, and the second he hit the top, a Sleeper lunged at him, knocking him back and down the entire twelve feet.

The pain of watching Danny land with a deadened thump shot through my being.

The first shot was fired by Alex, killing the Sleeper that sailed with my son to the ground.

It was the first time I realized the walls weren't safe, for at that moment, the Sleepers began to pour over the wall. My eyes were more focused on Danny. He wasn't moving.

Michael rushed Phoenix into my arms. "Get you and the kids into the barn for cover."

The barn was the only building close, and it wasn't as much of a barn as it was a storage building.

"What about you?"

"Go, Mera."

There were numerous Grace residents out there, all of them running. Some were screaming. It was pandemonium; everything was out of control. I wasn't certain the storage barn would be safe, but it was our only option. I had to put my faith in the hands of those who fought. I was sick to my stomach thinking about Danny. Was he all right? How badly was he hurt? I wasn't even sure if *I* were injured.

Making it into the storage barn was easy, but being in there was not. Once the doors closed, we were literally in the dark. No windows, no means to see what was going on outside.

With just the sounds of hysterical people inside, and gunfire and screams outside of the building, I held the boys close.

21
ALEX SANS

What a mess. Any opponents of Beck's Reckoning were going to be few and far between following the invasion at the back gate.

The Sleepers climbed over each other to get inside, jump the wall, and attack anyone they came across.

With just six of us, it was impossible to defend against them, and it was even clearer to me that we weren't as safe as I thought we were. How long had the Sleepers watched the wall? Why had they waited until that exact moment to attack?

If there were that many, there had to be more.

"Why did this happen, Alex?" Beck asked. "Why wasn't this area secure of Sleepers?"

Was he reprimanding me? Blaming me for a Sleeper onslaught?

"How did so many get to the wall?"

"I don't know."

"It was your job to keep these people safe!" Beck hollered.

"I know!" I blasted back. "And I did. For a year, I kept them safe! I don't know what happened or why they came just now. Why they waited."

"They didn't wait. They came yesterday. You should have sent men out to see where they were coming from."

"Yeah, I should have. I didn't," I argued. "I didn't ask for this shit, Beck. I did what I had to do to keep people safe."

"Yeah, well, today this community lost eight people. One was a child." Beck walked closer, so close that I could feel the heat of his breath. "A *child*."

"What the hell, Beck?" I shoved him away. "I'm not your peon here and I don't work for you. Who the hell do you think you are coming back and jumping in my face?"

Beck clenched his jaws so tight I could see the muscles. "I'm getting a scouting team together; we leave in ten. I expect you to be there." Beck turned and walked out.

He certainly wasn't the man I remembered or the man I intended to bring back. I guess a year acting as a military badass in the cave, wiping out Sleepers, does something to one's ego.

Admittedly, I was really down. I knew the people that died better than Beck did. I lived with them. It hurt. Not to mention, Danny was knocked out cold; fortunately, he only sustained a bruised back and a concussion. Mera had a huge-ass bruise on her face from having her mouth stretched further than it should have been. The medical folks didn't see infection in her blood but were watching her.

It could have been worse. There would have been no way six of us could have handled all those raging Sleepers if it weren't for Michael. He was a silent weapon. All he had to do was walk to a Sleeper and they'd stop. They'd freeze as if they were either in awe of him or didn't know what to make of him. They stopped; we shot.

By the time we cleared those that were inside the wall, the ones on the other side had fled.

We had to find them. They were gathering somewhere; we had to find out where. Other than finding the Sleepers, I wanted to find out what happened. I has been on my way back to the house when I heard the commotion. Someone said Mera couldn't find the boys, then another was screaming that they'd left the wall. We made it to the wall just as Mera and the boys made it back inside. I honestly didn't have a clue how many Sleepers there were. I heard them, but I couldn't see over that wall.

Mera was at the clinic and I headed there. I knew she was low risk, and they'd not have a problem letting me see her.

She didn't say hello; she stood and raced to me. "Where are the boys?"

"Home." I closed the door. "Michael and Jessie are there. Danny's home. He's fine."

"I know." Mera nodded.

I reached out and grabbed her chin. "You are gonna have one big bruise tomorrow."

"It feels like it."

"What happened, Mera?" I asked.

"I don't know. I don't. The boys were in the kitchen with me. A few minutes later Phoenix was holding Keller's hand and they were walking away. He said they were playing. Michael knocked on the door; I answered it. We spoke for a second. I thought the boys were in the other room but...they ran out."

"That's a huge haul from the house to the wall," I said. "I mean, for two little kids with one being blind. How did they get there?"

She shook her head. "Alex, I swear to you. I swear with everything I am that it was at most a minute from the time they left the kitchen until we ran out looking for them. They had to have run."

"And knew where to go. That's at least the length of two football fields." I scratched my head.

"Alex, this whole thing is weird. How did they know to go there? How did they know to run to the field? And they were just running when I saw them. Holding hands and running."

"To where?"

"The woods."

I looked up. "The Sleepers came from there."

She nodded. "Alex." She lowered her voice. "It was weird. It was like they knew. Like they *knew* where to go."

"They're babies, Mera."

"They're more than that together."

"Mera…" I shook my head in ridicule.

"He spoke again."

My eyes widened. "Who?"

"Keller."

I moved closer to her. "Keep that to yourself. Apparently, what you and I don't know is that there is this huge movement to kill all Sleepers. It's already in effect. We start mentioning weird stuff, who knows what the masses will think?"

"Well, then, should I keep my mouth shut about Michael? He saved me. He ran out and the Sleepers just stopped attacking when they saw me. I know this sounds unbelievable, but they seemed…"

"Scared of him?" I asked. "Yeah, I know. I saw it. They could see him as a freak. That's how we killed all the Sleepers inside the community. He walked up to them like a one man freeze gun."

"Do you think it's because he's a Sleeper?"

"No," said a voice from the door. "No."

I cringed. "Levi."

"I heard what happened; many people saw Michael's touch with the Sleepers. I saw it today with the baby. I had my own suspicions after that. But…" Levi stepped further into the room, "I ran tests."

"And?" I asked.

"He is not a Sleeper. Whatever ability Michael has over the Palers or Sleepers is a mystery. There is no rhyme or reason for it. It's bigger than us," Levi said. "Maybe we all need to rethink Pastor Michael's role in the Doctrines we so quickly dismiss."

22
MERA STEVENS

Beck.

There was something wrong. I know it was internally wrong because I felt as if I was swarming in a virtual realty game. What was real? What wasn't?

I watched him die. I watched them shoot him. I saw Alex's face when he couldn't save him. There I was, struggling with my own unresolved issues and demons, when Alex was doing the same. He just never said anything.

No wonder we fought so much.

Now here was Beck, a man of strength and conviction, a good man to whom I owed so much. Here was Beck...alive, his rebirth a product of Alex's rule-breaking. Of course, to look at Alex, no one would be surprised that he broke rules.

Beck rushed into the room at the clinic and embraced me. My God, I missed that embrace. So much comfort and safety was in his huge arms. I clutched him with gratefulness. I supposed I would do that for a long time.

Alex had left to get Michael at my request and ask Bonnie to stay with the kids until I got there. I was certain it wouldn't be a problem.

But with Beck, Alex, and a couple of other men going out to scout the area, they needed more protection than guns.

"I'm so sorry," Beck said softly. "I am so sorry you had to go through that."

"It's ok. I'm fine."

He pulled back, looking at my face. "You could have lost your entire face."

"I know." My finger clenched his arms. "Listen...I need to speak to you."

"I have to go. Can it wait?" Beck asked. "Mera, there's nothing more I want than to stay by your side, help with all this that you have taken on, but I can't do it until all of you are safe. This is not a safe place. I need to find where they are, where this hive is."

"Hive?"

He cocked back. "Yeah, I have told you about the hives. They gather in one area. Like bees. Hornets. That's why we're able to take them out like we have. We call them hives. Obviously, with how many we saw today, there's a hive around here."

"Why haven't we seen them before?"

"You haven't looked. Everyone here was in a sense of false security."

"Beck, Alex did all he could."

Beck blinked. "I'm not blaming Alex. He didn't think outside the box. He kept this area safe, and that's all that mattered because you guys were behind this wall."

"What if they just got there? What if your Reckoning caused them to migrate?"

"That's possible. We don't know. But I do know we have to get rid of them. I have a team on the Oklahoma border. We just keep an eye out and we can have them gone when I get the weapons."

I exhaled. "We've been peaceful here, Beck. What if people want blood? What if they want every Sleeper killed? They need to stop the Sleeper population in the future; that means—"

"No. I know where you're going with this. I will not let anything happen to Jessie." Beck grabbed my hand. "I promise you. No one is going to hurt her."

"There are others like her. What about them?"

Beck shook his head. "We will protect the healed. Okay? I have to go."

"Not without Michael." I grabbed his hand as he started to stand.

"What?"

"I want Michael with you."

Beck moistened his lips and sat back down. "Mera," he said softly, "everyone saw what happened today. It...it scared people."

There was a knock on the door. I looked beyond Beck to see Michael. He stood in the doorway then stepped inside.

"Am I interrupting?" Michael asked. "Alex said you wanted to see me."

"No," Beck said. "We didn't."

"Yes, *I* did." I slid from the bed and stood. "I want you to go with Beck and Alex on this scouting mission. You saw how many Sleepers there are. You need to go."

Michael chuckled a little in disbelief. "Mera, I don't know how I did what I did."

"Yes, you do." I stepped closer to him speaking with total seriousness. "You do. Don't you?" I looked deep into his eyes. "You've always known." I felt what I said to him. He knew. He had to.

Michael looked at me then shifted his eyes away to Beck. "What's going on?"

Beck lifted his hands. "I don't know. I have to go. As much as I'd love to have you there with that deflecting ability, I can't, Mike, I can't. People are gonna get weird about what you did. They'll get scared and know you're a Sleeper and you—"

"He's not a Sleeper," I interrupted. "He isn't."

Beck turned and looked at me. "He is."

I shook my head. "No, he isn't. Levi has blood work to prove it, so anyone who doubts it can see him."

Beck's mouth opened a little. "Levi did blood work?"

"Yes. Michael is not a Sleeper. Not one sign of infection or resistance to infection. Clean and clear, just like you and me. But he's not." I focused on Michael. "Did you know?" I paused and didn't give him a chance to answer. "Of course you knew. You just couldn't tell us."

Michael wiped his hand over his face and smiled. "Mera, I don't know where you are going with this, but there has to be a mistake. I have the virus."

"Mera," Beck said, "if he doesn't have the virus, then how does he control the Sleepers?"

"Why don't we read the Doctrines?"

Michael gasped loudly and stepped back. "No. No, I will not let you blaspheme like that. No. The Doctrines are bull. Made up. As flattered as I am, don't bestow the honor of the Doctrine's holy man on me."

"Then there's something about you," I argued. "Whatever it is—good, bad— could you please go with Beck and Alex?"

Michael lifted his hands. "I'll go, but Beck doesn't—"

"It's fine," Beck interrupted him. "Can you wait outside? I'll be right there."

"Yeah, sure."

I thanked him and waited until he was gone to look at Beck.

"Mera, do you know how crazy you sound?"

I shook my head. "You know what's funny? We can believe that people from the future are here. We can believe in time travel. A virus made by man to make humans better decimated our earth. We can believe in unnatural killing creatures, but it's impossible to believe for a second that something bigger than all this is here for us? That God—"

"Mera. No."

"Whatever." I folded my arms and turned my back to him.

"Whatever?" Beck asked. "Did you just say whatever?"

"I did."

"I have to go." He kissed the back of my head and whispered that he loved me, and that he'd be back.

I closed my eyes tightly, told him to be careful, and turned back around to see him leave.

I know they thought I was crazy. It *did* sound insane. But until someone offered another plausible explanation, my train of thought was going to another level. It had to. I said it from the beginning. There was something about Michael. Good or bad, I'd figure it out.

23
ALEX SANS

I have an unabashed irritation for Beck, and he felt it. I didn't hide it. See, here's the deal; I missed a year of my relationship with him. Obviously, I was his pal. His radio buddy. But as we tromped through the woods, I was his flunky, or at least I felt that way. Maybe it was total resentment because for a year, I was the man. Now he comes back and everyone looks to him.

"Stop it," Michael whispered to me. "Here, have a drink."

"Padre," I sniffed the bottle, "I didn't know you carried the moonshine."

"Only when I'm out with you and you get like this." Michael showed the bottle again. "One sip."

"Am I that transparent?"

"Yes."

I took a sip.

We were a four-man team. We didn't want to be so big that we'd be spotted; we were only scouting. Beck and another man named Stan were up ahead.

Beck stopped and turned around. "Can you keep up?"

"Can you get off my back?"

"Alex..." Michael said in a warning voice.

Beck shook his head. "Since when did you get so edgy?"

"Since when did you become such a dick?"

I saw it through the corner of my eye; Michael cringed as Beck moved my way. I wasn't scared of the big guy. In the time I knew him; he was pretty tame, just physically intimidating.

"A dick?" Beck asked.

I tugged my ear. "I believe that's what I said, yes."

Beck huffed out a hard breath. "Why...why would you say that about me?"

"Oh, am I hurting your feelings?"

"Yes."

"Really?"

"Yes."

"Wow." I tilted my head. "I'm sorry. It's just that you are so bossy now."

"Then I'm sorry. I don't mean to be that way. I'm just worried. I thought this place was safe. I did. Nothing that you did or didn't do, it's just that they're *here*, and I have a feeling it's bad. I need to take care of it."

"Save the world for humanity?"

Another heavy breath, Beck smiled, lowered his head, and shook it again. He dropped his voice. "Between you and me, I don't care about saving the world for humanity. I just care about saving enough of it for the people that I love. Mera, the kids, you. That's my concern. Get it?"

"Got it." I held up a finger. "I'll try to be better."

"Thank you." Beck turned and started walking.

"It's just that, fighting with…with my wife and all…"

Everyone who had been moving stopped.

Beck looked over his shoulder. "Your wife?"

"Yeah, you probably don't know. You were away."

Beck blinked a few times. "I would think you would have told me."

"Um…sorry?" I shrugged and followed.

Michael reached out, halting me. "When did you get married?"

"You would know. Did you marry us?"

"Who did you marry?" Michael asked.

"Oh, you know."

"Really, I don't."

Stan laughed. "Dude, I know you're trying to lighten the mood by joking, but you even have me convinced that you're married."

"I'm not? I mean…" I faked a laugh. "I'm not. Kidding you, Beck." After getting a glare from Beck, my mind screamed at Sonny. He told me I was married, and the only reason he would do that was if Mera told him about the time change.

I made a mental note to get them both.

Beck walked a little more, following the slight grade upwards. "The trail comes from this way. Look." He pointed to an impression. "This is a pathway. Just gotta follow."

"Can't Michael tap in?" I asked. "He is the Son of God."

"You're an asshole," Michael snapped.

"Wow, is that any way for the Son of—"

"Stop. Okay? It's not funny to me. I take my faith very seriously. I am a man like you and Beck and everyone else. My father sold electronics and my mother was a waitress. I wanted to be a musician. Where in all that do you get—"

"Gentlemen." Beck called out gently. A soft call that sent a warning to me. He waved his hand. "Come here."

Stan reached him first gasping, "Holy shit."

I arrived and was immediately breathless. "Oh my God." While we didn't get a full view of the town, we saw enough.

Michael asked. "Where did they all come from?"

"Have you been to this town?" Beck asked me.

"Yeah. Stan and I came through here last month for a Wal-Mart run. There were maybe three or four. We took them out."

"No more than that, Beck, I swear," Stan said. "Not this."

Beck slid his hand harshly down his face. "I can't even get a count. Our closest ground troop movement is a good four days away."

"Air support?" I suggested.

"We don't have it or the fuel for it." Beck looked at me. "We need to figure out something. This is big. This is…"

"Terrifying," I finished his sentence. I hated to, but I looked out again. The small area of the town, from what we could see, was covered by wall-to-wall, shoulder-to-shoulder, sauntering Sleepers. They moved aimlessly, except for a few of them that I saw skirmishing over something. A low hum of vocal moaning carried to us. I knew one thing: if they even slightly developed an ability to think, to storm our wall, we were in trouble. We were seriously outnumbered, and that was only what I could see.

24
SONNY

It was pretty early in the evening when we stopped. We didn't plan on it, but the skies were brewing a storm and, without power, without lights, the roads were going to get dark.

The trip was full of surprises.

We stopped in Bowie County on the outskirts of a town called Texarkana.

I expected to run into Sleepers, maybe groups of them. We didn't run into any or have any problems at all. We passed them as we drove; they walked west, as if they had a destination. Some walked alone, some in groups. The first leg of the journey I marked as safe. Dismal, but safe.

The highway had started to crack. Weeds lifted the concrete, and the cars abandoned on the road were weatherworn and had become planters for vegetation. I suppose in time they, along with the highway, would be buried beneath nature.

The town held Sleepers, and a pack of four came for us when we pulled over. Silent in the slaying, Miles took them down without alerting any others. We took refuge in an old drugstore just off the first exit of the highway. The building was clear, save a few deer that had their way in the parking lot. We secured the place for the night. I found cans of spray paint, three of which were red.

In the morning, if we were attacked or overrun, and the place was still secure, I'd mark the outside with a big red 'S' for safe. My sign for Mera.

I had a plan, because somewhere deep inside me, I knew I had to lay out not only a safe route, but an escape route. There was no reason for this other than a gut instinct. I was never psychic before and believed the feelings to be borne from paranoia.

I managed to make radio contact and reached Mera. The connection was bad and I wasn't counting on the radio contact lasting all that long, so I quickly informed her of my plan. I told her the route Miles and I were taking, my destination area in Ohio, and that I would mark things along the way. Any place safe to stop for the night would be marked. If a change of course was taken, we'd find a way to let them know.

I knew exactly where I wanted to go. I was familiar with the area of Ohio and the farms in the region. I grew up there. It wouldn't be as easy as Grace, but it would feel more free and less like a prison camp. I hoped that the rest of the trip would be like the first portion, a dead country, a decaying modern civilization, a world abandoned, but one with fewer Sleepers.

In Randy's time, he told of a civilization, a free zone from Sleepers beyond the Great Divide.

I prayed that held true in this time as well.

25
MERA STEVENS

I'd be lying if I said I almost forgot that Beck was alive, because he only returned briefly, apologized for not staying, and then took off again. There was a situation and he'd fill me in when he had a chance. It wasn't good. Beck didn't say that, but the urgency with which he moved and spoke told me that.

Even more so when he said, "Lock the doors."

Lock the doors?

Only in the beginning did I lock the doors, and that was only when I saw Sleepers. He might have been saying it so the babies didn't get out again. I know that was forefront on my mind.

Danny was awake when the radio call came from Sonny. It was good to hear from him and even better to hear that they were traveling safely. Sonny seemed to not only be heading home, but also setting up for all of us to leave. I saw the look on my son's face. He looked relieved to hear from Sonny.

Danny's head hurt, and rightfully so. He took a pretty good knock. He was sluggish and groggy, and I didn't want him to sleep. He said he didn't think he could.

"Remember when I returned home that day?" Danny asked. "I told you about the sleeping sickness. You didn't believe me."

"Yes, vividly. Why are you bringing this up?" I asked.

"I have that same feeling now. Scared of something, I don't know what, but I also feel I need to be strong and ready."

"Danny…"

"Mom, they climbed the wall. They used each other to climb the wall," Danny said emphatically. "There were about two hundred of them, Beck said. Imagine if there's more. Worse yet, imagine if they can *think* again."

"I don't want to."

"Yeah, well, neither do I. We keep forgetting things that Randy said. You know? We keep forgetting that he came to us to try to find the cure because kids in his time were dying. He called them the Palers and never said a word about how they were. But they had to be some way, Mom, because it went from mainly us to half us to them owning this world. That's scary. It's bad enough when they're mindless and dangerous, but make them logical and dangerous and we're in trouble."

I shook my head. "No. We aren't. Apparently, the uninfected still thrive for a while, in our lifetimes."

My son had a point though. I reached out, allowing my fingers to run down his face. It was pale and his eyes were tired. He had already been through so much in his young life. I hate the thought of him having to be so grown up. He was only eighteen.

I told Danny to rest, that I wanted to check on the babies. Last I looked in on them, they were sleeping. I heard footsteps and I wanted to check. Plus, I had a baby gate that I wanted to put on their door.

It was hard getting used to Keller being in another room. I arrived at the bedroom, gate in hand, and heard a voice. I knew exactly who it was. Jessie. I had adjusted to the fact that my daughter, despite being a full grown woman physically, was a mere child mentally. She reminded me so much of how she was when she was four.

Phoenix and Keller were her toys. She loved Keller to death. We all did. The child may not have made a noise, but he exuded personality and when he smiled, it melted you.

I leaned in the doorway, watching Jessie on the floor with Phoenix, and Keller was sound asleep on the bed.

"Mommy," Jessie smiled. "We're playing."

"I see. It's bedtime." I then noticed what Jessie was wearing. Miss May had made Jessie several summer dresses. Cool cotton and perfect for the weather. Childlike in a way, to match Jessie. Miss May was left over from the religious group that had survived on the land. She loved Jessie. Everyone did. Jessie loved that dress.

"Why aren't you dressed for bed?"

Jessie smiled widely. "I pretty."

"I see."

"I ready for tomorrow."

I flashed back to when she was really a child. She did the same thing. When she was excited about her day, the night before she used to get dressed so all she had to do was get out of bed.

"Phoenix talks, Mommy."

"I know." I walked to the bed to check on Keller.

"He's big in a small body…like me."

"He just talks very well for his age, sweetie." I told her. "Now go to—"

"So does Keller," she said.

This made me stop. "You hear Keller speak?"

She pointed to her head. "In here."

I just stared at her.

"He told me."

"Keller told you what?"

"They want the baby. They want the baby back."

"What baby, Jess?"

"The one they hide at the clinic."

My heart thumped hard in my chest and a knot formed immediately in my stomach. "Who wants the baby?"

"The bad people that came. They will go away," she made a crinkled face, "when they get the baby."

"Honey, I don't think you should worry about it." I extended my hand. "Now say good night."

Happily, Jessie darted a kiss to Phoenix and stood up. Her eyes shifted to the gate. I explained, "It's so the boys don't leave while we sleep."

Jessie shook her head. "They were bad."

"They didn't know." I kissed her and laid my hand on her face. "They didn't know."

"Still bad. He called them. Night, Mommy." She kissed me and left the room.

"Who called them, Jess?" I asked, but she was gone.

Was she making up stories? In her youth she did. I stared at the door for a second then held out my hands downward to Phoenix. "Come on. Bed."

He looked at me with an angelic smile and slowly stood, not accepting my offer to carry him. He walked to the bed and I helped him onto it. "Under," I told him and brought the covers over him. "Goodnight, sweetie. I love you."

"Wov you too." He grinned.

I walked to the other side of the bed and looked at Keller. He was curled up in a ball and sound asleep. I grabbed his little hand, brought it to my lips and to my chest, then to his. I knew he was sleeping but I had to convey that I loved him. "I love you little man, so much." I bent down and kissed him.

Once more I walked around and kissed Phoenix. He delivered another smile.

"Goodnight. I'm putting a gate up. Call for me if you need me. I am right next door." I adjusted the covers.

"Keller call them," Phoenix said.

"I'm...I'm sorry?"

"You ask Yessie. Me answer. Keller call them."

"Who?"

"The bad." On that, the little boy, still not even a full-fledged toddler, flashed eyes that seemed years beyond his age. Then he brought the covers to his shoulders, rolled his back to me, and closed his eyes with a smile.

26
ALEX SANS

"Now you've really lost it, Mera."

Heck, I had just taken a leak, still in my boxers, when she opened the bathroom door. At first, I thought she had to go. But then she started rambling.

"Can I have coffee? Can I brush my teeth?" I asked her, trying to gather my bearings. Beck and I had been meeting and discussing strategies all night. I was going on only a few hours sleep.

She gave me my peace, and I sensed she was impatiently waiting on me.

I stepped into the kitchen and, in a rare occasion, Mera had a cup of coffee for me.

She was anxious to talk to me, but that would wait until the seven or eight or nine little people filed into the kitchen for breakfast, all calling out their morning cheer.

Hi, Alex. Hey, Alex. Morning, Alex. Hello, Alex.

Admittedly, it was hard keeping their names straight, even after a year. Nick, Mary, Haley, Steve...

Jessie...

"Hi, Alex, Bye Alex." Jessie hurried to the door.

"Whoa. Hey, wait." I walked to her, grabbing that coffee from Mera on the way. "You look pretty today."

"I do." Jessie said brightly. "Bye."

I shifted my eyes to Mera.

"Where are you going?" Mera asked. "Aren't you waiting for Bonnie?"

"No. I'm a big girl." Jessie stepped back into the kitchen, kissed Mera, then me, and hurried out. I started to follow, but instead I watched. She walked in the direction of Bonnie's.

"Now..." I turned to Mera, sipped my coffee. "What's up?"

Mera dropped her voice. "Jessie hears Keller."

I slowly tossed my head back and then nodded. "And what did Jessie say he told her?" I immediately followed that question with an 'ow,' because Mera reached out and hit me. "What the hell?"

"I'm serious," she snapped. "Keller told her the Sleepers wanted that baby. That's why they came. And…and she said Keller calls them."

I grimaced, looked at the kids at the table and inched to Mera. "Keep that little bit of information silent. I don't believe it for a second, but after the attack yesterday, people will be up to believe anything. Okay?"

Mera nodded.

"I promise we'll talk about this when I get back. But I need to get to the clinic. Today is the day they…they put the baby to sleep."

She tightly closed her eyes. "And you want to watch it?"

"No, Mera. I want to stop it."

Her eyes opened and widened.

"A lot happened yesterday. Beck and I were talking about how clearing the hive was going to happen, and I thought about seeing that infant in Michael's arms. Mera…it's just a baby."

Her lips quivered and she threw her arms around me.

"I can't make any promises. But no one really has a good reason other than it's a Sleeper. There's no justification in doing it. It is still human and maybe…maybe we can turn it. Look what we've done for Keller."

"Thank you, Alex. Does Beck know?"

I hesitated in answering. "No. But…knowing Beck, I really don't think he's gonna fight me. His plight is not what we all thought."

Mera had a lost, clueless look on her face as she tilted her head in question.

"But I have to…" My attention was drawn to the sound of squealing brakes. Very near. Standing right by the kitchen door, I turned my head to the sound only to see that beat-up yellow school bus. The one that had carried us to Grace.

I was going to go out until I saw the driver step from the bus.

Danny walked up to the back door as if bringing that bus into our yard was completely normal. He walked into the house.

"What is that doing here?" I asked.

"It's parked there and will stay there. I have to get it ready," Danny replied.

"For what?"

"To go," he said nonchalantly.

I repeated, "To go." I looked at Mera. "He said, 'to go.'"

Mera asked, "Go where, Danny?"

"Anywhere. Out. To meet up with Sonny. I want to prep it. Pack it, have it ready to roll."

"Why?" I questioned. "Where is this coming from? If it's because of yesterday, I can understand. But Beck's Sleeper troops aren't far away and we're coming up with a plan to—"

"No." Danny shook his head. "After this morning, I have no doubt that things are gonna happen. They're coming and we're gonna have to go."

I shook my head. "How do you know this?"

"Keller told me. He told me this morning. He said '*We go. They come. We run.*' Just like that. That's what he said."

Mera gasped.

"Keller," I said. "The little boy there with no ears, no mouth, he told you?"

"Yep. I heard him. Here." Danny pointed to his head. "Weird."

"Yeah, it is. Okay. Good luck with your bus." I opened the door.

"Alex," Mera called. "What the hell? You still don't believe?"

I looked at her, Danny and then to Keller who happily and so oblivious enjoyed his cereal. "No," I said and left.

I pulled the door closed behind me and stopped. Looking at the bus gave me a twisted feeling inside my chest; it almost caused me to lose my breath. I had to get to the clinic, but seeing that bus made me realize, more than I wanted to admit to Mera, that I was starting to believe her about Keller.

And it was scary. Because if a little boy with no ability to verbally communicate was talking and warning us, then we'd better listen.

The clinic wasn't too far from the home front. So my 'thinking' walk, trying to figure out what I was going to say to Levi, was a short one. Almost there, I passed Bonnie. I waved but I slowed down some, because I didn't see Jessie with her.

I was going to ask, but fearful that Bonnie would think I was questioning her, I kept walking. Jessie was probably in Bonnie's house.

Taking a deep breath, words rehearsed in my mind, I stepped into the clinic, not expecting to see Levi and Javier right inside the hallway.

Levi gushed out my name as if he were relieved to see me.

"Hey, guys," I said. "I'm here to talk to you about the baby. Do you guys have a minute?"

"Alex, the baby is gone," Levi said.

A sickening feeling hit me. "You guys were supposed to wait. To talk to me. To tell me when..."

"No." Levi cut me off. "Gone. Disappeared. Someone took the baby."

We weren't talking modern day technology or hospitals with security bracelets. It was Grace. There really wasn't much of a clinic staff, no one watching to see a kidnapping. I stammered, "W-wait. Who would just take..." It started as a heaviness churning in my gut and it hit my chest when the revelation hit me. "Oh God. I'll be back."

I spun and rushed from the clinic. I hoped, I really hoped I was wrong. But it all hit me at once. Jessie in a hurry, being the big girl, running out. Bonnie and no Jessie.

JACQUELINE DRUGA

I ran as fast as I could back to the house, my mind begging with each step I took that the house was the destination. But just in case, I put out a radio call on a private channel.

27
MERA STEVENS

"And how exactly is he talking, Mera?" Beck asked me. He had come down right after Alex left and saw the bus. I took him outside to explain.

"Tele...tele...something."

"Pathic."

"Yes, that's it. I hear him, but not through my ears. Jessie does too, and so does Danny. My kids and I can't all be crazy. You don't believe me."

"I am not saying that. Not at all."

His words made me smile. That was the one thing about Beck. With the exception of the day he arrested me, he always gave me the benefit of the doubt.

"I know it doesn't make sense," I said. "But the whole baby thing doesn't. Something is up with those boys. Something beyond our understanding or control. Every child died, all babies were stillborn, but those two. Keller was born without eyes and ears and communicates. Phoenix, well, he's like...way up there. I don't know how he got so smart and advanced."

"Mera, he spent a year in a scientific environment. He didn't have a choice but to learn." Beck reached for the porch door and allowed me to go in first.

"So what do you think about what Danny is doing?"

Beck looked at Danny first. Danny was at the table with the boys.

Beck replied, "I think Danny should keep doing what he's doing. Get the bus ready, just in case we have to emergency evacuate. But Danny is in charge of that. You and the kids. Okay? If something happens and you have to run, you guys go. The bus is there for you."

I nodded and exhaled. "Thank you, Beck," I tiptoed up and kissed him. "I'm so glad you're alive."

He laughed. "Me, too."

I cringed. He didn't know why I said that, but I did. It was a slip.

To my surprise, Alex rushed in the back door and frantically blurted, "Tell me Jessie is here."

"No," I replied. "She has lessons with Bonnie."

After a single shake of his head, Alex lifted his radio. "Stan, that's negative. Keep looking. No one, repeat, no one in the community is to know but our guys."

Beck moved forth. "What's going on, Alex?"

"Jessie took the Sleeper baby, I think they're both missing."

"Oh my God." My hand shot to my mouth. "Alex, you don't think..."

"She has to be in this community somewhere. I have people looking."

Danny jumped up. "I'll go look by the creek. I hate that creek. It scares me when the kids go there." He moved to the door.

Alex pointed. "Do not leave the wall. Got it?"

Danny opened the door.

"Danny," Alex called. "I'm dead serious. Do not leave the wall."

"It's my sister."

"I know that," Alex said. "But if we need to look outside Grace, then we leave together and leave with a plan and armed. Got that?"

"What's out there, Alex?" Danny asked. "How bad did it get?"

"Check the creek."

Danny flew out.

Beck walked to the hall. "I'm gonna grab my weapon and do a perimeter outside the wall, just in case."

I turned to Alex. "I'll get Bonnie to sit with the boys. I want to help look."

"Mera, I don't think that's—"

"Baby," Phoenix said. "She took baby back."

I immediately looked at Phoenix and Alex raced to the door.

Then I heard another voice. Keller's.

"Hurry, Alex. Get her. Help her. Hurry."

Alex froze. He literally froze at the door then he quickly spun around. His jaw clenched and he moved to the table and stared at Keller.

Keller just sat there, he didn't move, cereal still in his hand.

"You heard him," I whispered. "You heard that too."

Alex's dark eyes shifted my way, then back to Keller. "I will," he said to Keller, then ran from the house.

It wasn't like the old days when I could pick up a telephone and call. I had to get hold of Bonnie. To do so, I had to gather the boys and take them. My heart raced with fear. Where was my daughter?

28
ALEX SANS

I knew. I absolutely positively knew Jessie wasn't in Grace. But where was she? My first inclination, because of the freakish incident with the babies, was the back area that led to farming. But we had men posted on that wall. Surely, one of them would have reported a young woman in a flowery summer dress carrying a baby.

Everything was freakish. A toddler who spoke like a three-year-old and a deaf, mute boy who delivered to me via a telepathic manner a plea to help his sister. I reeled in disbelief but determined that I would find Jessie.

I felt confident until I got the radio call from Stan stating they saw her in the Reflection Area.

Typically, I wouldn't have panicked, but it was the wooded area on the outskirts of the Reflection Area that Sonny and I found the baby.

Ironically, or possibly on purpose, she was heading there.

My stomach knotted and I radioed that I was headed that way.

Beck came on the radio. "Alex, wait for me."

"Negative. I'm by the gate."

"Alex, just wait."

"Negative."

There wasn't time to wait. Someone said they saw Jessie heading to the Reflection Area, no one said anything about her still being there and that scared me.

Grace from an aerial view was a big square. Center of the west wall was the main road, the main gate. From that were the town buildings—school, store, things like that, and also the main church. Random barrack-style buildings were set up around the community for housing, with a few big houses. We lived in the biggest of the houses because we had a lot of the kids. Grace wasn't huge; it was pretty compact. Except to the east.

The north wall had a small entrance, a gate that led to the Reflection Area. The east wall had a bigger gate for going to the fields just beyond that. The south, not a single exit.

The wooded area ran in circumference around the north and east, with the narrow portion being north...the Reflection Area.

I knew the second I got to the North Gate that Jessie wasn't in the Reflection Area.

No one was around. I closed the gate and started running toward the wooded area.

Sleepers be damned, I cried out her name. "Jessie! Jessie!" I called with every pounding slam of my feet to the ground.

Just at the edge of the Reflection Area where the empty area met the woods, Beck called for me.

I ignored him. I searched the ground looking for foot prints.

Nothing.

"Jessie!"

Over the radio, Beck barked, "Goddamn it, Alex, wait."

I didn't respond. I wasn't scared for me or scared of the Sleepers. I was well aware of how many had gathered a little over a mile away.

I ran into the woods, looking left to right. I headed northeast, knowing that was going to lead me eventually to the edge of the woods, just on the grade that overlooked where the Sleepers were gathering.

I didn't care.

Ignoring Beck's pleas over the radio, I saw it on the ground and it made me stop.

Blood.

A pool of it, a good foot in diameter. Fresh, bright blood.

An ache filled my chest. *No. No. No. No.*

I wanted to scream, cry out.

Oh, God, Jessie, where are you?

A small trail led from that bloody spot, and even though I didn't want to see where it ended, I followed it. Not twenty feet away, I saw the body. Had it not been for the blood trail, I would have missed it. It was so small.

My fault. My doing. What had I done? The myth of the animal killing the young after it being touched by a human was somehow proved true in a twisted turn of fate. The tiny Sleeper baby lay curled in a ball. Its body was a bloody, mangled mess. His left arm was nearly detached from the body, his stomach ripped apart and insides pulled as if a hand just tore into him.

The worst, the absolute worst, was the fact that the child's eyes were open and staring and his head had been crushed. Stomped upon until dead.

I suppose to kill him took mere seconds, but it was seconds of misery an innocent baby, Sleeper or not, did not deserve.

Heartbroken for the sadistic, cruel punishment the baby had endured, I dropped to my knees. My hands hovered over the body at a loss what to do. I removed my overshirt.

"Oh God," I heard Beck's voice and then heard his footsteps come to a halt.

My jaws locked and tightened and my face grew hot. I felt so much emotion over it, that I was literally frozen right where I knelt.

"Alex, come on. Leave it. We have to find Jessie."

I brought my shirt down to the baby. Before I could say anything, Beck had taken off.

Leave it.

It.

I would have to, but I'd return. Beck was right. We had to find Jessie. I covered the body of the infant and resumed my search.

29
MERA STEVENS

I grabbed an extra radio from the house and attached it to my belt as I took the boys to Bonnie's. She refused to watch Keller. What the hell? It was my daughter, and she was allowing her fear of Keller to stop my search? I had to rush to Michael. It was on the way that I heard Alex on the radio. Jessie had headed to the Reflection Area. I monitored the back and forth until I got to Michael's school.

I pulled him aside. "Jessie took the baby. We can't find them."

"Where are you going?" he asked. "Stay put."

"To find my daughter."

I was about to run out, when he told me to give him one second. I didn't have a second, but I waited. He was gone about a minute and returned with a gun.

"Just in case." He placed it in my hand. "Safety is on."

"Thank you." I put the weapon behind my back and turned for the door.

"Mama," Keller's voice called me.

I turned.

Michael looked at me. "What is it?"

Ignoring him, I spoke directly to Keller. "What, Keller?"

"Mera?" Michael asked.

A pause, then Keller said, "Help Jessie."

On that, I flew out. I could hear Michael calling my name, but I kept going. Beck had said something about a group of Sleepers in the town northeast of Grace, just beyond the woods. The 'hive' of Sleepers they needed to get.

That was my destination.

I hurried to the gate, just by the fields, the same area where the Sleepers had stormed. I saw Danny racing out. I called for him to wait. I felt more secure being with my son. He was as determined as I was.

I feared for my daughter, especially since I didn't see her at all.

We headed straight for the woods. I knew where the town was. I told Danny what Keller had said. He moaned, and his face screamed with worry.

"Why, Mom? Why would she do this?"

"She's like a little girl. She doesn't know."

"But she took the baby."

"She thought the Sleepers attacked because they wanted it back."

Danny stopped. His winced and bent over to catch his breath, then he started running again.

After a few minutes of running through the wooded area, I spotted the end of it at the top of the small hill. The sun peeked through the trees, and I followed the brightness and my son.

"Mera, stop!" Beck's voice carried to us. "Don't go any further!"

I looked to my left and saw him and Alex running our way. We didn't stop. It was my daughter; I had to find my daughter.

Once I reached the top of that grade, I had no choice. I couldn't move. I could tell Danny had the same reaction.

A gathering of Sleepers? A hive? No term whatsoever could even remotely begin to describe the magnitude of what I saw.

My body heaved. Between the shock and being winded, I felt as if I were going to throw up. It wasn't just a large group of Sleepers; it was a *sea* of them. I couldn't even comprehend what I saw.

Danny had a look of sheer horror on his face, and conveyed it to Beck when Beck arrived.

"Jesus, Beck," Danny gasped. "How did this happen? How did so many get here? This is more than were around the ARC."

Beck shook his head. "I don't know, Danny. It's more than I have ever seen. Too many for our ground forces."

I could hear them, the Sleepers. Their voices were a low-grade hum, like locusts. Then I saw Alex and the blood on his hands.

"Oh my God." I thought immediately that they had found my precious daughter. "Jessie's?"

"The baby," Alex squeaked. "The baby was killed. It was a Sleeper kill."

My eyes welled with tears and my body shook, "Where is Jessie? Oh, God we have to find her." I started to go back to the woods.

Beck stopped me. "She's not there. They got the baby, Mera. They killed the baby. I don't believe for one second that they killed Jessie."

"Then where is she?"

Slowly, Beck went from looking at me to the multitudes of Sleepers below.

"You think she's there?" I gasped and pointed.

"If they were hurting her, we would have found her. No," Beck said. "I think they took her."

I saw through the corner of my eye, Danny dart forward only to be halted by Beck's grip.

"Leave me alone, Beck." Danny swung out, fighting Beck. "Leave me alone, that's my sister. It's my sister!"

"What are you gonna do?" Beck asked harshly. "Rush down there? Storm into thousands upon thousands of Sleepers with a pistol? They'll tear you apart." Beck moved his face closer to Danny's. "Tear...you...apart."

"It's my sister."

"And that is your mother." Beck shook his head. "For her. No."

Alex stepped forward. "I'll take that chance."

"No one goes," Beck ordered. "Not without a plan. You hear?" He looked at all of us. "Jessie is a Sleeper. Sleepers don't hurt Sleepers."

"They killed the baby," I said.

"Yeah, well, I think it's a 'we had the baby' thing," Beck replied. "We know for a fact they don't touch Jessie. We saw it."

My throat closed and I tried to talk. "Beck, it's my daughter. My daughter. She doesn't know. She has to be scared. She has to be so, so scared."

Alex spoke my name softly and stepped to me. "Mera." He looked into my eyes like he had never done. Deep and with conviction. "I promise you, with everything thing I am, I promise you, I will get her. I will go down there. I will get her and bring her back."

"But it's..."

"I promise you," Alex said.

I saw it in his eyes and I believed what he said. But then I looked beyond him to the mass of Sleepers. So many. Too many. I was frightened for my child and my heart ached. It felt like someone had plunged a fist into my chest and squeezed my heart. I wanted to die.

My daughter. My poor daughter. What she was going through, what she must have felt and was feeling.

Emotionally spent, my legs buckled and I dropped to my knees. Yes, they said they'd have a plan. Yes, Alex said he'd get my daughter. But as I looked out below to the throngs of Sleepers, I had only one question.

How?

30
SONNY

A trip that should have taken four hours on a barren highway, no rules, no police, took six. Miles and I ran into a failed exodus just outside of Memphis. Cars were everywhere. It was a familiar sight in every city.

The exodus wasn't to leave, but to get help.

The day the children died, everyone sought assistance. Very few found it through the massive traffic jams; no one received the help needed.

There was none.

I was hoping to get a glimpse of the Great Divide, but that would take backtracking. We'd missed it by two hundred miles and headed northeast.

There were a lot of things we saw that first ten hours.

Cars, cities burned, small towns flattened by what looked like tornados. A world without technology took the world back in ecology. Trees didn't just grow; they crowded the road. Food grew as well; corn fields were wild but fertile. We even stopped at a plum tree.

Four times on our journey we stopped for fresh vegetables. It was amazing.

We stopped for other things, too. We needed to stock up. I hoped the place we were going had items remaining.

Yes, we saw a lot of things, except…Sleepers.

Like Randy had said, in his time, east of the Great Divide, was a free zone.

Once we passed Memphis, we didn't see a single Sleeper.

Had they left, or did they simply die?

Not seeing the creatures that threatened our existence was only one odd thing. The other was a radio call. Crackling with static, the signal was weak. It was the last radio call. I knew it. The distance would grow too far and I didn't have the means like the ARC did. I wished I would have known about the lack of Sleepers. I would have conveyed that.

I didn't place the radio call, Danny did. He radioed to tell me and rattle about how he was having the bus all ready to go. Packed with supplies. He wanted to know if I knew my destination.

I did. Eastern Ohio, a piece of property not only surrounded by a fence, but by farm land. A facility I knew well, the Indian River Juvenile Correction facility. It was one of two places I spent time as a youth. The other was in Kentucky. Ironically, the Ohio one was only about twenty miles, maybe less, from Alex's survival haven.

How cool was that?

The fence would safeguard us, but it wasn't a wall. It was far enough removed that we'd not run into the Sleepers. I envisioned Alex riding his motorcycle, feeling the freedom that he deserved, that all of us deserved. For those I loved; those who were no longer just my friends, but now my family.

God gave us this earth and we failed it. Perhaps we could set it straight.

Danny asked directions, as if he were leaving soon. I found the urgency odd and asked why and he said...Keller told him.

Why something so ludicrous didn't faze me, I don't know. Actually, yes, I do. Because I was one of the very few who still believed that the whole thing was God's doing.

It was too prophetic. All the children dying at the same time, the same day, the same way. Natural disasters swept across the land.

Those who claimed to be from the future were, I think, angels sent to lead us into a different way of thinking.

In any case, The Event led to faith with those who didn't believe. Suddenly everyone turned to God. I bet there wasn't a single parent out there, atheist or not, who didn't pray to a higher power as they watched their child die.

My wife prayed, and she always claimed there was no God. Then again, she died. Our child died.

Every child, born or unborn, died, except for those two babies.

One perfect and beautiful, the other marred and different, both with gifts. How can one even remotely not consider that a higher power didn't have a hand in it?

So Keller telling Danny to go didn't surprise me.

They were spared and had been spared for reason. To lead this world? To be the future? But if a higher power or God was the reason for it all, then like everything in the Bible, there was a balance. A yin and yang, a good and bad.

In a sense it was frightening. If the babies were saved by a higher power, I wondered if that balance applied to them.

Two babies. One perfect. One not. Yin. Yang.

Good...bad.

31
ALEX SANS

Physically, I was there. Mentally and emotionally I was a divided soul. I saw where Beck was coming from, calculating what he needed to do. All I kept thinking about was Jessie.

She had to be frightened. I know Jessie. She was crying. I could see her in my mind huddled in a corner somewhere, wondering why we had abandoned her.

"Alex," Beck called. "Are you with us?"

"Yeah." I nodded. A dozen men were in the room, planning a save and attack. I knew why Michael was there, not because he was security but because he was the only option. At least to Beck.

"Area spreads out seven, eight more blocks," Beck explained. "We assume they cover that area as well. More seem to be arriving by the hour. Our ground Reckoning forces are still two days away. We can't hit them by air, even though that would do."

"We can't hit them at all until we get Jessie out of there," I said.

"And we will."

"We're wasting time."

"Time has to work for us. Sleepers are most volatile at night and early morning. They seem to rest mid-day. That's when we go in. We're taking them out from within. Take them all out. After we get Jessie."

"Every second we stand here is a second Jessie could die."

Beck shook his head. "I don't believe that. They took her because she's a Sleeper. She's down there, probably lost within them. We just need to find her."

Another man spoke up. "With all those Sleepers it could be like finding a needle in a haystack."

I shook my head in disgust. "I'll find her."

"No," Beck said. "Michael will."

It took everything I had not to scream out loud. I wanted to go now, right now, and get her. I didn't give a shit about Sleepers or the dangers.

Beck continued, "Michael will set the explosives that will take out the town. After he plants them, he'll look for Jessie. He can slip in and out without notice."

"He scares them. I saw it, you saw it," I said. "No offense, Mike."

Michael waved out his hand. "None taken."

"Are you able to do this?" I asked Michael.

"I'm pretty sure I can," Michael replied.

"How are you sure?" I questioned. "Are you positive, confident? This is Jessie. I need to know."

"What do you want me to tell you, Alex?" Michael asked.

"Mera seems to think you're special. That you're chosen, some sort of prophet, son of God, savior. Maybe you are, maybe you aren't. Maybe you are bound by some sort of heavenly law that you can't say. But if you are any of those things, I beg you to tell me. I need to know."

"I'm...I'm sorry, Alex," Michael slowly shook his head. "I'm just a man."

"That's not good enough. Just a man can't do it alone. I want to go."

"No." Beck stepped in. "Alex, I know—"

"You know nothing." I swung out my arm, stepping back, fueled with raging emotions. "Nothing, Beck. You haven't been here. Yeah, you saved Jessie. Yes, you were there. But so was I, and I have been here. For a year. I was here when she was sick, read her stories every night, drew with her, nursed her through that broken arm when she took her first tumble from a horse. I have been here. She is my family. It is killing me that she's out there. Michael can't do this alone. He can't. No one can."

"Sending anyone else in there is taking a chance of losing that person. They outnumber us. They'll tear a normal man apart, Beck said. "Getting Jessie out, destroying the town can be done. It can. It also *has* to be done by Michael. I'm sorry, it's our only option."

"I don't believe that," I said. "I don't. I'm sorry. There's always other options." I turned. "Excuse me." I wasn't needed at the meeting. It was pretty much about what Michael was going to do.

Something Beck said struck a chord with me, a crazy, insane chord. I left the room and, late hour or not, I sought out Levi and Javier. Outlandish, stupid, possibly even suicidal. But I had an idea.

"Alex, my God," Levi stumbled back.

"It's insane," Javier added. "Really it is."

I knew that. They didn't need to reiterate it, because nothing they said would change my mind. Insane? Insane was what I was feeling inside. I couldn't even begin to verbally convey how twisted and emotional I felt. Guilt over the baby, sad and scared for Jessie. The inner turmoil was unreal, I was screaming inside with every beat of my heart, every breath I took. If what I felt was only a percentage of what Mera felt when she first was looking for Jessie, then I haven't a clue how she did it.

"Can it be done? Or am I asking for something impossible?"

Javier looked at Levi before answering. "Yes. But I don't know what the timeframe is. Hours, perhaps."

A single knock on the door brought Beck into the living room with us. I sighed. What was he doing there?

"Alex?" Beck walked in. "What's going on?"

I didn't want anyone to know. I suppose Beck had to know; I would ask him to keep it between us, though.

"I'm about to get an answer," I told him then faced Javier again. "So will you do it? Will you turn me into a Sleeper?"

There was a pregnant pause, and another exchange of glances between Javier and Levi, and then, finally, Javier solemnly looked at me. "Yes."

"What? No!" Beck blasted. "*No*. Alex, are you fucking insane?"

"Well, that's the million dollar question tonight, isn't it?" I smiled nervously. "I guess I am."

Beck shook his head. "Are you getting the virus and then hope they turn you back?"

I replied. "No. I'm getting it in hopes of not being sensed by them and getting Jessie back. I can't find that needle in the haystack if I'm a big pitchfork sticking out. I'll be the hay as well. Michael can't do this alone. He can't. He scares them, Beck; what if they turn on him?"

"I won't allow it," Beck stated emphatically. "Alex, my God, you're my friend. You're Mera's friend. A father to Keller. Come on..." He spoke from his soul and I felt it. "Please. Please. I can't let you do this."

"Beck, you don't have a choice. I have to get her. I have to be the one."

"Why?"

"Because we brought that baby here. It was my fault. I love Jessie, Beck, and this is crushing me. I'm doing this."

"Then what?" Beck asked and looked at Javier. "It takes hold and he turns into one of them? Then what, Alex?" He stared deeply at me. "I'm supposed to put a bullet in my friend? No."

"It may not happen like that," Javier interjected. "Alex has a very low resistance to the infection. We saw that with the bite. It takes hold rapidly with him. This will take hold. He'll probably start exuding the Sleeper pheromones four hours post-infection. It will embed immediately in his DNA. Hours after that, it is complete."

Beck tossed out his hands. "So for sure he's turning."

"Not really," Javier answered. "I spent a good part of the day extracting a different virus sequence. It's different, not like the baby or our infected. It's an evolved form. Evolution got a hold of this one. I'm hoping to make it a cure. I'll infect you with that. You'll still be a Sleeper, but I'm hoping not the type that runs around out there. But I can't guarantee it."

I asked, "Where did you get this from?"

"Michael."

I hurriedly looked at Beck then squinted my eyes in confusion. "Levi, you said he wasn't a Sleeper."

"He's not...technically," Levi answered. "He wasn't infected. Like our baby, he was born with it. I recognized the genetic markers. It is the same as the evolved Palers of our time."

Okay. I was confused even more. I couldn't even speak. What was going on?

Thank God, Beck asked, "How is Michael carrying a thousand-year-old gene sequence? I saw his baby pictures in a scrapbook. I saw all kinds of pictures of him and newspaper clippings."

Levi explained, "The Doctrines tell of a baby born that is the cure. The baby could be Michael. We know for a fact the Doctrines were misinterpreted. Time travel has been around a long time. It's possible that he was a mutant. He was shunned at birth by Palers and taken by our kind. I know that happens. It's possible he was sent back. Who knows? I'm guessing here. Only Michael would know. Or not."

Javier continued, "Maybe that is why Michael is never touched by the Sleepers."

"Well," I exhaled. "At least that mystery is solved."

"This is not a joke, Alex," Beck scolded. "This is serious. We don't know how it will react in you. This could be the end for you."

"But it won't be for Jessie. I'll get her. This is our only chance. Besides...it'll be fine. I feel it. I'm getting it from Michael." I repeated the name with a confident smile. "Michael. The dude is amazing. So how can something bad come from someone so good?"

I saw it in Beck's face. His eyes glossed over slightly. His jaw twitched. My big friend was overly emotional, and it moved me. He wasn't convinced by what I said, but he knew he didn't have a choice.

My mind was made up.

In a few short hours, I was going to be a Sleeper.

32
MERA STEVENS

Something was up. I felt it. I was hoping when I saw Beck and Alex walking toward the house in the still dark early morning hours that they didn't have bad news about Jessie.

They had been gone a good while.

I had been crying so much that I was unable to sleep; no amount of drinking was even soothing the pain I felt over Jessie. What must have been going through her mind broke my heart. Was she hurt? I prayed she wasn't. I know she was cold. All she had on was that flowery dress.

Watching through the window, I flung open the door as soon as I saw Beck and Alex step to the porch. I rushed to Beck, throwing my arms around him.

"I was worried," I said. "You were gone a long time."

"We had to get things ready. We're going in to the town in a few hours. I needed to set up a watch, cover the wall...Just a lot of details."

"I'm scared, Beck."

"I know you are. Just remember, okay? Remember that woman I met a year and a half ago. Remember her and how determined and strong she was. I need you to be that woman, right now."

I nodded.

"And...I'm going to let you two talk alone."

That was odd. It was my confirmation that something, indeed, was going on.

Once Beck stepped inside the house, Alex sighed heavily.

"What's going on?" I asked him.

"I just need you to hear it from me. I'm going in with Michael tomorrow to get Jessie."

Two emotions hit me at that second. Fear, because I knew Michael was immune from a Sleeper attack and Alex wasn't. And relief, because I believed with all of my heart if anyone could get my daughter, Alex could.

"Alex, I can't expect you to put your life on the line for Jessie."

"She's a part of my life, Mera." He scratched his head as if messing up his dark hair would somehow give him the right words. "When I met you, you were looking for her. We found her. I got this connection with her because I believed I could help her. I've watch her progress so much this past year. I can't sit by and put it in anyone's hands. I have to go, because I have to know it will be done right."

As he always did, Alex drummed up feelings in me, and that moment was no different. I threw my arms around him and held him.

"Forgive me for not trying to talk you out of this. Please forgive me," I whispered in his ear. "I know you'll do it. I honestly believe with all of my heart that you'll do it."

Alex pulled back from the embrace, his face close to mine. He placed his hand on my cheek and locked his eyes into mine, speaking with strong conviction. "I will get her back to you. I will. I promise you, if it's the last thing I do..." his voice cracked. "I'll bring her home."

33
ALEX SANS

I didn't want to go to sleep. I was scared to. Afraid that the Sleeper infection would kick in while I slept, just like it had to most of the world. Because of that I stayed awake. I spoke to Danny about staying behind during the rescue, just in case. I stopped in and saw every single one of the kids. Phoenix and Keller were last.

I prayed I could watch them grow up. While not related by blood, they acted like twins. Holding hands while the slept. Keller was precious to me; I couldn't have loved him more if he were my own flesh and blood. Phoenix was special too, but I'd spent that year with Keller.

It had crossed my mind, with a lot of guilt, that Keller was the cause of everything that was happening. After all, he was communicating with me, Mera and Jessie. Phoenix told Jessie that Keller called the Sleepers. After some thought, I realized that was wrong. If Keller was the cause, then why now? Why a year later?

No, it was something else. Something else summoning the Sleepers.

Or...some*one* else.

I said my goodnights and passed around kisses, fully intending to see them all in the morning before I left. That was before I took my walk.

Trying to stay awake, even with my adrenaline pumping, I walked out to check on things. We had guards on the back wall, on the gate, and I cut through the Reflection Area and headed toward the woods.

I knew Stan was up on the hill with another man, watching the Sleepers in case they moved. I signaled with a whistle then whispered it was me as I made my approach.

"What the hell, Alex?" Stan asked. "It's four in the morning."

"I know. I just wanted to check on things."

"They haven't moved our way, just moving about the town. But it's hard to see."

Stan was right. It just looked black out there. Moving shadows lit only a little by the moon.

Even though it was four in the morning, to me it felt like night. And the quiet of the darkness magnified sounds, making them clear and more audible. The moans and groans of the Sleepers, like always, meshed together as a single low hum noise. It carried to us and so did something else. A sound that flowed over the noise of the Sleepers, shot through my being, and broke my heart.

Sobbing.

Jessie.

I spun to Stan. "Do you hear that? Do you hear the crying?"

"Yeah, it's been going on for a little bit."

Enraged, I grabbed him and shook him. "Why didn't you call? Why didn't you tell me?"

"Alex, I...I thought we were just watching that we weren't—"

"Give me your weapons."

"What?"

Before he could say anything else, I took the rifle from his hand and grabbed his side arm. "Ammo."

"I need—"

"Ammo!" I growled.

Nervously, Stan handed me two clips. "Tell Beck I left. I had to."

"Alex, where are you going?"

"I'm following the sound."

"It's dangerous."

"I don't care."

And with that, I took the first jump down the grade and headed toward the town of Sleepers.

Keep making noise, Jessie. Keep crying, I beckoned in my mind as I ran as fast as I could. *I'm coming.*

34
MERA STEVENS

There was absolutely no air in my lungs when I sprang to a full sitting position in that reclining chair. I heaved in, fully convinced I wasn't going to be able to breathe. Because my esophagus closed and tightened, it was hard to inhale. I did, finally. I wasn't dreaming; by the time on the wall clock, I hadn't been asleep long. I'd merely dozed off in the chair.

As the grogginess left me, everything else started to register.

The noise outside the house. Men's voices. Bonnie was saying something.

The door opened and she walked in saying, "No, Beck, I'll ask her myself."

I stood from the chair and didn't even utter a greeting.

"Mera, what is going on? Please. Please tell me."

It wasn't that I didn't want to, I just didn't know how. In addition, it didn't even dawn on me that she didn't know.

Beck walked in and my eyes shifted to him then back to Bonnie.

She said, "Men are out there moving and armed. The bus is behind your house. Where is Jessie?"

"They took her," I squeaked out painfully.

"Who?" Bonnie asked.

"The Sleepers. She was in the Reflection Area and they got her. They took her."

Bonnie didn't react as I expected. A tough woman, the 'Cowgirl' as Alex called her, folded. Her hand went to her mouth and she dropped right there to her knees on the floor, immediately sobbing.

"Oh my God, not Jessie. Not my Jessie!"

I walked over to her and laid my hand on her back.

"Mera, tell me we're getting her. She's all I look forward to in this world." Bonnie gazed up at me.

"They're going in shortly."

Beck corrected, "Actually, now."

"What?" I asked in surprise.

"Michael is leaving to go in. Alex…Alex already left."

I gasped. "Why? Why early?"

Beck pursed his lips, swallowed, and his eyes glossed over. "He heard Jessie crying."

Instinctively, with pain, I closed my eyes. "I need to see Michael before he goes. I want to get the boys. They need to see him before he leaves just in case." I turned toward the hall.

"They aren't there," Danny said, entering the room.

"Where are they?" I asked.

Danny pointed backwards. "On the bus. Waiting."

"Did you put them there?"

Danny shook his head. "They went on their own. I asked them why and Phoenix said 'leaving soon.'"

Another spin of my body and I faced Beck. "Should we leave them there?"

"As a matter of fact, yes. Leave them," Beck said. "Danny, I want you to throw supplies in that bus as if we are leaving, okay? Make sure we have first aid, my field bag. Be ready. Be prepared, and be near that door. Get the other kids; have them near the bus at all times. Bonnie, too."

Bonnie looked at Beck. "We're evacuating Grace?"

"Yes. Just as a precaution, we should prep the two trailers we have and any and all vehicles. Get everyone ready to go."

Bonnie slowly stood. "Beck, we're surrounded by a huge wall. How many will make it over, really?"

"They don't need to make it over. They could storm the gate."

She gasped. "Are there that many out there?"

Beck said nothing; he just turned and walked out, telling Danny to 'get on it.'

"Mera?" Bonnie questioned. "Are there that many?"

"More than I would ever believe."

In a state of shock, Bonnie backed up. "I'll go gather everyone and pack some things."

After I said what needed to be said to Michael, I, too, would go pack. Get things ready. Not because of all the Sleepers, not because Beck said so, but because two very special and gifted babies were waiting to leave. If they were on that bus of their own accord, then something was going to happen. Something big.

35
ALEX SANS

The second the infection entered me I knew there was no turning back. No turning *it* back. I felt it go in. There didn't even appear to be much in the syringe, yet it felt like a never ending deliverance. It wasn't like getting a tetanus shot; there was no burning, no immediate painful cramping knot in the muscle. It was cold. Ice cold. I felt it move through every millimeter of my body; I even felt it hit my heart.

I knew I was turning. Nothing about my manner of thinking was different; my senses were the same, and I felt emotion, sadness, not rage. I didn't feel like ripping someone's throat out. I was normal except for my blood felt as if it was running cold.

The more my adrenaline pumped, the more I felt my blood move through my entire circulatory system.

My heart failed to beat properly. I noticed that right away when I ran into town. That was only three hours post injection. According to Levi, the pheromones hadn't kicked in, but it was a chance I had to take.

Jessie was crying. No...she was *sobbing*. Her high-pitched sounds of sadness conveyed no less than if she was screaming, 'Help me!'

I didn't get winded. I wondered if it was my imagination, but I ran without tiring. My heart felt as if it wanted to beat faster. I could hear Jessie all the way there, until I got to town.

Then it stopped. It was my only trail to Jessie, and without it, especially in the dark, I couldn't track her. I hoped and prayed she'd only cried herself to sleep and nothing worse had happened.

I positioned myself at a tiny store just on the outskirts of town, Windmans Stop-n-Go. The store windows had been busted out, the shelves were empty, and cans spread across the lot.

The entire place had been looted, and I guessed it was the Sleepers. They worked on instinct to eat, and I heard that instinct.

Slurping, sloshing.

As the light of dawn crept upon the town and I peeked from the confines and protection of Windmans and watched the Sleepers dine on deer and a horse, as well. The horse was still partially alive as they pulled at his flesh. He wouldn't be for long.

The deer…well, there was very little left of it. The Sleepers were covered in animal blood, guts dripping from their mouths and across their fingertips. I was engrossed in watching when a hand to my shoulder nearly caused me to jump from my skin.

"What the hell, Alex?" Michael whispered. "What were you thinking?"

"I heard her crying, Mike. I had to come."

"And you made it no further than if you'd waited." He shoved a headset radio to me. "Put the earpiece in your ear so they don't hear. Keep the microphone close to your mouth."

I adjusted the headset on me.

Michael hitched his backpack higher on his shoulder. "I have to go to the center of town. I'll radio you if I see her. I'm channel seven. Beck is monitoring. After I plant these devices, we'll go to the rooftop to look. Stay clear of them. They'll tear you apart."

"No, they won't."

Michael just looked at me. "Why would you say that?"

He didn't know. "I'm infected."

"With?"

"The Sleeper virus."

Michael's eyes widened. "Were you bitten? You need to run back and—"

"No, Padre. I was infected on purpose. Infected with a future strain of the virus in hopes that it wouldn't turn me into a monster. I'm six hours post injection now. I should be able to walk among them like you."

"Alex Sans," Michael said sadly, "I thought you were a smart man."

"I am. That's why I thought of this to help you."

"Where did they get the future strain? Did Levi bring it?"

"No. You did."

Michael blinked in shock.

"Hate to break it to you, Padre. You aren't the savior. Your blood carries the evolved strain of the virus from the future. Anything you care to own up to?"

Michael shook his head. "I don't believe that. I grew up here. You know that. I was a doorstep baby."

"Well, we know where you came from, or, rather, when."

"We'll discuss this later," Michael said. "Right now we need to find Jessie, set these explosives, get out, and get you help. Understand?"

I nodded. "Let's go."

Michael didn't move.

"What are you doing?" I asked.

"Give me a second. I'm praying." Michael held up a finger. "We're gonna need all the help we can get."

"Amen to that, Padre. Amen to that."

Michael walked out into the throngs of Sleepers, and they parted like the Red Sea—no pun intended—toward his holy man status. They watched him walk; it was freakish. I was actually scared for Michael. A part of me hoped at the end of the parting that Jessie would be standing there.

She wasn't.

Michael walked through them, slowly, staring ahead. He disappeared into the first building, giving me instructions in my ear to stay put, not to test the serum, just in case. I guess he wanted to plant the explosives in case I stepped onto the street and was immediately attacked.

Explosive one set at the library. Ten minutes later, explosive two was set.

I was getting antsy; I started not to feel well. I knew I was sweating, and it wasn't hot. Something was going on with me.

I knew where the third explosive was going to be set. When they went off, the entire town would blow and with it, the Sleepers.

"Wait for me, Alex. I just set the final one. On my way back."

It was defeating my whole purpose just to stand there. I had infected myself on purpose purely to get Jessie, I had gone into the town, and I was doing nothing but monitoring his progress.

It was time. Besides, when I looked out, the Sleepers weren't parting. Why weren't they parting if Michael was walking back down the street?

Screw it.

I stepped forward, away from the protection of Windmans, and into the street where the throngs of Sleepers meandered. They didn't move. It was frightening, because I wasn't sure whether I'd be noticed and attacked or if I blended in. My hand was on my pistol, just in case. Not that a pistol would do much. I was severely outnumbered.

Staying close to the buildings in case I had to dart inside, I inched down the street through the Sleepers. They stunk horribly. They smelled sour, rotting from the food they digested. Shit, piss, every smell you could imagine permeated the street. It took everything I had not to vomit.

"Alex, where are you?" Michael said in my radio. "I'm cornered. They're staring at me."

I hated to speak. I was really close to them. A male Sleeper brushed by me, his body bumping into mine. Right now I was silent, but if I made a noise...

"Alex."

"Walking down the main street among them," I whispered.

A Sleeper stopped. He turned and looked at me.

Fuck.

I looked beyond him, hoping not to make eye contact, keeping him in my peripheral vision. It worked. He moved over, and when he did, my heart sunk. It would have pounded faster had it not been inhibited. But there she was.

Fifteen feet away from me. *Fifteen feet.* Jessie's head hung low, hair flung over her face, arms dangled at her side and she just stood there. He face was scratched and bloody and her thin, white, flowered summer dress was in shreds across her half-nude body. Sleepers bumped into her, moving her around, and she didn't respond. She was a ping-pong ball. But at that second, she was something else.

A Sleeper. Not just a Jessie Sleeper of a little girl trapped in an adult body, but she had turned. At least I thought she had. I wanted to cry; it broke my heart. How did that happen? How? Scientifically was that even possible? Sleepers didn't hurt Sleepers.

Or did they?

In my ear, via the radio, an answer was given. Michael called out my name; it was a painful call, followed by, "They got me."

What? What? *No!*

I was standing in the middle of them, surrounded by thousands on every side. Where was Michael?

Crack. Hiss. *The radio.*

"Alex, what's going on?" Beck asked.

I was staring at Jessie, my heart broken. How could I tell Beck? How could I tell Mera I failed? That I'd failed them, failed Jessie.

I backed up, hitting against a building.

"Alex, we can set the explosives off from this end. You need to hurry and go."

I heaved out a breath. I was still safe, still not noticed. I lowered the radio and dropped it to the step of the store before me. I wasn't going anywhere. Michael was gone or trapped, Jessie had turned. I would turn as well.

No, I was at the finish line. I'd stay with Jessie. Whether I stayed with my conscience intact or became one of them, I'd stay with her. Overwrought with emotion, I internally folded, and, hands to my face, still holding my pistol, I slid down against the building.

Shoulders bouncing, knees brought up, everything rained from inside of me. There I was, the broken, crying man in the middle of the street and not a Sleeper took notice. No one noticed. Except...

"Alex!"

Jessie.

I heard her cry out my name with relief and enthusiasm, screaming it from the top of her lungs as if my name were her saving grace.

"Alex!"

I jumped to my feet and every ounce of breath escaped me. She hadn't turned. Jessie was just in a state of survival-shock. Seeing me had snapped her out of it.

"Alex! Alex!" Her frail arms extended, she pushed through the Sleepers to reach me, calling my name over and over.

"Jessie. Oh, God, Jessie." I pushed through as well. "I'm here. I'm here."

She seemed a mile away when she was only a few feet. Against the masses of Sleepers I reached between their bodies. "I'm here, Jessie!" I shouted. "I'm here, baby." Finally, fingers touched hers. I saw the look in her eyes. She knew it. I had her. I gripped on to her wrist, yanked her to me, and into my arms.

Jessie lunged at me with gratefulness, her arms clinging as tight to my neck as my arms held to her body. "Alex, help me. Mommy."

"I'll take you to Mommy, baby. I have you."

She cried in my ear, and her body shook. "Thank you, Alex. Safe now?"

"Safe now," I sighed. "Safe now."

With Jessie in my arms, I turned. My plan was simple: I had her; we'd go.

But at that second, we were discovered. I had stepped from the norm of the Sleepers' behaviors. My pheromones didn't give me away; my reactions did.

They were all around us, staring at me with Jessie in my grip.

"Alex, I'm scared."

"Don't be. I'm getting you out of here."

I meant it. I really meant it. All I had to do was push through. Most of the Sleepers were behind us. Push through. Clear a path. Run.

"Hold tight," I told her.

Still holding my pistol, I raised my hand, extended the gun outward and from left to right I shot at the Sleepers, unloading the entire clip. Even if they weren't hit by a deadly shot, they fell.

Jessie screamed; I cleared a path.

The first Sleeper lunged at me and I swung out my pistol, hitting him. Dropping the gun, I swept Jessie into my arms and as I did I felt the first blow.

A painful blow to my lower back. Then another, and another. It arched my spine and I stumbled. I held firm to Jessie.

Hands reached for me. I felt them grab for my back, my shirt, my skin.

I would not go down. I wouldn't.

I had Jessie. She was safe and I would, at all costs, get her out of there.

I just had to make that distance.

With Jessie in my arms, and all my intestinal fortitude, I forged ahead and broke free. I took off running. I knew they were in pursuit. I sensed and smelled them.

I didn't get winded on my way to town, and I prayed the same would hold true as I ran for our lives. Trust me, I ran. Focused on the wooded area ahead, I asked Jessie, "Do you see them?"

"They're coming."

"How close?"

"You're winning the race."

I laughed. She was right. As long as I had her, as long as she was in my arms and I was ahead of them, I was winning.

I was faster, smarter, and stronger. Most of all, I made a promise to bring Jessie home, and damn it, I would.

36
MERA STEVENS

In a matter of minutes, Grace erupted into pandemonium. People ran scared into the streets, and security men rushed them into trucks. Javier, Noah, and Levi ran through my house with boxes.

They thought Michael was dead. That's what Beck said. Then Michael radioed. The Sleepers left. They abandoned the attack on him and moved another direction.

"I know you're injured; can you make it to the highway? I have a truck going west," Beck said as he moved about. "All right, do that."

Beck reached out and grabbed one of the men. "Why are people still on the streets?"

"Some won't go," the guard said. "They won't get in the trucks."

"Then leave them. But tell them we're blowing this place."

"Yes, sir."

"What?" I asked. "You can't blow up Grace."

"Mera, listen to me. They're coming here. They're coming full force and these walls won't hold them. We have to go." He lifted a finger and listened to his radio. "Then retreat. Get off the wall. Retreat." He returned to me. "It's like a tidal wave. That's what I was told."

"I'm not going."

"Beck," Danny called, "all ready. Bus is loaded. Gas cans on top."

"Everyone in there?" Beck asked.

"Except my mom."

"Go," Beck pointed.

Danny nodded and raced out.

"Let's go, Mera." Beck grabbed on to me.

"No. Jessie."

"Mera, *now*," he snapped. "You hear me? Get your ass on that bus."

"No."

He grimaced then grabbed hold of me. Arm around my waist, he lifted me off my feet, carrying me out to the back door.

My hands reached for anything to stop him, but he was bigger and stronger.

I screamed, *No!*, over and over. But he didn't care, he didn't stop. When we got to the bus, he put me on the step, and I turned around. "Beck."

"Mera, I'm sorry, sweetie. It's over."

"Jessie...Alex."

He shook his head. "I'm sorry. He hasn't answered."

I felt my entire body tense up. Beck stepped up, nodded at Bonnie, and the doors to the bus closed. Oh my God, we were leaving.

My baby. My Jessie.

With my whole heart and soul, I cried out. I wailed, long, and from my gut as Beck lifted me further into the bus.

"Hit it," he told Bonnie.

The bus didn't just start to move, it jolted fast and sped forward. My body lurched and Beck grabbed me. I was hysterical and not registering anything at that second.

Danny asked Beck with such a sad voice, "What about the others?"

"Danny, my focus is you guys and getting you to safety."

I saw Danny plop down in the seat. I sat down next to Phoenix and Keller. My head went forward, hands gripping the metal bar of the bus seat in front of me.

"Take the back gate," Beck instructed. "Hit the field and then right before the corn, you'll see the road. Veer right for that."

"Got it," Bonnie said.

"Beck," Javier called from the back of the bus, "any word? What's the last you heard?"

"They moved like a wall," Beck replied. "Something was driving them."

Phoenix, sitting next to me, whispered, "Keller called them. Keller said, 'come.'"

I heard it; I don't think anyone else did.

"No," I told him. "No, Phoenix."

I raised my eyes to see Keller by the window. His hands pressed against the glass and his body faced it. "Mama," Keller said, "Alex."

Just as I heard him say that, Bonnie cried out, "Oh, dear God, hold on."

The bus jerked hard to the left and she gunned it.

"What are you doing?" Beck asked, charging to the front of the bus.

"Alex!" she screamed. "Alex!"

I glanced at the window, moved Keller over, and looked out. Alex was indeed running through the high grass of the field and in his arms, he carried my daughter.

The bus made a full turn, taking Alex from my view and I stood, so did Danny, to look out the windshield.

I screamed in excitement while Bonnie barreled the bus his way, and then I saw why. A virtual *wall* of Sleepers was running right behind them.

"How close can you get?" Beck asked.

"As close as I can," Bonnie said. "Grab them, and make it fast."

She was moving fast; thank God, she could drive that bus like no other. Alex saw us. Bonnie slowed down the bus, turning it as she did. She whipped open the door.

"Hurry!" Beck was off that bus, and before my son could go, I jumped out too.

I ran out after Beck, ignoring the call of my name, and charged to Alex and my daughter.

The Sleepers were close—we didn't have much time at all.

Beck arrived at Alex first, grabbing Jessie from his hold to free him so he would be able to run. The moment Beck took Jessie and raced back toward the bus, I saw Alex stumble.

"Mera! Come on!" Beck yelled.

I kept running to Alex. No way was I leaving him. Not when he had done that. Not when he had brought back my daughter.

I reached him and grabbed his arm. "Come on, Alex!"

"Go," he said weakly.

"No. I can't leave you here. Let's go." I grabbed his arm. "I'll help you."

Alex got back on his feet. I glanced back one more time. The Sleepers were close, too close. It was a race against time. Alex and I moved together toward the bus. I reached out, placing my hand on his back for support.

It was wet, thick, like mush. My hand virtually sank into his frame and then my heart sank into my stomach.

I couldn't look. I didn't have time to look. No... I didn't *want* to look. We just needed to make it to the bus.

At the door, Beck jumped down and grabbed Alex.

"Easy, he's hurt," I said. When my foot hit the first step of the bus, Bonnie took off.

It was a good thing she'd closed that bus door or I'd be out, gone, because I flew back against the door.

The bus erupted into screams. Those on the bus, the kids especially, yelled for Bonnie to hurry.

Then...*Slam. Slam. Slam.* The bus jolted with repeated impacts from the Sleepers' bodies hitting the outside.

"Keep going!" Beck ordered. "Danny, arm up!" He reached over and extended the rifle through an open window. "Hold your ears!"

He started firing. Danny started firing. I'm not sure if we hit any of them. But eventually we moved ahead and left them behind.

They chased us for a while. However, after a distance, we lost them.

When the excitement and rush of the moment was over and we hit the overgrown roadway, it was time to take it all in.

"Jessie?" I called.

"Mommy!" She was in the back of the bus with Javier. "Mommy! Alex!"

"She's fine," Javier said. "I'll examine her more when we can stop."

Then I looked down. Alex sat on the aisle between the seats. I crouched down. "Alex, thank you so much."

He lifted his head. His eyes were dark and filled with a pain.

"Alex," Beck softy called him, "what did you do to yourself?"

Alex chuckled once; it was more strained than real. "I think I lost a kidney."

"Let me look." Beck tried to conceal the look on his face when he checked Alex's injuries, but he couldn't. I couldn't, either. I wanted to cry. Alex was ripped apart. His entire back had been torn to shreds. His joke about losing a kidney wasn't funny, because I could see them. I could see many of his organs.

Beck's voice cracked. "Mera, get my field dressings."

"Big guy," Alex said, "I think you're gonna need more than field dressings this time."

"Yeah, well, that's all we have. We'll make do."

I handed Beck his pack. Alex had lost a lot of blood. I could see that. So much that I don't think he had any blood left to bleed.

How was he even standing? How had he kept going? I don't know. He lifted his head as Beck attempted to do something with the wounds. His eyes met mine and that's when I knew. His eyes. They were dark. So dark, they absorbed all his pupils.

I knew at that instant why he had made it. Alex, just like my daughter, was a Sleeper.

A little town called Brady sat in the center of Texas. It was the closest town we knew of and we hoped that Sleepers hadn't taken it over. We didn't run into a single Sleeper once we left them behind, but that was no guarantee we wouldn't run into more.

Brady, pre-Event, had a population of, I guessed, about five thousand. The Heart of Texas Memorial Hospital was smaller than my local Walmart. It sat in the center of the beaten town. It worked to our advantage that Brady was small. Most of the parents had run to the hospital on foot instead of driving. The traffic congestion was minimal.

I hated that Alex had to be treated in a raw, dirty environment, but it was better than nothing and better than any field dressings Beck could apply. The wounds were so bad, Beck didn't know where to start.

We arrived at Brady, and parked the bus next to the hospital.

We'd packed thirty people on that bus. Only half of the residents of Grace had made it out, Beck estimated. A tractor-trailer with more people arrived in Brady shortly behind us.

Beck made radio contact. They still hadn't found Michael, but he was calling out. At least he was alive.

We all were a mess.

Javier, with Noah's assistance, went to work on Alex. Alex didn't want to sleep. He was afraid to close his eyes. Levi assured him he wouldn't be a monster, and to rest. He claimed he felt nothing. Barely any pain, only pulling.

Sleepers lost the ability to feel pain.

That's why Jessie didn't complain about her abrasions or bruises. I cried when Levi told me that she had been beaten badly. She'd lost hair, one of her ears was half gone, and worst of all, he believed my daughter may have been raped.

Oh my God. She couldn't even comprehend what they were doing to her. It hurt to think of all that she'd endured. Such an innocent, and her innocence was brutalized in an animalistic way.

She curled into a fetal position against Danny, finding security with him while we waited for news of Alex.

Six hours later, Javier finally emerged.

He shook his head. "I don't know how he's still alive."

Beck was standing with me. He exhaled loudly, running his hand down his face. "I know it's bad."

"Bad?" Javier laughed once sarcastically. "His internal organs are shot. Shot, Beck. Punctured lung, one kidney left. They went through his back and tore him apart from behind. I counted five bite marks where chunks were taken from him. It is almost inhumane to let him suffer. I would deliver a dose of morphine to him and end it all if he wasn't telling me he felt nothing." He tossed up his hands. "I don't know what to do. Alex is dying. His body isn't processing fluids. He's drowning from the inside. But he's still fighting. I did the best I could to get everything in place and repaired but…it's a matter of time. Not much at that. I'm sorry."

I wept, grabbing on to Beck.

"Is there any way…" Beck said, "…any way that we can keep him stabilized for two days?"

Javier gasped. "I don't know if I can keep him stabilized through the night. Why two days?"

"That's how long it's gonna take," Beck said. "To take him home. Back to his home."

"We can try. Be gentle when we move him. Take what we can. Stop if we need to. But I'm gonna be honest, Beck, if he does stay alive, Alex is the one doing it."

Alex.

How much trouble I gave him. How much I fought with him. And for every mean thing I'd said, every time we'd fought, I wanted to cry.

He was sleeping for a while after surgery. I spent time with Jessie, getting her clean. Bonnie wanted to spend time with her as well. I couldn't deny her. I was so grateful my daughter was with me. She was alive, and it was all due to Alex.

About two in the morning, I decided to go see him. As I left, I heard Keller.

"Mama. Alex. Touch."

I knew what he was conveying. He wanted to visit Alex. Touch him. And more than anything, I believed Alex wanted to see Keller.

With the child in my arms, I went to where Alex rested.

A generator from a local hardware store, with our gasoline, powered the respirator. Alex was awake.

"Hey," I whispered as I approached his bed. "Look who wanted to see you."

"See me?" Alex smiled. "Well, I guess, in his own way, he does."

"How are you?"

"I've been better."

My lips felt huge. They puckered, and I fought the tears.

"Please don't cry, Mera."

I couldn't help it. I looked down to Alex. He was so pale, his arms were starting to swell, stretching those tattoos he was so proud of. I grabbed his hand. "Thank you. Thank you so much."

"Even though part of this was for you, this was for Jessie. You know I love her, right?"

"She loves you."

"Mera, when she called my name," Alex paused to close his eyes, "that moment... that moment hearing her call my name...like I was the one person she needed to see most, it was worth it. No one has ever called me or looked at me like she did. It was worth it."

My vision blurred from the tears that welled in my eyes.

"Tell her I love her. Tell Danny I love him. Okay?"

I shook my head. "You tell them yourself. Besides, you have lots of time to tell them."

"Who are you kidding? I know." He squeezed my hand. "You know, you and I, we fought. But you've been my best friend."

"You've been mine." A sob bigger than I was escaped me, and I bent down, Keller in my arms, and placed my face against his. "I love you, Alex Sans. Know that. I love you for who you are and everything you have done for me."

"I know that. I love you, too. We've had a journey."

"And it's not over."

Alex chuckled. "Yeah, it is."

"Not yet," I said. You have to hold on, Alex. You can beat this. If anyone can, you can. Please hold on."

"I'll try."

"You think I was a mess when I lost Beck? Ha! I'm not gonna be the same if you leave me. You drive me. So please keep driving me."

Weakly, Alex said again, "I'll try." He closed his eyes. I listened for the sound of his heart as it beat through the monitor.

When I prepared to leave, Keller reached out his tiny hand and I leaned him forward. Without my guidance, his hand laid upon Alex's chest.

Alex didn't open his eyes, but he lifted his hand and laid it on Keller's. "I know, buddy, I know. I love you too."

Alex went to sleep.

Oddly, I didn't hear what Keller conveyed, but Alex did. I suppose, at that moment, that was all that mattered.

37
ALEX SANS

I supposed people facing their death comes to the revelation in one way or another that, this is it. *This is the end of my life.* I knew mine was close, for a couple of reasons. I had a euphoric sense about me. No pain, no struggle to breathe. Levi said it was the Sleeper virus that was causing it. Or it was my sheer will to beat it.

My hands swelled and I couldn't even bend my fingers. I didn't recognize my own arm. This was me, positioned on my side, slanted, a tube in my arm.

A part of me wanted to call Beck, to have him put a bullet in me. I would slow them down. Then another part of me wanted to fight. People live with one kidney, a partial liver, and John Wayne, hell, he lived with one lung. Who was I kidding, though? They just tucked what they could back inside, sewed what was ripped, and hoped for the best.

There was no positive ending in all this, not on my end. I was virtually a Heston movie. Do something good, but it comes with a price.

Death.

Mera never left my side. She sat in a chair by me, staring. Every time I dozed off, I'd wake and she'd jolt and ask me if I needed anything. This was a woman who wouldn't fry me an egg in Grace and now she was offering a bottle to help me piss. I guess she forgot my body wasn't processing fluids.

That was another sign that I was a goner. Mera was being nice to me.

During the course of the night, a lot of people stopped in to see me. Jessie came in. It was hard to see her, but I was glad she was alive. She didn't seem to comprehend my condition and I was happy about that.

The hardest person to face was Beck.

Yeah, he was my friend, we went through a lot, and I loved him, but to see him like that killed me. A big man, strong and always in control, was broken. He couldn't look at me without his eyes filling up.

"I want to say it's going to be okay," Beck whispered. "I want to tell you, that you're gonna be just fine."

"I know better."

"This is just killing me." Beck closed his eyes. "It's breaking me up."

More than Beck realized, I knew how he felt. I knew what I felt like when he left us. At that moment, I was so glad I'd broken the rules and changed things. I couldn't imagine what would happen to Mera and the kids without one of us.

"I need you to do me a favor, Alex. I need you to hold on. With everything you have, hold on."

"It may be out of my control."

He shook his head. "No. I don't believe that. Not for one second. I believe, right now, you have the ability to hang in there. You, of all people, after all you've done for us, you don't deserve to leave us in a dirty small-town hospital."

"You have a better place in mind?"

"Yeah...yeah, I do. If God's gonna take you home, then I'd rather it be from *your* home."

"The Haven?"

Beck produced a sad smile and nodded.

Home.

They wanted to take me home. I would do my best; it was a goal to hang on to, and I'd try with everything I had to reach that goal.

But, if by some chance I didn't...I was okay with it.

I was okay with everything.

Even dying.

38
MERA STEVENS

Beck worked the whole night. He and Danny siphoned all the gasoline they could while intermittently trying to reach Michael.

Just before dawn, he made radio contact with Michael. A trailer from Grace had found him. Michael was a part of our group, not having him with us was hard, and that had something to do with Beck's insistence to speak to him. However, when I heard Beck, I knew why he wanted Michael.

"Alex is bad, Mike," Beck said with a shaking voice. "He is so…bad. We can't lose him. We can't, but I know it's gonna take a miracle." He paused and sniffed. "So if anything is left, any connection, any pull, please use it. We need a miracle."

"I'm praying, Beck. I am praying with everything I am."

"Thanks," Beck crackled out and closed his eyes. He brought the radio to his forehead. He gripped it so tightly I thought he was going to crush it. His arms tensed and he leaned forward to the side of the bus and slammed his fist hard into the side, causing a loud echoing bang that carried out across the street.

"Beck," I whispered and reached for him.

Shunning me, he just shook his head, turned, sniffed hard, and walked away without letting me see his face.

His physical actions epitomized every emotion we were all feeling. He stayed focused and about two hours later he found me and called me to the bus.

"Are they getting him ready?" Beck asked.

"Yeah, they are."

"I wanna get on the road. But I wanted to show you what I did."

First, he showed me the small generator strapped tightly to the roof of the bus, the power cord trailing through the last window. We stepped inside and Beck walked me to the back. He had laid a board across the two back seats, connecting them, and had placed a cot mattress on top. For privacy, he'd hung a curtain.

"We can hook his support system up without the generator getting fumes in the bus."

"This is good, thank you."

"It's fucked up," he said. "But it's the best I can do for him. It's a long trip." He exhaled. "I feel bad. I haven't even talked to Jessie."

"She's not talking much." I lowered my head. "Beck...she isn't saying what happened. I'm sick about it. Levi said..."

"I know what he said." Beck held up his hand and his faced tensed up in pain. "She'll get through it."

"How? How is she to understand what happened? How do we make her trust people again? How does she grow up knowing not everyone wants to take care of her? And Beck, she may mentally be a baby, but physically she's a woman. What if... what if the Sleepers did...you know, and she got pregnant?"

"Mera, then we'll deal with it. We'll face it together." He stepped to me, taking me in his arms. "One day. One step at a time."

"Beck!" Danny hurriedly called his name. "Sleepers!"

I backed away and Beck moved forward to the front of the bus and to Danny.

"Where?" Beck asked.

"Coming down the road. Just spotted them. I counted thirty. We can take them."

Beck shook his head. "No, let's get everyone on the bus and head out. You and I will keep a watch until this bus starts to roll." He looked back at me. "Get the kids, the babies, and Alex."

I agreed and left the bus. Bonnie had already heard about the Sleepers and was escorting the children to the door.

"Jessie has the boys," Bonnie said. "They're right inside the hospital entrance."

"I'm headed that way," I said. "I'll tell them to get on the bus."

We were parked right in front of the hospital, so it was only a few steps. I was taken aback when I saw them, all three of them. Jessie stood in the middle, holding both boys' hands, and when I stepped inside, they all faced me and tilted their heads the same way, the same speed, at the same time.

"We need to get on the bus now," I said.

"Sleepers," Jessie said.

"Sleepers, yes. Go to the bus now."

"We saw Alex."

"Good. Get on the bus." I waited until I saw them pass through the doors and Bonnie took over. Just as I turned to head toward Alex's room, Javier and Levi rolled a cot with Alex down the hall.

I hadn't seen him in an hour, and I swore he looked worse.

"Hey..." Alex called out sluggishly. "I'm ready to roll. I am rolling."

"Sick as you are, you're still making jokes." I walked alongside as they moved him. "Beck has a nice area set up for you on the bus."

"Are you gonna stay by me?"

"I'm not leaving your side."

"Good."

They moved him beyond me and to the bus. I was so glad they did so quickly, because not long after they placed him on the makeshift bed, I heard Beck shout.

"Danny, I need a headcount on the bus. Now!"

Within seconds, my son was on the bus. Even through the chaos of getting situated, he held out his hand, looking. "Where's Levi?"

I pointed behind me. Levi couldn't be seen behind the curtain.

"Beck!" Danny shouted out of the bus. "All accounted for." He walked on the bus. "I need everyone seated."

The Sleepers had to be close. I looked out the emergency exit and could see the group moving up the road toward us. What the hell? How did they get there?

I heard Beck talking to Bonnie.

"We're good. Drive," he said, his voice carrying back to me. I kept my eyes on the Sleepers. The bus door squeaked as it closed, and we immediately started to drive.

Javier exhaled so hard and long that I felt his breath hit my cheek. "I'm gonna sit down," he said. "He's all hooked up."

Levi flipped the switch on the portable respirator and monitor then checked the IV and scooted by me.

I closed the curtain and sat on the seat in front of Alex, facing him. "That was a rush. We're on our way now."

"I can tell." Alex's eyes were partially open; his head moved side to side with the motion of the bus. "Sleepers."

"Yeah, they're everywhere."

"No."

"No?"

"Got..." He reached and laid his hand on my wrist. He tried to grip it but couldn't. "...to get east. He can't call them once we cross the Great Divide." His hand slid from mine. "He can't call them anymore."

"Who?" I asked. "Who is calling the Sleepers?"

His monitor beeped steadily and Alex closed his eyes. He had passed out.

39
SONNY

We had been at our final destination for two days. We made great time, even though we stopped when we could and grabbed supplies. We didn't see a single Sleeper... alive, that is. When The Event happened, everyone ran for help for the children. After that, no one really left or went anywhere. They stayed put and turned. That made traveling easier with fewer cars on the roads.

I found what we were looking for. I wondered if someone else had taken haven where we stayed, but I knew it wasn't the case when we pulled up. The grass was so high around Indian River Correction that it buried the fence that ran the perimeter.

The positive thing was that corn grew in the field next to the facility. It looked like wheat did, as well. That was hopeful.

There were forty-seven Sleepers locked in on the property, most outside, some inside, all of them dead. Withered away by starvation and malnutrition was my guess. There really wasn't much left of the bodies outside. Inside, some were preserved and they hadn't eaten. The water was still in bottles, cans laid about the floor, unopened, but some had labels off, dents on the lid which could only be bite marks. The vending machine was broken into. They'd tried; they'd failed. They had perished.

We spent the first day, clearing bodies, and at first light on the next morning, foraged for food and supplies. I intended to start the clean-up process on the third day.

What I wasn't expecting was the radio call from Danny.

The connection was crystal clear, which let me know they were close.

A couple of hours, Danny said. They were hauling ass. So Miles and I did the same to get ready. Clearing up eighteen months' worth of dust, dirt, bugs, and animals wasn't an easy task.

There were thirty-plus arriving by bus and more in the tractor trailer. We prepped for that as best as we could, then took the pickup, opened the gate, and waited.

I screamed with joy inside when I saw that beautiful old beat-up bus roll toward our gate.

My smile was the width of my face when I stepped out of the way to allow the bus to pass through the gate.

It stopped.

The door opened and an outpouring of kids raced from the bus and encircled me as if they hadn't seen me in ages. I tried my best to hug them all. Then after them came Javier, Levi, and Noah, all extending a hand and thanking me.

Thanking me? I didn't do anything. A few more people I knew from Grace unloaded and that's when I started to get a sick feeling. They looked bad, scared, and worse for wear.

Bonnie stepped off. She hugged me, shook her head, and waited. Jessie then followed. Her face was bruised and red, her arms went around my waist and her head to my chest.

"Missed you, Sonny. Missed you."

"I missed you too, baby." I lifted her face. "What happened to you?"

She was about to tell me when Bonnie pulled her away. My eyes went from her to Danny. He looked as if he'd lost his best friend. Oh my God. *Mera.*

"Danny?"

His lips puckered and he tried to talk. I didn't want to ask where Mera was; I was scared of the answer. Beck stepped from the bus holding both babies. After setting them down, he joined their hands and told Phoenix and Keller, "Go to Bonnie."

"Beck, what happened? Where's Mera? Where's Alex?"

"We…we…" Beck choked up. "We had problems, Sonny. Bad ones. Alex isn't going to make it."

Oh, God.

"He wants to see you," Beck said.

I nodded and stepped onto the bus. Mera stood before a parted curtain that blocked off the back.

"Sonny, you found a place."

"Yeah." I walked to Mera and embraced her. "Are you okay?"

"I've been better." She wiped her face. "Alex has been better, too." She struggled with her words. "He wants to speak to you alone. He was very specific." She started to walk away but paused, grabbing my arms. "Make it count, okay?"

Those were her words of advice. *Make it count.* I wish she would have told me more. Perhaps I wouldn't have been so shocked when I stepped through the curtain and saw Alex.

My heart broke. His body was thick with swelling, some of it discolored. The rough, tough, no nonsense guy was weak. I couldn't take it.

"Hey, Boots."

Boots. Of all things. He was sick and he called me that stupid nickname he gave me all because Mera mentioned my boots a lot.

"Hey, Alex. What did you go and do to yourself?"

"I don't know. One minute I'm thinking I'm infallible, the next, I'm carrying Jessie and my liver."

I tried not to let it be heard, but a groan slipped from my throat. "How?"

"Not important. But something is."

Laced within his struggling raspy words was a dead serious tone.

"Sonny...I need to tell you something. Only you can know. Close the curtain."

Without asking any questions I closed the curtain and sat down.

40
MERA STEVENS

He wanted to go home with dignity. Alex wanted the children to see him get in the truck and have their last look be how they remembered him.

We washed his face, cleaned him up as best as we could and I straightened his hair into a neat ponytail. We put a crisp, clean shit over his bandaged torso and a bigger pair of jeans. As I put on his boots, I saw it. He cringed. Alex was finally feeling the pain.

With the help of Beck, he gave the appearance of stepping off that bus. Only three of us would go to the Survival Haven with him. We'd stay there until he got well, or...

Alex wanted to walk to the truck; it wasn't far from the bus. He did, with me on one side, Beck on the other and Sonny behind him.

The children and those from Grace lined up as he walked by. Sadness laced their faces. They waved as if he were embarking on a long trip. He stopped at Keller and Phoenix and told them to be good, then he paused at Jessie.

"I'm so proud of you," he told her.

"I'm proud of you, Alex."

He smiled sadly and laid his hand on her face as he took the last step to the truck. There at the open door he looked around.

"What is it?" I asked.

"Danny? I don't see him."

I searched around for my son and saw him a few feet away with his back toward us. "I'll be back."

"Let him go."

"No. I'll be back. Stay here." I walked to my son. "Danny..." He didn't turn around. "Danny. Alex is leaving. We're taking him home. Come say goodbye. He wants to see you."

"I can't, Mom. I can't." Danny lowered his head and I saw his shoulders bounce.

I moved closer to him placing my forehead against his back. "Danny, I know this is hard. But you need to do this. For you and for Alex, okay? Please."

"He's leaving us. I can't say goodbye to him."

"Then don't. Go over, wish him luck. Tell him you'll see him. But see him now."

Danny slowly nodded, reached behind him, and grabbed my hand. I turned him around and we walked to the truck.

He was trying. Danny was trying so hard not to break down. A few steps into our walk, he sobbed once.

Beck intercepted, stood before Danny. "It'll be okay."

"No, it won't," Danny replied. "It won't."

"You're right." Beck gripped Danny's shoulders and squeezed, stepped aside, and headed to the driver's side of the truck.

I guided my son to Alex.

An immediate explosion of emotional energy was generated between them just by a glance.

"Thank you for seeing me off," Alex said.

Danny pursed his lips, fighting his turmoil, anger, and hurt. "I can't say goodbye, Alex. I can't do this. This is wrong. I can't believe this is happening."

"Yeah, I know. But despite what you think, it'll be okay. I'm so proud of you. So proud. Danny…" Alex shifted his weight, "I need you to watch your mom. I mean it. Okay? You be there. You believe her when she tells you things. She is going to need you. I have a feeling this world has a big role in it for you. One only you can fill."

"You're gonna try, right Alex? You're gonna try to beat this?"

"Oh, yeah. I'm not gone yet. But I better go."

Then they embraced.

Alex grabbed Danny and Danny held onto Alex, arms wrapped tightly around each other for a long time.

"I have to go," Alex said emotionally.

Danny nodded within the embrace.

Alex stepped back, placed both hands to Danny's cheeks, and planted his lips on my son's forehead, leaving them there with his eyes closed. After a shivering breath, Alex pulled back and tried his damndest to climb into the truck himself.

Sonny helped, moving Alex to the middle of the bench seat.

"Wait!" Danny called out before I climbed in, and ran to the truck. He reached inside and grabbed Alex's hand. "I'm proud of you, too, Alex. Proud of you, too."

I led my son from the truck and kissed him. I knew what was going to happen next. I knew it by the way Danny waved once and walked away. He wasn't going to watch the truck leave, or, at the very least, let us see he was watching.

I knew my son. He was going to find a quiet place to break down. I felt bad for him. He was hurting. We all were.

It was *Alex*.

Alex was filled with a strange and energetic renewal as we drove closer to his home. Sonny sat outside in the rear, his side against the cab window, engaging in conversation with Alex who narrated every mile.

This is where this happened...

Oh, I remember this...

Turn here, Beck. Turn here.

He grabbed my hand and squeezed it. I looked over at Alex; he was smiling.

We passed that sign for the Survival Haven, the one we first saw almost two years ago. Weeds were grown over it and entangled around it.

"Almost there," Beck said. "I remember this road. Hopefully no Sleepers are out this way."

"Only me," Alex replied. "There are no Sleepers on this side of the Divide."

From the window, Sonny asked, "Is that it up ahead, Alex? Nice place."

"My pride and joy."

Pulling up to the Survival Haven brought back memories of that day when we arrived with Danny, looking for help, trying to let him heal from his injury. Alex helped him that day. The area around the Haven was dirt and brush back then and wasn't much different now. The place looked nearly the same.

Alex sighed. "I never thought I'd see this place again," he said softly. "Thank you." He squeezed my hand again. "I'm home. I'm...home."

I knew the moment was coming, and there was no way I was prepared. I knew the second his hand relaxed and his head fell to my shoulder.

I gasped, struggling to catch my breath.

"Let's get out, buddy," Sonny said, reaching through the window, tapping Alex.

Beck put the truck in park. "I'll give you a hand. I know you want to see..."

He stopped talking when I lifted my hand. I lifted it as if to tell him to stop. Just stop. At that second, he too knew.

Alex was gone.

Silence engulfed the truck and Beck's head dropped to the steering wheel.

I reached around Alex and pulled him into me, wrapping both my arms tightly around his lifeless body. I held him tight against me, burying my head into him, and I wept like I hadn't done in a long time. The pull of loss from my soul was great. It burned in my stomach, shot up through my chest, and literally choked me. I wanted to scream, to make a noise as I cried, as if that would release some of the ache I felt. But nothing would come out, just air laced with my agony.

I couldn't stop crying, I couldn't stop holding him. I didn't want to let go. My heart was broken. It didn't matter. No amount of holding him, weeping, praying would make a difference.

Alex was gone, and he wasn't coming back.

It was early afternoon. A cool autumn breeze swept in but with it came a sense of peace I did not believe would be there. The most surprising thing about being around someone that leaves this earth is the amount of serenity that surrounds him. It is the one thing that can make you truly believe there's a better place that we all go.

Alex just wanted to go home. So many times since we first met, he said he wanted to get back to the Survival Haven. He wanted to see it one more time.

Prior to meeting us, he had given up all of his normal life and put it into his dream of the Haven. Then he gave all that up to trek across the country with me to help me find my child.

It was only fitting that he made it home in more ways than one.

He'd be laid to rest in a place he loved.

I stayed with Alex in the truck until they were ready to bury him. Beck wanted to dig the grave himself.

I asked Sonny what it was that Alex had to tell him on the bus.

"I can't tell you," Sonny told me. "I promised him I wouldn't. You'll find out. It's something he needed me to put in the Doctrines."

"It's important?"

"Yes. Yes it is."

Beck returned, simply stating, "It's time."

I placed my lips to Alex's head and then stepped from the truck.

Beck reached inside, slid his hands under Alex's body, and lifted him. He exhaled an emotional ache as he adjusted his friend in his arms.

I couldn't watch them put him in the ground. It was hard enough to watch Beck carry our friend in his arms to his final resting place.

While they buried him, I went inside the Haven. I walked around Alex's home. When I was there before, I was so distraught over the loss of Jeremy, Daniel, and trying to find Jessie that I never noticed how much there was about Alex in that place. How much I didn't know.

I gathered things for me and for the children. Pictures, items that were probably important to Alex. Things that told a story about a different Alex, one that existed before the world turned.

A world before the Sleepers. A carefree man who laughed and lived life to the fullest.

I smiled at a picture of him in the Navy. He was thin and young and it was way before the long hair and tattoos. There was cigar box full of pictures. I took that. His music player was on the nightstand. What did he listen to? Country music, that's right.

Anything and everything I could think of, I took as my way to hold on to him. Preserve him. It hurt me more than I ever thought possible. Losing Alex was losing a part of me. He was my partner with the kids, my rock, my nemesis at times, my hero, and my friend.

There would forever be an emptiness no one could fill. I wouldn't let them. That spot was reserved for Alex Sans.

Alex was gone, but I had to remember, really, he wasn't. The Haven wasn't far from our new home. Perhaps I couldn't touch him or hear him, but I knew when I needed an 'Alex' fix and more than the items I retrieved, I could come here. I could always find a piece of Alex.

Things would forever be different. We were all changed people. Grace was behind us but still with us. Our struggles were far from over; the Sleepers were still out there, on the other side of the Great Divide, but still there, waiting, one day crossing over. One day challenging us. That day could be tomorrow, next year, no one knew. A war was before us and we were ill-prepared. It was one we didn't want to fight. Not yet. Eventually we would. Eventually.

How ironic that we had, indeed, in a sense, come full circle. Nearly two years ago, we arrived at the Haven lost and sad and in the throes of one heartbreak only to return in the throes of another.

Beck called for me.

Alex was placed in his final resting place. It was done.

It was time to go. Time to leave the Haven. Time to return to our new home.

Filled with sadness as we left the Haven, I had to remind myself, that it wasn't just the end of one man's legacy, it was the start of a new beginning, and I had to embrace and share the legacy Alex left behind.

As we slowly pulled away from the Survival Haven, I took a deep breath and braced myself for embarking on the next chapter of life, sadly, one without Alex.

All three of us were quiet. No one felt like talking. Laying my hand over Beck's, I glanced back, just one more time and watched that chapter, the chapter of the Survival Haven, get smaller and smaller as we drove down the road. I watched until I couldn't see it any longer.

Then I closed my eyes and a single tear rolled down my cheek.

It was over.

Time to move forward.
But not without remembering, always remembering.
Not without loss.
Goodbye, Alex. I will never forget you.

ABOUT THE AUTHOR

Jacqueline Druga is a native of Pittsburgh, PA. She is a prolific writer and filmmaker. Her published works include genres of all types, but she favors post-apocalypse and apocalypse writing.

PERMUTED
PRESS
needs *you* to help

SPREAD (THE) INFECTION

FOLLOW US!

f | Facebook.com/PermutedPress
𝕐 | Twitter.com/PermutedPress

REVIEW US!

Wherever you buy our book, they can be reviewed! We want to know what you like!

GET INFECTED!

Sign up for our mailing list at PermutedPress.com

PERMUTED
PRESS

KING ARTHUR AND THE KNIGHTS OF THE ROUND TABLE HAVE BEEN REBORN TO SAVE THE WORLD FROM THE CLUTCHES OF MORGANA WHILE SHE PROPELS OUR MODERN WORLD INTO THE MIDDLE AGES.

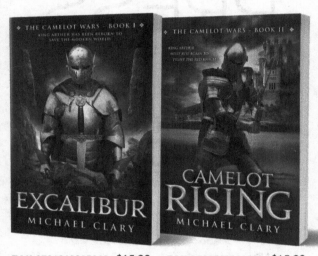

EAN 9781618685018 $15.99   EAN 9781682611562 $15.99

Morgana's first attack came in a red fog that wiped out all modern technology. The entire planet was pushed back into the middle ages. The world descended into chaos.

But hope is not yet lost— King Arthur, Merlin, and the Knights of the Round Table have been reborn.